A Life Found

A Life Singular
Book 2

Lorraine Pestell

First published in Australia in 2013
Second edition published worldwide in 2016

© Lorraine Pestell 2016
http://lorrainepestell.com

Paperback ISBN: 978-1-925151-11-4
E-book ISBN: 978-0-9875256-4-2
Amazon ASIN: B00HAVJEMC

Other books in the "A Life Singular" series:
Book 1 – A Life Singular
Book 3 – A Life Entwined
Book 4 – A Life Lived
Book 5 – A Life Tested
Book 6 – A Life Loved
Book 7 – A Life After

For Jed,
my ever-loving and much loved companion

The author supports two not-for-profit organisations which provide invaluable assistance to Australian children in need:

EdConnect Australia (formerly the School Volunteer Program)
(http://EdConnetAustralia.org.au) *"We're harnessing the wisdom and skills of older generations to enrich the learning experience of young people who are at risk of falling by the wayside in an often over-burdened school system."*

The Smith Family *(www.thesmithfamily.com.au). "The Smith Family is a children's charity helping disadvantaged Australian children to get the most out of their education, so they can create better futures for themselves."*

Prologue

Dannie's shift ended unexpectedly early at the leisure centre. The kids she had been expecting from the local children's home for their basketball coaching had not turned up, which gave her a free half-hour before the next bus home. Munching her way through the squares of a chocolate bar, she stared out of the window. It was a typically cold, wet, dreary day in Glasgow, and she decided to wait inside the building, hoping not to get too distracted and miss the bus pulling into the stop in the rain.

The ambitious youngster reached into her backpack and lifted out the book she had brought with her to school that morning. She had refrained from starting it while eating breakfast, predicting the definite danger of it making her late, unable to put it down once she had turned the first few pages. Now faced with thirty minutes to spare, she opened it with a distinct sense of excitement, at the place where her dog-eared bookmark stuck out: right at the very beginning.

The weighty tome was the combined autobiography of superstars Jeff and Lynn Diamond, published back in nineteen-ninety-seven. Somehow this famous story, which was sadly over before the young Scot was even born, had left an imprint so strong on her mind that she had read the bestseller four, perhaps five times already, and had decided to embark on it yet again.

"A Life Singular" had been the most important influence by far in the avid reader's short life. The first time she had read it, the sheer scale and impact of the couple's life had amazed her. On subsequent readings though, she had managed to sink deeper and deeper into the insightful rhetoric and comforting subtext, which had been so cleverly written that *La Grande Oeuvre* had won several literary prizes that season. Throughout childhood and adolescence, Dannie had used its candid lessons and uplifting messages to summon the motivation she needed to pursue her own lofty goals and to break out of a humdrum life in rainy Scotland.

Each time the senior year high school student immersed herself in the rich, humanistic language, she found yet more ideas and boundless inspiration for directing her energies. The paperback was a large volume, with four sections of photographs of the young woman's idol, his sublimely beautiful wife and their two children, Ryan and Kierney, who had since both become important world figures in their chosen careers. However, the magic of this book for the driven teenager from the southern highlands lay in the way the author challenged its many readers on topics of right and wrong, and the well-crafted chapters never failed to guide her when it came to making the best decision.

Snapping out of the daydream and once more checking outside in the dusk for the bus, the index finger of Dannie's left hand traced the letters of the iconic "JL" symbol in the cover's top-left corner, while she flattened out the pages and re-read the simple dedication.

> "To those we loved and who loved us, we give
> you 'A Life Singular'. JL"

She turned the page, and a strange but familiar shiver ran down her spine.

Golden Opportunity

Jeff arrived at work that morning a good twenty minutes early. He unlocked the door of the computer room and switched on the lights. Nothing unusual was afoot, with the three rows of gleaming, off-white cabinets flickering and whirring as they should, under the crude, deafening extractor fans.

His checklist complete, he went to the tea stand in the tiny office in the back corner and made himself a cup of instant coffee. This was Melbourne, he thought; the city famous for good coffee. *Oh, well...* He would buy a real one later from Pellegrini's on his way home.

The printed timetable affixed to the wall informed him that the Melbourne Academy class was due to commence at ten o'clock. That was still almost two hours away. The student settled down to work on an assignment which was due for submission the following evening. He had completed another very similar during the previous semester, and the boredom of regurgitating the same content for a second time rendered him easily distracted. He was brimming over with nervous energy, even more so than normal.

The lecturer arrived just after nine, flustered and bad-tempered. He was a quirky man, and Jeff was beginning to warm to him in spite of his idiosyncrasies. Professor Martin was his name, and he didn't care to be called anything else. He had lost his hair early, old beyond his years in most other ways too. His new offsider had regularly been able to prove him wrong when he came up with ideas and theories, which had sparked a rivalry from the outset.

Over the weeks however, Professor Martin had come to respect his younger colleague for his persistent attitude and ability to think laterally around problems of all shapes and sizes. He had been forced to admit that this upstart recently arrived from interstate was highly intelligent and personable, if a little too cool and hard-edged for his liking.

The Vice-Chancellor had impressed upon the university's staff, after receiving the undergraduate's glowing references and some startling details of his life history, that they were fortunate to have a brilliant mind joining them. According to his sponsored application, the teenager had been shepherded through the New South Wales education system as a case study for disadvantaged children who showed promise despite their circumstances. Therefore, there was considerable political mileage to be gained by the university from being seen to help this long-haired and loud-mouthed lanky lad, whose casual manner belied an immense intellect. And there were precious few in the Computer Science department who could be described as cool, making this enigmatic young man a definite asset when encouraging new blood onto its courses.

Today was a Tuesday, the fifteenth of February nineteen-seventy-two. Jeff Diamond had arrived at RMIT, the Royal Melbourne Institute of Technology, fresh from Sydney for the start of the new academic year. He had completed the first year of his Bachelor of Science degree at the University of New South Wales and had negotiated a deal whereby he could transfer his completed units for full credits towards the equivalent RMIT degree. The unlikely student had been the recipient of a tertiary scholarship from the State Government, which meant that the various authorities were also duty bound to help him succeed, just in case the country's press was watching.

The boy's passage through the state's school system had been an unusual one, and a string of teachers had either hailed him or loathed him. As long as the extremely talented but wild child chose to listen, so the rest of the unruly mob would be quiet. However, as soon as Jeff Diamond lost interest, mayhem would invariably ensue. The more astute teachers learned to capitalise on the tearaway's thirst for knowledge, along with his Pied Piper ability to corral the class, to help them gain control of their lessons. The less astute did not, and paid a high price for their ignorance. Most branded him a troublemaker, but certain others lauded him as an irreverent genius. Either way, this dangerous character from the Stones Road escaped no-one's attention.

It was due respect that the young man had been seeking all along; nothing more and nothing less. The way he saw it, the local high school was obliged to provide him with an education, regardless of his lowly beginnings and the bad reputation which clung to him and his older sister by dint of their memorable surname. If teachers gave some respect, they were given some in return, and against all expectations, Jeff systematically racked up a series of school certificates and other academic distinctions, finally graduating in December nineteen-seventy with the top HSC score in the state.

As a teenager, the swarthy, good-looking kid was hugely popular with girls and boys alike, despite spending hundreds of hours in the library and at home, garnering knowledge about anything and everything and constantly firing his imagination. Added to this were a solid sporting prowess and musical talent, leaving officials at the Education Department frequently flabbergasted at the youngster's natural capacity to lead his peers. And, as many people had found out along the way, once Jeff Diamond was on their side, he would look after them forever. Professor Martin was beginning to learn this too, much to his annoyance.

Only a year into his bachelor's degree, the restless student had jumped at the chance to make a fresh start in Melbourne when his close friend, Gerry Blake, was asked by his father to head up the Victorian state office of the family firm. The two lads had been best mates since Jeff was twelve years old. Another outstanding achiever, Gerry was three years older and had graduated with honours in Accounting from Sydney University a couple of years prior, having completed his Chartered Accountant qualifications straight afterwards, under his father's watchful tutelage. Born with the proverbial silver spoon in his mouth, the former Sydney Grammar School Head Boy had found himself a luxury apartment near Toorak Road, and he and his girlfriend had driven down the Hume Highway in his brand new BMW to start new chapters of their lives in Melbourne.

Jeff Diamond, on the other hand, had loaded all his worldly goods, which amounted to very little, into his dark blue, nineteen-sixty-two Ford Fairlane and had driven the seven hundred or so kilometres southwards on his own, past Canberra and into Victoria, finally ending up in a bed-and-breakfast in Prahran.

As soon as he could, the independent and solitary young man had rented a one-bedroomed flat in the run-down suburb of Richmond, about a kilometre from the majestic Melbourne Cricket Ground. Jeff was a budding songwriter in his spare time and had earned a lump sum in royalties for a couple of songs that had been recorded by some well-known artists. With these proceeds, he had been able to pay a full year's rent upfront and buy a few basic items of furniture, which had taken the pressure off student life for the time being. Gerry had told him he was mad to blow so much money at once and that he should look for shared accommodation, but his younger friend needed his own place. He had lived on his own since the age of fourteen, in spite of many attempts by Social Services, his grandparents and several interfering but well-meaning neighbours to make other arrangements on his behalf, and he was not inclined to forgo this vital sanctuary too easily.

Ten o'clock on this particular morning represented a most important milestone for the boy from western Sydney. It had been weeks, if not months or even years in the planning, depending on how he looked at it. He was anxious and excited, but desperate to remain calm and for nothing to go wrong. He had rehearsed his lines all the previous sleepless night, and even now his overactive mind was busy thinking of all the contingencies. What if there were a change of plan and the class were cancelled? They couldn't do that at this late stage, could they? The timetable was set in stone. What if the registered students didn't all show up? He cursed his own pessimism, knowing he should stop obsessing about all the things which could go wrong and focus on what he would do if events went according to plan.

Jeff looked at the clock again. Professor Martin was preparing his acetate slides for the overhead projector, making sure his notes were in order. The first Melbourne Academy class of the new year was a significant component of the annual marketing programme run by RMIT to attract the best and brightest to the university for the following year's undergraduate courses. Computer

11

Science was an emerging subject, and the staff typically struggled to leave a lasting impression on these students, who had received a very traditional education thus far. A very privileged education, in fact. One might even say an over-privileged education, if one was your typical, left-wing career academic.

'Let's see how this year's beautiful people stack up,' Professor Martin had resentfully shared with his technical assistant when they had left work together at the end of the previous day.

It was now nine-forty-five, and the young man's heart was in his mouth. He took a cigarette break and smoked two in quick succession in an attempt to calm his nerves. It was a warm day, and there were already many students milling around campus. He searched the crowd for the bunch of clean-cut kids in uniform whom he was anticipating. There was a bus in the car park at the far end of the quadrangle, but its signage was obscured by the wall of another lecture hall. With time running out, Jeff jogged back to the computer room to watch his fate unfold. Or not.

'Here they come, those lucky, lucky kiddies,' sneered the sarcastic lecturer, with a glint in his eye. 'Look at them, with their sun tans after their summer holidays down at Portsea and Sorrento, sailing around on Daddy's yacht, or visiting Granny for Christmas in the Home Counties. Oh, look there! I say, old boy! There's even one who went skiing in the French Alps on the way back.'

It was true, Jeff had to smile. A beanpole of a boy was struggling up the steps of the tiered seating on crutches, with a plaster cast from his toes to just below the knee. He laughed more to appease the professor than because he found it funny. If he were honest, he considered the bald man's frequent snide, political tirades a little tiresome, often goading him on subtly for a bit of sport.

After today's presenter had left to introduce the class, his impatient assistant peered through the window from the computer room into the lecture theatre. He scanned the rows of young faces, dressed in black blazers with red trim and the Melbourne Academy crest on their breast pockets. They all wore ties, and the girls with long hair had it tied up, away from their fresh, well-scrubbed faces. They were a noisy bunch, he thought. They didn't look particularly special either.

And then at last he spotted her. Three rows from the front, about six seats in from the left, chatting idly with a redhead who was sitting in the adjacent seat. Jeff scanned the class again to make sure he wasn't mistaken. Could it be someone who looked like her? A decoy to divert attention from the real thing? No, it was definitely her. His plan was working, heaven help him! Christ Almighty! Now he had to go through with it...

The dark-haired student stared at Lynn Dyson for what seemed like five minutes. In reality, it was probably less than thirty seconds. The radiant face wasn't exactly smiling, yet her gaze was wonderfully warm nonetheless. She had looked straight at him, through the glass. He hadn't been prepared for that, and his nerve nearly failed him. He managed to hold on to the pair of blue gems in a steely, purposeful gaze, and it had been she who had finally looked away. Eye contact was another step in the right direction, deserving of a small amount of self-congratulation. *Patience*, he urged his heart, which was now beating so hard he could almost hear it, not to mention the contortions taking place in his jeans.

Professor Martin droned on and on about the history of the computer, about IBM and the Americans, and about the evolution of tape storage and databases. Why in the world would anyone want to learn about this in an introductory session designed to encourage youngsters into a new and exciting profession? What a turn-off! This was the Sydneysider's main problem with the degree course; it was far too theoretical and dry. It completely failed to explain the promise of the many powerful ways in which computers would undoubtedly improve real people's lives over the coming years.

Yes, the dreamer would have loved to be a musician; the Pied Piper of Richmond. Or a philosopher perhaps, sipping liqueur coffees and poking fun at the pretentious characters who frequented Melbourne's laneway cafés. But needs must for a boy from Canley Vale, and he had decided on a practical qualification which would open up the world to him on a far more down-to-earth level.

Jeff Diamond had determined from a very young age that he was going places. He had come from nowhere, but had his heart and mind set on going somewhere and being someone. He had been this way all his life. Even as a three-year-old, as his mother had recounted to a friend when she thought her son was out of earshot, "That stupid kid asked Lena's teacher if she could tell him the difference between this and that. Why does he wanna know stuff like that at his age?" Unfortunately, mother and son had never been on the same wavelength. Not even on the same planet most of the time, for reasons the boy preferred to keep to himself. His elder sister, Madalena, was her mamá's girl, whereas the young Jeff was simply a tireless nuisance who asked too many questions and reminded everyone of his father.

The clock on the laboratory wall ticked rhythmically, but nowhere near fast enough for the young man's liking. Patience didn't come at all readily to the nineteen-year-old, since vices were so much easier to cultivate than virtues for people like him. Over the last few weeks, he had wondered how on Earth he might possibly get close enough to his dream girl to strike up a conversation, let alone to ask her out on a date. He had staked out her school a few times, as well as the sports centre where she and her family trained regularly, but until now he had never seen her in person and certainly didn't relish the prospect of getting sprung by security for stalking. He had even driven out to the family's enormous homestead, an hour due north of the city, not surprised at being confronted by wrought iron gates of corresponding proportions.

But then today's golden opportunity had truly landed in Jeff's lap. It ought to have occurred to him in those months of planning his southward migration that there would be a close tie between Melbourne's most prestigious schools and the local tertiary institutions of good standing. Yet he could hardly believe his luck when, during staff room chatter, he had discovered the Melbourne Academy Year Twelve induction programme contained several lectures at RMIT.

Back in Professor Martin's lecture hall, the class continued into its second half-hour. The anxious student attempted to concentrate on the newspaper while the boring man cycled through his slides. Every now and then, he glanced up to check if Lynn was still paying attention. She was. Admirable, he thought. A bizarre image flashed across his mind of the nerdy, tweed-jacketed academic being in his shoes and about to take on his challenge, which he dismissed with a lazy chuckle.

Jeff wondered how closely the real Lynn Dyson would resemble the television personality, or indeed the perfect being who had occupied his thoughts and sexual fantasies ninety-nine percent of the time over the last few years. He was hopeful but had realistic expectations. He could handle disappointment. He had no fear of that, but would rather not have his illusions shattered just yet. To him at this precise moment, sitting there in her school uniform, the famous blonde teenager seemed much younger than her public self. She looked as if she needed to be taken care of, as did he...

The troubled soul dismissed this foolish notion too, hating the way his insecurities always got the better of him. During personal appearances, at concerts or sporting events, the Lynn Dyson whom the dedicated fan recognised so fondly gave the impression of being mature and self-assured. Sitting in Professor Martin's class however, she looked exactly like she should: an attentive, sixteen-year-old private school girl scribbling in her exercise book, with a pencil case in front of her on the desk and surrounded by classmates.

Only sixteen... The young buck from New South Wales had keenly watched this significant birthday click over during the previous September, just before he, Gerry and Suzanne had become serious about their move down from Sydney. Was sixteen too young for Australia's most promising society girl to associate with a nobody from the western suburbs? He suspected so, but was determined to go through with his plan nonetheless.

The noise of creaking wooden benches jolted the songwriter out of his daydream. Suddenly the class was on its collective feet and filing out of the lecture theatre.

Here we go, Jeff murmured to himself, closing the newspaper.

No time to think about it any further. The man on a mission slipped out of the back door of the adjoining laboratory, which led directly into the main thoroughfare. He spotted Lynn's golden hair among a bunch of about eight uniforms, already heading down the corridor towards the car park. It was now or never, he vowed.

In less than twenty seconds, the long-legged man had caught up with the group and walked alongside for a few steps. Lynn looked over to her right and seemed to acknowledge his presence. Summoning every available molecule of bravado, he launched forth.

'Hi, Lynn. I'm Jeff Diamond. I work in the Computer Science department and I'm also a student here.'

The famous teenager appeared slightly startled but smiled graciously anyway. She must be used to people accosting her out of the blue, Jeff figured. How many young blokes like him were there, chasing their fantasies just the same as he was? Hundreds, he expected. Thousands, perhaps. Her friends looked at him suspiciously, awaiting his next move, and he felt a shield of protectiveness close in around the young star.

Undaunted, the single-minded student continued, as per his many mental rehearsals. 'I've got tickets for Thursday night's performance of "A Streetcar Named Desire" at His Majesty's Theatre. Would you come with me, please?'

Flawlessly executed, even if he said so himself...

Lynn was taken aback. Who was this guy? Should she know him? He was stunning looking though, whoever he was. Well over six feet tall, with hypnotising, dark eyes and a disarming smile. And "A Streetcar Named Desire" would be amazing to see as a play. Its new season had received good reviews as it toured around the Australian capital cities.

Before she knew it, the young woman was accepting the invitation. 'Why not? Thanks, Jeff. That'd be great.'

OK. So the impossible had happened! It was as if all the air had been sucked out of the corridor, leaving everyone in a sort of frozen limbo. The handsome man willed his mind to turn faster, but only his heart rate was heeding the call. Had Lynn Dyson really agreed to go out with him? Their walking pace had slowed to a virtual stop, yet it took him a while to figure this out. He had her attention. So what was he going to do with it?

'Fantastic, thanks,' he said, calming down slightly. 'It starts at seven-thirty. Where shall I pick you up from?'

On Lynn's face was a cautious smile. By the looks of things, she was none too sure what had transpired in the last few seconds either.

'Do you know the Dyson Administration building, just a bit further down St Kilda Road from the river? After the army barracks, on the corner of Coventry Street.'

Jeff nodded. 'Yes.'

He didn't, but would find out easily enough.

'Seven o'clock then?' he suggested.

'OK,' the schoolgirl confirmed. 'See you in the lobby there at seven. We have to go now. Bye, Jeff.'

'*Adiós*. Thanks again. See you Thursday.'

Elation threatened to lift the astounded student's feet off the ground, and his ultra-cool persona fought hard to counteract its force. Catching the eyes of a couple of the star's friends, Jeff could see he was not the only one to be surprised by the snap decision. As he watched the small group walk off into the distance, he could hear girls' laughter and tried to imagine what their *post mortem* analysis might contain. He turned and walked in the opposite direction, back towards the faculty building and the remainder of his mundane shift.

Did that really happen? Had his script really had the desired outcome? The master plan had been in abeyance for so many weeks but was suddenly obsolete, fully executed and closed. He now needed a new plan for Thursday, because he, Jeff Diamond, the no-good reprobate from Nowheresville, New South Wales, was taking the lovely Lynn Dyson to the theatre. How about that!

The worst thing about it though was the fact that he couldn't tell anyone. *Jesus Christ*, the young man cursed. How was he going to make it to Thursday without going completely crazy? He stepped outside for a cigarette. Sitting on the wall, he played and replayed the last few minutes in his head. Yes, it had definitely been Lynn. No, he hadn't asked the wrong girl out. He was positive about that. Well, then... It had to be true, and he would damned well be ready.

The dreamer reluctantly dragged himself back to reality, needing to return to the computer room as if nothing consequential had happened. There were another three long hours to be spent at work, after which he had a few classes to sit through and then had agreed to a squash game with Gerry. His stomach felt sick, and his head was aching. He hadn't slept for a number of nights, and his head was heavy at the best of times. Still, today was a good day. It wasn't every day that one arranged a date with the country's most eligible young lady.

***

The Melbourne Academy Year Twelve class filed back onto their bus. Lynn Dyson was, as always, surrounded by friends. She was a genuinely popular girl, and not just because of who she was. Several students in her year had famous parents or were heirs to successful businesses in Melbourne. Most of their cohort had been together since primary school and they were a close-knit bunch.

Sitting next to the young celebrity was her closest friend, Michelle England, who was particularly excited after the impromptu encounter in the corridor.

'Who is that guy?' she yelped.

'I don't know,' the smiling blonde answered, before seeing the disbelief on her friend's face and adding, 'Really, I don't!'

Michelle, together with Andrea and Jenny, who were sitting in the seats behind, were unable to fathom how a perfect stranger could have had the gall to approach their famous classmate and ask her out. Just like that! This was one brave man. They witnessed the pretty musician turn boys down on a regular basis, with ready excuses such as training commitments or too much homework. Occasionally too, they had seen young men retire hurt after their especially arrogant assumptions had been quashed simply for their audacity.

'So if you don't know him, why did you say you'd go out with him?' the redhead persisted.

Lynn had to agree that her action was more than a little impulsive.

'I know,' she shrugged. 'It's probably not the smartest thing I've ever done.'

'He was so cute though,' squeaked Andrea. 'So what about the ticket you've already got? Who are you going to give it to?'

That was right, the sixteen-year-old thought. The information to which her brazen suitor was not privy was that his date was already booked to see the same play on the same night with the music crew from school.

'Yes. I don't know. It is a weird coincidence, isn't it?' Lynn agreed, as much to herself as to her friends.

So who was this mystery man who had singled her out and made his move? He was courageous, that was for sure. He might not have gone through with it if Lloyd had been walking with them, the celebrity mused. Lloyd, the boy towards whom Professor Martin's scathing remarks about the French skiing holiday had been directed, was one of the sixteen-year-old's best friends and another well-known child actor, who of late had taken on the role of her unofficial bodyguard. Thank goodness for the crutches, she smiled to herself. The trendy lothario had been lagging behind the main group, most likely chatting up girls himself, and hadn't even noticed that he was neglecting his duties.

'What are you going to do about Dean then?' asked Michelle.

Dean Keller was Lynn's so-called boyfriend, from her older brother's group of sports-mad friends, and they had been out on a few dates over the last three or four months. He had been putting pressure on her to have sex with him, but she had refused, and his continued insistence was becoming tiresome. She had told him she was too young, but had also been thinking of calling it off with him altogether. Dean was good company, but there was no connection. Even though the prodigious starlet was only sixteen, she already had a keen idea of the type of relationship she wanted and definitely didn't see that developing with her current beau.

'I don't want to keep seeing Dean anyway,' she told her friends. 'I'll break up with him this afternoon.'

The girls looked at each other in amazement. Such topics were the stuff of grown-ups, with which their young lives had only just begun to come to terms.

It was rumoured that a few of their classmates had already had sex, both boys and girls, but none of Lynn's immediate circle had admitted to going that far yet. There was a great deal of curiosity but not much intent among the girls; and among the boys, an even greater deal of both curiosity and intent, but precious little success!

'So are you going to go through with it on Thursday?' Michelle egged her on. 'What if he asks to come up to your room?'

'I'll tell him he can't,' the pretty blonde responded. 'I'm lucky. I've got a security guard to help me.'

The friends agreed it would be quite safe, as long as she was sensible.

'Besides,' the sporty schoolgirl added suggestively, 'I might want him to come up to my room. It's got to happen one day, hasn't it? And he was so good-looking!'

A mixture of horror and excitement rippled through the foursome.

Theatre

"Thursday 17th February 1972, 7:30pm," the tickets read. That was tonight! Jeff checked the date on the top of the newspaper to make doubly sure. He had never known such an interminably long couple of days, filling far too many waking hours with as much activity as he could physically manage, in order to pass the time and tire himself out.

Disappointingly, and despite his best efforts, the student still felt terrible. He really needed to learn how to get some decent sleep. There were now only three hours left between finishing work and meeting Lynn to get himself into some semblance of good shape. He ate a huge meal of steak and chips, which left him feeling nauseous. He didn't want to arrive smelling of beer or cigarettes, which ruled that type of stimulation out of the question.

The nineteen-year-old lay on his bed, revelling in the idea of his dream girl finally being close enough to touch, and contemplated how the evening might unfold in her company. He mentally undressed her and then chastised himself for debasing the object of his affections before he had even properly met her. It must be the Catholic in him, he smiled. At least by masturbating now, he wouldn't have such an uncontrollable sense of urgency when he was with her. Well, maybe not anyway... That was a little too much to expect, even for someone as well-acquainted with self-discipline as he was.

The prospect of sitting next to Lynn Dyson for two hours seemed like a distant fantasy to the young man who had waited so long for this opportunity. The fact that they were actually going out on a proper date still hadn't sunk in, even though he had only a short time to wait before fantasy hopefully would morph into reality. As he pictured the gorgeous sixteen-year-old with his hands all over her, smiling the enticing, irresistible smile which had beamed down on him from the many posters on his childhood bedroom wall, the excited teenager let his imagination run wild.

The pressure release cleared the fuzziness in his head for the next half-hour, but it soon returned. *Wake up, man*, Jeff kept saying to himself. This could be the most important day of his life so far. He took a shower, ironed his shirt and put on his one and only suit. He had bought it for Gerry's twenty-first birthday party, the December before last, and it hadn't been worn since, despite having cost him several weeks' wages. He combed his hair and splashed on some after-shave. His shoes were polished, and his tie was straight. He looked good on the outside, and his rich boy costume would hide how he was faring on the inside well enough for this evening, before the malicious fairy godmother in his mind saw fit to turn him back into a lost boy from the Stones Road.

One thing the young student had never lacked was self-confidence. For all his many defects, nature had bestowed on him a striking countenance, a strong, lean body and a wit to rival any great satirist. He had also learned some hard lessons along the way to reaching the ripe, old age of nineteen, and they had left him wise beyond his years. Ever since he could remember, he had engineered those events under his control to deliver the best learning experiences he could lay his hands on. He had always nurtured his thirst for knowledge, because for him it brought independence. Knowing more than the next person could only be a good thing, as far as this unfortunate son was concerned. He had formed his alliances carefully and never abused their friendship. Life was all about fairness in Jeff Diamond's world.

In return, these alleged friends of his had teased him heartlessly about his crush on the young Lynn Dyson, child actor, musician and rising tennis champion. At just ten years old, she had impressed the prodigious intellectual to the core with her sensitivity and interest in the world when she had been given the role of hosting "Strong Current", a children's current affairs program on the ABC. There was something about her sincerity which captured Jeff's attention, beyond the obvious attraction normally harboured by young boys for hot television starlets.

Subsequently, when she turned thirteen, Lynn and the band with the unwieldy name of Melbourne Academy Chorale, or MAC for short, had made a special programme featuring folksongs from Mediterranean countries. They had travelled to Spain, Italy and Greece to research the origins of some of the songs, and the Sydney lad remembered vividly the singer's interpretation of the political struggle of peasant farmers at the turn of the twentieth century. He had no idea how much of her commentary had been constructed from her own ideas and how much was scripted by the producers, but the wayward adolescent was happy in his delusion. Even to him, Greek folksongs seemed weird fuel for an adolescent infatuation, yet he had not been able to get Lynn Dyson out of his head ever since. Or other parts of his anatomy, for that matter.

If only to satisfy his obsessive curiosity, tonight's date was the first step towards a well-planned destiny. With his head thumping and tension gathering painfully in his shoulders, Jeff approached the revolving doors of the Dyson Administration building, opposite the illuminated Shrine of Remembrance, full of apprehension and anticipation. It was not a particularly impressive building, probably about a decade old, with eight concrete steps rising from the street to the main entrance. Breathing deeply, he passed through the doors and walked up to the desk.

'Can I help you, sir?' asked the security guard, eyeing the young man up and down.

The student wasn't used to being addressed as "sir" and was at once very glad he had opted for the suit and tie.

'Yes, please. My name's Jeff Diamond. I'm here to meet Lynn Dyson.'

The guard fixed the stranger with a patronising stare, as if to say, "Are you sure?" Nevertheless, he dialled a telephone number, and the visitor heard a female voice at the other end of the line.

'Miss Dyson, I have a Mister Diamond here in reception to see you.'

The faint voice replied, but the man in the lobby was unable to make out her response. With any luck, she hadn't forgotten or changed her mind. The uniformed official replaced the receiver with a haughty sigh of disapproval. Par for the course, the young man smiled.

'Miss Dyson will be right down, sir.'

OK, Jeff thought. *Less of the condescending tone now, if you don't mind.* The quaintness of this situation reminded him of one of those period dramas imported from Britain, where upstairs rarely came into direct contact with downstairs. He waited in the entrance of the building, trying but failing not to pace around like a prize-fighter preparing to confront his opponent. He stared absentmindedly at the selection of uninspiring paintings on the walls, and trained his ears beyond the security barrier, where he had noticed three lifts.

While he waited, the tired teenager took a few more deep breaths and rolled his shoulders. He wished he could relax and simply enjoy the occasion, but his extreme physical reaction to this event was entirely predictable. He smiled to himself again at the irony, as he acknowledged the ease with which he attracted any other female company, and yet for the one who mattered, he was a total wreck. Perhaps that was the way it should be, he attempted to justify his own behaviour.

A bell sounded behind him, and the right-hand lift opened. Miss Dyson stepped out, and Mister Diamond's stomach flipped over. Inhaling and exhaling quickly to regain his composure, he stepped towards the turnstile to meet her. She was dressed conservatively, as was he. Her shining, golden hair was loose over her shoulders, her blue eyes commanded attention, and her face wore a friendly smile.

'Hi, Jeff,' Lynn greeted him and extended her hand politely, her voice cheerful and unassuming.

'Hello,' he replied, relishing the sensation of her hand in his. 'How're you going? Thanks for coming out.'

'You're welcome. I'm looking forward to it.'

The young man held out a chivalrous arm, indicating for her to pass through the barrier and onwards in front of him. He observed that whether the young star meant them or not, she certainly knew the right things to say.

'Actually, we should go out this way,' Lynn changed her mind, turning abruptly and pointing to the back of the building. 'We can get to the tram stop faster through the side entrance. Howard, please could you let us through again?'

The uniformed man obliged, giving Jeff a knowing nod. The impatient student responded with a voiceless "Up yours" and followed his stunning date to a door at the rear of the building. His long arm reached over her head and swung the door open for her, and she smiled as they passed through.

'Thanks. Have you had a good day?'

'Pretty good, thanks. About to get a whole lot better. You?'

They found themselves outdoors, in an open area which the general public was unable to see from the street. With meticulously tended lawn surrounded by flowerbeds, the area resembled an ornate English tea garden, complete with a stone fountain and quaint, covered picnic tables. A path led to a gate in the far corner, towards which the pair was walking. Jeff kicked off the conversation proper, itching to get past the pleasantries and on to something more constructive.

'So...' he began, anticipating the questions his new acquaintance must have. 'Who am I?'

Lynn laughed at the quirky opener from the handsome man at her side, dangerously close to her shoulder. Despite his very gentlemanly behaviour, he had an insistent air about him which was strangely exciting for the sixteen-year-old.

'Yes, well... It is a bit like that! I have to tell you that after you asked me out, we were talking on the bus going back to school. My friends asked, "Who is that guy?" and I had to say, "I have no clue!"'

'Not surprised!' Jeff responded with a flash of his dark brown eyes. 'I was going to ask you for a coffee there and then, but guessed you wouldn't be able to stick around. I just had to go for it. Anyway, I'm a second year student.'

'Doing Computer Science, obviously,' she interrupted.

'Yes, and I work some shifts in the computer room. Just keeping stuff ticking over, et cetera. I moved down from Sydney over the summer with some mates.'

The evening sun was particularly warm, and the young man felt the first few strands of tension slipping out of his neck and shoulder muscles. He took off his jacket and tossed it over his shoulder, where it hung, casually hooked on the index finger of his right hand. They had reached the tram stop just as one was pulling up, so they ran to jump in through the back door. There was only one seat vacant nearby, and Jeff motioned to his famous date to take it. He stood in front of her, wondering how competent he was at blocking the view of prying eyes, and watched as a light breeze from the open window blew Lynn's hair back away from her face. She was so beautiful, and making things extremely easy for him, he thought.

'Wow! That's a big move. Why did you come to Melbourne?'

Jeff inhaled deeply and smiled, leaning against the wall of the trundling vehicle. There was no way on Earth he was going to tell her yet that the main reason he had moved south was for this very moment.

'For a number of reasons really,' he explained. 'I wanted a change of scene, my best mate was taking over the Melbourne branch of his dad's company, and his girlfriend's come down to take over a boarding kennels business she inherited when a family member died. The stars were aligned, so we just decided to relocate. It was a spur of the moment decision that got legs very quickly. And here we are!'

'That's a good story,' Lynn told him, grinning at the drama in his outstretched arms.

The pair talked idly about their various experiences of Melbourne and Sydney, laughing at the different perspectives they held as resident and visitor of each city. Jeff's first-hand knowledge of other Australian state capitals was non-existent, of which he felt initially ashamed, but he soon realised that this rich vein of ignorance did not seem to count against him in the pretty sixteen-year-old's mind. In fact, she appeared particularly impressed by his academic achievements, despite his having omitted a number so as not to seem too boastful.

After only five minutes, the tram arrived at the intersection of Swanston and Bourke Streets, and the couple alighted to continue their journey on foot, heading eastwards to Exhibition Street and the theatre district. The student proceeded to answer the inquisitive young woman's detailed questions on university life and how different it was from school, most of which constituted safe ground for the man who sought to stay reticent about his own story.

'And have you had to start your degree again?' her bright voice asked.

'No,' Jeff began to answer, only to have the conversation cut short by another sudden change of direction.

The pair had reached the doors of the theatre, and the blonde star was being greeted and pointed at from all sides. Checking to see her companion was following her, the celebrity marched through the vestibule and over to a wide staircase of plush red carpet.

'To be continued!' the amused man shouted, revelling in the attention his famous date was attracting.

So this was what it was like to go out with someone famous... Having always been fascinated by the paradox of fame, her companion scanned the rows of entranced faces which swayed like corn in a stiff breeze, following the celebrity's every move. Lynn's success had no direct positive effect on the lives of these excited individuals, and yet she was quite clearly adored. Why? Perhaps due to the hope a sighting engendered that a portion of her success might transfer to those whom she touched or said hello to, he guessed. Or maybe her presence among them simply made people feel good about the world for a few minutes, the therapeutic value of which the afflicted student could most certainly appreciate.

Was this sufficient though to deserve such adulation? Or ought there really to be an obligation on these special somebodies to take their power a step further? He dared to wonder what it would be like to discuss his impudent theory with the young lady herself, dazzled by her smile and feeling his heart leap into his mouth again. Focussing back on more earthly matters, the new kid in town wasn't entirely sure what he was supposed to do now. The world had slipped into slow motion. This very scenario, which had only existed inside his head for so long, had precipitously become real.

Concentrate, he scolded himself. Lynn Dyson was his responsibility tonight. Should he help to push his precious charge through the crowd or allow her to be mobbed?

But he needn't have worried. The slender, dignified teenager was a professional crowd-pleaser. Born into the job, she handled the attention with grace and patience, while managing to keep moving at a steady pace. Jeff studied the tickets and found the number for the door they needed. A split-second later, his date caught his eye with the question for which he already had the answer, and he pointed over towards the left-hand side of the huge foyer. That was close, he blanched.

The inspired man handed both tickets to the usher on the door, who was also excited to see the child star. As he began to relax more, the ambitious songwriter was keen to observe how people reacted to her at close quarters, eager to absorb more of this world of celebrity. The usher gave them a programme and refused to accept any money, simply returning the ticket stubs to Lynn, who duly separated them and gave one back to her chaperone. He accepted it with thanks, searching this time for the seat number.

He needn't have bothered to do this either, however. They were receiving extra special service, shown right to their seats. The sixteen-year-old sat down and gazed around at the full auditorium, now appearing oblivious to the excitement she was generating. The cavernous space, with its modernistic *décor* and red velvet upholstery, was familiar territory for her, both peering out from and looking down at the stage. She watched closely as Jeff sank into the seat on her left, so tall that his shins pressed against the back of the chair in front. He was most unlike a regular university student; this guy wore after-shave and cleaned his shoes. He had put his jacket back on and looked very smart and handsome, with long, wavy black hair, mysterious dark eyes and a fantastic smile.

'I didn't even get a chance to buy you a drink,' the subject under observation apologised, handing his dream girl the programme. 'Are you OK?'

'I'm fine,' Lynn smiled. 'Thanks, but it's easier for me to avoid the public spaces. Sorry about that. My friends are used to it.'

The cool, young man shrugged. 'No apology necessary. It was quite exhilarating to be washed along in your wake.'

His evocative words were met with a look of amusement, emanating from dancing, aquamarine eyes. Jeff took this to be a token of appreciation, and it melted his heart. Any sign of approval at this early stage was worth its weight in gold.

'So carry on about your degree,' the beauty invited. 'You didn't have to restart when you moved?'

The handsome migrant was quietly impressed too. This girl, who must be so used to being the centre of attention, was prepared to take the time to find out about him. This was the Lynn Dyson he had hoped was real, and still hoped was real. She was evidently so practised at talking to strangers that he decided to reserve the right to some cynicism. It was among his well-honed self-preservation skills, yet he would remain optimistic for now.

'No. We struck a deal,' Jeff replied. 'I was at UNSW, and there are enough similarities between the two degrees that they gave me full credits for my first year. The job's not too exciting though. Prof' Martin and the other lecturers in the department haven't opened their doors to me yet, but I'm working on it. They're an interesting bunch. For a subject that's all about the future, they don't seem to be great visionaries.'

He received a sympathetic smile. 'That's disappointing for you. It must be strange being a student and a member of staff at the same time.'

'Yeah, it is,' the young man agreed, 'but there are a few of us around the place. Usually post-grads though. Not many like me.'

The lights dimmed, and the audience slowly fell silent. Jeff watched Lynn settle back into her seat and did the same, wondering how he would be able to concentrate on the play when his body was already intent on a whole different plot for the evening. As the curtain began to rise, he shot one last, loaded half-smile in her direction.

'Enjoy!'

The play unfolded before them, scene after scene. Fortunately, Jeff had read the gritty play not too long ago, courtesy of a sleepless night trapped in a random girl's house after a night out, and the characters he remembered were soon brought to life on the stage. He speculated hesitantly on what the privileged schoolgirl might make of the subject matter.

She seemed totally absorbed, and her companion was torn between maintaining his focus on the stage, as the most effective sedative for his rampant urges, and studying the young woman's facial expressions and body language for any signs that might inform him as to her level of tolerance for imperfect people. After a few exquisitely torturous minutes, he pinched the programme from Lynn's knee and scanned the cast list.

He pointed to a character on the stage. 'Who's that?'

To the nineteen-year-old's delight, his date playfully snatched the programme back and pointed to an actor in the gallery of photographs. His eyes flashed at her in gratitude, both for the answer and for the easy way she was interacting with him; not quite flirting, but with the same, tantalising result. The interval arrived more quickly than either youngster expected, and soon the curtain was descending again and the house lights were coming on. People immediately began to make their way to the bars and toilets, and the background noise deafened the pair until they became accustomed to it.

Lynn gave a sigh and turned to her mystery man.

'Good, isn't it?' she stated, her blue eyes so engaging that they almost distracted him completely.

'Yeah. Would you like that drink now? We've got fifteen minutes.'

Jeff could have really done with a cigarette too, but some things would simply have to wait. Most things, to be more accurate.

The young woman shook her head. 'Do you mind if we stay here? It's too much hassle to walk around out there.'

'Sure,' the compassionate man smiled. 'That's perfectly fine.'

This was the first sign of vulnerability he had detected, and his heart went out to the young beauty. Here was a chink in the armour of the public Lynn Dyson, and her new admirer could almost see through. He twisted round in his seat to face her, and she moved over instinctively to allow his long legs to extend a little.

'Let's stand up for a while. You need to unravel.'

Great idea, he thought, smiling at her metaphoric choice of verb. They stood together in the otherwise empty row and continued to get to know each other, finding conversation flowing readily between them. Jeff unravelled on command, stretching out his shoulders and twisting his back until it clicked. It was a relief to feel the tension leave his body, albeit gradually.

At a lull in their carefree exchange, he served again. 'So, tell me... What do you like to do?'

To his surprise, the sixteen-year-old seemed genuinely stumped by this question, staring into her companion's searching eyes for a few seconds before responding. In truth, she was also struck by how pleasant it was to find someone who was interested in her real self, rather than seeking trivia or gossip about her public life. She was caught off guard and didn't quite know what to say.

'That's an excellent question,' Lynn began to piece together her answer. 'What do I like to do? I don't get much time to think about what I like to do, because I'm always so busy doing what's on my schedule. I love what I do though, don't get me wrong. I love the music. I like spending time with friends. I'd love to read more but hardly ever get a chance to, except for school work. I like learning about anything, especially about people and different cultures. What about you?'

At her date's request, the celebrity sat down, and he followed, utterly captivated. She leaned forward in her seat and elongated her back too. Seizing the moment to focus his avid attention on her body, he rested his right arm across the back of her chair and made himself as comfortable as he could. This evening was turning out every bit as well as he had hoped, and certainly much better than he had dared to expect. He prepared to reply to her question, also struggling to find anything original to say.

'Well... Much the same, I suppose. Not the busy schedule part, but many of the same interests. I like to read, play the guitar and piano. I write songs, run, play football, tennis, squash, basketball. Any sport, really. And to get heavy for a minute, I'm into social justice and human rights, but not in any organised way yet. One day...'

The star's blue eyes told him again that she approved. 'Oh, me too. Well, I'd like to be, at any rate. Plenty of opinions and no power, that's me! I hate being so young.'

There was something very interesting about this man, Lynn decided. He was funny and outgoing, and yet introspective as well. She had the oddest sensation that this Computer Science student from Sydney whom she barely knew seemed already able to see inside her head, and she wondered whether she should trust him with her confidences so soon.

Her charming suitor chuckled kindly at her comment. 'You're not the only one who feels that way. Heaps of opinions and no power. That's a big percentage of the world's population you're describing.'

Out in the foyer, the tones of the five-minute bell had started. The good-looking pair watched silently as members of the audience filed back in to take their seats, each lost in thoughts of the other. Lynn reclined into her chair, bumping into Jeff's long arm. She didn't move away, and he left it in place for a few delicious, extra seconds. There was a definite connection. A spark which both felt but neither acknowledged in words. The young man pulled his hand away, his fingers gently but deliberately gliding across her back, and she chanced a tentative smile.

'Can I let you into a secret?'

There was a glint in her girlish eye, almost mischievous.

The inquisitive man urged her to continue. 'Absolutely.'

Lynn gestured over to the seats on the left of the auditorium, at a box further forward from where they were sitting. 'Can you see a group of kids over there, about rows three and four from the front?'

Jeff nodded, although he couldn't really tell at whom she was pointing.

'I had a ticket to sit down there tonight, with the music group from school.'

'Really?' the nineteen-year-old exclaimed, loud enough to make the snooty lady in the row in front cast a hard stare over her shoulder.

He raised his hand and mouthed an apology. Well, that was an unexpected twist!

'So you were going to be here anyway tonight?'

'Yes!' Lynn answered, laughing at the odd situation in which they found themselves. 'I was really looking forward to it. I'm surprised no-one blurted it out when you asked me to go with you, because some of those same girls are down there now.'

'That's amazing,' Jeff replied, flattered beyond belief to think that Lynn Dyson would choose his company over her friends'. 'Well, I have to say thanks again. That makes me feel damned good.'

The pretty teenager shrugged modestly, suddenly a little nervous. 'I was intrigued by you. I saw you through the window, looking at me. At least, I think it was you. Was it?'

Her date nodded. 'Yep. I was staring at you, and then you stared at me. You backed down first.'

'I know,' she affirmed, before playfully coming to her own defence. 'Because I had to pay attention to Professor Martin.'

'Yeah, right,' her happy companion teased.

Lynn slapped his arm gently, and he caught her hand on its follow-through, bringing it to his lips just as the lights went down for the second act. He released her fingers as she instinctively pulled them away, sensing her uncertainty. Such a cautious reaction was very appealing to the red-blooded male.

The couple lost themselves in the ensuing scenes. The performances were first-rate, and the abrasive Tennessee Williams story was appreciated by the cultured Melbourne audience. The plot unfolded slowly, and eventually the curtain fell for the final time to a thunderous ovation. Jeff exchanged a smile with his pretty neighbour, both applauding with enthusiasm, but then abruptly, with the clapping and many shouts for more still going strong, the famous patron placed her hands on her knees as if she were about to stand up, and turned purposefully.

'Let's get out of here.'

Before Jeff could agree or disagree, the young celebrity was already on her feet. He cottoned on quickly that she wanted to avoid a slow exit through the foyer, so he stood up straightaway and helped guide her past the other people in their row, who each gaped in turn. Out in the entrance hall, the march accelerated into a sprint, while admiring glances and shouts of recognition were launched from all sides. Her protector had to up the pace to stay close behind and was almost breathless by the time they reached the corner of Bourke Street.

'Whoa!' the student exclaimed. 'You're fast! Or I'm out of form.'

'Sorry! It would've taken us ages to get out of there, and I didn't want to give anyone the chance to stop us.'

Stop *us*? Nice touch, the boy from Sydney's west smiled. Sensing a little anxiety from the beautiful girl whose company was so intoxicating, he concluded that they shouldn't linger out in the street for long. He flagged down a yellow taxi and received a grateful smile for his unprompted action. Holding the door open while she climbed in, Jeff felt his head swim a little as a mixture of pride and relief curdled in his stomach. The serial womaniser was just about to drop into the back seat beside her when his conscience dealt him a sharp slap.

No way! his brain warned him. *This is Lynn Dyson, remember? Close the door and ride in the front, mate.*

Whether the schoolgirl was any the wiser to the battle raging between mind and body, the nineteen-year-old silently rejoiced that a social *faux pas* had been avoided. After giving the driver his instructions, he turned round to check that she was comfortable, and his eyes were met with yet another relaxed, smiling expression. Moreover, the suspense which now engulfed them was foreign even to the man who was no stranger whatsoever to encounters with good-looking females.

'It must be pretty frustrating not to be able to move at your own speed,' he offered, seeing her enquiring eyes. 'And you can't afford to piss anyone off, I guess.'

The young woman giggled, putting on an exasperated air. 'I'm not even allowed to talk about pissing people off.'

Foul language sounded clumsy emerging from such a refined mouth, and it made the Sydneysider laugh too. What was he doing? Bad boys like him didn't date nice girls like Lynn Dyson. But what the hell? He was here with her now, determined to make the most of it while it lasted.

'Who are you?' Lynn asked, disarmed by his insight again. 'Are you a reporter?'

'No. I'm a friend.'

Her enquiry was so cute however, that Jeff couldn't help but take the liberty of toying with the situation a little. His left hand grabbed the lapel of his suit jacket while he dipped his other hand into its inside pocket, as if to retrieve a hidden voice recorder. The star's face was a picture, intently following this short series of actions.

'It's OK,' he told her with a wry smile. 'We can turn this thing off now. I've got what I need.'

Lynn's eyes widened still further, not knowing whether to believe his soothing tone or his impish antics. The comic flamboyantly pulled out a battered, black leather wallet from his pocket, creasing his jacket in his hands to show her that the space was now empty.

'Oh, very funny,' she huffed, sounding a little perturbed and turning away to look out of the window at the tall buildings along the right-hand side of Flinders Street.

The taxi let its passengers out on the opposite side of St Kilda Road from their destination, leaving them to cross the wide, tree-lined boulevard along which flowed multiple lanes of car and tram traffic. In the fresh air, the young sportswoman waited under the cover of a nearby tram stop while her date paid their fare, and the cool breeze again blew her hair back from her face. Marvelling at how gorgeous she looked, Jeff slipped sideways, at her back, to shelter her from the wind, and his hands grasped the rail on either side of hers.

The aroused man was in no hurry to cross the road and deliver her home. No objections were raised by the sixteen-year-old either, and he moved in a little closer. His mind began to race ahead, though with no hope of keeping up with his body. He needed to take it easy, and yet that task was becoming more impossible with each passing moment.

'So do you live up there?' the nineteen-year-old asked, his eyes directed over her head at the Dyson Administration building on the far side of the street.

'During the week I do,' Lynn answered. 'Most weekends I go out to the farm at Benloch if I'm not travelling. It's near Lancefield, north of the airport. Do you know? Where do you live?'

Jeff leaned further forward, pushing into her back slightly, and raised his right hand as if to point towards the light towers of the MCG.

'In Richmond, about a "K" from the "G".'

The handsome stranger's mouth was now very close to the young woman's right ear, and she could feel his breath on her cheek. He smelled good too, like a grown-up. The joke at her expense now behind her, she realised she felt comfortable enough with the physical contact. In fact, she liked it a lot. This Jeff Diamond was a very expressive man, both verbally and physically, and she became aware of a strong desire to lean back into him, which conflicted with a sudden uneasy feeling inside. Her date showed no sign of moving away either, causing her to become slightly more apprehensive at their proximity.

Naïve to the world of dating, Lynn continued to make light of the situation, even though her heartbeat was quickening. 'Are you in a share house?'

'No. Just me. I value my freedom very highly.'

Caught out by his own honesty, Jeff kissed the back of the blonde's head, and her hair felt unbelievably soft against his lips. He briefly gave himself permission to consider how much he wanted her, but then banished the dangerous notion immediately, knowing that tonight was not going to be the night. The eager young man promised himself this would not be the last time he was so close to his dream girl.

Both immersed in the sublime moment, the student watched as Lynn's hand settled on top of his right wrist and squeezed it gingerly, mostly coming into contact with his watch under the cuff of his shirt.

'You're left-handed,' the famous schoolgirl said awkwardly.

The ladies' man nodded, smiling at the cute combination of *naïvetée* and nerves, while his date worked to cover her embarrassment. She was quite obviously in uncharted waters, and he took pity on her. Still facing towards the river, the young star failed to notice him nod or smile and continued ruefully.

'I'm really looking forward to finding out what freedom feels like.'

Exhaling and positively imbibing their closeness, Jeff closed his eyes and bowed his head to touch hers. The power of his reaction to her comment rocked him to the core. It was as if it finally validated the feelings he had inexplicably held for this woman over the last few years. For two people with nothing in common on the surface, they had certainly identified a connection on a very fundamental level. And what was more, it had happened after only a couple of hours in each others' presence.

An outlandish thought suddenly entered the young man's head. Was this how ordinary people turned into kidnappers? From where he was standing, with the girl of his dreams so defenceless, trapped by his large frame against the railings, it was but a short step to taking her hostage, such was his desire to wrap her up in his arms and transport her back to his flat, if only to explore this unfathomable attraction in more detail over the next few hours. And naked, of course…

'Shall we go?' he suggested, necessarily breaking the spell for both of them.

Lynn was grateful. 'Yes. It's late. We'd better.'

The confident student stepped to one side and allowed his quarry to escape onto the footpath. She turned and looked up into his eyes, still wearing the same uncertain smile. Time to put their connection to the test, he resolved. Was it one-way or two-? He undid the top button of his shirt and loosened his tie most deliberately, watching the delectable creature standing next to him scan him up and down.

Was Lynn Dyson really giving him the eye? What a deliciously sweet image for him to take home in his heightened state of arousal. The handsome stranger gave her a sly wink, and she looked away quickly.

It appeared she was, he dared to dream. The self-assured man knew the signs only too well, and he allowed himself a brief moment of arrogant pride before coming to his senses.

Bring it on, his body urged ever more forcefully. It was definitely time to call it quits for the night. There were by now far fewer people around, and Jeff had successfully hidden his secret snare from view while a bunch of rowdy tourists disembarked from the next tram. Sensing his new friend relax a little, he fixed her enquiring eyes with his and invited her to walk towards the nearest traffic lights, to cross over to the headquarters of the Dyson empire.

Still lost in his wild and lustful imagination, the boy from Canley Vale held out his hand without so much as a conscious thought. Lynn's eyes darted downwards, momentarily stunned and unsure whether to take it or not, and her reserve brought him back to reality also. Jeff Diamond didn't hold hands. What was he doing?

But before he had a chance to disguise the spontaneous gesture, slender fingers brushed across his palm. Electricity sparked between them, causing both to recoil a little, inhaling sharply and focussing on their conjoined hands in dismay.

'Sorry,' the sixteen-year-old gasped. 'I'm not quite sure what I'm supposed to do.'

Jeff exhaled too and flashed a reassuring smile. 'Me neither, but it feels great.'

As casually as he could, given the fact that his nerves were now tingling all the way past his shoulder and into his chest, the young man resisted his flight instincts and squeezed the smaller hand a little tighter. It did feel great, skin-on-skin, and his sex-drive growled in complicit agreement. His date glanced up as they strolled along and dared to swing her arm just a tiny bit, relishing the unfamiliar physical attraction of such a strong grip.

The pair was thus committed to walking the hundred metres or so back to the Dyson Administration building hand-in-hand. Unable to come to terms with either his behaviour or its inexplicable rightness, Jeff found his mouth launching into an equally natural conversation about his timetable for the next few days and other such harmless pieces of generality.

'Can we do this again?' he asked, realising they were almost at the gate.

'The play?'

'No,' Jeff chuckled. 'When's the next gap in your busy schedule?'

It was the celebrity's turn to sigh. How could she possibly have a proper boyfriend? There was no time.

'Well, I'm going to Sydney this weekend. Then most nights next week are booked up with rehearsals for Friday's TV special. The show's live, so it's got to be good.'

Undaunted, the young man pounced on an opportunity. 'There's a party at RMIT next Friday night, for the start of the new academic year. How about we go after your show?'

'Hmm... I wouldn't be able to get there until about ten-thirty or even eleven, depending on what sort of reception they throw for us afterwards,' she answered, not committing but not turning him down either.

'That's OK,' Jeff shrugged. 'It's at the Uni' Club on Swanston Street. You can't miss the place. Or I could pick you up from wherever you are.'

They had reached the unmarked side entrance to the Dysons' office building. Lynn removed a set of keys from her handbag and unlocked the gate. Her new chaperone hung back, not knowing whether they had reached the part where he was meant to say goodbye. Having spent such a mind-blowing evening together, he wasn't about to make this decision for her. Not if he could help it.

'OK. That sounds good,' she agreed, waving him through. 'I know the place you mean. My brother pointed it out to me. He's got friends at RMIT. I can ask someone to drop me off. Are you coming in?'

Jeff grinned, scarcely believing what he was hearing. 'Thanks, Lynn. That's fantastic.'

The couple walked through the manicured gardens, past a few sets of tables and chairs, their path lit by a line of waist-high lamps. To the dumbfounded young man, the scene was bizarrely similar to how he envisioned C S Lewis' Narnia, and he distracted himself by imagining them re-entering the building through a set of old, wooden wardrobe doors.

On a more serious note though, still fighting his libido, the boy from Sydney's west also realised that the child star was being rather too trusting of him. At sixteen, she of all people ought not to be out walking in the dark with a man she hardly knew, and she definitely shouldn't have invited him in through the gate. He was surprised at her apparent confidence and wondered if there were cameras located around the paths and perimeter, through which the security guard could keep an eye on her.

It also occurred to Jeff at the same moment that he already felt protective of this beautiful fledgling and vowed to convince her next time to take more precautions. No. On second thoughts, he concluded, this discussion must take place regardless of whether he was lucky enough to see her again. The prospect of Lynn Dyson being attacked in the dark filled him with horror. He would never forgive himself if something were to happen without having voiced his concerns and giving her a chance to reduce the risk.

'Can security monitor these gardens?'

'Yes. There are a few cameras strategically placed,' the naïve and light-headed schoolgirl replied. 'No guard dogs though!'

The tall, dark, handsome stranger smiled. The safeguards he employed for his own security had been learned on the downtrodden streets of Sydney's south-west but were equally applicable for susceptible female sporting heroes. Nonetheless, the last thing he wanted was to be accused of interfering.

'Good. I guess there's a fine line between sanctuary and prison,' he ventured, in an attempt to reinforce the point and hoping he wouldn't be overstepping the mark.

Lynn turned towards him as his words sunk in. Who was this man who looked so casual and relaxed, walking along with his hand in his trouser pocket and his jacket sexily thrown over his shoulder, as if he didn't have a care in the world? One minute he was smiling broadly and cracking jokes, and the next he was making keen and somewhat unnerving observations about her personal safety, as if she were the most important thing in the world to him.

'Thanks for looking after me,' the star replied. 'I should be more careful, shouldn't I?'

Jeff nodded and shrugged. 'I think so.'

The air thick with more unspoken thoughts, the pair continued walking towards the back of the building. Putting his arm around her, the nineteen-year-old lightened up by asking about her plans for the weekend. Lynn told him how nice it usually was to have the chance to escape the city on Saturdays and relax on the family's farm until Monday morning, but that this upcoming weekend held a non-stop itinerary of recording and filming.

This was exactly the type of light conversation on which they needed to end, and Jeff stopped his alluring companion before she reached the door, placing his hands on her shoulders and turning her round to face him.

'I've had a great time tonight,' he said, bending to kiss her full on the lips.

To his delight, Lynn didn't pull back this time, and he prolonged the embrace for as long as he could, lifting his left hand to brush her cheek. His mouth could feel the muscles in her face mould into a smile, and his rebellious sex-drive hastened. Once the kiss was over, he hugged the bashful woman in close and stroked her forehead for good measure. He didn't quite know why, but some altogether unexpected instincts had been awakened tonight, quite apart from the fierce and familiar passion kept hidden from the celebrity's view.

'So have I,' the breathless sixteen-year-old responded. 'Thanks very much for inviting me. You're great company.'

The very special young lady unlocked the glass door into the building. Pushing it open, she signalled for Jeff to step inside again. With his blood pressure so high that it rang in his ears, he had to call upon all his powers of deception to remain cool, calm and collected while he walked through the private area of the Dysons' city headquarters. The hot-headed teenager fought not to submit to the irrepressible urge inside, although he was unable to remember a time when he had felt more turned on.

Lynn was indicating up ahead, beyond the lifts and towards the security barrier. 'You'll have to go out the front door, I'm afraid.'

'You've got that the wrong way round, you know,' he quipped, following her through the large, tiled foyer. 'Usually secret visitors get ushered out the back door.'

The schoolgirl giggled again. 'That's true. We do everything backwards here.'

They crossed into the main lift lobby, and she pressed the button, stifling a yawn. This was presumably the clearest signal he would receive from this well-bred and unaffected teenager, who had yet to learn the correct protocol for dismissing a red-blooded paramour at the end of an evening. Jeff took his cue to leave, although this truly *was* the last thing he wanted to do.

'I'd better go. Sleep well, Lynn. Thanks again for a great evening. See you next Friday, or in class on Tuesday, if we get the chance. Hope the show goes well.'

The good-looking man kissed his dream girl again, deliberately in the security guard's line of sight, recalling his earlier patronising attitude.

'Goodnight, Jeff,' the young woman replied, stepping into the lift and leaning against doors which were anxious to gobble up their valuable cargo. 'See you next week.'

As he drank in the shifting mirage, the slender beauty took a pace backwards, and the lift doors were allowed to close. The nobody from New South Wales pushed the bar on the turnstile and nodded to the guard, whose expression didn't alter, and the revolving doors shunted him back out into the fresh air.

Jeff could have run home, such was the energy coursing through his system! Lynn Dyson's last words to him were, "See you next week." From every angle, that was a win. His headache had subsided, and adrenalin was pumping through his body, not to mention the testosterone. He walked past the Victorian Barracks, crossed the road and jogged into Alexandra Gardens, continuing all the way down to the river's edge. He sat down on the first bench he came to, resting his forearms on his knees and staring down at the grass between his feet. He smoked a long-awaited cigarette in the cool night air.

An hour must have passed on that bench, while the tired student replayed the evening several times in his mind, still not quite ready to believe it had actually happened. Another milestone achieved in this strange life of his. The most major milestone so far, in fact. Moving to Melbourne was proving to be an extremely good idea. Lighting another cigarette, he set off towards the Swan Street Bridge. His watch informed him it was eleven-thirty, and he needed to cross over to the north bank and make his way home.

The nineteen-year-old arrived at his second-floor flat, which was situated in a quiet Richmond street, not far from Bridge Road. Climbing the stairs, he steeled himself for the usual battle with his front door. Scarred by the traumas of his childhood, no-one but Jeff Diamond knew the extent of his ongoing personal struggle to overcome the demons he carried with him. Once inside, he jumped into the shower and stood under the cool water for a few minutes, waiting for his pulse rate to return to normal and exercising the many fantasies that were banked up inside his throbbing body.

The dreamer didn't go straight to bed. He stood in front of his bedroom window, looking out towards the city, his fingers playing idly with the souvenir ticket stub. He wondered what Lynn was doing now. Fast asleep, he assumed. He allowed his mind to wander once more over her face, her hair, her breasts, her long legs. He had been feeding forever off the images his memory had stockpiled from the television screen, album covers and magazine articles, and today he had added some new material to his mental inventory: her physical presence, her grace, her gentle humour and her touch.

Jeff Diamond had kissed Lynn Dyson. What about that! How many of her millions of fans could say that? And what was more, he had kissed her as an adult and with the promise of more to come.

Yet there was much more to it even than that, the dreamer realised, as he peeled back the sheet and climbed into bed. The strongest impression with which his dream girl had left him that evening was the apparent similarity in the way their minds worked. There was a woman of substance behind the international artist's polished and successful exterior. Hadn't he always known this though? He had sensed a connection on a level that was notably deeper than anything he had experienced before. Perhaps he was overstating it? And perhaps it had only been he who had felt it? He had no way of knowing, and the troubled teenager sparred with his natural pessimism for the benefit of the doubt.

What the elated man did know however, without a shadow of a doubt, was that his first date with Lynn Dyson had far exceeded all expectations. Plus, there would be a second date. Unless she pulled the pin during the week, that was. How the hell was he going to lead a normal life for eight long days and nights? The previous two had seemed like an eternity. Jeff lay down on top of the bed for a while before he fell asleep, enchanted by a strange, lingering sense of anticipation.

Two-and-a-half hours later, rapidly spiralling downwards, the exhausted man awoke, yelling and in a pool of sweat. Snatching a beer from the fridge, he sat on the couch until his heartbeat slowed, listening to Lynn's record for the millionth time, in an effort to distract himself and to assuage his desire-fuelled physical needs. One more night when his sleep account would slip further into overdraft, despite it having been a very good day otherwise. The music washed over him, and this time he heard a different voice; that of someone he liked very much.

***

Lynn arrived at school on Friday morning to a gaggle of giggling girlfriends, all excited to hear how the date with her mystery boy had gone. Much to their annoyance, she was not prepared to give anything away. Michelle England, her best friend, was the first to put the pressure on.

'Oh, come on, please! You've got to tell us. There must be more to it than "We had a great time."'

The famous schoolgirl sought refuge in some last-minute homework, unable to wipe the grin off her face. She had woken that morning full of joy at having met someone so interesting and secretly couldn't wait to talk about it. She knew it wasn't appropriate for her, the youngest and best protected girl in the class, to be playing in such a grown-up world, especially since this was an

Olympic year and therefore the first big chance she would have to show the world what she was made of.

'No. Nothing happened,' she insisted. 'He was the perfect gentleman. He's got lovely manners and a wicked smile, and you know how good the play was, because you were there. We talked, we had fun. That's it! He's a nice guy.'

'So,' Andrea took over, 'what's next? Are you going to see him again, this nice guy?'

'Maybe,' the starlet teased. 'I'm very busy. I don't have time for a boyfriend.'

The girls weren't buying it. They had never seen their friend enthusiastic about a boy before. Happiness was written all over her face, and they were determined to wheedle the truth out of her somehow.

'But he was so handsome! If you're not interested, can you give him my number?' Michelle asked.

Saved by the bell, the young ladies filed into class. As the day went on, Lynn found herself unusually distracted, often having to force her attention back to the lessons. Her mind was full of enticing images of this enigmatic stranger: those strong hands gripping her shoulders; his chiselled, southern European facial features; his deep, resonant voice and the body language full of temptation were all unexpectedly irresistible to the impressionable teenager. Nevertheless, she could ill afford the luxury of day-dreaming. Her life was planned out to the minute, and her goals were set by others for her to achieve, without regard for these new-found preoccupations. There was no way she would be able to have a proper adult relationship with this gorgeous find. How could she possibly get away with it?

Lynn reflected on the doleful comment she had made to Jeff about freedom. Had he understood? Is that why he had kissed her, or had he been intending to do that anyway? Why was she so affected by this boy? She had many good friends and was never lonely, but perhaps it was now time to find someone more consequential with whom to share life and develop her blossoming ideals.

The more she ruminated, the more Jeff Diamond presented as a conundrum for the celebrity. He was obviously intelligent, independent and impressive, but also inscrutable and intense. Dare she add integrity into the mix? Could he be relied upon to act in her best interest? Her parents had sent her and her elder brother to a series of self-defence training classes, to instil in them a sense of responsibility for their own safety, and she knew she owed it to them and to herself to be wary of this new arrival, about whom she knew absolutely nothing.

But above all, Lynn was sure she had made a real friend last night. Even with her limited experience, she considered they had got along much better with each other than two people usually do on first meeting, regardless of any physical attraction. She didn't really understand why, but somehow this new bond felt symbolic and important.

The dreamy sixteen-year-old focussed back on the teacher, shaking her head a little. Yesterday evening was the first time she had been on a date with someone she didn't already know reasonably well, since her handful of boyfriends to-date had all come from within their usual circle. These were easy friendships to make and break, uncomplicated and childish. The next few days would give her the chance to find out if this was all she needed, or whether she was ready for something more grown-up.

Between now and the following Friday night, Lynn Dyson trusted that she would come to know whether the heady euphoria brought on by her brief encounter with a handsome stranger would settle down, or if her novel desire to be half of a fascinating whole was here to stay. She hoped fervently for the latter.

Save The Last Dance For Me

On the other side of town, Jeff Diamond had spent the weekend seeking sex and sleep, the one to help with the other. He was utterly preoccupied with his dream girl, often finding himself transfixed by the memories of their chaste but auspicious outing to the theatre, and sought as much stimulation as possible in order to push the days along until he could see her again. He was pleased to receive two separate party invitations from university friends, and had taken his pick of female company at both events, walking home from a different suburb on both Saturday and Sunday mornings.

The sleep yield had been modest but better than nothing over the same period. Friday night had been the best, with a full three hours before his nightmares had forced him awake. Saturday night was a complete write-off, having only arrived home a short time before the young man was due at Gerry's, to help him move into his new apartment in South Yarra, and as the weekend finally passed, he had worked on an assignment through the early hours of Monday morning, after less than half an hour's rest.

The dejected student had sworn out loud when he looked at his clock, reaching for the bottle of whisky his mate had given him as a thank-you for his *pro bono* removal services. Great start to the week, he cursed. It always seemed to happen that way when it came to sleep. When he needed the most, he got the least.

Each ensuing weekday followed the same pattern. Jeff would drag himself either to classes or work in the morning, partake in some type of exercise in the late afternoons, grab a quick dinner and then meet up with friends in the evening. He would return home, after sufficient alcohol or sex or both, and fall asleep relatively easily, only to wake up soon thereafter and end up running the streets of Richmond and its surrounds until sunrise.

One benefit delivered by the endless nights, however, was that the inspired composer was able to churn out over thirty new songs in the one week. Inspiration was abundant, for which he was grateful, because it presented him with the potential for earning some much needed money.

The nineteen-year-old had had very little to drink on Monday night, so he postponed his run until sunrise, when he could drive over to Suzanne at the boarding kennels with his blood-alcohol level under the legal limit. They had taken twelve dogs out at once, all piled into her van. It was pandemonium, but Jeff liked to help her out every now and then. He and his best mate's girlfriend had known each other for many years. Similar to Lynn's situation, Suzanne's family moved in wealthy circles. Her parents were neighbours of the Blakes' in the affluent seaside suburb of Mosman, and the privileged couple's relationship had developed from teenage sexual experimentation to a steady, on-again-off-again saga.

In the proceeding years, through high school and into their respective tertiary courses, the gifted student from the bogan west had become firm friends with them both, after having gained a series of bursaries for summer camps normally only attended by private school children. He often found himself mediating between the two headstrong kids and even more regularly sworn to secrecy by one or the other.

Suzanne's great-aunt had recently died, and to everyone's astonishment, had left her boarding kennels to her niece in her will. The aimless twenty-two-year-old had been delighted to be given the chance to move to Victoria at the same time as the boys, and had taken surprisingly easily to the routine demanded by her four-legged guests.

'The Three Musketeers must stick together. All for one and one for all!' she had proclaimed one drunken evening.

Jeff was dying to tell the feisty young woman about his date with Lynn Dyson, but decided against it at the last minute. The endless ribbing he had received in earlier years had subsided once the trio had grown older and had each embarked on adult relationships, but he remained dubious of the reception he might expect from either of them. Despite being Suzanne's boyfriend in theory, Gerry was almost as promiscuous as his sleep-deprived mate, and the only daughter of a successful North Shore real estate agent had long harboured a crush on Jeff which had not been requited. Therefore, with his secret safe for now, the middleman kept quiet and listened to her sob stories about leaky plumbing and disgruntled owners who refused to pay, in return for an invigorating spell in the country air and a complimentary breakfast.

***

February's last Friday had finally arrived, after the longest week in history. The tired student had snatched a blissful, five-minute chat with his favourite schoolgirl, back in her uniform, at the beginning of Tuesday's American History class, before receiving a spiteful warning from the teacher for fraternising with the female students. Great customer service, the undergraduate staff member had thought. He couldn't afford to lose his job though, so allowed the beautiful vision to walk on into the lecture theatre with no more than a wave.

Jeff checked the newspaper to see what time Lynn's TV special was to be broadcast that night: eight-thirty. He wondered whose place he could crash to sit in front of a television.

'Hey, Gerry,' he said, when his friend picked up the telephone. 'Are you going to be at home tonight?'

'No, mate. I'm off to a dinner party with some prospective clients and their blisteringly hot daughter. Why?'

'There's something on TV I want to see,' the honest man confessed. 'Is it OK if I drop by?'

The accountant gave a caustic laugh. 'Does it have anything to do with a certain blonde singer, by any chance? I saw something in the paper today.'

'Might have.'

Not much escaped Gerry's attention, and he scoffed predictably. 'Isn't it about time you invested in your own bloody telly, mate? Then you won't leave any more stains on my new sofa.'

'Ah, come on. That's gross, and grossly unfair too, you bastard,' the younger man took offence. 'I'd hate to think how many bodily fluids have seeped into your couches over the years, and very few of them would be mine.'

'Be my guest,' the businessman capitulated. 'Fuck yourself out.'

'Cheers, mate. Enjoy tonight. *Adiós*.'

After work, Jeff showered, changed into his smart jeans and a collared shirt and ventured out to his car. Would he take it? If Lynn turned up, he wanted to be able to move around easily if he needed to. And if she didn't turn up, he would probably drown his sorrows somewhere closer to home. He looked at the old Ford and felt a pang of fear for what the privileged young woman might make of such a rust bucket. What choice did he have though? The blue beast was clean enough, and it was all he had. He was not about to start pretending to be someone he wasn't. He could easily borrow Gerry's brand new BMW, but then he would have to come clean sooner or later that it wasn't his. Provided there was a sooner or later, of course...

Parking near his friend's apartment was always difficult on a Friday night, owing to the wide selection of restaurants and night clubs concentrated in the area around the northern end of Chapel Street. The nineteen-year-old eventually found a spot about half a kilometre away and walked back to the flashy building, set back off Toorak Road. He opened the lobby door with no drama, given it was glass, but the front door to the apartment was an entirely different matter. It had three separate locks, meaning there was no way one could gain a quick entry. By the time Jeff made it to the other side, he had already broken into a sweat and was breathing heavily.

The impatient man helped himself to a beer from Gerry's fridge and noticed a bottle of champagne lying on its side. The schmoozer evidently had big plans for the hot daughter, he smirked. His smile then widened further when he entered the lounge room to see a set of shelves piled up on the floor and a rather ugly set of holes in the wall. Another failed attempt at home handyman! When would the idiot ever learn? Gerald Blake Junior was simply not cut out for manual labour.

Switching on the television and selecting the correct channel, Jeff settled down and waited for the show to begin. He recollected the disgusting remark concerning the couch; a revolting thought, but probably accurate. His fertile imagination soon drifted off into fantasyland, finding himself at one of the local night clubs that he had just walked past, where the golden-haired Lynn Dyson arrived with her entourage and singled him out in the crowd. "He's the one I want," he heard her saying, before that elusive commodity, sleep, swallowed him almost straightaway.

Fortuitously, something in his subconscious must have woken him, because the exhausted man became suddenly aware of orchestral strains playing a hit from MAC's recent record. He jolted himself awake and looked at his watch, which said eight-thirty-three. Thank Christ! He hadn't missed anything. Bloody hell! If a god really existed, surely he would never let that happen. Not tonight...

Jeff fetched himself another beer from the fridge. His evil twin thought to hide the champagne bottle, but his good side triumphed, and he resisted the temptation, launching himself back onto the sofa just as the announcer was introducing the stars. The familiar faces of John Betts and Richard Kerr, guitarist and keyboard player and Lynn's co-writers, were shown in close-up, along with the drummer, percussionist and a flautist. The avid fan knew them all from the album notes.

Then there she was, running onto the stage to vociferous applause. His Lynn, the girl he had kissed and held hands with, looking awesome in skin-tight pants and a glittery top. She sported a wide grin on her face and didn't seem at all nervous, quickly waving to the cameras before sitting down at the piano and bashing out a rhythm. The concert was underway, and the musicians worked through a mixture of old hits and new material.

From Gerry's lounge room, the superstar's mystery man didn't miss a beat. He liked what he saw, and even more than usual now that he had met her in the flesh. Better still, she was spending much more time at the front of the stage than she used to when the group first sprang to fame, and tonight she was in full view of the energetic audience for the majority of the show.

Jeff wondered if the stunning musician might be thinking about catching up with him later while she was on stage. He dared to think she might be, and hoped this might partially account for her apparent *joie de vivre*. *Don't be stupid*, he chastised himself. Lynn Dyson was a professional. She would be concentrating on her performance. And so should he...

Anxiety building, the young man calculated the time at which he would need to depart South Yarra, in order to ensure he reached RMIT before his date arrived. She had said ten-thirty would be the earliest she was likely to get there. It was nine-thirty now, and the show was still in full swing.

After four or five more numbers, the main set was over at about ten o'clock, sadly for every audience member bar one... There would be at least two *encores*, but the teenager was leaving nothing to chance. He needed to traverse the city and find parking on the eve of a warm summer's weekend, and the nightspots all over town would be teaming by now. Switching off the television, his heart began to beat faster, and he fleetingly regretted not having taken the opportunity to add to the decoration on Gerry's furniture.

Get a grip, the aroused man scolded his reflection in the hallway mirror. Locking the door behind him, he descended in the lift and wove through the back streets towards his car. It was a still, humid night, and he checked himself out again in a shop window while walking along the crowded footpath. Pretty good, he declared. How could she resist?

The mighty Fairlane coughed twice and sprang into action. Jeff meandered northwards through the backstreets of the inner east, which were no longer catching him out so frequently these days. He crossed Victoria Parade, turned left down Langridge Street, then into Brunswick Street and on up towards the suburb of Carlton, where the University Club was located. He was lucky to find a parking space within a hundred metres of the door. Perfect! The gods were back on duty.

The giant shindig was already packed to bursting point. The newcomer didn't know too many people there but soon hooked up with a few mates from his linguistics class. He found some mindless diversion by dancing with a group of highly animated girls for a few tracks and drinking neat Coca-Cola, before entering into a shouting match with the disc jockey, who was grateful for the company of a man with a trail of nubile dancers behind him. In exchange for a drink, Jeff persuaded him to play a particular song on his cue. All part of the next stage of the ambitious man's master plan, which had worked a treat so far.

And so on to stage two of tonight's plan he went. Thankfully, the likeable party boy already knew the blokes on the door. He had met them at other events he had attended during his short time in Melbourne, and had even backed them up a couple of times, when their numbers had been low in the face of trouble. As the kid from Canley Vale had learned only too well, it never hurt to make friends with security, even if one was already adept at defending oneself in a drunken brawl. They tended to stick by those they knew if the police arrived, which was fairly essential for a tearaway like him.

The burly quartet had laughed in the Sydneysider's face when he first suggested that Lynn Dyson would be rocking up later, requiring him to place a ten dollar bet with one of them to be assured of their attention. He made them promise to let him know as soon as she arrived. Not prepared to take any risks tonight, he put up with their jeers of derision. His optimistic side looked forward to seeing the incredulous expressions on their faces when he and the pretty, blonde superstar were leaving together at the end of the night.

With all the necessary components of his plan in place, Jeff went back into the main hall to find someone else to dance with. He had decided to take the hitherto inconceivable step of staying sober, preferring to keep a clear head in case the need for quick thinking arose. To compensate, he contented himself with another cigarette, and before he even had a chance to select a partner for his next diversion, he was accosted by Martina, a German girl with whom he had enjoyed a one night stand a couple of weeks ago.

'Jeff, what happened to you?'

'Hey!' the good-looking student shouted above the music. 'D'you want to dance? Having a good time?'

He could tell the woman from Düsseldorf wasn't at all happy with him, but she followed him onto the dance floor nevertheless. Women always did. "The Pied Piper of Sex", as Suzanne was known to call him. Either that or "The Love 'em and Leave 'em Kid". Both were well deserved.

'I thought you would call me.'

'I'm sorry,' Jeff sought to close the conversation down, on perennially familiar ground. 'Been busy. Didn't promise anything, did I?'

The jilted maiden shrugged and pouted. 'Whatever.'

The popular dancer's watch said ten-forty-five. Meeting the angry Martina had helped to pass some time at least, but after a few more dances with a few more forgettable girls, he unwillingly began to think he might be leaving with one of them after all. Trying not to give up hope, he fought the urge to down a few beers to ward off his creeping pessimism.

And then everything changed. All of a sudden, Eddie from the door was by his side, holding out a ten dollar note. Confidence restored in an instant, Jeff opened his left hand, and the blue note was slapped into his palm.

'Is she here?'

'Bloody oath!' replied the bouncer, as they walked back towards the door. 'Who are you, man?'

The long-time fan recognised Nick Mason, who had been a MAC band member for a while, and alongside him was the lad he had seen the other day on crutches. Excited beyond belief, he couldn't locate Lynn at first, probably because she was signing autographs or something, but then, from among the throng, he heard her voice calling his name, and his heart took flight.

The student found her and gave her a bear hug without really thinking. 'It's great to see you. Thanks for coming.'

Despite his normally cool exterior, Jeff's reaction couldn't have been more honest, given the deliverance flooding through his veins. He guided Lynn and the others towards the main dance floor and waved a hand to the open-mouthed disc jockey, who acknowledged him with a thumbs-up sign. Master plan once more in execution mode.

'Has it been good?' the young star asked, struggling to be heard above the music. 'How long have you been here?'

'Only about an hour,' her date yelled back. 'I watched the show. Good as ever! Are you happy with it?'

Dancing casually in their circle, which included the extrovert on sticks, Jeff again noticed the quizzical look he remembered very clearly from their first meeting. He hadn't quite worked out what it signified yet, but it seemed as if she was seeking information.

'You ask the best questions,' she smiled and squeezed his arm. 'Yes, thanks. It went well.'

'D'you hear what's playing?' he distracted her, pointing into the airwaves.

Obediently, Lynn listened to the music for a few seconds. 'Is it The Drifters?'

Jeff nodded and raised his eyebrows, as if he too was after more.

'"Save The Last Dance For Me",' Lynn completed her answer.

The sixteen-year-old giggled, gathering that her expressive mystery man apparently still wanted more. After another second or two, she eventually solved the puzzle and gave him a melting smile.

'Oh, yes! Did you request it? That's so nice! Yes! Of course I will.'

'Thank you,' the handsome stranger sounded relieved, lifting her hand and placing it on his chest, in order that she might feel how hard his heart was thumping.

The corners of Lynn's mouth drooped comically, pulling her hand away. 'Sorry! It's been a long day.'

'Come on. Let's get a drink.'

But Lynn hung back. 'Jeff, wait, please. I want to introduce you to my friends.'

The thirsty man halted in his tracks, for this was a stop worth making. He wasn't going to object to being dragged further into the world of Lynn Dyson. Her fellow musicians would be like an extended family for the young star. It was important to take the time to acknowledge this.

'Sure,' he agreed.

The two men stepped forward, and Lynn introduced Nick Mason and Lloyd de l'Enseigne. Nick was built like a rugby prop forward, with whom no-one would care to cross paths in the middle of the night. A gentle giant however, Jeff immediately got the impression that he was no fighter. Lloyd was tall and thin, with a quiff of styled hair which looked somewhat laughable on one so young. The actor also fancied himself as a rock'n'roll singer in his spare time.

'These guys brought me over here,' the young woman explained, watching the three men shake hands.

'What happened to your leg?' Jeff asked the taller of the two, keen to prove Professor Martin's theory wrong.

'Cricket, actually. Dull, I know! I dived for a catch and came down heavy on my ankle,' the gangly teenager laughed. 'It's fractured in two places.'

'Nasty!' the dark-haired newcomer grimaced. 'Well, thanks for driving Lynn over, guys. Are you staying? Can I buy you a drink?'

The university student bought a round of beers for himself and the two couriers, while their under-aged charge was happy with a lemon, lime and bitters. While waiting to be served, he reflected on how long it had been since he had last bought a non-alcoholic drink for a girl. Nick and Lloyd took their leave after a single beer, confident that their friend was in safe hands. The recent arrival from over the border in New South Wales seemed like a nice bloke, and the star of the show was obviously comfortable to be left with him.

For his part, the nineteen-year-old wasn't sorry to see them go, since he anticipated the walls they defended around their precious princess would have become considerably higher and harder for this peasant to scale once his plan for her began to unfold. He stood with his prize at the entrance of the dance hall and watched the boys disappear, under the bewildered surveillance of the official security team.

'Those two are my minders,' Lynn informed her date when they were finally alone and the volume of the music subsided between tracks. 'It's quite sweet, really. My dad didn't ask them to do it, but he told them they were saving him money, so they're chuffed.'

Smiling at the innocent tale, Jeff led her back to the dance floor. The skin-tight red satin pants the young star had been wearing on stage had been replaced by equally figure-hugging jeans, and the neckline of her top was cut just low enough for someone of his height to find interesting. The long-awaited night was about to begin at last, as his libido was keen to remind him.

'Do you ever have paid bodyguards?' he asked.

The lithe blonde nodded, frowning at the continued difficulty of shouting above the music. 'Yes, when I'm overseas I do. And occasionally at tennis tournaments, when we have to stay far from the venue. Hardly ever in Melbourne though.'

They danced through three or four numbers, doing their best to communicate over the noise. Spotting the young celebrity in the crowd, a number of people came closer to satisfy their curiosity. Some tried to ask questions, and Lynn responded in her usual gracious way, until a couple of drunken students became a little too excited to see her, and even rather free with their hands at one point, requiring Jeff to step in and send them on their way.

'Now *you're* my minder!' she laughed. 'I keep insisting I don't need one, but maybe I do.'

The young man looked at his watch: nearly midnight. 'What d'you want to do? Did you want to get something to eat?'

'Oh, yes, please. I'm starving, but where are we going to get food at this time of night?'

Her date chuckled. 'You can't possibly know how ironic that question is...'

The confused teenager gave her mystery man another enquiring look. 'Why? What do you mean?'

'Oh, nothing,' the young man dismissed her questions, regretting his impulsiveness. 'I'll tell you later.'

The disc jockey had chosen a big ballad to end the evening. From all around, couples were drifting onto the dance floor. Some were very worse for wear, after a long night's drinking, and needed to lean on each other to stay upright. Lynn pointed out some especially pathetic examples and laughed at their lack of coordination. She was delighted to be part of this very adult scene, especially in the arms of her handsome stranger. She guessed he had gone to a lot of trouble to make her feel at home in the unfamiliar environment, even though she still felt considerably out of her depth.

Completely and unusually sober, as Friday lapsed into Saturday, Jeff Diamond took Lynn Dyson's hand and led her to the middle of the floor. The song was "Stairway To Heaven" by Led Zeppelin, which had been a monster hit in the UK at the end of the previous year. The ambitious songwriter took a mental snapshot of the fact that he was about to have a slow dance with an Australian superstar, who herself had posted no less than five number one singles during the same year.

Mesmerised by swaying hips in front of him, the young man reached his hands out to his stunning dance partner and pulled her in closer to him, sliding his right hand past her left shoulder and down onto her back. He was so glad he hadn't been drinking, because this was surely a moment to savour with all his faculties about him. His actions were controlled and deliberate, and he was not going to push her too far. This was way too important an opportunity to ruin for the sake of instant gratification.

On the spur of the moment, Jeff took yet another atypical decision, to do something else he didn't usually do at discos: he danced. Married with his natural musical affinity, the ballroom dancing lessons he had been forced to take with Gerry and his sisters during his teens, with the express purpose of making up the numbers, had turned him into quite some dancer. He took Lynn's right hand in his left and held it straight down by his side, before leaning in and gently leading her in a very slow and artistic Latin ballet.

After a few bars, Lynn looked up appreciatively into the handsome face. 'Is this a tango?'

Jeff winked and said nothing, merely sweeping the unassuming temptress across the floor in time to the music. Happy to be led, it was as if she had become weightless, floating to him and away from him on command. Then before this enjoyable sensation had a chance to die away, he had whipped her round in a circle, and they came deliciously face-to-face.

'We are dancing a tango, aren't we?' the young performer persisted. 'You're a good dancer. You really feel the music.'

Her partner nodded and kissed her, temporarily suspending the dance while their heartbeats raced on ahead. He could really feel everything.

'You're worth it,' he whispered close to her ear. 'So do you.'

With the same intensity she had felt during their first date streaming through her memory, Lynn let the expert dancer glide her over the floor, appreciating the changes of tempo which he introduced regularly into the routine. She laughed in surprise when they almost bumped into other couples and were required to shift course without notice, each time being gathered in closer to this man's inviting body.

Eventually the music finished, and the pair kissed again, oblivious of all around them. Their chests rising and falling with the exertion, his hand felt divine against her ribcage, bringing her to a smooth stop while their lips remained connected.

'Still hungry?' Jeff asked, leading her off the floor.

'Yes, I am. Where could we go?'

The night owl knew of a couple of places open at such an hour, serving those who had finished serving others. However, the seeds of another plan were rapidly germinating in his head, prompted not unexpectedly from elsewhere. They walked outside into the warm night air, past Eddie and his mates, whose jaws dropped once again. The arrogant student cocked his head as if to say, "What did you expect?" but chose not to labour the point. He had what he wanted right here beside him. He hardly needed any further affirmation.

'Wow! Beautiful temperature!' Lynn cried out, spinning around girlishly.

Her equally euphoric companion pointed some way down the road, to where his car was parked. 'This way, please.'

Walking close to the kerb, the chivalrous young man guided his leading lady along the street, keeping half a pace behind her. He could sense she had become slightly nervous again, so deliberately avoided any direct contact. It made scant difference though, because the force-field generated from being so close was palpable for both youngsters.

Once alongside the old, blue Fairlane, Jeff opened the passenger door for the young star to get in, hoping she wouldn't take too much notice of its condition. Jumping in on the other side and flicking the gear stick into neutral, he caught his breath. Christ Almighty! Lynn Dyson was sitting in the passenger seat of his clapped-out Ford. What the hell was he doing? What if her father knew where she was? She was only sixteen. A child, but legal at least. Did *she* know what she was doing? Perhaps he ought really to drive her home...

Thankfully the engine fired first time, and the creaking sedan pulled out of its parking space and into the steady stream of traffic. Out of the corner of his eye, the driver saw his dream girl turn to look at him.

'You OK?'

'I'm fine,' she answered, while her eyes added, 'Why shouldn't I be?'

He grinned, desperate to play down his own, nervous excitement. 'Just checkin'.'

They drove in an easterly direction, down Victoria Parade and towards Richmond. Quite coincidentally, the radio station's late night disc jockey was in the middle of giving the MAC concert a rave review, and their fingers tangled in a duel, hers to turn it off and his to leave it playing.

'Where are we going?' the sixteen-year-old asked, looking up and realising they were heading away from the Central Business District.

OK, Jeff resolved. Now was the time to make a serious choice. He could relinquish some control in the hope that Lynn wanted the same thing as he did, but with the risk of his master plan being subject to negotiation and potential delay. Or alternatively, he could carry on driving and ignore her concerns, trading on his track record of winning women over with a few choice phrases and well-timed actions. The latter had a greater likelihood of short-term success, yet the former was the right thing to do. Short-term success he could procure any day and from any woman, but Lynn Dyson represented the long term, however foreign the concept seemed to his eager body.

'Lynn, say no if you want to, and I promise I'll drive you home, but I'm heading for my place,' he stated as plainly and unambiguously as he could. 'We could get some food there. Open a bottle of wine. It's the butler's night off, and the cook's sick, so we'll have to fend for ourselves, I'm afraid, but I'm sure we'll cope. Whatever you want. I just want to spend time with you. Is that OK?'

The pretty teenager stared straight ahead, watching some of the city's venerable, old hospitals pass her by as they drove eastwards. Food, wine and what else? Her heart was beating fast, in a wild maelstrom of heady excitement and fear of the unknown. Alone after dark with a man... As she had told her friends, it had to happen someday, didn't it?

Jeff could see the young woman considering her options, battling with her *naïvetée* despite his attempts to make light of things. Calling on his abundant and oft-used charms, he helped her out. At least if she requested that he drive her back to Dyson Administration, he would then be presented with another chance to have a crack at prolonging the date.

'I'm not going to force you into anything. You don't have to be worried, but if you want, I'll just take you home.'

'No,' Lynn sighed emphatically. 'Jeff, I really like you. You make me feel special. I'd love to see your Richmond apartment.'

The student's heart leaped into his mouth, and suddenly his plan was back on track. Even the car seemed to drive better with the choice made.

'Right answer,' he declared, smacking the steering wheel to dispel some of his own tension. '¡Vamanos!'

His tiny flat was on the second floor, with no lift. They climbed the six flights of stairs from the basement car park, engrossed in conversation about The Beatles, The Rolling Stones and Elvis Presley. The prodigious performer had met them all, several times of course, and the songwriter was fascinated to hear the inside information. They reached the top landing, and he handed her his key-ring with the house key already separated. She accepted it with a shy smile and unlocked the door, revealing a dark hallway. *Take it easy*, Jeff warned himself, reaching in and switching on the light. He was very relieved to have got past this latest hurdle without having to explain any suspicious behaviour.

'OK,' he announced, holding his hands out. 'Welcome to *Casa Diamond*! Now for the tour. Stand here, *s'il vous plaît, mademoiselle Dyson*.'

The host pointed to a spot at the end of the hallway and steered the gorgeous figure by the shoulders towards it. A little stiffly, the celebrity did as she was told.

Jeff took a deep breath. 'Quarter turn right... kitchen... again... lounge room... again... bathroom... again... bedroom. That's it.'

Having spun a full circle, Lynn was laughing and swivelling on her heels, first to one side and then to the other. 'Can I do it again?'

'No, you can't,' he joked. 'It's a once in a lifetime experience.'

Christ! The nineteen-year-old couldn't remember ever feeling this skittish, his pulse racing off the top of the scale. This girl's smile was hypnotising its willing subject. They headed into the kitchen, and the resident opened the refrigerator. The door creaked noisily, as it always did, exactly like his car.

'¡Bueno! ¿Qué podemos comer?' he asked rhetorically. 'I've got steaks, chips, salad or toast. Take your pick.'

'Steak and salad sound good but they'll take ages to make,' the young woman replied, enjoying his company too.

This man was so fascinating to her. In fact, he was unlike anyone she had ever met. It was as if he could read her mind, responding perfectly to her every emotion.

'No, the steaks won't take long,' her mysterious stranger countered with enthusiasm. 'Ten minutes, tops. D'you want a beer or some wine?'

'No, thanks. You have one though. Don't let my age stop you from drinking.'

Jeff laughed at her quirky response, leaning into the fridge for a bottle and twisting its top off. 'It won't, thanks! I'll open some wine in a minute. And I'll casually ignore your age if you make yourself at home.'

Whoa! There was that smile again… Against all the odds, it appeared his new plan was working.

The self-sufficient student grabbed a frying pan and placed it on the stove. His guest immediately grabbed the chopping block which was propped up on the draining board and, looking for a knife, opened the top drawer to find it very sparsely populated. She giggled, looking from the drawer to her host and then back to the drawer, with a look of consternation on her face.

'I think you've been robbed.'

Jeff smiled at her natural sense of timing and joined in the charade, sliding over and peering into the drawer with her.

'Apparently so,' he agreed, resting his hand on her shoulder and feeling her shudder in surprise. 'It's a dodgy area for cutlery thieves, Richmond.'

Selecting the one and only sharp knife, Lynn chopped the salad ingredients and spread them over two plates, having ascertained that the flat had also been visited by the phantom salad bowl thief.

'Let's have some music,' the distracted man suggested, already halfway into the lounge room. 'Have you heard of this mob?'

The opening track of the most recent MAC album began to play, still on the turntable from the previous week. Objecting, the superstar ran after him.

'Oh, not that! They're dreadful. What else have you got?'

Jeff laughed, reaching out to grab her but then thinking better of it. 'You choose,' he offered. 'I need to turn the steaks.'

He opened the bottle of *Rioja* which he had purchased opportunistically a few days ago. It had cost significantly more than his usual wine budget, but he wouldn't have had it any other way right now. He poured two large glasses and went back to check on the steaks, leaving the wine to absorb the warm night air. Lynn chose a Cliff Richard album and set it playing on the record player.

'Good choice,' the successful musician heard from the kitchen.

The strains of "Do You Wanna Dance?" rang out, bringing her host back in from the kitchen. This time, using the music as an excuse, he took hold of the performer's elegant fingers and rock'n'rolled her energetically. Her shoulders felt strong under his purposeful grip, and he appreciated the easy control in her movements, the result of a lifetime of physical training.

'Wow! That was amazing!' the visitor gasped, as the track faded. 'You're so different from all the boys I know. It's great. You're into the theatre and dancing, when they're just into football and being stupid.'

'Oh, I can do that too,' Jeff smirked, ecstatic at her compliments, 'but thanks anyway.'

The needle slid into the next track, which was a slow ballad entitled "Constantly". The perceptive man could tell it was a song Lynn really liked, and its lyric was uncannily appropriate for their circumstance. They were both pulled into its mood quickly, the rich baritone voice evoking a gamut of emotions in both dancers.

Without her shoes, Lynn Dyson seemed less imposing and more childlike, which was at once endearing and frightening for the boy from Sydney's west. She flicked a strand of hair away from her face and smiled up at him, and the vivid attraction made his insides jump. As the last verse repeated, Jeff slowed the dance right down and pulled her tight against his body. She stiffened again, so he relaxed his grip a little.

'Sorry,' he breathed against her face.

'That's OK,' Lynn replied. 'It's fine. You surprised me, that's all.'

'No more surprises, I promise.'

The tall, handsome stranger spoke with a sensitivity that made the novice feel safer. As the strings faded and the final phrase was sung, both became aware of their chests heaving as their lungs took in the shared air. "You're constantly deep in my heart," the British vocalist concluded, while the show-off deftly manœuvred his partner to one side, to enable him to lift the needle and play the last minute or so of the song again. *Never a truer word spoken*, he acknowledged silently, wondering what the woman in his arms might be thinking.

'I'm going to kiss you now,' he added, syllable by syllable, with a wry smile on his face. 'Just so you know…'

The beautiful young woman started to laugh, but the sound was soon consumed by his kiss, deep and passionate. They were no longer dancing, but still the expert moved their connected bodies in time to the music, gently stroking the bare skin around her neck and collarbones. She could feel him pressing against her. Not tightly, but enough to show her exactly what was taking place.

Both were scared that singing along, or even mouthing the words, would give too much away at this early stage, coming to the realisation that such communication was actually expendable. The connection that had been established the previous week remained alive and kicking, and was causing both hearts to race far faster than any song's beat. Jeff slid his hand up Lynn's back, until it was gently following the muscle across the top of her shoulder. It came to rest in the hollow at the base of her skull, and he felt her body relax into his insistent grip and her long hair brush against his fingers.

Tipping her head backwards, Jeff looked deep into those all-forgiving blue eyes and kissed her again.

'Stay?'

A razor-sharp silence rang around the room, slicing swathes through the atmosphere. The awestruck sixteen-year-old didn't hesitate for long, totally overtaken by the romance of the moment.

'Yes. OK.'

Her mystery man threw back his dark mane, eyes closed, and gave thanks to any and all gods who could possibly have had any influence over this latest, spectacular decision. The radiant face belonging to his dream girl now rested tantalisingly against his chest, and he placed his right hand firmly on the side of her head, kissing her hair. For such an impromptu plan, there could be no better result imaginable.

The song finished for the second time, and the speechless couple returned to the kitchen to serve dinner. The ambiance in the tiny flat was electric, refusing to be diffused by the light-hearted banter they both adopted to hide the myriad powerful feelings thrashing through their minds and bodies. With full plates and a large glass of tap water each, to accompany the red wine, the delirious pair left the kitchen to eat.

Back in the lounge room, Lynn proposed a toast, lifting her glass to his. 'To your burglars! Thanks for leaving us two glasses.'

Jeff leaned forward to kiss her again, as their glasses touched. This girl was so unbelievably cute. As they ate, he allowed his mind to wander far, far away into the potential of their unlikely situation. How far would they venture tonight? Would Lynn Dyson want to go where he wanted to take her? Would his dream girl really become his lover before the sun came up?

'I hope there's not a crowd of journalists waiting in the next room to report that I'm drinking alcohol,' the sixteen-year-old joked, jolting the dreamer back to the here and now.

'A crowd?' he exclaimed, waving his hands around theatrically. 'And where do you think a crowd could hide in this place?'

Enjoying her very late dinner, the celebrity took time to look around for the first time. There was a guitar pitched against the end of the couch, and a small electronic keyboard on the floor by the window. The room was not exactly messy, but there were books and newspapers everywhere. The walls were bare except for one picture of a yacht against a sunset. It was a boy's place, plain and simple.

Jeff saw her eyes fix on the gaudy print. 'Beautiful, isn't it?'

His guest couldn't be sure if he was being serious.

'Is it?' she chanced, not yet trusting her instincts about his taste.

The student smiled kindly. 'No, it's not. It's hideous. It was a gift from my landlord, and I should really take it down. The rest of my art collection's on loan to the National Gallery.'

'Oh, really?' the young star queried, laughing. 'And I thought it was burglars again.'

Jeff shook his head, enjoying their easy conversation. 'Great answer. You're a very practised diplomat.'

'And you're an expert manipulator,' the smart schoolgirl retorted.

Christ! The level of tension in the room suddenly ratcheted up another notch, and both pairs of eyes widened at a new and confusing pressure which had filled the room. This insightful observation had come out of the blue, the young man mused. Was this really what she was thinking? Bloody good pick-up actually, yet bad news though too. He certainly didn't intend to manipulate her in a coercive way, but had to admit it was a fine line. He was certainly guilty of assuming he could dictate the way the evening panned out, and his conscience got the better of him again.

'You don't have a television,' Lynn changed the subject, unaware of the wheels spinning in Jeff's head.

'No,' he replied. 'I need to get one though. It was an experiment when I moved here, to see how long I could last without one. But I think I've reached the threshold already. For example, I had to go over to my mate's place to watch your show.'

'Oh. Did you like it?'

The life-long fan shrugged. 'Not bad. Up to your usual standards.'

Lynn appeared to have already forgotten all about the previous evening's concert. Given how far the pair had come since he had sat in front of Gerry's television, watching the very same talented beauty performing inside, it wasn't difficult to see how that might happen. In a matter of hours, the superstar in the box had somehow found her way into his flat and was now eating from a plate on her knees, sitting on his couch.

Whatever forces were at play tonight, this was no longer a case of "singing sportswoman meets nobody from somewhere west of Sydney," the testosterone-charged philosopher acknowledged in silence. No way! He was quietly convinced that what they were currently witnessing in his tiny lounge room was the unavoidable collision of two matching souls.

'Gee, thanks! It seems like a long time ago,' the dreamy musician responded. 'Was that only today?'

Taking a mouthful of steak to refocus his mind, Jeff shook his head. 'No. It's tomorrow already.'

With a frustrated look on her face, Lynn threatened to whack his knee with her empty plate, and the nimble man quickly swung his legs out of the way.

'Think you're so clever?' she yelped. 'You know what I mean! We haven't slept, so it's still today.'

Laughing, the host again recognised an unwitting irony in her statement. And an innocence too. He sighed, as more guilty thoughts crowded his head.

'Incidentally, where should you be?'

'Not here,' the blonde starlet answered with a coy grin.

'Thought not,' the humble student nodded.

'My mum and younger brother and sister have already gone to the farm for the weekend,' she explained. 'I told them I was going to a party and then going back to Admin, which I will at some stage.'

Swallowing down his final mouthful of food, the handsome stranger winked at her, again hit by a chilling memory of the kidnap scenario he had pictured during their first meeting.

'You do have some freedom then,' he reminded her, 'compared to a lot of people your age.'

'People my age?' Lynn echoed, frowning slightly. 'You sound like my dad! But I suppose you're right. My parents trust me, and so far I haven't done anything to tell them they shouldn't.'

Jeff watched the young woman place her knife and fork together on her plate, sitting tall and elegant on his couch. So far? So what was on her mind? This angelic creature was much more open with him than he had expected, and it made him a little uneasy. It would be so simple to take advantage of her inexperience, only to have it all come tumbling down as soon as she or her parents wised up to him. He had to play it straight with this extra-special person. He needed an ally rather than a hostage; someone who would be complicit in her own capture…

'Well, I'm surprised you're here,' he admitted. 'Overjoyed, mind you, but still surprised.'

The starlet giggled. 'Me too.'

Empty plates deposited on the coffee table, the young man refilled their wine glasses and sat on the floor in front of Lynn's legs while she reclined into the couch. They talked about anything and everything, each new topic of conversation sparking another. He asked her about the professional tennis circuit, and she asked him how different he found Victorians to people from New South Wales. He described his keen desire to travel the world, and she gave him the grand tour of her favourite places.

'Excuse me for a minute,' the polite teenager announced after a while, standing up.

'Can you remember where to go?'

The young woman smiled at his absurd suggestion, melting his insides yet again. 'I should be OK,' she nodded. 'If I'm too long, send out a search party.'

'Oh, don't worry about that! I absolutely will,' the covetous nineteen-year-old replied, already feeling his blood pressure rise at the prospect of letting this new ray of sunshine out of his sight.

Slow down, the compulsive man scolded himself. *She won't run away.* Taking a large gulp from his glass, he lifted their plates and took them out to the kitchen, daring to let his mind wander to the way he needed this night to end and hoping above all that they both wanted the same thing. Out of the corner of his eye, he watched the slender blonde slip past the open doorway and back into the lounge room. He wondered if she had ever set foot inside such a modest home and what might possibly be going through her mind. Drying his hands, he returned to find her in her rightful place: on his couch, leafing through a car magazine she had found on the floor.

The ecstatic host brushed Lynn's shoulder lightly when he passed by, refilling his wine glass with the remainder of the bottle. She shivered and looked up into his eyes, as his tall frame walked around to face her. The alcohol was relaxing them both gradually, despite the apprehension still hanging in the air. The privileged teenager was obviously no stranger to wine, in spite of her tender age.

While they talked some more, the student noticed his mind drift involuntarily to her body several times. He initially pulled it back, until after a while it became virtually impossible to rein in his thoughts. Finally, he gave up trying, and instantly his most basic of instincts leaped into action. The driven teenager hadn't formulated this part of his plan in detail. He would have to wing it.

Jeff hadn't had a cigarette for over an hour and had scarcely even missed it until this moment. It was just what he needed to mellow out a little, keen to make the night last as long as possible. He walked over to the window, throwing it open wide to the night air. Lynn's eyes followed him, thinking how impressive he seemed; tall and strong, tanned and very Mediterranean-looking, dressed in blue jeans and a white shirt with the cuffs turned over a couple of times to reveal muscular forearms. He looked amazing, in fact.

As the young Casanova came back towards the couch, the weight of his guest's stare turned him on still further, boosting his ever-confident ego. He picked up an ashtray, the packet of cigarettes and his lighter from the coffee table and sat back down on the floor at her feet. He placed the ashtray on the floor by his right knee, to protect her as much as possible from the smoke.

Lynn declined his offered of a cigarette with a wave of her hand and a smile. 'No, thanks.'

'Do you mind if I do?' he asked, taking one out of the packet anyway.

'It's your flat,' she reminded him, and also reminding herself with a slight shiver.

Pretty soon, the nicotine hit the spot, and the student felt his nerves calm down sufficiently to marshal some semblance of composure. Up to a point, that was. This gorgeous woman's smile was completely engaging. And those tight jeans over her long, slim, never-ending legs... Jeff could make out the line of her breasts under her T-shirt, and his erection nagged unrelenting in his lap. He began to stroke her right thigh and received that same, mysterious look again. He couldn't decide whether she was scared or interested. *Take it slowly*, he nagged back.

The nineteen-year-old was in trouble though. His body was no longer the slightest bit interested in taking it slowly. His mind flashed back to Gerry's place and wished he had done what his friend had obviously expected him to do. At that stage, he had had no idea which way the night would go, but a pre-date ejaculation would definitely have bought him some time. Right now, he could really do without the screaming imperative which possessed him like a hellion.

Still their free-flowing conversation continued however. No matter which topic either teenager raised, the other would always seem to have an opinion for airing. Tips for making studying more effective were valuable lessons for the younger, while song-writing techniques were keenly lapped up by the elder. Until, that was, at one-thirty on Saturday morning, the hot-blooded young man's patience was finally shot.

'Lynn,' Jeff began, staring into her eyes with a serious expression that made her nervous again. 'I'm going to ask you something that you've got to promise to say no to, if it's not what you want.'

The blonde beauty gazed expectantly at him. 'OK. What is it?'

'As you can probably guess, I'd really like to take you to bed tonight,' his calmest voice continued, covering his inner agitation. 'But if it's not what you want, I'll stay out here, and you can have the bedroom.'

The well-bred young lady wilted, suddenly appearing confused and more than a little embarrassed. She paused before responding, clutching her wine glass with both hands and staring into it. After a few seconds, she ventured a reply with some trepidation.

'I thought I'd already answered that question, when you asked me to stay.'

The empathetic man felt sorry for her. He didn't want to make her uncomfortable. They were both scared, but for very different reasons.

'Well, yeah. I did, sort of,' the handsome man replied with a grin. 'I'd be more than happy for you just to stay here, but I'd *really* like to take you to bed. Like you wouldn't believe, in fact.'

'Well, why didn't you just say that?'

'I did!'

'Ha! Gotcha!' his stunning guest chanced a laugh, before adding with more reservation. 'I know you did. I just didn't hear it that way.'

Lynn felt slightly relieved that her honesty was not being abused. Her insistent and evidently much more experienced companion was prepared to give her some space to work things out, without making fun of her or taking the situation too seriously. So this was how things worked in the adult world...

Great, Jeff thought, looking directly into her eyes and seeing no objections. That was twice he had asked her now. What was that, if not a green light?

Sublime Encounter

Gulping down his last mouthful of wine, Jeff swirled it round his mouth to get rid of the taste of stale tobacco. He stood up and bent over the delectable human form on his sofa, sweeping her up in his arms with newfound strength and carrying her into the bedroom. He tried to flick the light switch with his shoulder but couldn't make proper contact, so Lynn reached it for him, giggling happily.

The amused man set his beautiful encumbrance onto her feet, and they stood together at the foot of his bed, kissing and drawing each other closer and closer. Lynn's arms looped around his waist, her grasp as loose and demure as his was tight and possessive, but in contrast, her lips were more than willing, and her blue eyes blinked with each new touch or shift of their combined body weight.

Jeff's eyes remained resolutely open, not wishing to miss a single cue to speed up or slow down. When he judged the time to be right, he lured the reserved schoolgirl down gently onto the mattress and began to undo her jeans, all the while caressing the sensitive skin under her ribs with his free hand. He almost didn't dare look at her.

'You're gorgeous,' he said, as the vision gradually became nude in front of him. 'Absolutely gorgeous.'

Deft fingers traced across her body, and his lips kissed every subtle undulation they alighted on. At each new sensation, the young woman became more aroused and yet more frightened too. She didn't know if she could trust her own feelings, let alone those of a total stranger. Things were moving very fast all of a sudden, and she needed to be honest with the amazing man who was all over her and making her feel so sexy. It was only fair to both of them that she let him know.

'You've done this before, haven't you?'

'Once or twice,' Jeff murmured, continuing to kiss and caress her smooth skin.

Lynn sat up and shuffled to the edge of the bed, tentative hands with painted nails unfastening his belt and jeans, and laughed as she tried to help him pull them off. He moved her hands away and began to slide his pants down his long legs, feeling her eyes burning into him as he progressively revealed himself too. His sense of urgency climbed yet further when she reacted to the sight of his engorged penis bulging in his shorts and then breaking free from its restraining clothes.

'There's just no elegant way to undress when you're wearing jeans, is there?' he tried to sound calm and laid back. 'It's one of life's true paradoxes. One of the few tasks made more difficult with the addition of an extra pair of hands.'

Lynn smiled at the rich, expressive language, and they both almost overbalanced. Jeff steadied her with strong arms, taking another opportunity to plant a kiss on inviting lips. She wrapped her hands around his torso with a little more force, but a hint of hesitation in her demeanour told him to pause.

'Are you OK?' he asked.

'Yes,' the sixteen-year-old stalled. 'Just so *you* know... This is the first time for me.'

A thunderbolt shot through the student's head, and this one simple statement landed him on the very precipice of self-control. One more thought, and their delicious encounter could already be over. But at least one more thought was called for right now. He wrestled with his conscience just enough to bring himself back from the brink.

'I see,' he answered comically, breathing hard. 'Well, that *does* give things a different flavour.'

'Sorry, Jeff. You promised no surprises, and I dropped one on you,' Lynn confessed, realising she was completely out of her depth and hoping that honesty was the best policy.

'You most certainly did!' the good-looking student laughed, nodding in agreement and rolling his provocative eyes.

The pretty songstress lay on her back, gazing up at the most attractive face she had ever seen. Those dark brown eyes were friendly, and his hands masterful, stroking her shoulders and neck while they navigated this latest sharp bend in their short road travelled. Although she could see his chest rising and falling regularly and understood his body was intent on much more, she no longer felt threatened. She had managed to slow him down when necessary. Maybe this game of sex was not so dangerous after all...

And for his part, Jeff had successfully regained control of his lascivious instincts and was also about to take charge of those belonging to the irresistible female form on his bed. Whyever hadn't the possibility of Lynn Dyson being a virgin occurred to him before? He was only too aware that she was nothing like the women he normally went home with after a party. This was his dream girl after all, for whom he had waited since as long as he could remember. He could only assume it must have been simply too much of a leap of faith to count himself as her first lover.

'Are you sure you want to do this?' he checked again, sinking back onto the mattress beside her. 'I mean it. We can stop.'

Hang on a minute, his libido was quick to oppose. What was he saying? How could he possibly stop now? But stop he would, sighed the boy from Canley Vale. Anything was possible for Lynn Dyson. He gently stroked her breasts and stomach through her top, trying desperately not to get too far ahead of himself. Stopping now would be insane, but entirely the right thing to do. He was stranded in limbo for what seemed like an eternity, waiting for her response.

Lynn was ready however. In her mind, she was totally comfortable, and further down, quite mysteriously, she could almost feel him inside her. She had decided that the splendid Jeff Diamond from Sydney was the one with whom she would like to take this huge, life-changing step. She already felt a real fondness for him, which she didn't understand any better but liked immensely.

Finally, the celebrity spoke. 'No. It's fine. I want to. I've had all evening to think about it and I'm sure. You've been wonderful and very considerate, in case you didn't already know.'

The nineteen-year-old couldn't help but empathise, sensing she was drawn to him even though she knew it to be unwise. His intrinsic Pied Piper gift might easily play against him tonight. He didn't want to dupe the classy teenager into thinking she was safe, because she wasn't. He was about to inflict irreversible change.

The practised lover sought to test his theory, marvelling at his hold over this sublime creature. His own, huge eyes drew her in with self-assured temptation, then soon enough warned her off with their urchin blackness. His new conquest trembled, like the stem of a flower that appears to waver a little before bending towards an admirer. So it was true. He ruled Lynn Dyson tonight. And, given time and the relentlessness of his addictions, she would doubtless turn the tables before too long.

Keyed-up beyond his normal limit, Jeff exhaled deeply as he closed his eyes, balancing on a tightrope both emotionally and physically. At one end of this important choice lay paradise, and at the other, fortunately fading further into the distance, was rejection. Someone up there was on his side tonight, and for what he was about to receive, he was already truly grateful.

'You won't regret it,' he said softly. 'I promise.'

The significance of the exquisite young woman's decision was acknowledged by slow, deliberate action from a man who wanted her more than anything. Jeff removed his shirt and boxer shorts and quickly rolled on a condom, before turning his attention to removing her remaining clothing. Moments later, Lynn lay on his bed in only her panties, framed in a soft glow from the window, through which shone the silver of the moon and the golden streetlights of the nearby city.

The nineteen-year-old was doing his level best to force himself to slow down, but to little effect. Using every trick in the book to distract his one-tracked mind, it dawned on him that not even his fantasies had ever brought him this far. The promise of sex with Lynn Dyson had only ever been a promise; never once daring to entertain the possibility of moving beyond his mind and becoming a physical reality.

His right hand massaging the inside of her thighs, Jeff lowered himself over her body and kissed her lips, with his left hand slipping behind her head and its thumb gently stroking the delicate skin behind her ear. Lynn couldn't help but moan quietly at the effect this subtle combination of sensations had on her awakening libido. His penis touched her stomach, and she shuddered underneath him.

'I warn you, this is not going to take very long,' her handsome man issued a wry smile.

Kneeling to one side, the patient lover removed the young star's underwear and placed her right hand on his erection. He didn't care that she didn't know what to do. He only cared that he helped her to enjoy her first time. At his command, like during their tango earlier, the naïve celebrity found herself touching and kissing, bending and caressing in a hot-blooded act of passion. Her wildest expectations were being surpassed at every stroke, as the man above responded to her subtlest attempt to reciprocate.

Yes, Lynn Dyson was ready for this. That made two of them.

Seeing her smile, the impatient teacher licked two fingers of his left hand and began to open her up. He closed his eyes and refused to listen to her shy sounds, lest her reaction were to tip him over the edge. However, he couldn't ignore the way her hips rose up as his fingers moistened around the lips of her vagina. It wasn't long before he was inside her, all the time fondling her breasts and kissing her uncertain mouth.

'That feels so good,' he whispered in her ear. 'You're fantastic.'

Holding her close and pushing himself deep inside the warm, tight space that had been saved for him, Jeff felt his dream girl begin to respond more freely to his touch, little by little. Making every possible attempt to prolong the special moment, he finally couldn't wait any longer. The level of tension which had been so exciting for so long was now becoming unbearable, and with virtually no warning, he groaned out loud and thrust into her more vigorously, rushing headlong towards orgasm. He could feel every last drop of energy course through his body, and it was all he could do to steal a breath to fill his lungs while he came into her like a steam train.

'Whoa! That was so good,' he shouted full bore, breathing heavily above his gorgeous lover.

Lynn looked up into his eyes, her face flushed. 'Yes, it was. You'll wake the neighbours!'

'Neighbours? There's no neighbours,' the satisfied man gasped, planting a kiss on her forehead. 'At this precise moment, there's only you and me in the whole, damned world. You are so beautiful.'

The shy woman smiled. 'That's such a perfect image. And thanks for teaching me.'

Jeff grinned back, his chest heaving for maximum air intake, inwardly digesting what had just happened. He bowed his head to hers and kissed her lips tenderly.

'That's the quickest lesson you'll ever get,' he confessed, sitting back and flicking away the sweat from his brow before it dripped onto his partner's face. 'I'd ask for your money back if I were you.'

Lynn frowned and shook her head. Drained but elated, the comic pretended that he was about to drop down on top of her, making her cry out in amusement. He then rolled over at the last minute to leave them lying side-by-side, both staring at the ceiling, and they lay still in a comfortable silence.

Jeff reached for her hand after several minutes and raised it up to his lips to kiss it, and the young woman leaned onto her elbow to reciprocate directly on his lips. It was well into Saturday morning by now, yet neither of them wanted the night to come to an end.

A while later, the student stood up and disappeared out of the room. Shortly afterwards, music came drifting through the air from the other side of the small apartment. It was classical piano; peaceful, cascading arpeggios. Chopin, the accomplished musician guessed but couldn't be certain. This man was so different from the other men she knew. Hearing the bathroom door click shut, she lifted her head and watched him return with a towel, which was duly spread over the wide ledge under his bedroom window.

Lynn looked around the dimly lit space. In the frenzy, she had barely had a chance to take a breath, let alone check out her surroundings. Irresponsible, she thought. She had been taught to always be aware of her environment and to look for escape routes. She vowed to be more careful and less caught up in the heat of the moment in future.

But her lover was beckoning to her. What was going to happen now?

'Come and sit up here,' he invited. 'This is my favourite place to think.'

The statuesque man reached down and picked up his shirt, which was lying on the floor where it had landed earlier. He handed it to his beautiful guest, who dutifully put it on. It was nice to see her wearing it. Carrying over their glasses of water, she climbed onto the windowsill in front of him, as he had suggested, and slid backwards between long legs, leaning back onto his chest, which she was surprised to find still so warm.

Unable to imagine a better end to this momentous night, Jeff's arms enfolded his dream girl, and so did his heart. Through the window, they could see the tall buildings on the fringe of the city, just a couple of kilometres away. There were stars in the sky, and the half-moon shone down onto the sparse skyline of Melbourne's CBD.

'So... What are we going to think about?' Lynn asked playfully, stroking the hair on his legs.

Sighing, the young man leaned his head back against the wall and closed his eyes, pleased that his partner was feeling so relaxed. He should have been relaxed too, but a complex cocktail of emotions had left him balanced dangerously on a knife-edge.

Jesus Christ! Life's a bitch, he cursed inside.

Jeff had waited his whole life to be in this exact situation, and now he was finally here, he was barely well enough to cope with it. He dearly wanted to tear down the walls he had shored up so high around his strange and solitary world, but he didn't dare. Trust was what he craved, and yet also what he couldn't give. Not even to the gorgeous creature in his arms. Not yet anyway.

Snap out of it, you idiot. These morbid thoughts were wasting valuable time. Who knew when he would next have the opportunity to spend time with Lynn Dyson? Regrouping, he wound his mind back to her question and turned it round with another.

'What would you like to think about?'

'How beautiful it is up there?' the tired teenager replied, picking up on his sombre mood and pointing out into the night sky. 'Tell me about you. You were born in Australia, weren't you? What's your family background?'

Now, Jeff resolved, *remember the rules. Stay at the superficial but don't lie.* After all, Lynn was entitled to know a little bit about the man to whom she had surrendered her virginity less than half an hour ago. This thought made him both glow inside and feel nauseous at the same time, as the arrogant, dragon-slaying knight he aspired to be wrestled with the lowly peasant who suddenly found it difficult to justify being in this situation at all.

'Well... I'm a real mongrel, to tell you the truth,' he began.

The man from Sydney's west opened the window next to him as he spoke, almost to distract the inquisitive guest from hearing his reply. A low rumble of traffic noise filled the room, along with a cool breeze. Instinctively shrinking from the fresh air, Lynn cuddled into him closer, and he inhaled slowly to welcome both in.

'My dad's parents were Polish Jews who came to Sydney via New York,' he continued. 'He was five at the time.'

'Wow! Your family has a habit of making long journeys.'

The student chuckled. 'And my mother's family's from Argentina. They came to Australia two generations ago and built a small import business in Parramatta.'

'That's interesting,' the young woman acknowledged. 'So are you Jewish or Catholic?'

He smiled and gave his standard reply. 'Was I baptised or circumcised, d'you mean?'

Lynn gasped, slightly shocked at his directness. 'Well, no. That wasn't exactly where I was going, but which is it then?'

Sweet, Jeff thought. Did he really have to explain that one?

'The former.'

The self-confessed mongrel left it at that, and satisfied with this answer, his partner immediately continued on her quest for further details.

'When's your birthday?'

'Second of June, 'fifty-two, Officer.'

Acting completely on instinct, Jeff hugged the beautiful woman closer to him. It had been a very long time since he had shared such an innocent conversation, and again he made his new friend giggle like a child. It was a refreshing change from the type of bland post-coital discourse he usually endured, for just long enough so as not to be labelled a complete rat, and most often dulled by alcohol or boredom or both.

'You're good!' Lynn declared. 'You should write comedy. Coronation day.'

'Indeed. And thanks. When's yours?'

'The twentieth of September, nineteen-fifty-five,' the star answered.

'Correct.'

No self-respecting Lynn Dyson fan wouldn't already have known this fact. Jeff heard the woman on his windowsill sigh dreamily and watched her run tender fingers along his hairy, muscular arm.

'So you're nineteen. You seem a lot older to me.'

The student scoffed somewhat sarcastically. 'I feel a lot older, believe me.'

Intrigued, Lynn turned her head round, but not far enough to see his face. 'What do you mean?'

Too much information, the tired soul realised. Time to change the subject.

'Oh, nothing. So what does your future look like? More of the same?'

He felt her warm body relax down onto his, and it was divine. The effects of their shared bottle of wine had completely worn off, and his head was clear. How right did this feel? And how long had he waited for this simple exchange?

'Pretty much! I want to go to uni', definitely,' came her emphatic reply. 'I'd love the lifestyle, I'm sure. To be in control of my own learning. Mixing with other people who like to debate stuff and who have very different views. One thing I'm bored with in my circle of friends is the sheer true-blueness of them all. They're really nice people, and it sounds terrible to criticise them, but they're only interested in things they already know. Richard Kerr... you know, the pianist in MAC... he's different, thank God. Did you know he was homosexual?'

Jeff found himself absorbed in the pleasing string of sentences enunciated by his very favourite voice and had to snap out of his trance to answer the question. 'No, I didn't know. But now you mention it, it doesn't surprise me.'

'Please don't tell anyone, will you?' his companion swiftly added, feeling guilty for such a casual betrayal of her friend's trust. 'He only confided in me six months or so ago. Even his parents don't know.'

The empathetic man squeezed her tight. 'It's more likely a case of especially his parents don't know. I won't tell anyone. Hey! I can think of a few things I won't be telling anyone from the last few days.'

'Ha, ha. Very funny,' Lynn responded dryly, seeming unbothered by her own tenuous circumstance.

The host decided against pursuing the topic any further, and to his continuing delight, the sixteen-year-old didn't seem to be in the least bit ready to call it quits. She remained full of questions.

'So what do you want to do once you graduate?'

Now here was a question the ambitious young man liked. He would have no qualms about answering this time.

'Well...' Jeff began dramatically, as if he was about to rattle off a long answer. 'My heart wants to be a rock star...'

'Really?' the superstar exclaimed, twisting as far round as she could.

Jeff caught a glimpse of the front of her naked body and almost lost his train of thought. He ran his right hand up her arm to rub her shoulder, inside the shirt collar, relishing the softness of her skin on his fingertips. He leaned down and kissed her cheek, as it lifted towards his lips.

'Yep. But my head wants to bring computers into the lives of everyday people. There's so much we can do with computing power to change governments and business. To improve communication. To improve everything really, if they can be made ubiquitous enough. And cheap enough.'

'That's so cool,' Lynn replied, sounding genuinely interested. 'I've never thought about that before. And I love the word "ubiquitous". I'm not sure I even knew what it meant until right this minute. You put it so completely into context. That's what I mean about my friends... We would never talk about something so extraordinary. I'd love you to tell me more.'

The man behind her exhaled, his companion's unexpected willingness to think widely engaging far more than his brain. Extraordinary or not, it appeared his libido had other ideas about to claim a distinct priority over technological ubiquity. He could feel a new wave of energy flowing into him, and his mind was firmly fixed on the corporal rather than the intellectual right now. He brushed Lynn's long, golden hair to one side, over her shoulder, and began to kiss the back of her neck with serious intent. The open shirt revealed just enough of her body for his imagination to savour that which his eyes couldn't quite see. His right hand was busy stroking the underside of her leg, reaching gradually higher with each deliberate movement.

'Again?' the young woman sounded surprised.

Jeff's breath felt warm on her neck, and the stubble on his face was halfway between tickly and scratchy against her delicate skin. The sensation of what the innocent teenager gathered was his penis hardening against the small of her back felt most unusual, and she was filled with a nervous anticipation once more.

'It doesn't take long for me to refuel,' he affirmed directly into her right ear.

Lynn tensed up a little, unsure of whether she was in any danger. Everything this man did felt amazing, despite her apprehension. Noticing her muscles tighten, the expert lover relaxed his grip a little.

'Let's go back to bed,' he suggested, placing his right foot onto the floor and hoping to tempt her away from the window.

Obediently, his dream girl swung round and slipped off the ledge in a single, graceful move. Her shirt, or rather his shirt, billowed open enough for Jeff to scan from her breasts and abdomen all the way down her long legs. She was a picture of human perfection, as far as he was concerned. However, despite her ready smile, he detected concern in her eyes, which cooled the flames in his loins more than he expected.

'Hey, if you don't want to do this, just tell me,' the nineteen-year-old insisted, taking hold of her hand and staring into enquiring, blue eyes. 'I'm not going to force you to do anything. You have to know that. There's no way I'd hurt you. You're way too important to me for that.'

The naïve young star leaned forward and wrapped her arms gingerly around him. This boy really knew what to say to make her feel wanted. As she came closer, Jeff backed off a little to stop his full erection from contradicting his previous assurances. He continued, encouraging her chin upwards to look him in the eyes.

'Do you believe me?'

Lynn gave a half-smile. She wanted to believe him, and she was almost sure she could, but everything she had ever been taught about protecting herself was telling her otherwise. What if this new man in her life was actually some sort of confidence trickster? She didn't know anything about his life in Sydney. For all she knew, he had probably attacked women and fled from the police. He might have even killed someone.

Don't be so sensationalist, the teenager told herself. She could just as easily be attacked by one of the boys she had known all her life. She had read the statistics about sexual assaults being more often perpetrated by people well known to their victims.

'Jeff, I really want to believe you.'

The patient student lifted his hesitant guest back up onto the windowsill and sat alongside her, aching to touch her but resigned to taking things at her pace. This woman was so absolutely worth it. He followed her eyes as they looked him up and down, obviously wondering what she had got herself into.

'Look, I understand. I really do understand. I'm asking for a lot, I know,' the kind man reassured her.

Lynn relaxed slightly, the pressure appearing to be off again. Although she was confused, there was something about this guy that drew her in. His deep, pleading eyes were hypnotic, and his empathy quite distinct. He was no longer touching her, but she oh-so wanted him to. He was everything she liked, all rolled into one: tall and strong, dark-haired and sallow-skinned, chiselled facial features and a broad smile, quick-witted and opinionated, and as sexy as anything. The list was endless, and to all these other qualities could she dare add trustworthy?

Jeff carried on, the remainder of this amazing night totally dependent on his powers of persuasion. 'Lynn, you know, in reality, whether you say yes or no now, if I was going to hurt you, I could. It would've happened by now.'

The young woman nodded slowly. Her captor was right. She was about as vulnerable as she could be, virtually naked in a stranger's apartment, where nobody knew how to find her. Yet still the respectful man refrained from caressing her, save with his eyes. Nonetheless, despite how exciting this situation was and how charming and friendly he appeared, the famous sportswoman began to realise just how far into the danger zone she had strayed. This man was totally in control, and she suddenly felt like a puppet awaiting the next tug on her strings.

'But I'm not going to attack you,' Jeff's voice interrupted her nervous thoughts. 'You're safe. Things were so frantic and rushed earlier. It was completely one-sided, and that's not how sex should be. I want to make *you* feel good too.'

Lynn wasn't quite sure what he meant, but his caring words made her feel slightly more comfortable. Taking a deep breath, she fixed the handsome face with a wide-eyed stare and slid off the windowsill. Turning towards him with outstretched hands, another unexpected question came his way.

'Have you seen the Kama Sutra?'

Surprise flashed across her host's face, causing the sixteen-year-old to recoil, feeling embarrassed. He laughed kindly and led her across the floor to the bed. The music had long since stopped, and even the traffic noise from the window had reduced to a dull hum.

'Yes, I have,' he answered. 'Why? What made you think of that?'

'My brother calls it prehistoric porn,' the young woman continued, laying down at his request. 'I've only seen a couple of pages of various positions.'

Jeff smiled at her innocence, starting to stroke her all over, this time able to fully appreciate her beauty. He loved how she had decided to seize control of her destiny in such an uncertain moment. That had taken guts, he admitted.

'Well, firstly, it's not prehistoric, to be perfectly accurate,' he corrected her, using an authoritative tone which made her smile. 'To the best of my knowledge, Miss Dyson, there are no dinosaurs in the Kama Sutra.'

The pretty teenager laughed out loud, her head filled with mental images too comical for words. Her mystery man kissed her lips while she was still smiling, making her giggle all the more. Being invited to sit up again, she felt the shirt being peeled off her shoulders and the fabric brush against her back as it fell onto the sheet. Now surplus to requirements, it was swiftly pushed off the edge of the bed by a strong, confident hand. Her senses were being bombarded from all sides with an almost overpowering intensity.

Her teacher continued. 'And secondly, there's much more to the Kama Sutra than just a bunch of sexual positions that are impossible to maintain for more than ten seconds. There's the whole spiritual side, and the link between sex and the senses, and how you can be at one with your surroundings, people or whatever. It's actually pretty interesting, once you get past the prehistoric porn.'

Lynn was utterly captivated by this enigmatic and eloquent man. Where had this good-looking Jewish, Argentinean intellectual come from? He had the refined, confident manner of a nobleman and the rough outer shell of a farmhand. Both were irresistible to the inexperienced teenager, and the combination even more so.

'You know so much,' she told him, with sincere admiration.

'I have a lot of time to read and a lot of questions to answer,' the modest student replied, his tongue coaxing her nipples harder, while he caressed between her legs with steady intent. 'Now… This is where you come in.'

The virtuous young lady was confounded again, and the blank canvas of his long-sought lover required Jeff to exhale sharply to counteract the ferocious desire welling up inside him. He hadn't dared afford himself the opportunity last time to take a good look at her body. Drinking it in now, while unwrapping another condom, he noticed how lithe and lean it was, and how her legs stretched out for such a long way down his bed. Every contour of her fresh face seemed so familiar to him, and it struck him once more just how unbelievable it was that Lynn Dyson was here with him, in his flat and in his bed.

'You're exquisite,' he whispered, gently sending one finger and then a second inside her.

The anxious woman squirmed, firstly out of surprise and then more from pleasure. The expert lover lifted her hand and placed it on his penis, guiding her to grip it harder and slip the sheathed skin up and down over its rigid shaft.

The couple lay side-by-side for several minutes, enjoying each others' bodies and the new experiences. Jeff could feel the intensity building up in both bodies and gently rolled his partner over onto her back. Lynn looked happy, he concluded, and not threatened any more. Soon he was inside her, continuing the work his fingers had started. She writhed upwards and inhaled sharply at his continued attention, before he felt her pull back a little.

'Hey. Relax, angel,' he urged, his mouth against her cheek. 'Just let it happen.'

Another minute, and it did happen. Her eyes gave it away, and seeing this, the ecstatic nineteen-year-old simply had to follow. Lynn Dyson let out a quiet moan, and Jeff Diamond let rip. After twenty seconds or so of pure heaven, he grabbed her upper arms firmly with both hands and swung themselves round, so that he was now on his back and she was lying on top of him. Her hair fell onto his face, and they shared a long kiss, lost in a lengthy, enchanted silence.

'That was fantastic,' the superstar said. 'I never knew it could feel that good.'

Her lover cocked his head, with a sly grin on his face. 'What did I tell you? Trust the master. Told you you'd enjoy it.'

The boy from Canley Vale smiled inside even more, listening to himself mouthing off. *What an arrogant arsehole you are, Jeff Diamond,* he thought. But man, was it good! It had been fantastic indeed.

By the time either partner wished to find out, the clock revealed it to be after three o'clock in the morning. In little more than an hour, the sun would be coming up over the inner east.

'Wow! Look at the time!' Lynn exclaimed, putting her host's shirt back on for warmth. 'I'll have jet lag tomorrow.'

It was Jeff's turn to laugh out loud. 'Jet lag? That's great! I like it.'

The irony wrapped up in his dream girl's throwaway line was not lost on him, quite apart from the humour. Little did she know, but he lived every day with the symptoms of jet lag.

Their euphoria soon gave way to tiredness. Lynn had her eyes closed, and Jeff could see her chest moving in a regular rhythm. It scared him. His usual *modus operandi* was never to end a date at his place, always leaving himself the option to escape whenever he was ready. Now he was trapped and would have to make another choice. Would he wake Sleeping Beauty and drive her home, so she could sleep peacefully in her own bed? Or would he allow her to stay in his bed, while he spent the few remaining night hours on the couch, reading and hoping not to fall asleep in her company?

The exhausted but completely satisfied nineteen-year-old stood up, put his shorts on and went to fetch some more water. He drank one glassful down in front of the sink and refilled it. What should he do? This perfect night had to end sometime. Back in the bedroom, he placed Lynn's glass of water onto the bedside table, just noisily enough to cause her to open her eyes.

'Oh, thanks,' she said, sitting up and drinking steadily. 'That's really good.'

Her host sat on the side of the bed, bare-chested and magnificent. At his unspoken but nevertheless expressive request, Lynn leaned forward to kiss his chilled lips. A wave of ragged emotion welled up inside him, and he once again cursed his predicament.

'You are gorgeous,' he told her, stretching out the first syllable of the inadequate adjective for as long as he could.

'Thanks. So are you. This has been a wonderful night.'

'Yeah. Pretty damned fine, if you ask me,' Jeff agreed. 'Any regrets?'

The star kissed him again and shook her head. 'Absolutely none.'

Looking at this man who had made her as a woman, Lynn watched with barely disguised dismay as his broad smile faded. What was he thinking about?

'OK... What would you like to do?' he asked. 'I'm happy to take you home, if you want. Or you're welcome to stay here, and I'll drive you back in the morning.'

'It is almost morning anyway,' the innocent beauty replied. 'I can't ask you to drive me home now. You must be ready to drop.'

Ain't that the truth, the troubled soul mused. She was considerate, he would give her that.

'You're right,' Jeff began to pull the bedclothes down. 'You stay here. I'm not too good at sleeping, so I'll probably end up on the couch after a few minutes.'

The lovers lay together in his bed, hand-in-hand. He stroked the long, golden hair which draped over his partner's soft breasts, kissing her shoulder idly. Lynn turned to face him, her head nestled into the pillow.

'Thanks. I hope you sleep OK.'

'That'd be good,' he replied. 'You too. G'night.'

The sixteen-year-old detected a note of sadness in his voice, but said nothing. Within a few minutes, she had drifted off to sleep in Jeff's bed and still wearing his shirt. The lowly peasant watched the princess fall asleep next to him and gave thanks for the short and incredibly sweet slice of life they had shared. For tonight, Lynn Dyson was his prize, and he could take comfort in the fact that he had won her all on his own. And beyond tonight? Who knew?

Eyelids heavy, Jeff knew he could easily follow her lead but was determined to keep sleep at bay until he was alone again. He did not want the girl of his dreams to meet the demons of his nightmares. They were his demons, and he wasn't prepared to share them with anyone. He would just give himself five minutes more to stare at her...

***

Lynn woke with a start. For the first time in her life, she had woken up in someone else's bed and was momentarily disoriented. The light was streaming in through the window. What time was it? Seven-thirty, Jeff's alarm clock told her. She should get up and take a shower. Her father was driving her out to the farm at midday, and she had arranged with her record company's office staff that she would sign a batch of souvenir items to be auctioned at charity events before she left town for the weekend.

The young woman looked across at the other side of the bed. No good at sleeping, her bedfellow had claimed. He looked like a professional from where she was standing. She wondered what he had meant, because he was out cold right at this moment. She went into the bathroom and helped herself to a towel.

There was still no sound from the bedroom even after her shower, and the sixteen-year-old would need to wake her picturesque lover very soon. She didn't want to ring for a taxi and disappear without saying goodbye. That would be a disappointing way to end such a perfect date. "Pretty damned fine" were the words her eloquent mystery man had used, and they were well founded. She was not the first among her classmates to have lost her virginity, but being two years younger than the rest, she hadn't yet made up her mind whether it was good or bad to be close to the first.

Lynn boiled the kettle and searched through the kitchen cupboards until she found what she needed to make hot drinks. She carried two mugs into the bedroom and put them down on Jeff's bedside table. He stirred and turned over onto his back. The sheet covered him from the stomach downwards, and she feasted her eyes again on his rugged facial features and hairy, muscular torso. How good was this man to look at? She watched his eyes open a tiny slither and then close again.

'Good morning,' his guest said, loud enough to stop him falling back to sleep.

The student opened his eyes fully this time.

'Hey!' he murmured.

For a fleeting moment, last night was forgotten, and the humble nineteen-year-old assumed he was still dreaming. Then the realisation hit him. *Hang on... Wait a minute...* This was real. He awoke to see Lynn Dyson's beautiful face floating above his head. It was an utterly surreal experience, and the pessimist inside wondered again whether he was snared in some sort of cruel hallucination, until the vision of loveliness sat down on the edge of the bed and he felt it give under her weight.

'It's eight o'clock, Mister Not-too-good-at-sleeping.'

The previous evening fast-forwarded through Jeff's head at warp speed, up until the point where they had said goodnight. Eight o'clock, the voice had said. Surely not? The visitor roused him out of his slumber, pointing at the mugs on his bedside table.

'I didn't know if you wanted tea or coffee, so I made one of each. Pick whichever one you want, and I'll have the other one.'

The dazed man hauled himself up to a sitting position and extended his hand towards her face. Gently pulling her head towards his and kissing her lips, he soon remembered exactly where he was and exactly how much he liked it. Predictably however, he found himself unable to speak, given that his jaw had locked up, as it often did. He picked up the mug containing coffee and toasted the attractive woman with it.

Before it reached his lips however, Lynn suddenly remembered something and jumped to her feet. 'Oh, I forgot! Do you take sugar?'

Smiling at her animated admission, Jeff nodded and raised two fingers of his right hand.

'Yes, please,' he managed to squeeze the words out of his throat.

Obediently, the teenager returned with a bag of sugar which she had tracked down in his kitchen. He helped himself and stirred the spoon around.

'Did you sleep OK?' he asked, his facial muscles finally relaxing.

'Yes, thanks. Did you?'

Jeff's eyes flashed, and he inhaled deeply as his faculties gradually reassembled themselves.

'Must've done. You wore me out,' he winked at her.

Lynn's heart soared, instantly transported back to their nocturnal adventures. She smiled coyly. Jeff kissed his own fingers, warm from holding the coffee mug, and brushed them across her cheek.

'D'you know? This is the first time anyone's brought me coffee in bed, so thanks a lot.'

'No worries,' his guest replied. 'I have an ulterior motive though, unfortunately, because I'll need to go soon. I could get a taxi, that's no problem, but I didn't want to sneak out.'

Christ, no, the student agreed silently. That would have been terrible.

'Thanks. You're very kind. What time do you have to go?'

Trying to hide his disappointment, Jeff's compulsions immediately ran riot. Even though he recognised them easily enough, they were hellishly persistent. What he really wanted was for Lynn to climb back into bed with him and carry on where they had left off, but not even he would have the audacity to suggest it now.

The famous teenager looked at his clock again. 'In about fifteen minutes.'

The student's heart sank still further. That wasn't long, he rued. Oh, well... He had to get moving. He was adamant that such a wonderful night, which had left him more fulfilled and re-energised than he could remember, would certainly not end with him loading his dream girl into a cab.

'You're not taking a taxi anywhere,' he insisted. 'I'll have a quick shower and take you. Are you going back to St Kilda Road?'

'Yes. I have to pick up my stuff and go to the record company. Dad's collecting me from there at noon, to go to the farm for the weekend,' the celebrity explained.

Her man was beginning to look much more human now. Lynn felt bad for waking him, since he evidently needed more sleep. Her memories of their evening together were clear and enticing, and she wondered what might be still to come. She was fairly sure he liked her, in part given away by the strange shape she could make out under the sheet, so hopefully there would be some sign from him before they went their separate ways. As yet they hadn't even swapped telephone numbers, but she wasn't game enough to initiate anything. This was completely new territory for the schoolgirl, and Jeff Diamond gave the impression of being such an expert at this dating game that she fully expected him to know what to do next. She fervently hoped his idea of what to do would match hers...

Jeff emerged from the bathroom, having pulled on last night's clothes again, as had his guest, of course.

'D'you want to grab breakfast somewhere before I drop you off?'

'I'd love to, but I don't really have time,' the young woman replied, wandering through to the lounge room to find her handbag. 'I don't want anyone to have missed me.'

Following her, Jeff placed covetous hands on her shoulders, turned her to face him and kissed her lips passionately, cherishing the sensation of her relaxing into his body.

'That's OK. I understand,' he said, hugging her close. 'So what's next week like for you? As busy as last week?'

Lynn glowed inside. Excellent, she thought. There would be more.

'No, not quite as bad,' she answered. 'Wednesday and Thursday evenings are free, as far as I know.'

The boy from Sydney's west liked what he heard. 'Great! There's a funfair on all next week in Carlton Gardens. Did you want to go on Wednesday? We could grab some dinner and scatter it all over the gardens later.'

The teenager laughed out loud. 'You're so funny! I love the way you speak. Sometimes you're deadly serious and then you go and say something like that.'

The young man grinned at yet another compliment from this very special lady. 'Thanks. You're pretty funny too. I'm going to use that jet lag line, with your permission.'

Lynn nodded. 'Permission granted.'

Regrettably for both lovers, the time had come for the party to end. With a heavy heart, Jeff let themselves out of his flat and followed his secret stowaway down the six flights of stairs, into the dark basement car park.

'Let's see how the mighty Fairlane's feeling this morning,' he said. 'We might yet be getting a taxi.'

The car started first time, and the couple joined the Saturday morning shopping traffic for the short drive south of the river. A hundred metres or so before the rear entrance to the Dyson Administration building, the driver pulled over. He yanked up the handbrake and switched off the ignition, smiling at the startled look which had appeared on his passenger's face.

'I just wanted to say goodbye properly, before we get too close,' he explained. 'I don't want to do anything that might cause trouble for you.'

Lynn hadn't really thought about it, but now he mentioned it, this was a good idea. They unfastened their seatbelts and embraced.

'Thanks. You're probably right,' she agreed. 'I had a great time, Jeff. You make me feel so normal.'

Normal? Now, the young man mused, from anyone else, the use of that adjective to describe one's lovemaking skills might have been a bitter blow to one's self-esteem. However, when one had been making love to Lynn Dyson, it was probably the best adjective one could possibly hear. She had also said "special" earlier, so over the course of last night he had taken his dream girl from special to normal. By his reckoning, this was good progress!

'Why, thank you,' he responded chivalrously. 'I'll take that as a compliment.'

The pretty teenager giggled. 'Sorry! Yes, that must've sounded a bit weird. I mean, because people usually wrap me up in cotton wool and daren't treat me like a normal person. You talk to me as an equal, and it's really great.'

Her lover smiled. 'It's my pleasure,' he told her. 'I'm glad you like it. I'm nowhere near your equal, and you're anything but normal, as far as I'm concerned, but I'll keep both in mind. So are we on for Wednesday?'

He restarted the car, and they drove the short distance up to the front of the building.

'Yes,' Lynn nodded. 'That sounds fun, except the vomiting part. What time?'

'Say six o'clock? *Ça marche pour toi?*'

The star grinned. '*Oui. Absoluement, monsieur.*'

'*Muy bien, señorita mía,*' the polyglot added, kissing her lips one last, lingering time. 'Now get out of my car.'

The passenger obeyed, smiling at his terse instruction and touching his left hand lightly as it rested on the gear lever.

'Thanks again.'

Jeff nodded. 'You too. *Adiós.*'

He watched the gorgeous, young athlete run up the steps, on through the revolving door and vanish within. He imagined the disdain on the security guard's face when he looked out and saw the old Ford littering his hooped driveway. Wouldn't the man with the uniform and snooty superiority sitting in his display cabinet be jealous to think of the things this reprobate had been up to with the precious heiress whom he was there to protect?

The student looked at his watch. Just before nine o'clock. What would he do now? He didn't want to go back to his flat. He felt so healthy after almost five hours' sleep. He couldn't remember the last time he had been granted this much rest in one stretch. The usual clouds in his head had cleared, and the drumming behind his eyes had subsided to the barest minimum. His legs, which were normally heavy and regularly cramped, felt as if they could run to Sydney. Perhaps he would, he thought, smiling in self-satisfaction.

The happy man opened the centre console next to his left elbow. He had left the flat without his wallet, but he had six music cassettes and almost a full tank of petrol. He also had twelve dollars in loose change, between what was in his pocket and the assortment of coins in the car. That would be more than enough for a coffee and a packet of cigarettes. So where could he drive to? He fancied losing himself on the open road, to give his mind a chance to relive last night and to make the previously inconceivable occasion stick in his mind once and for all.

Reaching for the street directory, Jeff thumbed the pages. His fingertips were alive with the memories of touching his dream girl. He knew this level of obsession was ridiculous but refused to care. It was as if life's volume level had been cranked up, and every sensory input was amplified. He found the map pages for the Mornington Peninsula. Which were those places that Professor Martin had mentioned? Those where the MA kids went on their holidays?

'Saturday morning in Portsea,' he decided, instructing his car aloud. 'My life is finally turning around.'

Fair

Lynn's last class the following Wednesday afternoon was dragging on way too long. It was Economic History, and the subject matter normally interested her greatly. Not so much today, however. All week, she had been trying desperately to put her cool but cultured, Argentinean Polish mystery man out of her mind. She had resisted the temptation to talk to her friends about her exploits on Friday night and Saturday morning, but had replayed them many, many times in her head.

The streetwise student had been right to exercise caution about causing trouble. Lynn was worried what her parents might think, and her coaches and musical director likewise. She had a large number of commitments which everyone fully expected her to honour. A serious boyfriend at the start of Year Twelve would be frowned upon, or probably downright disapproved of. Especially such an unknown quantity as Jeff Diamond appeared to be.

Lloyd de l'Enseigne, whom the blonde teenager had known since primary school, had been pleased to see his valuable friend had come to no harm after he and his fellow bodyguard had left her in a stranger's company at the University Club. However, he hadn't thought to ask a single question about the date, and Lynn hadn't offered any information either. That was the good thing about boys, she thought. They seldom connected events together.

The loss of her virginity had certainly been on the sixteen-year-old's mind too. Had she done the right thing? Should she have held out longer? Something told her that Jeff wasn't one to take no for an answer, but that was hardly a valid excuse for someone in her position. She had overheard a couple of girls talking during the lunch break on Monday about their awful first experiences of sex and how they both regretted giving in to their boyfriends' insistence. Had she given herself too easily? Should she have made him wait? But why did girls make boys wait anyway? Just for the sake of it? Because that was what nice girls did, or as a game of "oneupwomanship"? If it was to make sure the boy was interested in more than sex, this seemed like a forlorn hope for both genders. Like the rest of the animal kingdom, wasn't sex and perpetuating the species by giving life to the next generation the whole deal between boys and girls?

Lynn also wondered how this enigmatic stranger had come by so much sexual know-how. He had given the impression of being totally in command of the situation, but she was also prepared to believe it simply contrasted with her own *naïvetée*. Jeff was three years her senior, and she had always been told that boys matured later than girls. Most boys in her year were still awaiting their first female conquest, often voicing their frustrations at having been turned down. The teenager was also dying to share the joy with her mother, but was in grave fear of her father finding out and putting a stop to everything.

It was occasionally a disadvantage being ahead in school, the clever celebrity concluded. Her close friends were all around two years older than she was, and recently this had become a massive gap. Michelle and the others already had driving licences, and most had thrown extravagant eighteenth birthday parties and were constantly scheming about what to do with all the extra freedom which accompanied their newfound adulthood. And here she was, stuck in legal childhood for over another year and a half.

There was a thought, Lynn mused. She wondered if Jeff even knew she was sixteen and not eighteen. The university computing class was a Year Twelve option. Surely he did. He had claimed to know her birth date when they exchanged them, and there was more than enough publicity about her family for there to be no hiding their ages. It was a real pain to be constrained like this, and she cast her mind back to the comment her lover had made about feeling older than nineteen. What had he meant? She really wanted to find out more about him, and yet he had seemed rather distant when answering questions about himself. It was only fair to respect his privacy, but what might he be hiding? And why?

Life was complicated, she thought, and on this occasion, being Lynn Dyson didn't help one bit! When it came to dealing with major life events, fame and fortune lent no advantage whatsoever. In fact, there was far more at stake for her than for any of her friends if her affair were to leak out into the open. Leaving their class, the starlet walked to the sports centre with Michelle and listened to her best friend blather on about being unfairly marked for an English essay which was apparently perfect. Lynn had oozed the appropriate amount of empathy, and the redhead had gone home feeling better.

Tennis training after school was hard work too, especially when her mind was so keen to skip to later in the evening. Lynn was definitely earning her dinner, serving fifty or sixty times in quick succession and to all parts of both courts, at the behest of her coach. She hoped she wouldn't end up emptying her stomach on the fairground rides. Upon reaching her apartment, she had less than three quarters of an hour in which to get ready for the third date with her handsome Sydneysider. The evening was cooler than of late, so she decided jeans were appropriate. With her hair clipped back away from her face, she was excited and ready for whatever the night had in store.

Down at ground level, equally expectant, Jeff parked his car in one of the visitor's spots at Dyson Administration and bounded up the steps two at a time. There was a different security guard on duty this evening; younger and less condescending.

'Good evening, sir,' he said, as the tall, athletic man approached the barrier.

'Hi,' the visitor replied. 'I'm here to pick up Lynn Dyson.'

'Mister Diamond?'

His name was on the list. Excellent. Another step in the right direction, and his heart beat a little faster still.

Jeff nodded. 'Yes, that's right. Thanks.'

'You're welcome. My name's Michael.'

'Hi, Michael.'

'Let me give Miss Dyson a ring. Please take a seat, sir,' the security guard added, pointing to a row of leather armchairs along the window.

The visitor didn't sit down. He was far too full of nervous energy for that. He heard the telephone being answered and imagined the blonde teenager with the alluring smile answering it in as much anticipation as he was feeling. Christ! He hoped so. He couldn't remember ever wanting something so much.

Michael called over to him. 'Mister Diamond, Miss Dyson will be right down.'

'Thanks,' he acknowledged with a courteous wave.

Within a couple of minutes, the lift bell sounded and out stepped the said Miss Dyson. The sight of her standing in front of him, dressed casually and looking relaxed, immediately brought back everything Jeff had committed to memory, and his jumbled thoughts crashed into one another as they rushed towards his heart. The young man was seized by an overwhelming desire to hurdle the barrier but instead settled for a kiss on the cheek once his date reached the other side.

'How are you?' he asked. 'You look great.'

The teenagers walked outside to his car, keen to be on their own and away from further scrutiny. Jeff opened the passenger door and watched his date climb in, taking serious notice of her long legs and figure-hugging top.

The schoolgirl felt great too. 'Thanks. I'm well. What about you?'

'Glad to see you, that's for sure.'

The driver revved the engine, and they sped out of the driveway a little too quickly. Lynn hung on to the door handle while the car leaned over to round the corner. Nineteen-sixty-two Ford Fairlanes weren't built for negotiating tight bends at speed.

'Hey! What are you doing?' she exclaimed. 'We're not at the funfair yet!'

The testosterone-charged racer apologised, pulling over to the side of the road and stopping suddenly. He jumped out of the car and ran round to open her door, signalling for his passenger to step out onto the footpath. He took her hand and helped the stunned woman to her feet.

'This is what I'm doing,' he answered, hugging her close and kissing her. 'Hello.'

A passing car honked its horn, and they laughed.

'Hi!' the lively sixteen-year-old replied.

'I missed you so much,' Jeff told the smiling face. 'I never missed anyone before, and it hurts.'

Properly reacquainted, the pair climbed back into the car and continued their journey to the north side of the city. Swapping news of their respective weeks so far, they chatted eagerly. In fact, the conversation was so fluid that at several junctures Jeff found himself about to divulge a few too many personal details, checking himself just in time. He drove along Lygon Street, looking for a restaurant or a parking space, whichever came first.

Lynn spotted a gap in a line of cars. 'How about over there?'

'Yeah, thanks. That'll do nicely,' the driver affirmed, pulling the car over and reversing expertly into the space.

'So what type of food shall we spread over the gardens?' the impressed young woman asked him.

Jeff smiled. 'Take your pick. Somewhere you won't get mobbed.'

The pair found a pub with a rear courtyard full of empty tables. They weren't disturbed as they ate and drank, enabling the star to pretend to be a regular adult again. Her companion had bought her a glass of wine, which she ought to have turned down but didn't. His first pint of beer hadn't even touched the sides of his throat, and his heart beat outlandishly fast while he waited at the bar for a second, hoping his precious charge would be safe in his absence.

The couple shared without embarrassment their thrilling memories of the last time they had been together, both secretly wondering whether it was appropriate to be so open at this early stage. The newly protective veteran asked again if the schoolgirl had any regrets concerning her *début* into the world of sex, to which he received a coy shake of the head and a wide grin.

'Do you?' she giggled.

'What do you think?' he replied, blowing on his fingertips, as if they were still burning.

A filthy, white delivery van was parked at the end of the beer garden, not far from where the pair was sitting, which gave Jeff an idea. Putting his knife and fork down on an empty plate, he pushed his chair back and watched the gaze of the young woman opposite scan him up and down as he rose to his feet. He walked over and began to write on the side of the van. Lynn's eyes continued to follow him curiously, yet because he was left-handed, she was unable to make out what he was doing.

'What are you writing? "Please wash me"?' she guessed. 'Or "Also available in white"...'

The sophisticated accent tailed off to a whisper when the nineteen-year-old stepped casually aside, revealing three white words in the dirty, grey film on the paintwork.

"I LOVE YOU"

The young celebrity gasped, putting her hand to her mouth, completely dumbfounded. This man was so full of surprises.

'Wow! Thank you. I don't know what to say.'

Jeff returned to the table, where his sexy companion was welded to her chair in shock. He waved a blackened finger at her, threatening to smear grime across her cheek, before leaning over and giving her a slow, ardent kiss.

'You don't have to say anything,' he responded, 'although "Please wash me" does have a certain appeal.'

Lynn hugged him close, fighting back tears. 'I can't believe what you just did. It's so romantic!'

After spitting on his oily finger and wiping it clean on a paper napkin, Jeff raised his almost empty beer glass to his date. Romance was a new dimension for him too, but it sat well. All previous plans were henceforth out of the window for the smitten student, and now the ice had been broken so spectacularly on the next phase of their relationship, spontaneity had become his new byword.

'I was wondering how I was going to tell you, then it just came to me,' he confessed, pleased with himself.

Talking for a few more minutes, neither could stop looking at the graffiti which the boy from Sydney's west had left on the side of someone else's van. In the end, they finished their drinks and began walking back to the car. Her stomach churning, Lynn fixed him with another searching stare.

'Jeff, I've been thinking about you all the time since I last saw you. You're an amazing man. I was really looking forward to seeing you tonight.'

The object of her affection put his arm around her shoulders. 'Thanks. Me too. Completely obsessed, in fact. You make it very easy to for me to love you.'

The singer continued, feeling uncharacteristically shy. 'I feel too young, too naïve to know what love is. I don't trust my emotions, because everything's so new.'

Jeff understood what she was trying to tell him.

'It's OK,' he said. 'I have a lot more to compare this to than you do. I know what I feel for you is totally different to anything else I've ever felt. Plus, my added advantage is that I've loved you for about five years already.'

They had reached the car, and the well-mannered driver held the door open for his passenger again. Lynn stared up at his handsome face, intrigued at this most unexpected response.

'What do you mean?' she asked. 'How?'

'Get in, and I'll tell you.'

The car made a u-turn and headed back towards the city. The student explained how he used to watch the famous star as a girl on the television, either hosting "Strong Current", performing with the band or in interviews after her many successful tennis matches. He told her how much Gerry and his family always teased him about being bewitched by her, and how he had collected every snippet of information over the years.

'The defining moment for me,' he went on, pulling into the car park behind the Royal Exhibition Building, 'was when you guys did that TV programme on European folk songs and their history. You were explaining the research you'd done on the peasant farmers for "Power and Glory", and there was such truth behind your voice and in your face. That's when I fell in love with you. The trouble was I then had to wait for us both to grow up.'

Lynn's insides were melting. She had received hundreds, probably thousands, of fan letters telling her similar things, but this boy had actually moved his world to be close to her. How could she not reciprocate his expressions of love? But surely it would sound contrived if she were to say something now.

'That's an amazing story. I'm very honoured,' the pretty teenager replied, reaching for his hand and planting an emphatic kiss on the back.

Jeff turned his hand over in hers and stroked her cheek, thankful for the necessity of focussing on the road ahead, preventing his excitement from completely taking over and ruining the activities they were about to enjoy.

The sixteen-year-old continued dreamily. 'I have this picture in my mind of a young you watching me on TV. I'd love to see a photo of you at that age, so I can picture you better. If only I'd known... I would've loved to meet you. It would've been so nice to talk to someone about those songs. They did mean a lot to me. Still do, I suppose.'

The next two hours flew by, literally, on various rides and side shows. The elated couple competed on the rifle range, shooting guns with sights that were decidedly crooked, and the Rotor made them come close to losing their dinners, just like Jeff had promised. They were as high as kites. Conversation ebbed and flowed easily, covering both the serious and the strange aspects of life. Nothing could possibly have dampened their enthusiasm for the evening or for each other.

'I'd better get back soon,' Lynn announced, stifling a yawn and twisting his right wrist round to check the time. 'It's after ten. I've got training at six tomorrow morning.'

With the late-night crowd having consumed greater quantities of alcohol, the celebrity was also beginning to receive more recognition from her adoring public than was comfortable. Reluctantly, her date wheeled his precious companion round and pointed her towards the car park.

'OK. Sure. Let's get going. They're starting to pack up for the night anyway.'

Hand-in-hand, the pair picked their way in between two caravans, dodging noisy generators and lines of cables connecting to the fairground equipment, until they found a gap in the fence. They broke into a jog and reached the car without drawing further attention, and the blonde sixteen-year-old breathed a sigh of relief.

'I'm sorry,' she said, with a sad face. 'I always have to spoil the fun.'

Jeff laughed. 'You don't need to apologise. D'you think I mind being alone with you in my car?'

'That's good. I've had another fantastic evening. I hope we can see each other again soon,' Lynn told him, now more confident that they had started something which would continue beyond tonight.

The Fairlane made its way, as slowly as its driver could get away with, over Princes Bridge and back onto St Kilda Road. Turning into the narrow service road running parallel, he didn't stop before the driveway to the building this time. It was a dark, moonless night, and he guessed there would be no-one around. He got out of the car and went to the other side to let his passenger out. They walked up to the top of the steps at the front of the building and paused before they reached the doors, which had stopped revolving by this time of night.

Lynn gazed at her handsome chaperone, wondering what to do next. She knew she oughtn't to invite him upstairs on a school night, since she was tired and needed to be up very early, but neither did she want to seem disinterested. As it turned out, she didn't have to make the choice. Jeff enveloped her in his arms and pulled her close up against him. She clung to his lean, muscular frame willingly, and they kissed.

'Don't ask me in,' the nineteen-year-old told her quietly, as if he were reading her mind. 'It's late and it's been a perfect evening. Let's not spoil it.'

The young woman nodded and kissed him again. Perfect indeed. Her doubts during the week about giving herself to her mystery man too quickly were unfounded. Not only did he not expect sex tonight, but he was positively dissuading her, even though she could tell he was keen.

Breathing heavily, Jeff reluctantly pulled away. 'But if we stay here like this for too long, you're going to make me change my mind.'

Lynn's insides swooned. *You're not the only one*, she dearly wanted to say. Her mind was very much for changing too. The aroused man walked backwards towards the steps, holding his left hand out towards her.

'G'night. I'll ring you on Friday. Thanks again for tonight. You are gorgeous.'

Seeing the tall, athletic student walk away, the famous schoolgirl felt a distinct hollow in the pit of her stomach. She really didn't want to see him go, so turned to face the non-revolving doors and waved to the security guard on duty inside.

'Goodnight, Jeff.'

'Hey, Lynn!' he called after her.

The enchanted teenager spun round again to see the long-haired clown balancing on the bottom step, flexing his ankles as if he were about to dive off backwards.

'I still love you.'

Amused and flattered, the blonde blew a kiss and waved. She was crying with happiness and didn't want her date to see, wondering if she should risk calling him back up the steps. She watched him get into his old, rattly car and drive quickly away. The extent of her feelings for this man surprised her, and she couldn't think of anything about him she didn't like. He was funny, good-looking, expressive, strong, intelligent, kind and empathetic. The complete package, in fact.

And what had he said earlier, when the car had screeched to a halt not a minute away from home? "I never missed anyone before, and it hurts." Such a beautiful observation, rendered even more poignant after his surprise declaration later on. Plus, now Lynn knew exactly what he had meant. She missed him, and it hurt. This must truly be the right man for her, she concluded on her way up in the lift, resolving to find a meaningful way to let him know.

Soon back in Richmond, the blue car pulled into the car park of Jeff's apartment block, and the blue boy walked up the stairs from the basement, his spirits sinking with each step. Faced with his front door again, he stood staring out of the landing window for five or ten minutes, dreaming about Lynn and their evening together and steeling himself for the nightly battle with his flawed mind. Nothing for it... He couldn't stay in the hallway all night. He had to go in and settle back into normality, needing to try once again to get some sleep before the week continued. He mustered all the mental strength he could find to insert the key into that lock and turn it.

Once he was finally inside, Jeff crouched down on the hallway floor, breathless and angry, feeling sweat prickling the skin on his forehead and on the back of his neck. After a while, his legs cramped, and he slumped back against the wall. Pent-up emotion overtook him, and the dejected man wept like a child.

'Please, for Christ's sake, someone... Anyone... Take this shit away,' he begged to nobody in particular. 'It wasn't my fault. None of it was my fucking fault. Just stop this happening, so I can get on with my life.'

His heart rate eventually slowing, the exhausted teenager hauled himself up off the floor and moved to the couch. He really had no idea why he was feeling so sorry for himself. He had spent another few blissful hours with the girl of his dreams. He should be feeling on top of the world. Nevertheless, the way he was reacting was totally predictable. He was sick to death of his cruel, overactive conscience punishing him yet again for daring to be happy.

After all these years, and with the prospect of this new chapter unfolding, the nineteen-year-old figured he had already endured more than enough pain, repeatedly being thrown straight back into the chasm out of which he had only just managed to crawl. And here he was, yet again, poised to tip back over the edge.

'Gimme a fuckin' break,' he pleaded with his poisoned mind.

The furious student tried his best to focus on the positives from spending another wonderful evening with Lynn Dyson. Just one peaceful night was all he was asking for, so that he could let his imagination run away with him and seek the physical and emotional gratification he so desperately needed.

'Let me enjoy something for once,' he begged. 'Piss off and leave me alone.'

Jeff Diamond had never told anyone he loved them before, and it hadn't felt awkward or embarrassing at all. Furthermore, he didn't mind that Lynn hadn't returned the sentiment. Her reaction had been totally honest, and this was the most he could expect. She didn't laugh him out of town and she hadn't run scared. Not yet, anyway...

The teenager resolved to be patient and let the relationship develop further of its own accord. Having been born into such an unusual family, self-discipline was a skill he had developed very early on in life, and without which he would have never regularly attended primary school, not to mention being fed or clothed. Hopefully, after a few more dates with his new friend, his mind might come to terms with things and stop playing such wicked games. Jeff longed to stop lurching uncontrollably from higher-than-high to lower-than-low. Who knew what would happen tomorrow? For Christ's sake, Lynn had been untouched until a few days ago. Her emotions might well be as mixed up as his own, although he doubted it.

The solitary student forced a smile, recalling the young woman's innocent "Please wash me" comment. It was so refreshing to spend time with someone who was untainted by adult cynicism. He had succeeded in surprising her, which was his intention, and she had told him she hoped to see him again soon. Everything was sweet. *Just deal with it*, he urged his tormented brain.

Thick clouds of tiredness gathered in his head, bringing with them a renewed wave of depression. The boy from Canley Vale was so fed up with being alone. He spent plenty of time in the company of others, but it was mostly a one-way street. Relationships of no consequence, where one party used the other to serve a particular purpose and then walked away. Why was it always he who checked in on people, picked up the telephone and shared their stories? *Don't be so ungrateful,* Jeff scolded himself. Gerry was a good mate, and Suzanne often asked after him when they were together. But just once he wished the telephone would ring for him.

How the teenager longed for those parental conversations about which his friends often complained: mothers calling to ask how they were doing, whether they were eating enough or if they had a supply of clean socks and undies; and fathers providing unwanted but probably much needed advice. Even his sister, whenever he could be bothered to track her down, would be quite happy to impart all her news but never once asked what had been happening in his world. Just occasionally it would be nice to hear, *"Olá, chico. ¿Qué tal? ¿Algo pasa con tigo?"*

Tears pricked the back of the young man's eyes again. *Grow up,* he taunted. *You don't need them.*

Jeff missed his grandmother on his father's side. She was the only one who had shown any interest in him during his childhood. He remembered sneaking out to her flat for another bowl of that revolting beetroot soup she always made. Her place had been a sanctuary where he had felt welcome, maybe even loved. It was his Polish grandmother who had arranged for him to take piano lessons, and it was probably she who had passed on the empathetic genes which the dark Diamond possessed in spades. His grandfather had died when the boy was only nine years old, after which he and Bubshka had shared an unspoken bond of loneliness until she herself had passed away a few years later.

Self-diagnosing again, Jeff concluded that the reason he felt so depressed after one of the three best nights of his life must be the unfulfilled promise of returned love. He had declared his deeply-held feelings for Lynn tonight, and he so craved her company. A kindred spirit with whom to share the world was all he ever wanted; someone who would believe in him and make him strong enough to accomplish all the wildly ambitious goals he had set.

This new relationship was something the gifted adolescent must learn to take slowly; an exercise none too easy for a man whose mind had been conditioned to work in such destructive ways. His love for Lynn was to be nurtured and allowed to form its own shape into the future, taking account of all the many constraints that the young celebrity's life necessarily incorporated. The intelligent young man's rational self understood this well enough, and now it was up to him to convince his irrational, compulsive alter-ego to cease the "Fuck me now" mentality that had ruled his life up until this point. His normal attitude would not work in this new, forward-looking scenario, and certainly not with someone as sophisticated as Miss Dyson. That type of irresponsible behaviour must be restricted to the days in between, while he waited for the next opportunity to act like a normal human being.

Shaking his head, the student levered himself to his feet and went into the bathroom, his legs aching almost as much as his heart and his head. Standing under the shower, his mind continued to tease him. *You idiot! You should have chosen an easier target to crave.* He had probably fallen in love with the least accessible woman in Australia.

'That'd be right,' he scoffed, looking at himself in the mirror.

***

Sunday, Jeff thought, looking at his watch. It was two-thirty in the morning, and he had just crept out of a girl's room without being caught. A group of RMIT students had gone to see a band together, ending up at a dilapidated worker's cottage in Brunswick. The party boy had no idea where he was and no cash to pay for a taxi.

Never mind. It was a nice night to run through the empty city. Again. Money was becoming scarcer by the day, which had been weighing heavily on the student's mind. He was receiving small royalty payments for the four songs he had managed to sell last year, but his income surely needed boosting if he was planning on entertaining Lynn Dyson in a style presumed customary. Also, he had noticed the muffler on his car was becoming noisier, a clear sign that it would need to be replaced soon.

New songs were coming thick and fast however. The prolific writer had a few that were almost ready, but he would need to sell something fairly quickly in order to see some cash flowing in before the current semester finished. Gerry had helped him negotiate a good deal with the publishing company which had picked up the earlier songs, and they had figured out how to work the exchange rate in his favour when bringing the money into Australia. Purging the residue of lactic acid and last night's drinks from his body, Jeff decided to go home right now and package something up to send to the US of A.

It took almost an hour to reach home, and the night owl was sober by the time he arrived and commenced the long climb to the second level. Crashing through the front door, he made straight for the guitar. His demo' tapes were very basic, a single vocal accompanied by guitar or keyboard, but so far they had been good enough. He smiled to himself as he thought of Lynn in the recording studio, surrounded by state-of-the-art equipment and skilled sound engineers. Another world...

At dawn, the restless teenager left the flat in search of Suzanne and her boarders, finding them in the usual spot behind her run-down property, which was nestled in the rolling hills, north-east of the city, beyond the fringe of

Greater Melbourne. She had only five dogs with her this time, all different breeds and ages, who burled up to the new arrival boisterously.

'Business not booming this week?'

His best mate's girlfriend hugged him. 'Hi! Nice to see you. I wondered if you'd be here this morning. What have you been up to?'

'Oh, nothing much,' he lied. 'Saw a band last night with some mates. Had a few drinks afterwards. What about you?'

'Similar,' she answered. 'Gerry and I saw "A Clockwork Orange" and then drank far too much. I drove home though. Shouldn't have, but I made it. God knows how! My head's pretty fuzzy.'

'I've read about that film. What did you think?'

Suzanne screwed her face up. 'A bit weird and gruesome. Decadence gone mad.'

'It's going to be a classic though.'

Jeff was jealous. He wished he could see this new movie which was receiving such critical acclaim, but the cinema was another no-go zone for him. He smiled as he saw the young woman looking disparagingly at the way he was dressed.

'You haven't been home, have you?'

'No, Mum,' he answered petulantly. 'What's it to you?'

Suzanne did have a habit of playing the big sister sometimes.

'I hope you're being careful. You're going to get someone pregnant soon and then you'll be stuck.'

Jeff threw his hands in the air in frustration, tired and not relishing another lecture. He bent down to play with one of the dogs, who was bouncing around and looking for attention.

'For Christ's sake! No, I won't. I know what I'm doing. I haven't got anyone pregnant yet, have I?'

The former city girl shook her head. 'No, I s'pose not. But you wouldn't tell me anyway, so how would I know? You could have your pick of steady girlfriends, you know.'

Jeff gave the prude an impish grin. 'Well, how do you know I don't already have one?'

This piqued Suzanne's interest. For as long as she had known the solitary ladies' man, he had seldom dated the same woman more than once and had certainly never owned up to anything that might be termed a relationship. In truth, she was very keen on him herself, were it not for an apparent inability to curtail his extra-curricular activities which, coupled with a complete lack of attachment, served to warn her off. Gerry was far from the perfect partner but was a whole lot more reliable than the handsome love-god standing in front of her.

'Have you? Good! That's really good, Jeff. Peter Pan grows up, finally. When can we meet her?'

They paused for a minute to retrieve one of the dogs, who had managed to slip through a hole in the fence. Jeff took up the chase, and panting like her charges, the twenty-two-year-old eventually caught up with him, intrigued to find out more. The enigma was not volunteering any information however, leaving the gossip-hungry woman to press the issue.

'So tell me more!' she urged. 'What's her name? What does she do? A uni' student? You know I want all the gory details.'

Jeff grinned. 'OK, OK! Now, are you sure you're ready to be open minded?'

'Open minded?' Suzanne shot back. 'What the hell do you mean by that? Is she a he?'

That would be the biggest surprise of her life. Her long-time friend couldn't possibly be gay, could he? Jeff was equally astonished that she had wandered off on that particular tangent.

'Fuck, no!' he exclaimed. 'Not that open minded! Have a guess.'

'Oh, for God's sake, I don't know. Just tell me!'

'OK, if you insist. I, Jeff Diamond, do solemnly swear, on my heart...'

The joker paused mid-sentence, laughing at the woman's expression of anticipation and miming a drumroll in the air.

'Don't stop!' Suzanne shouted, her fists beating his broad chest in mock fury.

The dogs jumped up at them on hearing their raised voices, keen to muscle in on the excitement. The tired young man left the kennel owner in suspense once more, standing his ground while the animals vied for position. She groaned in exasperation, which only made him delay further.

At last, he put her out of her misery. 'I'm going out with the one and only Lynn Dyson.'

The country girl stopped in her tracks, spinning round to face her old friend, who looked as proud as Punch. If she had been a cartoon, her bottom jaw would have dropped all the way to the ground.

'What?' she squealed.

Jeff continued. 'I said open minded, not open mouthed... It's true. I've been out with her three times actually.'

'Three times? No, I don't believe you,' the indignant woman objected. 'You've never gone out with anyone three times. How could you even meet Lynn Dyson? There's no way she'd go out with you just like that. Isn't she surrounded by security men? Have you been smoking too much dope?'

Typical, the street kid thought. The Mosman *débutante* didn't believe him. Her reaction was not unexpected, and he began to regret letting her into his secret. Feeling anger boiling up inside, he was in half a mind just to turn around and go home, when her tone softened a little.

'How did you ask her out?' Suzanne asked, desperate to find out more. 'Where did you take her?'

Jeff sneered in jest. 'Oh, so now you believe me?'

Well, half in jest anyway.

'I don't know. I'd love to believe you, but how could it possibly happen?' she replied, sensing his disappointment.

'I asked her out when a Melbourne Academy class came to the uni' for a Computer Science lecture. I chased her down the corridor and just asked her out there and then. There was no other way. You know... *Carpe diem* and all that... We went the theatre, to see "A Streetcar Named Desire".'

'Wow, Jeff! That's amazing. And she said yes?'

'Well, obviously... Otherwise I would've been there on my own, wouldn't I?'

'Sorry! Yes, obviously. So what's she like? Is she friendly or haughty?'

Jeff's heart leaped into his mouth as he remembered his first tentative but rewarding attempts at initiating conversation, and how patient Lynn had been with the people competing for her attention. What was she like? He had never had to put these words together before, and it made his pulse race even to consider their articulation.

'She's gorgeous,' he responded casually. 'Very friendly and down-to-earth. No airs and graces whatsoever.'

'You're joking!' his friend disputed. 'How could someone so famous have no airs and graces?'

The young man shrugged at the dismissive response. It was up to Suzanne what she chose to believe, and her opinion made little difference to him. He continued to paint the picture, as much to remind himself as anything.

'We got mobbed wherever we went, but she's very generous with people wanting to talk to her. We've had a great time so far, and I hope there'll be more. She's as clever as all hell, and funny too.'

The country girl was spellbound. Was the arrogant ladies' man telling the truth? Her boyfriend's mate had been harping on about his infatuation with the chart-topping singer for so long that she had grown out of the childish hope that one day they might actually meet. As it happened, the former private school student from Sydney's north shore was a huge Lynn Dyson fan too, and would be absolutely rapt to make her acquaintance. She didn't say anything, but her eyes must have egged him on.

Jeff obliged, his head now replete with fond memories. 'Last Friday night we went to the start-of-year party at the Uni' Club, and on Wednesday we went to a fairground behind the Royal Exhibition Building.'

However, before he had finished his sentence, the testy woman seized on something. She raised her hands triumphantly, convinced she had caught him out.

'Aha! But MAC were doing a TV show on Friday. I watched it.'

The handsome man smiled and raised his eyebrows. Of course her old friend was more than ready to tackle this ambit claim, and also ready to cover once again for Gerry who, as he remembered full well, had been keeping company with another woman that night.

'Yeah, I know. We met up afterwards. Do you want to hear more or not?'

'Sorry, Jeff. Yes, I'd love to hear more. So do you think you'll see her again? Has she given any clues whether she likes you or not?'

'Whoa! From the ridiculous to the sublime all of a sudden! Enough with the questions already,' the student begged, reeling back. 'Yep. I'm seeing her again tonight, as a matter of fact. We're going to the library to work on our homework.'

'The library?' Suzanne yelped. 'Last of the big spenders! Jeff, you'll have to come up with something better than that! At least take her out to dinner, for God's sake. You can't take a girl to the library!'

Again the young man shrugged. 'When I need dating advice from you, I'll ask, Suzie. OK?' he sneered. 'So far she keeps saying yes when I ask her out, so that's good enough for me.'

'OK. You're right. That's wonderful,' his friend admitted, hugging him and getting caught up in his enthusiasm. 'Wow! So you really know Lynn Dyson, after all those years of talking about it. I have to confess, I never thought you'd even get close. When do you think sex'll rear its ugly head? That'll be a big deal, even for you.'

'Yes, it was.'

The young woman screamed again. 'Yes, it was? Jeff, you haven't?'

He nodded, feeling surprisingly sheepish and guilty.

'We have. It was fantastic.'

The twenty-two-year-old was beside herself. 'Jeff, for God's sake! You can't just fuck Australia's most famous schoolgirl? She's only sixteen and she's our darling. What about her parents? Where did you go?'

'Slow down, Suze,' her indignant friend answered. 'I didn't *just fuck* her. Please! Give me credit for some class, at least.'

Suzanne hung her head a little in apology. 'Well, it sounds like it. You haven't known her five minutes and already you've got her into bed. This is Lynn Dyson we're talking about. Surely she's expecting to be wined and dined a bit before putting out. I can't believe you were so brazen.'

'I took her back to my place after the disco,' Jeff explained, shrugging his shoulders as if it were the most natural thing in the world to do. 'And one thing led to another.'

'Oh, my God! As it does... With Bart Dyson's daughter... You're mad! And I thought you never entertained at your place,' the young woman gestured quotation marks around the word "entertained".

The nineteen-year-old laughed. 'No. First time actually. And it was her first time too, by the way.'

Suzanne screamed yet again.

'You're kidding! Was she a virgin? Oh, my God! What have you done? You've deflowered Australia's first daughter! I don't believe you! Oh, my God!'

This was more like the response the modern-day Don Juan had been looking for. Yes, it was a huge deal, and he wanted to celebrate it with his long-time friend. Eventually she regained her composure, and they walked on, by now almost back at their vehicles.

'So what was it like? The sex, I mean.'

'Quick!' the student snapped, smiling and slightly embarrassed, both by the unmanly concession and the knowledge that his irrepressible erection must be highly visible by now. 'But not so quick the second time. She's fantastic; sensitive and intelligent, and so unbelievably hot, in a cute kind of way.'

The young man plunged his hands deep into his pants pockets, hoping to disguise his predicament. Suzanne hugged her handsome friend again and pecked him on the cheek.

'I hate you!'

They both knew the meaning behind those three words. Gerry's girlfriend loved Jeff deeply, and he knew it. Now the shock was wearing off, he could see she was happy for him regardless, because she knew how much he had wanted to go out with Lynn ever since the Sydney trio had first met as young teenagers. After all, this was the only reason he had moved to Melbourne with them, truth be told.

'So what's it worth for me not to go blabbering to the press?'

'Your life,' the deep voice answered dryly, right next to her ear.

He waited for her to open the back door of her van and helped her to load the dogs in one by one. Suzanne laughed, turning to slap his shoulder.

'So have fun at the library,' she joked, hopping up into the driver's seat and starting the engine. 'No nookie between the bookcases. Mummy and Daddy won't want to read about their little darling in the tabloids.'

The kennel owner wound up her window, and the van disappeared up the track which led to the main road. Jeff turned the Fairlane around and headed for his flat, to shower off the previous night's sins in preparation for the next appointment with his dream girl. Somehow he would need to focus on an assignment this morning, plus fit in a shift at the university and play squash with Gerry. His eyelids felt heavy as he drove back towards the city, but the thought of being busy between now and the evening comforted him.

***

Lynn threw her suitcase onto the bed, back in her suite on the top floor of the Dyson Administration building. Her weekend had been a full one, and she was quite tired. Nevertheless, she was very much looking forward to seeing Jeff again. She had felt very grown-up when he had requested they exchange telephone numbers. This was a proper relationship now, with all the anticipation and excitement of a romantic movie. She was no different from the next girl in this respect.

Her handsome stranger had rung her on Friday morning, before she left for school. He had sounded exhausted too, and his voice had been scratchy, but he wished her a good weekend and asked if they could see each other on Sunday evening for a few hours. Against her better judgment, with another hectic week ahead, Lynn jumped at the chance.

The other four-letter word beginning with "L" had not been spoken again during their brief conversation, but the sixteen-year-old had spent the whole weekend mulling over the subject. How would she recognise love anyway? Yet Jeff had, or at least he thought he had. Unless he was spinning her a line for other purposes, whatever they might be? She also remained rather anxious about the difference in their sexual experience. He was obviously not a new starter! She wondered whether she ought to have chosen someone who had seen a little less active service.

Nevertheless, her new lover's worldliness, particularly when it came to sex, was just one of the many multi-faceted pieces which made up the interesting puzzle that was Jeff Diamond. His was a great name for a would-be rock star too. Was it even his real name? The celebrity had so many questions, and he appeared to know so much about everything. Quite apart from the physical attraction, this aspect of his personality was especially seductive for the energetic young woman. She too was hungry for knowledge, and delighted that this man seemed willing to see past her youth and treat her with so much respect. She couldn't help laughing when she remembered the dinosaurs that weren't in the *Kama Sutra*.

The teenager took a quick shower and dressed in appropriate study wear: her favourite underwear for a start. She then chose a skirt that was below knee length, but which was full and swung as she walked. It made her feel very feminine, especially compared to the shorts and t-shirts she had lived in all weekend on the farm.

Her date arrived at the Dyson offices early, so he drove around the back streets of South Melbourne for a few minutes. He had thrown his pile of books onto the back seat and was feverishly looking forward to seeing the girl of his dreams again. In fact, certain parts of him were looking forward to it a little too much.

When he reached the building, Jeff parked the car on the end of the row of reserved spaces, as inconspicuously as possible. He didn't know which other members of the famous family might return to the city in advance of the new week, choosing to take his chances. He climbed the steps to find yet another security man in the usual spot.

'Good evening, sir,' the guard said politely, not offering his name.

He was between the ages of Michael and Howard, with a weathered face and a large pot belly. What a boring job this must be, the visitor mused.

'Good evening, sir,' he replied, accustomed to the routine these days.

'Is it Mister Diamond?'

'Yes, it is. Thanks.'

Well, that was new… This time he hadn't even been asked whom he had come to see. Was his face on file already? This supposition disturbed the lad from Sydney's rough western suburbs, even though he shouldn't be surprised that his anonymity was not assured in the Dyson world. Perhaps he would be prudent to open up a little to Lynn in advance of any questions her family might be prompted to ask. At least her allegiance might count on his side of the ledger when it came time for him to defend himself.

The telephone receiver was replaced, and the uniformed man pointed towards the lifts.

'You can go up, Mister Diamond. Top floor, last door from the end, to your right out of the lifts. Number six.'

Shit, Jeff cursed under his breath. *This could be interesting too.* The inclusion of a girlfriend in his singleton life was becoming less and less simple every day. He entered the lift by himself and ascended to the penthouse level. He could feel the hairs standing up on his neck as he quickly planned how he should deal with arriving at a closed door. By the time he reached the top, he felt nauseated and his head pounded.

To his relief, the door to apartment number six was already open, and the lift bell brought its occupant out to meet him. The anxious man breathed a sigh of relief. Lynn reached out her hands to greet him.

'Are you OK?' she asked, before even saying hello. 'You look very pale.'

Jeff gave her an impetuous hug, all nerves summarily tossed aside. 'Hey! I'm fine. It's so good to see you.'

In other words, it was so good to see her outside and with the door open… Ironically, his panic attack had done him a favour, having taken his mind off his caveman instincts and buying the pair time to ease into the evening.

Lynn took the handsome man at his word and stopped worrying that he looked as white as a sheet. And indeed, after about five minutes, the colour returned to his face, and he was back to his old self, kidding around with her and being generally irresistible.

'So... Shall we go?' she suggested, pointing to her schoolbag which was already fastened shut and ready to be picked up and taken to the library.

The nineteen-year-old stared into her blue eyes. 'Not yet. Come here.'

His smiling host did as she was told, seeing a hungry look come over his face.

'Why? What do you want to do?'

The schoolgirl had been wondering when she would be asked for sex again. Jeff had been the perfect gentleman during the week, and she was almost relieved to find that he still wanted to. Still not in the least *au fait* with the politics of sex, she had even begun to wonder whether she had done something that she ought not to have done, or *vice versa,* in her *naïvetée*.

'Well...' the guest smiled, taking her left hand in his and twisting her round so that her back was against his belly, cuddling her into his eager body. 'Aren't you going to give me the tour?'

The joyful young woman giggled, instantly excited by the feel of his erection against her back.

'Of course! I'm terribly sorry. How remiss of me. Please step this way, sir.'

Lynn started to walk forwards, but her man restrained her playfully for a second or two, before relaxing his grip and following her through the apartment. It was as if a network of interlaced electric currents criss-crossed the room, through which their individual anticipations were woven.

'Sitting,' she began, pointing to the lounge suite, about three paces from where the tour kicked off.

'Check,' Jeff responded.

They then walked up a single step into a small dining area, with a kitchenette against the far wall.

'Food.'

'Check.'

At the back of the room was a door to a bathroom, and to the right, a queen-sized bed, divided from the rest of the room by a row of built-in wardrobes.

'Watery things,' Lynn continued, waving to the bathroom, 'and...'

She looked around at her visitor, who was grinning at her choice of words, feeling very apprehensive at what she was about to do. Their first time, until now vividly remembered with great accuracy, suddenly seemed like a blur to the naïve teenager. Her partner, on the other hand, again appeared totally in control.

'*Muy buen,*' he smiled. 'Thanks. I'd like to use the "and" room with you, if I may. It'll help us concentrate later.'

'Us?'

Jeff shrugged, sprung again. 'Well, at least one of us.'

He pulled the sexy, pouting sixteen-year-old in towards him and kissed her wantonly. She remembered how good this felt and did not object. Why was she afraid? In fact, she realised she felt safer, if anything, wrapped in this tall man's arms, with his warm breath against her cheek drawing her in.

'I *still* still love you,' he reminded her. 'You look so good and feel so good. Can we?'

'Thank you,' she answered, blissfully powerless in his embrace. 'OK. Since you put it so nicely.'

Straightaway, Jeff began to remove her clothes, his fingers caressing her collarbone from neck to shoulder before passing temptingly over her breasts and on to the hem of her top, which was soon lifted slowly over her head. Even though she felt nervous, Lynn decided to make an attempt at reciprocation. During her previous lesson, her expert lover had encouraged her to do whatever came naturally, because it would probably be the right thing to do. He had explained that he was a great believer in instinct, so she used hers to unbutton his shirt and kiss the dark hair on his chest. She then slipped her hands around his ribcage until they came to rest over his kidneys, just above the waistband of his pants.

Her man groaned. 'That's so perfect. Keep going, please.'

While enjoying the sensation of Lynn's lips on his skin, the hungry man had managed to undo her skirt, and the stylish garment slipped to the floor, having already served its purpose. The slender blonde followed suit, undoing his belt and starting on his jeans. They laughed as they had last time at the awkward spectacle that was removing a pair of jeans. The more invention she applied, the more she was encouraged by his willing response, and her nerves began to dissipate.

'Teach me something,' the schoolgirl asked of her breathless Polish Argentinean. 'What would you like me to do?'

Jeff groaned again, cupping her face with loving hands. 'You are too good to me.'

He gently invited his innocent partner to sit down on the edge of the bed, before taking off his shorts and throwing them to one side. Standing in front of her, he rubbed the end of his stiff penis against her cheek and moved it slowly across to her lips. Although this all seemed very strange, Lynn's instincts encouraged her to open her mouth. Her tongue tentatively traced around the bulbous tip, and she felt him shudder. After the initial unfamiliarity of the act, however, it began to feel pretty good to the young woman.

The patient but highly aroused teacher gently held her head and coaxed her to move backwards and forwards, to let her mouth travel up and down the length of his erection. He could hear her breathing quicken, and before long felt his own self-control weaken. Scared that carrying on would cause things to accelerate way too fast, the nineteen-year-old exhaled sharply, feeling her lips close around the head of his penis as he pulled out. Buying himself some time, he crouched down to kiss this beautiful and brave young woman, whom he was coming to adore more and more with each passing moment.

'That was fantastic,' he whispered. 'Thanks, but let's slow things down.'

At his direction, Lynn lay back on the bed while her mystery man put on a condom, and he climbed onto her slowly, kissing her all over. His hands were strong, and his movements purposeful. She could feel herself becoming more turned on and hoped he would bring her to orgasm again.

Jeff Diamond wouldn't have done anything else. He was so excited by the way his dream girl was behaving with him, his mind obsessed with how much he loved her, and vowed to make sure she enjoyed her time with him as much as possible. Leaning forward until their faces met, he entered her, gently laying down onto her body and kissing her passionately.

'Do you like this?' his lips whispered against her face, working his magic with the fingers of his left hand.

Lynn nodded, her face flushed. 'Oh, yes. You know I do.'

'That's good,' he smiled, feeling her come at his hand. 'So do I.'

They stared into each other's eyes as the extreme sensation overtook the young celebrity and then subsided gradually. Although Jeff had given this sort of pleasure so many times before, in so many different circumstances and to so many different women, somehow this gorgeous creature's enjoyment was much more fulfilling than anything else. This was Lynn Dyson he had brought to orgasm. Lynn Dyson!

'You're the best,' the sixteen-year-old told him, running her fingers up his back and stroking his neck as he climaxed inside her moments later.

Jeff let out the longest moan she had ever heard, bending his arms slowly and dropping his body down onto hers.

'So are you. *Y que era increíble, señorita.*'

'Thanks. What did you say?' the young woman laughed. 'Are you sure you're OK?'

'No. Much better than OK, I assure you,' he replied. 'I said, "That was amazing."'

The delirious pair lay stuck together for a good few minutes, kissing and talking about their weekends. After a while, Lynn dared to remind the satisfied man that this evening was originally to be used for catching up on their studies. Reluctantly, following a few feeble attempts to convince his young love that she had already learned quite a lot this evening, they made themselves ready for the library.

'Shall we walk?' Jeff suggested. 'It's a nice night, and it's not too far. We could grab some dinner in Chinatown afterwards.'

'OK,' the schoolgirl replied. 'As long as I get some work done, I don't mind. I've got so much to do.'

The happy couple set off on the three kilometre walk to the State Library, on the north side of the CBD. When they arrived, there was hardly a soul inside, and they took up residence at a table in the Modern Sciences section. Hoping his famous study-mate wouldn't be disturbed while he was gone, the undergraduate disappeared to find some books from another section, leaving Lynn to settle down to her homework. He returned after ten minutes with two large tomes on philosophy, along with a copy of the *Kama Sutra* that was dropped dramatically on top of her notebook.

'Let's see if we can find the dinosaurs,' his kind, sonorous voice sounded suggestively close to her ear.

The young woman giggled. 'Are we going to borrow this?'

'Yeah. Why not? It's ed-ya-kay-shunol,' the Sydneysider answered in his best bogan accent.

The two diligent students resigned themselves to more serious pursuits and began to concentrate on their individual assignments. Occasionally one would share a morsel of interesting information with the other, but on the whole they were very conscientious. Stealing a sly look at her lover's handsome face, Lynn concluded this to be a very good way of having a boyfriend. Her parents would definitely approve of the main part of the date, if not the *prélude*!

The celebrity quietly turned over the page on which she had been writing and began to scribble something on a new sheet of paper, ending with a flourish. Jeff glanced over, noticing a change in her writing style, just in time to see her tear off the bottom of the piece of paper. She folded it in half, kissed it and gave it to her study partner.

The note was addressed to "JD". Raising an enquiring eyebrow, he accepted it and opened it out.

"To Jeff, I definitely love you too. Lynn xx"

Initially, the young man had taken hold of the note rather casually, expecting it to be a joke or a secret remark about someone else in the library. As soon as he read it however, his whole body language altered. The starlet watched as his eyes read her simple message and saw his Adam's apple gulp in his throat. As he leaned over dangerously on his chair to kiss her, she could see the lights hanging from the library ceiling reflected in shining eyes.

'Thank you,' he whispered.

The boy from Sydney's west was transported instantly to Cloud Nine. It was quite the most perfect reply to his white van declaration, and he could scarcely believe his eyes. The tortured tearaway was learning, at long last, and his newfound forbearance had already yielded a priceless dividend. *Good things come to those who wait.*

So there was truth in that old saying, Jeff reflected, fighting back tears and kissing the pretty teenager again. Last week's decision to ignore his instinctive impatience and anxieties and to put his faith in the future had paid off. Maybe there truly was some higher force pushing the two of them together. It didn't really matter, did it? He should get over trying to understand every nuance of life and concentrate on enjoying this incredible journey.

'I'm sure now,' Lynn added, somewhat nervous. 'I love you, Jeff.'

'I know you do. I can feel it, and I love you too.'

Breathing in deeply, the humble student folded the note in half again and inserted it into the breast pocket of his shirt, holding his hand over it for a considerable pause, both to protect it and to show the famous beauty how close it was to his heart. Between them, they had generated such an emotionally charged atmosphere that neither could concentrate on work any longer.

'Let's get some food,' the sixteen-year-old suggested, closing her text book and tucking her notepad inside. 'My shout. You paid for me last time, so it's my turn.'

Jeff didn't argue. He was in fact extremely low on funds, and taking up Lynn's offer now would certainly save potential embarrassment later. He wondered what assumptions the rich girl had made about his financial status. He hoped it wouldn't matter, but expected this not to be the case.

'OK. If you insist,' he replied with a grin. 'That'd be great, thanks.'

They packed up their belongings and made their way to the bookings desk. Jeff slid the copy of the *Kama Sutra* onto the top of the young lady's pile, only to have her shift it smartly back to his before the woman behind the counter saw it.

'Don't!' she whined like a child.

Her expressive companion magnanimously took the offending title back, and the librarian dealt him a filthy look as she stamped the books out. He shrugged towards his pretty, blonde companion, making surreptitious gestures that the book was really hers. The student was disappointed that the clerk didn't appear to realise whose books she had just stamped, unless she was simply behaving like a pillar of Melbourne discretion with Australia's favourite daughter. His vivid imagination feasted on the possibility that the prim librarian would hardly be able to wait until her next staff coffee break to share the juicy gossip of Lynn Dyson reading the *Kama Sutra*.

The couple laughed all the way to the front doors, almost breaking into a run. Swanston Street on a Sunday evening was virtually deserted, even though the temperature lingered in the high twenties and there was only a trace of humidity in the air. A perfect Melbourne summer's night was in the making, in more ways than one, as they walked the two blocks to Little Bourke Street and turned under the red-painted gateway into Chinatown.

'Have you been to the Banana Palm restaurant?' Lynn asked.

Jeff shook his head. 'The only one I've heard of is The Flower Drum, and only because I hear it's bloody expensive.'

'Yes, it is bloody expensive,' his well-bred companion laughed. 'The Flower Drum's nice but not that nice. The Banana Palm does Malaysian curries. Is that OK?'

Was that OK? The hungry student was ready to agree to dinner on the Moon if it meant spending more time with this captivating woman. They arrived at the small establishment and requested a table in the corner. The manager scurried around, making sure his special guest was shown to their best table. Jeff thanked him and stood by until Lynn had been seated properly. Still on a natural high after receiving her note, he was totally unable to concentrate on the menu.

'What's good? You choose for me.'

They prepared to dine well, sharing three main courses between them. The nineteen-year-old drank beer from Singapore, and his under-aged partner ordered a non-alcoholic cocktail which arrived ornately decorated, with pieces of fruit threaded under a miniature umbrella.

'Hey, look!' Jeff exclaimed, as the waiter brought it to the table. 'It's Marlene Dietrich. Come up and see me sometime. She said that, didn't she?'

'I think so,' Lynn shrugged and nodded, rendered shy by the thrill of his suggestive eyes.

The celebrity was thoroughly enjoying this latest escape into normality as well. She was glad her quickly scrawled announcement had made her good-looking man so happy. Inexplicably, she felt very close to him already, as if they had been friends for years. She still had no idea who he was and was bemused as to why the absence of information didn't bother her more. They delighted in each other's company, which perhaps was all that mattered for now.

The temperature had chilled down by the time the lovers left the restaurant, so they jumped onto a tram heading down towards Flinders Street. Jeff pulled out Lynn's note with his ticket and slotted it into his wallet for safekeeping. He signalled for her to sit next to the window, in order that he might shield her from onlookers.

Unabashed, the star allowed herself to be kissed on the tram, caught up in the romance once more. So what if people saw? This was her life, and she was determined to enjoy it. The rattling vehicle dropped them off on the edge of the gardens, and they walked the rest of the way back over the wide thoroughfare to the Admin building.

'Would you look at the time?' Jeff exclaimed, with a theatrical bow. 'I must leave you to sleep.'

'Oh, OK. Did you want to come up?' the young woman blushed, feeling disappointingly torn.

The chivalrous young man shook his head. 'Yes, of course I do, but I won't.'

Again he exercised uncommon restraint, and again his dream girl was impressed. Smiling, Lynn thanked him for thinking of her need to rest before the start of another busy week, and Jeff thanked her for returning his expression of love so beautifully. They embraced once more for luck, outside the glass doors and in full view of the new security guard.

Then, as if she had suddenly remembered something but wasn't sure if she should mention it, the pretty blonde looked up into her chaperone's dark eyes with a worried stare.

'That new guy,' she began, gazing in through the window. 'He's Scottish, called Alastair, and he makes me uncomfortable. There's something weird about him. Did you notice?'

Jeff looked over at the bloke in the box. 'No. He seemed OK to me. What kind of weird?'

'Oh, it's probably my imagination. He just gives me the creeps.'

'Trust your instincts,' her new guardian advised, as he had the other day. 'Say something. Get your people to check him out. Promise you will?'

The young star nodded and smiled at his humorous but caring suggestion, and they kissed again. Out of her line of sight, the larrikin reached the copy of the *Kama Sutra* from his bag and slotted it into hers, without even coming up for air.

'Do me a favour, please, angel?'

Lynn looked at him expectantly, her heart flipping at the pet name he was beginning to use for her quite regularly.

'Yes. What?' She was surprised at how serious the student had become, clearly concerned for her safety.

'When you're back in your room with the door locked, would you leave a message on my machine? I don't want to leave you here and not know you're OK.'

Lynn hugged him again. 'You're so gorgeous.'

'Hey! That's my line.'

'Sorry, but you are,' she insisted. 'Goodnight. Have a good week.'

'Thanks. And for dinner too, and especially for your note.'

Jeff watched the exquisite vision go through the security barrier and step into the lift. He then gave Alastair a stern glare, but the portly Scot didn't react. Hopefully Lynn's instincts were wrong this time. He decided to use some of the money he had saved from dinner on a taxi, still worried about his new friend's uncertainty. Once home, his heightened fears acted as a good incentive to get inside his flat, and he managed to open the door relatively quickly. He rushed into the lounge room to find a welcome red, flashing light on his answering machine.

"Hi, Jeff. I'm fine. Locked in my room and thinking of you. Thanks again for a great evening. See you soon. Love you heaps. Bye."

The nineteen-year-old slumped heavily down onto the couch and played the message again. What a contrast from the last time they had parted at the revolving doors! He couldn't remember ever feeling this happy. Lynn was as romantic as he was, and he loved it. He who had remained determinedly unattached until now could tonight feel justified in calling her his girlfriend. Lynn Dyson and Jeff Diamond had become "an item". How about that? Moreover, he was beginning to feel the type of bond he had always longed for: mutual love and respect.

And great sex! Man, sex with Lynn was good. It must be the combination of love and sex that made the physical act so special. Jeff had always hoped this might be the case, but his innate cynicism had invariably crept in and lampooned any optimism up until now. Feeling extremely horny, he went straight to bed, entrusting his new, fulfilled state with warding off the nightmares.

He was wrong. Two hours later, the tortured soul was on the couch again, his hopes for a miracle cure baseless. The cruel reality check didn't surprise him, but it was frustrating nonetheless. He clasped Lynn's note in his hand. It was enough to keep him sane for the rest of the night, and tomorrow would be another day. It always was.

Tennis

The umpire stepped down from his chair, and the Master of Ceremonies for the evening, Bill Kingdom, waved his hands to arrest the applause. The occasion was the annual charity tennis knock-out tournament, featuring various members of the Dyson family and several other local players, held at the Kooyong tennis centre, home of the Australian Open. This year was the first that Lynn's younger sibling, Richard, had been included in the line-up, and the blonde teenager found herself having to work hard to win shots against the twelve-year-old, who had grown much stronger in the space of the last few months.

Waiting for the intermission, Lynn sat on the sidelines while a men's doubles game captured the audience's attention. Shaking her legs to keep her muscles warm, she began to daydream. She smiled to herself, remembering an indignant Michelle, who had arrived at school that Monday morning after succumbing to the charms of one of her brother's workmates. Apparently, they had ended up under a tree somewhere in the Botanic Gardens, far from the ranger's prying headlights, and the long-awaited deed had been done in a fluster of excitement and inexperience.

'It was disgusting!' the redhead had declared to her classmates, quickly covering her mouth in case she was overheard. 'What the hell's the fuss all about? All I got out of it was a crook back and marks where sticks and stones had been stuck to my bum. And then he didn't talk to me all the way home.'

The schoolgirls had all giggled in sympathy with their irate friend. Surprisingly little had been said between them since witnessing the superstar in their midst being asked out by a certain tall and utterly gorgeous university student a few weeks ago, and neither had Lynn volunteered any of her own secrets. She was dying to, however, but was only too aware that she was much younger than the others and had perhaps embarked on this treacherous adventure a little sooner than the others would condone.

One by one, those girls with something to confess gradually agreed with Michelle that they were in no real hurry to have sex again, and even the ones with steady boyfriends had laid down some unofficial ground rules concerning the minimum number of dates on which a boy should be required to take them out, before he had earned the right to some more physical contact.

Lynn was momentarily distracted by a rogue ball, which came whistling past her right ear and landed in the front row of the press gallery behind. Lifting her gaze, she looked up to where her guests were sitting, hoping she would get the chance to speak to them during the break. Her mind quickly drifted back to the discussions at school, and she remembered listening patiently to the other girls' woeful tales, deliberately keeping quiet about how well her own love affair was progressing. How lucky she was that her memories were so sweet! Perhaps because she had not immediately divulged every last detail at school, Michelle and the gang had assumed the date had been a one-off and that nothing had come of her mystery man.

At some point she would have to come clean, the sixteen-year-old realised. Her diary was the sole accomplice, and her face reddened as she recalled how much she had written about Jeff and their four pretty damned fine encounters. For the first time in her very public life, she had separated her personal diary from her coaching records and had hidden it in the base of her weekend bag. She would be mortified if her little sister were to find it and show their mother.

Up above the players' box, on the far side of the court, Lynn could see the cause of her distraction, with his long, wavy dark hair and wearing his suit again, conversing with another man with light brown hair and a woman with fair, shoulder-length hair. She guessed that they must be the couple who had driven down from Sydney with him. She couldn't wait to meet them.

Phew! The athlete felt herself blush again. This was crazy! She attempted to focus on the tennis, clapping with great enthusiasm when her younger brother successfully lobbed a ball high above his opponents' heads. Jeff was not at all like the boyfriends about whom her mates complained, and he also treated her differently to the other men who had courted her affection, almost as if he didn't care who she was. Not a bit like Dean, her brother's footballing buddy, who had always made sure they bumped into his friends while out on dates, so that he could show her off, and who would frequently exaggerate how far he had gone with the pretty sportswoman.

The man who had stolen her heart, by contrast, had done so silently, with minimal fuss and maximum impact. The celebrity realised the recent arrival didn't yet know too many people in Melbourne, but even so, he regularly spoke of friends and spending time with other students. To her joy, it appeared he only wanted her for himself. "One on one, and I love it!" she had written in her diary, after their recent trip to the library. "Jeff makes me feel so wanted, and just as me. For my inner self, not how I look or what *kudos* I can bring him with his mates."

Therefore, tonight was a bit of an experiment, the young woman admitted with some shame; a test to see if her boyfriend's behaviour would change when they were together in the company of his fellow Sydney migrants. Would he treat her like a trophy to be arrogantly paraded past Gerry and Suzanne? It was probably to be expected, given who she was, she acknowledged, feeling guilty.

Was it fair of her to be so clinical and judgmental so soon? Perhaps her friends' derision was rubbing off?

Lynn allowed her eyes to wander up to the row behind the players' box again, this time finding those of her boyfriend. Did he just wink at her? Oh, God! That was so sexy! Her stomach turned over, and a shiver ran the full length of her body. She dared to give him a small wave, hoping her father wasn't watching.

And from his vantage point some thirty metres from where his dream girl sat, the tall student fixed her blue eyes in his avid stare for as long as he could. After a couple of seconds, he noticed her glance across at the Dyson patriarch, who was serving for the game. For how long could their sublime liaison endure under the weight of this powerful man's influence? How long would he enjoy this beautiful champion's association, before her parents cottoned on to the incongruity of their match?

To alleviate his poor financial situation, Jeff had accepted a part-time job at a pub around the corner from his flat. He wasn't sure how long this would last either, since by solving one problem, he was most likely about to make another one a whole lot worse. On his first night, having quickly memorised where everything was and after swapping a few light-hearted jokes with his boss, he had expected his ever-present craving for alcohol would get the better of him, surrounded by bottles of spirits and cans of beer, all within easy reach.

However, to his surprise, their abundance had quite the opposite effect, and the clever conversationalist had been a hit with the customers, even finding himself amused by other people's drunkenness for a change. It wasn't until after his shift had finished and the manager had invited him to get stuck into whatever he fancied that he followed their lead, and now had only vague memories of ending up in bed with one of the other members of staff.

The boy from Sydney's west was well-practised at hiding his addictions from those who mattered, relying on his brain's considerable powers of concentration while at school, coupled with the intelligent humour and adept sexual techniques he had employed since his early teens at various other times. There had been several teachers at his high school with drinking problems who had eventually confided in the streetwise teenager, of whose blind eyes he remained assured as long as the favour was reciprocated.

Also, as with several other part-time jobs over the years, he had provided the landlord with a false name and address, just in case the rough public bar was frequented by gangland thugs with connections in New South Wales. The adult Jeff Diamond bore more than a passing likeness to his father, whose notoriety might not be as localised as the young man hoped.

At least he didn't need to lie about his age anymore, Jeff smiled, winking at the stunning teenager who was looking right at him from the court below. He wondered if Lynn Dyson ever masqueraded under a different identity to preserve her anonymity. For other reasons, obviously! She had complained that her age was becoming a handicap these days. Perhaps, in that case, she would understand his world on some level, so dissimilar to yet no less unusual than her own? Would he ever find the courage to put this theory to the test?

Christ! How the hot-blooded man could hardly wait to spend more time with this goddess! His paradise, his guardian angel, as his songs chronicled; his oasis in a world of phobic sleeplessness, hangovers and the struggle both to make ends meet and to make sense of his weird lot in life. He felt his penis beginning to swell and quickly distracted himself by looking around the arena.

Jeff couldn't afford to get carried away with thoughts of where or how he and the singing tennis star might end this evening's date, knowing it would only result in an extreme level of discomfort, which he would then need to endure throughout dinner with his implacable mates. Each time he ventured into fantasyland, picturing Lynn's lithe body and imagining seeing even more of it than he could see right now, he managed to force himself back to more mundane things, such as Suzanne's kennel duties and Gerry's tax returns.

Then suddenly, courtside, the other resting tennis players were all on their feet. Breaking out of her *rêverie*, Lynn jumped up with them and waved cheerfully to the audience, following her father along the net to thank the officials. Bill Kingdom was a long-time friend of the family, together with his brother Mike. They were television executives these days, having earlier been news readers and presenters, and they had also become property developers on the side. They were like uncles to the Dyson children, and often lent their support to these charity events. The sports stars responded to the applause by waving and thumping their racquet strings in appreciation, before disappearing into the changing rooms.

'I can't believe my script here says we're now going to let the players take a rest,' Bill spoke into the microphone, pointing to a piece of paper in his hand. '"Hard-earned rest," it says here on my running sheet! Can you believe that? Volunteers will be moving through the arena to collect any money you might have spare for our worthy causes. Please give generously, and we look forward to seeing you back in your seats in twenty minutes' time. Thank you, ladies and gentlemen.'

Lynn had sent her new boyfriend three tickets in the stands, for himself and his two *compadres* from Sydney. They were great seats, almost directly in line with the net. Feeling very privileged, the young man had needed to work hard to conceal his pride and excitement at being given an opportunity to show off to his friends that he really had met and won the heart of Australia's darling.

The student was determined to play it very cool during the mini-tournament, and for their parts, Gerry and Suzanne had been suitably impressed with the invitation, still reeling in amazement that their enigmatic friend wasn't lying about his success at snaring the teenaged celebrity. To his relief, their doubts were further moderated, when on a couple of occasions during the first half, Lynn had picked the good-looking man out in the crowd to give him a cheerful wave.

With the intermission now announced, the nineteen-year-old Sydneysider was glad of a break from his private battle to concentrate on the quality of the tennis, having repeatedly found his dream girl's long, tanned legs, athletic contortions and very short tennis skirt much more compelling viewing. From time to time, he had snuck a glance sideways at his mate, who had responded with a knowing nod, thereby revealing exactly where his thoughts were straying also. Jeff glowed inside to think that it was he, among a stadium full of equally distracted men, who was looking forward to getting a whole lot closer to her divine body than the rest.

With the floodlights over the court dimmed for the break, the crowd began to chatter and stretch and move around. It was a balmy March night, following a hot, sticky day, and patrons were already making their way to the bars and refreshment counters. The threesome in the stands watched the players head off into the locker room for their break.

'OK!' Gerry stood up and stretched. 'Who wants a drink?'

'I can't be bothered to move,' Suzanne sighed and stayed seated. 'You two go, if you want.'

'It's only twenty minutes,' Jeff agreed, determined to keep his head clear, at least until dinner. 'Hardly worth getting in the queue. I'm with you, Suzie. Let's just stay here.'

'Whatever you say, boss,' moaned the older man, lifting his arms above his shoulders and swivelling to loosen his spine after a long day at work.

Gerry sat back down and offered his cigarettes round. The close friends began to discuss their days at the office, kennels and university; about awkward clients, difficult employees and general run-of-the-mill stuff. They knew each other so well that the conversation never faltered. "The Three Amigos", as Gerry's mum was known to call them.

A few minutes into the interval, Suzanne tapped Jeff's knee. Making eye contact, he followed her gaze across stage right, to the blonde bombshell who was about to open the gate to the players' box, only a few metres in front of them. His heart skipped a beat or two, before he quickly pulled himself together and got to his feet.

'Hey!' he smiled at Lynn, who had put on a tracksuit top over her tennis outfit and was still looking flushed from the last hour's play.

The tall man had to bend nearly double to greet her, and the agile athlete hopped up onto one of the seats to meet him halfway. Without looking around, Jeff sensed all heads turning as the celebrity greeted him affectionately. Man, this was good for his reputation!

'Don't get up,' she said, as his mouth met hers.

It was the type of deep and meaningful kiss they were beginning to perfect, and they both drew breath loudly enough for each other to hear.

'Are you kidding?' her boyfriend whispered suggestively in her ear, making her giggle.

With his hand on the tennis star's shoulder, helping her balance on the wobbly seat, the proud man introduced his dream girl to his wide-eyed and unusually speechless friends.

'I can't stay long. I just wanted to come and say hello.'

'Lynn, this is Suzanne and Gerry.'

'Great to meet you, Suzanne,' the superstar added, leaning forward to shake each hand.

'Nice to meet you too,' the other woman replied in a shy voice.

'And the notorious Gerry.'

The accountant gave a comic shrug, as if to say he had no idea what the stunning celebrity might be talking about. He hadn't, in fact, but liked her style nonetheless. She was confident and cute; just the type of girl he favoured. All four sat down, the three guests in their seats, and their host perched on the low wall at the back of the box which normally separated the players' family and friends from the rest of the viewing public.

Drinking in her beauty, Jeff could feel his girlfriend's warmth even though they weren't touching. Her hair was tied back in a ponytail, which he hadn't seen up close before, and her jacket had a scripted "D" embroidered on the breast pocket, with her name underneath it. As if anyone needed reminding, this was Lynn Dyson. *Amazing, huh?*

Yet despite her label, Lynn Dyson looked every bit the schoolgirl she was, with no fancy attitude. The young pretender fleetingly allowed himself to believe he had every right to be with her, regardless of the difference in their backgrounds. *This is really happening*, he marvelled. His heart was pumping wildly, but otherwise he felt strangely calm. After all these years of clinging on to the wild dream about which the Blake clan teased him relentlessly, he was at last able to make this new "item" a reality right in front of their eyes. He felt proud of himself in a startlingly childlike way.

And trust Lynn to surprise him like this... It made the moment all the sweeter, and he transmitted his thanks over the telepathic airwaves.

'So!' the tennis star asked, engaging directly with Jeff's companions. 'Are you enjoying it? Thanks for coming.'

The schooling the celebrity had received from a very young age had left her with an easy manner that came across as completely genuine. She was as gracious with her words as she was graceful in her movements.

'It's great,' Suzanne answered, thinking how beautiful the famous girl was in the flesh. 'Thanks for the tickets.'

Lynn's bare legs were strong, tanned and flawless, and she seemed to hold herself effortlessly straight, like a ballerina. The older woman felt very envious.

'Good to see you all hamming it up,' chuckled Gerry.

The elder of the two men looked at his mate with this new girlfriend and saw something utterly right. Lynn was leaning leftwards over towards Jeff, and her hand rested gently on his right knee. This girl was for real, the accountant thought, doing his best to read her body language. Against all natural odds, it appeared the pin-up princess really liked his wayward, vice-ridden buddy.

The sixteen-year-old laughed. 'You're welcome. Yes, it's nice not to have to take ourselves too seriously once in a while. Even Dad relaxes a bit, and that's pretty rare.'

'Are we still on for dinner?' Jeff enquired of the pretty teenager.

'Oh, yes. I hope so,' she replied, rubbing her stomach. 'I'm starving.'

'I've booked Lynch's,' Gerry announced.

The small establishment was a new, up-market restaurant, fashionably expensive and suitably trendy. The young businessman had entertained some important clients there and knew it ought to make the right impression on the new *Dartagnan* in their midst. He had a feeling there would very soon be a fourth amigo in their tight little clique. He welcomed it, since Lynn Dyson was ticking all the right boxes so far.

'Mmm... Good choice,' the aristocratic young lady indicated her endorsement.

Truth be told, she would have approved of fish and chips in the park that night, so happy was she to be spending more time in the company of the handsome stranger with whom she had fallen in love, yet this was definitely an excellent choice of dinner venue nonetheless. Her parents had taken her and her older brother there after a school event, and she recalled how tasty the fare had been. Gerry looked pleased with himself, subconsciously puffing his chest out.

Less interested in the food, Jeff drew his girlfriend's attention back his way, running the middle finger of his right hand along the length of her thigh, from her knee to just underneath the hem of her tennis skirt, and leaving it lingering dangerously, a fraction too high. The delicate skin on the inside of his finger, between the first and second knuckles, was so sensitive that the infinitesimal friction gave them both goose-bumps.

'Are you wearing this to dinner?' he asked, without a smile but with a flash of his dark gipsy eyes.

Still reeling from the thrilling sensation, the object of his tacit lust looked down her nose with mock disdain.

'No,' she responded, like a schoolteacher disappointed at being let down by her favourite pupil.

'Shame!' Gerry piped up, with a lecherous grin.

In an instant, the star's surprisingly possessive lover took issue with his friend's predictable reaction, instinctively tightening his grip on her thigh. She flexed her muscles to counter the pressure, which he read as a sign to remove his hand. Jeff looked at Suzanne and knew she would be grateful for his coming to her rescue, since the older of the two lads was rarely the chivalrous gentleman she longed for.

'No, you don't,' the smouldering man snapped, only half joking. 'Not "Shame," mate, but "Thank Christ," so as not to piss off your girlfriend, who's sitting right here, in case you hadn't noticed.'

Gerry stared his friend down, as he always did, while Lynn looked on with interest at the two bucks going head to head. Their behaviour was no different to that of her many male sporting colleagues, where every aspect of life was a competition, and yet somehow Jeff's words did not appear to be borne out of *machismo*. Rather it seemed to the young woman that he was defending her and Suzanne.

'Or me,' Jeff added, 'your best mate.'

Gerry raised a sly middle finger, and they all laughed. The sixteen-year-old found the dynamics in the relationship between these two alpha males fascinating and wondered who had the upper hand. Given the way Jeff had described his long-time friendship, she had expected the older man to be dominant. However, now sitting here with both, the younger of the two seemed to be in charge, but most subtly. Her mystery man continued to surprise her, almost with every sentence he uttered.

'I see what you mean,' Lynn motioned a theatrical aside towards the tall, handsome stranger, who winked back.

Jeff's hopes of the brand new duo being in tune with each other tonight were thankfully well founded. Dinner was going to be fun, he mused. The banter continued for two or three more minutes, until the celebrity pointed towards her man's right wrist.

'What's the time?'

'Just coming up quarter-to,' he answered.

Lynn straightened up. 'I'd better get back to the team. I have to do rev-up before we come back out.'

Rev-up, she explained to a row of blank stares, was the Dyson term for the pre-game pep talk. She and her siblings took it in turns to motivate their fellow team members, in order to build their leadership skills. Jeff's right arm steadied the sexy sportswoman as she stepped back down onto the tilting seat and dropped lightly onto the floor. He felt so protective towards her already and definitely didn't want to be responsible for her sustaining an injury and spoiling the rest of the evening's entertainment for the crowd.

'Where'll we meet?' he asked, feeling Lynn's hand slide down his forearm and grasp his strong fingers.

For a man who hadn't previously seen the point of touching someone unless there was sex involved, the headstrong teenager was amazed at just how good all these small demonstrations of affection felt, how naturally they came to him and how amenable he was for them to continue. He squeezed her hand, which now seemed so small in his.

His girlfriend smiled into inviting eyes, feeling butterflies in her stomach again. 'Either stay here or wait out there, by the entrance to the seats. I'll come up as soon as I can escape. Might be a while though, because of the press photos and interviews, *et cetera*. I'll be as quick as I can.'

'OK. Sounds good,' Jeff nodded. 'Play well.'

Lynn turned back to the others. 'See you later. It was nice to meet you.'

Suzanne and Gerry waved and echoed her words. The athlete turned back to her man, who had sat back down in his seat. Their heads were almost at the same level, and he leaned forward to plant a soft kiss on her forehead.

'Thanks for coming up.'

With a quick grin back, the young star turned and headed for the gate. The three friends watched her leave, only to be immediately accosted by several fans, before eventually managing to disappear behind a door marked "PRIVATE". How exhausting must it be to constantly have to act politely towards people who obstructed one's path? Jeff wondered whether the brief encounter the foursome had shared had been an oasis for Lynn in the anonymous desert of onlookers, or whether her grace and poise with his friends merely constituted another public appearance. He preferred to think she had found their company relaxing and resolved to ask her later, as much for his ongoing research into being a "someone" as to feed his ego.

The second half of the exhibition was as entertaining as the first. Junior Dyson and Evonne Goolagong were playing Lynn and her father. Jeff watched keenly how father and daughter interacted and noticed how she hung off his every word. The implications were becoming slowly clearer to the young man, contemplating how the introduction of a serious boyfriend into the child star's life would change this relationship over time. Assuming there would be an "over time", of course. And assuming said serious boyfriend were he...

At one point, Suzanne slapped both male companions on the knee quite hard. 'Oi! Your tongues are hanging out. Do you want me to leave?'

Jeff sat back apologetically. 'Sorry, Suzie-Anna. It's hard to watch and not drool.'

'You're entitled to,' she replied, before sneering at her own boyfriend. 'He's not.'

She slapped Gerry's leg again, since he hadn't moved from his bug-eyed, leering posture. The Three Amigos remained in their seats and watched the tennis centre empty quickly at the end of the tournament. Suzanne had shared her private envy at Lynn's physique and glowing beauty, neither of which had been disputed by the men. After fifteen minutes and no sign of their fourth musketeer, Gerry suggested they wait outside the stadium, where hopefully the bar would still be open. Desperate for a cigarette to calm his nerves, Jeff readily agreed.

'Will Lynn find us?' Suzanne asked, picking up on her friend's anxiety. 'She might think we've gone.'

The younger man looked at her comically. 'No, she won't. I very much doubt she's that insecure,' he teased. 'Come on. Let's go. I'll keep a lookout. Don't fear! I have a vested interest in finding her.'

Gerry laughed. 'I bet you do.'

They reached the bar with seconds to spare, since its shutters were already partially in place. They convinced the staff to pour them two beers, and Suzanne contented herself with only her cigarette. Making the most of the overdue hits of nicotine and alcohol, Jeff began to flip his lighter over and over in his hand.

'You're so jumpy,' the young woman observed, slapping him on the arm. 'Someone's very keen to get to the next stage of the night...'

The nineteen-year-old finished his cigarette with a long drag down to the filter and inhaled as much into his bloodstream as he could. It was true, he was a wreck. His own insecurities had seized on Suzanne's comment and sent panic signals to his fragile mind. He swallowed down the last of his beer and laughed in agreement, keen to make light of the situation.

As insensitive as usual however, Gerry was thinking quite differently. 'He's just hanging out for the *final* stage of the night.'

'Oh, for God's sake!' Suzanne exclaimed. 'Not everything revolves around sex, you know.'

Jeff gave them both a look designed to give his mate's girlfriend the impression that she held the minority opinion again, even though he actually agreed with her in this instance. Sometimes Gerry's crassness was a welcome diversion, and he used it to his best advantage. With the cleaners busily collecting rubbish from the floor and emptying bins, the suburban arena began to resemble a ghost town. There were another six or so people finishing their drinks at the bar, but that was about it for patrons.

Then finally, from around the corner, Lynn Dyson appeared, walking briskly towards them with an apologetic look on her face. She was wearing a cream woollen cardigan over a floral summer dress, and her hair was still damp from the shower. The vision coming towards them was by far the most welcome sight the stressed out student had ever seen.

'Sorry, guys!' the celebrity shouted, as she came within earshot. 'Thanks for waiting.'

She made straight for Jeff, and he draped his arm over her shoulder lovingly. Her hand slipped around his waist in response, and they kissed tenderly. He wondered whether she was truly empathetic enough to have picked up exactly what he needed, or would she have done this to any dinner date? Regardless, the anxiety began to drain out of his sore shoulders and down his back, until it trickled away across the concrete. Good riddance, he swore under his breath.

'Suzanne thought you'd given up on us and gone home,' the younger man joked, covering up his relief that it hadn't been the case.

Lynn smiled. 'No. I'm sorry I took so long. We had to do a TV interview at the end, which took ages. Are we ready to eat?'

'Sure thing,' Gerry agreed. 'Let's go. I hope they hold our table.'

The gold-coloured BMW was all alone in the car park by the time they reached it. Suzanne had already claimed the seat behind the driver, so Jeff opened the rear passenger-side door for Lynn to climb in and then took his position in the front. The junior partner started the engine, and wide tyres crunched on the loose gravel as he drove quickly towards the exit.

'Nice car,' Lynn remarked from the luxury of the back seat. 'It looks new.'

Its proud owner was pleased to receive some attention from their famous guest. 'Indeed it is. It was a Christmas present from me to me. Glad you like it.'

Jeff turned around, looking hurt.

'Nicer than mine?'

The sixteen-year-old smiled. 'Yours is nice too. It has character.'

Gerry scoffed. 'Yeah, that's about all. Sounds like you, mate.'

'It *is* like you,' Lynn agreed, smiling at her companion's forlorn expression.

'Old and blue, but with plenty of character,' the accountant embellished, amusing himself at his friend's expense.

Jeff appreciated and understood both comments perfectly. They were accurate enough, despite the continual ribbing.

'That's so mean,' Suzanne leaned forward and punched the boisterous driver's shoulder. 'You pompous bastard!'

The young tennis player said nothing, enjoying the spirited exchanges between her boyfriend's friends. It was clear they knew each other very well, and she identified with the closeness as similar to her own circle.

'No sweat, Suzie-Anna,' Jeff joined in. 'He's just compensating, as you well know.'

They all laughed. Within ten minutes, they had reached the quiet street, with its line of high-classed eateries along one side of the road and the darkness of the parkland on the other. The majority of buildings in the area were owned and run by Melbourne's most prestigious schools, and hence it was familiar territory for the celebrity.

Parking on Domain Road, just a short walk from the restaurant, Gerry led the way with Suzanne. Lynn took Jeff's hand as soon as it was offered, and he kissed it eagerly, feeling the residual tension finally slipping away with the renewal of their connection. He almost allowed himself to believe this beautiful woman was as happy to see him as he was to see her.

'You look fantastic,' he said. 'It's so good to see you. Thanks for coming up during the interval. It boosted my credibility no end.'

'You're welcome. It was a good way to break the ice,' his girlfriend smiled. 'Your friends are very nice. They're exactly how I expected them to be, so you must've described them accurately.'

Jeff nodded. 'We've spent a lot of time together. Gerry doesn't give a damn about what people think. He just says what he thinks and lets people object if they want to. He's extremely thick-skinned, so you don't have to worry about offending him either. And Suzanne gets so embarrassed sometimes as a result.'

Up ahead, the businessman was holding the door open for them.

'Come on, laggards. Dinner awaits.'

Jeff stood back and let Lynn pass in front of him through the narrow doorway, watching her every move. He caught Gerry's eye as he took hold of the door and acknowledged their shared appreciation for the hot starlet. Luckily their table was still waiting, and the ambitious executive's reputation with the *Maître d'* remained unblemished.

After ordering a round of drinks and some wine for the meal, the latecomers focussed on selecting their entrées and main courses. While they were flicking through the menu, Jeff placed his right hand on Lynn's left thigh, and the simple act sent shivers through her. A few seconds later, he felt her fingers come to rest on top of his, the delay making her tentative response all the more tantalising. He felt himself becoming aroused again. The newest member of the band had become fully engaged in the lively banter about the evening's entertainment, and yet the new lovers had their own private conversation going on under the table. It was very erotic.

'So, Lynn...' Gerry started, with an impish smile on his face.

'Ah, here we go!' his friend jeered, anticipating either an embarrassing revelation or an intrusive question.

The blonde teenager squeezed his hand again to signal she was ready for anything.

The accountant continued. 'What's it like going out with such a control freak?'

Jeff rolled his eyes at Suzanne, who grinned back. Any hope of some charity from his long-time mate was evidently too much to expect. His girlfriend wasn't fazed though.

'It's great,' she replied. 'It's just like my father. I'm used to it.'

'Good first serve, but equally good return,' the student joked, relieved but fully expecting more. 'Over to you, Blake-san.'

The older woman attempted an intercept. 'Gerry, can't you talk about the weather or something? Don't go straight for the jugular. Poor Jeff!'

Both men scoffed, quite disappointed that the rally was broken so soon. The nineteen-year-old shook his head as the volley plunged straight into the metaphorical net.

'I believe that'd be love-fifteen. Wouldn't you agree, Miss Dyson?'

Lynn gave him a high five. So far, her handsome stranger was more than passing the test. He was positively drawing her into the tight-knit trio. Again she was struck by the power of his suggestive orchestration, almost as if the others were stringless automatons under his dominion. The feeling of inclusion was uncommonly powerful.

'Absolutely. Please serve again, Mister Blake.'

'OK, then. If you're intent on playing hardball,' Gerry threatened his dark-haired adversary, before turning his eyes on the blonde beside him. 'Miss D, how do you cope with him always having to have things his own way?'

'I don't!' Jeff volleyed, annoyed but not surprised.

'You do so!'

'I haven't noticed,' the naïve star added, not wishing to concede the point on her boyfriend's behalf, like Suzanne had done before. 'So there's no coping!'

'He does, actually,' Suzanne cruised in with the killer blow, calmly staring at the smouldering Adonis opposite her. 'Fifteen all, I believe, Mister Diamond.'

The Mosman couple high-fived each other triumphantly, and Gerry refilled everyone's wine glass. He flagged down a passing waitress and requested another bottle. Lynn restricted herself to a single glass, knowing full well that there were inquisitive eyes all around her, some of which she recognised as belonging to acquaintances of her parents and to personages high up at school. It wasn't worth joining in the grown-up fun too much, even though she was sorely tempted.

'Why then?' the tennis champion went back to the other woman's definitive rebuke. 'Not that I'm challenging the point, but I'm interested in why you say that. Doesn't everybody want their own way?'

Jeff squirmed in his seat, not sure what further incriminations might to come to light. This was the downside of introducing his girlfriend to those closest to him. Neither was particularly discreet, but he had no choice but to learn to roll with the punches if this beauty was going to become part of his life, rather than sitting on the periphery. Gerry and Suzanne were the nearest thing he had to family, therefore it was no different a challenge to making room for Bart Dyson.

'Perhaps this'd be a good time for me to leave?'

'Oh, no, you don't. You coward! Stay right there,' Gerry told him, waving his hand, palm downwards, and forbidding his friend to move.

Entrées finished and cutlery set on their empty plates, Lynn had placed both elbows on the table and was resting her chin in her hands, waiting for the information she had requested. She looked phenomenally attractive, and the nervous man steeled himself to face the music.

Suzanne deferred to her boyfriend. 'It's still your serve.'

'Because, fine lady,' Gerry answered, 'he's so fucking clever that he can manipulate every scenario to whatever he wants to get out of it, before you've even realised it's happening.'

'Really? So it's a skill that makes you jealous, you mean?'

Seeing his date looking at him so fondly, Jeff's heart glowed at the way the captive celebrity had chosen to defend him, and his mate chuckled in appreciation of her accurate analysis. The more he heard from this special lady's mouth, the more he was driven to acknowledge the similarities between these two compassionate people.

'Damned straight I am! But it's bloody annoying for the rest of us. She's quick, this one, mate.'

The proud student nodded, unable to put his feelings into words. He had shivers running down his spine.

'I think that's our point then, Mister Diamond,' Lynn adjudicated, patting her boyfriend on the back. 'Is that Game yet? When do we get the chance to serve? If this was badminton or squash, we'd be in the lead by now. Tennis is such a stupid game.'

Everyone laughed. Jeff leaned over and kissed her, and his hand returned to her thigh for safekeeping.

'What's going on under there?' Suzanne asked, putting on a disapproving tone.

'Nothing,' the innocent man answered. 'I'm just resting my hand in a comfortable spot.'

Taking advantage of the break between courses, Lynn pushed her chair back and excused herself from the table. Suzanne immediately got up too, not wanting to miss an opportunity to have a girl-to-girl chat with their famous new friend. Their boyfriends stood briefly, gentlemanly behaviour warranted in honour of the aristocrat in their presence, who thanked them with a smile and made it clear that going to such lengths on her behalf was quite unnecessary.

'Mate, she's gold,' Gerry confessed, when the women were out of sight. 'I can't believe she's only sixteen. She's fucking gorgeous.'

'You don't have to tell me that,' the younger man laughed. 'I'm surprised she's so game. She must be used to dealing with her dad.'

The businessman nodded. 'She's hot too. Looking forward to later?'

116

'What do you think?' Jeff laughed out loud, tilting his chair on its back legs and stretching. 'It's killing me, in fact. And the more I drink, the more excruciating it's going to get.'

Meanwhile, in the ladies' restroom, the kennel owner couldn't wait to quiz their guest about what she thought of her beau. She was inquisitive to find out how this unlikely pairing might pan out.

'Lynn, I hope you don't mind me asking,' she began, while they washed their hands, 'but what did you think when Jeff asked you out? You mustn't have had a clue who he was.'

'No, I didn't,' the sixteen-year-old replied, intrigued by her circumstances too. 'I still don't. Did he tell you what happened? It all happened so fast that I didn't really stop and think. My friends told me I was mad just to accept an invitation from a total stranger, but he looked so determined.'

'That's exactly what we mean about always getting his way,' Suzanne explained. 'He's so irresistibly charismatic that people just fall at his feet. But even you!'

Lynn was taken aback. 'What do you mean, even me? I'm no different to anyone else. He's good-looking and charming and intelligent. Why wouldn't I want to go out with him? Are you trying to tell me I shouldn't?'

Suzanne laughed. The celebrity was indeed very friendly and just as Jeff had described her. It wasn't hard to imagine why her boyfriend's best mate felt so strongly, for there was a distinct similarity in the way the two lovebirds interacted with people. The fresh-faced star didn't appear to be at all spoiled, and there was a genuine excitement in her tone when speaking about her new relationship.

'Oh, no reason. I'd like to go out with him too,' the older woman admitted. 'He's got nothing though. He's been Gerry's mate for years, but they're from completely different sides of the railway tracks. At first I didn't know really how they came to be such good friends, but since I got to know Jeff, I realise he's not that different from Gerry. They're both so competitive and ambitious. He's always been on his own though, which is sort of weird for a teenager. I don't even know anything about his parents or anything.'

Lynn looked at Suzanne's reflection in the mirror.

'Neither do I,' she affirmed. 'I don't think they're around. He talks about a sister, but they don't seem to have much to do with each other either. He's a mystery man. That's part of the attraction though.'

'Don't you worry about not knowing more?' the twenty-two-year-old asked.

'Yes, a bit, but we're not getting married or going into business. We're just dating. And, as I said to my friends the other day, I have a security guard at the end of the 'phone at all times, so unless he stabs me or strangles me, I should be OK.'

Suzanne shivered. 'Oh, don't say that. Poor Jeff! If he heard us talking this way...'

'Yes, I know. It's no big deal for me. My parents would kill me for saying that! What I like about him the most is how expressive and kind he is,' Lynn explained dreamily. 'And how ready he is to pass on all that knowledge. I can't believe how much information he's got in his head. Did you know he hardly ever sleeps? That's another odd thing.'

'Yes. He does often complain about it,' Gerry's girlfriend confirmed. 'And he often meets me at six in the morning when I'm walking all my dogs, saying he's been up all night either partying, studying or running.'

The sportswoman nodded, frequently burning the candle at both ends herself these days. 'I don't know how he keeps going. He must just crash and sleep for days, I suppose.'

'Can I ask you something else?' Suzanne asked, suddenly looking serious.

Lynn's hand was on the door handle, about to pull it towards her and walk back into the restaurant. She let it go and turned back to discover the reason for her companion's earnest question.

'Of course. What is it?'

'Do you mind that he's been with so many women? And I mean heaps!'

'I don't really know,' the celebrity confessed, not much appreciating the inference. 'Jeff's my first proper boyfriend, so I don't have much to compare him with, but I get the impression that the mix of compassion and strength he has is fairly special. I'm not surprised girls find him attractive. He's a good teacher too, which I need! Friends of mine who've slept with their boyfriends all complain that they don't much enjoy it, so either I'm unusual or Jeff's very good at it!'

The older woman gasped, reaching out and putting her hand on the superstar's arm. She felt guilty for alarming her and for pouring cold water on her first romance. The mean streak in her wondered whether, if she were to speak more candidly about Jeff Diamond's promiscuity, Lynn might have second thoughts and open the door for Suzanne herself to make her move on the gorgeous man, now that she and Gerry were living so many kilometres apart.

Mercifully, the jealous friend thought better of it. How could she do that? What sort of a mate would that make her? She would be likely to lose her two *amigos*, were she to follow that line of thinking.

'Or both?' she smiled instead. 'You can be sure though, Lynn, that Jeff's so unbelievably in love with you. He's been fantasising about meeting you for years. We take the piss terribly over it, but he's always been deadly serious about meeting you.'

The singing star stared at herself in the mirror this time, absorbing the corroboration of her mystery man's own story.

'I know. He's told me. It's very flattering, but how did he know? I feel very close to him, so it's weird to think we're so well suited despite having such different lives. It's as if I've known him forever, and then I'm reminded that I hardly know him at all. Very strange...'

'Do you love him?' Suzanne asked outright.

'Yes, I do,' Lynn responded, blushing slightly. 'I don't feel old enough to be qualified to love someone, but I'm sure I do.'

'Have you told him? And has he told you?'

Lynn laughed. 'So many questions! It's like the press conference all over again! Yes and yes.'

'Oh, wow!' the fair-haired Sydneysider almost screamed. 'That's fantastic! I'm really pleased. He must be so over the moon. He told me once that you were the only person he'd ever have a serious relationship with. He said he'd only ever sleep with one woman he respected, and that would be you.'

'I'm not sure I even know what that means,' the honest teenager replied, 'but it sounds good, doesn't it? Or is that just more charisma talking?'

Suzanne shrugged. 'Probably. How should I know? All I know is that Jeff's twice the man Gerry is, and Gerry's quite a catch. Jeff's got all the intelligence and sophistication that Gerry has, but... you're right... he's kind. He takes time to understand other people.'

'Well, that counts for a lot, as far as I'm concerned,' the younger woman agreed, reaching for the door again. 'My mum always says to look for kindness in people.'

Realising they had been absent from the table for a long while, the excited pair went back into the dining room to find their men discussing the rugby and VFL results from the previous weekend. The second bottle of wine was already nearly empty, and another one was on its way. Their voices were louder too, and the language more colourful than when the girls had first left.

Sobering Lesson

'Ladies, welcome back!' Gerry exclaimed at the top of his voice. 'Enjoy your holiday?'

A woman at a nearby table shrieked with laughter, twisting round to see who had made the funny comment. Suzanne scolded her boyfriend for drawing attention to them, but Lynn enjoyed the joke too.

'You had a lot to talk about, evidently,' Jeff smiled.

The beautiful teenager put a hand on her man's shoulder as she sat back down. He took it as a signal that all was well, which was a relief after so long in the restroom with the world's greatest gossip merchant. Their third bottle of wine arrived at the same time as their main courses. Gerry immediately refilled his and Jeff's glasses, complaining that the girls weren't drinking fast enough.

'All the more for us, mate,' the younger man retorted, sounding inebriated for the first time since Lynn had met him.

'Shhh!' the polite patron warned him. 'You're very loud. We'll get kicked out.'

'Sorry, angel,' he replied, kissing her cheek. 'How's your food?'

Everyone agreed the food was sensational, cooked to perfection, and the portions were exactly the right size. It was late to be eating on a weeknight, but all four were hungry, particularly the tennis player. The conversation lulled while they savoured their meals.

'So, Gerry,' Lynn began after a while. 'Which do you prefer to do business in, Sydney or Melbourne?'

Good question, Jeff thought, particularly since it diverted the attention nicely to the other side of the table. Finishing his mouthful, the young entrepreneur answered quite seriously, much to Suzanne's astonishment.

'It's interesting,' he responded, waving his fork in the new arrival's direction. 'I find far more of a class distinction in Melbourne than I do in Sydney. Much more of the old school tie, if you know what I mean.'

Lynn nodded. 'Oh, I definitely know what you mean.'

Gerry laughed. 'Yes, well... Coming from a Melbourne Academy student, that makes perfect sense. But otherwise it's the same. Suck up to the right people and business dribbles in. Piss off one person and business marches out. Have to be careful, you know, what you say in posh restaurants...'

'You're getting drunk,' Suzanne complained.

The wine was beginning to go to her head too. Since moving into the kennels, miles from civilisation, her alcohol consumption had dropped considerably from the steady quantities she had been drinking while socialising in the New South Wales capital. The man opposite grinned and aimed his girlfriend's attention towards the glazed look on the other woman's face. She was staring at his right hand, in which he held his fork, being left-handed. Then she did the same to her own man's hand.

'What's up, Suze?'

'You know, you guys have got such big hands! Look at the difference between ours and theirs, Lynn.'

The accountant laughed, raising his hands to eye level and turning them around to examine them more carefully. 'You know what they say: big hands, big ...'

'Gerry!' Suzanne shouted in frustration. 'Be quiet.'

'Size isn't everything, they tell me,' the brave teenager added, looking at all four large hands, which had duly been spread out over their empty dinner plates.

It was true. Jeff's and Gerry's fingers extended almost the whole diameter of their plates. Silence descended on the table, and a smirk spread over the older man's face. The professional entertainer had set yet another priceless rally going, and both men revelled in it.

'Who's they, pray?'

'Friends of mine, obviously,' the songwriter answered flippantly, smiling at his girlfriend's comic timing. 'I've had to do some nifty marketing over the last week or so. She was going out with Dean Keller before me, so I'm bloody glad you didn't get far enough to make a direct comparison.'

Gerry looked disbelieving. 'You were going out with a Richmond player? What would your big brother say?'

The youthful celebrity wasn't perturbed, casually turning to her gorgeous partner.

'Ah, but you know how to use yours better,' she smiled.

'Lynn!' exclaimed Suzanne.

The older man gave his mate a look which told him he was a very lucky man, and the compliment's grateful recipient leaned back on his chair and put his right arm expansively around his favourite person in all the world.

'What can I say, mate?'

What a sublime, easy *répartée* this was turning out to be, Jeff thought. Lynn had figured out exactly how to fit in with his friends in less than an hour, and already she was feeding him what he needed. This was really too good to be true, and he made a mental note to temper expectations. Leaning forward again, he reached into his back pocket for his wallet and peeled off a twenty dollar note, handing it to his pretty stooge, who giggled and refused to take it. Instead she kissed him, allowing him to take hold behind her head with his huge, right hand. The alcohol-fuelled student made their kiss last for as long as he could.

'Jeff, please,' Suzanne hissed.

'Yes, Jeff. Please!' the celebrity reinforced, able to break away for a brief moment before being drawn back in. 'Someone'll tell my parents!'

'Yeah, mate. Not in front of the children,' Gerry cackled. 'Oh, yes. That's right. She is the children.'

Without coming up for air, Jeff kicked his friend under the table, his shoe accurately making contact with the accountant's shinbone, like they used to do as teenagers at Blake family dinners. The older man didn't even flinch, as they had also learned not to over the years. They were all laughing.

'And Jeff, you're not so jumpy anymore,' Suzanne made another accurate observation.

'No,' his mate agreed, 'but he does have to stand on his head to pee.'

'Gerry!' both women exclaimed in unison, before collapsing in more fits of laughter, wondering if they were causing a disturbance.

'No, I'm not so jumpy anymore, thank you very much,' the younger man replied, no longer embarrassed. 'Suzie-Anna, you have Tourret's Syndrome today. All you've contributed to tonight's conversation so far is a tirade of name-calling.'

'Now *you're* being mean,' the stunning celebrity came to the defence of her fellow female diner, who was grateful for the support. 'We're only trying to retain some decorum at the table, while you blokes drink yourselves blind. God! I sound like my mum!'

Suzanne looked deflated, and Jeff reached out his hand for her to smack it. He moved his feet well back under his chair, expecting to receive a kick too, but it didn't materialise.

'Sorry. You're right,' the handsome student replied, smiling broadly. 'We might want to come back here one day, with Blake-san's cheque book again.'

Gerry wasn't listening, ready to launch forth on a new and equally odd topic of conversation. 'So if you guys start attending official functions together,' he mused, 'your names are close enough together alphabetically that you'll almost always appear together on guest lists. That's very convenient.'

Jeff looked at his drunken friend quizzically, wondering where on Earth this was leading:

'That's good, mate. So?'

Lynn took up the slack. 'Oh, yes. That's true. Jeff's always going to come before me though. Not very good for equal opportunity.'

The gregarious executive howled. Dangerously close to spitting out his mouthful of wine, Jeff did his best to stifle a laugh too. The teenager was embarrassed, realising what she had accidentally inferred. Gerry gave his friend a look that said, "naïve but so cute."

'That's a damned shame,' the businessman coughed, shaking his head. 'Mate, you've got to do something about that problem of yours.'

Lynn sighed. 'Sorry, Jeff. You know that wasn't what I meant.'

'I won't check with *Herr Doktor* Freud,' her intelligent lover shrugged and replied in a melancholy tone, 'because he's sure to find against me. But listen... We'd have been even closer alphabetically if your grandfather hadn't changed the spelling of your name, wouldn't we?'

'You know about that?' the starlet cried out in astonishment.

Gerry shot his old friend a mischievous grin, knowing exactly how many statistics the fanatic had memorised about the girl sitting next to him. He had lost track of the number of useless facts that had come his way over the course of their teenage years, some of which he remembered, but the majority not.

'There isn't much he doesn't already know about you. His anal-retentiveness is world renowned when it comes to the facts and figure of Lynn Dyson.'

'I hope that's not the case,' Jeff countered, turning to his right with a wry smile. 'How boring would that be?'

'Yeah,' agreed Lynn, rising to the occasion yet again. 'When I was six I got my first horse.'

'I know.'

'And I had my hair cut on the fourth of March.'

'I know.'

'My toothbrush is yellow.'

'I know,' the ardent follower said for the third time, winking at her having alluded to the fact that he had managed to get close enough to know this.

The sixteen-year-old leaned against him playfully, and Jeff pulled her in close to kiss her left temple, feeling an enticing resistance. His right hand wandered up her thigh, threatening to keep going right to the top, and all the time watching while her expression failed to register the spirited objection her fingers were dishing out under the table.

'I've never seen you so affectionate,' Suzanne teased. 'Lynn, you've brought out a whole different side to this boy. I've known him for all these years and I've never seen him kiss or hug anyone.'

Gerry laughed. 'You obviously haven't been to some of the places I've been with him.'

'Fuck off,' the nineteen-year-old sneered at his friend, suitably restrained in volume fortunately.

'You know...' Lynn changed the subject, unworried by the revealing comment or her boyfriend's blunt rebuke. 'I've always liked the word "indomitable", and tonight I've finally found someone I can use it on.'

The others laughed as the older man played up, proud to receive a backhanded compliment from their famous guest. He made up a headline for tomorrow's newspaper.

'"Indomitable Melbourne businessman, Gerry Blake, successfully rescues beautiful, singing tennis star from fate worse than death."'

Lynn grinned, beginning to feel rather tired. 'Why? What's going to happen to me?'

'You're going to have to try to escape the clutches of the horny bastard sitting next to you,' the indomitable one enlightened her, before quickly desisting for fear of another dressing down from Suzanne. 'Who's for dessert or coffee?'

Jeff wasn't going to let him away with this however, the wine taking the polished veneer off both men's humour.

'Wait a minute,' he menaced, the alcohol also causing him to slur his words a little. 'Are you surmising that Lynn wants to escape my clutches?'

'Tonight I think she might,' the third amigo ventured, becoming annoyed at their behaviour. 'You're not going to be capable of anything, either of you!'

Jeff scowled, tapping his finger on the table in front of his supercilious friend. 'Ring her in the morning.'

The waiter arrived to take their order for dessert, which was declined all round. The two men ordered coffee and a glass of brandy each. They lit cigarettes and leaned back in their chairs, feeling very mellow indeed.

'I've got a question for us over our coffee,' the kennel owner announced, changing the subject. 'I was asked it today by a client.'

'What's that?' the blonde teenager asked.

'Lynn!' Jeff exclaimed, impersonating the scolding voice Suzanne had previously been using.

'Shut up!' was the response he received, together with a kick from a pointed court shoe, for which he was unprepared this time.

The smiling man winced but made no sound. 'You're right. I'm hammered,' he admitted, reaching down to rub his shin. 'My reactions are way too slow. So what's your question, Suzie-Anna?'

'It's nice how you say Suzie-Anna,' Lynn praised her handsome but obstreperous partner, seeing he was in pain.

'Don't pander to him,' Gerry chided. 'He's only doing it so he can get in your knickers.'

Jeff gave his mate a strange look as if to say, "Why would I use a pet name for one woman to get into the knickers of another?" They had definitely had too much to drink, he thought.

Suzanne continued, despite the others' apparent disinterest. 'If you met a new partner who was a vegetarian, would you turn vegetarian if they wanted you to?'

Both men put their hands to their heads simultaneously, dissolving into a fit of giggles.

'Brain ache, Suzanne,' the Sydney Grammar old boy complained.

The kid from the Stones Road laughed. 'That's not a question about cars, sex or football. Do you really expect us to answer it at this stage of the evening?'

'Yes,' Lynn interjected, thinking how sexy her boyfriend looked, now that he was more relaxed. 'It's an interesting question, and you'd be right into it if you hadn't drunk so much, wouldn't you? I think I would, if it were a deal-breaker and I really liked him. If it was a moral question for the other person and not just a fad.'

'See... I don't think I could,' the older woman opined. 'I couldn't give up my steaks and fish. And what would you have at barbies?'

'And you're supposed to be the animal lover,' Jeff joined in, unable to resist a good debate. 'There must be meatless food that you could yearn for instead.'

'Crap!' Gerry objected. 'There's no meatless food I could yearn for.'

'Ice cream,' Lynn offered. 'And chocolate, of course. Women would be fine.'

Her boyfriend leaned in and kissed her. 'Cigarettes and alcohol. We'd be fine too. What about blow jobs?'

'Jeff!' all three exclaimed, causing people on other tables to look their way.

'What?' he shouted back, raising his hands to proclaim his innocence. 'It's a fair question. If you were vegan, you couldn't swallow.'

'Jeff!' they yelped again with raucous laughter.

Gerry signalled for the bill, and the head waiter brought it over to them almost immediately. Clearly he was anxious to have the noisy upstarts leave the other diners in peace. To spite him however, Gerry ordered two more cognacs.

'So what do you want this bloke to give up, Lynn?' the accountant asked, winking at his friend.

The caring teenager paused for a few seconds, genuinely trying to think of something.

'I don't know.'

'Cease all relations with you guys, after tonight,' her lover suggested, telepathically willing Suzanne not to say "other women".

'No!' Lynn replied. 'Definitely not. This is fun! Although I'm sure I'm going to be shopped by someone tomorrow for conduct unbecoming. I can't think of anything I'd want you to give up.'

'Ugh!' Gerry moaned. 'That's no good. Not even barracking for Richmond?'

'That's for Junior to say, not me,' the young blonde answered. 'Maybe running in the middle of the night, in case you get knocked down by a drunken motorist.'

Jeff kissed her again. 'OK. Done. I won't hit the streets in the middle of the night ever again. Just for you, angel.'

'Oh, for Christ's sake!' his mate blurted out, picking up his brandy glass. 'Where's your independence now, man? You're selling us down the river. Next think you'll be swearing celibacy.'

'No way,' Jeff objected instantly, crossing his hands over each other in total abrogation. 'Every man has his limits, and you've found mine. Sorry, baby!'

Suzanne gave the younger man a half-smile that he knew meant, "You got away with it this time." He was well aware of the dim regard in which Gerry's girlfriend held people who cheated on their partners and quickly dismissed the urge to inform her just how often it was happening right under her own nose. His loyalty to his mate was unfailing, but sometimes the matronly nagging he received was almost enough to burst his *amigos'* bubble.

'Thanks, Suzie,' he acknowledged. 'I owe you one.'

Lynn gave the pair a questioning glance but didn't pursue a clarification. Gerry picked up the leather folder containing the bill and wrote a cheque. Jeff didn't object. He couldn't afford to. The celebrity thanked her host with sufficient understatement to avoid embarrassing her date, for which he was grateful once again.

'Shall we make a move?' Suzanne asked. 'It's after midnight. Thanks for dinner, Gerry. That was delicious.'

'Yeah. Thanks, mate,' the struggling student added.

'Any time,' Gerry replied with a wave of his hand. 'It's been very interesting. We should do it again. Somewhere quieter next time.'

Standing up, the tall, handsome gentleman pulled Lynn's chair away behind her as she got to her feet. The raucous foursome thanked the restaurant staff profusely for putting up with them, and Suzanne led her man past the other tables and towards the door. Lynn smiled sweetly as she watched Jeff swallow down the last few drops from his brandy glass, before beckoning her to go ahead of him.

***

The warm summer evening had cooled down substantially while the hours had passed in eating, drinking and being very merry. The two couples stepped out of the narrow doorway and headed towards the car. Jeff put his arm around his girlfriend's shoulders as they traversed the short distance, the fresh air flushing the alcohol quickly through his brain and on down towards his feet.

'Whoa!' he laughed. 'It's cold out here! Anyone would think we'd been drinking.'

'I hope you're not expecting me to hold you up,' the young woman replied, seeing him stagger slightly.

'You're beautiful,' her handsome stranger said in return. 'So beautiful.'

The lovers walked on in silence, one nervous about what lay ahead and the other with only one thing on his mind. However, when the new BMW came into view, the loyal friend's inbuilt duty of care overrode his drunkenness once again. Jeff looked ahead at Gerry and Suzanne, slowing almost to a stop.

'Hold on a second, angel,' he requested, suddenly serious.

Leaving Lynn confused on the footpath, he jogged up to the couple, who turned round towards him, wondering what was going on.

'Gerry, give us your car keys, mate,' he demanded, slightly out of breath.

The older man looked affronted. 'You're not driving back. You're just as pissed as me.'

'No,' Jeff insisted and grabbed the keys out of his friend's hand rather more easily than he expected to, causing him to reel backwards and almost lose his footing. 'It's Suzie-Anna's turn to drive tonight.'

It was true that Suzanne had drunk significantly less than the men, but she seemed reluctant.

'Oh, I don't know. I've never driven this car before, Jeff.'

'It's OK,' he reassured her. 'Get in, and I'll show you where everything is.'

'You see?' Gerry shouted at Lynn, who had caught them up. 'He *is* a control freak. What did I tell you?'

The sixteen-year-old smiled politely and looked at her watch: twelve-twenty. She was very tired and had a busy day tomorrow, yet she didn't want to spoil this party for the world. The enigmatic RMIT student had taken the upper hand again, just moments after his best friend had paid for their very expensive night out. Her new world was growing more and more intriguing as time passed.

The owner of the luxurious, metallic gold automobile had already accepted his fate and settled into the front passenger seat. Jeff was always so darned sensible, he had to admit. It would be very bad for business if he were to lose his licence, and he had certainly had way too much to drink. He would pay for it in the morning, as usual.

The younger man opened the rear door behind Gerry and motioned to Lynn to jump in. She smiled at him gratefully, and her hand brushed his on the top of the window frame, as if to support him for doing such a good deed. He closed the door with a secure click and went around to the driver's seat, where Suzanne was puzzling over the complicated dashboard of the BMW.

The intoxicated passenger began to chant over and over again. The responsibility of driving relinquished, he had happily succumbed further to the alcoholic haze.

'Give us a song, Lynn! Give us a song, Lynn!'

'What would you like?' asked the starlet. '"Three Blind Mice"?'

Jeff looked up and grinned at her from over Suzanne's shoulder, between the headrest and the door pillar. This very special woman could give as good as she got, which was fortunate in this boisterous company.

'The lights are here,' he explained patiently to Gerry's long-suffering girlfriend, switching them on.

The tree-lined street lit up beautifully.

'There'll be no-one on the road. You'll be fine. And the indicators are here,' he flicked the handle up and down. 'That's all you'll need. The rest you can figure out.'

After several attempts, Gerry had found the volume knob on the car stereo, and Lynn's voice rang out from the speakers instead. It was a cassette of MAC's recent album, and their lead singer groaned from the back seat.

Her objection was ignored. 'Well, if you won't sing to me, maybe this bird will?'

Suzanne flung her left arm out and slapped her boyfriend across the wrist. He dutifully turned the music off. Reverting to the controls, the reluctant driver remained uncertain.

'What about the wipers?'

The younger man stared at her kindly but also as if she were a little crazy. He didn't know if she was being serious or not.

'Suzie, it hasn't rained in three weeks, you idiot.'

Jeff closed the heavy front door and climbed in behind the driver's seat. The car moved slowly forwards into the deserted, leafy suburban street. Content that he had done enough to ensure Suzanne would be alright, he turned to his date and pretended to introduce himself.

'Hi. My name's Jeff. How are you?' he said, shaking her hand. 'Do you come here often?'

'No, I don't, but I like it very much. It's very entertaining here.'

'Oh, for God's sake,' groaned Gerry. 'Enough already with the corny chat-up lines. I want a song. What happened to "Three Blind Mice"?'

'Where am I going?' a stressed voice piped up from the driver's seat, seeing an intersection up ahead.

The empathetic man in the back leaned forward. 'Blake-san, will you shut the fuck up and give your lady some help with the directions?'

Too far under the influence to deliver any more instructions for the time being, the student slumped back into the leather luxury and pulled his fellow passenger in closer. It was a long time since he had ridden in the back seat of a car. He *was* supposed to be a control freak after all, he chuckled to himself. Perhaps he was? He had never thought about it before and was too groggy to think about it much now either. It was a question for another time.

Before long, the sleek sedan had turned into St Kilda Road and was heading into town, towards the river. Gerry was gazing out of the window and mumbling something about the number of new apartment buildings being constructed. The weight of Lynn's body against his side reignited Jeff's sexual urges through the fuzziness, and he looped his fingers through hers. Not too long now, he reckoned, until this gorgeous girl would be denuded and all his.

'Hey, Suzie,' he began again, loosening his tie and opening his shirt's top button. 'You want to turn left just before the next set of lights, please.'

'Thanks.'

'How do you like the drive?' he asked, breathing deeply to clear his head a little, grateful that she had agreed to take on the responsibility.

'It's actually not too bad. I feel very safe in a tank like this.'

How the Sydney girl wished Gerry had more of Jeff's charming qualities. He really was the perfect man. In the moment, that was... The twenty-two-year-old had always thought so, and often told him so, but it hadn't made any difference. They had both started out as Gerry's friends and became firm friends themselves, but the good-looking bad boy had never responded to any of her overtures. He had dated almost every girl she knew and reportedly many, many more whom she didn't, but still she remained under his spell. Anyway, it was all kind of moot now, with Lynn Dyson sitting in the back, her hand resting on his thigh as if it belonged there.

Glancing in the rear-view mirror, Suzanne caught the Latin lover's eye. He smiled and winked at her, and she looked straight ahead again smartly. She was often convinced he knew what she was thinking, and felt herself blush.

'Left here, please,' Jeff directed, pointing up ahead, 'and then left again into that driveway.'

The circular car park behind the Dyson Administration building was still illuminated, and Lynn immediately reached into her handbag for her keys. The car came to a smooth stop at the bottom of the steps.

'Thanks very much, Suzanne,' the celebrity said, gathering her handbag up to her chest and reaching for the door handle.

However, the door swung away from her hands, because Gerry had got there before her.

'And thanks to you too, Mister Blake,' she added, looking up at the man who was as tall as her boyfriend but not nearly as heart-stoppingly handsome.

The hapless accountant made a valiant effort to help their famous friend to her feet, although it was probably he who needed the more help. He took the celebrity's left hand in his and raised it to his lips.

'It's been delightful to meet you, Miss Dyson,' he recited. 'I look forward to the next time.'

Jeff had also opened the door for Suzanne, who jumped out and gave him a big hug.

'Drive safely,' the kind man urged. 'Get this ugly bastard home to bed.'

The older woman kissed Jeff on the cheek, momentarily overcome. 'She's lovely, Jeff. I'm very proud of you.'

The humble student smiled at his long-time friend but said nothing. He knew he was very lucky, both to have met Lynn and also to have friends like Suzanne and Gerry. The trio had been through quite a lot together over the years, and he was beginning to wonder how much longer the couple had, before their very separate lives completely disentangled. He foresaw the inevitable, even if they didn't yet.

Looking away, he whispered, 'G'night. I'll ring you.'

Round on the other side of the car, the agitated man rescued his dream girl from Gerry's drunken clinch and turned to his mate. They shook hands and embraced each other strongly. The accountant slapped his friend on the back twice.

'I always knew you could do it,' he blurted out.

The businessman winked at Jeff and looked up at the tall building, hinting at how much enjoyment would be found up there.

Then turning to Lynn, he yelled, 'Look after this bloke, won't you. He's a good one.'

The young woman nodded and smiled at his mate, who continued to play up.

'I had every faith in you, mate.'

Jeff scoffed. 'Bullshit!'

The two men embraced again, both knowing that what the nineteen-year-old really meant was that he was grateful to his friends. The impassive accountant poured himself back into the car, and it drove off. After a quick wave, the good-looking couple climbed the steps up to the revolving doors, which had been switched back on for their return and quickly swallowed them inside.

'You have very nice friends,' the young star let on, sighing and leading her boyfriend toward the barrier.

'Thanks,' Jeff nodded.

'They obviously think a lot of you,' she continued, before greeting the doorman cheerfully. 'Hi, Howard. Goodnight.'

'Goodnight, Miss, Sir. Nice evening, I hope.'

The uniformed man was pleasant enough but gave the young man a stern look, as if to say, "I hope you're not up to no good." Feeling unsteady from having left the cold outside for the stuffy air of the lobby, Jeff nodded back, giving nothing away, but probably thereby giving everything away. His unruly thoughts had already moved to what was about to happen behind the closed door of apartment number six, and fuelled by the self-satisfaction that alcohol induces, he could feel a massive rush surging through his whole body. The pair made its way to the lift, which obediently opened. Lynn pressed the button for the top floor, and they prepared to be propelled to the family's city residences. Jeff leaned against the back wall and yanked the stunning young woman in towards him.

'Are there cameras in here?' he asked, kissing her mouth hard.

The cocktail of beer, wine and spirits he had consumed during the course of the evening had certainly taken the considerate edge off her mystery man's touch, and Lynn was forced to pull away to breathe.

'Don't ask me a question and then kiss me. How am I supposed to answer?' she responded, a little perturbed. 'No, there aren't any cameras.'

Once at the top, the lift doors parted, and they stepped out into the hallway, turning left towards Lynn's door.

'I wonder who else is here?' the sixteen-year-old said, mostly to herself but also as a caution to her intoxicated visitor. 'I think Dad and the boys are all here after the tennis.'

Jeff leaned heavily on her as she unlocked the door, so much so that they nearly fell into the room when it opened. His breath smelled of spirits and tobacco, and the heat of anticipation radiated from his body. He grabbed at the door and closed it noisily behind them, steering his quarry inside and up against the wall. He wanted her so badly and was going to have her right now.

Lynn was startled by his importunity and began to feel uncomfortable. Was this what they had referred to in her self-defence lessons? The male on a mission? She tried to push the tall, heavy frame backwards, but he kept on kissing her, all over her face and neck, and with his body pressed hard against her. She couldn't decide whether it felt exciting or frightening. His hands pushed inside her dress and started fondling her breasts roughly. This was too fast, she decided. They were hardly inside the apartment. She had to slow him down.

'Hey, wait,' Lynn instructed sternly, turning her head sideways, away from his demanding mouth. 'Please?'

She was being squashed against the wall and scarcely had any space to move. Or even to breathe. Through what the young woman figured was a drunken haze, her formerly attentive lover didn't appear to have heard her request, and if anything, was becoming more aggressive. Where was the romantic, patient teacher who had taken such good care of her on the previous two occasions?

'I want you,' Jeff muttered and leaned harder against her.

Lynn pushed back again, with more force this time. Still the boozed-up student didn't react. She tried to squeeze out from his strong grasp, and it crossed her mind that she could scream. Her father or brothers would hear her and come to her aid. But no, that had the potential of turning ugly. Her dad would be angry and throw Jeff out, and then she might never see him again. Screaming must be reserved as a last resort. She had to try to deal with this herself first.

'Jeff, STOP! STOP!' she persisted, trying to push his broad chest away from her.

The teenaged celebrity was now shouting directly into her boyfriend's face, but he simply wasn't listening. He had taken her cardigan off and had undone the hooks of her bra, and was by this time attempting ham-fistedly to undo the tiny button at the neck of her dress with his left hand, while his right had already lifted her skirt to waist level and was inside her panties. Finding extra strength, the athlete pushed him with all her might and yelled again to stop.

The aggressor reeled back, unsteady on his feet. Lynn raised her voice further, glad at last to be free of his grip.

'Jeff, wait a minute! What the hell's going on?' she continued at the same volume, relieved to have got through to him. 'Take it easy!'

A confused expression spread across the lost boy's handsome face, as it dawned on him what had been happening. The tension in his balls matched the desperation in his head, and yet something in the depths of his conscience was telling him that he was in the wrong. Why was he in the wrong? Why didn't Lynn want him anymore? He would show her a good time. He always showed women a good time. He was famous for it.

'Don't you want to?' he growled, somewhere between angry and embarrassed.

The starlet held her ground, maintaining as forthright a tone as she could muster. Her parents' investment in self-defence classes had been a wise one, and she wondered if she should grab her bag and run. Even though her heart was beating at an alarming rate and she didn't feel the least bit in control, she was intent on diffusing the situation herself by utilising the techniques she had learned. And they appeared to be working, thankfully.

'No, I don't want to. Not like this. I don't want to make love to Jeff-the-drunk-ego. I want Jeff-the-man, like the other day. Sit down for five minutes and calm down. Please?'

Exhaling loudly, the student staggered to his right and removed his suit jacket, suddenly overheating. He murmured something Lynn didn't understand, probably in Spanish, ripping off the tie which had already been loosened in the car. The pretty teenager immediately felt sorry for him, watching him deflate like a punctured balloon, but she was also full of renewed confidence that she had done the right thing. She headed for the sink to fetch them both a glass of water.

'Do you want some coffee or tea?' she asked, attempting to cut through the thick atmosphere they had brought into the room.

'No,' Jeff replied, following her. 'No, thanks.'

He lunged slightly in her direction, and for a moment Lynn was frightened that he was about to grab for her again. However, the insistence had disappeared from his eyes, and his breathing had slowed. Leaning on the refrigerator door, the normally self-assured man seemed unable to make eye contact with her.

'Lynn, I'm sorry,' he croaked, after several seconds.

The young woman could tell he meant it. The colour had drained from his face, and his usual smile had been replaced by what could only be described as a sickly scowl. He took the glass of water on offer and gulped it straight down.

'I'm pissed,' he continued, accepting a second glass. 'Do you want me to go?'

'No, I don't want you to go,' Lynn responded, motioning towards the couch. 'I just don't want to be mauled.'

Mauled? Jeff rolled his eyes at the destructive image this foul-tasting word conjured up. Very fitting, he thought. It was the perfect description. He had been mauling her like a tiger. Disgusted with himself, he was sobering up very quickly. Jesus! This wasn't at all how he had hoped the night would end, and he could feel the usual rage boiling up inside him. He turned to pick up his jacket and tie.

'I should go,' he hissed, finally finding the courage to look his stunning new friend in the eyes. 'I'm really sorry. I'm drunk and I shouldn't be here.'

'Yes, you are drunk! Very drunk. But please, I don't want you to go,' the brave young woman repeated. 'Jeff, I've had a great time tonight. Your friends are lovely, and you've been such good company. I want to be with you too. Just not so pushy. Not so aggressive. It wasn't sexy. It was horrible. Frightening.'

His head reeling and at a loss to know what to do for the best, the sickened nineteen-year-old slumped down onto the couch and threw his head back. What the hell had come over him? How much had he had to drink?

'You're right,' he apologised. 'I was an animal. You were right to stop me.'

The young sportswoman sat down beside him, having refastened her clothing and straightened her hair, far enough away that he couldn't reach her in the time it would take to spring out of the way. She smiled at the dejected heap of manhood into which her antagonist had transformed during the last few moments.

'It's OK. For a while I didn't think I was going to be able to stop you.'

Without speaking, her tall mystery man stood up again, and the room spun around, making him feel decidedly queasy. 'I'll be back in a minute,' he announced, making his way to the bathroom.

Once inside the small, windowless room, Jeff didn't really even comprehend why he was there. He splashed some water on his face and allowed his reflection to chastise him for behaving so badly. He stood leaning on the vanity unit for several minutes, trying desperately to sober up and reorder his tangled thought processes. Had he really been on the verge of raping Lynn Dyson? What the fuck had got into him?

When the subdued student returned to the lounge, his dream girl had disappeared. He dropped back down onto the couch, with his head in hands, still disoriented and furious with himself. Why did he have to drink so much? He should know better than to throw all this away for a few glasses of wine and cognac.

'Fuck,' he muttered under his breath.

Jeff sat quietly hating himself, wondering if he should get up and walk out of the door. Had Lynn gone to bed and assumed he would sleep on the sofa? He wasn't going to do that, regardless of the desperately alarming final message that running away would send. If he stayed, his nightmares would almost certainly be lurking just beyond his impeded consciousness, eager to punish his stupidity.

Through the confusion scrambling his head, the hot-headed student discerned the sound of a wardrobe door banging shut behind him, as yet unaware that Lynn now stood in the opening between the bedroom and the rest of the apartment.

'Are you coming to bed?'

At first, Jeff didn't even look up. How could he think of going over there? Did this fragile creature have any idea what she was doing? Could he trust himself, he who had been so protective of her earlier? He certainly couldn't be sure of his ability to perform when he reached her in this spaced-out state. Shit! He was a joke. Suzanne would be proved right after all. He laughed softly to and at himself, and took a deep breath in.

Where's your ego now, chico? the voices in his head taunted. *You're a fucking mess. No longer the great lover you thought you were... You got close enough to paradise, only to completely ruin your own chances. Great job!*

So his bluff had been called. The nobody from Sydney's west had nowhere else to go, and not only physically speaking. By rights, Lynn should have thrown him out. Yet here she was, calling him into the bedroom. What a rollercoaster he was on lately! Feeling old and heavy, Jeff heaved himself to his feet and turned towards her voice, wondering how on Earth he was going to rescue this night and his future.

The young woman waited patiently for her boyfriend's addled brain to engage properly. She watched with a mixture of curiosity and trepidation, as he seemed to battle with some subconscious force, and speculated as to the intentions he now held for her. It was as if he was on autopilot, his body moving independently, dragging his overactive and highly conflicted mind along after it.

However, all thinking came to an abrupt halt as soon as Jeff's tired gaze met the dazzling spectacle which now stood before him. He stopped in his tracks, upon lifting his shameful head upwards from her tanned legs, all the way to her exquisite smile.

'Oh, my sweet saviour,' he growled, raising his hands to his head.

Scarcely believing his eyes, the nineteen-year-old's legs began to buckle, and he could almost have fallen to his knees. If his mind hadn't already been blown, the scene which greeted him in the entrance to the bedroom completely finished the job. He rocked on his heels, taking in the amazing sight that confronted him.

Lynn stood there, dressed in her tennis outfit again, bathed in the subtle light from a bedside lamp, with her long, blonde hair loose around her shoulders. She was staring her hungry man directly in the eyes, willing him towards her. How the tables had turned! The seasoned playboy was about to be seduced by the same sporting temptress who had fed his fantasies so well earlier in the evening.

In one fell swoop, all Jeff's emotional chips were cashed in. His dream girl looked fantastic, and he was immediately and seriously aroused, despite his impaired state and his guilt at the loutish behaviour he had displayed.

'OK,' he smiled sheepishly, raising his hands in surrender. 'You got it, lady. Anything you want.'

The mesmerised young man walked towards the blonde beauty, gently cupped her face in his hands and kissed her for a long, long time. No doubt about it, Jeff Diamond had met his match. He had been thoroughly humiliated, and his punishment was exquisitely painful.

'I want you,' Lynn whispered, 'but slowly, like before.'

She stepped a few paces backwards to the bed, and her partner followed like a puppy, levering off his shoes, removing his shirt and letting his suit pants fall to the floor. They made love in breathtaking, electric silence. The effects of the alcohol counteracted the urgency built up over a long evening of keen anticipation, and Jeff somehow found the presence of mind to weave his usual magic. And for her part, Lynn was almost overcome with his response to her courageous and probably reckless idea.

The naïve teenager had taken a huge risk by inviting such a potentially dangerous man into her bed so flagrantly, but her instincts had proven sound. With renewed confidence, brought on by recognising the fact that she could now hold her own in very adult situations, she stroked his body all over. She was beginning to understand her man's actions and reactions a whole lot better, and the sincerity he had shown was pleasantly reassuring.

'I don't think I can hold on much longer,' her lover whispered against the soft skin of her face, feeling the end rapidly approaching. 'You are sensational.'

Lynn kissed him. 'So are you,' she replied. 'Jeff-the-man's back.'

He was, thankfully for both of them, and they orgasmed together in slow motion. Long after the intensity had died down, they continued to lie beside each other without speaking, both drained of all energy. It was almost one o'clock. Friday morning was well and truly upon them, but neither wanted to break the peculiar and perilous spell they had cast for themselves.

Several minutes later, feeling drowsiness encroaching, Jeff took a deep breath and sat up on the bed. Lynn had already pulled the covers up and was drifting off to sleep. She looked very peaceful, and the tortured soul felt jealous of her ability to switch off so easily. He had no doubt that what lay ahead of him was yet another sleepless night of soul searching and self-deprecation.

'I have to go,' he said, gently touching the quilt covering her right shoulder.

The young woman stirred and sat up. 'You don't have to. You can stay here. It's fine.'

But Jeff was already nearly dressed.

'Yeah, I do have to,' he insisted. 'You need to rest, and I'm going to be awake all night, so I'll just take off.'

Lynn was far too tired to argue, and her mystery man seemed determined. 'Call a taxi,' she suggested, motioning to the telephone on the dressing table.

'No, thanks. It's OK. I'll walk. It'll be good. Clear my head,' the exhausted lover smiled and sat down on the edge of the bed, as she began to get up. 'Don't move. Stay there, gorgeous. I'll let myself out and say goodnight to Howard for you.'

'Stay safe,' the schoolgirl urged him. 'I love you.'

Jeff bent down and kissed her softly on the forehead.

'I will. And I love you too. I will never maul you again, I promise. You are far too special for that, and I don't deserve you. I'm really sorry. I'll ring you in the morning. Well, you know... Later in the morning.'

Lynn gave a muffled chuckle and lay her head back down onto the pillow. Christ, she looked so beautiful. It was all he could do not to change his mind. Finding resolve from somewhere, the student picked up his tie and suit jacket from the couch, walked through the lounge area and out of the apartment. The door closed quietly, and the sleepy schoolgirl jumped up to fasten the lock, just in case.

Wow! That was one wild night. She glowed and cringed alternately as she remembered pieces of the evening's events. It was an adjustment, this grown-up stuff, that was for sure. She had always wondered if life became boring once a child turned into an adult, but if tonight was anything to go by, clearly not. She filled another glass of water from the tap in the kitchenette, climbed back into bed and turned out the lamp. Within a few minutes, she was lost in sleep, to prepare for another busy day being Lynn Dyson.

***

Back out in the cool air, Jeff chose to walk home along the Yarra River again, but on the northern bank this time. The path was well lit, and there were still quite a few die-hards and tourists out, mostly well-behaved but some fairly rowdy. Everyone was good humoured, and it was nice to be among them, anonymous and unaccounted for.

He too cast his mind back to the overwrought situation he had left behind. Boy, he had learned a few lessons tonight... He had learned that there was most definitely such a thing as too much to drink. He had learned that he couldn't always dictate the play. He had also learned that a heartfelt apology was a powerful tool. Being a hot-blooded, testosterone-charged, obsessive-compulsive male had its challenges. For fuck's sake! He thought he had put all that first-rush-of-blood behaviour behind him. Wasn't he meant to be the mature, experienced one; the one who always scoffed at his mates bemoaning their sexual shortcomings and romantic rejections? The Been There, Done It Kid, as one long-forgotten woman had dubbed him.

Up until the early hours of this morning, these stories had all been true. Jeff Diamond was the archetypal stud; the man with whom every female at university was keen to be seen. He knew how to pick the girls who wouldn't want more, the ones who just wanted to say they had been with him, or those who simply wouldn't remember. They were normally as drunk or as stoned as he was, or more so. Such stringless encounters were perfect for him: no expectations and no exchange of telephone numbers, no fights and no hate-mail. Occasionally there would be a tearful or angry girl in a bar, wondering what had happened and what she had done wrong. He would tell them straight, but always kindly, that it was just the way he was. He wasn't interested in a relationship.

But now look! Life was all of a sudden extremely complicated. The student scolded himself for always over-analysing. Why did he feel the need to consider all the angles and answer every question that came into his head? Despite his arrogance, he had to face it: a naïve sixteen-year-old had got the better of him tonight, and he was reluctant and embarrassed to admit it. Lynn had known how to deal with him and executed her plan masterfully. He felt as if he had been turned inside out.

And why had the well-bred teenager forgiven him so quickly for his aggression? How could she forgive him, when he couldn't forgive himself? Jeff wondered if his dream girl might think differently in the morning. What if tonight was the last time he ever saw her? A shiver ran down his spine, and he unleashed a loud roar into the empty street, feeling suddenly very sick. He stopped walking and leaned against a tree, groaning aloud. *For Christ's sake, man, stop wondering what'll happen next.* There was no point in trying to second guess the future.

With his emotions see-sawing up and down, the troubled man resolved to be patient and leave circumstances to take take their course. He had no choice. This aberration had been entirely his fault, and he knew it only too well. No-one else to blame. A rare error of judgment, brought on by way too much alcohol and an over-inflated ego in front of his two friends, and his own domineering stupidity may well have let the future he had worked so hard to create slip through his fingers. He kicked the tree hard and yelled out in anguish.

By the time Jeff reached home, it was after two o'clock in the morning. He jumped straight into the shower and stood under the warm water for a few minutes, fighting to keep Lynn and her tennis skirt out of his thoughts. What was on tomorrow? No, today; Friday? Working at the university all day, then out for drinks with his classmates. And Saturday? Finishing two assignments which needed to be submitted by the following Friday, then he had arranged to go to a pub to watch a band in the evening. He and his mates would probably go on to a nightclub afterwards, depending on how much money they had left.

Resigned to the inevitable, the western suburbs teenager turned off the taps and towelled himself dry. Standing in front of the mirror, he stared again at his reflection and wondered what his dream girl had seen while he had been "mauling" her. Feelings of guilt and embarrassment returned with a vengeance, and he snarled venomously at his own image while unsavoury footage of his mother and sister filled his head.

He hadn't struck Lynn, had he? Jeff shuddered. Had he crossed that unforgiveable line? Mental torment fuelled the possibility of his memory blocking something his conscience could never support. He would have remembered hitting her, surely? If he found out he had committed such an unspeakable act, his ingrained self-loathing would never, ever let him off the hook. Not in a million years...

Shaking himself out of the destructive spiral, the exhausted man put on a t-shirt and a pair of boxers and opened the fridge door, more out of habit than purpose, before closing it again without helping himself to anything. He didn't need another drink. That much was perfectly obvious. Instead, he made a mug of strong instant coffee, scooped in three large spoonfuls of sugar and went to sit in the living room.

His acoustic guitar was lying against the couch next to him. Lighting another cigarette, the morbid songwriter picked out a melody and began to fashion a lyric from the incessant jumble of words in his head. This was how songs always came to him, through life's experiences. Oftentimes, it wasn't really the song which was the end product, but more the mood it captured and the therapeutic catharsis it provided for his tortured mind.

Weird Present

Marianna Dyson, her daughter and Michelle England entered the lift lobby of the Dyson Administration building, coming up the stairs from the car park underneath. They had been to a meeting at the girls' school about an upcoming interstate netball carnival in which they were to participate. Michael, the daytime security guard, waved to them.

'Miss Lynn,' he shouted. 'I have a parcel for you.'

'Ooh!' whooped the feisty redhead. 'A secret admirer!'

Lynn's best friend was "in the know" about the younger woman's dangerous liaisons with a certain Catholic Argentinean Polish Jew, but hadn't received the update that Marianna had since been let into the secret too. Feeling embarrassed, Michelle bit her lip and tried to act normally. The three women approached the security desk, where a long, narrow box wrapped in brown paper was waiting.

'I don't think you should open it, Miss,' the solemn man advised. 'It might be better if you allow me to open it, just in case.'

'It looks like a bottle of wine or champagne, in a presentation box,' her mother said.

'It can't be,' Lynn replied, longing for a message from the boy who was occupying her every thought, dream and waking moment.

'Who would be sending a sixteen-year-old a bottle of wine? I'll have to confiscate it,' Marianna joked to the girls.

'Who's it from?' asked Michelle. 'What does it say? It might be a bomb.'

The uniformed guard courteously scolded the schoolgirl. 'You shouldn't joke about that sort of thing, Miss. It's not a bomb. And it's not a bottle of wine either. It's not heavy enough.'

Michael looked to his employer's wife for her instruction. 'Will you allow me to open it, Missus Dyson?'

'Who delivered it?'

The conscientious former soldier racked his brain, taking a while to recall. Lynn's eyes scoured the package for any clues, hoping the adults wouldn't see fit to deny her the opportunity to open her own gift.

'Ah, yes. It was the tall lad who came to take Miss Lynn out last week. Dark hair… He's visited a few times. I remember him now. I was just going off shift. He made eye contact with me, which is rare these days. Mister…'

That was definitely Jeff, Lynn thought with glee. Those friendly, dark eyes had made a formidable impression on her too.

'Jeff Diamond,' she said proudly. 'Please let me take it. It's not a bomb. I know who it's from, and it's private.'

Marianna looked from the guard to her daughter and back again. Sixteen and wilful, she had noticed a definite change in her daughter's behaviour over recent weeks, and all had become clear to the elegant lady after the teenager had divulged certain details about her precipitous entry into the adult world. The Dysons had always allowed their children a fair degree of autonomy, in exchange for the huge commitment they made to their education and training, yet the mother remained hesitant about passing on Lynn's news to her husband.

'Alright, darling. Take it, but be careful opening it. Thank you, Michael, for your vigilance.'

The excited starlet picked up the parcel, feigning nonchalance and trying not to snatch it from the man's hand. How intriguing! What was inside? It rattled a little but gave her no clues.

'Thanks, Mum. Let's go, Mish.'

Upstairs and inside the top-floor apartment, the two girls couldn't wait to open the package. There was no indication on the outside as to the sender's identity, and Lynn had no idea what might be beneath the wrapping. Its contents moved slightly when she shook it, and they couldn't feel or hear the sloshing of any liquid.

'It's definitely not booze. What do you think it is?' asked her friend. 'Is it from Jeff?'

'It must be. No-one else has picked me up from here and taken me out,' her friend replied, hugging the parcel to her chest protectively. 'Anyway, it's private, so that means I open it and I might show you.'

'Ooh! Hark at you, Miss Precious!'

Michelle got the message loud and clear and went to switch the television on. Lynn carried the mysterious item onto her bed, facing away from the rest of the apartment, and carefully started to undo the packaging. Inside was indeed a wine bottle, but an empty one. What on Earth? That was odd, she thought.

The empty bottle was in a box, under some cling film, and beside it there lay a single red rose with a two-year-old boy's birthday card next to it. The curious young woman spied an envelope inside the card as well, or maybe two envelopes. She recognised the label on the wine bottle, and there was now something written on it: "L&J 26/2/72". It was the bottle of Shiraz she and Jeff had shared that first night they had spent together at his flat in Richmond.

Thinking back to that fantastic adventure gave the young woman butterflies in her stomach again.

Lynn chuckled quietly to herself, elated and bemused, quickly understanding that her boyfriend was seeking to make amends for the other night's dreadful behaviour. The dark green bottle was tied to the back of the box with two tennis shoe laces, presumably to stop it moving around too much. Very funny, she smiled. Only Jeff's idiosyncratic sense of humour could possibly have dreamed up this gift.

The teenager peeled back the transparent plastic covering and lifted out the card and the rose. The cartoon on the front of the card was of a boy in a red car, with a big figure two on the top. The pair of envelopes dropped out onto the bedclothes, leaving the stem of the rose stuck to the inside of the card. She inhaled sharply and drew back a little when she opened the card and saw what looked like a bloodstain next to one of the thorns, and then gasped still more on reading the solitary line in the middle of the page.

"Lynn, your beauty on the inside shines even brighter than on
the outside. I love you. Jeff"

Tears welled up in the impressionable youngster's eyes. The various pieces of her gift were beginning to make sense, and she re-read the line, trying to imagine her mystery man speaking the words. Reading it for the third and fourth times, a teardrop escaped and ran down her cheek. This was a very special peace offering; an apology incarnate.

Hearing nothing for such a long time, Michelle was bored with waiting and was now loitering next to the wardrobes, anxious to release the suspense.

'Lynn, what's going on? Can I come in?'

The blonde schoolgirl quickly put the gift's various pieces back in the box and wiped her eyes, before turning round to invite her friend to join her.

'Yes. Sorry, Mish. Come in.'

'So?' the older teenager's curiosity was written all over her face. 'What is it?'

She looked down at the bottle-in a-box which had been hastily reassembled and noticed that her previously animated friend had become particularly reserved. There was clearly something worth hiding here...

'It *is* wine!' Michelle exclaimed. 'Did you tell him you were eighteen?'

'No! Of course not. How could I get away with that? Anyway, it's empty.'

The ginger-haired girl looked incredulous, standing with her hands on her hips, waiting for more. However, her famous classmate felt no inclination towards clarifying why a man might send her an empty wine bottle tied up with tennis shoe laces. There was no way she was going to risk her future with Jeff by telling her excitable teammate that she had narrowly escaped being sexually assaulted by the sender of this obscure collection of objects. It was all too difficult to explain and way too personal to share, even with her closest friend.

'It's just a joke.'

'Weird joke!' laughed Michelle. 'So when are you seeing him again? Is he going to Robert's twenty-first?'

Lynn nodded. 'I hope so. I invited him.'

The sixteen-year-old cast her mind back to her nervous suggestion that Jeff might attend a birthday party her family was hosting for the son of family friends. She still didn't completely understand what was expected of her in the protocol of boy-meets-girl. Was it acceptable these days for a girl to ask a boy out, once they had declared their feelings for each other?

Her mystery man had behaved awkwardly too, the star recalled. He had confessed to being equally inexperienced at navigating the dos and don'ts of relationships. She had been extremely surprised to learn that he had seldom dated the same girl twice and was still unsure as to whether she ought to approve of this fact or not. What was he trying to avoid with all those other girls? Not sex, obviously! Parents, perhaps? Jeff never spoke about his own family, so perhaps he didn't know how to behave around other people's parents? And there was the sleep thing too. He had mentioned several times about not sleeping during the night. What was the deal with that? Everyone needed to sleep, didn't they?

Nevertheless, Lynn had been relieved to hear Jeff enthusiastically accept her invitation to Robert McLean's swanky birthday party. The student had told her in typical, eloquent fashion that he was very unlikely not to want to accompany her anywhere, as long as it was appropriate. What had his funny example been? Oh, yes! He had described a time when Gerry's older sister had insisted he join a group of her friends for music practice, and when Jeff had arrived, he had been the only boy in amongst eight or so giggling girls whose only apparent objective was to stare at him.

Her perplexing boyfriend was certainly cavalier about the way he looked, the sportswoman smiled to herself, but with good reason. After all, had his looks and charm not been the primary reasons why she had extended her invitation too? She couldn't wait to show off this gorgeous specimen of modern manhood to her friends!

'Wow! He'll have to meet your mum and dad,' Michelle continued, waving her hand in front of her friend's dreamy face. 'That'll be scary for him. Do they know about you two yet?'

Lynn nodded again. 'Mum does. I told her on Saturday, and she knows we've had sex too. Helen gave me some really good advice on what to say and what not to say. It worked, thank God!'

'Oh, my God! Did you?' the redhead exclaimed. 'What did she do? Was she angry?'

'No, not really. Surprised, I think. I told her we'd been careful and that Jeff's a uni' student. You know... serious about his studies... blah, blah, blah... All the good bits,' the teenager realised her words sounded less than convincing this time around. 'Mum wanted to know all the gory details about him, but I don't know any details. She said she was worried that I didn't know more about him and that she'd have to tell Dad. I mean, I knew she would anyway. It's no big deal. They haven't told me to stop seeing him.'

The eighteen-year-old looked down at the bottle-in-a-box again. 'Maybe they will now... That's one strange present!'

'I hope not,' Lynn smiled, half to herself.

Michelle was right. Her mother was bound to ask about the package's contents and would probably want to see it. This would necessitate a much better explanation than the one she had just provided to her friend.

'Does Jeff do drugs?'

'Hey! I don't know,' the young woman replied indignantly.

'Well, an empty wine bottle... Come on! Maybe he's an alcoholic?'

That was enough. Why was everyone intent on filling her mind with negative thoughts concerning her new beau? Was Michelle jealous that her best friend was experiencing romance before she had? Or was she simply pointing out the pitfalls of jumping headlong into a relationship with a man so unlike anyone else who had come into their short lives so far? Lynn coaxed her friend out of the bedroom and into the living area, shoving her shoulders gently to make her move forwards.

'He's not an alcoholic,' she insisted, although not entirely convinced of this fact after the other night. 'And so what if he takes drugs? That's up to him. He's over eighteen. He can't force me to take them. I'm not interested.'

The sixteen-year-old didn't really want to push her friend out but she did really, really want to telephone Jeff and thank him for the special gift. She was dying to know how he was feeling and to hear that sonorous, deep voice of his again. Her heart began to beat faster just thinking about it.

'What time do you have to go home?'

The older girl looked at her watch. 'Oh, God! Now, actually. It's late. Can I get a lift home from someone?'

Secretly pleased, Lynn picked up the telephone and dialled the security desk.

'Hi, Michael,' she said in her usual, sweet manner.

The redhead stood and listened to the brief conversation. The guard was apparently asking the celebrity about the parcel.

'It was a present,' she told him. 'Yes, perfectly harmless! Yes. Please could you call a cab to take Michelle home?'

The amused eighteen-year-old mimicked her friend once the call was over. 'Yeah, Michael. Perfectly harmless, but weird, weird, weird!'

145

The two schoolgirls left the apartment and proceeded downstairs to wait for the taxi. As it turned out, the elder had more of her own boyfriend stories to tell, and they laughed and carried on like two normal teenagers until the car arrived. As soon as it had driven off, the impatient starlet hurriedly pushed the lift call button and waited to be taken back upstairs to the telephone.

Answering machine. Damn!

'Hi, Jeff. It's Lynn. I'm just ringing to say thanks for my gift. It's beautiful. Michelle thought it was weird, but I don't. Actually, I think it's a work of art. Or a work of heart, as my teacher would say. A physical representation of your emotions; like a song or a sculpture, I suppose. He'd be pleased to know I pay attention in his classes! I think it's lovely and I really get it. At least, I think I get it. Don't worry about ringing back, because I'm hardly going to be here until Wednesday afternoon. Please would you explain it to me then, in case I've missed anything?'

The joyful young woman was about to sign off, and then remembered she hadn't yet explored all the parts of the puzzle yet.

'Oh, I forgot! I haven't opened the two envelopes yet. Is that what "2 4 U" means in the card? Anyway, I'm using up all your tape. Can't wait to see you on Wednesday. Any time after five-thirty should be OK. I'm going to cook you dinner, so come hungry! I love you. Bye.'

The rapturous young woman replaced the receiver on its hook, content with her long message. She couldn't think of anything she had omitted.

So now for the envelopes... They were marked "1" and "2". Dutifully, the teenager opened them in sequence. Number one contained a single sheet of paper on which was a handwritten poem. No, a song lyric, she decided. Jeff had told her he wrote songs. Either poem or lyric, she didn't mind, because the exotic idyll in the verses instantly transported her high up into the clouds.

Evocative and poignant, the lines spoke to its recipient of an ancient love which had only now been given life, and how their author dared to believe in its future for the first time. At the bottom of the lyric was a signature: "JMD, 9/3/72".

Lynn read the group of romantic verses again, wondering what sort of melody might complement them. She wanted to believe in their relationship's future too, even though she didn't even know what the "M" stood for in her boyfriend's initials. She was crying with happiness. The starlet had received hundreds of letters and poems before, from her many ardent admirers, some of which had been decidedly unsavoury and others very dubious, leading the office staff or her parents to throw them away.

However, this latest offering had a completely different effect on the young star, because of the unfathomable connection she was beginning to feel with her new boyfriend. Suddenly feeling very special and mature, adulthood was looking brighter by the day.

Envelope number two was the same: a single handwritten sheet of paper, signed at the bottom with the identical code. As passionate as its predecessor, this second poem had a harder edge and spoke of painful realisation that her shamed man had been conquered by a superior force. Lynn dared to think Jeff meant this to be her. Was she his superior force? She *had* succeeded in averting a situation which might have spelled disaster for their relationship, so maybe she was. Wow!

"Until you, there's been nothing I couldn't leave behind. Until you.
This proud man stands here, naked and unarmed. It's up to you.
Until you, I steered the game to win or lose. Until you.
Command and care, hand-in-hand, I promise.
Give and take, unite or divide. You choose."

So the strange gift was fully revealed. Her heart racing, and with tears running down her face, Lynn was confident she understood the different levels of two which Jeff was trying to convey. But "command and care"? What did that mean? She shivered when recalling the risk she had taken in assuming control of the potentially harmful scenario her drunken poet had created, and now realised that she had done exactly the right thing. Without knowing how or why, she had chosen the best way to pitch her counterattack and appeal to this particular man's keen sense of right and wrong. The weird present, as Michelle had put it, demonstrated to the young woman that her lover knew this too, and by all accounts he was truly sorry.

Make no mistake, Lynn said to herself, this was no ordinary boyfriend for a sixteen-year-old schoolgirl. There was real depth to this man, way beyond the norm for someone who was only nineteen himself. It also scared her though, because this sort of depth would surely be more than her parents would support at her tender age and at this vital stage in her development.

The thrilling, romantic future they both sought was sadly also out of her hands for the next few days, for Lynn was shortly to be leaving for Sydney to compete in an Olympic qualifying event. Feeling overwhelmed, she packed the pieces of her enigmatic stranger's artistic creation back into their original box with a fanciful sigh. She would have to wait until Wednesday evening to ask the dozens of questions which were queuing up in her curious mind, and also to see if the songwriter would play his songs to her. She longed to find out more about this complex intellectual who professed to have been in love with her for so long.

***

Jeff arrived home late on Monday evening, after working a double shift at the university to earn some extra money. He had only managed two or three hours' sleep over the previous weekend and was completely shattered. He desperately needed to get some rest that night, but didn't hold out much hope.

Still, the dedicated student had achieved an excellent mark for his recent assignment and had succeeded in functioning pretty normally over the last few days, despite the tiredness and dread hanging over him. Gerry had appeared genuinely impressed, after having met Lynn in the flesh, and was treating him with a newfound respect. Suzanne, on the other hand, remained in a jealous rage, on his case about the constitution of fidelity.

The student saw the conservative woman's point of view but was not yet prepared to cede to what would almost qualify as celibacy, especially relative to what he had become used to, given his new girlfriend's distinct lack of leisure time. He had refused to relent and make an attempt to convince his old friend that his promiscuity was purely for medicinal purposes, because to pursue that argument would mean he would be required to give too much of himself away. Having managed to live a double life for so long, now was not the time to expose his darker side.

The light on the answering machine flashed in the dark, giving the young man a jolt. In the frustration at his inability to solve his sleep deficit problem, he had almost forgotten about delivering Lynn's present earlier that day. His heart began to beat very fast, and the veins in his head immediately pulsed loudly in his ears. Shit! He wondered what she thought of the eclectic box of tricks, his usual self-confidence rapidly deserting him. This was the moment when he would find out whether his mindless, drunken behaviour had cost him his life's dream. Had it been an inexcusable mistake which not even the most heartfelt peace-offering could rectify?

To negate his light-headedness, Jeff tried to convince himself there was nothing to worry about. The message was probably from someone else: the library book he had ordered was ready for collection, for example. *You complete moron*, the nervous man scolded himself. One little red flashing light had succeeded in putting him right back on the rollercoaster all over again.

Nothing for it! The strung-out student lit a cigarette and pressed the "play" button.

'Hi, Jeff. It's Lynn.'

A smile spread gradually across his washed-out face, as the innocent message played itself through. It appeared miraculously that he remained forgiven, and the bright white light once more shone in his life. The lost boy listened to the message five or six times, head thrown back onto the couch and eyes closed. Each time he heard, "I love you. Bye," he pressed "rewind", without even having to look at the buttons on the machine, and listened again to the voice he adored. By the sixth time, he was aching to be with her.

'I get it,' Lynn Dyson had committed to his answering machine.

That was all Jeff needed to know. Even if she didn't completely get it, at least she understood there was something to get. The gamble had paid off, and their relationship would live to see another day.

The inspired songwriter guessed that by now Lynn would also have opened the envelopes and read his lyrics. He checked the clock: nine-fifteen. Not too late to play music. Not in this noisy neighbourhood. He sat on the floor, with his cheap, electric keyboard across his knees, and picked out the chords to the first of Lynn's songs, tasting the meaning of each word and picturing her hand in his, her body next to his.

A whole new set of emotions were triggered when the novice performer assumed he would be asked to play the two gifts for his dream girl on Wednesday: fear again, but this time laced with excitement and pride. He knew his work was good. How? He had no idea, but he just knew... The prospect of playing his own compositions to Lynn Dyson was quite something! He wondered if she would be a tough critic. Hundreds of songs must have been sent to her over the years, but with any luck she might attach some value to two from him. Two out of a very large number, in fact.

The restless but more consoled student retired to bed with his happy thoughts. What a change from the last few days! Images of Lynn were good company for a while, each one committed to memory in minute sensory detail. *Please sleep*, he begged himself, *and no dreaming*.

Too soon Jeff was woken by the sound of his own yelling, drenched in a pool of sweat and panting as if he had run the hundred metres sprint. What time was it? Still before midnight. Little more than an hour since he last looked at the clock. Angrily, he switched the light on and went into the kitchen for a tin of beer. *Oh, well...* Even an hour was better than nothing. He slumped back onto the couch and opened a book. Perhaps he could bore himself to sleep, he sneered.

Try as he might, the nineteen-year-old was unable either to concentrate or to relax. He played Lynn's message another three times, before realising that the tape would soon wear out if he wasn't careful. He decided to remove it from the answering machine and replace it with another. Afterwards, he went back to the book for a few minutes, then returned to bed for a few minutes, before giving up on both and heading out for a walk.

It was a mild night, and the exhausted man had the streets to himself. He couldn't run on the road, because he had promised Lynn he wouldn't. Where would he go? He already knew Richmond like the back of his hand after just a few months, but only in the darkness.

And how the hell was he going to solve this turbulent problem? This constant state of sleep deprivation was completely unsustainable and appeared to be worsening. For Christ's sake, he should be relaxed tonight. He was no longer afraid and was looking forward to his next date with Lynn. Such was his contorted mental state, that often the more relaxed he was, the more violent the nightmares would turn out to be. It was a desperate paradox which needed to be resolved somehow, and fast.

***

It was hard for Jeff Diamond to believe it was already over a month since he had first climbed the steps to the front doors of the Dyson Administration building, and he couldn't possibly have foreshadowed a journey like the one he was now travelling. He remembered how badly his head had ached that first evening, with the tension of five years' worth of anticipation. It was much the same right now, riddled with guilt and shame, but hopeful.

Tonight, the gallant suitor was dressed in student attire, blue jeans and a collared shirt that had seen better days. He had brought some beers and a full bottle of wine. Michael was on the door, and the two men greeted each other.

'Evening, sir,' the security guard said politely, waving the young man straight through the barrier.

'Good evening.'

The nobody from New South Wales felt uncomfortable addressing even a security guard by his first name in response to being addressed as "sir". People like Jeff didn't belong on the "sir" side of life, but he wasn't challenged as he made his way to the lifts. At the top, he walked to the end of the corridor, the hairs on the back of his neck bristling in a cold sweat, and knocked on the door. Even though he was thankful it was half open, still a chilling shiver ran down his spine. Was it an omen that his dream girl had left the door ajar? He nudged it cautiously to let himself in, finding his guardian angel walking towards him with a friendly smile. Relief flooding through him, they kissed and embraced for a long time without saying a word, the residual pressure from their last encounter obviously still playing on both minds.

'How are you?' Jeff broke the ice.

He brushed Lynn's cheek with his thumb and felt her weight sink into his chest. That was more like it. Both were on edge, although neither wanted to be, instinctive reactions never failing to reveal greater wisdom than any conscionable act.

'Well, thanks. I've missed you.'

'Jesus! Me too. You can't imagine how long these last few days have seemed,' her boyfriend answered, determined to keep things light but already not wholly succeeding.

The young man had contemplated long and hard the previous night, while walking the streets of Collingwood and Fitzroy, about how this implausibly blooming relationship should work from now on. Somehow the two excited lovers must find a way to cultivate it, allowing it to develop into whatever it needed to be, and with as little interference from his freakish tendencies as possible. There was no need to rush into anything, demanding everything right

150

here and right now, even though this was the only way his erratic mind knew how to operate. His sage heart knew what he needed, and the challenge now was to see how that fitted in with Lynn's ideas.

'What's cooking?' Jeff asked, leading her by the hand and walking over to the stove. 'Smells good.'

'Just pasta and some sauce. I'm not much into cooking. Still learning the basics really.'

'Basics is good,' the self-sufficient student approved. 'Peasant food's what I call it. I'm sure it'll be delicious, just like you.'

Seeing the coy teenager blush, he paused, straight-faced. 'And if it's not, we can ring for *pizza*.'

'Huh!' Lynn scoffed, disgruntled.

She flicked the tea towel at Jeff's hips, and he caught it, pulling her towards him. But before he could wrap his hungry arms around her, she broke away, eager to start a conversation about the present.

'So... Are they song lyrics or poems?'

'Either, at the moment,' their writer replied with a mischievous grin, 'until there's music.'

'Smart-arse!'

The sixteen-year-old was glad they were back to this type of light-hearted banter too. She had become unusually worried, waiting for her date to arrive, and was unsure how they would tackle the aftermath of the other night. Jeff's humour was perfect, but now she was about to risk spoiling it by turning serious.

'Can I test my understanding of the rest of your present, please? I'm dying to know if I'm close or way off.'

'Sure. Do you want some wine first? I thought we could have a glass over dinner, go to the library and work, and then finish it off afterwards. How does that sound?'

'Great,' the young woman replied, reaching a couple of wine glasses down from the cupboard above the sink.

'I'm going to have a beer first up,' her guest told her, helping himself to a bottle-opener from the drawer. 'Do you want one? I promise not to drink too much tonight. Or ever again, actually.'

Lynn shrugged, determined to move on. 'Thanks! Let's not talk about that. I don't like beer. Yet, anyway. Michelle says she's beginning to like it lately, so we must grow into it. I'll have some "OJ".'

The pretty blonde, dressed also in jeans and a sports top, began to lead the way into the bedroom area but paused halfway there, feeling her blood pressure rising fast. Caught between wanting him close and fearing for her safety, she turned around to see if Jeff was following her, the uneasiness refusing to leave either of them. He raised his hands well clear of her body, as if to let her know that he didn't plan on touching any part of her, and she giggled.

'I relieved some pressure earlier,' he confessed with a suggestive smile, 'so I've got a few hours until you'll need to turn me back into Doctor Jekyll again.'

Lynn was shocked, hoping she was interpreting her boyfriend's meaning correctly. Such preventative strategies hadn't crossed her mind at all. Yet another adult concept she hadn't been required to consider before. The young woman thought better of responding, swept out to sea once more.

'So Michelle thought this was weird?' her man asked, pointing to the reconstituted gift on the chest of drawers.

'Yes,' the nervous schoolgirl nodded. 'Although I didn't let her see it properly. She saw the wine bottle was empty and the kid's birthday card, so I suppose that would look pretty weird to someone else.'

'Yeah, you're right.'

Jeff didn't much care about Michelle's opinion. The present hadn't been constructed with her in mind. He was very keen to hear what Lynn had to say though. The idea had come to him during another of his nocturnal outings, and it had taken shape slowly over the weekend. Quite apart from being the key to restoring his place in her good books, he was extremely interested to discover whether their two artistic minds would be in tune.

'So, what's your theory, Miss Einstein? You can be the art critic, and I'll be the precious creative, so go easy on me.'

Still refraining from touching each other, the couple sat down on the end of the bed, and the gift's recipient began to make the case for her work of heart.

'The bottle is you, and the rose is me,' a tentative voice offered, searching for clues in her mystery man's eyes.

'Right so far,' Jeff affirmed, with an expectant look on his face.

He took a long, slow gulp from his beer bottle. Very sexily, Lynn thought.

'OK. Good,' she continued. 'The rose has thorns, which I was annoyed with at first, but then I matched it with the blood and realised that it represents my way to protect myself. And the blood means I succeeded. But you were hurt, so that's not so good.'

The humble artist nodded. 'Not so much that I was hurt *per se*. More that I needed to get hurt to understand what was going on.'

'Oh, OK. I like that better. Cruel to be kind,' Lynn ventured, smiling and gaining in confidence. 'Now, the two thing... That's complicated because there are two twos. You and me...'

'Yep.'

'And the two yous that night. The drunk you that was dominating and aggressive, and then the normal Jeff, gentle and caring. Ego-man and Jeff-man...'

The sixteen-year-old checked again for confirmation. The ferocity of her boyfriend's stare unnerved her slightly, but his tone was friendly and encouraging.

'Yes, still right. You're good!' the philosopher was genuinely impressed.

'But there's a twist in the second two because you went from Jeff to ego-man and back to Jeff again.'

'Well, yeah. I guess I did. See what you mean. Shit! You've uncovered a flaw in my design then, because I didn't think of doing a reversing two,' his long left index finger drew an imaginary scoreboard on the quilt and made a mark in his girlfriend's column, before springing to his feet. 'You're too smart! I'm going to get another beer. Want anything?'

'Sorry!' the young woman shouted after him. 'No, thanks.'

His loud voice came straight back. 'Don't apologise. It's great! Keep going.'

Lynn looked back at the display and selected the next component to analyse.

'The shoe laces,' she shot back. 'They're funny. That's the control freak bit, because they're stopping everything from moving. And there are two laces, so you must think there are two control freaks here. Do you?'

'Yes!' Jeff exclaimed, now standing behind her and looking over her shoulder at his carefully-crafted peace offering.

He slapped her firmly on the back, his strong hand drifting round to squeeze her shoulder and neck lovingly. The physical contact was overdue and its effect took them both by surprise. Neither let on, of course.

'Fantastic! I love it!'

'Explain then,' the young woman invited, leaning back onto his thigh and pouting her indignance. 'I'm not saying I disagree. I just want to hear what you say about it.'

'OK. I will, but you have to remain open minded.'

The young pretender considered himself on dangerous ground here, since it had been he who had committed the offence in the first place, but their discourse was way too enjoyable to curtail now. What he was quickly discovering, to his utmost delight, was that this beautiful superstar was wise beyond her years, as was he, and was also someone who could see life from many different viewpoints.

Jeff caught his breath. What had they stumbled on, these two strangers? Sitting down beside his dream girl, he offered a little more.

'When I was mauling you... for which I apologise again, by the way,' he began, once more sheepish.

'Shut up! You don't have to apologise anymore.'

'OK. I know, but I still feel bad. I was way too aggressive, which meant you were losing control and you didn't like it. Fair enough. Completely right, in fact. But then to turn things round and get dressed in that tennis skirt again was downright nasty.'

The romantic student watched for a reaction. There was none, so he carried on.

'You're a master manipulator too, because you used sex to win me over, just the same as I'd tried with you. But you knew I wouldn't be able to resist you, so you gained back control by default.'

Lynn hung her head. 'I see what you mean,' she murmured.

Jeff hooked two fingers under her chin and lifted her face upwards. They looked into each other's eyes, and he kissed her open mouth.

'It doesn't matter. I deserved it,' he told her. 'It was the most excruciating humiliation I've ever felt, and it turned me on so much. There was no way I was going to back off, and you already knew that. You know the saying "There's a fine line between pleasure and pain"?'

'Yes, I've heard it.'

'Well, you hit that line so hard at that point. Like one of those fast first serves down the middle of the court. Could've gone either way, but it worked, because I can't resist you. Hence the second song.'

Jeff leaned forward and rested his forehead on hers, accepting a shy kiss on the cheek. 'You see... You made me *need* my punishment,' he explained. 'That's the ultimate in control freakdom.'

Lynn dropped her shoulders in capitulation. Her man's hands were roasting hot as they gripped hers, and she could see the blood vessels in his neck bulging. She wondered whether her own heightened emotional state was quite as visible to him.

'You're right. I can see it now. I'm sorry.'

'You're sorry, I'm sorry,' the handsome man laughed. 'We're quits then. *¿Comprende? Más no se disculpa, mi amor.*'

The schoolgirl struggled to translate the Spanish phrase that was uttered so quickly and without warning. 'No more something love? Hey! That's another control freak moment,' she pointed out, quietly proud of her growing understanding.

'Damn! You're right,' Jeff admitted, both annoyed at his lapse in concentration and buoyed by the way this conversation was going. 'Good pick-up. I said, "No more apologising." OK?'

'OK. Deal. So what's left? Oh, my God! The pasta sauce!'

She leaped up and ran out of the bedroom.

'Told you we'd be ringing for *pizza*,' the amused man yelled after her.

'No, it's OK,' came the reply. 'We'd better eat soon though, because we'll run out of time to work.'

'It's only quarter-to-seven. Plenty of time yet.'

'The songs are what's left,' Lynn continued, pouring overcooked pasta shells into a colander and boiling the kettle. 'And I didn't know you kept the wine bottle from our first night together. My mum thought you were sending wine to a minor. She was keen to confiscate it.'

'Ha! I'll bring her a full bottle on Saturday, I promise,' Jeff replied, walking over to help serve up the dinner. 'If I'm still invited, that is... Yes, the songs. The lyrics were born while I was walking home, then they grew up overnight.'

'Of course you're still invited. Are the melodies grown up too?' the celebrity asked, placing two large, steaming bowls on the table. 'Can I hear them? Please?'

As they ate, the nineteen-year-old plunged into a daydream of the time when he was a child of around ten or eleven years old, coming to terms with the fact that he could write poetry and songs. This gift had started out as something secret; something he felt compelled to do, but with no idea why. Normal boys didn't do that sort of thing. Normal boys were tough cowboys and soldiers, played football and spoke with outrageous certainty on topics they knew little about. It wasn't that his young self had been ashamed of being musical or appreciating art in all its varied forms, but more that he hadn't come across any other boys who shared his interests. Plus, it just wasn't cool at that age to hang out with girls.

The clever but wayward primary school kid had been given an old guitar by his grandmother's neighbour, who had heard the old Polish woman was paying for his piano lessons. However, his mother had been totally nonplussed when he brought the large, wooden object home, telling him they didn't have enough room in the flat. He never really found out why she hadn't liked it, suspecting a lethal mix of jealousy and ignorance to be at its root. Their relationship was already fairly distant by that time, so the boy had simply never bothered to ask.

Later, when he moved up to high school, Jeff finally met some other young lads who played musical instruments. Some even liked to sing, and the good-looking boy took advantage of free trumpet lessons as a way into the combined schools orchestra. The satisfaction of being part of a larger, albeit rather discordant experience fed the lonely youngster's need for belonging. The school's music department had been small and underfunded, but the teacher was dedicated and easily recognised his talent. This was the first time the prodigious student had had access to a piano outside of his grandmother's flat, and he made a habit of hanging around after school to play it, at least until the caretaker came to lock the music room and would send him home.

During this period of intense adolescent creativity however, the troublemaker had never played one of his own compositions for anyone else. Songwriting had developed as a method of escaping the grotesque life which was unfolding around him. His father was in much bigger trouble, and the boy only saw him fleetingly every now and again. His mother became increasingly depressed and would often drink heavily and take sleeping pills, leaving her two children to fend for themselves. Madalena, nearly three years older than her brother, already spent most of her time out with boys. She tended to flit in and out of their tiny flat, only stopping to change her clothes or to help herself to some food, on the rare occasion when there was any.

The black sheep didn't remember, looking back on those days, feeling particularly sorry for himself. He hated seeing his mother in this pathetic, self-destructive state, but the family's meagre existence carried on in a regular rhythm, and he lived from day to day, deliberately lost in a wild, imaginary refuge. He became increasingly introverted and was more than happy to spend hours on end sitting in a park with his school work and his guitar, and with a growing set of worthy goals to fend off the growing darkness in his heart.

At twelve, the boy from the western suburbs met a fifteen-year-old Gerry Blake, and shortly afterwards, the two Blake sisters, who were both avid music fans. The affluent family boasted a full-sized grand piano in their large lounge room and another baby one in their den, which the composer seized every opportunity to play whenever the rest of the family was elsewhere.

Thirteen had been a lucky age for Jeff, comparatively speaking. So much had happened to him that year, and mostly related to girls. It had all started with being thrown a very small *bar mitzvah* by his grandmother. As expected, his mother and sister had refused to go, despite pleading and crying from the old woman. For his part though, the outlawed boy didn't care one way or the other if the rest of his family was in attendance and hadn't even particularly wanted a *bar mitzvah*. Organised religion made no sense to the intelligent youngster, regardless of its flavour, and he had previously turned down a Catholic confirmation. He had done his best to turn this down too initially, but in the end obliged the elderly widow, only because he knew how much it would have meant to his grandfather, who had passed away a few years before.

A matter of weeks after the Jew in him had become a man, the rest followed. Although the teenager still spent the majority of time on his own, he enjoyed being in company and could be very social when he felt like it, particularly when drink and drugs were on offer. Girls flocked to him, especially those in the music room, who harboured not-so-secret crushes on the handsome boy with the nifty dance moves and the dangerous reputation. Jeff Diamond thought he had really made the grade when he managed to get his former mathematics teacher to take him home, in exchange for showing her how to dance the rock'n'roll. Gerry's older sister, followed closely by the younger one, also fell for his charms, unbeknown one to the other, and the young lover was sworn to secrecy by each not to tell his mate or their parents.

Jeff's entire adolescence passed slowly by, in a long series of sexual encounters; anywhere, anytime and with anyone. Even when his mother died and through all the drama that ensued from that terrible event, his next female conquest was never far away. It delivered the arrogant and angry teenager much needed power and attention, which he had no way of securing otherwise. And throughout this time, he had been prolifically writing songs and poems, borrowing records from friends and learning as much as he could about composing, lyric structure and performing in front of an audience. He had planned it all with specific aspiration, deciding that capitalising on this inner and unending compulsion would be a judicious way out of his dead-end, poverty-stricken, low-down life.

Towards the end of his high school years, the gifted youngster had frequently been enlisted to accompany Gerry's sisters on the piano, whenever they pretended to be pop stars or rehearsed for school musicals. He even joined in occasionally, much to his sports-mad friend's disgust. The two girls were huge Elvis Presley fans and loved to encourage the boy with the mop of black locks to impersonate their idol. Only when they added alcohol to their list of impure incentives did Jeff find the resulting freedom from inhibition and agree to indulge them.

Gerry's mother had even suggested he try out for a scholarship to drama school, but the ambitious student hadn't been inspired by a showbusiness career at that point. It wasn't serious enough for him, except as a conduit to the rich and famous. Music and girls were consigned as hobbies, while he worked part-time wherever he could, learned as much as possible about everything and fought doggedly for his liberty.

Where was this *rêverie* going? Jeff continued to ponder, munching on the dinner rendered especially delicious by the fact that it had been prepared for him by the ultimate prize, whose company also caused the years of struggle to pale somewhat. The Blake girls' extra brother's crush on a certain young star by the name of Lynn Dyson had been known to the musical family for a couple of years, and the sisters would often urge him to send her some of his songs. He had laughed their comments off at the time, yet secretly swore that one day he would indeed have the opportunity and the courage to play for the rising star.

Now wouldn't Jacinta and Tamilla be flabbergasted to know such an opportunity had actually arisen!

'Jeff,' Lynn said, her fingernails drumming on the table beside his wine glass. 'Are you listening? Please will you play the songs to me?'

The dreamer shook his tired head and brought his mind back to the here and now. 'Sorry,' he replied. 'I was off in another time. I used to dream of how scared I'd be to sing you one of my songs. I'm still scared, but after the library, I promise I'll do it.'

'Excellent!' the pretty teenager smiled, thrilled with his response.

She was only too accustomed to the fortitude required to perform in front of people she knew, even now occasionally nervous to try something new with the band or her music teachers. The first attempt at cooking for her boyfriend was no different, she realised, but the simple meal had turned out to be perfectly edible, and the pair chatted easily about their weeks until their bowls were empty.

After dinner, they grabbed their bags of books and prepared to vacate the apartment. True to his word, Jeff had not issued a single hint about sex, and the oppressive atmosphere had by now drifted far away.

'Are we walking or shall we catch a taxi?' asked Lynn.

'I brought the car tonight,' the student answered. 'I hope you don't mind. The Aston Martin's in the shop, getting some more gold-plating done, so it's just the old Ford, but it'll be quicker than walking.'

They parked the trusty Fairlane a street away from the State Library. A little Italian coffee shop nearby was still open, from which the exhausted nineteen-year-old purchased a double espresso. He swallowed it straight down. The caffeine would help his concentration. Something had to...

The young couple found itself a table in a small alcove near the Politics and Current Affairs section. Lynn had a history essay to complete and wanted to choose a suitable subject on which to base it. Jeff was tasked with constructing a philosophy argument that couldn't be solved with logic. Fascinated by the idea, his inquisitive girlfriend asked him to explain how this assignment related to computers, and the natural-born teacher enthusiastically explained the absolute logic required when one was trying to make machines do what one wanted them to do. They laughed about ending up back at the subject of control freaks, before shushing each other.

Two-and-a-half productive hours went by in a flash, before the inner monster's patience began to wear thin.

Jeff looked at his watch. 'Did you want to get going?'

The teenaged star had yawned a few times but was still writing fluently. She had chosen Oliver Cromwell as her protagonist, and there was a great deal of information to include. History was probably her least favourite subject, much preferring science or languages. She also had some French homework outstanding, but that would need to wait until the morning. She would grab half an hour before class to finish it off, so eager was she to return home and sit in the audience for the new songwriter she had uncovered.

'So did you grow up speaking Spanish?' she asked her mystery man, as they walked out of the library.

'*Sí, cierto*,' Jeff replied. '*Mi madre siempre habló en español con mi hermana y migo. Mi padre lo odiaba.*'

Smirking at the confused look on her beautiful face, the self-nominated mongrel surmised that his final sentence hadn't been understood.

'My dad hated it,' he repeated.

'Oh! Thanks! What did he speak? Polish? Was he Australian?'

'I don't know. I only heard the odd Polish word from him, but he would've understood more, I guess,' the student answered, trying not to sound dismissive but keen to stem the flow of these questions. 'Maybe he became a citizen, but he was born in New York. My mum was born in Australia. Crossing a Polish Jew with a South American Catholic did not produce a very good result, as it turned out.'

'Oh, that's a shame. You've got a sister, haven't you?' Lynn pressed, having no idea how uncomfortable this was making her boyfriend. 'Older or younger? Suzanne mentioned her over dinner, didn't she?'

Jeff stiffened. 'Yep. Madalena. She's twenty-two and lives in Sydney. We hardly ever speak. She only 'phones me when she needs an abortion.'

Gasping a little, the young woman was appalled by his flippant reply but was also intrigued for him to continue. Yet another gory detail to be kept as far away from her parents as possible. How many more were there?

'What? That's terrible.'

The nineteen-year-old shrugged. 'We have nothing in common. We always were a weird family. Don't like each other much and tend to leave each other alone. To tell you the truth, I don't even want to talk about it, if that's OK? Do you mind?'

The celebrity was not surprised to be shut down. She could tell her boyfriend didn't enjoy being questioned about his family, which only made her want to ask more.

'OK,' she complied. 'Sorry. I didn't mean to pry.'

Jeff took the pretty sixteen-year-old's bag and slung it over his own, putting his arm around her shoulders. The end of the weekend had descended on the city, and a thick layer of cloud obscured the moon and the stars. The metaphor was not lost on the reflective student.

'They're perfectly good questions,' he assured her. 'You're not prying. It's just that I'm not ready to tell you all my stories yet. No-one knows about that stuff. Gerry and Suzanne don't even know. I'd just like to leave it all behind, now I'm in Melbourne.'

'Oh. No problem,' Lynn agreed. 'You can stay the enigma. I don't mind. It's mysterious!'

'Glad to be of service,' the young man laughed, knowing full well he was unlikely to be allowed to maintain this level of secrecy for long.

The pair had reached the car, and he opened the passenger door for his gorgeous study companion. They kissed tenderly as she began to get in. Mister Hyde was calling, and both knew it. Refusing to allow himself to give into the chemistry, he threw their bags onto the back seat and jumped in. The car took a couple of turns of the engine to start and stay started.

'Come on,' the impatient man shouted melodramatically, taking his frustration out on the steering wheel. 'Don't let me down now! It's not even cold, and we said we didn't want to walk home today.'

Jeff revved the motor hard, and they sped off down the lane. While Lynn chatted happily about her older brother's footballing career, they circled their way through the city's one-way streets, completed a final hook turn, crossed the river and were soon back at the Dyson Administration building.

'Park in the driveway,' she instructed, pointing up ahead. 'No-one else'll be arriving at this time of night, and security's here to look after it.'

'Ha! I don't think it needs looking after. I'd be pleased if somebody stole it.'

'Don't be mean! Cars can hear us,' the schoolgirl chided. 'I bet it doesn't start in the morning now.'

Her boyfriend smiled and shook his head. 'Well, there's a pretty good chance you're right, but it won't be because of any insults I've hurled at it.'

'How do you know?'

The perfect gentleman fetched their bags from the car and motioned for Lynn to climb the steps ahead of him, his eyes firmly fixed on her body as it made its way to the revolving doors. He managed to resist the temptation to steal more than a kiss in the lift, both afraid of rekindling the stilted, stumbling climate from the beginning of the evening. Instead, the aroma from their pasta dinner hung in the air when they opened the door to the apartment.

This time there was no leaning heavily on his dream girl in the doorway and no pinning her against the wall. Jeff didn't want her any less, but things were different now. He had learned his lesson well. Dumping their bags onto the couch, he walked towards the kitchenette.

'Would you like the rest of this wine?'

'Mmm. Yes, please,' Lynn answered. 'Are you going to play your songs?'

The young man chuckled. 'I was hoping you'd forgotten.'

'No chance of that!' she exclaimed. 'There's a piano in the ballroom. No-one'll hear us. It's on the first floor.'

Private Audience

'Ballroom?' Jeff's heart leaped into his mouth. 'No-one said anything about a ballroom! It's alright for you. You do this all the time.'

The impish schoolgirl grabbed the two wine glasses from the table and stamped her foot on the floor in determination. Her exuberance was infectious, and it turned him on even more.

'Bring the bottle. It'll be great. Come on,' Lynn urged.

The nervous man followed obediently. No time like the present, he thought with trepidation. The lift let them out on the first floor, directly into an enormous function room, complete with a stage with full-length velvet curtains at the opposite end and a bar off to one side. It was as big as the average Town Hall.

'Whoa!' he gasped, looking around at the impressive surroundings. 'I had no idea there was one of these in this building. It's magnificent.'

Up ahead, the celebrity was striding purposefully towards a grand piano, situated at the foot of the stage, left of centre. She dragged the heavy tarpaulin cover off and opened the lid, then sat down and played a few bars of the "Moonlight Sonata", as if to warm the majestic instrument up. The sound rang out around the room while her boyfriend refilled their wine glasses, enjoying the soothing melody of the well-known Beethoven piece.

Setting the wine bottle on the floor underneath, Jeff leaned against the piano's concave wall, looking in at the strings. He raised his glass to the skilful pianist and took a much needed gulp of the deep red tonic.

'Don't stop.'

So here he was... Jeff Diamond had been granted an audience with Lynn Dyson, albeit with some work of his own to do. This was a circumstance he could never have envisioned just six weeks ago, yet strangely it now seemed the most natural situation in the world.

The accomplished musician was keen to make the newcomer feel at ease. She played extracts of several classical pieces and then launched into one of her recent hit singles. While she sang and played effortlessly, Jeff moved round and sat beside her on the piano stool, taking stock of exactly where he had ended up. He wondered if he dare ask her to reach back into the past and give him a private rendition of the old folksong which was partly responsible for bringing them together.

'Do you still remember "Power and Glory"?' he asked at an appropriate hiatus, placing his fingers on the keys and picking out a meandering refrain of thirds, as accurately as he could reproduce from memory.

Lynn smiled. 'Not sure. Probably. It was in "E", I think.'

Playing too high up the register for such a plaintive sound, the entranced visitor removed his hands from the keyboard while the star pieced the accompaniment together. He leaned back in amazement, stoked that she might actually try for him. After a couple of false starts, the child star reconstructed the introduction, which had originally been recorded on an acoustic guitar.

'Wow. I'd forgotten all about this song until you mentioned it the other day. I love it but I haven't played it for so long. I don't want to mess it up, because the words are so beautiful.'

The lost boy nodded, closing his eyes as she began to sing. His chest tightened with the emotion evoked by her crystal clear alto voice, not only in himself but as also revealed in the beautiful entertainer's eyes when he dared to reopen his. By the third line, she had entranced him all over again, and he clenched his jaws tight to mask the depth of his reaction. However, by lines five and six, they were both singing with tears in their eyes, seeking solace in the brighter chorus.

'And rich men don't grow old,' they growled in unison, laughing as the tune was banged out tune as loud as possible on the stupendous instrument.

'I love you, Lynn Dyson. So much.'

With a quick peck on his smiling girlfriend's cheek, the unsung songwriter's hands returned to the keyboard. He started big. There was no other way, after the impromptu watershed he had initiated. Del Shannon's "Runaway" came to mind, for some unknown reason, and he began to play the jingling treble riff. To his delight, he glanced across to his left to see and hear Lynn's hands thumping the bass part out really hard, several octaves lower down the keyboard. They grinned at each other, appreciating their combined musicality, coming in with the chorus together.

> "I'm-a-walkin' in the rain
> Tears are falling, and I feel the pain
> Wishing you were here by me
> To end this misery, and I wonder
> I wo-wo-wo-wo-wonder why?
> Why-why-why-why-why she ran away?
> And I wonder where she will stay
> My little runaway"

This performing lark was actually quite easy, Jeff realised. He was pleasantly surprised at how comfortable he felt. All those years spent hamming it up with Gerry's sisters had stood him in good stead for this very important moment. The unlikely duo replayed the same song, but more quietly the second time. Surely the room wasn't fully soundproofed? They joked that Howard, the night-time security guard, would soon feel compelled to check the melodious intruders out.

Remembering his promise with a renewed attack of nerves, and before the chorus started for a third time, Jeff slid a little further to his left and began to play the introduction of "Until You", the song which had only been written a few days ago, after the notorious tennis skirt episode. He hoped he would remember all the words, trying to convince himself that it didn't really matter if he missed a verse, because Lynn wouldn't know the lyric off by heart. Or would she?

The sensual singer looked up at the object of his long-held affections, who had slipped away to listen from the far end of the piano. He stared into her eyes, and it felt so good to be communicating with his dream girl like this; in exactly the same way as he had fantasised so many times over the years. He carried on singing, finding the words flowing easily from his memory and feeling a surge of genuine adoration glowing inside.

After the first two verses, the spellbound starlet sat back down on the edge of the piano stool. She remained silent, but her eyes spoke volumes to her modest minstrel. Inviting her closer, Jeff reached around her body, and she squeezed up further, in order that his right hand might stretch all the way round and back onto the keys. This trick didn't work too well, and they laughed as the sixteen-year-old's torso jerked from side to side as he moved through the chords and accentuated the beat deliberately.

Finally giving up, the ecstatic songwriter flicked an ornamental flourish with his right hand and hit a final bass octave to bring the song to a premature end, leaning his head onto hers while the sound gradually faded. Lynn reached her hand up to turn his face, and they kissed passionately. And as she did so, the young man recognised this as the first real kiss she had initiated. Breathing deeply, she swung round to sit across his lap, and they embraced.

'Jeff, it's fantastic. Thank you. I feel so special that you'd write those lines about me.'

'*You're* fantastic,' the composer replied, 'and I mean every word. Every word.'

The pair remained locked in each others' arms for a good while, their chests moving together as they took in air between long, sensuous kisses. The ballroom was completely silent apart from their laboured breath. The highly aroused student was more than ready to adjourn to the apartment, but he knew he would never get away without playing the second song from his weird work of heart.

'This one's in the style of Elvis,' he explained, lifting long, slender legs off his lap and letting them drop gently beside him. 'There's supposed to be an orchestra in the background, but I forgot to pay the deposit, so only the piano player turned up. You'll have to use your imagination.'

Lynn gave a sunny laugh. 'Cheapskate! Piano players always turn up.'

As he had expected, the expensive instrument reproduced the mellow chord structures much more evocatively than his tinny electronic keyboard at home, and Jeff played the opening bars twice to conjure up the romantic mood he sought. No longer harbouring any inhibitions, he played slowly and sang soulfully, in as good an impression of Elvis Presley as he had ever given. When he finished, his girlfriend wiped a tear from her right eye and clapped her hands.

'Wow!' she whispered. 'That's a brilliant song, Jeff. I mean it. I love it.'

The rank amateur nodded his thanks for the compliment. Indeed, he had to admit to being particularly proud of this composition. He was happy with both, and there were plenty more where they had come from. Furthermore, if he played his cards right, tonight would give rise to yet more inspiration before too long. Having fulfilled his duty, he played a couple of minor chords and closed the piano lid.

'*Vamanos*,' he beckoned, a little embarrassed by Lynn's enthusiasm but also greatly buoyed by her genuine display of emotion.

They stood up and hugged each other tightly, leaving the young woman in no doubt as to why he was so keen to go. Between them, they replaced the sun-bleached piano cover and grabbed their wine glasses, which had not been touched in all the excitement. Jeff took care of his in two gulps as they walked to the lift. He was then given his companion's to finish, and polished this off too, in a single slug. On the way up, he tipped the wine bottle towards the ceiling and provocatively swigged down what was left, full of egotistical relief that he had successfully accomplished another of his life's goals.

'Seriously though,' the charitable celebrity said, looking up at her sexy partner, 'you should send that second one to Elvis.'

With his head still slanted upwards, catching the last few drops, Jeff's eyes angled down to hers, and his mouth released from the bottle. He coughed, incredulous.

'Right! No worries. I'll give him a ring tomorrow.'

At first, his enthusiastic agent stared him down, before dissolving into laughter and shrugging. 'Why not? He's a human being, just like us, you know. Our record company could easily get it to him. MAC are working with him next year on a project.'

Like us? The boy from the Stones Road frowned, caught by an inescapable bout of anger. *Like we're the same, lady...* One day they would know exactly how far she was from the truth.

The lift doors opened on the penthouse landing, and Jeff signalled to his girlfriend to walk out in front of him, still clutching two empty wine glasses in one hand and the now empty bottle in the other. Send his song to Elvis Presley, he smiled to himself, begging his inner brute to relax. Of course! Why hadn't he thought of that?

'Thanks, by the way,' he said, after a short pause.

The independent student had resolved long ago that if he were to seek success as a songwriter and musician, it would be through his own efforts and not through Lynn's connections. He needed to find a way to tell her this without causing offence, but that was a conversation for another time. He hung back, waiting for her to reach the apartment first.

'That would be amazing. Let's talk about it later though.'

Lynn opened the door, none the wiser to any of the competing forces occupying her boyfriend's powerful mind. They walked straight through the living area and towards the bedroom, leaving the empties on the table on their way past. Jeff disappeared into the bathroom and emerged clothed only in his boxer shorts. He looked so mature and seductive, the young woman thought, very fit, and at six-feet-four, in perfect proportion; not muscle-bound but very strong nevertheless. The handsome specimen had told the sportswoman that he and Gerry had become quite religious about training regularly, and his shoulders, arms, chest and legs bore the results of many hours spent lifting weights.

The songwriter approached the blonde beauty with his arms outstretched, desperate to claim his reward for waiting so long. 'Come here, you gorgeous thing.'

He began to fondle her breasts through the fabric of her top, but without urgency this time. Although his partner could hear his breathing turn heavier, the caring teacher was back. She felt unbelievably relieved that the evening had gone so well, and couldn't wait to be taken to heaven again in the welcoming arms of a fellow musician. She hadn't realised until this evening how important this factor was in their compatibility.

'Thanks for being so easy on me,' her eager lover said, referring to the performance in the ballroom.

'You were great,' she replied between kisses. 'I don't know what you were worried about. You have a good voice and you play really well.'

'You too,' he laughed, peeling her t-shirt over her head and letting it fall to the floor. 'Did anyone ever tell you that?'

Shaking her head comically, Lynn undid her jeans and took them off too. They were soon both standing in their underwear, and Jeff took a moment to enjoy her youthful figure once more. He nodded over her head towards the bed, pushing her shoulders gently with his two index fingers. Obliging, she walked backwards, knelt on the bed, and to his pleasant surprise, stretched out the elastic waistband of his shorts and let them drop to the floor. As he stepped out of them, she held onto his hard penis and put it straight into her mouth. The naïve young lady hadn't dared to be this forward before, yet was clearly starting to feel more confident with this new game she had learned.

For his part, the nineteen-year-old had to battle to control himself, such was his level of excitement. He steered his mind back to Elvis Presley, but it made little difference. Reluctantly, he encouraged Lynn to stop for a while. They lay on the bed and played with each other's bodies, laughing and talking.

This is the way it should be, the grateful young man realised.

'Lay back for a while, angel,' he suggested, running his hands all over her skin, as she loomed over him. 'Let's try something new.'

The agile duo switched places on the mattress, and the smiling pupil reclined, awaiting her next pleasurable lesson. Jeff put his hand on her firm buttock, casually slipping a long, piano player's finger between her legs and feeling her tremble again. His tongue began to trace around first one nipple and then the other, wandering down her abdomen to take over from his thumb. His willing partner came for his tongue, crying out much louder and freer than previous times. It was all he could do to stop himself immediately doing the same, saved only by her fingertips digging into the painful muscles in the hollows of his shoulder blades. There was true passion in this woman, and amazingly it belonged to him.

'You are gorgeous,' he whispered, wiping the juice of her orgasm onto the back of his hand before kissing her smiling mouth.

Jeff was not surprised to feel the recent initiate withdraw a little, coming to terms with her own taste. Her education was by no means complete, but the expert lover was pacing themselves nicely, and making love while sober was so much better than the alternative. Kissing her lips feverishly, he encouraged her to climb on top and plunged deep inside her. He could savour their every move and hear her every whisper and moan, all five senses engaged and bombarded with patent stimulation. If ever there were an incentive to stop drinking, this was undoubtedly it.

His dream girl was beaming, and her slender fingers moved over his body fluently too. She looked fantastic above him. Her taut abs and supple breasts aroused him still further, and Jeff felt the point of no return rapidly approaching. Praising her exquisite instincts with a long, satisfied moan, as soon as he turned his mind to his own climax, he felt Lynn's subtle hand slip between their bodies and take hold of his balls. There was no waiting left in his white-hot desire, but she wanted to come again and was making sure he did something about it.

Pulling back and exhaling loudly, he interlaced his own fingers with hers between her legs, his eyes shining as hers opened in surprise, before a desperate rush tipped them both breathlessly over the precipice. He grabbed her hips, and they began to move in unison, orgasming together almost immediately.

'Whoa,' Jeff groaned in pleasure. 'That's so amazing. Perfect timing! You're getting very good at this, angel.'

'Thanks. It was amazing,' affirmed his girlfriend, who had lowered herself gently down to lie on his heaving chest. 'Really amazing.'

The flushed teenager lifted her head and placed a tender kiss on the outer corner of each dark brown eye. The awestruck man felt electricity course down his spine and radiate through his sore shoulders. He could easily get used to this affection. Addicted, even. He ran his fingers down her back and felt her muscles twitch under their magical contact.

After a few minutes however, the tired man was forced to move, a panic attack suddenly gripping him, caused by the fear of being trapped slamming up against the need to be subsumed into a world where he could finally belong to someone special. Using the condom as his excuse, they separated, and Lynn lay down with her head on the pillow.

Fulfilment and confusion vied for pole position in his head, and once out of sight, Jeff slumped heavily onto the bathroom floor, the tiles cooling his steaming skin.

Stop resisting, he goaded his brain.

You'll only get hurt, it retaliated. *You don't deserve her.*

But she loves me, doesn't she?

The tormented nineteen-year-old turned the shower taps on full pelt and roared into the jet of water, hoping his dream girl wasn't listening. Why was it so hard for him to be happy? As post-climactic euphoria subsided, the value of the disguising effects of drugs and alcohol became all too apparent again, and the young man cursed the sudden deprivation with which he was filled. He took a long series of deep breaths in and out, in an effort to calm himself down and force the oxygen through his veins as some sort of substitute.

Determined to prove himself better than his addictions would have him believe, the handsome man, wet hair combed back off his face and skin still shining from the moisture, feasted his eyes on the way back from the bathroom. He counteracted his sadness and consequent cravings with the absolutely divine view, bathed in a half-light shining through from the living room.

The young woman held her hand out, welcoming him back, levered herself up onto one elbow and turned towards her lover.

'I've got something to tell you.'

'What's that?'

'You know I told Mum all about you and us over the weekend.'

Jeff nodded, immediately feeling the anxiety returning. He decided to make a sortie into the living area, on a vital mission to turn out the lights.

'It's OK. It went well, honestly,' the schoolgirl reassured him. 'She's worried about me being distracted from everything, but I told her all the good things about you.'

The student chuckled, lying back down beside her. 'That wouldn't have taken long.'

'Anyway,' Lynn continued, jokingly slapping him across the face. 'She made an appointment for me at the doctor for tomorrow morning, to go on the pill.'

Her boyfriend's eyes widened. 'Really?' he exclaimed, not knowing what to say. 'Jeez! I'm glad you didn't tell me that a few minutes ago. Everything would've come to a very abrupt conclusion. Whose suggestion was it?'

'Mine, but Mum agreed it was a good idea,' the proud sixteen-year-old answered. 'She asked me what we were doing to protect ourselves and said the pill was more reliable.'

'That's amazing. Thanks! Alright! Skin-on-skin.'

The young woman was pleased that her news obviously met with her experienced lover's approval. In fact, he struggled to think how long it had been since he had enjoyed skin-on-skin, so preoccupied had he been with preventing accidental parenthood. Three years at least, he figured.

'You'll love it,' he told her. 'When's your next period?'

Taken aback by his directness, Lynn blushed slightly. 'I've never spoken to a man about that,' she laughed. 'Not even my fitness coach, and he knows most things about me.'

Jeff's doleful, dark eyes asked again, ignoring her embarrassment.

'Next Monday or Tuesday, I think. They say it takes two weeks to be safe.'

'Yeah. I've heard that too,' he nodded. 'But you'll be safe after your period anyway, so *c'est pareil*.'

'*Oui*,' the happy teenager agreed. '*On va dormir?* Will you stay?'

As she had come to expect, her enigmatic stranger hesitated. Why did he always want to leave after they had had sex? Was it purely because of this fabled insomnia, or could it be that he was going home to someone else? His apparent desire to disappear after getting what he wanted seemed so out of kilter with the affection he purported to hold for her.

'Please?'

The exhausted man closed his eyes, inhaled and held his breath for a long time. His right hand found his dream girl's left and gripped it tightly. It was at least a minute before he spoke, but eventually a reply came.

'You don't know how much I want to say yes.'

'Then say yes then,' the young woman stated matter-of-factly, as if there couldn't possibly be anything complicated about it.

Jeff lifted heavy eyelids and smiled, but his voice remained serious. 'It's just not that simple, angel,' he told her. 'I can't sleep like you can. I'd disturb you and get pissed off with myself, and just end up leaving later anyway.'

'I don't mind if you disturb me. Really,' Lynn assured him. 'I'd so love you to stay until the morning.'

Looking into her inviting eyes, the Stones Road native knew he owed his princess a better explanation but was unsure as to how far to go. He had never discussed his sleep patterns, or lack thereof, with anyone except psychiatrists. He had never even considered how he might explain it. Had the time come to bare his soul to the girl of his dreams? If he wanted this relationship to last, he would have to start being totally upfront with her at some point. But could he trust her to understand? And if she weren't to understand, could he trust himself not to get angry with her and ruin everything?

A muted sigh escaped from Jeff's lungs, while his mind raced. Which was the less risky strategy? To keep seeing each other casually, for light-hearted evenings peppered with romps in bed, where Lynn never found out what lay behind the eyes of the man who arrived to entertain her and then left her to dream peacefully until the next rendezvous? Or to confess to some home truths in the spirit of honesty, only to watch her elegantly bring the curtains down on their future?

The peasant boy from Sydney's west had realised earlier this evening that he was but a stone's throw from becoming addicted to the physical presence of his newfound vision of loveliness, to the affinity developing between them and to the amazing sexual chemistry they shared. But it was an addiction nonetheless, and therefore dangerous. Jeff knew that if he were to open his soul to her, he ran the risk of losing all control over their relationship. His already long list of dependencies would extend to include their shared secrets, and he could see himself becoming reliant on any support she might give him emotionally too. Lynn would then have the power to choose at any time not to continue seeing him, thereby leaving him stranded with a string of enslaving habits which could no longer be satisfied.

As frightening as this prospect was, his lonely heart was desperate to move past the arm's length, fuck-and-run scenarios to which he had restricted himself with every other, throwaway girl. This was Lynn Dyson, who deserved so much more from him. And Christ, didn't he deserve much more as well? For too long he had let his demons rule his life, and at last he had the potential of experiencing something different; something the old soul was convinced he needed more than anything.

And it was clear that Lynn wanted a meaningful relationship equally as much. She didn't want her lover to leave, any more than he wanted to go. But surely she would prefer a meaningful relationship with someone who wasn't all screwed up inside? How far would her tender first love stretch across the endless screaming nights and in the face of his compulsive behaviour, before she realised there must be someone else who would be infinitely easier to love?

So Jeff Diamond had a decision to make: to try passing each nightmare off as a freak incident, conceivably every night they spent together? That wouldn't wash for long. Or to give Lynn a full confession and risk her labelling him as the madman he was, and then watch her head for the hills? Would she have the compassion to listen and understand? And even if she listened and understood, would she then be prepared to take a chance on a future with someone so scarred and conflicted?

In a way, the nineteen-year-old reflected, pulling his silent lover's hand to his lips and kissing the fine skin over her knuckles, if this new nirvana was going to cave in… and the realist knew it had to at some stage anyway… it would be better to end sooner rather than later. Logic told him it would be much easier to rid himself of a few weeks' worth of memories than a few months' worth, or even a few years'.

Come on, man, make your choice, his mind chastised. Life wasn't about taking the easy option. Life was about doing the right thing and facing the consequences.

Jeff Diamond made his decision. One which he hoped would change his life for good.

'OK, angel. Let me tell you something about me,' he started, taking a deep breath and faltering a little.

Somewhat surprised by her partner's apparent change of tack, the young star fixed his eyes in hers, encouraging him to speak further. His heart was once again pumping in his throat, and his mind worked frantically to select the best possible words to explain his strange situation. He exhaled slowly, feeling the weight of her stare bearing down on his aching forehead.

'Things happened in my family that no kid should have to live through,' he told her, trying not to sound too melodramatic. 'Violence and other shit that I'd much rather forget, but which my mind won't let me forget…'

'Wait, Jeff,' Lynn interjected, raising her finger to his lips. 'You don't have to tell me all that, if you don't want to. That's none of my business. Just tell me how I can help.'

Tears welled up in the adolescent's eyes without warning, even sooner than he had feared. There was nothing he could do about it. He tried to fight them for a few seconds, but seeing the look of concern on his dream girl's face and being so, so tired of living a lie, the lost boy surrendered.

He had waited so long to hear someone say those simple words to him; someone other than the string of clueless doctors and counsellors, who one by one had treated him like a lab' rat to no avail. The brilliant but discarded teenager had spent his whole life giving, trying desperately to repay a debt that he didn't believe was his. Perhaps now it was finally his turn to do some taking?

And of all the someones who could have said, "Just tell me how I can help," the fact that it had been Lynn Dyson who had chosen to utter this open and non-judgmental phrase in response to his tentative first confession was the answer to all his life's prayers at once. Jeff couldn't quite believe what he was hearing, and hence neither was he about to let her off the hook.

The tortured Sydneysider had been through hell for the last ten or so years, hanging on to his sanity by the thinnest of threads. The only thing to have kept him from committing suicide during his mid-teens was the dream of one day meeting Lynn Dyson. He had worked his guts out to overcome the obstacles blocking his path to the very place where he found himself right this minute. If he owed anything to anyone, he owed himself the chance to share his pain.

'Angel, I'm sorry,' he muttered with difficulty, sitting up and struggling to maintain his composure.

The blonde champion was dismayed by the veritable force she had unleashed and wondered whether she should have left well alone. Jeff was gripping her hand so tightly that it had started to sting. She had never been in the company of a man who was crying, and he seemed to need her more than anyone had needed her before. Perhaps this late night conversation would go some way towards revealing the conundrum that was her new boyfriend?

She flexed her hand inside his, and he released it slightly. The handsome stranger looked directly into her eyes, almost pleading.

'Angel, I don't expect you to understand what I'm going to tell you,' he explained, 'but I've been left with the after effects of all the stuff I experienced back then, and it's driving me absolutely fucking crazy. There's a medical term called Post-Traumatic Stress Disorder that they're trying to get officially recognised, and it looks like that's what I'm stuck with. Do you know what it is? I apologise for the bad language, but it's killing me not being able to be who you want me to be.'

The singer had moved to sit facing him on the bed, wearing a pure white, silk bathrobe. She had tied her golden hair back off her face, which was reddened and full of concern. Jeff's fists were clenched with rage, and his eyes bloodshot. Whatever he was hiding, it was obviously deadly serious, and she was ready to help him. The young woman didn't really know why, but she felt compelled to do everything she could for this gorgeous man who had come into her life out of nowhere to make himself at home in her heart. So far in her sixteen high-achieving years, all around had existed to pander to *her* needs. Now it was she who was needed, and the calling didn't scare her at all.

'Yes, I do know what it is,' Lynn answered calmly. 'Well, not by that name, but I think I know what you mean. At school, we spent some time last year studying the effects of war and actually visited a few veterans, so we could talk to them about their experiences. All those fine men ruined by something they can't control.'

Instinctively, she leaned over and turned out the light, and the room became almost pitch black.

'Lay down, Jeff, please,' her soothing voice requested. 'We don't need to see each other to have this conversation. I love you and I promise I'll do anything I can to help you.'

Those words, together with being granted the refuge of darkness at his most vulnerable, were exactly what the drained young man craved. "Fine men ruined by something they can't control." This warm-hearted woman hadn't said whether she included him on her list of fine men, but her compassionate tone was good enough for now. By this time, tears were rolling down his cheeks, down his neck and probably onto the pillow, but he didn't care. His guard was down, and it was going to stay down until they had played this out. This gorgeous creature couldn't possibly know the hell he went through night after night, and yet she was giving him what no-one else had ever even tried. She had taken away the pressure and was inviting him to open up and let her in.

Overcome, Jeff struggled to speak. 'Lynn, I love you too. I never knew how much I could love you, and never dared imagine what it would feel like to have you love me like this. Whatever happens to us in the future, you've already helped me more than you know.'

The wretch from Sydney's west reached for her aristocratic hand in the darkness. The slender teenager lay on her side next to him, propped up on her elbow, and he could hear her soft, rhythmic breathing. Holding his right hand in her left, she stroked his face gently with the other. She could feel tension in his whole body, like a spring ready to release, so she kissed his right temple and tasted his salty tears.

'Talk to me.'

Her man sighed deeply. 'Christ, do you know how much I need you right now?' he asked, his voice deep and throaty from crying.

'Well, I'm here and I'm not going anywhere.'

The nineteen-year-old took a huge deep breath in and pressed his head back into the pillow, in an effort to rid his head and neck of the blinding pain. Through the haze however, he was beginning to feel a weight being lifted.

'You can't begin to understand all my shit, and I'm not about to burden you with it either, but I'm so fucking desperate to break out of this endless cycle of nightmares and sleepless nights. My head pounds all day, my whole body aches, sometimes my jaw completely locks up, and yet every day I carry on being Mister Life-and-Soul. Nobody has a fucking clue what's going on in here, and it's bloody knackering.'

He prodded his forehead with an angry finger as he spoke, only to have it lifted off his face and set to rest on his chest by a phantom hand that was apparently intent on relaxing the muscles around his jawline. He had never felt anything so therapeutic in his life; even seductive in a faraway, ethereal way.

His voice cracked. 'Jesus, that feels good. I've waited my whole life to be with you, Lynn. That's the absolute truth. I'm supposed to be the one who protects you from dragons, yet all I can do is bring you my own bloody dragons! So now I've met you and, believe me, right now I want nothing more than to fall asleep with you in my arms, but I'm too fucking scared that two hours later… or sometimes less… I'll wake you up, kicking and screaming.'

His princess had tears in her eyes now too. She raised his hand up to her eye and wiped a tear onto his fingers.

'Oh, that's awful. I had no idea.'

Jeff took a moment to absorb what this exceptional young woman had done, since it truly amazed him. In Lynn Dyson, just as he had always assumed he would, he had found someone who understood the power of communicating via one's senses. He rolled over towards her, and his mouth searched for hers in the dark. They kissed like they had never kissed before.

'And,' he continued, breaking away and cupping her face in his trembling hand, 'd'you wanna know the funny part, my gorgeous angel?'

'There's a funny part?'

Her man was laughing and crying at the same time. He felt so close to her. This facing up to one's own vulnerability was peculiarly liberating.

'Yeah, there damned well is. D'you know what the craziest thing is about me?'

His girlfriend tapped his forehead gently. 'You're not crazy.'

The distressed man scoffed. 'Oh, yes, I am! The funny part is that I can't even open my own bloody front door without freaking out. Can you believe that?'

The pretty teenager cast her mind back to when they had arrived at the Richmond flat, after the party. Yes, that was right. Her mystery man had handed his key-ring over and asked her to let them in. She hadn't thought anything of it at the time, but on reflection, it had been an odd thing for him to do. She wondered when she might discover the real reason why.

Lynn sighed. 'I have to believe it, if you're telling me it's so, but I don't understand how it could happen. I do remember you giving me your keys that night, but I'd never have made a connection. Anyway, that doesn't make you crazy in my eyes. Is it just your front door or other people's front doors too?'

Jeff was battling to come to terms with what was happening. He switched on the bedside light, which had been extinguished with such perfect timing a short while ago, and focussed on the sixteen-year-old beauty lying beside him. Her eyes were red, and there remained a worried look on her face. He leaned over and kissed her again.

'Thank you,' he said. 'I love you so much. I never thought I'd be having this conversation with anyone, and especially not you. But I'm glad we are. I promise I'll tell you everything over time, if you want to hear it. I hope you can understand that these things are buried deep inside of me, mainly because even I don't want to hear them. I just want to be able to forget that stuff.'

The distressed schoolgirl was relieved that her boyfriend had recovered and was now sounding a little optimistic. She definitely wanted to hear more. What a fascinating story! Given the whirlwind that had swept across her life in the last few weeks, she oughtn't really to be surprised that there would be more to this handsome and intelligent Catholic Argentinean Polish Jew than she first suspected.

'When you're ready to talk, I'm ready to listen. I love you too and I don't think you're crazy. Should we try and get some sleep? And if you wake me up, it won't matter. I'll just go back to sleep again.'

'Yep. OK,' Jeff answered slowly, still feeling unsettled about the prospect of the next few hours, even though he was determined to see it through. 'And by the way, it's mostly my own front door, but any closed, solid door has the potential to freak me out. So watch out!'

His smile was a welcome sight for the tired champion. 'It's good to see you looking happier again. Goodnight, Jeff.'

The anxious young man turned out the light and wrapped his dream girl up in his arms. It felt so completely right, and he begged to any god within telepathic earshot for a nightmare-free night. He was pretty sure his prayer would go unanswered, but right at this minute, absolutely anything was worth trying.

'G'night,' he whispered from behind her head, 'and thanks for listening.'

Lynn leaned her head backwards, feeling her skin tingling as he kissed her neck. 'Thanks for letting me listen.'

Less than a minute later, Jeff noticed his new confidante's breathing slow. Soon she was out for the count, and a new wave of apprehension rushed into his head. This was normally his cue to leave, but this time he was staying, and it occurred to him that physically he felt unusually relaxed. He turned his mind back to the start of the evening, and Lynn's accurate interpretation of his peace-offering. A lot had happened since then, and they had successfully navigated yet another minefield in this incredible relationship.

The grateful songwriter pulled his arm gently out from underneath Lynn's already dormant body, feeling tiredness washing over him too. He turned onto his back and allowed himself to drift off to sleep, more comfortable in his own skin than he could remember. Could there really be a light at the end of this long, dark, claustrophobic tunnel?

***

Sure enough, Lynn woke a couple of hours later, vaguely aware of movement next to her. Within seconds, the conversation about Jeff's nightmares seeped back into her consciousness, and she listened to him with interest. There was no doubt he was dreaming now. His breathing was

174

shallow and rapid, and muffled words were becoming louder. He was beginning to struggle with whomever or whatever was with him in the dream, punching the bedclothes and then seeming to dodge out of something's way.

Tentatively, her fingers brushed his forehead, which was boiling and damp, just as the dreamer let out an incensed, bloodcurdling cry. The disconcerted teenager recoiled, not knowing if she should wake him. She hadn't got around to asking him about such practicalities, so concerned had she been with his emotional outpouring. Perhaps if she tried to jog him out of the nightmare, he would return to peaceful sleep? She gently placed her hand on his right arm, which was by this time flailing wildly.

'Jeff,' she whispered. 'It's OK. Stop, please.'

The curious young woman repeated the process a few times, gradually putting more pressure on her boyfriend's biceps and speaking more forcefully. After a few minutes, his abrupt movements calmed down, and he stopped trying to shout out. He continued to breathe heavily but appeared much less aggravated, as if his opponent had disappeared. She was hopeful her intervention was working, and it made her cry. She so wanted to help this poor man whose story she was dying to understand. What a revelation it had been to discover that the funny, cool and intelligent man whom she had had such difficulty pushing away the other night could turn out to be so tormented and afflicted by the ghosts of his childhood. Trusting that the bad dream had abated, Lynn rolled over, leaving her boyfriend to his own devices. He seemed calm enough. Sleep returned to her quickly too, content that a good deed had been done.

Not very many hours later, the superstar woke again and checked her clock: five-forty, and time to go for her early coaching session. She glanced over to her left to see her man still sleeping soundly and didn't have the heart to wake him, slowly pushing back the quilt and standing up. She put a pot of coffee on, before getting dressed in the bathroom for training. Still no movement from the other side of the bed. Good, she thought. She wrote a note and left it with the thorny rose on her pillow. Grabbing her sports bag, the athlete left the apartment as stealthily as she could.

Jeff stirred eventually. He was only half awake, yet soon remembered where he was. Slowly gaining full awareness, he looked to his right, only to see Lynn's side of the bed empty except for the crimson bloom and a piece of paper. He was disappointed to find himself alone but also felt uncharacteristically at peace. He cast his mind back to the way the previous night had ended and wondered how his new friend was feeling about his strange admissions in the cold light of day.

Could he smell coffee? Was she still here after all? No, she couldn't be. She wouldn't have left a note if she was still here. How stupid of him! The bewildered student reached for the piece of paper.

"Good morning! Hope you slept well. Have to go early to training and didn't want to disturb you. Coffee's ready – help yourself. See you here on Saturday morning at 10. You are a great songwriter and, as far as I know, an even greater lover. Huge love, Lynn xx"

The relieved man smiled, his brain recreating the star's soothing voice reading the note to him. How had he got so lucky? His morning erection responded within seconds to the positive endorsement, demanding attention most insistently. As far as Lynn knew, as this latest priceless souvenir described, he was the greatest lover walking this Earth, and he vowed to prevent his dream girl from ever having the inclination to disprove this theory. Lost in the growing stock of memories easily conjured up by both mind and body, the tortured soul reached orgasm in no time, basking in sufficient invincibility and arrogance to set him up for the day.

The sun was already risen, and the alarm clock on the bedside table read seven-fifteen. What time had they gone to sleep? Midnight, maybe? Not much later. That was seven hours' sleep. Seven hours! No wonder the student felt so refreshed. He should get up and go for a run. His mind performed a quick body scan, and none of his muscles was aching. Unbelievable!

Jeff jumped out of bed, pulled his shorts on and poured himself a cup of coffee. He stood at the window, gazing out southwards towards the bay, which was also waking up to a hazy summer's morning. Bushfires had been burning in northern Victoria for the last few days, which had left the sky with a reddish-brown tint. Standing there alone in Lynn Dyson's apartment, he wondered how long this unfamiliar mental clarity would last. He realised his mind wasn't galloping at full tilt, like it usually did. No morbid thoughts were feeding his underlying pessimism about the world, and he didn't have his usual compulsive urge to storm through life, keeping himself distracted and busy.

The nineteen-year-old didn't need to be at work until after lunch. He would go home and get ready for a long run, before the weather warmed up too much. He was also ravenously hungry. Suzanne might be up for breakfast somewhere, he guessed, after her morning kennel duties were out of the way. He finished his coffee, dressed and left the apartment, feeling very positive indeed.

The door to his flat loomed in front of him as large as ever, but the buoyant teenager almost felt contempt for it as he got his key ready. OK. This was new, he thought. He pretended his dream girl was beside him while he opened the door, telling him there was nothing behind it and that everything would be fine. The forced delusion didn't help, but he was always prepared to try new techniques. Anger mounting again, he slammed the door shut as hard as he could, swearing at the inanimate object's ludicrous ability to transfix him.

In spite of the predictable setback, the world's greatest lover wasn't about to let anything spoil his new outlook. This was the first ever day he could remember waking up invigorated. He dialled Suzanne's number. It rang a few times before he heard the clicking and whirring of her answering machine.

'Hey, it's Jeff. Suze, you remember a while ago you were talking about how much you'd like to go to one of those posh cafés in South Yarra, by the Botanic Gardens, and have breakfast during the week, when it's not crowded? You know... Spend some time reading the 'papers and looking sophisticated? Well, d'you wanna do it this morning? I'm not working 'til after lunch, so give me a call if you want to. *Adiós, amiga.*'

Less than five minutes later, the telephone sprang to life in the Richmond flat.

'Hello,' Suzanne sounded quite breathless.

'What's up? Did you listen to my message about breckie?'

'Yes, I did and I'd love to.'

'*Bueno.* Is someone else there this morning who could hold the fort for you?' the young man enquired. 'It's just that I need to celebrate getting seven hours' sleep last night.'

'Go, Jeff! That's an achievement. Congratulations!' Suzanne joined in the enthusiasm she could detect in his voice. 'Were there drugs involved?'

The young man scoffed. 'Only a couple of beers and two glasses of wine. Anyway, I'm going for a run now, because I feel fantastic. Tell me what time, and I'll drive over and meet you. We can work out which café when we get there.'

'That sounds great. What time is it now?'

'Just after eight,' he answered.

'Is nine-thirty too early? I can pretty much leave in fifteen minutes.'

'OK. That works for me. I'll see you there at nine-thirty-ish,' her friend confirmed. 'And be sophisticated...'

'Oh, I've forgotten how to do that. It's been so long since I was a city chick.'

'Don't be an idiot! It'll come straight back to you. Gotta go. *Adiós.*'

Arrangements made, the energetic teenager was soon on the road and pounding towards the river. He ran away from the city, eastwards, lengthening his stride as the lactic acid worked its way out of his system. *Look forward*, he kept telling himself. *The past doesn't matter anymore.* He rejoiced in the knowledge that there was finally someone special in his life and that he had taken the first few hesitant steps towards trusting her. Each time he saw Lynn, he was left with an even sweeter feeling than the time before, and last night had surpassed his wildest hopes.

The runner reached the end of the towpath, turned round and ran back westwards, following the track through the city and as far as it went. He continued onto Spencer Street and passed by the Grand Hotel, tossing up which route to take home. He couldn't believe how clear his head was, nor how he no longer had that horrible stale taste in his mouth and the constant humming in his ears. His legs weren't aching either, his muscles seeming to be strung with more elasticity. No doubt about it. Human beings were definitely designed to sleep.

Jeff ran as far as the Queen Victoria Market, still full of energy, and past the host of old hospitals on the northern edge of the city, then along the strip of Vietnamese and Korean restaurants, where East Melbourne met the borders of Collingwood and Richmond. He felt at home among the diverse population which had colonised this little section of the Victorian capital. His senses were being treated to a feast of different faces, different languages, different food smells and very different driving habits.

Nearing home, the student was determined to arrive at his flat in as elated a mood as he could, in order to maintain the optimism all the way through the front door. An incredible lightness of being, the philosopher thought. He was back to the *Kama Sutra* again! He played with a new image in his mind: it was as if his soul had been hosed out, cleansed of all the *débris* which had been cluttering it up while the windows had been shuttered. The only items left after his spring clean were those he needed for forward motion. The long-suffering nineteen-year-old harboured no illusions that this euphoria was most likely only transitory, but was keen to extract the goodness from it for as long as possible.

'Come on, angel. Help me out here,' he implored under his breath, panting hard on his landing. 'Save me from this crap.'

Another door opened behind him. His neighbours, a retired Italian couple, were leaving the flat across the hallway, and he gave them a casual wave. They would guess he was out of breath from his run. He inhaled deeply, turned the key and pushed the door open. Violent images crashed through his mind, and he mentally ducked and weaved to get past them. No change. He kicked the wall in anger and yelled out to no-one.

A shower and the expectation of a hearty breakfast managed to drag the young man back into his prior optimistic state. In this new trusting mode, did he dare tell Suzanne what had led to his seven hours' sleep? Probably not. She wouldn't understand.

The Fairlane needed petrol, so Jeff pulled into a service station nearby and filled up. Standing at the pump, he noticed he still felt free. Somehow taller, he thought, and his eyes seemed to be wider open. The endorphins continued to race through his nervous system, and his limbs felt strong and agile. Whoever said mental illness was all in the mind had obviously never experienced it first-hand.

Gerry's girlfriend was already waiting for her breakfast companion on the corner of Domain Road and Park Street, busy making a fuss of a yappy Maltese terrier belonging to a well-heeled South Yarra resident. She stood up and waved to the noisy, thrumming vehicle pulling up on the other side of the road.

'I hope you gave her your card,' its driver said, kissing her on the cheek.

'Oh, shit! I didn't even think of it,' his friend replied, frustrated at herself.

The student gave her a stern look. 'How are you going to run a business like this? And that wasn't a very sophisticated start, by the way...'

Suzanne laughed. 'You're right. I need to pay more attention to these opportunities. Anyway, where shall we eat?'

The pair chose the café with the fewest people and the most comfortable chairs. The waitress took their coffee orders while they studied the menu.

'What are you having?' the country woman asked.

It was kind of Jeff to invite her out like this. She and Gerry would often "do" breakfast on weekend mornings, but the crowds made it a far less pleasant experience. The restaurateurs needed to turn their tables over quickly, and there was never enough time to linger over the newspapers or watch the world go by. Seeing her inquisitive look out of the corner of his eye, her handsome friend glanced up from the menu and gave her one of his typically disarming smiles. Suzanne thought she detected a glint in his eye, struck by the way those long legs were stretched out towards her and that he looked unusually relaxed. Her boyfriend's normally highly-strung buddy wasn't fidgeting in its seat like it normally did before his first coffee. He hadn't even lit a cigarette since they had been seated.

'What have you been smoking?' she confronted him. 'You're behaving differently. I can't put a finger on it, but you're like all laid back.'

The personable, dark-haired student looked up again and grinned from ear to ear. 'Nothing. I'm just being sophisticated,' he lied.

Suzanne wasn't satisfied. 'No, but look at you... On any other day, you'd be champing at the bit to place your order and get your coffee.'

'I'm just happy and ready to enjoy the morning with you,' the charmer responded, edging slightly closer to the truth. 'Let's order anyway though. I'm starving.'

The good-looking man caught the waitress' eye, and they ordered two Big Breakfasts with "the lot". He picked up a copy of The Age, Melbourne's daily broadsheet, and began to read the front page. Their coffees arrived soon after, and Suzanne was temporarily quiet, immersed in a glossy magazine. Her languid companion spread the Green Guide out on the table and searched for the music pages, wherein he found a review of the new MAC album, which was to contain live tracks from the recent show he had watched on television just a few weeks ago. He read with a strangely possessive pride the critics' comments on Lynn's performance.

Jeff realised he must have been smiling again, because his nosy neighbour leaned forward to see what he was reading. Playfully, he pulled the paper off the table and scolded her.

'Hey! Being sophisticated means you read your paper and I read mine.'

'Shut up!' Suzanne goaded. 'Did you see that show? Gerry said you were going to watch it as his place. Was it good?'

'Fantastic. Did you see it?'

'Yes. I thought it was great too. So, how are things going with little Miss Perfect?'

The student wasn't going to be drawn into her teasing, still in his newfound cosmic calm. He didn't even look up to answer.

'Lynn's fine, thanks.'

'That's not fair. You haven't told me anything since the middle of last week.'

Their breakfasts appeared at the table, delivered by the same swooning waitress, and Jeff folded the newspaper and dropped it onto the couch beside him. He picked up his cutlery and began to eat, deliberately evading his friend's unasked questions.

'I told you I was happy. That should tell you how it's going,' he replied after a short time, relishing the fact that he at last had an opportunity to tease her back.

'But you're always happy,' the woman whined. 'Today you seem so happy, you're melting all over the sofa.'

Jeff chuckled at the apt image. It was true. He did feel somewhat lethargic.

'It's a combination of seven hours' sleep, a long run and the love of a good woman,' he listed without ceremony.

So Suzanne reckoned he was always happy... The teenager's thoughts turned back to the previous night and his conversation with Lynn about playing his signature "life and soul of the party" role. The act was obviously credible if his best mate's girlfriend thought he was always happy. He would be happy with her problems, he cursed bitterly. They were infinitely preferable to his.

Don't get angry, the young man convinced himself. *Not today.* He didn't need to feel sorry for himself, because he was now facing forwards and everything looked bright in that direction. He opted to give his breakfast partner a morsel of gossip after all.

'Hey, guess what?' he opened, catching her with a large mouthful of bacon and scrambled egg.

The woman frantically swallowed her food, eager to hear what he had to say, and wiped her napkin across her mouth.

'What?'

'I'm going to a twenty-first birthday party at the Dyson homestead this Saturday.'

Suzanne became instantly excited at this news, as her old friend fully expected she would. Like most other women, she was obsessed with how the famous family lived, what they wore and which parties they attended. If she played her cards right, Jeff would soon be able to feed her with inside information, making her the envy of all her friends.

'Really? Wow! That's amazing. I'm so jealous.'

'Yeah. Should be good. It's a mate of Junior's; Robert somebody. I don't know who he is.'

'Ooh! That means you'll meet Mummy and Daddy,' his companion stated the obvious. 'Are you ready for that? That's not like you either.'

The nineteen-year-old smiled and shrugged. 'No, it's not. You're right. I'm scared shitless,' he admitted. 'But it'll be worth it. It's my one shot at gaining their approval before they forbid her to see me anymore.'

The young woman looked suitably forlorn. 'Do you think that'll happen?'

'Hope not. You know… Hope for the best but expect the worst.'

'I wonder what their house is like,' Suzanne mused, his plight already forgotten. 'Massive, I'd think. With stables and everything.'

'S'pose so. It *is* a farm.'

She stuck her tongue out at her impudent friend. 'Don't forget your camera,' she pestered. 'Take plenty of pictures so I can see what it's like.'

'Suzie, I don't own a camera. And even if I did, I'm not going to go sleuthing around their house like some sleazy tabloid news reporter. Gimme a break!'

The country bumpkin was a little hurt by the abrupt dismissal of her request. Jeff took her hand from across the table, and squeezed it.

'I'm sorry.'

She smiled. No-one could never stay mad at Jeff Diamond for more than ten seconds.

'That's OK. I know I'm such a sticky-beak,' she told him. 'I'd be opening every door in that palace, if I ever got a chance to go there. You better invite me one day!'

Their table had been cleared, and more coffee had been ordered. Shaking his head at her request, Jeff spread the paper out again, open at the sports pages, the diversion designed to mask the lack of faith in his own ability to secure a second invitation to *Château* Dyson, let alone having the family grant him licence to put on guided tours of the famous Benloch property. He was not about to give the gossip queen the satisfaction of capitalising on Mister Life-and-Soul's self-doubt. Not after he had slept for almost seven hours.

'Footy's good this weekend, Richmond and Essendon,' he read out loud, knowing how poorly his friend would react to his diverting onto her least favourite subject.

'You bastard!' she swore, as loud as she could get away with.

'So-phi-sti-cayded,' her companion reminded her slowly, syllable by syllable, waving a finger like a schoolteacher.

She sniffed at him. 'Shut up. So what *are* you going to be doing then, apart from going to the birthday party?'

Jeff shrugged. 'I don't know. Going with the flow. Having long episodes of rampant sex.'

The shock on the young woman's face was genuine. 'Jeff, you can't have sex in their house! Don't you dare! They'll definitely forbid her to see you again. Can you imagine what would happen if you got caught? They'll throw you in jail!'

Exactly the reaction the joker had hoped for. Suzanne was so easy to wind up.

'You'll have to come and visit me then,' he replied with a sensual half-smile. 'In jail, that is.'

Languishing in the café, the pair was the picture of youthful refinement from that point on, smoking cigarettes and sipping coffees, leafing through the piles of magazines. The university student allowed his mind to fast-forward to Saturday morning and tried to imagine what the weekend had in store. He was confident that Lynn and he would have a marvellous time, as long as no-one interfered. She had invited him before their relationship had developed to its latest, closer stage, and his instincts were doing their best to convince his warped psyche that she might keep last night's promise.

It was nearly lunchtime by the time the two friends said goodbye on the footpath next to Suzanne's car, and she was now in a hurry to get back to the kennels to relieve the early shift. As for Jeff, there were several ideas for songs wandering around in his brain which needed to be set free, in advance of having to focus on the afternoon's classes. As soon as he reached the university, he scribbled down some lyrics into his notebook, before attempting to concentrate on his latest assignment.

Frantically purging his mind of the latest ream of poetry, he became somehow fixated on his beautiful best friend's need for a new beginning. What was that all about? She had never expressed any regrets about her life, save for the freedom she lacked. He could give her a new beginning, if that was really what she wanted. He could create their life story. Nothing would give him greater pleasure, if only he could believe his own absurd rhetoric.

Without question, the genius freak from Sydney's west was different to the others, as his dream girl had already impressed upon him, with nothing to substantiate her claim except a handful of conversations and some great sex. Jeff Diamond was not just another Lynn Dyson fan, among the millions of lusting males. He could give her anything her heart desired; she only had to ask. The final word would be his.

***

The nineteen-year-old looked up at his father, who was gazing thoughtfully at a photograph of their happy family, taken some five years ago in the dining room, here at Benloch. His parents had been jointly awarded the Companion of the Order of Australia in that year's Queen's Birthday honours list, bestowed for their services to peace negotiations in South Africa and Northern Ireland.

The distinguished medal had been a hot topic of conversation at the dinner table on the evening when this particular picture had been taken, since the hard-working couple had gone a step further than Bart Dyson, who was a mere "AO". Regardless, the memories captured by this souvenir were a far cry from the simple and raw accounts over which the young man and his sister had been poring just moments ago.

'Dad, I never thought before about how daunting it must've been for you to have to play something for Mum for the first time.'

Ryan and Kierney had been leafing through Lynn's nineteen-seventy-two diary, marvelling at the naïve and sometimes shockingly honest accounts of her adventures in the wild, romantic, messed-up world of Jeff Diamond. It was late on Christmas Eve, and they were doing their best to keep their father's spirits up, now that the rest of the Dyson clan had retired to bed.

'You were the same age as me,' the young cricketer continued. 'That's really weird, actually. I could almost be in the same scene, reading some of these things. I hear the girls at uni' talking the same way. Not much has really changed about teenaged life in all that time.'

'In all that time?' Jeff scoffed. 'It's not that long ago, mate. Do you mind?'

The dark-haired gipsy girl sitting on the floor at her dad's feet smiled sweetly. 'Well, I think what she wrote is beautiful. She was right about Elvis Presley. He was just a human being, and you all found that out a few years' later. Just like we did.'

All three sighed together, before laughing at their familial synchronicity. The billionaire songwriter had met their childish demands to provide his own, blow-by-blow verbal diary of those early days, happy to oblige in return for a homemade song from each teenager. He had found it surprisingly easy to reproduce that same acute sense of anticipation at being asked to sing his brand new compositions for the girl of his dreams, and had cried buckets while piecing together the words and music for "Power and Glory", almost twenty-five years after its resurrection that night in the capacious ballroom.

'We take performing for each other in our stride,' the seventeen-year-old added, 'but I do understand how you might have felt, Papá. I still get nervous when I play for Youssouf or Annie Lennox, or any other really famous songwriters.'

'How did you make your first demo' tapes?' her brother asked, picking out another old melody on the piano.

'Crudely,' his father answered with a half-smile. 'On a normal music cassette. You know... C60 or C90, whatever they are. The proverbial shoestring. But before I left Sydney, for a while I got really flash, because my grandmother left me money that I had no idea she had.'

'*Bubshka*, you mean? I thought she was poor as.'

Jeff shrugged. 'Me too, son. It was only just under three grand, but you can imagine what a fortune that would've seemed like to me, at sixteen. She must've been squirrelling it away from her pension, for a rainy day, as they used to say.'

'But then she died before it rained,' Kierney mused. 'That's sad, but I like the image. What did you do with it?'

The forty-four-year-old frowned, struck by the old guilt again. 'Jesus, *pequeñita*, I was a real piece of shit back then. I divided it into three, I remember. A thousand bucks went on a ten-week sex, drugs and rock'n'roll binge. She died right at the end of Year Eleven, the day after my last exam, I think, so I had the whole summer to fuck myself over before I went back to school. The second thousand was set aside for general living expenses and clothes, in case I was too pissed or stoned to go into work, and the rest went on my old electric keyboard, microphone, heaps of guitar strings, a cassette recorder and an enormous supply of blank tapes, which actually lasted me until I moved to Melbourne.'

The celebrity shook his head in consternation at these old memories, seeing the look of wonderment on his children's faces. 'I remember growing some ridiculous number of inches that year, so none of my clothes fit me. That money couldn't have come at a better time. I should've been much more grateful. I did visit *Bubshka*'s grave once, I think, to say thanks.'

'With a bottle of beer in your hand,' his son chuckled. 'Is that where that song came from?'

'Perhaps, mate. Or more likely my mum's. I bought a two-year gym' membership too, that's right...'

'Did you know these existed when you and Mamá were first going out?' Kierney asked their dad, lifting one of the leather-bound diaries in the air.

'No. No idea.'

'Makes me wonder what girls have written about me,' the confident sportsman interjected, laughing at his own ego rearing its ugly head. 'One girl did write to her sister all about me. Then she came to visit at uni', and we got off at a party. It was a bit embarrassing, but she was awesomely hot!'

His sister chuckled too. 'Now *you're* the chip off the old block!'

Jeff high-fived his son. 'That's the type of thing I was getting up to the rest of the week, whenever I wasn't seeing Lynn. Your mum and I... That was like a parallel existence. Two completely different lives I was living those first few months. Gerry was the same with Suzanne, so we didn't really think anything of it. I was totally faithful to Lynn in here…'

The widower pointed to his heart, tears welling up in his eyes but forcing a smile nonetheless. In all the years the Diamonds had been married, his gorgeous wife had never challenged him on his early promiscuity, despite the many diary entries proclaiming him as her "one and only". In recent months, he had taken great solace from the fact that she had at first been completely oblivious to his playboy antics, and therefore thankfully untroubled.

'Totally, one hundred and fifty percent faithful,' he insisted. 'But just not further down!'

Kierney frowned. 'But women can't separate the two,' she lamented. 'Mamá would've been really hurt if she'd found out.'

'The hard way,' her father appended onto the end of his daughter's sentence. 'Yeah, I agree, which is why I confessed. And by some amazing piece of undeserved good fortune, I got away with it. She loved me, gorgeous. There can be no other reason to put up with such poor treatment, and Christ Almighty, am I grateful! Even to this day.'

'What would you have done if you found out Mum was sleeping around too?' Ryan asked, instantly wondering if he had overstepped the mark.

Jeff flinched and rubbed his chest absentmindedly. 'Hated it, I expect. But I wouldn't have stopped her. That would hardly have been right, would it? Thank you, angel.'

The two teenagers looked at each other, the twinkling lights from the Christmas tree reflecting in their watery eyes. Ethereal communication between their parents appeared to be coming thick and fast in recent weeks, signalling the imminence of the next episode in their life singular.

The older Diamond child was the first to break the sombre silence, pointing at the nineteen-seventy-two diary. 'But you guys hadn't known each other long when she wrote these pages. I'm not sure I'd be staying all night either. It's not that bad to call it a night after sex, is it?'

'No, mate,' his father chuckled. 'Ordinarily I'd agree, but it felt to both of us like I should hang around. Can't tell you why, and maybe it'll be the same for you too, whenever the time comes. Neither of us said anything at the time. It probably wasn't until years later that we even really thought about it; that what we'd been feeling made sense…'

Ryan and Kierney nodded, spellbound by these intimate assertions which had led eventually to their births. Rarely did the next generation have as clear an insight into the solid foundation of its immediate heritage. Their lives were not the result of some casual, fly-by-night liaison. They were the product of love; of the complete devotion of one man to one woman. In the face of what they were soon to go through, they were both comforted by this knowledge.

'Guys, it was always like we belonged together,' Jeff continued, wiping a new batch of tears from his wise eyes. 'Before I met your mamá, there was only one equation: "touch woman" equals "have sex". Then it all changed. We both felt it right from the beginning, even though neither of us knew that was what we were feeling. I don't know... It's probably all bullshit. We didn't know we knew, if you know what I mean. Not for a long time.'

'You "just knew",' Kierney offered, reminded of something the everyman philosopher had said a few months ago. 'Like in the trial, Papá. Instinct, gut feel...'

'Prior knowledge?' her brother interjected.

An ominous silence descended over the trio, and the youngsters watched their father flinch again.

Research

The library slept like a ghost town on Thursday afternoon. Lynn searched the Medicine and Psychology sections for any information she could find on the treatment of trauma victims. She was preoccupied with Jeff's late night revelations and sought to discover more about this condition he had described: nightmares every night, headaches and jaw locking, all coupled with a peculiar inability to open solid doors. What a strange combination of symptoms this was!

Eager to learn, the smart schoolgirl found an article in a medical journal which traced the lives of two young men who had committed suicide in their early twenties, both having been abused as children. What caught her attention was a new definition of the word "trauma" that didn't refer to physical harm, such as the loss of a limb or other severe injury. This definition referred to trauma as damage to the rational mind. Of course, she had come across the adjectives "traumatic" and "traumatised" before, but had only really considered their meaning frivolously, as in an exaggerated expression for a shocking or upsetting event. The boys profiled in the paper she was reading had experienced horrific violence, and in one case, sexual abuse in early childhood.

Lynn longed to find out about the kind of trauma her boyfriend had endured but was also keen to respect his privacy. She had noticed several scars on his right side, underneath his ribcage, which looked suspiciously like stab wounds. He had hinted last night that his problems stemmed from his family, and that they didn't much like each other. In light of this new research, such a simple phrase now sounded like a distinct understatement. If she hadn't seen his raw emotions with her own eyes, it would be impossible for her to imagine how the funny, easy-going and loving Jeff she had known up until now could be the same person, saddled with all these burdensome afflictions.

What an effort it must be to put on a show every day... No wonder Jeff took refuge in alcohol from time to time. The busy performer had some experience to draw on in this regard, having several times been on stage after a particular sporting event and having to summon up every last reserve of energy to entertain the crowd, when all she wanted to do was fall asleep.

Another article outlined other clinical symptoms which Jeff hadn't explicitly described, such as depression, anger, anxiety and an acute fear of betrayal. These were more than just words to the caring sixteen-year-old. They were also the unspoken curses of the war veterans she had met the previous year, during their school project. Moreover, she hadn't related to them closely enough before meeting her mystery man to truly comprehend how these mental scars would affect their everyday lives. Did these symptoms apply to Jeff too, as well as the nightmares and the door phobia?

Was her boyfriend really crazy, as he had insinuated? How could someone so perfect on the outside be crazy on the inside? And what exactly did he mean by crazy? Did he mean out of control? Was she in danger? This was the information Lynn needed to find out, but she continued to draw blanks. Was she looking in the wrong section? Perhaps the information she was hunting for might be more easily tracked down in the Crime section?

A shiver ran down her spine, as the fascinated teenager moved her belongings to another table. Could the man she had invited into her room with barely a second thought flip out at any moment, like the time after dinner with Gerry and Suzanne, when he had almost raped her? She soon uncovered a report which suggested that violent criminals were often found to be victims of violence themselves. This hardly sounded like the profile of the ideal boyfriend either.

The young woman's thoughts reverted to the first night they had spent together, in Jeff's pokey flat. How much danger had she really put herself in that night? The awful admission filled her with dread. What was it he had said to her? "If I really wanted to attack you, I could," or words to that effect. Had he assaulted someone before? A woman? Someone like her? He certainly spoke as if he knew what he was talking about. But then again, he always did. He might have even raped and killed his last girlfriend... Was that why he moved from Sydney? Far-fetched though these notions were, it was beginning to look like her mystery man did indeed have something sinister to hide, which was a possibility she couldn't bear.

It would break her heart to say goodbye to this gorgeous boy, just when they were getting to know each other properly. All those beautiful gestures of love he had given her, and the songs he had composed. Not to mention writing "I LOVE YOU" on a dirty van! Lynn was experiencing romance and passion for the first time, and with an intensity her friends had never described. She didn't want to give that up.

The various journals put back in their rightful places, the celebrity returned to Admin on the tram, as usual badgered for autographs and photographs by tourists on their way to St Kilda. Her head was spinning with unanswered questions, and on a subject she certainly couldn't discuss with her parents, for it was guaranteed to put an immediate stop to her relationship with the man she loved. Her head wouldn't blame them, she admitted, with a sinking feeling in her stomach. It was the responsible thing to do, being who she was and with everything she had ahead of her.

Lynn resolved to telephone her dark stranger as soon as she arrived back, to see if he would shed some light on her murky uncertainty. By the time she reached her apartment, it was after six o'clock. She didn't know if he would be at home, but there was only one way to find out. Her heartbeat was racing as she dialled his number.

'Hello?' the warm voice sounded rich and smoky.

'Hi, Jeff. It's Lynn,' she greeted him, trying to sound cheerful. 'How are you going?'

'Hey, angel! I'm fine. How are you?' her boyfriend responded, delighted to hear her voice again, and unexpectedly too. 'This is an extremely pleasant surprise.'

The young star swallowed nervously. How would she steer the conversation to where she wanted it to go? She could already feel herself falling victim to the hypnotic persuasion in his tone, the appeal of which was now tinged with a certain alarm.

'I just wanted to see if you were OK after last night.'

'Yeah. Mighty fine, thanks,' he replied. 'You've given me a new variation on my theme.'

Lynn giggled, amused by the musical reference. 'Oh, yes? What do you mean?'

'I've gone from *staccato* to *legato*.'

'Really?' she responded brightly. 'That's a lovely analogy. I can picture you lounging around all relaxed, instead of full of nervous energy. Is that what you mean?'

Jeff smiled. Of course it was what he meant. This girl always knew what he meant.

'*Sí. Exactamente*,' he answered. 'When I left your place, I went for a long run and then met Suzanne for a long, drawn out breakfast on Domain Road. I felt so good. Liberated and no headache. She told me I was melting all over the sofa.'

The imagery was powerful. Lynn felt her heart melting too.

'I'm glad. I'm sorry I had to go before you woke up,' she said, seeing if he would respond with how it made him feel.

She mustn't let him charm her out of her quest, mindful of Gerry's comment about his buddy always getting his own way. All the separate comments she had initially taken as throwaway banter were now beginning to coalesce into a complex web of intrigue, which threatened to trap her if she didn't wise up to the danger.

'That's OK,' the nineteen-year-old replied. 'The rose was a nice thought. I was disappointed when you weren't there but felt so healthy after seven hours' sleep that I refused to let it matter.'

'Seven hours? What time did you wake up then?' Lynn asked, remembering having stifled his nightmare but not ready to tell him she had done so.

'About seven-fifteen, I think. What time did you go?'

The pretty teenager wasn't receiving any of the information she needed. Her man was completely gorgeous, as per usual, and not giving anything away. Was he putting on the charm on purpose? Above all, she now found herself questioning why she needed to know, which annoyed her. After all, Jeff Diamond *was* the master manipulator.

'Just before six,' she replied flatly.

The super-sensitive student honed in on the hint of hesitation in his girlfriend's answer. His heart sank, dragged down by the pessimistic alter-ego living in his mind, ever intent on sabotaging his happiness and ready to pounce at the smallest hint of negativity. *Don't go there*, he desperately tried to convince himself. He could save this.

But it was too late, he was already sliding. What was the real reason for her call? What was she about to tell him? Jeff's head began to spin, so he sat down on the couch and prepared for the worst.

'Lynn, what's up? Is there something you want to talk about?' he asked, doing his best to sound casual.

His innocent and inexperienced lover sighed. This wasn't easy. She didn't want to subject her new boyfriend to an inquisition, but it was impossible to weave her questions into normal conversation.

'Jeff, I've been trying to research into your trauma effects and couldn't really find anything out.'

OK. That made sense. *Think quickly*, the young man implored. What did she want to know? Which credible facts and figures could he furnish to put her mind at rest?

'Were you? That's great. Thanks for trying,' he started. 'It's not surprising you can't find much, because there isn't much. Especially in Australia. Believe me, I've looked everywhere. There's some good stuff coming out of France recently. I can give it to you if you want to wade through it. It's hard going, because the arguments aren't very well formed, in my opinion.'

Lynn admitted defeat. This well-read, highly intelligent man was too good. Was it practice or sincerity? She wondered if she would ever know for sure. All she knew was that he was very convincing. Or maybe she was too keen to be convinced.

'I'd love to read it,' the schoolgirl capitulated. 'I'd have to have my dictionary close by.'

Jeff breathed a secret sigh of relief at the conciliation in her tone. Disaster averted, for now at least.

'I can help with the translation. You can trust me, Lynn. I'm not going to lie to you about anything and neither am I going to hurt you. You probably read a whole lot about violence and anger and irrational bitterness.'

'Yes, I did,' his girlfriend replied, slightly frustrated that since she had given up trying, he was suddenly giving her what she was looking for. 'Some of it was quite frightening.'

The student wished he was there with her, to read her face and to find out what his dream girl really needed from him. And to touch her once again, he had to be honest.

'Yeah, I agree. And I can't dispute any of that. It's real in many cases, but it's not who *I* am. I don't have split personalities or answer to voices in my head. That's the real scary stuff, and I wouldn't put you, of all people, in that position, believe me. You don't have to worry about staying safe, angel.'

'But what about the other night?' the young star interrupted, determined not to be walked over. 'I didn't feel very safe then.'

She heard her man exhale and again her love for him overrode her own good sense. This was ridiculous, she thought. It revealed to the naïve sixteen-year-old how easy it was to be taken advantage of, where dangerous predators played with the empathy of compassionate people because someone had preyed on theirs during their childhood or adolescence. Perhaps she should never have ventured into the Crime section after all. Could this really be her boyfriend's story?

'Sure,' Jeff answered after a short pause. 'I get that, and I'm still sorry. I wouldn't have hurt you that night. I just wasn't going to give you any choice. That's what I did wrong, and it won't happen again. I would never have hurt you, angel. I've seen the result of that sort of hurt, and you're the absolute last person I'd inflict it on.'

Lynn felt tears pricking at the corners of her eyes. His words sounded so sincere, so utterly believable. And he had stopped mauling her eventually, hadn't he? Someone with real intent to do her harm would have kept going, she presumed. A man of Jeff's size and strength could easily overpower her, despite the years of physical training. It was a sure-fire physiological fact.

Her mind went back to the first set of journals she had unearthed at the library, the ones which chronicled the lasting effects of mental trauma, such as depression, fear of abandonment and a tendance toward suicide.

'Lynn, are you still there?' her boyfriend sounded worried.

'Yes, I am. I was just processing what you said. I do believe you.'

'Jesus, angel. Don't freak me out like that,' the young man attempted to make light of a situation which had put him on a knife-edge. 'I thought you were going to hang up on me.'

'No, I'm still here. Sorry. I wanted to find out more, so I can help you with the nightmares, but I only found stuff that scared me.'

The boy from Canley Vale sighed audibly. Life had been much simpler before he had followed his path to paradise. Who was he kidding? Had he really assumed he could get away with remaining obtuse about his objectionable behaviour with someone who was protected by security guards and surrounded by an influential and well-meaning entourage?

'I know it looks bad,' he continued. 'I want to leave all that behind. Get over it and move on, you know... That's why I moved down to Melbourne and miraculously managed to meet you. Lynn, I'm in control of my actions, and no-one's going to come to any harm. I promise.'

'OK. Stop,' the famous songstress began to laugh. 'Mister Control Freak! That makes two of us, remember?'

The student sniffed, grateful for her light-hearted quip. 'Lynn, I'm not a lunatic, I'm not dangerous and I don't make bad decisions. I love you, and there's no way I'd ever let anything bad happen to you.'

'Thanks. I know,' his girlfriend responded with some relief. 'Jeff, I have to go. I believe you, and I love you too. I want to help you stay *legato.*'

Her fellow musician chuckled in appreciation. 'I'd love that. I'm looking forward to Saturday. I can't wait to see you.'

'Yes. Me too. It'll be fun. Don't forget to bring swimmers. There's a pool party after the main event.'

'Right. Sounds great. Are you OK?'

The young woman sighed. 'Yes, I'm fine. I'm sorry.'

'What for?' he asked, knowing full well.

The anxious man needed to hear her tell him. Two days in limbo between now and Saturday stretched long and bleak ahead of him, and some positive reinforcement might help rid his heart of the thick, black, strangling pessimism and allow it to float back up the happiness scale in the interim.

'Jeff, I had a whole heap of questions, but now they seem irrelevant, and I don't really know why,' Lynn admitted honestly. 'I was hoping to find out that there's nothing that could go wrong with us, but all I found out was that neither of us wants anything to go wrong.'

The ambitious philosopher took a few seconds to ingest these words, impressed with the way the privileged young lady dealt with complex problems. Silver spoon or not, Lynn Dyson's mind was wide open and ready to be self-critical. This observation presented as a welcome glimmer of hope, which his brain instantly transferred to his libido.

'That's a very interesting statement,' he told her. 'Maybe that's enough? All we can ask of each other is to keep talking honestly. Ask the questions we want to ask, and respect the answers we get back.'

His girlfriend laughed.

'What's so funny?'

'You can see through me, and I'm annoyed,' the sixteen-year-old replied. 'I did have a hidden agenda, but it didn't do me any good. I've learned a good lesson. I'm just going to be straightforward in future.'

Now that the pressure of the uncomfortable topic had subsided, Jeff was engulfed in fervour of a whole different nature. Ever since he had passed puberty, the tortured young man had relied on sexual gratification to clear his head of depressive thoughts. His genitals felt as if they had burst into flames, and the Testosterone Kid really, really wanted to be with his dream girl right now.

'Jeez! Don't tell me that,' he groaned. 'That's the sexiest thing you could possibly have said to a control freak.'

Lynn didn't completely understand but pictured her boyfriend sitting at home, breathing heavily, pupils dilated and his penis hard inside his trousers. His slow, sultry tone gave away the fact that he was aroused, and it had the same effect on her.

'I'll say it again on Saturday,' she teased, relieved to be ending the call on a happy note.

Jeff groaned again. 'And you think I can wait 'til then?'

'We have to,' the impressionable schoolgirl replied. 'I'm sorry. I'd better go. I have to go to the studio.'

'Yes, you had better go,' he agreed. 'See you at ten on Saturday. I love you, gorgeous.'

'I love you too. Bye, gorgeous.'

Jeff replaced the receiver and sat on the couch, overtaken by the longing in his body. He had two assignments to complete for Monday, and with the weekend already reserved for his trip to Benloch, tonight was the only night this week when he wasn't working. Nevertheless, after such stressful discourse, he detested the idea of satisfying himself at home on his own. A girl at university had been flirting wildly with him that afternoon, and he had left things open-ended with her, as usual. Now, with conflicting emotions jangling in his head and his sexual urges heightened, he needed someone on whom he could act out his fantasies and restore his equilibrium.

In his mind's eye, the hungry young man could see Suzanne's wagging finger and hear her nagging words, telling him it how wrong it was to be playing around while purporting to be in love. Yet what was wrong with a meaningless hour or two spent in the company of a willing accomplice? That which Lynn didn't know couldn't hurt her, and the girl he was going to meet would be well satisfied, having no idea that he was thinking of someone else. He would be satisfied too and able to concentrate better on his assignments. Such was the superficial veneer Jeff had constructed over his life to help him cope. Everyone would be happy enough on the surface. He was always happy, Suzanne had confirmed. On the surface...

Not dangerous, the persuasive man had told his beautiful lover, and she hadn't challenged him when he had maintained that he did not make bad decisions. However, just a few days ago, he had come extremely close to proving himself a liar. Did Lynn believe him this evening on the telephone, or was she merely biding her time? They both knew it was a fifty-fifty chance whether he would have crossed the line if she hadn't stopped him, but he hoped the famous teenager believed he wouldn't have hurt her, even in his extreme and obsessive state of predilection.

Jeff growled, once more racked with guilt and shame. Never had he hurt a woman in pursuit of sexual gratification, regardless how casual, anonymous or spontaneous their tryst had been, and no matter how much he had had to drink. No-one could ever accuse him of that. The damaged young man was once more furious that he had laid himself open to ready comparison with the clinical accounts his girlfriend had found in her research, and furthermore, he had committed this potentially heinous act in the presence of the one who meant the most to him in the entire world. Perhaps he was a lunatic after all. What other explanation could there be?

Jeff picked up his car keys, left the flat and drove back to Carlton, to find carnal satisfaction and to obscure his guilt with illicit substances. Bitter? No, not him.

Inner Sanctum

At ten o'clock precisely, the athletic student ran up the steps at the rear of the Dyson Administration building, two at a time. He had successfully resisted his obsession to call Lynn once an hour, on the hour, since their last conversation, to make sure there was no change of heart, thereby hoping to con her into thinking he hadn't been thinking about it either. The latest university assignments were completed to his usual exacting standards, submitted in plenty of time and awaiting review, and his wallet was stuffed with four nights' worth of cash-in-hand wages and tips earned from his shifts at the pub.

And now, finally, a weekend away with Lynn Dyson. How sweet it was to be Jeff Diamond today!

'You look fantastic,' the delectable blonde told him, when they met outside the lift. 'I can't believe how bright your eyes are.'

'Really?' the young man asked. 'I feel good, I must admit. And it's all your fault.'

Jeff swung the beautiful woman round in a circle, feeling her breasts against his forearms as he propelled her into the air. Her smile was teasing his eager libido quite unwittingly, which was half the attraction. Her *naïvetée* was a huge turn-on for him.

'Are you still *legato*?' she asked, once back on dry land.

'*Si, signorina,*' her boyfriend responded, bowing with a sweeping arm across his body. '*Signor Molto Legato, à vôtre service.*'

'I've never met someone called "Very" before,' the clever teenager ribbed him. 'What a weird name to give a child, even for an Italian.'

'*Ta geûle!*' Jeff scolded, putting his fingers over her mouth. 'Have we got time to mess up your bedclothes before we set off?'

Huge, dark, pleading eyes bore into hers, and Lynn's heart flipped over. Nevertheless, she couldn't possibly let her handsome control freak get what he wanted less than five minutes after he had arrived. With all her recent research, the celebrity was determined to ascertain whether he was genuine, and therefore worthy of her help in fighting the negative effects of his afflictions, or whether he was simply using these symptoms as an excuse to always have things his own way. Whichever it was, she was beginning to understand the reason for Gerry's boisterous opening gambit very well indeed.

'No. I've got a better idea.'

'A better idea?' her man repeated in abject disbelief. 'Is there a better idea?'

'Yes, there is,' she insisted. 'Trust me! It'll be worth the wait.'

The red-blooded nineteen-year-old felt the ache of urgency well up within him, despite having given himself a head-start in the shower this morning. No way! Nothing was worth the wait, faced with this gorgeous female form and the thought of being in her presence for two whole days. Maybe he wasn't quite so *legato* after all.

'Are you sure?' he begged.

Lynn slapped his arm. 'Yes! Come on, please. The sooner we leave, the quicker you'll find out.'

'OK,' Jeff raised his hands in resignation. 'You win. I'm on dangerous ground as it is, I know. It better be worth the wait. You're testing me to the extreme, I'll have you understand.'

'Shhh!' the sixteen-year-old stopped him. 'I want to hear about being *legato*. It sounds like a nice feeling.'

Together, they loaded the sportswoman's suitcase into the boot of the trusty Fairlane. Although Jeff kissed her wantonly as he held the door open for her to get in, she sensed the pressure had already relented. She was learning how to de-manipulate herself, and the change in his demeanour reassured her that this particular subject seemed less compulsive than those featured in the case studies she had read. This morning, at any rate.

'You're a very alluring tease,' he told her with a wry smile. 'We're going to have a fantastic weekend. I can just tell.'

The driver turned the old Ford onto the road, and they tracked northwards over the river and through the city. He began to describe how different he felt since he had broken his silence about the nightmares; somehow taller, as if he were looking at the world from a different angle. He no longer fidgeted constantly, agitated by his overactive mind, and his movements were generally slower. Lynn commented that his voice also sounded slower and deeper too.

'Is that what you meant by feeling a lot older?' she asked the mystery man who was taking her to her parents' home.

'In a way,' he replied. 'I feel old because I'm always so tired, but it's all part of the same picture.'

The car sped on past the airport, through Sunbury and towards Lancefield, with the radio blasting out their morning's entertainment. The man from New South Wales noticed they were driving through real farming country now, beyond the smallholdings and rich people's weekenders which lined the roads leading into the city, close enough to civilisation to reassure the would-be men and women of the land that they were not too far from the nearest wine bar or petrol station.

'We're not in Kansas anymore, Dorothy,' Jeff joked.

He wasn't about to tell the stunning temptress sitting in his car that he had already driven this route once, shortly after first moving to Victoria. He had taken to the road one Saturday afternoon, on the spur of the moment, to see where his dream girl hung out whenever she wasn't teasing him mercilessly from the television screen.

'Indeed, Toto,' Lynn smiled. 'I like it. It really lets us be a family, especially now we're all up to our own thing. It's still home, even though I've never really lived there full-time.'

'Yeah, I guess so. It'd be tough always having to remember to bring what you need to whichever house.'

'Exactly!' she cried out, joyful that her boyfriend could relate to one of the hassles which had frustrated her throughout childhood.

'At least it's made you very organised, so it paid off,' Jeff added. 'I had to really check and double-check what I was bringing this weekend, because I never have to pack to go anywhere. This is a holiday for me.'

The sixteen-year-old giggled. 'But you moved down from Sydney?'

'Yes, I know, but that was a no-brainer. I had to bring everything, so no organisational skills involved with that. Just threw it all in the car.'

'S'pose not,' she agreed, smiling at the image of the sum total of the student's worldly possessions piled into the back of this rattly, blue sedan.

She patted the faded plastic fascia under the windscreen, looking over her shoulder and out of the rear window. Old and blue, with plenty of character. Just like its owner, as his old friend had reported.

'You drove a long way, old car. Well done!' she congratulated it.

The young man scoffed gently and rolled his eyes. She was cute. Seriously cute, as his body was making him only too aware. This was going to be a superb holiday.

'We need to turn right just before the top of the hill,' Lynn instructed, oblivious to his sublime agony and pointing ahead of them. 'We'll go in the back way rather than through the main entrance. It's less hassle getting the car through.'

Jeff nodded, deciding against bringing her attention to his interpretation of her choice of words. One-tracked mind, he scolded himself.

'Sounds good.'

Heaving the car around the tight corner and onto a gravel track, the impulsive teenager double-declutched in second gear and accelerated quickly, spinning the wheels and fish-tailing along the track. He and Gerry had often schemed about buying a rally car, and the slippery road surface was altogether too tempting for the keen rev-head.

'Hey! What are you doing?' his co-driver shouted, hanging onto the door handle.

The boy racer grinned. 'C'mon. Let me play a little. I haven't seen gravel in a while.'

'OK,' Lynn relented, shaking her head. 'Boys!'

'And anyway,' her charming guest continued with a wink, 'the car likes it.'

'Hmm... *Touché.* Very funny. Left up there.'

The sixteen-year-old gave in and held on tightly, as Jeff slid the car round the next corner on the loose stones. He straightened it expertly and sped up to the tall farm gate at the end of the lane. The car stopped with very little room to spare.

Looking around, the driver spied a metal box on a post to the left of the gate, and then heard the door open beside him. The daughter of the house sprang out of the car and went to punch a code into the keypad inside the box. The gate jerked and swung open away from them, and she waved the blue Fairlane through with a flourish. The car lurched forward, and she watched carefully as it came towards her, standing her ground. The front wheel passed less than five centimetres from her toes. Shrugging as if to say, "Not even close," she pressed another button on the control panel and the gate began to swing shut behind the old Ford.

The tearaway from the Stones Road took a moment to absorb the scene, following his girlfriend's every move in the mirrors. The gates had closed him inside the sanctum of Dyson greatness. He forced himself to give the significance of his circumstance sufficient attention, rather than focussing on the very short shorts currently walking towards his car. How long had he been waiting for his luck to change? How much did he want to be part of this woman's life? And to be someone significant, important and respected?

The dreamer was jolted back to reality by a two short beeps of a horn behind them. Lynn wasn't yet back in the car and ran off to re-enter the code.

'Hi!' she shouted, waving.

Her boyfriend raised his head and looked in the rear-view mirror, seeing a silver sedan covered in a thin layer of red dust, similar to the make-up his own car was sporting. He couldn't see who was inside or even what type of car it was. Maybe a Mercedes? He pulled his wreck of a vehicle further over to the left, yanked up the handbrake and got out. He figured it was time to start meeting the family.

The student could see the wearer of those short shorts leaning against the silver car, with her head and shoulders inside the driver's open window. He wandered over and stood close by, sensing that he ought to be on hand for the inevitable introductions.

'Mum, this is Jeff,' the young woman declared proudly.

The sexy teenager stood back from the car and gestured towards the tall, dark-haired man who had brought her home. The handsome student stepped closer to the window, and Marianna Dyson opened the car door. She stood up and extended her hand towards him, blonde, tall and slim, and the visitor registered the definite resemblance between mother and daughter.

'Nice to meet you, Jeff. Glad you could make it for the party.'

'Thank you, Missus Dyson,' the young man replied, shaking her hand. 'It's great to be here.'

'You can call me Marianna,' offered Lynn's mother. 'It's much easier for everyone. We're pretty informal out here in the country.'

The dignified woman turned to get back into the car. Jeff hadn't realised that her other daughter, seven-year-old Anna, was sitting in the back, until he heard a young voice pipe up from inside.

'Mum, is that Lynn's boyfriend?'

'Yes, it is,' he heard the driver answer while refastening her seatbelt. 'Let's get up to the house and we can all say hello together.'

Jeff exhaled through pursed lips and shoved his hands into his pockets. The girl of his dreams stood right next to him, tantalisingly close but not touching, and the temptation was at once agonising and peculiarly comforting to the man who suddenly found himself on so many levels of unfamiliar territory. The giant Mercedes began to hum its favourite tune, gliding past the teenaged lovers on its own private cushion of air, and vanished into the distance, leaving a trail of red dust behind it.

'Let's go!' shouted Lynn, walking back to the car.

The gate clunked shut with a metallic ring, and Jeff took off slowly, emulating the lady of the house. He drove suitably regally along the gravel road until the homestead rose up before them. There were several buildings at the end of a wide driveway. He took in the vista and fixed on the house, which was in colonial style with low, bushy hedges around the ground floor and four grand pillars surrounding the front door. Three storeys in all, the house was impressive, though not too ostentatious.

Marianna's sleek vehicle was nowhere to be seen. The visitor looked to the elder Dyson daughter for his instructions.

'Where do we park up?'

'Go over there, to the right, between the house and the gym',' she responded, pointing towards a large, barn-like building next to the mansion.

The narrow opening gave into a far-reaching courtyard with a bank of garages to the right and another, even larger barn behind. Straight ahead was an enormous swimming pool, beyond which were golden paddocks that stretched as far as the horizon. The poor boy from Canley Vale was careful not to let his jaw drop. He had always considered the Blake residence as luxurious, but this place was in a new league.

Some of the garage doors were open, and the Benloch native was pointing in their general direction. 'Pick any open door. It doesn't matter which one.'

The unassuming, dark blue Ford took its place alongside the Jaguars, Mercedes and Land Rovers which Jeff's mind's eye pictured behind the row of closed doors. All these beautiful automobiles in one place! He would need to buy a better car if he was going to be visiting here regularly, the young man resolved. Time to sell another song or two?

The guest switched the engine off, and to his delight, Lynn leaned over and gave him a welcoming peck on the cheek. He was nervous, he had to admit. Marianna had seemed friendly enough, but their meeting had been necessarily brief. Her daughter was already out of the car and waiting for him. Dutifully, he opened the boot and started to gather all his belongings into his arms, while Lynn picked up her one, neat suitcase.

'What can I carry?' she asked, watching him struggle with several separate items.

The joker pretended to dump the whole lot into his patient girlfriend's outstretched arms, before retreating and dumping it all back into the boot. They laughed, and he began to gather it all up again, but more systematically this time.

'Thanks,' he said. 'I didn't plan this very well, did I? Told you I wasn't used to being organised.'

Jeff hooked the curved head of the coat hanger which held his suit, shirt and tie for the party with the index finger of his right hand, then looked back into the boot for something else that wouldn't load Lynn up too heavily.

'Can you take these?' he asked, holding a pair of freshly polished black shoes.

Lynn took them. 'Sure. What about that bag?'

'No. That's OK. I can take the rest.'

With his car keys in his teeth, Jeff pushed the boot lid down with his chin and made sure it closed with the right cheek of his bottom. He was about to enter the Dysons' home. Was he ready for this? *You betcha.*

'Let's go, baby!'

The teenagers' feet scrunched across the gravel, towards the back door. The large, glistening pool was separated from the house by a manicured lawn and an outdoor bar and barbecue area. It was quiet and private. The house itself was in the shape of an "H", Lynn explained, designed to maximise the amount of window area lighting the many rooms it comprised. The famous family's home was even bigger than it looked from the front, Jeff reckoned. He scanned along the windows on the first floor and wondered which one belonged to his beautiful host's bedroom. And where exactly would he be spending the night?

A little girl with two bunches of long, blond hair ran out to meet them.

'Anna!' shouted her older sister. 'Hiya!'

The seven-year-old sprinted towards the couple, excited to see them. The sisters embraced energetically, before turning to their guest.

'Anna, this is Jeff.'

'Hey, Anna! What's up?' the nineteen-year-old greeted the littlest Dyson. 'Are you looking forward to the party tonight?'

'Yes, I am, thanks,' the girl answered. 'Are you Lynn's boyfriend?'

The recent arrivals looked at each other and laughed at the youngster's directness.

'Yes, I hope so,' the tall man replied. 'Is that OK? Is your big sister allowed to have a boyfriend?'

Anna looked puzzled for a moment. 'Yes!' she replied indignantly. 'Of course she is. As long as she doesn't kiss and do all that yukky stuff.'

The horny student laughed and glanced awkwardly again at the woman with whom he hoped to be engaging in such yukky stuff very soon indeed. He decided not to enter any further into this particular topic of conversation, deferring to his eminently better qualified chaperone.

'Anna! What yukky stuff anyway?'

'Oh, you know. Lovey-dovey talk and kissing. It's gross!' the child grimaced.

'Take these, please,' the elder sister held Jeff's shoes out. 'Let's go inside and get rid of all these things.'

A pair of half-glazed doors led into a hallway next to the laundry. Further down the corridor, Jeff discerned a large kitchen, judging by the clanging noise of pots and pans and female voices chattering. Anna and Lynn were already making their way up a straight staircase to the first floor, so he followed. At the top was a long, long landing with a row of white doors on both sides, all closed. This was something Jeff Diamond always noticed, and he felt his brain freeze involuntarily.

Anna pointed to one of the offending doors. 'That's my room,' she announced proudly to their special guest.

'Thanks. I'll remember that.'

The trio continued past quite a few more white doors and round a corner which led to still more white doors, until the girls both turned at once. Perhaps they sensed his blood pressure rising?

'You need room numbers,' the young man joked.

The seven-year-old pulled a face. 'Mum won't even let me put my name on the door,' she lamented.

'And this is *my* room,' Lynn informed her boyfriend in the same childish tone.

Her sister looked annoyed. 'Stop taking the piss.'

'Anna! Shhh!' Lynn was startled by what she had just heard. 'Don't say that. It's not nice.'

Jeff made a vain attempt to keep a straight face, although the youngster's comment was pretty funny. He fixed Anna with a stern gaze, wondering if it was appropriate to help the older sister out in such situations.

'Who've you been hanging out with at school?'

'No-one,' the defensive child responded.

And that ought to be the end of that, the guest concluded. He couldn't remember the last time he had shared a conversation with such a young child. Many, many years ago.

Lynn Dyson's bedroom was large and bright, with a lounge and TV area, an upright piano against one wall and a desk on the other side. The bed was at the far end, partitioned off by a bank of cupboards and bookcases. There was an *en suite* bathroom to one side and three full length windows. It was remarkably similar in layout to her city apartment. Probably deliberately, the visitor decided, given their earlier conversation about homes away from home.

'Anns,' the sixteen-year-old asked. 'Is there lunch planned or anything, do you know?'

Her sister shrugged, her eyes following the interesting male's every move.

'Please could you go and ask Mum or Helen?' Lynn persisted, looking for a way to get rid of the little hanger-on.

But Anna was wise to the ploy, planting her feet firmly on the floor and pouting.

'Can't you ring?' she replied scornfully, her gaze alighting on the telephone not two metres from where her sibling was standing.

The older girl opted for the plain instruction, delivered with a twist of boredom. 'Please go downstairs. We'll come and help in a minute. We're only going to unpack.'

Anna appeared a little downcast at first but then obeyed the big sister whom she idolised. She left the door ajar, and her running footsteps could be heard tripping lightly down the stairs.

The two who remained stood stock still for a few seconds, simply staring at each other. Lynn seemed unusually strung out, and Jeff wondered whether he was projecting his own feelings onto her. His arrival was obviously eagerly anticipated, at least among the female family members. While on paper he had by far the higher score in the dating experience ratings, in reality this was far from the case. Sexual conquests were not to be confused with relationship maturity, he concluded. He was a fish out of water, beginning to feel the pressure acutely, and so far he had only had to deal with a seven-year-old.

The celebrity broke the ice. 'So,' she exhaled, spinning round. 'Do you like it?'

'Your room?' asked her boyfriend, giving his surroundings another quick scan. 'Great!'

'Yes. My room. Or the house, or being here, or meeting my mother, or anything really.'

The student was right. His girlfriend was nervous too. He stepped forwards with his arms outstretched, and she walked into them gladly. He gave her a bear hug, as much for his own benefit as hers.

'Relax,' he whispered, kissing her cheek and immediately feeling a stirring down below. 'We're stressing each other out. Told you we should have had sex before we left!'

Lynn wasn't sure how she should take this latest remark. Was this yet another well-known adult fact which he was passing on to his naïve, school-aged host, or was the control freak in him simply making sure she knew what he wanted again? The look of consternation on her face made the young man laugh.

'Everything's fine. A bit overwhelming for both of us, isn't it?'

'But why are we *both* nervous?' the pretty woman asked in exasperation. 'I live here!'

She couldn't understand her own reaction. It was fair enough for Jeff to be apprehensive about meeting her family, being who they were and all that went with them. But she, nervous in her own home? Perhaps she was too keen for her family to like her new boyfriend as much as she did; to receive their blessing or, worst case scenario, to be allowed to keep seeing him.

'Hey, I need to ask the obvious question,' the new arrival ventured gently, wanting to get one thing straight from the outset.

The sixteen-year-old looked up at him, ashamed that she didn't understand.

'Which obvious question?'

'Well, this is *your* room, as you've already told me,' he replied, imitating the kid sister too. 'So where's *my* room?'

Immediately, Lynn's concern returned, and she hesitated a little. 'Oh, yes. OK. I actually thought you'd stay here. Don't you want to?'

'Are you kidding? Of course I want to,' her boyfriend smartly dispelled this myth. 'It's just that this is your parents' house, you've got a very young sister who's highly inquisitive, and from their perspective, we hardly know each other. I don't want to do something that's going to cause either of us any trouble.'

The celebrity was happier on hearing his response and took his hands.

'Oh. That's good. I was worried.'

'I'm serious though,' Jeff insisted. 'Some parents go weird when their kids want to sleep with someone under their roof. Even when they know full well it's going on somewhere else, it's like they can no longer deny it if it's happening right next to them. Gerry's parents were like that for a long while.'

'Oh, right. I get it,' his girlfriend nodded. 'Should I ask them specifically? It'd be embarrassing for all of us if they expect you to be in here all along, because then they might feel obliged to behave like you just described.'

'Good point,' the uncertain student owned up. 'What the hell? You've told your mum we're sleeping together. Jesus! She's already put you on the pill, so she's obviously not expecting it to stop. And she didn't throw me out earlier, therefore I can't have made too bad a first impression. My vote says we just face the music. Whaddya think?'

Lynn smiled, relieved. 'That sounds perfect. Let's put everything away, and I'll find out what's going on with lunch. Sometimes we all sit down to eat together, but I'm not sure everyone's here yet. Junior's playing footy this afternoon anyway, so he won't be here 'til much later. Not sure about Sandy. He's probably here. That only leaves Dad.'

She led Jeff towards the bedroom area, her heart in her mouth.

'You can hang your stuff up in here,' she instructed, pointing to an array of wardrobes. 'I'm just going downstairs to find out what the go is with lunch.'

The lithe, young celebrity left the room before her anxious man could suggest any other activity, and he hooked his suit hanger over the wardrobe door knob, not wishing to explore any further into her domain just yet. The rest of his clothes were then dropped onto an armchair to the right of the bed, beneath which he slotted his shoes. That left the bag with his university assignment material, which he placed on the floor, leaning against the chair.

The guest hadn't realised at first that there were balconies outside two of the three windows. He opened one of the French doors and stepped out. It was a pleasantly mild morning, not too humid and no breeze to speak of. Jeff pushed the windows shut behind him, lit a cigarette and leaned over the railing to smoke it. He could see the row of garages where they had left his car, and there looked to be a second bank of garages beyond these. To his left was a large building, the entrance to which must have been at the other end of the garden they had walked through earlier, and he recalled Lynn had also pointed out a gymnasium to the right.

The longer the young man lingered on the balcony, the more the calm became noisier. He could hear many different bird songs, the sound of farming equipment engines, some children playing behind the garages and, straining to make out the detail, the sound of a busy kitchen. They must be getting ready for tonight's party, he thought, under Helen's supervision.

Helen, Jeff remembered, was the family's housekeeper. She was the one from whom Lynn had garnered advice on telling her mother about her boyfriend. A smile flashed across his face when he remembered Anna's bad choice of language earlier. This was really quite a normal family, all things considered, and he began to relax. It had been a good move by his canny host to spend a few moments apart. His cigarette finished, he returned inside.

The bathroom was bright. There was a skylight in the ceiling. The guest could have sworn he saw three storeys when they had originally approached the front of the house, and yet he only remembered climbing a single flight of stairs on his way to Lynn Dyson's bedroom. He freshened up quickly and lay down on the bed. Looking around at the tasteful floral wallpaper and a select group of cuddly toys sitting on top of the chest of drawers, he imagined Lynn as a young girl, thriving in these idyllic surroundings, never wanting for anything and having a solid set of family values with which to grow up.

The boy from the Stones Road felt no jealousy, as such, because he had long since come to terms with his own lot in life. He had made a conscious decision at a very early age to break out of his suffocating and limiting family situation. He had deliberately sought out, watched, read about and listened to people from whom he could learn the finer aspects of life, and it had reaped substantial dividends. He had developed an easy self-confidence around the few affluent people he knew, never having to worry about which knife and fork to use or which "P" or "Q" to mind. He didn't fear meeting Lynn's parents for that reason, not overawed by who they were or how they lived.

Jeff stretched out on top of his girlfriend's queen-sized bed and gazed around the room some more. His disquiet stemmed more from being accepted as their daughter's lover, which was more complicated in so many ways. He knew all too well how the cards were stacked against him. First of all, Lynn was only sixteen and still at school. Her parents were expecting her to go on to university, to have years of *élite* sporting success and to carry on building her career as a superstar entertainer and actor, all at breakneck speed. He had a fairly good idea about the type of man with whom they would prefer her to be associated and could draw very few parallels with himself. At least, not the type of man he was at the moment.

Being his usual, over-analytical self, the intelligent student was accustomed to looking way into the future and planning his path through life in terms of the qualifications he would need, jobs he could do and where his ultimate ambitions lay. Yet he had never dared, either consciously or subconsciously, even to dream about a future with Lynn. Why was that? Probably because he had convinced himself that the odds were too steep and that he feared the devastation if it didn't come true. However, reclining on the famous star's bed now, Jeff's mind endeavoured to conjure up an appealing impression of what the next few months or even years might hold, and how their relationship could survive while they were still so young and both with much to achieve. The last thing he wanted was to be seen by the young champion's parents, coaches and management as someone who would get in her way. He didn't want that at all, despite the depth of his feelings for her.

Almost asleep, the tired man heard the door open and shut, followed by some light footsteps running over the carpet.

'Where are you?' his girlfriend cried out.

'In here,' he replied, getting to his feet. 'What's the plan?'

The pretty teenager sat down on the end of the bed, and the visitor gladly slumped back onto the mattress again, making her bounce upwards and in towards his waiting body. His arms enfolded her slim torso, and she cuddled into him briefly, before leaning back and preparing to speak. He raised his eyebrows expectantly, trying to pull her back in.

'Well...' she began, laughing happily.

Jeff kissed her before she could say anything else. 'I love you,' he said. 'Thanks for bringing me here. It's great.'

Lynn smiled. 'I love you too. I hope you're not too fazed by all the fuss. I don't really know what's got into all of us. The atmosphere's got a life of its own.'

Being granted a few minutes to sort out his messed-up head had made all the difference. The young man had honed his social skills at Blake family parties and other company events to which Gerry had invited him from time to time. Family chit-chat was irksome, but no big deal. He was ready for anything.

'We'll just take it as it comes,' he assured her.

The celebrity continued. 'Lunch is soon, in about ten minutes. Dad's downstairs, by the way.'

Jeff instantly felt his pulse quicken again at this announcement, almost as if his subconscious had picked up a cue from the great man's daughter to be prepared. Bart Dyson was a well-known formidable force. Was he still sure he was ready for anything?

'What I thought...' Lynn's eyes were questioning, and her tone tentative. 'What I thought was that we could take a ute out after lunch to my favourite spot. You know, when I mentioned a better idea, before we left?'

Her boyfriend nodded with renewed interest. 'Oh, yeah?'

'We could take our swimmers and school work and go out there for a while. I have to come back to the gym' for a two-hour meeting with some sports psychologist Dad's invited to talk to us, so you could stay out there or come back. Whatever you want.'

'*Suena bien,*' the young man responded.

He didn't really have any say in the matter, but this plan sounded perfectly fine anyway. The way his insides ached right now, if there was sex to be had at the gorgeous enchantress' favourite spot, he would agree to anything.

'As long as it means we can kiss and do yukky stuff.'

The schoolgirl laughed out loud. 'She said, "Taking the piss"! Can you believe that? I don't think I even knew that phrase when I was seven. She knew what it meant too. So funny! Thanks for keeping a straight face.'

'It *was* funny,' Jeff agreed. 'I was thinking about it while you were gone. Anyway, we'd better get downstairs and get the rest of the introductions over with, then we can relax. I'm hungry. Are you?'

Lynn nodded. Her eyes glanced down at her boyfriend's crotch, easily able to make out the line of an erection in his pants. He raised his eyebrows again, this time much more suggestively, and the sixteen-year-old blushed.

'Downstairs,' he smiled, straightening himself out and beckoning for her to walk in front of him. 'Or I'm taking you now.'

The kitchen was huge, almost the same size as the guest's entire flat, made up of two adjoining sections. The main room was filled with an enormous farmhouse table and about twenty chairs, and the working area was off to one side, through a door and with a large serving hatch into the dining area. The table was adorned with plates of bread, cheeses, cold meats and antipasti, with bowls of salad and other condiments.

Marianna Dyson was behind the serving hatch, handing still more platters out to Anna and a slightly older boy. A rather plump lady was busy taking cutlery out of a drawer on the far wall. She turned just as the youngsters entered the room.

'Ah! Here you are!' she exclaimed excitedly, placing the bundle of knives and forks onto the table and wiping her hands on her apron.

It was like a scene from a television sit-com, the student mused. All the regular actors seemed to have their roles to play, while he and his beautiful companion had become the unlikely stars of the show. He found it hard to believe that someone like him could cause such a stir in the celebrity household, concluding that it must be a big deal when the newly eligible young lady of the house brings home a boy for the first time.

'Hi, Helen,' the young lady in question greeted the housekeeper with a hug and a kiss on the cheek. 'How are you?'

'I'm well, dear, thank you,' she answered, her eyes quickly turning to the long-haired, statuesque man, 'and you must be Jeff.'

He was indeed very handsome, the housekeeper approved, having been treated to an extremely detailed appraisal by the love-struck girl a few weeks ago. Tall and strong, with big, brown eyes and a smile with the potential to cause heart palpitations in a woman of her age. She could easily see why the impressionable teenager would be attracted to this man. And *vice versa*, she imagined.

'I am.'

Jeff leaned forward to shake her hand, and the friendly woman presented her left cheek. He obliged, and she giggled like a girl. It was strange for him to think of her as Lynn's adviser on matters sexual, and embarrassing too. Had she chuckled because she could guess his nefarious intentions for the weekend in this grand house?

'Nice to meet you, Helen.'

Lynn was already preparing for more introductions when the guilty man focussed his attention back on the rest of the room. Marianna had entered, with arms laden, and was walking towards them with her other two children.

'This is my brother, Sandy. Richard. Whoever you are!' the host informed her boyfriend.

'Hi,' Jeff said, waiting to find out which name he should use.

The twelve-year-old looked so much like Lynn, yet seemed reserved, which was unlike either sister. The newcomer shook his hand.

'You're up for the weekend as well?' he asked, hoping to ease Sandy's apparent awkwardness.

The boy smiled, grateful to have been asked a noddable question. He liked his sister's boyfriend already. There was an inviting air about him, as if he wouldn't judge who he was or what he said.

'Anna and Mum you've already met,' the older sister continued, receiving nods and smiles all round.

'OK. What can I do to help?' the dutiful visitor asked, slapping his anxious palms against his thighs.

'Ooh! Isn't he the perfect guest?' cooed Helen, gesturing behind her, at the dresser on the far wall. 'You two can get the plates and glasses out.'

'How many are we?' the young woman asked, mostly to herself.

She counted those in the room and included her absent father.

'Seven?'

'Eleven,' Marianna corrected her. 'Rick and Sue and co' are joining us. They're with Dad in the office.'

'Oh, OK,' her daughter nodded, before turning to give her boyfriend an explanation. 'Rick Pelten's Dad's right-hand man when it comes to the farm. He and Sue are the managers and live here full time. They've got two kids, Brett, whose real name's also Richard, and Pete. Except Pete's a girl.'

Jeff put on a deliberately confused face, raising both hands to his head and making the younger children laugh. 'OK. I can be cool with that. There are too many Richards around here, aren't there?' he joked with Sandy, who was helping to lay out the plates and cutlery.

Another smile and nod. The nineteen-year-old was intrigued by the dissimilarity of this boy's personality to the rest of the mob, never having heard him interviewed before. Another black sheep? He could identify with that... When the table was laid, Helen asked Anna to run and fetch her father and the others. Lunch was ready.

'Marianna, you sit down,' the housekeeper offered, motioning to the recent arrivals to do the same. 'It's a shame Junior isn't here. We'd have a full set. It's been quite a while since you were all together for lunch.'

'Probably not since New Year,' the mother agreed. 'Sit down, kids. What would you like to drink?'

Lynn poured everyone a glass of iced water, sneaking a quick hand onto Jeff's shoulder. He winked and watched the cheery, overweight employee swoon once more in the background. Within a few minutes, in walked Bart Dyson and the Peltens, throwing the luncheon proceedings into disarray once more. The two young children ran round to greet their playmates.

The newcomer stood up again, quickly followed by his excited host, who was itching to introduce him to her father. Bart was a huge man, a couple of inches taller than the Sydneysider, but also much broader, with a tanned, weather-beaten complexion. He had immense presence. Just by entering the room, the guest recognised that the Olympian had changed the whole ambiance. *Watch and learn*, he reminded himself.

'Hi, Dad! This is Jeff Diamond.'

The Dyson patriarch gave his daughter a quick hug and waved to the rest of the room, his gaze already fixed on the visitor and his sweeping arm making a large, majestic arc towards the guest's outstretched right hand.

'Jeff!' his voice was larger than life too. 'Good to meet you. Welcome to Benloch!'

The big man gripped the student's right shoulder with his left hand as their hands clenched. Jeff fought to stand his ground, reading his girlfriend's father's posturing body language. The younger man wasn't going to let himself be pushed around, however good natured it was. That much he had already learned, long ago.

'You too, sir,' he replied, and their hands broke apart. 'Thanks.'

Bart was impressed. 'Good man,' he said, patting him on the back as he walked towards the serving hatch.

The patriarch kissed his wife warmly and opened a low cupboard door to reveal a refrigerator. He reached out four bottles.

'Beer, Jeff?' he boomed.

'Great. Thanks, sir.'

Thank Christ, in fact, the teenager thought. He caught Lynn's gaze, and she gave him a sly thumbs-up. He hoped he was behaving suitably, feeling uncharacteristically at sea. Her smile relaxed the grateful man a little, and he accepted the beer and poured it carefully into a spare glass. He had assumed Marianna's rules would be similar to those of Gerry's mum when it came to beer at the dining table, until he realised the other men were drinking straight from the bottle.

The drama having subsided, Lynn resumed her introductions. 'Jeff, this is Rick and Sue. They're long-time friends of the family.'

The young man nodded and smiled, following her moving hand to where the couple's children were chattering happily with Anna.

'And those are their kids,' she added, waving casually in their general direction.

More hands were shaken and pleasantries exchanged. Marianna urged everyone to sit down and start eating. Anna and the other children loaded their plates and went to sit at one end of the long table, but Sandy looked a little lost, having reached the in-between age. Jeff cocked his head towards an empty chair on his right, as if to say, "Come and sit down here, buddy," and the boy eagerly took his place.

Lynn overheard Marianna remark to Helen about how empathetic their guest was. *Yes, he is,* she agreed silently, giving her handsome stranger the eye and smiling sweetly. It was her turn to receive a thumbs-up sign, which was followed by another suggestive attempt to draw her eyes downwards, into his lap. The young woman turned away, stifling a giggle.

The meal was delicious, with everyone passing round platters and helping themselves to the rich selection of food which Marianna and Helen had prepared. After a few minutes, Rick went to fetch the next round of beers, and his boss returned his attention to his elder daughter's beau.

'So you're at RMIT, I hear.'

'Yes, sir. That's right,' Jeff replied. 'Computer Science "B Sc", second year.'

'Good thing to be into, computers,' Rick added, handing the visitor a full bottle and removing the empty one from his hand. 'I haven't got a clue. Sue's better at that sort of thing than me. I always think I'm going to stuff the bloody thing up.'

The student gave a polite chuckle, raising the bottle to the farm manager. He was about to explain a little more about the subject, to make safe, impersonal conversation, when Sandy's voice drifted tentatively from between him and Bart.

'I lost a program at school last week. It was annoying as hell. Two hours' work,' the boy moaned.

'It's actually very easy to stuff them up, mate,' Lynn's boyfriend supported her brother's foray into the discussion. 'They're not very resilient.'

He presumed the cautious lad was dying to impress his father, being so far down the pecking order and somewhat overshadowed by his elder siblings. Surely not everybody in the same family would automatically be blessed with such natural sporting talent. Perhaps this particular Dyson was destined to make his fortune in a different sphere from the others, although the technologist envisaged a whole host of problems with this possibility.

'I expect you remembered it pretty easily when you came to write it again though,' the undergraduate continued.

'Yes, I did,' Sandy replied, growing taller in his chair.

Bart and Rick gave each other a knowing look, as if they too had picked up on the perceptive student's attempt to include the quiet lad. Lynn offered round a plate of cold meats, and her boyfriend accepted it gratefully, finding himself with an unexpectedly large appetite after their stressful morning. He managed to snatch a few long-awaited sentences with his beautiful companion, before Marianna continued the inquisition of her daughter's new suitor.

'And you're from Sydney, Jeff, we hear. What made you move down to Victoria?'

Fleetingly, the nobody from north of the border wondered how he ought to answer this question. Cards on the table? No, not now. A need-to-know basis would suffice for today. He looked Lynn's mother straight in the eye and provided a superficial answer.

'Yes. Born in suburban Sydney. I have a mate who came down here to head up the Melbourne branch of his father's business, and I felt like a change, so we came down together over the summer holidays.'

'But you said you were in your second year at uni'?' Bart looked mildly puzzled.

'Yes, sir, I am. I managed to get enough credits for prior learning from UNSW,' Jeff explained, not about to allow Big D to catch him on any technicalities.

The big man nodded.

'It's proving interesting though,' the confident teenager went on, 'because the curriculum's quite different here, after all. There are a couple of units this year that I did last year, so I'm replacing them with one first year and one final year unit. It's causing some confusion.'

'Jeff works at the uni' too,' Lynn piped up, keen to paint him as industrious. 'He looks after the computer lab' and helps the other students with their assignments.'

'Stopping people stuffing things up too much,' the humble man shrugged, glancing over to Sandy, who laughed.

The others did too. So far so good, the newcomer thought. Eager to turn the heat off himself, he turned to his girlfriend's father.

'Lynn tells me you've got a sports psychologist session this afternoon.'

Bart tilted the top of his beer bottle in the direction of the young couple, swallowing down his mouthful. 'Yes, indeed. Should be instructive,' he boomed. 'I heard the man speak at an Olympic Committee conference. He's an Aussie studying at Berkeley, California. They're doing some ground-breaking work around motivation techniques and self-leadership that I'm keen to test on ourselves.'

Jeff glanced at his stunning partner, who appeared unmoved by her father's comment. She must be accustomed to being experimented on. The story of Josef Mengele suddenly drifted into his head, but he quickly dismissed it in case there were any mind-readers in the room. Then, still tangled in his distraction, he briefly allowed himself to wonder what this psychologist might conclude when Lynn turned up at their meeting, fresh from the pleasant outdoor escapade she had planned for them after lunch. He dismissed this particularly enticing fantasy too, for precisely the same reason.

'I look forward to hearing about it,' the visitor responded seriously. 'I'm fascinated by all that stuff.'

'You really are a people person, aren't you?' Marianna said, looking from her daughter to the teenager's new boyfriend. 'You pick up on everything.'

The nineteen-year-old refrained from answering, flashing his dark eyes rather too flirtatiously, in hindsight. He took her statements as compliments but was still determined to deflect the attention away once and for all. However, before he had a chance to suggest a new topic and completely without warning, Big D addressed his wife with the strangest of questions.

'So darling, is everyone clear where they're sleeping tonight?'

A stunned silence gripped the whole room. Caught unawares, neither Lynn nor Jeff dared look at each other, anxious to hear what was coming next. Marianna was also somewhat taken aback.

'Bart! By everyone, I assume you mean these two?' she replied, with a slow emphasis on the word "everyone" and turning her eyes on her elder daughter again.

The man of the house signalled in the affirmative, and Rick Pelten gave a deep chuckle, shooting a sideways glance at the dark-haired pretender. Jeff felt sorry for his girlfriend, who had been sorely embarrassed, but thought better of reaching for her hand. Instead, he sat up straight in his chair and waited for the dignified lady to make her proclamation.

'Well, as far as I'm concerned,' Marianna declared, 'it's up to them what they do. With the number of people staying over after the party, there probably aren't many empty beds anyway. It's going to be a madhouse in the morning. Sorry, Helen!'

The distinguished mother figure finished off the last few morsels from her plate, rested her cutlery on it with care and stood up to clear the table. That was apparently that. Lynn breathed a sigh of relief which drifted as far as her man, who was now hanging out for the opinion of the instigator of this particular awkward scene. It wasn't long in coming and was delivered in the same bombastic manner as their guest had already come to expect.

'Good on ya, Jeff,' Bart winked theatrically. 'If my daughter's happy to sleep with you, then I'm fine with it too. You're as solid as a rock, as far as I can tell.'

As one, the young couple inhaled sharply to counteract the relief which surged forth from their bodies. Anna piped up with her familiar primary school theme, talking mostly to her partner in crime, the girl called Pete.

'Ew! They're going to kiss and do rude things. That's gross!'

'Be quiet, young lady,' scolded her father. 'You wait 'til you're sixteen and see how you are.'

Anna pulled a disgusted face, convinced that such nastiness would never happen to her, and the other children couldn't help but agree. Lynn left the table and busied herself with clearing the food into the servery. Her boyfriend went to help her and to check that she was OK, only to be summarily commanded by Helen to stay put.

'You know, Jeff,' Bart turned again towards the handsome student. 'There may be a couple of blokes you'll know here tonight, for the McLeans' party. I'm sure some of my older son's mates are at RMIT, and they'd be second year too. You never know.'

Jeff considered his response, caught up in the inevitable competitiveness developing between the two men in the young beauty's life. There were a large number of students at RMIT, but if he were to play Bart down, he ran the risk of having his bluff called as soon as one of his classmates arrived at the splendid function.

'That'd be good,' he nodded gratefully, and left it there.

Marianna issued her instructions. 'So... Let's get the rest of this food cleared away. Sandy, kids, please help carry the plates through.'

Everyone pitched in until Helen shooed them away. Lynn was quick to slip a conciliatory arm around her man's waist, when they both ended up at the pantry door at the same time, and he sneaked a quick kiss for the same purpose. The jolly housekeeper caught his hand as he was leaving.

'That was a good result,' she affirmed. 'You did well to stand up to him. Full marks, dear.'

The sixteen-year-old nodded in agreement. 'He gets so pompous sometimes, doesn't he?'

The housekeeper couldn't possibly comment on her employer's behaviour, simply landing a kindly pat on the celebrity's shoulder, and Jeff smiled at the two women looking out for his welfare. Their support was welcome, and not something he was used to.

'It's fine. It's his house. I wouldn't have expected anything less.'

When the kitchen spoils were finally packed away, Lynn led her mystery man around to the front of the house, where there was a wide, sweeping staircase and a sumptuous cream and navy circular rug by the grand set of double doors in the entrance hall. She then pointed past the stairs, providing a virtual tour of the grand mansion. Suzanne would be insanely jealous right about now, the young man smiled to himself.

'Down there's a lounge and the formal dining room, and a couple of offices and a TV room,' the musician explained, pointing to the other vertical of the "H".

Fighting off her boyfriend's lustful groping, she spun back around leftwards, her eyes passing the front entrance again and coming to rest on a door they had walked past earlier.

'Hey, wait! I forgot about that room. That's another room for hanging out... another lounge... where we go mostly if we're here during the week.'

The guest took it all in, still reeling from Big D's apparent approval of their physical relationship. Lynn began to climb the stairs, looking round to check if he was following.

'Are you OK?' she asked.

Jeff leaped up the first ten or so steps two at a time to catch her up, keen to establish whether they were any closer to the trip in the ute. He had surprised himself with his own ability to dampen his sex-drive this far, but had his doubts that his resolve would last much longer, especially since his girlfriend's family had left them alone.

'I'm fine,' he answered, grabbing her playfully around the waist.

'They like you.'

'Apparently so,' her boyfriend laughed, kissing her long and hard. 'I hypnotised them. They're under my spell, just like you are.'

The pretty star looked over her shoulder and down the stairs, almost making them overbalance. Her arrogant suitor nudged her chin sideways, towards his mouth, and kissed her again until she leaned herself backwards to take a long overdue breath. Their nerves had finally subsided, now that everyone had had a chance to get used to each other, and the renewed sexual tension that supplanted the anxiety was utterly intoxicating.

'Hope Anna can't see us,' Lynn giggled.

As they climbed the remaining stairs hand-in-hand, she turned to look Jeff in the eye. 'You're really good with Sandy, by the way,' she told him in a more serious tone. 'He's struggling with Dad at the moment. I don't know why, but he's become really scared of him recently, and Dad isn't helping. You see how he is... Junior's so much the golden boy, and Sandy's more gentle and not so competitive.'

'Thanks,' the empathetic man appreciated her observation. 'I sense there's something going on. He's a smart kid though. He's trying hard.'

The perennial misfit was hit by a sudden, silent epiphany, as he processed the kind sister's remarks. He was willing to bet that Bart Dyson's younger son was in the process of figuring out that his sexual orientation may not be quite what anyone expected. Not a thought for airing now, but Christ Almighty! He had it easy being Lynn's boyfriend, in that case. How difficult would it be for Big D to accept a homosexual son, even in the progressive nineteen-seventies? Once back in the upstairs corridor and not wishing to interfere with Lynn's happiness, the young man forced his mind back to the present.

'I have no idea how I'd find your room by myself,' he confessed in amusement, resisting being dragged along the long corridor. 'The doors are all identical.'

Lynn laughed. 'Everyone says that! When Michelle first used to stay for weekends, I always used to stick a magazine out from under the door. Trouble was, if Helen came up here, she would put it back inside! Junior does too, for fun, or so he thinks. Mine's actually easy. It's the second from the end. The very end door's just a cupboard, so you won't make that mistake twice.'

Inside the spacious bedroom suite, Jeff slumped down on the couch, feeling quite tired after the dramatic familial experience. Meeting Bart Dyson had been every bit as daunting as he had expected. Not quite a bully, but close. The great man had a distinctive method of commanding respect, which had evidently been honed over many years at the top of his profession, yet it was not a technique the aspiring leader particularly sought to emulate. Watching and learning didn't necessarily mean he was obliged to adopt every trait demonstrated by this legendary "someone".

'*Digame,*' he mused, holding his hand out for the sportsman's beautiful daughter and pulling her down next to him on the sofa. 'How come there's a skylight in your bathroom when the house has three storeys?'

'Aha!' Lynn threw her hands in the air. 'It's a good trick, isn't it? Only the front half is three floors, the back's only two. I'll show you later.'

'*Excelente,*' her boyfriend smiled, another conundrum clarified. '*No me volvo si loco pero.*'

His host looked at him, bemused. 'That's funny.'

'Why? What do you mean?'

'Do the Spanish put "but" at the end of their sentences, like Sydneysiders?'

Jeff had to think back to what he had said. 'Ah, yeah... See what you mean,' he replied after a couple of moments. '*Pero* can be "yet" or "but". It's a good point though. I never thought about that before. Perhaps there's something there, in how the immigrants have shaped Sydney's language. That'd be a good case study for our linguistics class. Cheers, angel.'

Lynn smiled, being smothered once more in desirous kisses. She loved how clever her boyfriend was, and also that he gave her credit for the few occasions when she managed to rise to the challenge.

'Oh, that's OK. So you said you're not going mad yet. Is that it?' she checked.

'*¡Eso es!*'

The tall man levered himself to his feet out of the low couch by putting his hands on his knees and flexing his thigh muscles. The feat was harder than he had hoped, after only a handful of hours' sleep all week. He vowed to push some more weights, having since seen how strong Lynn's father was in the flesh.

'So when are we going to your special place for some outdoor sex that your dad approves of?' he urged, reaching for her hungrily again.

'Now, if you like,' the celebrity answered, pushing him away. 'What shall we take?'

Jeff laughed. 'Take? Well, you and me, for a start!'

Without waiting for a more sensible answer, Lynn grabbed her school bag and put it on the couch, before proceeding into the bedroom. Her guest was right behind her, instantly fired up by the delightful prospect. The slender woman chuckled as she dodged out of his way and pointed towards the bathroom.

'Shall we get into our swimmers now? Then we don't need to carry too much stuff.'

The young man nodded eagerly. 'Yep. That works.'

He quickly changed and donated his books to their growing pile, to which a battered guitar case had also been added. Lynn had fetched two towels, and Jeff could see she was now wearing a bikini top under her sports shirt.

'Hey, nice! And the guitar's a nice touch too,' he approved.

His playmate gave a quick curtsey, batting flirtatious eyelids at her re-energised lover. 'We'll take a rug and some water from the garage. Let's go!'

Wild horses and all that, the nineteen-year-old seized the moment. Arms laden, the happy pair headed outside into the hot sunshine. There were catering staff everywhere, preparing for the evening's party, all of whom stopped and stared when they caught sight of the famous and popular teenager.

In the cavernous sheds, Lynn picked out a rug, two water canteens and two large sticks from a storeroom in the corner. She handed the canteens to Jeff and waved towards a sink at the back of the building. Suddenly, a golden Labrador came bounding up to them out of nowhere, barking excitedly.

'This is S'malo. Do you like dogs?'

She smiled at the sight of her boyfriend already crouched down, making a fuss of the affectionate animal.

'Love 'em,' he replied, continuing towards the sink.

'Do you mind if he comes with us then?'

'Is he a spy for your folks?' her lover shouted back in jest. 'No, of course not. It'll be good. Hope he has his own protection.'

Lynn's eyes widened, still not totally accustomed to her boyfriend's whacky sense of humour.

'You're terrible!' she laughed. 'I never know if you're being serious. I suppose I should know better by now.'

The happy youngster led her guest towards a white ute covered with the customary layer of red dirt. It had led an active life, judging by the dents and scrapes all over it. To Jeff's surprise, Lynn approached the driver's door and climbed in, ushering the dog in ahead of her. This was novel, he thought, reeling round and making for the other door. Once inside, she flicked the gear lever into neutral and started the engine.

'What?' she exclaimed, amused by the stunned look on his face. 'Control freak!'

His bluff called again, the student closed his eyes and shook his head in defeat. 'Whatever! It's your house too.'

The ute reversed steadily out of the garage and drove off, round the front of the house and across into a golden paddock. With the breeze blowing in her long, blonde hair, and her legs extending from under her shorts all the way to the pedals, Jeff drank in the truly magnificent sight. He was being driven to paradise by the girl of his dreams. Why should he worry about losing control? What was he thinking?

'You never told me you could drive,' he said, impressed. 'You're good.'

'We all learn to drive really young out here,' the nonchalant teenager replied. 'It's the best way to get around. That or horses. I can't wait to get my licence though. Only six months to go.'

Of course. Why not? Why wouldn't this privileged young lady already know how to drive? She was on private land, and there was a great deal of it to cover. The smooth-haired Labrador lay happily on the floor of the cab, his tongue lolling out of the side of his mouth. Jeff kicked his thongs off and buried his toes in the soft, golden fur.

'So why S'malo?'

'It's from Saint-Malo,' his host answered. 'You know? The old town on the north coast of France. It just gets shortened to S'malo. Mum and Dad went on a golfing holiday there, about the same time as we got him, so it just stuck.'

Jeff was content with the reasoning behind the dog's name, as if it were any of his business anyway, and divided his attention between the tanned legs that were transporting him to his long-awaited heaven and the breasts bobbing inside her t-shirt, which would soon be fully revealed in the sunlight. The vibrations from the stark, functional vehicle only added to the intense sensation, as Lynn drove quickly down a gravel track and then entered another paddock of knee-high corn.

The blonde beauty was at home here, the visitor could tell, relaxed and away from the pressure and adulation she encountered during the weeks. They weren't too different, these two people travelling with the dog named after a golf resort, both enjoying an escape from their everyday lives and both seeking happiness in simple pleasures.

'There's not much growing on this part of the farm,' the farmer's daughter explained. 'This crop's mainly for hay to feed the horses. Tomorrow I'll give you a proper tour, if you want?'

'Yeah. That'd be great,' her boyfriend responded, not really caring what they did, as long as they were together for this precious weekend.

'D'you know the rules? About gates, I mean?' she continued, without taking her eyes off the road, since the ruts had become quite deep and the ute was tightrope-walking along them. 'If it's open, there's no livestock; closed, there is. If you find it closed, close it after you. *Et cetera, et cetera.*'

'Got it,' Jeff answered, smiling. 'Roger, ten-four.'

Lynn giggled, launching a misguided fist at his knee but missing by a few centimetres, largely due to the vehicle veering suddenly to one side of the track. Jeff caught her wrist and held onto it, hanging on resolutely until she jerked it away. All control surrendered, he understood this to be her territory and that he was but a mere transient. He reached over again and placed his right hand on her strong and unblemished thigh.

'This is fun, angel, and you are totally gorgeous.'

The ute had skated round the perimeters of three paddocks and soon came over the brow of a hill, for its occupants to find an oasis of gum trees and willows in the middle of nowhere. The water shone in the dam, and the small copse was completely secluded. The city boy immediately became further aroused at the thought of why they had come here, feeling the ute slow to a stop close to the trees. He hardly had the door open, and S'malo had pushed past him and jumped out. The impetuous gundog ran around in circles, barking and causing a number of large birds to take flight.

'Whoa!' Jeff exclaimed, with his arms held out from his sides. 'This place is fantastic!'

Pleased that her handsome stranger liked his new surroundings, Lynn grabbed the rug and the water canteens from the back of the ute and placed the keys on top of the driver's side front tyre. Her boyfriend's quizzical expression was priceless.

'They can't get lost. In case something happens.'

The young man nodded, wondering what she might be insinuating. Paranoia in paradise? Again, not so different. What could possibly happen to them out here? Or did she just mean to her? He realised he must have come across as worried, because all of a sudden his empathetic girlfriend doubled back to the car and collected the keys from the wheel.

'Relax,' she smiled, throwing the jangling bunch to him. 'Put them in your pocket, if it makes you feel better. I feel safe, Jeff, and I won't run off. It's just what we do here.'

The nineteen-year-old exhaled sharply, feeling ashamed. 'Sorry. Old habits, I guess.'

'Can you bring the sticks, please?' his stunning tour guide requested, shrugging and blowing him a kiss. 'They're for the snakes, if we see any. Hardly ever do though, but it's a hot day.'

218

Jeff assumed she wasn't joking about this either and guessed the stout poles were for flicking the snake out of the way, rather than for bludgeoning it to death. He was a townie. He didn't know about such things. Lynn was already running towards the water's edge, closely followed by S'malo. He watched as the various props she had carried from the car were dropped onto the ground and wished he had a camera after all, to capture his dream girl in her natural habitat, so carefree and uninhibited.

'Are you coming in?' the animated young woman was looking at the water. 'Beware! It'll be freezing cold.'

Carrying the rest of the paraphernalia, her boyfriend watched keenly as she removed her shorts and top, to reveal a lemon-coloured bikini and her taut, tanned athlete's body. He dropped the ute's car keys onto the rug, then took his wallet and his own set of keys out of his shorts' pocket and left them there too. What the hell! He was on holidays. Normal rules need not apply.

The sixteen-year-old hadn't brought any such quotidian trappings with her to this idyllic location, and now he understood why. Money was not important in a place like this, and neither was time. The lascivious man watched her wind her hair into a bun and tie it up, her breasts quivering while her arms reached behind her head. She moved like a dancer, and his body ached wonderfully. Just a short swim to prolong the suspense, he agreed. He peeled off his t-shirt, and they both ran to the edge.

'We have to go on three,' Lynn challenged. 'Otherwise it's agony.'

It would be agony anyway.

'¡Uno, dos, tres!' Jeff chanted, taking her hand.

They leaped off the side and plunged into the dam. The deep water was icy, even at the end of March and after a whole summer of sunshine. Their heads burst back up through the surface of the water, and the Sydneysider shook his long fringe out of his eyes. The temperature had certainly reduced the size of his ardour. The breathless pair embraced in the beautiful scene, kissing and sinking under the water again. Gasping for air, they laughed and splashed around like children. Meanwhile, S'malo barked at them from the top. He wasn't about to get so cold.

Feeling wonderfully alive, the tormented young man looked around. His body had already become used to the chill, and the setting was completely peaceful. He could well understand why Lynn would love this place so much. He floated on his back and gazed up through the trees, squinting in the bright sun, while his girlfriend swam lazily around, lost in her own thoughts. They had arrived at the paradise he had been sold, and he didn't much care if they never left.

After a short while however, Jeff's mind turned back to the tiny lemon bikini, those long, slender legs and that which connected them all. Scanning the banks along the steep sides of the dam, he wondered how they were to climb out of the creek. The long, dry summer had caused the water level to fall about two metres from the lowest vegetation. He hoped his sexy tour guide had the solution to this latest conundrum.

'Hey! Are you ready to get out?' he yelled.

Lynn looked over. 'Yes. OK.'

'So how *do* you get out?' he asked, unable to hide is concern.

'Aha!' she replied again, obviously anticipating this question too. 'You've spotted that particular challenge then? Over here!'

Bursting into an effortless front crawl, the sportswoman swam over to the side, where some sturdy boughs hung over the water. Against the wall of red earth, attached to one of the thick branches at the top, was a simple rope ladder. She started to climb up. Panic over, Jeff feasted his eyes on her graceful agility.

'Are you staying in?' the perfect physical specimen shouted down from the top, flirtatious hands on gyrating hips.

'No way!'

The young man grabbed hold of the ladder and climbed out to join her, finding hidden strength to heave his tired body up out of the water, as if he scaled such heights on a daily basis. The drenched nubile form handed him a towel, and her eyes danced as they alighted on his wet shorts, which were clinging to the outline of his hardening penis.

'You said you had a better idea,' he shrugged. 'You should know I take you very seriously.'

Unabashed and unapologetic, Jeff walked over to where his girlfriend was drying herself and threw his towel down on the ground. He then stole hers from her innocent hands without resistance and wrapped them both up in it. He pressed himself hard up against her body, and she kissed him passionately.

'You're totally gorgeous too, by the way,' his dream girl said into his ear.

'Thanks. Why are you whispering?'

'YOU'RE GORGEOUS!' she restated, at the top of her voice, laughing at her own foolishness.

'Much better,' her man smiled, before adding, louder still, 'I LOVE YOU, LYNN DYSON!'

They kissed again, their hands ranging over each others' bodies voraciously, while Jeff attempted unsuccessfully to scoop up the rug with his foot. Eventually, he admitted defeat and broke away from her luscious lips long enough to take hold of one edge of the bulky item. Between them, the couple spread it out on the softest piece of grass they could find. S'malo continued to run around, chasing birds and insects, not taking any notice of their change in activity.

The handsome city boy laid the farm girl down gently on her back and removed her bikini top. Her eyes were closed, and shining droplets of water glistened all over her skin, complementing the rivulets snaking down the dark hairs on his chest and abdomen. He kissed and stroked her breasts, while her hands took hold of his penis through the wet shorts.

'Take these off,' she urged, her voice husky with excitement.

Jeff didn't need to be asked twice. He then slipped her bikini bottoms down her legs, looping them off her feet, and they lay together naked, under the scorching afternoon sun. The apprentice was beginning to perfect the art of applying his condom, and he struggled to contain himself simply watching her do it. After several minutes of caressing every part of each other, he entered her gently, and they moved slowly in rhythm. As slowly as possible, the ardent lover cautioned himself with great difficulty, captivated by the serenity of their surroundings.

Outdoors in the fresh, warm air, their intimate act seemed utterly surreal; both feverish and soothing at the same time. Lynn orgasmed quietly, writhing against his rigidity, and they shared a long kiss before Jeff's time also ran out. He came with a sudden rush that made him cry out loud enough to catch S'malo's attention. The excitable dog came bounding over and started to lick their faces.

'S'malo, no!' the young woman laughed, trying to push him off. 'Get away!'

Her boyfriend rolled to one side, and the celebrity rose onto her knees, making S'malo even more excited. Chivalrously, her lover called the dog to leave her alone, fighting him off while he put his board shorts back on.

'Thanks!' she said. 'Sorry about him.'

By the time the nineteen-year-old could reply, the agile nymph had jumped back into the water. He heard her scream from below and ran to look over the edge in amusement, watching as she ducked under the water a couple of times. He imagined the freezing water cleansing the very erogenous zones which had brought them such pleasure just a few moments ago.

'Is it nice down there?' he laughed.

'Come in!'

'No, thanks!' Jeff objected. 'Climb up. I'll check what the time is. You'll need to go soon.'

The content and fully satisfied visitor jogged over to the ute, where he had left his watch in the glove box. Two-thirty-five. Perfect, actually. As much as he didn't want Lynn to go, he was also quite looking forward to spending time on his own in this beautiful place. It was indeed a shame he didn't possess a camera. And not for Suzanne's benefit either.

Lynn was drying herself again when he returned.

'You've got plenty of time,' he said, wrestling the towel off her and taking control of the vital task. 'It's nearly twenty-to-three.'

'Good,' the sportswoman didn't seem overly keen, 'though I'd rather stay here with you than be psychobabbled.'

Jeff chuckled at her made-up terminology. The truth was that he would really like to be psychobabbled himself, to hear what this Californian academic had to say. He knew his way around the human brain quite well, after years of reading about and practising various psychiatric techniques for influencing one's own behaviour. To hear the psychology of self-leadership expressed in the context of sport would be a new angle which he would welcome.

'It'll be interesting,' he encouraged. 'And if it gets boring, you can cast your mind back to what we've just done. Your dad'll see you blush and know what you've been up to.'

'Yikes!' the young woman riled. 'That'd be horrible. He's probably going to be thinking that anyway.'

'Yeah, I expect so. Your parents were young once too, you know. Or were you immaculately conceived?'

Grimacing, Lynn got dressed in clothing suitable for experimentation, provocatively looping the wet, lemon bikini over her fingers and having it snatched from her hands. The pair walked to the ute and threw it and her other belongings onto the passenger seat.

'I'll drive back over straightaway after it's finished,' she told him. 'Two hours, I think. But if you get fed up waiting, it's only about one-and-a-half "K" in that direction. As soon as you get to that track up there, you'll be able to see the house.'

Jeff smiled, his eyes following her finger to where it was pointing. 'I won't get fed up,' he assured her. 'I'm going to work for a while, then I might write some songs for you. I've got a couple of ideas floating around at this very moment. And S'malo'll keep me company.'

Two doggy ears pricked up at the sound of his name, his tail whipping Lynn's bare legs.

'OK,' the sixteen-year-old nodded, standing on tip-toes to kiss her lover's parched lips. 'I'd better go. Have fun, and don't forget to drink heaps.'

'You too,' he replied, pushing strands of wet hair back off her forehead and kissing it goodbye. 'Happy brainwashing. I trust your mind not to be too much altered when next we meet.'

Smiling more at his poetry than his mocking tone, the pretty teenager climbed into the cab, turned the vehicle around and drove away. Jeff watched her negotiate the ruts in the track, thinking he could teach her a thing or two about where to position the wheels, before turning back to face the dam, slapping his thigh and calling the dog. They both ran back over to where the guitar and his work were waiting. He lay back on the soft terrain and stared once more at the azure expanse above, which stretched as far as he could see in any direction.

After a couple of minutes extracting and arranging some lyrics from his unusually clear head, the songwriter reached for the guitar. With it balanced on his chest, he strummed some chords and sang. S'malo began to bark along and licked the singer's face, evidently angling after co-writing credits.

'Get away, boy,' he demanded, gently pushing him off. 'This is serious business. I need money, so leave me alone.'

LORRAINE PESTELL

The Pretender and the Débutante

Two hours slipped by extremely quickly in paradise. Jeff heard the sound of the engine before he saw the dust, peering across at his watch in the sinking sunlight. Five-fifteen. They would need to get ready for the big bash soon. He wondered what Lynn might wear to the *soirée*, about which he had all but forgotten in the tranquillity of his oasis. Something sexy, he hoped; something he could spend the whole evening knowing he would have the pleasure of removing when the party was over.

The novice suitor wasn't exactly sure how he should play this evening yet. He was expecting it to be rather more difficult than Gerry's twenty-first birthday party, where he hadn't quite melded in as part of the family, but at least most people had met him before at some point during the prodigal son's formative years. And neither would he be on neutral ground here. The Dysons' guest could hardly monopolise their elder daughter among her own family and friends. He would be wise to stay in the background and bide his time, talking trivia with some unknown bloke's aunties and uncles, while his gorgeous girlfriend drove him wild from afar.

'Hi, Jeff!'

Lynn waved from the ute, pulling the handbrake on and launching herself out onto the loose, sandy ground. S'malo bounded over to her, closely followed by her boyfriend, who wrapped her up in his arms and hugged her tightly. She didn't object, relishing his vehement affection more and more.

'Hello, boys,' she giggled, as the hound jumped up and tried to lick her with equivalent fervour. 'Are you OK? I had visions of you being fried to a crisp, but you just look brown and healthy.'

Jeff smiled and shrugged, trying to distract the dog in order to stop the young woman's irresistibly long and slender legs from being scratched by eager claws.

'It's the Argentinean in me, I guess,' he responded, pointing behind him. 'S'malo and I spent most of the time under that tree. It was nice, but he's not my type. Can I tempt you back onto the magic carpet?'

The pretty teenager didn't even try to evade her boyfriend's grasp this time. He looked fantastic, bare-chested and replenished by an afternoon in the fresh air, and far from the angst-ridden man who had struggled to reveal his inner self just a few days ago. She hugged him, soaking up the attention he seemed compelled to heap upon her.

'Don't you ever stop wanting sex?'

'No,' he replied in an bewildered tone, pulling a fresh condom packet out of the pocket in his board-shorts. 'Why would I want to do that? Especially with you here, looking so ravishable, and with all the images from earlier swirling around my head. You gotta be joking, lady.'

Lynn dropped to the ground, pulling the expressive poet's hands downwards with her. He resisted for all of two seconds, before letting her down gradually onto the rug and lying on top, covering her with tender kisses. Her hands gripped urgently under his ribs, and it felt so good. This potent desire was not one-sided, the grateful man realised. His dream girl wanted him too.

'I missed you,' she whispered, feeling his body react to her hands. 'Am I holding too tight?'

'Never. It's perfect. The tighter the better. It makes me feel like you really want it.'

'I want *you*,' his lover corrected. 'The man from Berkeley told me I should go after what I want, and that's you.'

Her words invaded Jeff's nervous system like a drug, sending both brain and libido into overdrive. Why shouldn't she want him? He could make Lynn Dyson happy. She sure as hell made him happy. To his delight, the willing body beneath him came almost immediately, in response to the rhythmic, gliding strokes of his fingers, and then again only a few minutes later, once his full length had worked its magic inside her. He watched closely as the pleasurable sensation reached her face, maintaining the perfect amount of pressure only until she could take no more. It was the most beautiful sight he had ever seen, causing the same reaction in himself within far too short a time.

'You are the most wonderful thing ever created,' the emotional man whispered in her ear, kissing the side of her neck and massaging her strong right shoulder. 'There's nothing else on Earth that feels this good.'

The teenager's eyes shone as she squinted into the early evening sun, before her boyfriend's considerate hand reached up to shade them. He rolled her over until they were both lying on their side and reached behind him to where he remembered his towel having been abandoned in an untidy pile on the grass. Jeff draped it over the exquisite female form, as he carefully released their connection and stood up.

'Thank you,' the sixteen-year-old said. 'I love you. That was amazing.'

Pulling his shorts and t-shirt on, the tall, dark, handsome man smiled cockily. 'Of course it was.'

'Hey!' Lynn cried, jumping to her feet and wrapping herself in the towel. 'You're awfully full of yourself, Mister Diamond.'

Jeff shrugged. 'It takes two, baby. But yeah, I am. Take it or leave it.'

Shaking her head but without further dispute, the young star set about collecting her various items of clothing, which had been strewn all over in their hurry to get naked, and she was soon also dressed. With her hands on her hips, she fixed the arrogant man with a triumphant stare.

'I'll take it, thanks. Can't think why, but I will.'

The Sydney boy began to pack everything up, grinning quietly to himself but refusing to rise to the bait. He had a fair idea of how far he could push his luck, and it was not much farther. Unable to stand the silence, Lynn joined him and helped him to fold up the rug.

'So how was it?' he asked. 'The psychobabble?'

'You were right,' the tennis champion answered, her blue eyes still shining.

'About blushing because your dad knew what you'd been doing or that it was interesting?'

'Probably both,' she confessed with a smile. 'The guy had some good ideas that are definitely worth trying. I've got the info'. You're welcome to look at it.'

They piled all the gear into the back of the ute. Jeff called for S'malo to jump in, climbing up after their four-legged friend, lighting a cigarette and blowing smoke into the breeze. Lynn turned the car around, and it trundled back over the deep trenches once more, driving at a steady speed until the big homestead appeared in the distance. They were back in the garage in no time. The driver handed her relaxed passenger the canteens and sticks, which he took back to their rightful places, and the dog ran off as invisibly as he had arrived, with the day's outing clearly over.

The ecstatic pair walked back into the house through the same door as before, up the stairs, across the middle of the "H" and in through the second door from the end.

'Thank you for an amazing day so far,' the young man grabbed his girlfriend around the waist and pulled her close into him. 'I've got three more songs to play you.'

'*Excelente*,' she impersonated her Latin lover. 'When can I hear them?'

Jeff looked at his watch. Too late now.

'Maybe tomorrow morning?'

His girlfriend pointed to a pile of papers lying on the coffee table. Jeff picked up the various documents gratefully and sat down on the couch to leaf through the psychologist's material. He felt a little guilty, being made privy to confidential information reserved for the Dyson family and the Olympic movement.

'I'm going to make some tea,' the athlete announced. 'Do you want some?'

'Why not?'

The nineteen-year-old felt unusually mellow and could very easily doze off. To think he was in Lynn Dyson's bedroom, after spending a day at a picturesque and deserted oasis, making love to the most beautiful girl in the world and having already completed a good chunk of his homework! A more perfect afternoon he could not imagine. He would just give himself five minutes' rest, before showering and preparing for the festivities. He leaned his head into the back of the couch and closed his eyes.

The next thing the young man knew, Lynn was gently stroking his right shoulder. He came to, pressing his head into her hand. Surprised at how far his newly-trusting subconscious had sunk into the situation, his uncertain waking self jumped immediately to a sitting position.

'Your tea's cold,' she told him, kissing his forehead lovingly. 'Do you want another one?'

Jeff frowned. 'No, thanks. Sorry about that. We need to get ready, I'm guessing?'

'Yes. Soon. No rush though. I'll have a shower now, so there's enough time for my hair to dry. Go back to sleep. I'll wake you when I get out.'

'You're an angel,' her mystery man sighed, turning round and lying down across the couch. 'This is very comfortable.'

He recalled how stressed they had been when they first arrived this morning and contrasted it to having just woken up in the same room, with his lover's smiling face bearing down over him and her soft breasts brushing his shoulder while she leaned in to kiss him.

'Jeff, wake up.'

Déjà-vu! The sleep-deprived student shook his head and sat up. This time, his dream girl was crouching down at his side with her hand on his stomach, rocking it gently to tempt him back into the land of the living. Jesus! Again? He could most definitely get used to this treatment.

Almost on autopilot, the dazed man rose to his feet and made his way to the bathroom, eventually waking up properly once the cool water hit his head. By the time he had dried himself and was putting on his clothes in the bedroom, the visitor felt human again. He looked at himself in the full-length mirror, hung on the inside of one of Lynn's wardrobe doors, while he tied his tie. Not bad, he thought.

Having worn his suit only once in eighteen months while in Sydney, this was now the third time he had needed it in five weeks. He liked how it made him feel; a costume to disguise his lowly roots and which allowed him to mix indistinguishably with men of substance. He combed his thick, wet hair back off his face and went to find his date for the evening, who was sitting on the couch watching television in her undies.

'Is that what you're wearing tonight?'

'Yes,' the young woman giggled. 'Do you like it?'

Jeff stood behind the couch, bent over and kissed the back of her neck. He slipped the fingers of his left hand inside the cup of her lacy bra.

'*Sí, me gusta mucho.*'

He felt her shiver as he continued to kiss her. She smelled of a perfume he didn't recognise, and it aroused him no end. He liked the idea of feeling horny all evening, knowing that he could claim her at the party's conclusion.

'That was lovely,' Lynn said, hunching her shoulders when he stopped.

The expert lover stroked her neck and gave her one more kiss for good luck, groaning lustfully in her ear.

'So you're feeling better then?' she chuckled, reaching up and running her hand across the front of his suit pants.

'Oh, yeah! Ready for a wild night. I'm going to rip your clothes off in front of everyone and make wild, passionate love to you on the dance floor. Is the party here, or do we have to drive somewhere?'

Laughing, Lynn realised she had failed to give her guest any details about the proceedings. The event had been in the family's calendar for six months, and she had known Robert McLean for as long as she could remember. She felt ashamed of the rude omission and that she should have helped him feel more connected to what was going on.

'I'm sorry. I meant to show you. I completely forgot when we got back here. It's about fifty metres from here, outside and through the garden.'

This made sense. The function must be in the building Jeff had seen from the balcony before lunch, whence all the haste and commotion had been emanating. The near-naked beauty stood up and began to walk towards the bedroom area.

'Not so fast, baby,' Jeff said in an American accent, catching her arm as she passed by.

They hugged each other close, and the smartly-dressed suitor slid his hand around her back, locking her in a deep kiss. Lynn moaned quietly before pulling herself away. How quickly she was growing up and becoming comfortable with the physical side of their relationship. She no longer felt shy and full of tentative *naïvetée*. And with each bold move she made, her enigmatic stranger would ratchet up the tension just that little bit higher, letting her know she hadn't reached her limit yet.

'I have to get dressed,' she smiled, astounded that he would be ready for more so soon. 'You look amazing, by the way. Very suave.'

With a hangdog look, Jeff let her go and watched the youthful vision disappear out of view. Suave, huh? He would accept that descriptor! No-one had ever labelled him that way before, probably because he was wholly unaccustomed to such formal attire. He returned to the sports psychology paperwork, taking up where he left off. The subject matter fascinated him, and he began to see a whole host of other uses for such mind-over-matter techniques. He had registered for an additional elective in psychology for the next university semester, and wondered whether he might have the opportunity to get to grips with such advanced concepts in an introductory unit.

Around the corner, out of sight for now, Lynn lifted her party dress off its hanger and held it up in front of her body. She liked what she saw in the mirror and hoped her handsome chaperone would too. Tonight was her first official *soirée* as an honorary adult... her *début*, in a way... complete with a man on her arm and three packets of contraceptive pills in her bag to take back to the city tomorrow. She could still feel the after-effects of Jeff's hard penis being inside her twice in quick succession; a dull ache between her legs that was accompanied by exquisite memories and a definite quickening of her heartbeat every time they were recollected.

The young star slipped the dress over her head, zipped it up and sat down at the dressing table to apply her make-up, still lost in a dream world. Her appreciative boyfriend whistled loudly when she returned, gift-wrapped in a mid-length dress of swirling, red chiffon and finished by delicate strapped sandals with stiletto heels. She was wearing dark red lipstick, and her hair was tied back away from her face, making her look much older than her sixteen tender years.

Jeff drank in the view longingly, ruing his previous vow of restraint.

'You look fantastic!' he praised, holding his hands out towards her. 'You are the most beautiful woman ever.'

Lynn thanked him coyly. 'That's a big call.'

Her boyfriend shrugged. 'Yeah, it is, and no contest. Let's go, before the dress comes off, and we both have to start again.'

He followed his sheer, crimson vision down the back stairs, past the kitchen and into the enormous drawing room at the front of the house. The entrance hall doors were open, and Bart and Marianna were busy receiving guests. Another couple stood with them, presumably the birthday boy's parents. The lady of the house spotted the young lovers and cheerily waved them into the front room.

'Junior!' Lynn cried, clapping eyes on her older brother. 'This is Jeff.'

The elder Dyson son was as big as his father in every dimension. Perhaps even a little bigger. He broke away from the cluster of older men with whom he had been discussing the week's sporting diary and covered the ground in very few steps.

'Hi, Jeff. Nice to meet you,' the blond colossus responded, shaking the hand of his sister's new boyfriend.

The guest had seen this well-respected sportsman many times on television and had watched the Melbourne Demons play a couple of matches at the MCG. Face-to-face, however, Junior Dyson didn't give the impression of being the aggressive player he was on the football field. Like Lynn, he had a ready smile and an easy manner.

'Did you win today?' the visitor asked. 'I haven't seen any scores.'

Junior handed the newcomer a glass of beer that he had purloined from a passing drinks waiter, swapping his own empty glass for another and picking up an orange juice for his kid sister. She frowned comically, before clinking glasses with both men. Jeff invited her to stand in front of him, and like on that first visit to the theatre, she swore she could feel his chest against her shoulder even though they were separated by a thin buffer of electrified air. Her body tingled all over with anticipation.

'We did, thanks,' the footballer answered, raising his own glass. 'Not by much though. We were bloody lucky. Welcome to the family!'

Lynn's brother's toast to the couple was laced with friendly sarcasm, and the newcomer warmed to him instantly. This enormous, fashionably-dressed giant was much more like his dream girl than he had expected: smart, good-looking and gracious. He raised his glass to Big D the Younger and took his first gulp. The cold liquid slipped nicely down his gullet, so he quickly followed it with some more.

The student looked around, wondering if it would be acceptable to smoke. There were guests of all ages, shapes and sizes. People were flocking towards Lynn, inducing an instant pang of jealousy which he fought to suppress. He couldn't expect to hang on to her tonight, and in response to an apologetic flash of her blue eyes, he let her excuse herself. He was her guest, and would have to take it easy and await his cues.

Jeff helped himself to another beer, lit a cigarette and discussed the rest of the day's sporting results with Victoria's Best and Fairest. On the other side of the large room, his lady in red had become the centre of attention, continually glancing back to see where her boyfriend had got to. She was being kissed by old and young, men and women. Not wishing to hamper the enjoyment of her first ball by causing her to feel guilty, he caught her eye and winked his permission for her to abandon him. Less than ten minutes gone, and the persecuted boy had already lost his lifeline.

'She's quite something, isn't she?' Junior asked rhetorically.

The disappointed man gave a single, slow nod. He was not going to allow anything to spoil this evening. Simply watching Lynn was a veritable feast, and the night was yet young. After the special day they had shared, even someone as anxious as he felt sure it was only a matter of time before he would have the young beauty back in his arms.

'Your dad said you've got a couple of mates at RMIT,' the nineteen-year-old continued to make conversation with his girlfriend's brother. 'I'm doing Computer Science.'

'Yes, I have. Do you know Adam Lawley? Or Geoff Knight? They do some Comp Sci units. Oh, and Al Lewis. He'll be here.'

Jeff took a breath. 'Does Adam Lawley have a twin sister?'

'Yes. Alison. Why? Is this something Lynn shouldn't know?'

'Yeah, probably,' the ladies' man gave a sly grin. 'As long as she's not here tonight.'

'No. You're safe,' his girlfriend's brother scoffed. 'Adam's not here either. I think they're out of town, on holidays in Europe. They would've been here though. It's a small world.'

The two men swapped stories of university life, and Jeff dared to ask for some inside information on which teams the star player expected to reach the finals of the minor premiership, which marked the end of the pre-season competition. However, his concentration soon drifted from the recent cricket scores, when he saw the blonde in the red dress approaching, having managed to shake off her many admirers.

'Quick, hide!' the dark-haired stranger joked as the dazzling teenager came within earshot.

He reached out to her slim waist and pulled her in close, kissing her on the cheek. He was very pleased to reclaim his prize, his fingertips sliding the fine fabric of her dress across her hips. Junior's eyes followed his every move, the young man noticed. It was nice to see someone else taking care of the young woman's interests, except he hardly needed such protectiveness to extend to his own actions.

'I'm sorry I left you,' Lynn said. 'I got caught in a tide of Robert's rellies.'

'It's fine,' her mystery man whispered in her ear. 'Please don't worry about me. Just do whatever you need to do, and I'll be watching you looking so sexy. It's a tough gig, but I can handle it.'

His tight grip on her hand belied his nonchalance however, and Lynn leaned into him. Jeff was grateful for her sensitivity and relaxed a little. He was desperate for another drink, but realised there were many hours ahead of him. He couldn't afford to overdo it at such a swanky affair. Paranoia was already lurking just behind his eyes, waiting to leap on any innuendo or supposition, and more alcohol would only magnify its effect out of all proportion.

'You don't have a drink,' he noticed Lynn's hands were empty.

At that moment however, Bart Dyson's booming voice announced that the party would be continuing in the reception room behind the house. It appeared the batch of guests gathered in this drawing room constituted only the family invitees, and all the birthday boy's friends were already in the main venue.

Junior caught Jeff's eye, offering some sound advice. 'We should charge our glasses here, because there'll be a run on the bar when we get in there.'

'Good plan,' the guest agreed. 'Angel, what'd you like?'

'"OJ", please,' the young woman requested, stuck once again with the downside of being an under-aged celebrity.

The reception centre across the way was buzzing with conversation and activity, backed by upbeat rock music coming from the far end. The stream of guests from the house swelled the numbers, and the party was soon well underway. Lynn introduced her handsome man to a number of random people, all of whom swooned over her, causing the proud nobody to pause and take stock of where he was standing. Melbourne's *élite* surrounded him, and he was drinking beer out of a crystal glass, in a sumptuous function room on the Dyson family farm. It couldn't get much better than this for the ambitious *maladroit* from Sydney's west.

Yet after half an hour, the newcomer still hadn't met the guest of honour.

'So where's Robert?'

'Don't know,' his date answered. 'I haven't seen him yet. His parents and brother are here. As soon as I see him, I'll introduce you.'

The hall was huge, with high ceilings and white walls shrouded in long blinds that billowed in the breeze from open windows behind them. At the back of the room was a live band playing a variety of covers, sounding tight and professional. It was a courageous band that accepted a gig playing at a Melbourne Academy establishment affair, the young man hinted to his beautiful companion, who smiled in agreement. Junior left the happy couple, to talk to some mates he saw at the bar, and Jeff was once again in direct contact with his dream girl.

Hand-in-hand, they strolled through the throng. Onlookers parted like water cut by the bow of a boat, and from all sides they could hear people whispering. The lowly student realised this must be "situation normal" for the stunning young star, who waved and answered everyone in turn.

'There he is,' Lynn turned suddenly, pointing with her glass of juice. 'Over there. Red tie. Brown, short hair. There's a girl in a dark green dress with him. That's Natalie, his girlfriend. She went to MA too.'

Again the sea of guests cleaved to let them through, and Jeff saw they were making for a group of about ten young people, all impeccably turned out. Natalie caught sight of her friend and shook Robert's arm.

'Lynn!' she shouted above the noise. 'Rob, it's Lynn.'

The friends hugged each other one by one, and the younger woman introduced her date for the evening, who stepped forward and shook the men's hands and received excited pecks from each woman. The level of chatter resumed, and the dark-haired dreamboat read the lips of the lady in green, while she whispered about him to her famous friend.

'Wow! He's sensational! Where did you find him?'

The attractive pair laughed like naughty schoolgirls, the observation soon being shared by a number of other former classmates. Jeff said nothing, on similar ground now to Gerry's twenty-first, where his mate's giggling sisters had shown the anonymous heartthrob off to all and sundry. After the introductions, the conversation in the group quickly divided along gender lines; the men discussing the weekend's VFL results, and the girls mostly talking about the men.

Before long, the band went on a break, leaving the disc jockey to play some fill-in music and prompting the whooping bunch of females to depart for the dance floor. Again Lynn sought permission to leave, and again her boyfriend was at pains to dismiss her concern.

'So who do you barrack for?' Robert asked the recent arrival.

'Well, I used to follow the rugby when I was in Sydney and was an Eels man. But I live in Richmond now, so I've sort of adopted the Tigers.'

'No shit!' one of the others bellowed. 'I s'pose someone's got to support them.'

The birthday boy laughed, pointing to a large hulk opposite. 'He plays for Richmond.'

Jeff raised his glass to the unnamed footballer. 'Yeah? Go Tigers!'

The face was familiar actually, now he thought about it, and within a few seconds, a sudden realisation hit him. This massive forward was Dean Keller, Lynn's ex-boyfriend; the one she had dumped for him. This could be interesting, he mused.

'Have you two met?' asked Robert innocently.

The newcomer gave the birthday boy a glare which was meant to indicate that connecting these particular dots might not have been his smartest move. Too late. They were all now committed.

'Dean, this is Jeff. He's here with Lynn. Sorry, I don't even know your surname.'

The dark-haired stranger stepped onto the front foot, quite literally, leaning forward and standing as firm as he could. His practice at posturing with Bart Dyson earlier would now stand him in good stead. This bloke might be big but he was the "ex", and Jeff had also been in this situation many times before.

'Jeff Diamond,' he introduced himself, extending his hand. 'Dean, how are ya?'

The bulky sportsman had been drinking heavily since he arrived, Richmond having drawn the Friday night game this round, and he lurched forward to grab the smaller man's outstretched hand. Beer slopped over the top of his glass and splashed onto the floor.

'Nice one, mate,' Robert chided, hearing his friends jeering.

'So you're the prick who stole my girlfriend?' Keller snarled back. 'I've been waiting to meet you. Who the fuck do you think you are?'

A ring of startled faces stood back from the sparring duo. One of the others tried to silence the aggressive footballer.

'Mate, that's not very sporting. Shut up and chill out.'

Keller went on undeterred, transferring his glass into his left hand so that he could use his right to point a stubby finger at his adversary.

'You low-life shit. She's mine, so leave her alone.'

The surly drunk pushed the newcomer in the chest with both hands, causing more beer to spill. The Sydneysider reacted quickly, jumping back so that the liquid didn't land on his clothes and keeping Dean's eyes locked with his. Using a similar technique to the one which he had used on Lynn's father, the young man braced himself to absorb the contact that followed from the footballer's left fist on his chest. The bigger man recoiled angrily, the resistance having jarred his wrist.

'Lay off, mate,' Jeff gave him a firm warning. 'This isn't the time. If you've got something to say to me, let's pick a time during the week, and we can sort it out. This is Rob's night, so back off.'

'Well said, sir,' Robert acknowledged, although somewhat excited at seeing a potential fight break out.

Out of the corner of his eye, the handsome pretender glimpsed Bart Dyson, who had appeared from nowhere and was overseeing the developing fracas like a security guard. Jeff wondered how much their eminent host had seen and what he would make of it. He imagined the star forward to have a long history with the father of modern day Australian sport, and he had also been courting the big man's daughter for a few months. There could well be some loyalty between the pair which might easily affect the older man's eyesight.

Keller wasn't finished however, unaware of the Olympian's arrival. He pushed the birthday boy roughly to one side and focussed on the long-haired nineteen-year-old, who quite clearly was not for admitting defeat, as most people would in front of the tanked-up thug.

'Piss off, Rob. I don't know who you are to tell me to lay off, pretty boy. You better get out of her life and leave her to me, or you'll be heading back to Sydney with a fractured skull, you fucker.'

He lunged forward and took another swing, this time aiming for his adversary's head but missing by a few inches. Jeff scoffed subtly and took a step closer, confident in his reflexes against the clumsy oaf.

'Mate, Lynn's the only one who can decide who she goes out with. You've had your time, and I'll probably not be long after you, so leave it alone, eh?'

Bart stood by, watching intently, with his arms folded across his chest. He was keen to avoid a scene but also interested to see how his daughter's new man would handle himself against the hapless brute, Keller. For his part, Jeff was thankful his dream girl wasn't around to witness them sparring over her.

Another slew of choice words came tumbling out of Dean's mouth, his behaviour rapidly spiralling out of control. He lunged once again, threatening the stylish student with a clenched fist.

'Get out of that slut's life and teach her a lesson. It's one bloke at a time, and that's one me.'

Smiling at the jumbled phrase, the experienced street brawler continued to move forwards until their faces were less than thirty centimetres apart and raised his voice a little too.

'That's enough, mate,' he said sternly, raising his hand. 'You can call me all the names you want, but you DON'T talk about Lynn that way. It's her choice. She chose me for tonight. End of story.'

The aggressor swung his right fist at his vocal opponent once more. His reaction time not yet impeded by too much alcohol, Jeff caught the strong wrist and pushed it down. There were some advantages to being a southpaw after all, he thought. Dean went to punch him again, and this time the younger man chose to walk away.

'Come on then,' he beckoned. 'Outside. You're embarrassing everyone, mate.'

Bart Dyson intervened. He avoided eye contact with his daughter's boyfriend altogether and rested a heavy, persuasive hand on the footballer's left shoulder.

'Mister Keller, come with me, please.'

The impressive man's voice was loud and authoritative, and Dean instantly registered who was talking to him. His bravado dissipated, and he seemed to shrink in size at the older man's words. Big D was like a god to him, and even through his drunken anger, he was humiliated. Like a scolded dog, the footballer followed Lynn's father out of the room.

The rest of the group watched the host and their forlorn friend disappear into the fresh air. Out of other guests' earshot, Bart gave the younger man a thorough dressing down, shaking a thick finger menacingly.

'How dare you put on such a show? You should know better, Keller. You do not come to my house, drink my beer, embarrass my guests and insult my daughter. Understand?'

The footballer was sobering up fast and looked around sheepishly to see if anyone he knew could overhear.

'But, sir,' he began offering excuses. 'What would you have done? That bastard…'

Bart Dyson cut him off. 'That *bastard,*' he stressed, 'is my daughter's guest this weekend. And that makes him my guest too.'

'But you know, sir, *I* was meant to be Lynn's guest at this party,' Dean continued, whining like a child.

'Go home, Keller,' the sporting hero snapped. 'There's a taxi coming for you. It'll take you home. Accept your fate and move on.'

Petulantly, the subdued Richmond player mumbled something under his breath. At any other time, Bart would have demanded he repeat it, but the big man had heard enough. He watched Dean trudge across the courtyard and disappear round the front of the house, before picking out a passing member of the catering staff and stopping him.

'Excuse me, David,' he began, reading the name on the young man's badge. 'Would you mind doing me a favour?'

The youngster stood rigid and nodded. His work instructions hadn't included being asked to do Mister Dyson any special favours.

'Do you know Dean Keller, the Tigers' midfielder?'

David looked confused. 'Yes, sir?'

'I'd be grateful if you could stand at the front door of the house and watch him get into his taxi, and then let me know when he's gone. He's a bit drunk but harmless enough.'

'Yes, sir. I'll do that,' the staff member responded, quite excited, since an element of espionage was more than the local schoolboy's part-time catering job usually entailed.

Back inside, at the party, nobody moved for a few moments. It was as if their host had frozen the frame while he dispatched the villain. It was Natalie, Robert's girlfriend, who brought them all back to life, having returned from the dance floor in search of diversion and another glass of champagne.

'What's going on?' she asked, seeing an array of stunned faces.

'Oh, nothing,' Robert answered. 'Someone got too drunk, so he's been asked to leave. There was a bit of a scene brewing but it's over now.'

'Oh,' the brunette replied, bored already. 'Who's going to get me another drink?'

Bart re-joined the group just at that moment, and the extrovert woman swallowed the last few words of her request. She knew she had probably consumed enough already and was more than a little bit scared of Junior's dad. The huge man shot her a quizzical look but said nothing, turning to the others instead.

'Keller's on his way home.'

It was Jeff who was first to thank the man of the house, with the rest quickly following suit. Lynn's father walked up to the bar, signalling for the Sydneysider to follow him. They stood next to a middle-aged, distinguished gentleman whom the visitor had noticed there earlier, minding his own business with a scotch whisky on ice.

'Angus,' Dyson said, shaking his hand. 'How are you doing? Enjoying the evening, I hope.'

'I am, Bart. I am,' he chuckled. 'And you are too, I see! You're too much of a penny-pincher to hire security, so you have to do it yourself.'

The three men laughed, looking round at the group of long-time friends.

'And who is this young man with the impressive temperament?' Angus asked, as if said young man were not capable of introducing himself.

Surprised, the student wondered if this latest question was truly referring to him. He stayed silent, interested to see how his girlfriend's dad would answer. "Impressive temperament" was indeed a compliment for a seasoned, hot-headed fighter like him, but the arrogant teenager considered it well deserved under the circumstances.

'Angus, this is Jeff,' Bart replied. 'He's my daughter's guest for the weekend.'

'So I gather,' the grey-haired man nodded. 'I haven't met you before, son, have I? Angus Donaldson.'

At last, thought the teenager, offering his hand. One of these stalwarts had actually spoken *to* him instead of across him, which was a good thing. The use of the familial identifier stuck in his craw however, at once habitually condescending and annoyingly welcome, since he had missed out on such terms of endearment from his own father.

'No, sir, you haven't. Jeff Diamond. And this is my first and probably my last Dyson party,' he smiled as the words came out, but deep inside he realised his prediction was a distinct possibility.

'Nonsense,' his host objected, slapping the young man generously on the back.

Jeff was grateful, but didn't give his emotions away. The big man could hardly say anything else in front of a third party. Surreptitiously, he glanced around the huge hall to see if he could spot his dream girl, judging it to be about time they were reunited to enjoy the party together.

Angus continued. 'You did well, son. Not many people would've put up with that sort of provocation. Did you hear the foul language he used about your lovely Lynn, Bart?'

'Yes, I did,' the father replied, shaking his head.

'You did a good job not decking him too, by the way, mate,' Angus added to his old friend. 'I'm assuming Lynn and he were an item before this young bloke came along. Am I right?'

Both other men confirmed the assumption in unison and laughed. Bart made a gallant gesture in deference to the pretender.

'Changing of the guard,' the regal gentleman stated. 'I get the impression my little girl won't be my little girl for much longer. It's a crime, mind you. Sixteen. I didn't even know what sex was at sixteen.'

The friendly exchange served to nourish Jeff's flagging confidence, and he shot his girlfriend's famous father a disbelieving look.

'I highly doubt that, sir.'

Bart chuckled and stared at his feet. 'Yes, well. You're probably right.'

Angus was about to say something facetious in reply, but Bart interjected, obviously remembering where he was and to whom he was talking. He had standards to uphold, especially in front of his daughter's long-haired suitor.

'But I never did anything about it, you understand. It wasn't the done thing, not like these days.'

The grey-haired man ordered another scotch for himself and one for Jeff, who accepted willingly. The host declined, however.

'I must get back to work,' he scoffed, and the two men shook hands.

'Thanks for sorting the situation out, Mister Dyson,' the nineteen-year-old offered again for good measure, painting quotation marks in the air around the word "situation" and wondering what had befallen his drunken rival.

'You're welcome. I'm supposed to be co-hosting this party, so must away and find the McLeans. I'll see you later.'

'Certainly,' the student nodded, raising his whisky tumbler to the man of the house.

The party continued in the large function room. Food was passed around by young people carrying trays, and a good time was being had by all whom the amazed man surveyed. His beautiful best friend remained nowhere to be seen however. While Angus rabbited on about some local event from last year, about which he knew nothing, Jeff zoned out and put his recent memories in order. What a bumpy ride this life was turning out to be lately! Who would have thought that after the interesting interlude with *messieurs* Keller and Dyson the teenaged yob from the Stones Road would have ended up drinking at the bar with an Assistant Commissioner of the Victoria Police, who had in fact been standing right behind him during the whole exchange.

The two men talked cricket for a while, until the erstwhile bad boy's curiosity about the inner workings of the police force got the better of him. He managed to engage the seasoned officer on a few sensitive topics around the quest for solving serious crimes and the difficulty in finding credible witnesses. Responding to each hypothetical with unexpected patience and candour, the senior policeman appeared to enjoy the stimulating conversation and let it be known that Jeff had impressed him a great deal with his maturity and understanding of the subject. *Little do you know*, the Sydneysider mused.

From the other end of the room, the band struck up the classic rock'n'roll number, "Jailhouse Rock", which presented the perfect opportunity for the young man to take his leave. Bidding farewell to the high-ranking officer, the eager lover searched the sea of faces for his rose-coloured goddess, finally locating her in among the crowd, and deposited his empty glass on the bar.

Lynn turned round to see her boyfriend almost sprinting towards her, flamboyantly throwing his jacket over the back of a nearby chair and loosening his tie. She too excused herself gladly from the ladies with whom she and her mother had been talking, instantly transported to heaven by the gallant man's sweeping approach.

'Come on. Let's dance!'

Jeff grabbed her outstretched hand, and they sped over to the dance floor on a cushion of ecstasy. Again the waters parted for the celebrity and her dashing partner, who marvelled at how surreal it was to be dancing with Lynn Dyson in the midst of Melbourne's *glitterati*.

'You wouldn't believe what's just happened to me,' he whispered in her ear as their heads met. 'Tell ya later. I need to let off some steam. Just follow me.'

The expert dancer whisked his lady through a string of jive and rock'n'roll moves and swung her in circles until nearly all the other dancers had stopped to watch. The two were as one, moving freely and enjoying being immersed in sensuous physical activity. Lynn surrendered to his lead, responding to each flick of the wrist and nudge of the thigh transmitted from leader to partner, almost devoid of the need for verbal instructions. There seemed to be no end to this man's creativity as they covered the whole dance floor, and the couple hardly noticed the band had segued into "Rock Around The Clock".

'When does it end?' Lynn remarked to her handsome stranger, out of breath.

Everyone was clapping from the sidelines when the second song came to a close, and the dancers joined in to thank their audience. They were both panting really hard but had been delivered a huge endorphin high, hugging each other and bowing comically to the appreciative crowd.

'You're not only a great lover and a great songwriter,' the spellbound teenager gushed as they wove their way to a table at the side of the room. 'How did you learn to dance like that?'

Jeff squeezed her hand and leaned forward to kiss her on the lips, only to be interrupted by a couple of Robert's young cousins, who rushed up to the dancers, squealing in delight. The sixteen-year-old role model was gracious with the girls, giving them an autograph each, and they went away completely elated.

'Let's go outside,' her boyfriend suggested. 'I need to have you to myself for a few minutes.'

The pair left the table and made for the nearest door. The night air was cool but refreshing after their exertion, and there were quite a few people gathered outside, smoking. The addict sucked in some second-hand smoke and ushered Lynn through to a quieter spot near the house.

'I'm so impressed by how well you can dance,' the beaming celebrity told him. 'I thought you were good the last time, but that was just brilliant! Where did you learn to dance like that?'

The tall, striking enigma chuckled, leaning against the wall and inviting her to cuddle into his body. 'That's what comes from being mates with a boy with two sisters. Gerry and the girls were given ballroom dancing lessons, and I was drafted in to make up the numbers. I didn't mind though. It was good fun, once we all got over ourselves.'

Lynn kissed her gorgeous man, relishing the force of his strong arms around her. Excited by the whole evening, she chatted away without a care, and the tired student absorbed it all like a sponge. Gradually he felt some more tension leave his shoulders, and he lit a cigarette to help it on its way. Their peace was short-lived however, because Marianna was walking towards them with her arms outstretched.

'There you are!' she called out. 'We've been looking for you two. That was a great show you put on in there.'

Lynn thanked her mother, who had been a professional ballerina in her younger days. It had been she who had convinced Bart to include the arts into the young sportswoman's packed itinerary, noticing a musical talent from an early age.

'Was that rehearsed?' the elegant woman asked.

Her daughter laughed aloud, smiling up at her handsome boyfriend. 'No way! I didn't know what was going to happen next. Jeff just said, "Follow me," so I did!'

The nineteen-year-old found himself explaining the story of the Blake family's ballroom dancing classes once again, much to Marianna's amusement.

'Sounds like something we'd put these kids through too,' she chuckled, before turning to the young musician. 'Are you going to the pool party after this, darling?'

'Yes, Mum. Is that OK?'

'Yes, alright,' her mother replied. 'As long as Jeff's there with you, and you don't go too mad on the champagne.'

The guest said nothing, more than happy to take responsibility for his dream girl for the rest of the night. In fact, he couldn't wait until her parents were out of the picture and they could relax. Nevertheless, Marianna turned to him with a concerned air.

'I know you have my daughter's best interests at heart. I can tell,' she said. 'But please be careful, both of you.'

'Thanks, Marianna. Lynn'll be perfectly safe.'

The watchful mother was pacified but added a final warning, just in case. 'They do tend to get a bit wild in there sometimes. And watch Natalie, Lynn, please. I think she's already had too much.'

'I will, Mum,' the sixteen-year-old affirmed, now becoming a little embarrassed at the amount of mollycoddling to which she was being subjected, in front of her very independent boyfriend. 'We'll all be fine. Really.'

Finally satisfied, the dignified woman clasped her hands together and announced it was time for them all to go back in to the party. Lynn hugged her mother and thanked her again. Jeff was now well aware that, by complete co-incidence, he had shown up at Benloch for his young lover's "rite of passage" weekend. Yet another amazing milestone to have witnessed in this dreamlike, new world of his.

'We'd better go back in too,' the teenager said to her handsome partner. 'Please will you dance with me some more? Except not to such fast ones.'

Jeff threaded his left hand round the back of her head and kissed her smooth brow tenderly. He was beginning to comprehend the strong pull towards freedom which preoccupied the girl of his dreams, watching her being slowly strangled by her youth. Hers was a perfectly normal adolescent complaint, he realised, but one he had never known. How would he have reacted to such restrictions, as such a free spirit himself, had he been born into a family who looked out for each other like most did?

'Sure. I'd love to,' he replied, kissing her. 'It'd be my honour.'

Resisting impishly against Lynn's tugging hand, the statuesque man lit another cigarette and took a long drag on it. His heart was still pumping quite rapidly, and the nicotine hit the spot in an instant. After he had finished, the pair walked back in through the front doors of the reception hall and helped themselves to a jug of cold water, four glasses and just one more whisky for the nineteen-year-old.

'Why four glasses?'

'Just thinking ahead,' Jeff replied, stepping back and letting the beauty in the enticing red dress walk ahead of him.

He spotted two of his fellow RMIT students, one of whom Junior had mentioned earlier, and deposited the drinks on their table. After shaking hands and exchanging pleasantries, he then went to retrieve his jacket, which was still looped over the back of the chair a few tables away, where he had dumped it in his rush to whisk Lynn onto the dance floor. He took off his tie, folded it roughly and inserted it into one of the jacket pockets. He then removed his watch and cufflinks and dropped them into another pocket. Finally, he rolled the cuffs of his sleeves over a couple of times to reveal muscular, hairy forearms.

Unwittingly, Lynn had become transfixed, simply standing and staring at this hypnotic series of sensual moves. Twelve hours' growth on his face made Jeff look even more devastatingly handsome. All her friends, together with a good many older ladies who should have known better, including her mother, had complimented her on her choice of companion. His hair was long, jet black and more than a little messy after the dancing. His hands looked strong and capable, and his shoulders and chest were broad, under what had been a crisp, white shirt at the start of the evening. It was hard to envision a more appealing example of the male species, especially when he gave her one of his disarming smiles or showered her in poetic language.

Aware that his girlfriend was far away in a dream world, the self-assured lover sat down in front of her and waited for the trance to break. She didn't move a muscle, and her gaze didn't waver either. Looking around at their audience, with his long legs splayed out on either side of hers, he inched forward a little.

'Ahem,' he coughed in jest, tugging on her hand. 'Can I help you?'

The others laughed, leaving Lynn embarrassed when she realised that she had been staring in such a star-struck manner. She felt as if her thoughts had been running across her forehead like share prices on the Stock Exchange ticker board and made herself busy by picking up the water jug and filling people's glasses. Jeff thanked her with a sympathetic smile, as she placed a glass in front of him. They were both tired. Reporting today as a big day would have been a substantial understatement.

After a few minutes of idle chit-chat, the sixteen-year-old stood up and excused herself, saying, 'I'll be back in a few minutes.'

The men at the table stood up, with varying degrees of success, and then quickly sat down again. Robert and Junior had joined the group, and they all began to swap an assortment of drunken stories, not including Dean Keller's earlier misadventure. The Sydneysider watched proudly as each male pair of eyes followed his girlfriend's form disappearing into the throng.

'Are you and Lynn joining us for the after-party in the pool?' Junior addressed his sister's boyfriend.

He nodded. 'Yep. That's the plan.'

'Great!' Robert cheered. 'She's looking fantastic, by the way. You lucky bastard. After years of trying to go out with her, we're all really pissed off you've come out of nowhere.'

'I'd rather you didn't talk about my sister that way,' joked the blond sportsman.

Someone whom Jeff didn't yet know piped up, slurring his words. 'So is tonight the night you're going to try and get your leg over?'

'Matt!' Junior smacked the idiot around the scalp playfully, and they watched his drunken head wobble on its shoulders. 'Can we stop talking about this, please?'

The new kid in town shut them all down, in defence of the gorgeous *débutante*'s honour. 'The official line is "No comment." You guys' imaginations are going to make up whatever you want anyway, so go right ahead.'

The young man's ego continued to lap up the apparent adulation until the subject of their lewd conversation returned. The exquisite celebrity sat down on the chair next to him, and he curled a possessive arm around her shoulders. He knew the gesture would not go undetected and rejoiced inwardly at his good fortune. The group carried on talking about nothing in particular, with tiredness and alcohol loosening both their tongues and their inhibitions.

Meanwhile, Natalie was nagging the birthday boy to come and dance again, and he did as he was told after a few half-hearted objections. To keep her friends company, Lynn hauled her very own dancing partner up from his chair too and led him back towards the wooden flooring. The band had finished for the night, leaving the disc jockey now permanently in control. The familiar and evocative strains of "Bridge Over Troubled Water" had started, and Jeff allowed the majestic opening piano chords to spirit him along.

'This one's for you,' his dream girl murmured, as he pulled her close to him.

The man with the tormented soul threw his head back, and as his chest immediately tightened with pent-up emotion, he inhaled noisily to counteract its force. He knew every well-chosen word of the Simon & Garfunkel hit record from the year before and could barely contain his appreciation for the simple gesture. It was beyond his wildest dreams that Lynn Dyson would dedicate this song to him, knowing how much he needed her help. Mister Life-and-Soul felt tears pricking at the back of his eyes and fought to hold them back, concentrating instead on how tightly she was holding him.

He kissed the delicate skin on the side of her face, close to her ear. 'You are absolutely the most beautiful woman who ever lived. Thank you.'

Lynn's smile, in return, was at once intoxicating and calming, and it had taken this moment for the intelligent man to acknowledge how much more seductive it was to dance with someone he loved, even though his senses prompted him that he already knew this well. As the music swirled around, the young couple began to drift away into their own private world. Jeff had his eyes closed, with the heel of his left hand resting against his girlfriend's back, inconspicuously kneading the sensitive area between her shoulder blades, and his right arm hanging loosely by his side. Guiding her only through subtle signals from his hips, every now and again their movement caused his fingers to brush her thigh, sending shivers coursing through her body.

Lynn's hands alighted around his waist, her thumbs and index fingers tucked inside his belt, and her head settled lightly on his collarbone. Both were vividly aware of the current running between them at each touchpoint. She could hear Jeff's heartbeat clearly and could even feel its dull thudding through her ears and temples. Swaying to the slow rhythm while the song reached a crescendo, onlookers could have been forgiven for thinking something beautifully pornographic was taking place.

And inside Jeff's head, this wasn't so far from the truth. He dipped his knees slightly when the drums broke in, and his heart soared when his partner changed gear a split-second later. His mind was half in the moment, savouring the undivided attention of the world's most beautiful woman, and half back at the creek, where they had worshipped each others' bodies in the open air. He could hear Lynn singing along to the well-known song and bent his neck to swallow the words being sent his way by her heart.

'See how they shine. When you need a friend,' the music continued, carried to him by the gifted songstress whose arms now slipped from his waistband to grip his muscular arms while she sang, 'I'm sailing right behind. Like a bridge over troubled water, I will ease your mind.'

Now fully cognisant of each others' existence and temporarily lost to the world, the two teenagers reached independent conclusions that their lives would never be the same again. Invisible magnets drew one to the other, intensifying as the days went by. This particular dance was ending though, and subconsciously upon hearing the orchestral strings bringing the song to its conclusion, both dancers drifted back to Earth for the last few bars, slowing to a virtual standstill while the music faded to silence. They could feel everyone's eyes on them, yet neither cared at all.

A guest on the far side of the dance floor broke into spontaneous applause, and a small number of others followed suit. It quickly subsided however, the enthusiasts who assumed the couple had intended to put on another show now embarrassed for having invaded their privacy. Slowly, the chatter picked up again, and Jeff steered his partner back towards the table on which they had left their drinks, where the group around them had swelled to around twenty young adults, all sensing the main party was about to come to an end.

Natalie for one, high on champagne, was not ready for the dancing to finish and entered into furious negotiations with the disc jockey. She yelled over everyone's conversations, desperate to get her friends' attention.

'What's a good rock'n'roll song, someone? Let's keep dancing! Come on. What's a good rock'n'roll song, you guys?'

The exhausted dancer looked at his girlfriend as if to say, "Could you do it again?" Her face told him, "No, but we'll have to." Smiling, he exhaled through flared nostrils and shook his head in consternation, before yelling out a suggestion for the excitable brunette.

'How about CCR's "Travelin' Band"?'

The birthday boy's gregarious girlfriend jumped up and down with glee, and Jeff's choice met with general approval. The disc jockey obliged by searching through his record collection, and after a few minutes, he pulled out a long-player and cued the track.

'Come on, everyone!' Natalie shouted. 'Let's rock!'

She ran up to Lynn and Jeff and grabbed their hands.

'Come on, guys, please! Rob, come on!'

The in-demand pair walked slowly onto the dance floor, hand-in-hand, to a much more enthusiastic round of applause this time and egged on by Lynn's friends.

'What are we going to do?'

'I'm fucked if I know,' her boyfriend whispered, pretending to wilt and buckle at the knees. 'If I try half the stuff we did earlier, I'll bring us both down.'

'Me too,' the young woman agreed.

'OK. ¡Vamanos!' Jeff announced, loud enough to convince himself that it was a good idea.

The opening bars of John Fogerty's hit from nineteen-seventy rang out, and the couple made themselves ready. Racking his brains for a series of moves to go with this rocking tune, Jeff cursed Gerry's mother for her part in turning him into the evening's entertainment. Lynn giggled and shrugged, guessing that the arrogant exhibitionist must secretly be revelling in the attention. She was right, of course.

The expert dancer took his dazzling, red chiffon partner's right hand in his. They took two or three steps, and then he whipped her round, stopping her suddenly on full circle and pushing her back out. After only a few bars, the adrenalin had started to flow again, and they quickly fell into a rhythm.

The young lovers had very little time to look around, but soon gathered that no-one else was dancing. They could see a ring of people around the edge of the dance floor clapping along to the music and, summoning energy from somewhere deep inside, gave it their best shot. Lynn screamed when Jeff grabbed her round the waist and hoisted her high above his head, catching her on the way down and immediately spinning them both around. People from the other end of the room overheard the commotion and migrated *en masse* up to the dance floor. By now, everyone seemed to be involved, cheering with great enthusiasm.

As their faces came close, Lynn grinned at the man she was coming to love so much. She raised flirtatious eyebrows, tempting Jeff to dip in and steal a kiss. His lips barely made contact with hers, but it felt good nonetheless. Feeling every last drop of energy draining from his limbs, he held her hands and raised their arms high above their heads, weaving his partner under his right wing and turning her round to face the same direction as he was. He pulled her in close against his body, then lifted her high up and somehow collected her falling body safely on its return.

He let out a loud groan and shouted. 'Turn it off, for Christ's sake!'

Their audience laughed. With the song almost over, the leader slowed the dance down to half speed. The slender beauty fell into his arms, and he pretended to collapse under the strain. In truth, they were both happy to put on an exhibition, emitting a huge sigh of relief when applause erupted around them.

Natalie ran up to hug them. 'Hey! That was amazing! Thanks so much. You guys are so amazing!'

Bart and Marianna Dyson, along with several other older guests, had also heard the whooping and cheering above the music and had arrived to watch the spectacle. The former ballerina watched their daughter and her new boyfriend in the midst of the adoring crowd. Happiness was written all over Lynn's face, and her mother realised this was a very special time for her. She remembered her own first love and its all-consuming effect. One of her friends had mentioned how good the young couple looked together, and she had to agree.

Now safely off the dance floor and having recovered their balance, Jeff divided the remaining water from the jug into their two glasses and gave one to his breathless partner. Winking at her, he raised his glass in a toast, and she gave a demure curtsey in return. His chest was still rising visibly too, trying to take in as much oxygen as the air would surrender. The youngsters sat down side-by-side and shut everyone else out of their private exchange. The handsome stranger straightened Lynn's hair with his right hand and flicked his own away from his face with his left, remarking on how wet it was. The sixteen-year-old tousled it up again, telling him how sexy he looked.

Smiling, Jeff dipped the index finger of his left hand into his glass and wrote the letters "L", "O", "V" and "E" on the table cloth. Without speaking, he pointed to Lynn and then dipped his finger into the water again. He drew an arrow from the edge of the table in front of his body to the "L", which of course was no longer visible except to the two of them. He then repeated the same action, drawing his finger down from the "E" to the top edge of the table in front of his beautiful best friend.

She smiled and kissed his right cheek smartly. 'Thank you.'

Then still without uttering a word, the young woman took a turn to dip her finger into the water and drew an arrow from her side to the "E". Jeff feigned confusion. He pointed at each of her breasts in turn to discover the origin of her message, and she rapped his knuckles playfully. She then drew another line pointing towards where the word "LOVE" had been written.

Jeff shrugged in confusion again. He mouthed "EVOL?" and frowned, dragging his finger from right to left across the imaginary word. Lynn laughed out loud and began to draw another arrow from her edge of the table all the way to the "L". Now Jeff was on his feet and pushing her leftwards to swap chairs, but the blonde bombshell refused to move. In the end, he gave up and sat back down again, leaning back and toasting the beautiful teenager with his almost empty glass of water, most of which had been slopped out onto the tablecloth.

Blissfully unaware of anything or anyone else, the student reached his right arm lovingly across his girlfriend's back, and she leaned into him until their shoulders touched. His hand slid across to the centre, in the gap between her shoulder blades, and he ran his index finger lazily up and down, feeling her tremble at his touch every time it skipped over the edge of her dress and onto bare skin.

Becoming aroused, the hot-blooded male kissed her hair and whispered into her left ear. 'I love you, Lynn Dyson.'

'I love you too, Jeff Diamond,' the delirious sixteen-year-old replied. 'So much. I'm having the best night of my life.'

Lynn's father and mother had observed this whole, beautiful scene from their nearby vantage point and felt very happy for their hardworking second child. This boy was clearly besotted with her, and she appeared to be responding in kind. It reminded them of their own romance, well over twenty years ago, and Bart put his arm around his wife. The mood was infectious.

It was now after midnight, and many guests were beginning to drift away from the party, bidding their hosts and the birthday boy goodbye. The last of the queue filed past, until only about fifteen people remained at the tables and a few more at the bar.

Robert slapped Junior on the back. 'Party time!' he proclaimed, clapping his hands.

'Good idea,' agreed the eldest Dyson sibling, looking at his watch. 'I'll go and open up. Let's say fifteen minutes to get ready?'

The group of youngsters stood up together and made its way to the doors, with the catering staff taking this as their signal to move in to clear the tables and break them down. Jeff picked up his jacket and threw it over his left shoulder. He took Lynn's hand, and they started back through the courtyard.

'You go on ahead,' he suggested. 'I'm going to have a ciggie.'

'OK. See you in a minute.'

The overwhelmed visitor watched his dream girl intently as she walked into the house with her friends and family, still having difficulty believing where he was. He stood in the warm night air and lit a cigarette, inhaling a long breath and sending a jet of smoke up into the sky. The stars were out, but there was no moon. The lights in the courtyard were bright and they lit up the house beautifully.

The Dysons, the McLeans and a few other, more mature partygoers came out of the reception centre a few minutes later, chatting noisily after a long evening of eating and drinking. These must be the people to whom Lynn's mother had referred when she had let on that there would be no vacancies at the Benloch mansion tonight.

'Goodnight, Jeff,' Marianna turned, as the group passed him.

'G'night,' he called back. 'Thanks for a great party.'

Bart raised his arm in acknowledgement, ushering his wife through into the house. The young pretender wondered if the sophisticated lady had been informed of the Dean Keller incident yet. At least he wouldn't have to contend with Lynn's ex at the pool party, where Jeff presumed the alcohol would flow even more freely. Cigarette finished, he made his way to the doors too, only to find Junior running up to him from the direction of the gymnasium.

'Hey, Jeff!' he yelled. 'Can you ask Lynn if she can lend Vanessa a swimsuit, please? I'll come up and get it in a minute.'

'Sure,' the student agreed, perplexed.

'Thanks,' the sportsman replied, and quickly darted away again.

Vanessa? Who was Vanessa? The newcomer had spent a good part of the evening with Lynn's brother, and he hadn't had a woman in tow. This bloke worked fast, he mused.

After-Party

Lynn's bedroom door had been left open for the laggard smoker, and its gleeful occupant was already changed into her bikini, over which she had thrown an almost see-through sundress. Immediately enslaved by the arresting vista, Jeff grabbed her and spun her round in a circle.

'Swim's cancelled,' he joked. 'You're staying here with me.'

'Oh, no, I'm not!'

The fierce teenager was deadly serious. It was the first time she had been allowed to play with the big kids, so she wasn't going to miss out for anything; not even for her passionate dancing sensation. Just in time, and now with other, much more distracting things on his mind, Jeff remembered the question he had promised to ask on behalf of Junior's mystery girlfriend.

'Oh, yeah! Junior asked me if Vanessa could borrow some swimmers from you.'

'Oh, OK,' his girlfriend replied. 'I didn't even see her tonight. She's in the Australian Ballet. She must have been dancing tonight and only just got here.'

Mystery solved. 'Right! That explains it. I hadn't seen him with anyone all night, and now he's suddenly hooked up. I was impressed!'

'Vanessa's been Junior's friend since they were about ten,' she explained with a smile. 'She's his "sex-toy", as he puts it, or sometimes more crudely than that actually. They're not really going out. They just get together when neither of them's going out with anyone else.'

Jeff nodded, reminded of his own dubious past with Gerry's sisters. 'Very sensible.'

'Why were you impressed?' Lynn enquired, with a glint in her eye. 'Were you put out that my brother was quicker than you at getting hooked up?'

The arrogant nineteen-year-old shrugged. 'No, of course not,' he lied unconvincingly.

The young woman shook her head in resignation, and they headed into the bedroom together. Jeff climbed out of his suit trousers and put on his board-shorts, which had dried to a crisp since the afternoon at the dam. Lynn rifled through a drawer and pulled out two swimsuits, just as there was a knock at the door.

Junior's voice rang out. 'Lynn, can I come in?'

'Yes,' his sister replied, and ran out to meet him with the loan items.

The footballer thanked her and left quickly. Tired but highly-charged, the couple slotted their bare feet into thongs and made their way downstairs, back out through the door, past the garages, across the courtyard and into the large building they had passed on first arriving, more than twelve hours ago. The lights were very bright inside the gym', and Jeff's eyes took a moment to adjust, so that he could take in the scene. The space was enormous, with several, multi-purpose court markings painted on polished wooden floorboards, a huge weights room and some exercise bicycles, rowing machines and treadmills in a separate room with large windows and a mirrored wall.

Beyond all this, they came to a set of glass doors which were completely covered in steamy condensation, and the teenagers could hear a cacophony of music, animated voices and splashing sounds as they came closer. Jeff extended his arm around Lynn's head and pushed the door open ahead of her. The pool area was equally large, with a Jacuzzi against the left-hand wall and a fully-equipped bar, behind which stood Robert, mixing cocktails.

'This is so bloody good,' Jeff said to his girlfriend, whistling his appreciation.

She nodded innocently. 'I've waited ages to be allowed to go to one of these parties.'

A full-sized competition swimming pool stretched away to the right, with tiered rows of bleachers on either side. The roof was high, and the main lights were off. Instead, the area was softly lit with a range of different coloured lights above and below the water line. The boy from the western suburbs marvelled at the luxury facility. He had never seen anything like it. A rough semi-circle of plastic chairs had been set out in front of the bar where a few of their friends were sitting and drinking. Another half-dozen people were in the pool, either swimming back and forth or simply messing around.

Lynn signalled to her guest. 'Drink or swim?'

Natalie was standing at the bar with a plastic champagne flute in her hand. She hadn't changed out of her party dress, although she was looking slightly dishevelled, as if she had tried to undress but had given up. She and her birthday boyfriend had already had a great deal to drink, but for them the night was still young.

'Lynn, want a glass of bubbly?'

'Yes, please.'

'Jeff?' Natalie shouted over, having trouble remaining coherent. 'Do you want a glass of bubbly too?'

'No, thanks,' the confident newcomer declined. 'I don't do shampoo. I'll have a beer, thanks.'

The older woman shrieked. 'Hey, Rob! Did you hear that? He called it shampoo!'

Robert scoffed, clearly not finding the expression nearly as funny as she had. In truth, he was a little peeved at the attention this new bloke was attracting, particularly from his own girlfriend. And even more particularly, on *his* twenty-first...

The interloper helped himself to two tins of beer out of the cooler to which Junior directed him. He emptied the entirety of the first one down his throat in less than five seconds, tossed it casually into the bin and opened the second. From this, seeing the tacit disapproval on the almost sober schoolgirl's face, he took only a couple of big slugs before putting the can down again, feeling guilty for succumbing to his usual vices in such a rarefied atmosphere.

'C'mon,' he winked, lifting Lynn's glass out of her hand and placing it on one of the tables next to the bar.

The couple kicked off their thongs and removed their outer clothing, ran towards the water and jumped straight in. It was much warmer than the creek that had frozen them earlier. After a long, underwater embrace, from which they came up laughing and gasping for air, Jeff ducked back down beneath the surface and pushed himself off the wall. He swam off to the other end of the pool in a leisurely freestyle, while the sixteen-year-old went to say hello to the other girls.

'Lynn! So what's the go with the new boy?' asked Louisa, one of the usual crowd. 'Where did you find him? He's such a hunk.'

Catherine, another former Melbourne Academy student, who had been in the year above Lynn and was now taking a year out to enjoy life, joined in the friendly interrogation. The celebrity imagined they must have been gossiping about her and her new boyfriend before the pair had decided to take a dip, feeling very special to be able to speak from first-hand experience at last.

'How long have you been together? You never mentioned him last week when I saw you.'

The famous daughter was excited to tell her story but didn't want to stir up too many personal questions, especially when Jeff was so secretive about his past. She so wanted to spill the beans about everything, but two problems prevented her: first, her new boy would probably think it none of their business; and second, she genuinely had no scuttlebutt to share about the hunk she had invited to Rob's party.

'We've only been going out just over a month,' she dismissed their curiosity. 'I met him at RMIT, when we went for our first MA class there, at the start of term. There's really nothing else to say.'

'Nothing else to say? That's not good enough,' Louisa teased. 'Look at you! You're grinning from ear to ear, and he's all over you. Is he a dancer?'

'Where did you go on your first date?' one of the others interjected.

'To the theatre,' the young woman replied, looking from one to the other and frowning at their barrage of questions. 'No, he's a student. "Streetcar Named Desire". Funnily enough, I was there with him when I had a ticket to go with you guys.'

'You bitch!' Catherine poked the pretty celebrity in the arm. 'You never told us you dumped us for a boy!'

'Sorry.'

Lynn ducked underwater in the hope they would give the inquisition a rest, but these girls were relentless. Out of the corner of her eye, the blonde could see her man swimming at an easy pace, about to reach the far end of the pool. She hoped he couldn't hear the fuss they were making.

'Thanks for the loan,' Vanessa put her two cents in next, pointing to the swimsuit. 'How old?'

She burst out laughing. 'Jeff or the bathers? Nineteen. You're welcome, by the way!'

'Only nineteen?' Louisa shrieked. 'He looks way older. Are you sure?'

'Yes, I'm sure! What does it matter anyway?'

'Has he asked you for sex yet?' Catherine asked bluntly.

Lynn protested. 'I'm not telling you that!'

'Why not?' Louisa wasn't going to give up. 'Just say yes or no.'

Laughing, Catherine goaded, splashing water all over their famous friend. 'Has he asked you for sex yet? You have to tell us.'

Might as well get it out of the way, Lynn thought. What was the big deal anyway? They were all doing it, or at least that was what they would have each other believe. And she definitely did have something substantial to write home about on this subject...

'Yes.'

All the girls shrieked simultaneously. 'Did you say yes?'

'Yes, I said yes.'

An even bigger cry went up.

'When's the big day then? Tonight?'

'Shhh!' Lynn held her hands up in front of her, pretending it was all a big bore. 'That's not a question I'm prepared to answer. Whatever! Let's just enjoy the pool. I don't want to spend the whole time talking about my sex life.'

She sank under the water again and kicked away from the other girls. Jeff had been listening to the screaming from halfway up the pool and had left well alone. However, now that he spied Lynn breaking away from the others, he swam towards the hubbub and picked his dream girl out from among them, sprinting over towards her. From about five metres away, he dived under and grabbed her hips, sending her flying up out of the water.

'Hey!' he gasped, hugging her tightly. 'What was all that girl noise about?'

'Have a guess,' his dream girl huffed.

The young man looked crestfallen. 'Us?'

'They want to know everything, but I didn't tell them anything.'

'Good,' her empathetic companion smiled, inviting her to swim with him to the poolside. 'Keep 'em guessin'.'

Loud music blared out from the bar, and a few people were up dancing on the white tiles, in their bare feet. The lovers looked over at their friends' antics and then back at each other, comically shaking their heads in abject denial. They had had more than enough dancing for one night.

'Let's do a couple of laps and find our drinks,' Lynn suggested.

'OK. Race ya.'

The pair swam back to the wall at the shallow end and pushed off almost at the same time. As Jeff set off up the pool, he could see the streamlined, long-limbed female keeping up with him, stroke for stroke. Why the hell did he challenge Lynn Dyson to a race? He was bound to lose. He was a strong swimmer however, and they turned together at the top and swam back towards the bar end. Neck and neck, he wondered if she was even breathing hard. This had been an exhausting evening, all in all. He put on a final spurt and hit the wall a fraction of a second ahead of her. A very small fraction.

Hauling his heavy body out of the pool, the young man watched the pretty nymph spring from the water effortlessly and stroll towards the table on which they had left their drinks, barely troubled by the exertion. The sexy athlete had let him win, no question. He could live with that. He and his hungry eyes followed the tanned, lithe woman in the lemon bikini to re-join the crowd, and he slumped down into one of the chairs, attempting to convince himself that he could continue looking at her without stimulating an erection.

In the meantime, Lynn diverted towards a pile of towels. Already proving himself wrong, Jeff willed her to pick one up for him, using his best powers of telepathy. She did, of course. But she would have done anyway.

'You're an angel,' the grateful man said, when his caring girlfriend dropped the fluffy, white bundle onto his lap.

He stood up next to her and began to brush the water off his body. He could sense all female eyes in the immediate vicinity glued to his every move, safe in the knowledge that he had his own firmly fixed on the stunning creature standing right next to him, whose steady breaths he could almost feel on his skin. The force field between their two bodies was active again, setting his blood simmering nicely, and thereby reinforcing the necessity of diverting his attention to another subject without delay.

'Drink?' he asked, downing the last couple of mouthfuls of his warm beer.

Lynn looked pensive, clutching her towel to her chest in concentration. This was all such a new experience for the sixteen-year-old, and she was keen to learn as much as possible.

'Mmm... Not champagne. I don't know what to have. Whatever you're having, except if it's beer.'

'*¿La señorita no quiere el champán?*' Jeff raised his voice dramatically, throwing his towel onto a chair and making for the bar. '*¡Madre de Dios!*'

The group had embarked upon a sing-a-long to the radio station playing in the background. A medley of Beatles hits rang out, and with alcohol flowing freely through their veins, everyone soon lost their last remaining inhibitions. As he was mixing the drinks, Jeff surveyed the scene. He was no longer surprised to feel so relaxed, given how well the night had gone, but wondered why he wasn't feeling the effects of his steady alcohol intake, especially when all around him were. He didn't mind at all, but it was strange that he was able to keep such a clear head through all the excitement of this amazing evening. Was it the swim? Perhaps. But then again, perhaps it was just because he was so keen to capitalise on every second of this new chapter in his life? He returned to Lynn with what looked like two large glasses of Coca-Cola.

'Thanks,' the young woman said, taking a sip. 'Oh, wow! That's really nice! What is it?'

The highball cocktail was sweet but with a definite kick, and the flavour hit the taste buds all around her mouth. She took another elegant sip and grinned broadly at her enigmatic stranger.

'Is there alcohol in it?'

Jesus! Jeff's raging sex-drive spiked up another notch. That naïve smile could knock him out as well as any drug!

'Certainly is! It's a *Cuba Libre*. Rum and Coke, that's all,' he explained, taking a large mouthful and sitting down in the chair beside his favourite girl. '*¿Buena, no?*'

'*¡Sí, muy buena!*'

Lynn was staring at him again, although not quite so mesmerised this time. There were dozens of minute waterfalls tumbling down his muscular chest, and the hairs that covered his body stuck to his swarthy, Argentinean skin. Her handsome lover had pushed his long, wavy hair back off his face after getting out of the water, but a lock of his fringe had flopped forwards onto his forehead. The blonde reached over and shaped it into a kiss-curl. He played along, turning one corner of his mouth upwards, Elvis Presley style, for a couple of seconds, and then pushed his hair back with a large, strong hand.

'You're like a beautiful black stallion,' his girlfriend whispered so that no-one else could hear.

The object of her undivided attention hinted a slight smile but said nothing, stoked to receive such unsolicited praise. Their powers of non-verbal communication were becoming more and more varied, and also easier and easier to interpret.

'All the others are still colts,' the happy teenager continued the analogy. 'Well, maybe not Junior, but he's my brother, so he doesn't count.'

The chart-topping singer's very own carnal beast leaned over and kissed her open mouth with passionate intent, and it took her breath away. When it was over, he smacked his lips at the sweet taste from her tongue.

'Mmm… *Muy, muy buena,*' he murmured, catching Louisa's envious gaze as it quickly averted.

"Proud Mary" by Creedence Clearwater Revival had been playing for the last few minutes, and Natalie and Catherine were on their feet again, singing hopelessly out of tune. The famous singer looked at her boyfriend and grimaced in mock disgust. Nodding, he held his hand out and beckoned with his eyes for her to come and sit on his lap. Marvin Gaye's "Heard It Through the Grapevine" followed, just as the bikini-clad teenager sat down and put her arms around his shoulders.

They all began to sing at the top of their voices. 'You know a man's not supposed to cry…'

As the song continued, Lynn shifted almost imperceptibly in time with the music on Jeff's lap, the subtlety playing utter havoc with his self-control, as he tried to discern without asking whether she had any clue how irresistible her movements were. Determined to return the favour, his right hand stroked her side, hidden from view. Every now and again, he would let his fingers brush the underside of her breast, feeling her shiver a little at his behest.

'Don't you dare stand up,' he whispered, kissing the back of her neck.

Lynn continued to sing, with merely the tiniest of smirks appearing at the edges of her mouth. She was no longer as naïve as her friends might think, the horny man smiled to himself. The intelligent and sensual starlet was as quick a learner as he was a keen teacher, and the nonchalant lack of eye contact right at this moment set fire to his soul.

'I heard it through the grapevine, not much longer will you be mine. I heard it through the grapevine…'

'And I'm just about to lo-o-o-o-se my mind,' her musical boyfriend joined in theatrically, great anguish on his face.

The blonde star laughed, knowing full well that his agony was genuine. She loved how expressive he was and could feel him hard underneath her. She also felt a distinct tingling sensation building inside, and not so very far away.

'You really taste every word you sing, don't you?' she told him.

The songwriter and would-be rock star hadn't thought about his style this way before and took a moment to evaluate the image, liking it a lot. His libido was urging him to take his woman upstairs, unable to quell the passion with a cigarette in this super-clean environment. They didn't need to hurry, he countered vainly. Simon and Garfunkel's "The Boxer" was up next, and the harmonies sounded pretty good between the duo, both able to recite every word. He hugged her close and kissed her left shoulder, where his chin had been resting, doing his level best to pacify his one-tracked mind.

'You're spiky,' Lynn smiled, her voice at once raspy and childlike.

'Sorry,' Jeff replied, dragging his chin across her shoulder. 'I assume you're referring to my face.'

She ran her glossy, red-painted fingernails across his cheek, before slapping it, once she figured out what he had meant.

'No, I like it.'

Laughing out loud at her disgruntled air, the joker grabbed her hand and pushed it away. He knew the other women would be watching their every move, judging by the excitement earlier in the pool.

'Hey! You've got to stop that. You're driving me crazy,' he warned.

Lynn frowned, blushing slightly. She could feel exactly what he was talking about and gave him a shy grin. 'OK, sorry. I'll leave you alone.'

'Thanks,' her boyfriend sighed, keeping his voice down. 'You're turning me on so much, let me tell you... I couldn't even look at you when you came out of the pool just now. Just the idea of looking at you almost pushed me over the edge.'

The pretty sixteen-year-old kissed his forehead quickly, glowing inside. Again, she had no real idea about the typically male phenomenon he was describing, but remembered the high octane urgency of their first few encounters only too fondly.

With great reluctance, Jeff took his hands off her smooth skin, finished his drink and tried his utmost to focus his mind on what was happening with the others. Most were slowly collapsing in a heap, due to tiredness and excess alcohol consumption. He stared over at the coloured lights underneath the water level and reminded himself again of where he was. Wouldn't Suzanne be green with envy if she could see through his eyes right now?

'Shall we go soon?' he asked his dream girl. 'Can I be mean and take you away from your first pool party yet?'

She nodded and snuck a quick kiss. The Rolling Stones' "Satisfaction" played over the speaker system, prompting a very worse-for-wear birthday boy to grab a nearby mop and use it as a microphone stand. He was serenading Natalie in his own drunken, tuneless way, while the others jeered madly.

'I can't get no satisfaction. I can't get no satisfaction. And I try, and I try...' he sang, waving the long handle wildly.

'You're going to have someone's eye out, Robbo,' Junior shouted.

Taking his responsibilities as host seriously, the bigger D appeared to have stopped drinking and had been quietly supervising everyone else's descent further and further into inebriation. Vanessa was asleep on a pile of towels on the floor, as was Catherine. The new boy smiled at the spectacle.

'He ain't going to be satisfying anybody tonight,' he remarked to his dream girl, who was also wilting.

Anthony, who was within earshot, laughed heartily. 'Ha! Did you hear that, Rob?'

The crooner turned around but couldn't make out who had spoken or what had been said, so he carried on singing.

'Shut up, guys,' Lynn interrupted in a surprisingly stern voice. 'He's having fun. Don't cause trouble.'

'He won't remember anything,' Jeff assured her, although more quietly this time.

The clock on the wall said one-fifteen in the morning. Exhausted, the youngest partygoer smiled at her friends and sighed, now considering it safe to stand up without causing her boyfriend any embarrassment.

'Shall we make a move?' she asked.

'Yes, ma'am!' the handsome stranger answered readily, to anyone who cared to listen. 'There's only so much time a man can sit with you on his lap. Let's hit the road.'

Natalie perked up on hearing the suggestive comment, watching the chivalrous young buck pick up his girlfriend's dress and drop it carefully over her head.

'Are you leaving?' she asked, seeing them collecting their towels and shoes.

'They're going to have sex,' Robert blurted out. 'Lynn, don't do it. Don't give yourself away.'

Too late, thought Jeff, but he said nothing. Natalie came up to the couple and kissed both of them.

'So, *are* you?' she slurred.

'Goodnight, Nat,' her friend responded, shutting her down with a frustrated smile. 'See you in the morning, everyone.'

The rest of the girls crowded round the couple, kissing each other goodnight and promising to get together to catch up on the latest news before too long. Catherine pointed to Jeff's hand, which was possessively planted on his girlfriend's shoulder.

'You guys are so natural together,' she cooed.

Lynn glanced up at the rugged, unshaven face she loved so much, unable to keep her mouth shut. 'I know. I feel like I've known you forever.'

The tall, sultry nineteen-year-old raised his other hand and placed it firmly on her other shoulder, slowly wheeling the gorgeous blonde around.

'Maybe you have,' he bent down and hissed in her ear.

A huge shiver ran down Lynn's spine, feeling his warm breath against her face. What a delicious thought! The romantic notion obviously struck a chord with the rest of the throng too, because an eerie, pin-dropping silence had descended while time was suspended for a second or two. Very happy with the magic moment he had conjured up for his dream girl in front of her friends, Jeff turned to the menfolk and raised his hand to bid them farewell.

'Enjoy! Cheers, Junior. *Adiós a todos.*'

To a chorus of cheerios, the good-looking couple walked out through the glass doors, running through the sports hall and into the courtyard. The night had chilled down, and the weather had turned quite windy. Bracing themselves against the cold, they sprinted into the house and climbed the back stairs as quietly as they could.

'I'm so tired,' Lynn admitted, groaning as they let themselves into her room. 'I can't believe we only got here at lunchtime. So much has happened. Are you tired too?'

Jeff nodded. 'Yeah. Running on empty. I know what you mean. It's been a wild ride.'

He drew the young woman in close, and they kissed tenderly. His fingers ran along the straps of her sundress, tugging them gently and enlivening the sensitive skin on her shoulders. He exhaled, feeling her lean into him willingly.

'Let's go to bed.'

The student was already in bed when his girlfriend emerged from the bathroom, her hair loose, and her face glowing from having removed her make-up. She was still wearing her sundress, but the bikini was gone from underneath. He greatly appreciated the silhouette of her contours behind the thin fabric as she walked towards him in the lamplight. He pulled back the quilt from her side of the bed, and she began to remove her dress.

'Leave it on, please, angel,' he requested. 'You look incredible. I want to feel you through it.'

The sixteen-year-old flicked off the light and climbed into bed, basking in the satisfaction of being exactly where she wanted to be. Her boyfriend enveloped her in his arms, and they lay still together, spooning. She could feel his rock-hard penis against her buttocks and pushed back onto him. She must have sighed, because there was a guilty tone in his voice.

'Can we? It won't take long, believe me,' he requested, his voice sounding as smooth as dark brown velvet. 'Christ, you turned me on down there. It was all I could do not to wrap you up in the towel and take you right there on the chair.'

'I loved sitting on your lap, hiding you,' the young woman confessed with a giggle. 'I'm so glad you were here for my first pool party. I don't think it would've been half as much fun without you, and feeling so loved in front of all my friends. I'm whacked, but you feel so amazing. I don't want to say no.'

She exhaled and reached her hand round behind her back, taking hold of his erection and fondling his balls, which felt as if they were ready to burst. In return, breathing slowly, Jeff's left hand stroked her breasts and abdomen, gradually making its way towards her waiting vagina. He groaned deep and low, finding her moist and receptive, despite being ready for sleep.

'Thanks, angel. I enjoyed myself just as much. Having you sitting on top of me in there was an unbelievable ego boost. One that's going to make sure you'll get to sleep very soon. So if you want to come, you better tell me now, or we'll have another race on our hands. And this time I'm gonna have to let you win.'

The young star laughed, sending shockwaves through both their bodies, and he pushed his whole length into her and set his fingers to work. The pair made love, in the true meaning of the word, in silence and barely moving, until the elated man kissed the back of her neck and they came together, holding on so tight. He let out a long, slow moan, reverberating through his lover's bones.

'That's so good,' he whispered. 'Selfish though. I'll make it up to you in the morning.'

'Yes, it was good,' she confirmed, breaking free of his unyielding clasp, 'except I do need to breathe! You don't have to make it up to me.'

The young woman was already asleep by the time her boyfriend returned from the *en suite* and climbed back into bed. Not wishing to disturb her, he lay staring at the ceiling, drinking in the silence. She looked so peaceful, and her breathing was slow and almost inaudible. He could just about make out the sounds of the others still partying in the gymnasium and wondered for how long they would make it last. They would all have sore heads in the morning, he smiled, glad he and Lynn had checked out when they had. It occurred to him that this was the first time he had quit a party for a sexual encounter and not returned to take full advantage of the free alcohol. Was he growing up or was it his new friend's influence? Both, he hoped.

The impoverished student from Nowheresville ran through the events of the day once more, fastidiously committing each one to memory. He was anxious not to lose a single second of this amazing experience. His mind dwelled on the altercation with Dean Keller and speculated on the possible ramifications. Assistant Commissioner Donaldson had been complimentary, which comforted him somewhat. He *had* behaved himself. A few years ago he might not have done, but he had learned a lot about controlling anger during his difficult metamorphoses from child into adolescent, and on into adulthood.

Sleep continuing to elude him, Jeff tried to rationalise the stir he was causing simply by being with the young celebrity. He hadn't counted on his presence being such a disturbance to everyone. It clearly didn't worry the star herself, although she appeared to share his aversion to being made the centre of attention so often. She had a great way of dealing with people however, simply brushing invasive comments off with good-humoured circumspection.

Classy, he thought. There was an elegant, aristocratic quality about the whole Dyson family which he was beginning to appreciate and vowed to emulate.

The next thing the weary visitor knew, he was struggling to catch his breath. Gasping for air and shaking violently, he slipped out of bed and crept into the living area. His temperature having shot through the roof, salty, chlorine-tainted sweat ran from his temples and stang his eyes. He opened the balcony door as quietly as possible and stepped outside, glad he hadn't woken his bedfellow. His demons this time had been mostly faceless, but as his heart rate settled, he began to recollect several personalities from the party in their midst: Keller, Robert, Angus.

A few minutes later, beginning to feel the cold, Jeff heard the hinges on the glass doors squeak behind him and became instantly furious. *Fuck this*, he muttered under his breath, turning round to see his precious girlfriend standing there, still wearing her seductive, translucent dress. Her eyes were only partially opened, and she looked like a child.

'Are you OK?'

'Lynn, I'm really sorry. I hate myself for waking you.'

'Don't,' the sweet-natured celebrity countered. 'I didn't hear anything actually. I must've subconsciously felt you go, because I rolled over and knew you weren't there.'

She stood next to him, leaning over the balcony rail and shivering a little also. Jeff moved closer to shelter her from the stiff breeze, putting his arm around her shoulder.

'Can I do anything to help?' she asked with genuine concern, snuggling into his side. 'Wow! You're so warm.'

Jeff was upset as well as angry, frustrated that even the best of days were marred by his nightmares. Why couldn't he just be normal for once? Lynn deserved a peaceful night's rest after her successful sortie into the party scene.

'You are helping,' he told her through gritted teeth. 'The only decent nights' sleep I've had for years have been with you. I'm so effing sick of this though, I've got to tell you.'

The teenager sighed. The thought of regularly missing out on a good night's sleep was hateful, and she felt very sorry for her gorgeous boyfriend, keen to make amends.

'On Wednesday night I managed to stop you dreaming though.'

The incredulous man stood back and fixed her eyes in his. 'What? Did you?'

Lynn continued with a gentle laugh. 'Good! You don't remember. I'm pleased about that, but now I'm sorry I told you. You were trying to shout, in a muffled sort of way, and you were moving around a lot. Breathing really fast and hot, hot, hot... Like now.'

She reached up and wiped the lingering beads of sweat from his brow. The nineteen-year-old's expression hadn't changed, not yet knowing how to react to this revelation. His girlfriend continued regardless.

'So I just sort of nudged you and said, "Wake up" several times, louder and louder. You gulped, and then within a couple of minutes you were sleeping again.'

The naked student, who had switched from glorious to pitiful in the space of an hour, crouched down on his haunches, unable to stand up any longer. His hands clung on to the bars of the railing, and his head was bowed between his arms. He let out a long groan.

'Come back to bed,' Lynn urged. 'You're exhausted.'

'I'm exhausted. You're exhausted,' he sighed in frustration, rising to his full height. 'This is exactly what I didn't want to happen to you.'

The young woman reached for his hand and led him back through the French doors. They slowly walked back into the bedroom, and her erstwhile magnificent lover stood staring at the bed like a frightened toddler, as if it were going to swallow him up and spit him back out again. His head filled with images of himself at fourteen or fifteen years of age, petrified of the fate each night-time was likely to deal him.

'You're gorgeous,' Jeff told her, as they lay together, waiting for the shaking to die down. 'I'm really sorry to wake you like this. Can't say I didn't warn you. And thanks for what you did last week too. It amazes me, but it also gives me hope that one day all this shit'll stop.'

Lynn yawned. 'It's OK. I don't mind. I want to help. I'm not saying this to prise information out of you, but perhaps talking more about it would help?'

'Yeah, maybe…' her mystery man sounded sceptical. 'You may be right. I'll take you up on that offer one day.'

'Good,' she said, cuddling into his side.

A few minutes later, they turned away from each other, and the *débutante* pulled the sheet over her shoulder. The confused boy looked across at the sight of Lynn Dyson lying right next to him, eternally grateful for her sympathy. They had spent almost the whole day together, and still she spoke of a desire to help him. This was more than he could have expected but exactly what he had always hoped for. And tomorrow they would wake up together. Or later today, rather. Or, he feared, much sooner than that.

'Enough of the psychobabble,' Jeff replied, his spirits slightly higher. 'Sleep well for what's left of the night.'

'You too,' a drowsy voice agreed. 'Thanks for a great day. I love you.'

'I love you too, and thanks again for everything.'

***

Lynn awoke at around seven-thirty and slid out of bed. When she emerged from the shower, Jeff still hadn't moved. *Excelente*, she thought, remembering her wonderfully grown-up evening with the Catholic Argentinean Polish Jew who presently occupied one side of her bed. Grabbing some clothes and dressing in the living area, she wondered what condition her friends might be in. Her head was slightly fuzzy, but otherwise she felt no ill effects from her big night. She decided to go downstairs to see if there were any further signs of life.

As the barefoot teenager padded across the landing, sounds of conversation, coupled with cutlery and crockery colliding, emanated from her parents' suite, which was situated in the middle of the "H". She knocked on the door and entered.

'Morning!' she greeted whomever was there.

Marianna, Bart and the two younger children were having breakfast with Robert's parents, Joe and Pat.

'Sleep well?' she enquired of the guests.

'Yes, thanks, Lynn,' Pat replied. 'Did you?'

The elder Dyson daughter smiled. 'It was a short night, but yes, thanks. Is anyone else up?'

'If you mean pool people, haven't heard a peep,' her mother answered. 'Junior was planning to put on a barbecue breakfast. You could go and see if he's up yet. What time did you get to sleep?'

'Not sure,' the sixteen-year-old replied honestly. 'We left the pool a bit after one o'clock. The others were all still there, so I don't know what time they finished up.'

'Where's Jeff? Has he gone home?' Anna piped up, pretending she was dancing with her very own handsome prince.

'No. He's still asleep too. I'm going to find Junior.'

'May I go with Lynn, please, Mum?' the youngster asked her parents.

'No, darling. You two've got to do some homework this morning if you want to go shopping this afternoon.'

The little girl seemed satisfied with this compromise, and Lynn took her leave. Before she reached the door, Pat stopped her, hugging her and planting a sloppy kiss on her cheek. Why was everyone treating her differently this weekend? Perhaps it had something to do with how special she felt inside. Was she radiating the extra happiness that now engulfed her?

'We're going to pack now, so we'll come and say goodbye before we go,' Robert's mother told her.

The sixteen-year-old waved from the doorway and was gone.

'Well... She seems to be bearing up well,' Joe said to Bart.

'Hmm...' the grumpy father responded. 'Still doesn't make it any better.'

Pat scoffed at him. 'It was always going to happen one day. She's such a pretty, charming girl. She'll have men crawling all over her from now on. And it's better under your roof, where you can at least keep a bit of an eye on her.'

Marianna agreed. 'Lynn knows what she's doing, and this boy's completely head-over-heels for her. Did you see them dancing last night? If she wasn't so young, you'd think she was playing a part in a romantic movie.'

Bart snorted. 'Porn movie, more like.'

They all laughed, sympathetic to the big man's reticence. His eldest daughter was doing fine, so what did it matter?

The young star didn't find her older brother in his room. From the top of the back stairs, she could hear him and Helen talking in the kitchen, so decided to return to her handsome guest. She had a good deal of homework to do too and would wait for Junior to ring for help, which he invariably did.

There was still no sign of life from the sleeping giant in her childhood bed. Jeff looked fantastic, and the teenager stood watching him lovingly for a few minutes, before spreading her school books out on the desk. It was after eight o'clock. She would work until eight-forty-five and then wake him for breakfast. He would be starving. She was starving.

The man in question woke of his own accord shortly before half past eight. He reached for his watch and checked inside his head for damage. Miraculously there was none. *Nice work*, he said to himself. Unusually positive for first thing in the morning, he was ready for another fun day on the farm. So where was Lynn? The curtains were still drawn, the bathroom door was ajar, and no noise was coming from the shower. Full of energy, he almost sprang out of bed and searched around on the floor, in the dim light, until he found his boxer shorts.

His girlfriend was engrossed in her studies at the desk. Dressed in a short, denim skirt and sleeveless top, and with her hair tied in an untidy ponytail, she looked fresh, relaxed and extremely comfortable in her own skin. Jealous, Jeff walked up behind her and gently put both hands on her shoulders. She didn't jump and sank delightfully back into his large, radiating palms.

'G'day,' he said, kissing the top of her head. 'Working already?'

'Good morning. I was going to wake you in ten minutes. Feel OK?'

The young man squeezed her neck and ran his left hand across her back, first in one direction and then the other. Lynn swung her chair around to look at him. He looked well.

'Yep. I can feel OK, thanks,' he answered, examining his fingertips and touching them on each other. 'Surprisingly hangover-free too.'

Lynn laughed. 'Good. Me too. A bit of a heavy head when I first got up, but I'm OK now. Junior's cooking breakfast on the barbie, according to Mum.'

'Mmm, perfect. I'm ravenous. Or as Gerry's dad would say, I have the nous of a raven.'

The schoolgirl giggled again. 'That's funny. Sounds like something my dad would say too.'

Jeff was on a high after having woken up in Lynn's bed after five hours' sleep. He levered his sexy companion out of her chair effortlessly and hugged her close. His erection pressed against her abdomen, and she looked up into his eyes, almost pleading.

He grinned. 'Sorry. Just ignore it. It'll go away after a while. I'm going for a shower. How does one dress for breakfast *chez vous*?'

The blonde schoolgirl was relieved at his response, but felt guilty for disappointing him too. Adult, control freak games were riddled with doubts and double bluffs. What did he really think about her turning him down? She hoped it wouldn't put him off in any way. She was beginning to wish she could hang around this boy all the time, and the thought scared her a little.

'Thanks. I just don't think I could just now.'

The young man put his hands up in front of him, as if to silence her.

'It's fine, really. You've indulged me enough already this weekend,' he replied, kissing her gently but longingly, instantly regretting his last comment. 'I'm sure I'll soon get another chance to make you scream. You only have a temporary reprieve.'

'No special breakfast dress code,' Lynn answered his question, rolling her eyes at his presumptive tone, 'except we have a "no shoes" rule on Sundays.'

Jeff nodded in approval. 'That I like.'

The telephone rang, just as he disappeared into the bathroom. As predicted, it was Junior.

'I'm going to be putting the meat on the barbie in a few minutes. Are you guys coming down?'

The celebrity assured her brother they were on their way. She continued with her homework, listening to the sound of someone else in her bathroom. It still felt weird to be sharing her private quarters with a male companion. Michelle and other friends had spent weekends at Benloch regularly over the years, but since the beginning of their teens, the girls had always been assigned their own rooms for the night. True sleepovers had become a thing of the past until this weekend.

Jeff reappeared ten minutes later, wearing a tight, black t-shirt with the slogan "BUILT TO LAST" across the front and fresh blue jeans adorned with several abstract creases left by his rapid packing. His hair was damp, shining and combed back, and he had omitted to shave. His feet were bare, as per instructions. Lynn's heart skipped a beat at the tantalising sight, and felt her insides clench invitingly. Her self-confidence growing in leaps and bounds, she felt totally comfortable around this perfect embodiment of manhood. She thought back to her parting comment at the pool party. It was true that she felt as if she had known Jeff Diamond for every bit as long as all the other friends from last night's gathering. Longer, even?

'Wow! You look all scrubbed up. That's an interesting t-shirt.'

'Thought you'd like it,' the self-confident ladies' man smiled, flexing his well-trained muscles. 'It's an aspirational goal. Gerry's older sister got it for me a while ago. It's from a construction equipment firm she was working for.'

The young couple left the room and ran down the back stairs to the kitchen, hearing more voices in the vicinity than Lynn had noticed previously. When they arrived, Marianna was sitting with Louisa and Natalie. Anthony was also at the table but was in danger of slipping off. He was not at all well. Catherine sat at the other end, nearer the hatch, looking none too healthy either.

The Dyson matriarch glanced up at the new arrivals framed in the doorway and felt suddenly very old. The appearance of a boyfriend in Lynn's life had been the subject of much discussion among the older guests at last night's twenty-first birthday party, and her husband had been teased about his reaction to the pretty teenager's precocious coming of age. And if proof were needed at all, here was their daughter coming down to breakfast with a man. Not a boy, but a man.

'Good morning, you two. Feeling alright?'

The handsome guest looked around the room and laughed. 'Thanks. Yes, Marianna. Not like these walking wounded. Tony, what's wrong with you, mate?'

Anthony didn't even lift his head. Natalie and Louisa wished the couple a good morning, with a mixture of curiosity and wonder on their faces, and Catherine briefly looked up and issued a sickly smile. Feeling surprisingly self-satisfied, Lynn strolled over to help herself to two cups of coffee from the filter machine on the dresser, just as Junior came in from the outdoor entertaining area, tongs and a large knife in hand.

'Jeff, how are you?'

'Good, thanks, Junior. You?'

The athletic heir grinned, reading the words on the dark-haired man's t-shirt. 'Are you qualified to wear that? That's a lot to live up to.'

The lean, strong student nodded and shrugged. 'I'm working on it.'

'It's good to have a goal,' Lynn added.

Everyone laughed, and her boyfriend tried to kick her butt but missed. The sixteen-year-old feigned innocent surprise.

'What? That's what you said earlier. Very aspirational,' she refuted, keeping a straight face.

The chatter had quietened down again by the time Bart arrived with the McLean parents. Like yesterday, his presence changed the dynamics of the room, even those with hangovers feeling obliged to perk up a little.

'What's so funny?' the big man enquired.

Marianna pointed at Jeff's t-shirt. 'Your daughter has some keen observations on the slogan,' she explained.

Bart raised his eyebrows at the words written on the new suitor's chest and then at Lynn. Again he was reminded that the young woman had spent the night with a grown man in her bed, yet he played along.

'My dear, give the man a break.'

Those who could bear it laughed some more. Once again the centre of attention, Jeff decided it was time to make himself scarce, so he ducked outside to find Junior and the barbecue. Robert was already sitting with the footballer, under the canopy, also looking decidedly worse for wear. The likeable sportsman was glad of the extra assistance.

'This bloke's useless,' Lynn's older brother joked, pointing menacingly at the poor wretch draped over the table.

An almost empty jug of water was evidence of the birthday boy's attempts to return to full working order. He looked up at the new arrival, squinting in the light even though they were under cover.

'So... Did you get your wicked way?'

The friendly student scoffed. 'You're in no fit state to be talking about that sort of shit.'

'Answer me, you bastard,' Robert insisted, his face turning green from having to concentrate. 'Did you take her virginity away from the rest of us?'

'Get out of here, mate,' the impatient Sydneysider replied, annoyed that he and his dream girl were headline news out here too. 'Let's change the subject, shall we? It's not about you guys or me. If it was taken away from anyone, it was taken from Lynn herself.'

Junior agreed. 'Leave it, Robbo. That's between Lynn and Jeff. And it's my sister you're talking about, remember? I don't really want to hear about it this morning.'

Jeff picked up a set of tongs and started turning sausages, his back to last night's guest of honour. The smell rising from the hotplates was fantastic, and he was indeed very hungry.

'You've pulled up well, mate,' he said to the blond Adonis, amazed to find himself flipping snags with Junior Dyson.

'Not bad,' the footballer acknowledged. 'I was feeling a little seedy first thing, but I'm good to go now. How's Lynn?'

'Great,' the newcomer replied. 'She said the same actually. She'd done an hour of homework before I got up.'

'Ha! Vanessa's still sparko! Hey, Rob?' the chef turned to the queasy one, who was feeling sorry for himself. 'Could you do me a favour?'

'Fuck off.'

'Whatever,' Junior smiled at his sister's new boyfriend, to whom he was warming rapidly.

The first-time visitor grinned back. He felt sorry for the sickly guy, knowing he had yet to earn the right to impose himself on this tight group of friends. He should be grateful they were even talking to him, given the animosity they obviously felt towards the man who had stolen their pretty starlet's virtue.

'Hangovers are bastards,' he said aloud.

Robert flicked a middle finger at him. Jeff shrugged, his sympathy perfunctorily rejected.

'What do you need, mate?' he turned to Junior.

'Can you pick up the 'phone over there and dial sixty-two, please? I need to make sure Vanessa's on her feet.'

Jeff did as he was asked, and a sleepy voice answered after a few rings.

'Vanessa? Hi. It's Jeff. Fine, thanks. You? We're downstairs making breckie. Junior wants to know if you're coming down. OK. Great. See you soon. *Adiós*.'

'All OK?' asked Junior.

The visitor nodded, going back to the barbecue and the delicious aroma.

Robert struggled to his feet. 'Hey, Jeff. I'm sorry, mate. I'm out of order.'

'No worries,' the tall man assured him, picking up a large sausage and waving it under his nose. 'Apology accepted.'

Yesterday's party boy's face turned a greener shade of pale. 'Very funny,' he groaned.

'That's me, mate,' Jeff placed the sausage back on the hot plate and picked up a limp, half-cooked piece of bacon, fluttering it before his eyes again. 'This is more like you.'

'Arsehole,' sneered Robert, this time in jest.

Junior was amused. 'Good one.'

The door from the house swung open, revealing Lynn and Natalie, who were coming out to see how their men were getting on.

'Your mum and dad are leaving,' the brunette imparted.

Heaving himself to his feet, Robert gave the pretty sixteen-year-old a big hug, almost drooling on her and looking like he was ready to dissolve into tears. She pushed him away in disgust.

'Ugh! You look terrible.'

'Why did you do it?'

'Why did I do what?' the celebrity asked, looking concerned. 'What's going on?'

Junior butted in. 'It's OK, Lynn. He's sick as a dog and still pretty drunk. Can you take him inside to sit down, Nat, please? Get some coffee in him or something.'

The older of the two women took her sorry-looking boyfriend inside to say goodbye to his parents. Jeff smiled at his gorgeous lady and explained the situation, trying not to gloat with pride as he told the story.

'He's a sick puppy over you.'

But Lynn remained perplexed. 'What do you mean?'

As usual, her *naïvetée* was refreshing and most appealing to her normally cynical boyfriend.

'The little green man's in love with you, angel. He hates me for what I've done to you.'

'But what have you done to me?'

'Jesus! I'm gutted. You don't even remember?' the handsome, dark-haired lover whined and shook his head in mock exasperation, making Junior laugh out loud once more.

'Earth to Lynn! You're dense today. You see, Jeff, we've been in the same circle of friends all our lives. It's sometimes difficult for this one to tell between "friends who are boys" and "boyfriends". Sis, did you seriously never know wee Robbie had a thing for you?'

The blonde teenager seemed genuinely shocked, looking from her brother to her man and back again. 'Oh, my God! No, I didn't. Well... He did ask me out a few times, but I didn't think he was for real, because of Nat.'

She went over to her smiling boyfriend and took his hand, embarrassed to be having this conversation in front of someone so eminently keepable.

'Sorry about that.'

Jeff chuckled, bending to kiss her pouting lips. 'No need to apologise to me. I've come off best. So far, anyway.'

The sixteen-year-old hugged him. 'So far? What are you talking about? I'm not going to dump you for Rob. God, no!'

Their breakfast was ready, and the threesome filed back into the kitchen with platters piled high and covered with tin foil to retain the heat. Helen had recently arrived, supervising the setting of the table and making sure everything was in order. The two camps, those who were hungry and those who were hung over, sat at opposite ends of the table. One set was quiet and subdued, the other animated and noisy.

Vanessa arrived just in time to eat, to a chorus from the regulars.

'Shoes!'

The graceful ballerina had forgotten the Sunday breakfast rule. Enjoying the camaraderie, Jeff sat back and watched Lynn in her familiar *milieu*. Was it really his business to change all this? At least he was doing his bit to curtail inbreeding in the country's aristocracy.

'What are we all doing this morning?' Junior's long-time bedroom buddy asked of the table.

Everyone looked at each other and shrugged collectively.

'Driving back to the city later, otherwise just hanging around,' Natalie answered for herself and Robert.

'I promised to take Jeff on a tour,' added Lynn. 'He hasn't seen much of the farm yet.'

Yesterday's birthday boy muttered under his breath.

'Pardon?' Junior checked, preparing to shut the petulant man down again if things got nasty.

The good-looking lovers rolled their eyes at each other and then smiled at their synchronicity. It seemed as if anything they said would be pounced upon by someone. The pretty celebrity felt uncomfortable and began to wish they could return to the city as soon as possible, in order to avoid any further scrutiny and speculation about her burgeoning relationship.

Finally, Robert struggled to his feet. 'Let's go, Nat. I want to go home to bed. I don't feel well.'

'You'll throw up in the car,' piped Catherine from the sick end of the table.

'No, I won't.'

After kissing their friends goodbye, Natalie gathered up the pathetic remains of her boyfriend, and they left the kitchen and disappeared back towards the staircase. Helen wandered in again and chuckled at the assembled throng.

'What a bunch of lily-livered constitutions we have here today! I'm going to put another pot of coffee on. Is anyone interested?'

'Yes, please,' Lynn answered brightly. 'Jeff?'

'You bet. That'd be great, Helen. Thanks.'

The newcomer was glad last night's guest of honour had had the good sense to leave. Things were hardly going to improve for the poor bugger here, and he was looking forward to having time on his own with his irresistible tour guide, maybe even going back to yesterday's magical location. Helen put the fresh pot of filtered coffee on the table, and Jeff did the honours for those who wanted some.

Junior returned to their previous topic of conversation. 'Thanks, mate. So when are you heading back to the city?'

'We haven't discussed it, have we?' the tall, dark-haired man answered, looking at his girlfriend. 'I'm entirely flexible.'

Lynn nodded in agreement. 'Yes, you are indeed. Especially on the dance floor!'

They all laughed. The atmosphere had become much more relaxed. Catherine and Anthony were beginning to come out of their stupors and switched chairs to join the sound end of the table.

'So have you had sex then?' Lynn's former school friend blurted out, to the astonishment of the rest of the table.

Surprised to receive such a direct question, Jeff made a handball gesture towards the woman to his left and launched forth a mischievous wink. 'You got yourself into this predicament. Over to you, Miss D.'

'Oh, for goodness' sake!' the sixteen-year-old answered. 'What's this obsession with my sex life?'

Catherine was pleased she had provoked a reaction. 'Because we're dying to know. You look so happy.'

Lynn sighed and gazed at her man, who by the look on his face had chosen to remain adamantly unhelpful. He was trying not to come across as smug but was failing miserably, and his quietly confident demeanour was extremely attractive to the impressionable teenager, who realised she had been backed into a corner.

'OK, then. If you must know, the answer is... Melodramatic pause... Yes!'

Both Vanessa and Catherine screamed. For his part, Jeff feigned innocence, looking up towards the ceiling and denying all involvement.

'That's just too bizarre,' said Junior, unable to believe the girls' overreaction. 'Surely you knew anyway? What's the big deal about getting the confirmation? I just don't understand you females.'

'This is all your fault!' Catherine exclaimed, pointing to the new boy in their midst. 'If you weren't such a spunk, it wouldn't be such a big deal.'

She swallowed her words, embarrassed at having aired her innermost feelings in public. Left with nowhere to go, the man at the end of her accusing finger simply fixed the young woman with a forthright stare and continued to drink his coffee. Arrogance personified, as Lynn was later to commit to her diary! He had been in this situation several times before and knew it didn't make sense either to deny or dispute the obvious facts. Nevertheless, his inner being soared to new heights when he dared to acknowledge his assignment as Lynn Dyson's spunk on this occasion. No other accolade, past or future, would ever compare to this.

'Cat!' the starlet's protective brother was truly astonished. 'This is my sister we're talking about. Let's move on, shall we?'

Helen had been listening in on the conversation from the servery, chuckling to herself in the background. She popped her head through the hatch, waving a small saucepan for effect.

'You kids are terrible! If your mothers could hear you, they'd be ashamed. Some decorum, please. What one does in private should stay private.'

'What happens on tour stays on tour,' echoed the blond sportsman, shaking his head.

'Precisely,' the friendly housekeeper agreed. 'Well said, that man. Conversation closed, please, ladies and gentlemen.'

Suitably reprimanded, the tight-knit group of friends began to talk about other things; such topics as football, shows or movies they had seen recently, whose eighteenths and twenty-firsts were coming up and any other events befitting their status. The interloper reflected on the homely situation from his position on the periphery and let the privileged chatter wash around him. So this was how the upper echelons of society stayed up... It was the Helens of the world who continually reinforced the behaviours and obligations which their social standing demanded. It was a good lesson for everyone, but not many received it, he reckoned.

Once their coffee was finished and the breakfast *débris* had been dispatched, Lynn and Jeff said goodbye to the rest of the guests. Everyone was tired from the previous evening's exigencies and had eventually decided that arranging something to do together was beyond their capabilities this morning. After much kissing and hugging among the close friends, the newest couple was finally alone.

The ecstatic young woman took her boyfriend's hand as they walked along the upstairs corridor. 'I bet you'll be happy to get out of this madhouse!'

'No, not at all. It's great. Although it'll be nice to have a few hours on our own, if only to stop being constantly on the defensive. How do you do it? They just never let up.'

The celebrity laughed in agreement. 'This weekend has been kind of tough, I must admit. I can't believe my virginity is such a big issue.'

'It *is* a big issue! It was a big issue for me when you told me,' Jeff confirmed half seriously and pointed to the slogan on his t-shirt. 'You gave me a hard time that night.'

The suddenly shy teenager smiled. 'I've still got a lot to learn. I know I should understand but I don't really.'

The compassionate nineteen-year-old put his arms around his beautiful conquest, and they stopped in the middle of the corridor. He kissed her so hard that they both ran out of breath.

'I'll explain it, all in good time,' he mocked. 'Don't you worry your pretty head, little lady. Right after I fleece you out of all your worldly goods.'

Back in Lynn's bedroom, they bundled their swimwear and some towels into a bag, grabbed the guitar and headed off to borrow another ute. No sign of S'malo this morning. The younger control freak offered her boyfriend the wheel, but he turned her down.

'You know where you're going. It'll be easier than telling me, "Turn left, turn right" all the way there,' he told her. 'Besides, I want to look out the window, like I'm on holiday.'

They drove through the courtyard and set off in a northerly direction, beyond the reception centre and out past another set of buildings which Lynn described as Farm Management. Jeff had lost count of the number of vehicles on the settlement, wondering idly about the extent of the assets accumulated by the Dyson family. Wouldn't Gerry like to get hold of the Olympian's business! Such a significant cashflow boost would ensure the young executive stayed in his father's good books, fair compensation for the endless parties and business functions he hosted at Blake & Partners' expense.

'That's where Rick Pelten can be found most of the time,' the teenager explained.

After this latest clump of outbuildings came the staff accommodation, the riding school, the stables and a four-hundred metre athletics track, which doubled as a cricket pitch complete with pavilion. They passed paddocks with competition and stud horses, huge numbers of cattle and sheep, and acres and acres of crops, each of which Lynn painstakingly catalogued. The place was enormous, yet nothing excited the tourist more than the prospect of reaching the oasis she had shown him yesterday.

'Can we go back, please?' he begged.

His host shook her head blithely, counting up the nine hours since their last sexual encounter. It didn't surprise her that her insatiable lover was ready for more. And judging by the effect his arrival was having on her friends, her baptism of fire into the world of adult relationships was evidently worthy of greater significance than she had initially given it, in her determination to downplay her own feelings.

'Please?' Jeff implored. 'I won't lay a finger on you. Oh, no. What am I saying? I lied. I can't possibly commit to that. But it'll be great. Honest, gorgeous. I've got more songs to play you.'

'Oh, yeah!' Lynn remembered, instantly more interested. 'I've got one for you too.'

'Then we have to go,' the wannabe rock star declared, slapping the dashboard.

'OK. We'll turn around.'

Obediently, the ute drove back past the house and on down towards the creek. The air temperature was cooler than the previous day's, making swimming in the icy water far less appealing. The lovers sat on the grass and played each other their various compositions, conversation flowing freely. They were totally relaxed in each other's company, and the splendid isolation was perfect medicine after the madness of the last twenty-four hours. They talked about the need to keep their relationship light, Jeff discussed his concerns about achieving success independently, and Lynn countered that her contract meant she could only do certain work on other artists' recordings anyway. It was a "no secrets" discussion, and one that had the potential to continue for hours.

'There's so much I want to tell you,' the handsome man looked up suddenly. 'Like you said last night, I feel like we've always known each other. You have a right to know why I wake you up in the middle of the night.'

'No. Don't,' his girlfriend stopped him. 'I love you and I seriously don't mind if there are things you're not ready to talk about. It's entirely up to you what you tell me. Nothing's going to change how I feel about you.'

The boy from western Sydney wasn't so sure. 'Look, my gorgeous angel, some bad stuff happened in my life that your parents would go spare if they knew about. You just can't say nothing'll change.'

There were tears in his eyes, which he was fighting to prevent her from seeing. Lynn touched his hand, perturbed again at how quickly the sufferer's emotional state switched from high to low.

'Stop, Jeff. Let's leave it and get naked.'

The nineteen-year-old exhaled sharply, and his eyes changed just as quickly from doleful to playful. Mister Life-and-Soul was back, and the famous teenager couldn't help but doubt his sincerity, much as she would prefer not to think about it. Which Jeff was the real one?

'Now you're talking!' he said, lifting the guitar out of the way.

The eager lover gently lowered his playmate to the ground, his lips locked onto hers, and the fascinated woman watched through the narrow space between their bodies to see his penis fill the space in his board-shorts right before her eyes. She wanted him badly too, she realised.

'I love you so much,' he told her, hoping she could still tell he was tasting every word.

She sighed. 'I love you too. I wish it were easier, but I suppose it can't be. We are who we are.'

'Shut up,' Jeff urged, and a lone tear fell from his right eye onto her left cheek, making Lynn jump and thus providing her with the answer she was hoping for.

The black stallion rolled onto his back and pulled his dream girl over on top of him. Their lovemaking was slow, caring and intense. With nothing but nature around them, they were free to do whatever they chose. These were precious moments to be stored away in their memories for the many days and nights they would have to spend apart, once the young athlete embarked on her pre-Olympics training regimen.

As the sun gradually descended in the late afternoon sky, the air began to cool down at the dam. Agile eddies were whipping up the loose, red dust, and dark clouds had formed overhead.

'It's going to rain,' Lynn guessed.

She was lying on her back beside her replete lover, staring upwards at the ominous sight. They had both fallen asleep for a short while, and the wind whistling through the fine branches had woken them. Small leaves from the gum trees were floating down and alighting on their exposed and rapidly-chilling bodies.

'We'd better get back to the house.'

The couple dressed and gathered up their belongings. The first few distended drops of rain started to fall just as they were climbing into the ute, and it was steadily pouring down by the time they reached the garage. They parked next to Jeff's old Ford, which he had almost forgotten was there.

'Hey, my car's clean!'

'Yes. That happens,' Lynn laughed. 'The staff kids clean them for pocket money.'

'Nice, thanks! But who pays them?'

Lynn shrugged. 'I don't know exactly. Whoever's here at the time, I suppose.'

The boy from Canley Vale fell silent for a moment, deep in thought while they walked back through the house. Listening to his girlfriend's happy chatter about teachers she respected and other aspects of school life which came to mind during their casual exchanges, he wondered how she rationalised her exalted position in life with such a simple existence on a working farm.

'You know... I haven't spent a dollar this weekend,' he mused aloud. 'I suppose that's another reason why coming here for you is so important. Money isn't necessary to be happy, is it? In the city, we spend, spend, spend... feeding our insatiable appetites for doing stuff... whereas here it's just the simple life. It's a great model. Your dad's a very clever man.'

Lynn smiled, appreciating her enigmatic stranger's random insights. Their creek-side conversation topics had ranged from politics to history, from classical music to modern art, and from the Russian occupation of Eastern Europe to amusement parks in California. It was enormously satisfying for the young star to find someone so reflective and concerned about the world, and who shared her desire for knowledge.

'He'd like to hear you say that. In fact, it happened more by accident, I think. My grandfather owned this farm originally, so Dad lived here as a boy. It's got a lot bigger since then too, buying up neighbouring land parcels, *et cetera*. Dad's never lived anywhere else on a permanent basis, except when he was in the RAAF. Mum's the one who insists we do "normal" things, like helping in the house and getting a rounded education.'

'Well, they're both clever,' Jeff changed his argument.

Inside his girlfriend's room, they packed up his suit and other items of clothing and left the pile sitting on the couch, before tracking down the people to whom they needed to say goodbye. Marianna had left for the city at lunchtime with the two younger siblings, for their shopping trip and school the next morning. Bart was in the office on yet another international telephone call and therefore could only wave, and Helen was off-duty at this late hour on a Sunday.

'Time to go then,' the nineteen-year-old announced with an air of finality. 'Last one out turns off the lights.'

His companion giggled. 'Yes, it is a bit of an anti-climax.'

After its weekend in the crystal clear country air, the student's old car started first time in the garage, and its owner backed it out onto the gravel. It rolled slowly along the main driveway, down which they had travelled in the ute earlier on his tour, and Jeff looked back at the majestic house in the rear-view mirror. He had spent quality time at the Dyson settlement in Benloch. For how many years had he been dreaming about that?

The gatekeeper opened the huge, double wrought iron gates which marked the main entrance to the property. The rattly, blue Fairlane turned out onto the highway, and the driver increased the radio volume. Neither occupant spoke for several kilometres, savouring their own memories of the preceding thirty-two hours. This had certainly been a weekend of firsts for him, for sure. And they spoke of Lynn as the virgin!

He had enjoyed meaningful discourse with the second highest ranking police officer in the state.

He had swum in a pool with underwater lights.

He had also had sex five times in twenty-four hours, which even for Jeff Diamond, the greatest ever love-god, was a lot.

And stranger still, it was five times with the same woman.

He also wondered, had Lynn's parents been present when the youngsters departed, whether they would have invited him back. He hadn't quite worked Bart out yet, but he liked Marianna. She possessed many of the human traits she had recognised in him and which Lynn had also inherited.

Junior and he could be good mates too, the young man decided, and Sandy was in need of some help. Anna was Anna!

It began to rain again, more heavily than before. The old Ford's windscreen wipers each beat at a slightly different rate, throwing out a syncopated rhythm. Almost immediately, the musician's natural drumming instincts kicked in, and her hands tapped a complementary rhythm on her knees. Turning the radio off, she hummed a made-up melody, and Jeff searched the back of his mind for some poetry that was in need of a tune. Between them, their mobile jam session quickly yielded a song about unsuspecting soul-mates, all of which wove a veritable incantation between the two travellers.

The harmonious duo sang out strong. Their creative outpouring was cathartic, ridding themselves of any last stresses from the weekend and preparing themselves for the week ahead. Lynn quickly learned the songwriter's spontaneous lyrics and added inventive harmonies, the brand new song reprising over and over until they got it right. After about six or seven goes round, Jeff looked across at his beautiful passenger, concerned to find tears rolling down her face.

'Hey, are you OK?' he asked, breaking the spell. 'What's wrong?'

She wiped her eyes and smiled at him. 'Nothing. I can't believe I can be this happy,' she shrugged. 'Being with you makes me so happy, like we belong together. Now I really know I love you.'

The young man was overwhelmed by her emotional response, at once heartened and frightened by the independent energy their relationship could harness. He pulled the car over to the roadside and switched off the wipers, dragging up the handbrake roughly. He was a good driver, but rain on the inside as well as the outside was a recipe for disaster. Plus, there was that searching look in his dream girl's eyes again.

'I want to fix you,' Lynn told him. 'I don't want you to have nightmares anymore. I never imagined what it would be like to have someone sing to you that you're their soul-mate, or to say maybe I've known you forever. I just don't know if I can live up to that.'

The fortunate student held her right hand in both of his, and his blood pressure pounded through his temples. It appeared that a weekend in each other's company had cemented a bond which was going to be difficult to put aside, now that their lives were set to resume their respective singularities over the coming days.

'You are already fixing me, angel,' he insisted. 'Perhaps one day you'll completely fix me. We've got a long way to go, and who knows what's going to happen to either of us? All I know is I love you more than I ever thought I could love you, and that I love how it feels to be loved. You know what? I've never had anyone really listen to me before, or believe in my crazy ideas. You make me very happy too, Lynn. *Muy, muy feliz.*'

Having purged the sudden rush of emotion, the pair recovered their composure, and the Fairlane re-joined the road. The rain on the outside had eased too, and the wipers were downgraded to intermittent. The resultant rhythm wasn't the least bit infectious, and the percussionist passenger pouted her disappointment. She seemed tired. Jeff was too, but it was a pleasant, contented sort of tired, and not the desperate and deprived exhaustion which formed the normal background of his life.

'I don't mind if you want to get some sleep, you know. We've got at least another hour.'

Lynn nodded, then yawned as if on command. 'I feel guilty, but I am sleepy. You have to stay awake, so I should too.'

'Don't worry about me,' the driver told her with a straight face. 'I'll drift off as soon as we hit the open road.'

Looking horrified, the schoolgirl took a couple of seconds to realise he was joking.

'You're so funny,' she said, 'and so interesting and so sexy and so musical and considerate and...'

'Hey!' Jeff stopped her, embarrassed yet stoked by what he was hearing. 'That's enough. You're delirious. Get some sleep.'

Lynn agreed this was a good idea, although she was consumed by a compulsive wish not to miss anything, which she quickly banished as childish.

As if reading her mind, her empathetic boyfriend added, 'I promise to wake you if anything exciting happens.'

But the sixteen-year-old had already begun to drift away, which was fine for the time being. The philosophical introvert had been gradually losing himself inside his own mind, as he was wont to do far too frequently, and felt ashamed that he wasn't paying his gorgeous girlfriend the attention she deserved. Lynn settled down, with her face leaning towards the passenger-side window, and nodded off within a couple of minutes, leaving the driver all but alone.

The young man was disturbed by the profound effect that transporting a sleeping angel in his ageing chariot had on him, as if the "pause" button had been pressed on their relationship. Feeling strangely unsettled, Jeff took stock of the last few days. For the first time in his life, he had opened himself up to someone. Bared his soul... Had it been the right thing to do? Had he given too much away? The thought of Lynn having an insight into his very private world suddenly unnerved him, since he had been completely self-reliant for so long. What would happen if she abused his trust, even unintentionally? He had never taken this chance before.

Gazing sideways at his beautiful co-pilot, the young man's heart melted. Her long, golden hair fell over her shoulders, and her profile was full of youthful innocence and beauty. Her chest rose and fell gently with each breath. What was he worried about? He could take care of himself. Surely it was the celebrity who was taking the bigger chance? She hardly knew him and yet was sleeping soundly in his car, travelling further from home and with no way of contacting her family.

But wait... Was there more to this than he realised? Jeff had first been worrying about his own vulnerability, and now he was more concerned for Lynn's. Perhaps this was the key? The more he analysed the psychology of this scenario, the more he became convinced of its veracity. In the solitude, with the car radio playing and the noise of the engine's monotonous droning, the two teenagers were actually in the same boat. A most unlikely combination, they had found each other.

Was he being excessively romantic? Jeff sighed and dismissed his appetising theory. Lynn Dyson did not need him. However, this weekend they had both shared secrets which nobody else knew. That much was true, and because of this a bond had been formed. A contract sealed at the edge of an oasis, somewhere north of the airport.

Before long, the old Ford was turning into the circular courtyard behind the Dyson Administration building. Its sleepy passenger stretched and invited her man upstairs, but both knew better that they ought to part for a while, after thirty hours of such intensity. Both had work to do and were badly in need of more sleep before the next busy week rolled around. Jeff got out of the car, and they embraced as if they may never see each other again.

The famous schoolgirl waved from the top of the steps, as her boyfriend swung the car out of the driveway and into the narrow lane. It was a bittersweet feeling. This was the first time she had experienced the true power of this peculiar word, instantly finding a perfect appreciation for it.

And back in his parallel world, once the handsome student reached the front door of his apartment, he was just as instantly hit by a familiar wave of uncontrollable anxiety. He glared panic-stricken at the solid, matt black barrier for a good five minutes, and it took him several attempts to bring himself to open it. Once inside, he slammed it shut and breathed a sigh of relief. Everything was normal, as his rational self knew it would be.

His angel hadn't fixed him yet then, he lamented.

Recharging

It was hard for both Lynn and Jeff to leave the excitement of the weekend behind and focus on the routine of the next few days. This coming Friday, the head-over-heels celebrity was due to fly to London to record a televised concert and to participate in a tennis coaching camp which had been set up by her father with the All England Lawn Tennis Association. She was scheduled to be away for just over a week in total, and neither teenager was much looking forward to the separation.

As for the tormented, self-absorbed loner from Sydney's west, it felt good to be able to give his girlfriend something back for her love and respect, and above all for the non-judgmental way in which she had listened to his plight and committed to fixing him. It was now a full seven days since he had taken the first tentative steps towards trusting in his dream girl and provided her with a glimpse into his secret world, and he was surprisingly comfortable with how she had responded so far. Since then, to his delight, his very own superstar had also begun to realise that having someone to confide in was a source of strength rather than weakness. "Stronger Together", she declared, should be their motto.

The pair had spoken by telephone on both Monday and Tuesday evenings, catching up on each other's news and stoking the furnace that was their romance. The young woman had let on to her formidable intellectual that she was worried about the effect her travelling was having on her school work, and he had promised to put some creative thought into ways he could help her catch up with lessons she missed. This was dangerous territory, because he knew he couldn't be seen to cross the line into interfering and risk alienating her parents, and therefore it would necessitate a particularly artful plan of attack.

Sleep had continued to be a scarce commodity in a certain second-floor flat in Richmond. Despite a growing happiness shining from the new windows in Jeff's mind, the nightmares remained every bit as ferocious as before, and the unrelenting physical symptoms persistently took the edge off his euphoria. Money remained a very limited resource too, even after he had picked up some evening bar work and factored in as many extra shifts at the university as he could fit in.

The amazing trip out to Benloch had given the poor boy from New South Wales some valuable insight into the type of lifestyle Lynn and her friends enjoyed, and the student was concerned that he would be unable to keep pace without becoming increasingly parasitic. This was something his pride found difficult to rationalise. Jeff had lived through a similar humiliation with Gerry's family during his adolescent years. Therefore, now approaching his twentieth birthday, he was desperately seeking ways in which he could enhance his self-sufficiency while also showing his gorgeous new partner the good times to which she was entitled. He consoled himself with the fact that her busy schedule shielded him from this dilemma to a certain extent, affording the young star precious little free time to live the high life.

During the long, dark waking periods, the songwriter attempted to analyse his feelings for Lynn as objectively as he could. The last few weeks had dealt up a maelstrom of mixed emotions. Her absences left him feeling empty and aching, and the times they spent together rendered him at once carefree and intense.

It was not the sex. Sex was sex; a physical act which was either good or bad, or somewhere in between. The handsome young man had been there before, across the whole spectrum, more frequently than he cared to remember.

Neither was it the fact that Lynn was famous. He was certain of this too. A brief affair a few years ago with a television news reporter on the outer fringes of celebrity had not affected him anywhere near as deeply as this.

Try as he might, Jeff could not deny the hypothesis which continued to bug him: that he and Lynn had found each other. Why they were so driven to find each other remained a mystery to him, and probably always would, but at least now he understood how the expression "falling in love" had come about. No doubt about it, he had fallen. He had always hoped he would, and the result was a sublime, agonising and also fairly overwhelming state for such an unstable mind.

In reality, the romantic poet had been in the process of falling for a number of years, and now, somewhere between "A Streetcar Named Desire" and his bedroom windowsill, he had hit the ground and was still bouncing.

The demons came to call early on Thursday morning, true to form, attacking him with blades and fists which sunk into their mark's dreaming body like warm knives into butter. He fought back, hurling abuse at them in his sleep, eventually waking himself up with the noise and exertion. He sprang out of bed and straight into the shower, standing under stone cold water until his heart slowed down again.

'Leave me alone!' the student yelled into the air. 'It's not my fault. It's not my fucking fault.'

Jesus! When would this stop? Maybe it would never stop. Why was he still being punished by these monstrous representations of people who were no longer part of his life? All he had done was try to defend his family. Surely they would have behaved the same way if the situation had been reversed. Couldn't anyone see that? And they had won anyway. He had no choice but to live with the scars, so why couldn't they just fuck off and leave him alone to pick up the pieces?

To distract himself onto more pleasant thoughts, Jeff worked on a couple of new songs that were coalescing nicely. Two hours passed in a smoky haze, gently tapping chords out on his small, electric keyboard or strumming the steel-stringed acoustic guitar, scribbling lyrics onto paper as they fell into place. This particular batch of songs was more hard-edged, with driving beats, reflecting his bitter determination to rise above the past and soar on the wings of his newfound support system. Lynn had suggested booking some time in a recording studio with a real, live band, which he was really keen to do but only if he could manage to fund it himself.

At five o'clock, Jeff put on his running gear and left the apartment. Mindful of his promise not to get knocked down by a car in the dark, he stuck to the pathways along the river and made his way down to the Botanic Gardens, across St Kilda Road and through Albert Park, to the Sportsdrome. He assumed the hard-working champion would be attending her regular Thursday morning training session there, so planned to take her by surprise and encourage her to have breakfast with him before school.

Running on tired, aching legs was hard yakka, but the reluctant athlete forced himself to keep going. His increased workload had meant he had been forced to sacrifice a few weights sessions with Gerry, and he could already detect a reduction in the strength and size of his muscles. Having seen Junior Dyson up close at the pool party, the student had noted the many attributes of a dedicated sports body and resigned himself that such aspirations were well out of his reach while his time was necessarily split over so many activities.

A red Datsun Skyline GT-R swept around the corner and into the Sportsdrome car park. Jeff recognised it as the footballer's, and sure enough, out stepped his beautiful best friend and her brother. They were deep in conversation and had not thought to look around for potential breakfast companions waiting on recreation centre walls. He watched with a hunger of a whole different nature as Lynn came closer and closer, dressed in sports clothes and runners and with her hair thrown loosely up into a bun for the morning's workout.

He coughed, causing both Dysons to look up.

'Jeff!' Lynn exclaimed, running up to him. 'What are you doing here?'

The young man leaned forward on the wall to kiss her, dropping off slowly and landing on the ground on weak legs. His antics made her laugh, and he imbibed the positive energy like cool spring water on a hot summer's day.

'*Buenas días.* Just thought I'd swing by to say hello.'

'You look terrible,' Junior observed.

'Cheers, mate,' the student scoffed and turned to his girlfriend to complain. 'Who's he?'

Lynn shrugged and rested her hand on his arm, sending shockwaves through his flagging muscles. Junior was right, she silently agreed. Although still devilishly handsome, with his broad smile and swarthy, Mediterranean complexion, the dark rings around his eyes made them look sunken and his cheekbones seemed to jut out as a result.

'Rough night?'

'Ah, yeah,' Jeff brushed off her concern. 'Nothing a good breakfast won't fix.'

Junior waved and walked on inside the Sportsdrome, leaving his sister in private. Her feelings for this man were plain to see. Once they were alone, Lynn hugged her favourite insomniac.

'Are you alright? You look completely exhausted.'

'I'm OK,' he assured her. 'Don't worry about me. I won't hold you up. I was just wondering if you had time to catch up for breckie before you fly out.'

The celebrity hesitated. 'Breakfast this morning's a bit tight,' she admitted. 'Did you want to come over tonight instead? You look like you could use some sleep.'

The young sportswoman felt torn, excited to be able to spend some extra time with her boyfriend and keen to help him to stock up on some elusive rest. On the other hand however, her parents had made it quite clear that they would take a dim view of visitors staying overnight during the week, given her hectic schedule and training commitments.

Her gorgeous walking zombie knew this too, having done his best to sound simultaneously obedient and sympathetic when his girlfriend's new house rules had been passed on over the telephone. He was under no illusion that one trip to Benloch would count as sufficient status to see him climb the sixteen-year-old's list of sanctioned priorities. Receiving this bonus invitation, he rocked backwards on aching feet, and his eyes lifted skywards in thanks for his saviour's generosity of spirit. She truly was an angel.

'That'd be amazing. Only if you've got time.'

Lynn cuddled into him tightly, sensing she had done a good thing by the tired soul inside an even more tired body, which also felt thinner and didn't seem to have its usual steadfastness. She was filled with sorrow for his situation.

'As long as you don't mind having to watch me pack.'

'I don't mind having to watch you do anything,' the charmer laughed. 'How are you getting to the airport? I could drive you there.'

'OK. Sounds great,' the cheerful schoolgirl agreed. 'Thanks. We'll order *pizza*.'

Jeff was very happy, having secured a far better outcome than he had expected. He pulled the strong, slender frame of his beloved champion closer into him, and they kissed. He noticed she had one eye on the Sportsdrome entrance at all times, as if checking for Barts Senior or Junior.

'Fantastic. You're so good to me.'

'Jeff, I want to see you too, you know. This isn't all selfless on my part.'

'Of course not,' her boyfriend mocked, inviting her to look him over, from top to toe. 'How could you resist spending the night with this glorious physical specimen?'

'Stop it, you idiot!' she chided. 'You just need recharging. You look gorgeous, and I just want to come home with you right now.'

The young man held his hands out to accept her proposition, smiling because he knew it wouldn't happen.

'So what are we waiting for?' he tried half-heartedly.

Lynn put on a sad face. 'I can't. I'd love to, but I really can't.'

'I know, angel. What time?'

'Six, six-thirty? Are you working late?'

Jeff shook his head. 'No. Only 'til six. I'll come straight from there.'

They embraced and kissed passionately while a bunch of early morning swimmers yelled across to their famous friend, whistling to egg the couple on. Lynn squeezed his arm as she turned to enter the Sportsdrome.

'Have a good day. I love you.'

'You too, squared. See you later, you gorgeous thing. Train well.'

The nineteen-year-old watched his compassionate vision of loveliness disappear into the building before tracking homewards. It was not yet six o'clock. Twelve hours to wait. Still, much better than the alternative, for after tonight his beautiful best friend would be out of reach for nine days. He summoned the energy to jog back through the city but ran out of steam crossing the river. He jumped onto a tram heading down Bridge Road.

A very plump lady in the seat in front of him made a snide remark about the fact that he would be unlikely to increase his fitness by riding on the tram. Jeff nodded in tacit agreement, smiling as he imagined his fellow passenger being struck by a bolt of lightning from his guardian angel.

Don't mess with me, lady. I just need recharging.

The dejected man greeted his front door like a long-lost enemy, swearing under his breath as the demons returned right on cue.

'Don't mess with me,' he repeated.

Why did his threatening words sound so ineffectual when battling the monsters inside his head? The self-assured and imposing Pied Piper had no trouble convincing real human beings to do his bidding, and yet the ghosts from his past humiliated him effortlessly, taunting him like a worthless street kid. Didn't they know there was someone special looking after him these days? The shaft of light shining through the keyhole dared him to open the door, and he fought his rebellious mind with the few, remaining drops of dirty fuel sloshing at the bottom of his empty tank.

'For Christ's sake, let me in, you bastards.'

After ten minutes or so, Jeff walked away, cursing how small and downtrodden he felt. He stood on the landing, staring out of the window and becoming angrier and angrier. He fought the overwhelming impulse to kick the door down, an expensive solution to which he had resorted on several occasions over the years. This morning however, he wasn't sure he would even have enough strength to do this, so braced himself once more to enter in the conventional way. Sleep deprivation played tricks with his mind, and he suddenly saw Junior Dyson's face among the usual suspects.

'Fuck off! Don't mix the present with the past,' he begged. 'Don't do this to me.'

Taking a huge breath, the tormented teenager turned the key in the lock and opened the door slowly. He knew from bitter experience that if he were to shut it again without going inside, this would turn out to be a long, extremely tedious day of reproachful self-loathing. *I'm fucking better than that*, he swore again. He swung the door away from him and stepped into the apartment. Screaming female voices rang in his ears, and he quickly slammed the door shut, running into the bedroom to flee the mental movie footage intent on persecuting him in the hallway.

Jeff stared at his bed, longing to be able to fall down onto it and sleep peacefully. Instead, he jumped into the shower and prepared for another day working on the university computers and completing his latest assignments. Fantasising about seeing Lynn later that day brought some welcome optimism, and he leaned against the tiles under the warm water until relief was upon him. He pictured Lynn partaking in a similar act after her training session, before dispelling such erotic thoughts in a fit of Catholic guilt. Nice girls didn't do that sort of thing, but it was an appealing image nevertheless... Expending the extra energy left him dizzy and nauseated, but at least a little less strung out.

Checking his wallet, the undergraduate counted up the various expenses he was likely to incur today. He hoped he would find a free parking space somewhere which wouldn't attract a ticket. He couldn't afford any additional imposts on his finely balanced cashflow.

Jeff was famished, as was normal when overtired, and knew he couldn't last until the evening's *pizza*. He gave himself permission to take a cooked breakfast out of his contingency fund to tide him over. Parking the car in Little Lonsdale Street, he strolled round to "The European" on Spring Street, to read the newspaper and fill his empty stomach before work. The waiter greeted him in flamboyant French, to which the polyglot replied in kind, purposefully leaving the other patrons wondering who he was. It felt empowering to practise being a "someone", putting some of his recently acquired learnings into action.

Breakfast lasted an hour, during which Jeff read nearly all of the day's edition of The Age. Finishing his cigarette and swallowing the last mouthful of strong coffee, the nobody itching to be a somebody walked back to his faithful, old car. It started on the third attempt, and he revved it hard all the way up Rathdowne Street towards RMIT. It needed recharging too.

***

Howard, the oldest of the Dyson Administration security guards, ushered Jeff through the barrier with a cheery smile. The now regular visitor waved back courteously and pressed the lift call button. Looking at his reflection in the mirrored walls of the lift, he examined the dark circles around his eyes. He wondered if reflections could pick up headaches or sore necks and shoulders too. He shook his head, wondering where on Earth such a weird, metaphysical idea had sprung from.

Lynn was waiting in the corridor, holding her apartment door open, still dressed in her school uniform. She was indeed a sight for sore shoulders and sunken eyes. Jeff handed her the bottle of red wine he had brought and followed her in.

'How was the day?' the young woman asked. 'You're looking a bit healthier than earlier.'

'Am I?' he asked, surprised but grateful. 'That's good. My day was long. How about yours?'

The tall man held his arms out towards her, and the slim schoolgirl walked into them. Their bodies attracted each other like magnets, almost involuntarily. They stood locked in a kiss for a long while, both very happy to be alone together again. His erection pressed against her abdomen, instantly bringing back fond memories of their last rendezvous at the creek in the fading sunshine.

'Busy! That about sums it up,' Lynn answered eventually, pulling away. 'I have a suggestion for tonight.'

Jeff sat down on the couch, watching her passing the wine bottle from hand to hand.

'Oh, yeah? What's that? Juggling lessons?'

'No!' she laughed, hiding the bottle behind her back. 'That we have an evening free of artificial stimulants.'

'What?' her boyfriend exclaimed, launching expressive hands into the air. 'You've gotta be joking! I'd never have come if I'd known.'

The sportswoman smiled, believing him to be only semi-serious. Among the research she had been conducting on this strange condition her troubled man described, she had found many references to addictions and substance abuse. Michelle's innocent comments about alcoholism and drug-taking were proving to be distinct possibilities, the better she got to know her mystery man.

'Can you agree to it?'

His host's tone was adamant, and the nineteen-year-old paused, pensive for a moment. It would do him good to refrain from the constant poisoning to which he subjected his vital organs in the name of substitution, and one clean night in Lynn's company would surely not be too hard a stretch.

'It's a great idea,' he responded, pulling a frightened face. 'I hope I can, but I'm not sure. Can't I even sneak a ciggie in the bathroom?'

'No! Just healthy, natural stuff.'

'No *pizza* either? Sex is a natural stimulant, in case you're wondering.'

The secret addict knew he was a basket case, and had assumed Lynn's youth and privileged isolation would preclude her from too accurate an insight into the true depth of his problems. Yet she had divined enough to want to help without judging, and it appeared this successful, whiter-than-white starlet really cared. He so wanted to let her in, even though he wasn't at all used to such openness, and his gut reaction advised him to back away. Seeking to acknowledge her good intentions however, he dropped the humorous banter and attempted to relax.

His precocious girlfriend sat down on the couch beside the nervous guest, obviously determined to sort him out. 'No pressure,' she added, smiling and stroking his thigh. 'I just think it would be good for us to have a healthy evening.'

'For us, or just me?'

'For us,' Lynn reiterated, unable to keep a straight face, seeing his doubting raised eyebrows. 'Really! I'm tired too, and it'll do us both good.'

Jeff shrugged, sufficiently drained to be compliant in the company of the woman he adored. 'Fine by me. I'll try anything, the way I feel today.'

'Great! Thank you,' his girlfriend kissed his cheek, getting up from the couch. 'I'll get the *pizza* menu, and then we can talk.'

'Don't be long,' her boyfriend warned playfully.

The sixteen-year-old returned within a couple of minutes with two glasses of orange juice, a saucer of tablets and the menu. She handed one glass to her patient and transferred the other onto the coffee table. She then counted out four different tablets each.

'Pills?' the eager man joked, holding his left hand out. 'Have I slipped into a parallel universe? I spy artificial stimulants and I like it.'

Ignoring him, Lynn described each of the tablets in turn. They were a mixture of vitamin C, a magnesium-potassium combination for muscle healing and two others that she called electrolytes.

'We'll give each other shocks,' she laughed. 'I've no idea why they're called electrolytes.'

Jeff smiled at her unabashed innocence. 'They're supposed to adhere to cells in the blood and introduce minerals, I think. For rehydration and tissue regeneration. Sounds mighty artificial to me, but I'm not complaining.'

Admiration swam in her bright, blue eyes. 'Is there anything you don't know?'

'Yep,' the student sighed, swallowing all four tablets with a single gulp of juice. 'How to get rid of door phobia and nightmares. Any ideas?'

To his amusement, his morose reply was glossed over. An intuitive therapist was revealing herself tonight, and one who wasn't going to pander to his desolate ramblings. His dream girl was fixing him, little by little and quite systematically, whether she knew it or not. She straddled the stunned man's lap and handed him the menu, taking her own pills one by one in a much more ladylike fashion.

And then, just when the visitor reckoned he had lost the opportunity to feel sorry for himself, his amateur counsellor assumed a hangdog expression. 'That's not good. Are they worse then?'

'Yeah, but let's not talk about it,' her boyfriend changed his tune, feeling particularly strong all of a sudden and running his hands up her thighs, beneath her skirt. 'I want to explore what's under your uniform. It's very sexy.'

'Shut up,' Lynn scolded him. 'That's for later. I want to help you recharge first.'

Jeff felt instantly very guilty. He had misused the escape hatch she had opened for him so masterfully. The cute schoolgirl sitting on his lap had designed the evening with the objective of making him feel better, and he was as usual trying to steal as much selfish pleasure from the situation as he could.

'You're very kind,' he smiled, pulling his hands back and hugging her in close, 'and I'm an arsehole. Sorry, angel. Let's have a beautifully superficial evening, eating *pizza*, drinking juice and watching TV. It'll be good for us. You said so.'

Appreciating his contrition, the happy celebrity laughed, flapping the menu in front of her mystery man's face.

'Aha! I think I've hypnotised *you*, for a change. What are you going to have? I'll ring the order in. Then we can collect it from downstairs. Junior uses this place all the time, so it must be good.'

They were both starving, choosing a variety from the wide selection, and Lynn disappeared to make the telephone call from the bedroom. Her boyfriend turned on the television and began to watch the evening news, but by the time she had placed their order and returned to the couch, he was fast asleep. She stared at him lovingly, wondering what it must be like to be Jeff Diamond. She left him snoozing through the world's recent events and started to pack for her trip.

After about twenty minutes, the telephone rang on the young woman's chest of drawers. She leaped for it, not wanting to disturb the calm mood. Her exhausted guest only stirred when she walked through the apartment, bound for the door.

'Hey. Is that the *pizza* already?' he asked, coming to. 'I'll go. You stay here.'

His determined saviour instructed him not to move, already with money in her hand. Jeff objected, saying he should pay at least half. His host wouldn't have a bar of the argument, so he gave up quite easily, knowing he couldn't afford to pay for their takeaway food anyway.

'Next time,' he insisted.

The sixteen-year-old closed the door behind her, and the sleepy student lay down across the couch again, feeling spoiled and mellow. In just enough time for him to slip back into unconsciousness, she returned with three large boxes.

'This looks like heaps! What did we order?'

Jeff hauled himself off the couch and pitched in to open the boxes. 'One of each, I think. Where's the horse-flavoured one? I could eat that one.'

'Ugh! That's horrible,' Lynn grimaced, slapping his arm. 'Oh, by the way... Do you want to come to Benloch the weekend after I get back?'

Her boyfriend nodded, grappling with a large mouthful and some very stretchy *mozzarella* cheese. A twisted smile spread across his face, and the young woman rejoiced in the way his eyes instantly began to dance again.

'Sure. I'd love to. I'll have to swap some shifts, but shouldn't be a problem. Thanks!'

A second visit to the Dyson homestead, and it didn't sound like there was a special event on this time. The happy man was stoked that the star was these days asking him out, as if it were a forgone conclusion that she wanted to be with him, especially choosing to spend another whole weekend together. This was an even bigger deal, he concluded privately, with three Grand Slam tennis tournaments and the Olympics fast approaching.

'I have to be at the airport at six in the morning,' the celebrity moaned, as they ate and watched television side-by-side. 'I can get a taxi. It's no problem.'

'No. I want to take you,' the young man insisted. 'I like six o'clock in the morning. I'm very familiar with it.'

Lynn giggled again, leaning over until their shoulders touched. 'So am I! I love the way you speak. You speak like you sing.'

The nineteen-year-old looked puzzled. 'Speak like I sing? What do you mean?'

'Like you really mean every word,' the schoolgirl replied, suddenly bashful.

Jeff kissed her greasy lips with his own and dealt her a disarming wink. 'Thanks! That's a nice thing to say. I don't see much point in speaking if you don't mean what you say. I wrote some more songs last night ack-tcher-lee. I've got quite a few for our recording session now. Just have to save up to pay for it.'

At first smiling at his phony bogan accent, the celebrity then frowned thunderously. The pair had spoken at length over the telephone about gaining access to Melbourne Academy's recording studio, and the proud songwriter had refused to make use of the ultra-modern facility without stumping up the required fees.

'Mate!' she exclaimed, summoning her best indomitable Gerry Blake impression. 'Don't be so stupid! You don't have to pay for it. I don't pay for it. It's there for us to use. We'll just have to pay for any other musicians' time, if we need them.'

The independent student shook his determined head. 'I don't want to argue about it now, baby, but there's no "*We'll* just have to pay." *I* shall pay, and *ça y est*! End of story.'

Lynn shrugged. 'OK. *Comme tu veux*, baby.'

They both chuckled. Already feeling much healthier, Jeff jumped up off the couch to refill their glasses.

'Which wine was this?'

'Very funny,' a sarcastic voice answered. 'The one that's open. It's in the fridge, filed under orange juice. Can I have mine diluted, please? Half and half?'

The deprived addict laughed again, rolling his eyes. 'Jesus, Lynn! First you deny me alcohol, and now even the fruit juice is half-strength. What are you doing to me?'

The sixteen-year-old athlete followed him to the kitchenette with the dinner *débris*. 'But don't you feel calmer already? You're acting calmer.'

Her boyfriend took a few seconds to consider his guardian angel's remark. She was right. Barely discernible, but he did feel more relaxed; less jumpy, as Suzanne would have said. Nodding his confirmation to the gorgeous creature, he hugged her and thanked her for caring so much. He was impatient to rip her clothes off but redirected his libido to wait until later. If his dream girl was prepared to go to these lengths to help him out, he and his power-hungry sex-drive should damned well go with the flow.

'Don't let me stop you if you want to get packing,' the young man told her, returning with their drinks.

'Too late. I've almost finished.'

'OK,' he smiled, already guessing the answer to his question. 'When did that happen?'

'While you were asleep.'

'Right! Good. Glad I was so helpful. Let's go to bed then.'

'Already?' the teenager objected. 'It's not even eight o'clock.'

Jeff grinned. 'Well, if you won't let me have a cigarette and there's no more *pizza*, what else is there to do?'

'Just relax,' the persistent woman answered, closing her eyes and leaning on the wall. 'You know, do nothing. Veg' out. Chill.'

Laughing, the handsome visitor fixed her with a vacant stare which was aimed at conveying that he had no idea what she was talking about, not expecting for one moment to be believed.

'*No comprendo, chica. ¿Qué dices?*'

Unable to resist his charms, Lynn stood on tiptoe to kiss his mouth and was instantly snaffled up into his arms.

'What's "relax" in Spanish?' she asked.

'I'm not telling you, because that would mean admitting I knew what you were saying,' the comic evaded, hugging her close. 'OK. Let's watch TV for a while. I have to warn you though, I might get very distracted.'

Jeff had to admit that his gorgeous new friend had created quite the most perfect *bon voyage* tryst before their week apart. No pressure, no hard conversations and plenty of humour. It was without doubt recharging him very quickly. He forced himself to concentrate on the television, which was showing a documentary on the Vietnam conflict. He motioned to Lynn to roll off the cushion temporarily, so that they could both lie longways across the sofa. Propping his head up on his right elbow, he put the other arm round her ribcage and drew her in against his front. It felt very close, and he vowed to stay in the same position for as long as possible. Following her slow and regular breathing pattern, as his teacher instructed, he consciously made an effort to reduce his heart rate accordingly. The meditative technique worked a treat, much to the cynic's surprise.

With the programme's closing credits rolling, Lynn swivelled round onto her back and looked up into the handsome face. She suspected her man had nodded off again, due to the abnormal lack of verbiage behind her. His eyes were closed, and there was a faint smile on his face.

'Are you asleep?'

'*Sí,*' came the response, while his expression remained unchanged. '*Me relajo.*'

'*¡Bueno!*' his girlfriend cheered. 'You look gorgeous.'

Jeff opened his left eye and stole a kiss. 'So do you. Now be quiet and stop disturbing me.'

The schoolgirl sat up. 'I'm sorry. I have to disturb you, because I've had too much orange juice to lie here any longer.'

'Me too,' he confessed, 'but I've been trying to ignore it. Can I have a cigarette while you're gone?'

'No, you can't,' his nubile personal trainer forbade him forcefully, already heading towards the bathroom. 'What about some tea?'

'Woefully poor substitute, nurse, but OK,' the reluctant patient agreed, getting up to put the kettle on. 'I'll make it.'

The couple sat drinking tea on the couch as the clock ticked round to nine-thirty. Jeff yawned, triggering one from his partner too.

'I forgot to tell you my plan,' he smiled, stretching.

'What plan?'

'You know... When I said I'd think about how to help you not fall too far behind with school next week, while you're away...'

Lynn looked interested. 'You don't have to do that. It's my problem.'

'Yes, it is your problem, but you don't have to solve it on your own,' her boyfriend suggested, putting his right arm around her shoulder and hugging her in towards him again. 'Look how much you're helping me. I'd like to do something in return.'

'OK. Thanks. So what is your plan?'

'Well... How about if you give me a list of the subjects and exercises you're supposed to cover in the classes you miss, or I can ring Michelle and get it from her,' the student outlined, 'then I can do some research and find what you need to read, or whatever, so that you can just do the work when you get back. You'd save time searching for source material at least.'

The young sportswoman kissed him. 'I can't ask you to do that for me.'

'Why not?' he replied. 'It'd be interesting. And I wouldn't be putting pen to paper, so whatever you produce'd still be all your own work. You'd still have to learn everything and deduce your own answers. I'd just be giving you some shortcuts as to where to find stuff out.'

Lynn laughed, nodding emphatically. 'I've got a better plan,' she teased. 'Why don't you wear my uniform and go to school as me? No-one would ever know.'

Jeff dug her in the ribs and tickled the temptress mercilessly, making her scream. Taking her empty mug out of her hand, he lay down on top of her and kissed her warm lips.

'That's the dumbest idea I've ever heard, Miss Dyson. Call yourself intelligent? I'm not shaving my legs for any damned cause. Not even your VCE.'

They lay in the same position for a few minutes, and the sixteen-year-old could feel her enigmatic stranger becoming quickly aroused on top of her. She loved how freely he played with her, so keen to make him happy. She hoped it was not her imagination giving her the impression that he was much more content now, after being forced to slow down and leave his dependencies behind.

'Shall we go to bed?' she asked, slipping her hand between their bodies to stroke his erection. 'Something's happening here.'

The hot-blooded man kissed her again, pressing his groin firmly against her hand, as her fingers gripped him.

'Oh, you noticed finally?'

'What do you mean "finally"?' the indignant teenager replied. 'Get up. Let's get naked.'

Never one to pass up such an invitation, the tall student was on his feet in no time flat. It was such a turn-on when his exquisite *protégée* took the initiative, and this whole evening had been such sublime, innocent foreplay.

'Yes, ma'am! Walk this way...'

With only the gentle, flickering light from the television shining through into the bedroom, Jeff slowly removed Lynn's school uniform until she was completely nude in front of him, her tanned skin flawlessly stretched over the most exquisite set of body parts ever to have been constructed. She proceeded to remove his t-shirt by jumping up onto the bed and tugging it over his head, before kneeling in front of him, kissing his chest and stomach while unfastening his pants.

'How are your sore muscles? And your headache?'

The expressive lover lifted a long finger and stroked her lips gently. 'Shhh... I forgot about them. Don't remind me. This is so perfect.'

Seeing her eyes apologising for bringing him back to reality, he took hold of her shoulders and slowly lowered her down onto the mattress. Willing hands grasped his penis, stroking its whole length, while his left hand traced its way from her breasts to her vagina and back again, increasing and lightening the pressure as she responded to each well-timed stimulus. Before long, Lynn's erratic breathing let him know that an orgasm was brimming, and she came almost as soon as he entered her.

'I'm going to miss you so much,' the young beauty told him, as they made love in the blue-white glow. 'I wish you could come with me to London.'

Jeff's tender kisses were perfect counterpoint to the fever burning down below, and he slowly drew them both up and let them both down, time and again. Caught unawares, however, he was quick to withdraw when he heard these last few words. Their theme evoked danger and bliss in the same moment, a sure-fire formula for instant climax.

'Good God, woman! Don't say that kind of thing at moments like these. I need to retain some sort of self-control here.'

The young man lay down beside the teenager's flushed body and regrouped, fighting back his excitement. After a few minutes of gentle caressing, she came again enthusiastically for his fingers, and they lay side-by-side, their breath carnal, just enjoying the feeling, before he showed her in no uncertain terms that he was waiting no longer.

'Tell me you want me to come with you to London,' he pleaded, thrusting inside her. 'Please?'

Lynn kissed his chest and moved against him to maximise the sensation, with her pelvic floor gripping his penis each time he pulled back. He groaned and kissed her lips hard, his insistence commanding her to speak the words.

'I wish you could come with me to London,' she repeated, feeling his back arch above her. 'But it's rainy in London, and it's a long, boring flight.'

Jeff laughed out loud as he tipped over the edge, sinking down heavily onto her in absolute ecstasy. Tears were falling from both pairs of eyes, and their arms grabbed tightly around each others' torsos, with the unpalatable lament of nine days apart playing at full volume through the telepathic airwaves.

'I don't care,' he almost shouted. 'I just want to be with you. Anywhere will do. Siberia, Afghanistan, Ballarat... I don't care.'

The stunning blonde kissed the corner of his left eye, before shifting her partner's weight so that she could do the same on the other side. 'Thanks. When we next go on tour to Siberia, I'll be sure to invite you.'

'This has been such a great night,' her boyfriend sighed. 'You are very good for me. I wish I could pay you back for all the goodness you're feeding into me. It's so much more than I could hope for, and I'm very grateful.'

Lynn put her hand over his mouth. 'Be quiet. I can tell how grateful you are, and I love being with you so much too. It's nice to be needed, actually. It's a new experience for me.'

'I do have one request,' a more sheepish voice spoke to her closed eyes, after a brief pause.

'Oh, yes?'

'Can I *please* have a cigarette before we go to sleep?' he begged, putting his hands together as if in prayer.

The nurse feigned ignorance. 'Why? You've waited all this time. Why do you have to have one?'

'Because I'm weak,' Jeff confessed, knowing full well he should just push through the cravings and leave the expensive habit behind.

The fresh-faced young athlete freed herself from her beseeching boyfriend's long limbs and sat cross-legged on the sheet. Without taking her eyes off him, she reached for the quilt and laid it half over him, while wrapping the rest around her shoulders. He marvelled at how unbelievably cute she looked.

'You are perfect. D'you know that?'

Lynn smiled and deflected the compliment, her mind fixed on the cleansing mission. 'How old were you when you started smoking?'

Jeff shrugged. 'Don't know. Just always have. Five, maybe.'

'Five?' the teenager cried out, incredulous and more than a little saddened. 'That's even younger than I thought! Much younger, in fact. My guess would've been eleven or twelve.'

The young man laughed. It was ridiculously young, now he came to think of it.

'I'm sorry,' he said, feeling guilty. 'I can't go back and change it. I mustn't have smoked many back then. I didn't have any money, so I just used to take them out of my mum's packet. My sister smoked, and all my school friends too, so it was just something everyone did. Have you ever smoked?'

Lynn nodded. 'Yes, I've tried it but I didn't like it. And my dad'd kill me if he knew.'

'What about drinking?' Jeff asked. 'Do they allow you to drink?'

'Not officially,' the celebrity answered gingerly. 'But my parents have served us wine for years. As long as I don't do it in public and not too much, it's OK.'

'What about heroin?' the inquisitor continued, straight-faced.

Lynn burst out laughing, both shocked and amused. 'Heroin? I wouldn't have a clue what to do with it! Do you smoke it or inject it?'

'Any way you want, sweetheart,' he answered in his best Mafia thug accent, ashamed to have even spoken the word. 'I hate the thought of those hard drugs, to be honest. Marijuana's cool. That's a good drug, if there is such a thing.'

His girlfriend kissed him. 'I always get an education when I'm with you. How do you know so much? And how have you done so much? I think you must be twenty-nine, not nineteen.'

The Been There, Done It Kid rolled onto his back, groaning. 'You're onto me. I'm an old man. I'm forty-nine, to be exact.'

'Really? That explains everything. That makes you older than my dad, you cradle-snatcher!'

'Most likely,' the student smiled wryly. 'If I look like him when I'm in my forties, I'll be very pleased.'

'You said you felt older than nineteen when we first met. Do you remember?' Lynn reminded him. 'Why did you say that?'

Jeff turned onto his side and looked into her gorgeously inviting eyes. 'For precisely the reasons you've just mentioned. I know so much and I've done so much. And because my body feels like it's been dragged around the ring like a prize-fighter for a hundred years, especially these last few days.'

'That's terrible,' she said, stroking his face. 'Are you going to be the same next week?'

296

The uncertain confessor slipped off the bed and headed into the bathroom, mostly to avoid this particular line of questioning. Although he longed to talk, he also didn't want to dispel the light-and-easy ambience his dream girl had created this evening.

'Who knows? Probably. Every silver lining has a cloud.'

The young champion listened to the bathroom door closing while her brain processed his last phrase. It was as sad as it was funny, and there had been nothing malicious about the way it had been delivered. No sense of being hard done by. And neither did she detect any resentment from him towards her privileged lifestyle. Envy maybe, but not resentment.

Jeff meant her to laugh at his misfortune, and she did, but with reservation. There she was, jetting off to London, preoccupied by falling behind in a few lessons but otherwise without a care in the world. And here was the world's best boyfriend, struggling for life's bare essentials like money, food, and worst of all, sleep. Lynn didn't quite know how she should respond, hoping he would give her a clue when he returned and took his place beside her.

'You OK?' her handsome bedfellow asked, kissing her lovingly. 'You look deep in thought.'

The celebrity cuddled into him. 'I am. At first I laughed at your comment about the silver lining. It's really funny, and your timing was spot on.'

Her entertainer chuckled. 'D'you like it? I often say it. I'm surprised I'm not already repeating myself. It happens when you're fifty-nine, you know.'

'Fifty-nine now?' the young woman challenged, temporarily suspending her previous train of thought. 'You're ageing alarmingly quickly.'

'Indeed,' he kissed her again. 'By the time you get back from London, I'll be a hundred-and-nineteen.'

'Yikes! You'll be older than Australia itself.'

'True. Federation, anyway. Try that one on the aboriginals, I dare you… Maybe they'll constitute a new public holiday in my honour. The world's fastest ageing man,' the student joked. 'So, are you going to take me up on my offer to help with the schoolwork?'

'Jeff, I'd love to, but it's too much to ask,' Lynn replied. 'The library isn't open in the middle of the night. You're busy enough as it is.'

'Bloody crap, woman! No, I'm not,' he objected, becoming more animated. 'And, you see, if computers were connected in the way they should be, libraries *could* be open in the middle of the night. Once that happens, I won't want to sleep. How's that for ironic? Anyway… Let's see how it goes for this trip and we can re-evaluate upon your return. You might find I'm no help at all, so you'll want to sack me.'

The grateful starlet hugged him. 'OK, thanks. I doubt it! That's wonderful, but you don't have to… I've already got a list of everything I should be covering next week. It's a lot.'

'*Excelente.* I like lots, as you well know. And leave me Michelle's 'phone number, or anyone else who's reliable, so I can get any updates.'

Lynn sat up, remembering her unfinished business. 'Hey! You distracted me from what I was going to talk about.'

'Shall we go to sleep?' Jeff asked, pretending she hadn't uttered a word about his sorry situation. 'We've got to be at the airport before six.'

He received a sharp prod in the stomach from a determined finger. 'Stop it! I wanted to acknowledge the sadness in your comment. Are you going to let me?'

'No,' her boyfriend put his hands over his ears. 'You already did. Lynn, I can't help but know you care. I love it, but it makes me feel unworthy. I'm not accustomed to the attention. And I love you. You don't need to say anything else.'

'That's good,' Lynn was content to take him at his word, 'because I do care and I do love you. I'll try and ring from London, but I'm not sure when I'll be able to, with the time difference and everything. I definitely don't want to wake you up in the only hour's sleep you manage to get.'

The young man kissed her again. 'I'd much rather be woken up by you than by the usual people.'

'Who are the usual people?' she asked, instantly regretting her question. 'Sorry, I shouldn't have said that. Ignore me.'

'It's OK,' the student sighed, rolling over again. 'Look what you've done! I'm more relaxed than you now. I'm even volunteering confidential information. I *will* tell you who they are, or rather who they represent. Let's not bring them to life, please. I just can't tell you yet, if that's alright?'

'That's fine,' Lynn agreed, relieved that she hadn't caused offence. 'Did you have a cigarette after all?'

'Shall we go to sleep?' Jeff changed the subject again, barely stifling a laugh.

'Well done!' his girlfriend nudged his shoulder, sincere in her congratulations. 'You're amazing. You really do love a challenge, don't you?'

'Wait and see what I'm like in the morning,' he threatened. 'I recommend you stay out of my way until I've had one, or you might not like the consequences.'

'OK. Thanks for the warning. And can I make another observation, please, sir?'

'Observation?' the student raised his eyebrows once more. 'How come I suddenly feel like a lab' rat?'

'Oh, no,' she lamented. 'I don't want you to feel like that. Tonight wasn't some clinical experiment for me to see how I can control your smoking and drinking.'

'Wasn't it?'

'No!' Lynn insisted, receiving a tender kiss in forgiveness. 'Well, maybe a bit of curiosity, I s'pose.'

'Go on. What's your observation, doc'?'

The young woman blushed slightly, recalling their intense sexual encounter. 'I don't know if I'm right, but something tells me I am…'

Jeff nodded, circling his left hand, as if he were trying to extract the information from her timid mouth.

'OK. Sorry. It's just that when you asked me to repeat what I'd said about you coming with me to London, when you were about to finish…'

'Finish?' the amused man scoffed. 'That's a very private school way of putting it. Come. Blow. Orgasm. Ejaculate. Take your pick, Miss Scientist.'

Lynn scowled. 'OK, all of the above. Whatever! When you were about to let rip…'

The poet's eyes flashed. 'Hey! That I can go for. Good save.'

'Oh, for God's sake! I wish I'd never started,' the sixteen-year-old moaned. 'You said, "Tell me you want me to come to London, *please*," like you were asking. Any other time, I'm pretty sure you would've put another "tell me" at the end of the sentence, instead of "please". More like a demand.'

The boy from Canley Vale laid his head back onto the pillow and felt his jaws clench in anger, the usual response to being exposed. His eyes stared up at the ceiling, and he forced himself to consider his dream girl's findings as constructive, being sure it was the way they had been intended. Out of the corner of his right eye, he watched her lie down and pull the covers up, probably thinking she had annoyed him again. She had, but it was his ever-unreliable overreaction that was at fault.

'I think you're right,' he replied, after a long pause. 'I can quite easily hear myself yelling, "Tell me" when I'm so hyped up. A night off the drink's made me into a nicer person to be with, you mean?'

Lynn bit her lip without thinking, obviously nervous. 'Sort of. Although I love being with you, regardless. I love your rough edges too. It's hard to explain. You're just different when you're calmer, that's all I'm saying.'

Jeff rolled onto his right side, reached a long arm over and placed a hand on the brave woman's cheek. Her lips immediately puckered up, as if they were about to brush its palm, so he leaned forwards and kissed them tenderly.

'You are right, angel. Alcohol induces aggression. Well-known fact. I know I drink too much, I smoke too much and I swear too often. I promise I'll behave myself around you.'

His caring girlfriend smiled. 'Thank you. It's not a problem, honestly. I'm not trying to force you to behave differently. And whatever the root cause is for why you need so many artificial stimulants, we're only fixing a symptom, aren't we?'

The guilty man nodded, exhaling slowly.

'And until you're ready to share the root cause, we can't work on it,' she continued. 'That's what I was reading in some of those medical journals I found. People find the memories too painful to deal with, so there's no hope of getting rid of the symptoms. I get that, Jeff. I really do. And so tell me to stop if you want, if it's all too invasive. Just be truthful. I won't think badly of you.'

Once again, Lynn found herself battling tears, which she didn't bother to hide, and wiped her eyes childishly with the empty top edge of the quilt cover. The evening's patient lay back, feeling both secure and unmasked at the same time. Where had this gorgeous saviour come from? He could think of no words he would rather hear than these.

'I do feel better for a night off, even though I'm gagging for a cigarette right now. You deserve the best of me, Lynn... what there is of it... and I'll make sure you get it. We can declare your sneaky experiment a success, and it's taught me a lesson too.'

The drowsy teenager slipped her hand out from under the quilt and took hold of his. 'Really? What did it teach you?'

Jeff gave one of his most irresistible half-smiles. 'That you're unusually perceptive for one so young.'

'Wow! High praise indeed,' the young woman accused her pretentious genius. 'Patronising though...'

'And that you know what you want, as much as I do.'

'You know what I want?'

'No, I know what *I* want,' he sneered, knowing full well she was making fun of him. 'But I do know what you want too.'

Lynn sat up, indignant. 'Do you? What do I want?'

'Sleep,' Jeff cocked his head, daring her to dispute him. 'You want us to go to sleep, because we have to be at the airport before six o'clock. Am I right?'

The teenager flopped back down onto the bed, huffing and giggling at being smothered in a loving embrace and showered in kisses. 'Yes, you're right. Again, smart-arse. Let's go to sleep then.'

'*Gracias, gorgeousita. Te amo. Buenas noches.*'

'Sleep well, Jeff. *Te amo* too. Thanks for being here tonight.'

They kissed for a long time before saying goodnight for the final time. The tender sixteen-year-old turned over onto her side and instantly fell asleep, with the knuckles of her sober boyfriend's right hand resting against the small of her back. It was a most intimate feeling, as if they were permanently connected. Staring at the ceiling, he felt her breathing slow to a regular, much deeper rhythm. This was the life he had been seeking all these years; love and laughter with someone who could understand the differences and the similarities between the two. Tiredness overtook the grateful man after a short while. Off to the airport tomorrow. That was something different to do. He had enough petrol to get there and back…

**

As soon as he reached his building, Jeff could hear the piercing cries of a woman upstairs. He ran up the filthy steps two at a time, like he did every day after school, as fast as he could. Turning the handle of the scratched, dark brown door, his imagination already saw the familiar scene which would confront him on the other side.

'Get out of here!' he was shouting. 'Get the fuck out of here!'

The student landed a weedy twelve-year-old's punch into the gut of one of the men, stupefied by the screams in the background. He lashed out again and knocked a knife out of a gloved hand. The other man yelled at him, picked the pearl-handled weapon up off the floor and began to lunge at the boy.

'Fucking Diament kid. *Pozostawiacie teraz*. Get the fuck out of here.'

'*Pozostawiają jej jedyny! Wychodzą tutaj!*'

'Jeff!' Lynn shouted in his ear. 'Jeff, wake up! You're dreaming! Jeff!'

She shook the writhing body violently, no longer worried about how she woke her man out of a nightmare. There was abject horror written all over his face, and it gave her chills. Whatever was he dreaming about? And which language was he speaking? It certainly hadn't been Spanish this time.

'Jeff! Wake up!'

The star watched the sweating, contorting body struggle and listened to a few more emphatic but indistinct phrases, waiting for another opportunity to break the dreamer out of his ordeal. A half-hearted punch came out of the blue, and his long arm lifted and then slumped down onto the mattress. Good, she thought. He was waking up.

'Jeff!' she shouted again. 'You're dreaming. Wake up!'

The wild man beside her let out a horrible growling noise and gasped for air, suddenly sitting bolt upright. His eyes were wide open, but he wasn't seeing his girlfriend's bedroom. Slightly fearful, she continued to shake his straining arm back and forth, now rocking him quite hard.

'Jeff, are you awake?' the young woman yelled, kneeling on the mattress beside him and staring directly into his face.

Receiving no response, the persistent teenager kissed his cheek, which was boiling hot and tasted salty. The unexpected move made the haunted man jump, and his eyes instantly began to refocus, as if he was searching for her.

'I'm here,' Lynn said more quietly, holding on to his right arm as tightly as she could. 'Wake up. You're dreaming. Wake up!'

'Fuck,' he whispered through gritted teeth, gradually returning to the real world. 'I'm sorry. Fucking hell, Lynn. Are you OK?'

The relieved schoolgirl kissed his mouth. 'Yes, I'm fine. Are you? It took a long time to wake you this time. You were swearing a lot.'

Jeff swung his legs off the bed, stood up and shook his limbs to loosen their muscles, which had cramped up solid during the nightmare. Generating a bizarre series of cracks and pops, he rolled his shoulders forwards and backwards and twisted his neck from side to side, gazing into the darkness of the room. Then, feeling dizzy, he almost fell back onto the bed, groaning long and low. It was a plaintive, primitive sound which resonated right in the core of the impressionable celebrity. She said nothing, simply watching his recovery with a mixture of fascination and unease.

'Well, I now know it's not nicotine that gives me nightmares,' the bitter student eventually said with a sarcastic chuckle.

Lynn chanced a laugh too, seeing her angry boyfriend leave the bedroom, presumably to fetch his cigarettes and lighter. She followed after a few seconds, covering herself with a bathrobe, and found him slumped down on the couch, smoking. The drug hit his brain quickly, and his heart rate climbed back up. Not the smartest move, Jeff knew full well, after going without for some hours. The dazed schoolgirl sat down next to him and leaned against his arm in silence, with her hand resting on his thigh. She could feel his quadriceps muscle twitching.

'Thanks,' the young man muttered. 'Are you OK? I didn't hit you, did I?'

Lynn shook her head, trying not to let on that she was crying again.

'No.'

Her effort was unconvincing. Jeff could tell by this one simple syllable that something was wrong. Remorseful, he lifted her chin and kissed her mouth, eliciting an unconscious sob. The thirsty, smoky kiss registered as a hallmark deep within the sixteen-year-old, and she worked hard to maintain her composure, not wishing to add to his anguish.

'This isn't fair, is it?' he told her, his heart heavy when comparing their current situation with the playful humour of their pre-sleep mood. 'I shouldn't be doing this to you.'

'No, it's not fair,' his girlfriend agreed. 'But it's far less fair on you than it is on me.'

'What time is it? I'll go. You need to sleep. I can come back and take you to the airport.'

The tall man got to his feet to read the clock above the stove. He couldn't bear the prospect of leaving, knowing he wouldn't see his dream girl again for over a week, yet it was the right thing to do. The princess had been so kind to her lowly surf this evening. He couldn't be selfish any longer. He sat back down on the edge of the sofa, looking at the amazing sight of Lynn Dyson beckoning him back into her bed.

'Two-ten,' he reported. 'Actually, that's not too bad for me. That's three-and-a-half hours. But it's disaster for you, because you have to get going so early. This is what I meant about leaving you to sleep in peace. I wouldn't blame you if you reconsidered. Shall I go?'

'No, please don't,' Lynn replied, taking his hand. 'Come on. I don't want you to go. Let's go back to bed. Let's hope they've gone to persecute someone else now.'

Jeff stood up and held out a grateful hand. 'Yeah. Nice thought.'

He liked this idea, although he didn't hold out much hope. The pair had to be up and about in another three hours' time. Lying down, he drew his dream girl close into him and wrapped his arms around her. The determination in her voice buoyed his heart, because in it he thought he heard a common need; inexplicable, but inescapable too.

'Thanks again, angel. You'll be glad to be on that 'plane, so you can get some more sleep.'

Saying nothing, Lynn's strong hand reached across his chest and massaged his aching shoulder, feeling him wince each time she located a knot. Was it too much to hope that this enigmatic stranger would ever relax in her bed? She continued to knead the muscles around his collarbone and upper arm, occasionally drawing her fingers up his neck, filled with joy when she saw a smirk of guilty pleasure on his face.

'You really need to learn to receive as well as give, you know,' the sleepy woman murmured.

'What?' the student objected in astonishment. 'I've done nothing but receive since I got here.'

His loving girlfriend sighed. 'Yeah, for the first time since I've known you.'

A shiver ran down Jeff's spine. How insightful this exquisite godsend was, to pick up on this nuance where other women would consider his demands for sex to be borne purely out of selfish motive. Did Lynn somehow know sex didn't count? Had she already figured out that for him and those like him sex was not a gift? Rather, it was a means of redressing the balance of power in his David and Goliath battle with the world.

These all-consuming molecules of love and affection, so tightly woven into their sexual chemistry, were absolutely a gift however. A wonderful, potent and extremely dangerous gift, the tormented soul was coming to believe. And tonight, by devoting an evening to their joint wellbeing, Lynn had unearthed the cursed trust issue, probably totally by accident. How right had he been to seek this woman out? And how right was she to test him!

'Thank you,' he whispered. 'I promise to try harder.'

His partner raised her head and kissed the end of his nose, sniffing kindly in amusement. 'Very good. 'Night, Jeff. I love you.'

'I could get used to you, you know. I love you too.'

'You could get bored with me,' Lynn extrapolated sleepily.

Her boyfriend chuckled. 'I'd love to get bored with you. That'd take centuries! G'night, angel.'

The nineteen-year-old released the hold on his beautiful waker-upper and resumed his quest for a few more hours' rest, meandering his brain back through the amazing evening they had just shared. If their last night together before this forced absence had turned out to be an average, run of the mill date, perhaps he would feel her loss more acutely? A hopeless attempt at self-deception, the young man smiled to himself. Fortunately, they both fell asleep quickly and slept until the alarm woke them at five.

'Whoa,' the young man groaned, leaning over to greet his sleepy bedfellow. 'Short night. Sorry, gorgeous. I'll make some tea.'

Jeff's head was clearer than usual in the mornings, which he attributed partly to the lack of alcohol and only the one, solitary cigarette. Despite the nightmare's rude interruption, the calmness had not left him, and this was comforting at least. He heard Lynn turn on the shower. A week apart. The prospect didn't stress him out as much as it used to, now that their relationship was strong and dependable, and particularly when he had an invitation for another weekend at Benloch on which to focus his intrinsic, and shortly highly-latent obsession.

If anything, the intellectual was looking forward to the novelty of receiving international phone calls at various times of the day. He would be interested to hear the seasoned traveller's reports of this historic, far-off city, which only revealed itself to the landlocked teenager in photographs or on the television. He jumped into the shower quickly, while Lynn was getting dressed. He decided to go straight to the university without shaving or changing. No-one would mind, and it meant he wouldn't have to deal with his front door until the evening.

At five-twenty-five, they were ready to go. Jeff examined the traveller's airline ticket carefully, with its waxy, red carbon-backed pages and the cryptic codes he didn't understand. It was the first he had seen up close. They also shared a laugh at the starlet's passport photograph, which was now three years old and no longer bore too accurate a resemblance. Lastly, she showed him her British currency; the five and ten pound notes she had been given for emergencies, in the event that whoever was meeting her at the airport was delayed.

'Does your passport also say you're a virgin?' he asked, on their way down in the lift.

'No!' Lynn cried, slapping his arm. 'I hope not! I don't want to answer those sorts of questions at immigration.'

'I'd like to see how they'd test for it,' her boyfriend mused. 'That'd be a good job for someone.'

The pretty teenager laughed. 'Yeah, perverts mostly.'

'I'm frightfully sorry, Miss Dyson,' the comic rambled on in a passable English accent, throwing her luggage into the boot and opening the passenger door. 'We regret to inform you that we're afraid we cannot let you into Great Britannia, because of an irregularity in your immaculacy status.'

'My immaculacy status?' the tennis star exclaimed, getting into the car. 'What's that?'

'Yes, Miss,' he nodded, pointing to an imaginary document. 'It says 'ere that you are an intact female. You kindly agreed to submit to an examination, duly conducted by our resident pervert, whereupon we discovered evidence that you enjoy sexual intercourse, which of course is against the law in this country. On behalf of Her Majesty, we have no alternative but to deport you back to the house of nocturnal screaming.'

Jeff pretended to stamp her passport, before running round to the other side of the car and letting himself in. Lynn was still laughing heartily, fastening her seatbelt.

'You're so funny! I love being with you so much.'

'Take me to London then,' the impulsive peasant suggested to his princess, turning the key in the ignition. 'I'd smuggle you in somehow.'

The confident student smiled at her, steering onto bitumen which was shining yellow from the mix of streetlights, tyre grease and overnight rain. They continued to play around with other outrageous questions the young traveller might be asked at Customs, while they drove through Flemington and on towards the northern suburbs.

'You'll get to London soon enough,' the caring teenager encouraged him. 'When I get back, we'll record some of your songs. You'll be a rock star in no time.'

'I like your style, Miss Dyson. I don't even *have* a passport,' the student from Sydney's west confessed.

Lynn tried to cover up her surprise. 'Oh well... I suppose you've never needed one. You should apply soon. When you become an overnight success around the world, it'll be very frustrating not to be able to go anywhere.'

The ambitious songwriter nodded and smiled. Joking aside, it was another sound observation, and her optimism was hard to ignore. Apart from a steady stream of taxis, the roads were practically empty, and they were soon at the airport, beating the regular morning traffic by an hour or so. Jeff lifted the suitcases out of the boot and set them down onto the tray of a waiting trolley, feeling predictably desolate.

Lynn spied her tennis coach up ahead. 'There's Stuart,' she pointed and took hold of the trolley's handle. 'Don't worry about coming in. It's just standing in queues and a lot of waiting around from here. Thanks for the lift, Jeff.'

'No worries,' the young man agreed, disappointed at having been dismissed like the chauffeur. 'If you'll be OK.'

The couple walked together as far as the doors of the Departures terminal. After a brief introduction to Stuart Heywood, a former professional tennis player who had been drafted into the Dyson camp a few years ago to coach the promising youngsters, Lynn turned and hugged her boyfriend *con gusto*.

'I'll miss you heaps. Try to get some more rest, and I'll see you next weekend. We'll have a relaxing time out at Benloch, I promise.'

Jeff wasn't sure how he should behave in front of the young star's trainer, given her father's stern warnings about overnight visitors and his own role as "chauffeur with benefits" suddenly on display. However, Lynn seemed unabashed, and throwing caution to the wind, he kissed her full on the lips. He echoed her sentiments, at pains to make light of how hard it was to say goodbye.

'I love you, angel, and I'm going to miss you too,' the candour oozed out of him without prompting. 'My heaps'll be bigger than your heaps.'

The teenager giggled. 'I don't know how to measure a heap. That's a new challenge for you. Is it by diameter, circumference or volume?'

'Get out of here, you gorgeous idiot,' her boyfriend jeered. 'Just fly safe and hurry back, OK?'

'Thanks, Jeff. I will,' she reassured him, waving as she walked towards the check-in desks. 'See you soon.'

The student waved once more and took his leave, catching a familiar laugh behind him as he walked towards the exit doors. Sixteen and flying around the world without a second thought, and not a parent in sight. He and his dream girl weren't too dissimilar in that respect, the young man realised. Lynn made her own way through her tactical life, with others dictating the strategy. Pretty much the same as for him, except the people dictating his strategy weren't really people at all.

Jeff turned up the volume on MAC's cassette as he drove back into the city, picking up the first wave of the morning rush hour as he got closer. Revitalised by his healthy evening, he reached the Science Faculty by six-thirty, only to find it completely deserted. Most students didn't know that such a time even existed. Letting himself into the computer room, he sat down with his tepid takeaway coffee and yesterday's editions of "Le Monde", "The New York Times" and "The Times" itself, all of which he had picked up with a boyish excitement at the airport. Up until now, he had only come across these revered broadsheets in novels or watched people reading them in movies. This morning, he was sure he could feel all manner of ancient wisdom transferring from the paper, onto his fingers and into his brain. This was one up on Suzanne for sophistication!

***

Two days later, Jeff arrived home in a mad rush after a very long day, hoping he hadn't missed Lynn's call. He had been caught up in a heated discussion between Professor Martin and a final year student, where he had been called upon to mediate between two men with extremely poor social skills. Neither boffin would relent, both believing their opinion to be the right one.

The well-liked technical assistant had looked at his watch for what must have been the twentieth time and had eventually resorted to pointing at the clock. He was due to meet Gerry for a quick beer, to exchange information on a proposed song-writing deal, before making a fleeting stop at his flat to speak to the tennis champion in advance of the day's gruelling training schedule.

The pair had also snatched a five-minute chat twenty-four hours earlier, on her arrival in Wimbledon, with the promise of longer the following day. This evening, to add to his frustration, the young buck had forgotten how low he was on fuel. He hadn't counted on a queue at the petrol station either, so by the time he reached the apartment, his blood pressure was dangerously high.

Tonight was the second night in succession when Jeff would end up hiding the truth from his dream girl about his whereabouts, and for the first time in his life, he felt guilty for doing so. Yesterday, he and some classmates had been fraternising with some attractive Norwegian backpackers in a bar on Chapel Street when the handsome nineteen-year-old had made his excuses and sped home to talk to Lynn for however long she could spare, after which he had driven back to the bar to pick up where he had left off.

The tortured teenager's need for sexual gratification appeared to be spiralling frighteningly out of control, compensating for the lack of sleep and the gaping void in his heart, and then magnified further by the endless rounds of Schnapps that the Scandinavian holidaymakers insisted on buying for their Australian hosts.

Sure enough, arriving at his flat, the telephone was already ringing behind the front door, at which Jeff growled when his key refused to go into the lock without a fight. Lynn was just about to leave her message when he hurled himself onto the couch and snatched up the receiver.

'Hello?'

'Hi, Jeff. Wow! You sound out of breath. What are you doing?'

'Hey, Lynn. Yeah, sorry. I could hear the 'phone from outside on the landing. How are you? Thanks for ringing again.'

The distant voice was laughing as she tried to make out his words through the heavy breathing. She didn't understand why she felt so suspicious. Surely if her man had company, he wouldn't have answered the telephone, and she couldn't hear anyone else's voice. She should stop being so paranoid. She had no reason to believe her boyfriend would be unfaithful, and he was always so glad to hear from her. Including now.

The couple exchanged their news, and Jeff asked endless questions about the city he was so keen to visit. Most of the information he was seeking however, concerning the music scene and the nefarious sins which surrounded it, were beyond the boundaries of the young woman's experience, given her age and innocence.

'Just because you were smoking by five doesn't mean I've been hanging around blues dens since I hit double digits,' she insisted, after yet another monstrous speculation went unsubstantiated.

The student laughed. 'Of course not. At least you know blues dens exist. I'm sure your mum'd be horrified.'

A delightfully salacious image of Lynn Dyson dressed in black leather and fishnet stockings flitted across his tired eyes, with her blonde hair and red lips enticing him up onto a smoky stage. Easily aroused, he slipped his right hand inside the front of his trousers and began to masturbate, entranced by her prose and excited by his kinky inventions, while his blissfully ignorant, faraway girlfriend described her highly reputable and drug-free day at the All England Lawn Tennis and Croquet Club. The insatiable man was almost looking forward to arriving back at the Chapel Street pub, as the expensive call ticked by, drawn by the magnetic prospect of enacting his fantasies on a real, live ring-in.

'What are you doing tonight?' Lynn asked, after their sublime ten-minute conversation.

'Going back to find Gerry and have a drink with some mates. I left him on Chapel Street. I've got news for you, by the way.'

Lynn tensed up again. 'Male mates or female mates?'

'Mix of both.'

He could hear the disappointment all the way from the northern hemisphere. Was it more due to his incessant consumption of alcohol or to the fact that his dream girl suspected he was playing around? The former was bad enough, but he despised the thought of her putting two and two together. He didn't want to hurt her, and he sure as hell didn't want to lose her. The realisation that Lynn's values were likely to be a lot better aligned with Suzanne's than with his own hit the reprobate between the eyes, fairly and squarely, and he felt his erection soften. Something had to change. He was beginning to understand what was wrong with this picture. It had taken a while, but things were different now.

'I won't do it tomorrow, angel. I need the company tonight. I don't expect you to understand, but it's true. We'll talk about it next weekend. I miss you so much.'

'OK, then. I promise I'll try to understand, but can't you do something healthier with your time? Come home and we can have a clean weekend.'

Jeff smiled. He was getting plenty of exercise at least, but he could hardly own up to this either.

'Clean-ish. We'll see,' he replied. 'I can't wait to see you. I want you, you know, regardless of the drink, or the company or the cigs. It's you I really need. D'you believe me?'

'You're drinking your rock star money,' she persisted, determined not to get sucked in by his charms.

'I know, angel. Not much of it. I get people to buy me drinks. It's a game I play when I'm out. I'm very resourceful.'

'Hmm...' Lynn didn't sound too well sold. 'That's what I'm afraid of. I do believe you though, and I love you. I don't mean to lecture, sorry, and I can't wait to see you either. Have a good time, and I'll try and ring again on Thursday, just before I fly home.'

LORRAINE PESTELL

Confession

It was Jeff Diamond's second weekend invitation out to the Dyson family farm. He had been unable to arrange cover for his shift on the Friday evening, so Lynn had gone ahead with her father and younger brother. Early on Saturday morning, the student eagerly embarked on the long solo drive north out of the city, windows down and music blaring.

A Boeing 747, the "Jumbo Jet", nearly left tyre marks on the old Ford's roof, as it careened past the end of the runway at Tullamarine Airport. It had been just over a week since the nineteen-year-old had dropped his girlfriend at the Departures terminal, and seeing the gigantic aircraft overhead and hearing the roar of its engines put him in mind of travelling again. How he would love to jump on a flight and jet off to some far-off land! New York, Paris or London… Or even New Zealand, he grinned shamefully.

The handsome party boy had spent the early hours of that morning in the company of a Kiwi girl, who had been intent on cataloguing the many woeful characteristics of Australians, in her brazen opinion. Giving it back to her in spades, he had originally tried to avoid the obvious sheep jokes, but as the beers slipped down one by one, even these had been given a run for their money.

Jeff's head was a little fuzzy still. He had bought coffee from a truck stop just outside the CBD, but it had been weak and tasteless and had been thrown out a few kilometres later. The empty paper cup was all that remained, rolling around in the passenger footwell.

The separated lovers had spoken virtually every day that week, stealing valuable minutes from Lynn's hectic schedule. In fact, they were settling down into a nice rhythm with each other, despite the sportswoman's absence. After the frantic and guilty conversation early on in the trip, Jeff had taken it upon himself to curtail his drinking relatively well, particularly considering the amount of time he was left to his own devices. Suzanne's lectures had begun to sink in, and the free spirit was gradually becoming better able to appreciate the different perspectives from which he and Lynn viewed their situation. The benefits of a steady relationship with someone with whom he could talk freely and have nightmares, and who would help open doors for him, were plain to see. And as a further bonus, new songs were tumbling through him thick and fast.

Indeed, the talented songwriter was arriving with glad tidings to impart to his privileged girlfriend on this subject. Three of his compositions had been accepted by Columbia Records, and furthermore the publishing group had written to him suggesting two other companies in the famous Brill Building which he might try. He was stoked to receive such a helpful response, cautiously optimistic to be slowly breaking through on his own. It would also then be much easier to accept assistance from the MAC crew, thereby having the big-time boys at his disposal, for Jeff was too proud to take Lynn up on her offer until he had established some sort of reputation of his own. The songwriter from the western suburbs had far too much to prove.

The Fairlane pulled up at the main gates of the vast Benloch settlement. The gatekeeper had viewed it suspiciously to begin with, but Jeff's name was on the list, giving him no choice but to allow the rattling, blue jalopy onto the property. The skilful driver resisted the temptation to spin the wheels on the gravel and drove sedately up to the house. At about a hundred metres from the end of the driveway, he became aware of the sound and vibration of galloping hoofs behind him.

Two horses and a pony slowed to a trot and soon drew alongside the car. The surreal sight of Lynn's bare left foot floated outside the driver's window in a chromed stirrup, and he followed the lines of her suntanned leg up as far as they went, to reveal her complete beauty encased in white shorts and a pale blue sports top. Jeff stopped the car and jumped out, recognising Sandy on the second large, snorting steed, and little Anna on a daintier pony. All three Dysons were breathing as heavily as their mounts, obviously having chased after the car from quite some distance away.

'Hi!' Lynn called, scissoring her right leg over the horse's withers to dismount.

Slim hips slid off the saddle, and Jeff's dream girl landed by his side, as if she had descended from heaven only for him. The overjoyed young man thought better of touching her, despite an overwhelming urge to do so, since the youngsters were already giving them the eye. Both lovers contented themselves with a kiss, breathing in the dust thrown up by tyres and hoofs as they leaned into each other.

'Ew!' whined a voice which could only be the seven-year-old's. 'Stop doing that!'

Anna and Sandy's mounts stood on the other side of the car, scuffing at the ground impatiently. The new arrival walked around and patted their whiskered noses. He had never understood the attraction of horse-riding but had spent enough time at Gerry's luxurious family home to have become quite familiar with the sights, sounds and smells of the equine world. He smiled up at the pair of bronzed, outdoor children.

'Hi, guys!'

The three riders flanked the car as it completed its journey up the long driveway, and Jeff parked it in the garage like before. He walked with the others to the stables, and they all chattered together happily while the horses were unsaddled and rubbed down. The dark-haired guest was reminded how idyllic a way this must be to grow up. They worked hard, these next-generation Dysons, but they had each other and a healthy routine to rely on; a good, wholesome upbringing which was so unlike his own.

Sandy seemed more cheerful this weekend. The visitor made a point of walking back to the house with him, sensing the boy's need for some safe male company. It was not his place to interfere, and if the twelve-year-old was anything like Jeff remembered being at the same age, he would be reluctant to accept any explicit help. The amateur psychiatrist made a mental note to keep an eye on the boy for as long as he remained *persona grata*.

To Jeff's delight, the two kids ran on ahead into the house, leaving the lovebirds to linger in the sunshine and reacquaint themselves properly in private. Lynn leaned into his body eagerly and wrapped her arms around his waist. The power of this first embrace in ten days caught the young man by surprise, being forced to push her away when his abeyant libido immediately snapped into action.

'Jeez, you turn me on so fast.'

The sixteen-year-old looked up into pleading eyes, feeling coy all of a sudden. 'I noticed,' she giggled. 'I missed you.'

'I missed you too, as you can see. Hugely. So when do I get you all to myself?'

'Soon.'

A shiver ran down Lynn's spine. This audacious man was so divine; so utterly irresistible, never leaving anything unstated.

'After lunch? Is that OK?'

Jeff gave her another hypnotising smile, leaving his prize in no doubt as to the desire he held for her. The superstar glowed inside, feeling exactly the same way. They both laughed awkwardly as the young man adjusted himself, to allow them to walk into the house without embarrassment.

'And what do you want from me?' he asked, breathing softly on the side of her face while holding the door open for her.

Lynn stopped in her tracks. She hadn't expected this question at all, having become more used to her control freak boyfriend's frenzied demands, always coated in charm and charisma but uncompromising nonetheless. She knew exactly what she wanted from him. She wanted him to ask this very question, and butterflies took flight in her stomach.

'I want you all to myself too,' she made her confession to enquiring eyes.

'*Excelente*. Your wish is my command. Let's go then.'

Scarcely able to maintain the patient, carefree act any longer, the student made a grab for the gorgeous, fresh-faced woman and tugged her close again, just as his stomach let out a loud rumble. She could feel it too, through both sets of clothing.

'Your insides are noisy,' she chuckled, hearing another growl.

'Yeah? I'm hungry.'

The blonde host wondered when the cash-strapped student had last had a proper meal. Her mind flashed back to their telephone conversations and couldn't recall him ever describing what he had eaten for dinner, in contrast to the regular updates about how much beer and whisky he had consumed and how many packets of cigarettes he had gone through.

'We'd better have lunch quickly then. Do you want something to eat?'

'Only you,' he leaned over and kissed her mouth before it had finished her sentence.

His girlfriend pushed him playfully. 'Well, you can't have your Lynn and eat her too.'

'D'you wanna bet?' Jeff cocked his head to one side, kissing her again. 'You'll regenerate. A whole lot better than cake will, anyway.'

The couple strolled down the long corridor, and Lynn suggested her handsome guest leave his weekend bag at the foot of the stairs while they went in search of comestibles. The farmhouse kitchen was welcoming, as was Helen. She made a beeline for the new arrival, hugging him tightly.

'Lovely to see you again, Jeff. How are you?'

The tall, young man gave the Dysons' housekeeper a kiss without having to be prompted, and she was clearly chuffed. The pretty teenager rolled her eyes, knowing full well that her boyfriend was once more playing to the crowd. Jeff issued a multi-purpose wink for effect, and both women swooned.

'I'm fine, Helen, thanks. How are you?'

The plump lady giggled. She liked this boy a great deal. There was something very appealing about him, a combination of hedonistic and vulnerable, she hazarded. And he was looking a little tired too.

'Too much high living for you!' Helen declared, patting him on the chest.

This time, Lynn gave her man a warm smile, and he felt a pang of guilt. He didn't wholly deserve her compassion, truth be told. This double life he had been leading for the last couple of months was showing signs of needing to merge into one, and the admission made him uncomfortable. This would not be a straightforward process, if even possible without significant collateral damage.

'Helen, please may we grab some lunch?' the polite teenager asked.

'Absolutely, dears.'

The jolly, mature woman was like a favourite auntie to the Dyson children, having watched them grow from happy toddlers to responsible, committed and successful young champions, fulfilling their father's intentions. Junior and Lynn were turning into well-mannered, genteel young adults, and Helen was especially pleased to witness the pretty sixteen-year-old enjoying her first real romance.

'Help yourselves. I'll put a round of coffee on, shall I?'

The young couple made themselves sandwiches from chunky slices of freshly-baked bread, while the housekeeper prepared something for the younger children. Jeff was certainly starving, and the strong coffee replenished his energy levels. His dream girl looked on with interest, instantly reminded of their last evening together, when the nineteen-year-old had demolished at least two large *pizzas*.

While she marvelled at his capacity to eat and drink, it appeared her man was keen to share some good news.

'Hey, guess what?' he announced, seeing everyone's eyes turn his way. 'I've sold three more songs.'

'Wow! *¡Excelente!*' Lynn exclaimed. 'To whom?'

'Columbia, and maybe some others in New York too. You know, Tin Pan Alley factories. They sent me some names. They've got some big acts on their books.'

Genuinely excited for him, his girlfriend jumped up and gave him a big hug. She detected a strange air of destiny about the matter-of-fact way the songwriter had imparted these developments. It was not overconfidence or arrogance this time, but more that his lofty ambition to become a rock star was simply proceeding according to plan. For Jeff's part, his mind was already on other things, and he tried to pull her onto his lap.

'That's fantastic!' she praised, resisting his grasp and using her eyes to tell him, "Not in front of the children."

The horny student understood the subliminal message and calmed down again. There was a new and positively independent light in Lynn's piercing, blue eyes which promised him the Earth, and his heart leaped into his mouth. He would get what he was after in due course, he was sure. In the meantime, here was an opportunity to see how her little brother was faring.

'Any more computing disasters, Sandy?'

The shy boy was happy to have been engaged in custom-made discourse by his sister's new friend. By the animation in his expression, Jeff's earlier suspicions were further validated, and the nineteen-year-old realised he would need to be careful not to have his usual Pied Piper tendencies misconstrued by a sensitive and quite possibly confused child. The last thing he wanted to do was to attract unwanted attention and hurt the youngster's feelings by promptly turning those affections away. It was occasionally a burden to be so likeable, the enigmatic egotist scoffed to himself.

'No, not lately,' the quiet twelve-year-old answered. 'I wrote a pretty complex program that worked though. I'm starting to get the logic of it now.'

'Great news,' Jeff replied, giving a little. 'I could help you, if you like. We could go over to the uni', and I'll show you the computers there. They don't do anything particularly exciting, but it's impressive to see and hear them in that big space. Up to you, mate.'

Sandy's eyes gave his enthusiasm away, despite his cool response. 'Yes, that would be interesting. Thanks.'

The weight of expectation on this lad was far too high, the visitor decided. He wondered whether Bart and Marianna had asked as much from Junior and Lynn at that age, or had they simply forgotten to go back and start again with their two youngest children? He looked across at Lynn and caught her eye, making her blush. *Jesus!* His brain froze for a split-second. He had better back off. The stakes were high for him as well. With neither Dyson parent present, the guest feared he was already assuming too much control, and all apparently effortlessly. What was going on?

Over the last few weeks, since he had begun to lay himself bare to his beautiful angel, Jeff had noticed a distinct clarity of mind developing where the dark clouds had gathered before. His thoughts were somehow freer to roam around, unfettered by the boundaries of self-preservation he had previously put around them. *We can only be who we are at any point in time*, he mused, feeling a lyric pushing its way through his psyche. There were lessons to be learned here. For everyone.

The lunch cleared away, Lynn took her thoughtful boyfriend's hand, and they made their way up to her bedroom. In the fifty metres between the kitchen and the door before the linen cupboard, both teenagers found their pulse rates climbing through the roof and a distinct stirring inside. As soon as they were behind closed doors, Jeff dumped his bag on the floor and whisked the gorgeous young woman up in his arms, swinging her in a circle. Lynn whooped in childish delight, ecstatic to be alone again with this superb powerhouse of a man, who was in turn so enamoured by her.

'Can we go to the oasis again?' he asked, placing his girlfriend's feet back on the floor and looking deep into her eyes.

At first, Lynn provided no response, deliberately staring into space and keeping him waiting on tenterhooks. She watched him shove his hands into the pockets of his jeans and tried to make out whether he was already hard. During her nine-day overseas trip, she had found herself indulging in endless sexual fantasies that had taken her by surprise, and her diaries had been filled with the type of explicit language which she hardly recognised as coming from her own vocabulary.

'Can we, can we?' Jeff badgered. '*¿Por favor, señorita bellissima?*'

Stepping forward on tiptoes, Lynn kissed him tenderly. '*Sí, señor*. Yes, we can. You beat me to it. I was going to ask if you wanted to. Shall we take some homework?'

Jeff nodded, a grin spreading across his face. 'Good idea. I've got a tonne of stuff to do, plus heaps of information for you. What about you?'

The travelling champion walked over to her desk and lifted her school bag. It was obviously very heavy, and the young man smiled in sympathy. The weather was not as warm this weekend, so they elected not to bother with swimwear. The guitar came with them though, and the rug and sticks, of course. Down in the garage, the Testosterone Kid was happy to let his host take the wheel again and soon found his imagination wandering until it had her driving on his lap across the paddocks. He stared out of the window as they bumped along, letting his mind run wild.

'Can we work later?' the hot-blooded man almost begged, as they were spreading the rug out on the grass.

Lynn laughed. 'Why does that not surprise me? You're incorrigible!'

'It's your fault,' Jeff quickly shifted the blame. 'You've been away for over a week, remember? That's a bloody long time, as far as my self-control's concerned.'

He removed the guitar from its case and started to strum some chords, finding it almost impossible to concentrate, with the object of the previous week's fantasies reclining sexily on the rug. He couldn't believe how much the naïve schoolgirl had grown up in the few weeks they had known each other, now fully aware of how attractive she was and so comfortable expressing herself sexually. Her fingers wandered to her lips, which kissed them before they tripped lightly across the rug and made their way up his leg, starting at his bent knee and winding their way behind the body of the guitar, until they found what they were hunting for.

The blue eyes were most insistent that he keep singing, and it was all Jeff could do to remember the words to his own song. Sensing himself becoming further and further aroused, he unleashed his strongest powers of telepathic persuasion and leaned his head back to encourage Lynn towards him. Smiling, she knelt on her haunches and planted a kiss on his lips, and pretty soon they were precariously balanced by each other's weight while the guitar continued to ring out against their chests.

In the end, the singer could take no more of this earthy, artistic foreplay, sliding the instrument from between their bodies and laying it on the grass next to the rug. His strong hands gripped Lynn's arms and gently coaxed her body down as he lay back. After a few more minutes with their hands threaded inside clothing and their mouths hungrily covering each other with kisses, the beautiful blonde sat across his hips and began to peel off her t-shirt at her boyfriend's bidding. Taking his cue, Jeff did the same, before reaching up to help remove her bra.

'Let's stand up,' the young woman requested, jumping to her feet.

Obediently, the eager man sprang up as far as his knees and lunged for the waistband of Lynn's shorts. 'You are stunning,' he told her, kissing her abdomen and the hair in front of her vagina, while her panties slipped easily down her thighs.

'So are you,' she replied.

The lovers were both soon naked and caught in a slow-burning embrace, under the bright sunshine, with the natural beauty of the creek surrounding them and nothing but bird song and the rustling of leaves to drown out their passionate moans and cries. Lynn crouched down and took Jeff's erection into her mouth, her tongue caressing it while she moved backwards and forwards slowly. She heard him let forth a long, low snarl and felt his hands reach down to stroke her breasts.

The resolute man began to walk his gorgeous girlfriend backwards and turned her round, so that she could lie on the cool, soft grass. She let her hair out of its ponytail and arched her back, pressing her head down into the ground. The young man exhaled deeply, drinking in her perfection and feeling the desire welling up.

'I have to be inside you,' he murmured. 'It's been so long, and I love you so much.'

The sixteen-year-old smiled shyly, inviting him down and slipping her hands around his sides. The sensation was almost overwhelming as their bodies joined, and they both knew that time was running out. Oblivious of all else, the two kindred spirits voiced their pleasure, loud and uninhibited, across the paddock, climaxing together only a minute or so later.

Over the next hour or more, the musical pair traded songs with each other, with the sounds of nature in the background, then made love again much more slowly before trading more songs. Lynn had written two to Jeff's five, but who was counting? They played and replayed his new compositions, working on harmonies and mimicking swirling string arrangements, all in preparation for the budding rock star's trip to the recording studio. And after they had crafted Jeff's songs as well as they could without the assistance of technology, the experienced superstar introduced him to her own new numbers, which had of course been inspired by their thrilling, new love affair.

'I'm in danger of taking this for granted,' the young man confessed, suddenly serious.

'What do you mean?' the sixteen-year-old looked up at his handsome face.

'These bursts of creative energy, and having you motivate me like this. It's almost like we're getting *blasé* about all these beautiful things our relationship's giving rise to.'

'Hmm...' Lynn nodded in agreement, fascinated at how the formerly fluid, passionate movements of this man's irresistible body had been replaced by rough, twitchy spasms. 'What's wrong? You're so tense all of a sudden. Relax.'

Jeff exhaled and inhaled deeply several times, doing his best to hide his concern at how dizzy he felt. The fear of no longer having this gorgeous creature in his life had seized him and was refusing to let go. What the hell would he do if she called it a day? He would be absolutely lost, so deep had he fallen under her spell.

'Jesus, Lynn, I just don't want anything to go wrong, but there are so many things that could go wrong.'

'Like what?'

'Like you knowing more about me and where I came from.'

The innocent teenager frowned, ripping a handful of tips off the surrounding blades of luscious grass and sprinkling them over his knees. 'I only care about where you are now.'

The young man brushed the cuttings off his legs, and smiled. She was nervous too. Was paranoia contagious?

'For the moment...' the Sydneysider sighed, casting his eyes far into the distance. 'Us being here, away from everything and everyone in our day-to-day lives, it's too much like paradise. Almost as if we're using up an allocation of playtime hours that might run out at any moment, when the other priorities on your time take over.'

'I hadn't thought of it that way, but I understand what you mean. I am definitely going to be much busier for the rest of the year. Do you keep a diary?'

Before the thoughtful student had a chance to respond, their peace was shattered by the whining sound of a farm vehicle's engine struggling up the hill in the next-door paddock. The naked teenager reached for her t-shirt, which was thankfully laying only a short stretch from the edge of the rug. Jeff's eyes flashed in a mixture of appreciation and amusement, watching her breasts dance in the hasty lunge and then disappear under hurriedly-assembled clothing.

Chuckling, the city boy made a swift decision to cover his own modesty too, with the only object that came to hand: the trusty guitar. The tractor continued past however, its driver completely unaware of the inconvenience he had caused, and both lovers burst out laughing at their sudden fear of being discovered *in flagrante*.

'It's alright for you. You don't have to live here!' Lynn gasped. 'Sometimes the aboriginals come out here for a swim. I don't want to get caught, even by them. So... Do you keep a diary?'

Jeff shook his head. 'Why would someone want to keep track of a life like mine?' he answered with another question, mostly to himself.

The celebrity continued, deliberately choosing not to ladle sympathy on her boyfriend. She had taken another book on mental trauma with her to London, and was slowly beginning to understand the difference between sufferers' needs and wants. Overindulgence, she determined, was definitely a want her loving but exacting stranger didn't need.

'You should,' she urged. 'I do. That's where I think back about what's happened to me and realise how lucky I am. Occasionally, when I'm away from home or really busy, I re-read it before I go to sleep. It makes me humble.'

The young man's eyes showed he was impressed. Here was another clean habit he ought to consider on his journey to becoming a "someone". One day he might need to be reminded of his humble origin. This idea made him cringe, as ingrained traits of arrogance and self-loathing simultaneously drew their weapons inside his head.

'That's a mighty fine thing to do. Maybe I'll start one. My songs are my diary, I suppose.'

'Jeff, you're going to be really rich. Do you know that? These songs are *muy, muy bien.*'

He leaned over and kissed her. Lynn Dyson liked his work. That was worth starting a diary for, and this time his mind remained clear.

'*¡Gracias! Muy buenas,*' he corrected her Spanish. 'But I'm not interested in being rich.'

The teenaged superstar stared at him in surprise. Her family had always been well-off, and she automatically assumed that everyone aspired to wealth.

'Why not?'

Jeff smiled at the look of consternation on her face. 'Do you ever see any of the money you make?'

Lynn shook her head and smiled an innocent smile which made her boyfriend wonder if she had the slightest clue about the health or even the composition of her personal balance sheet. Given his knowledge of other private school girls, namely Gerry's sisters and their friends, he found it hard to believe that the Melbourne Academy girls wouldn't also regularly indulge in comparisons of wardrobe contents, jewellery and the sorts of cars their parents might buy them for their birthdays.

'Sometimes,' the young beauty shrugged. 'I can ask for money for a specific purpose, if I want. It goes through a trust. It's not my money anyway. It's MAC's. And a lot of it's to fund our uni' and other things in the future.'

The nineteen-year-old frowned. 'Are you happy with that? You need to take control.'

'Do I?' the young star grinned.

'Sooner or later you should. Don't you want to make sure you get your share?'

Lynn giggled. 'There's that "C" word again! But you're right. I suppose I should pay more attention. Dad's always taken care of things with school, but hearing your stories about negotiating royalty payments with Gerry has prompted me to take more interest, I must admit.'

Jeff winked. 'I don't want it, by the way. Just in case you're wondering.'

'My money? No, I know. I'm not worried about that.'

'Good.'

'I feel so young, compared to you,' the starlet added, changing the subject. 'You have to juggle every part of your life. I don't even think about buying food or where I live, *et cetera*. How long have you been running your whole life?'

The student sighed, reaching for his cigarettes and lighting one. He really didn't want the conversation to veer off in this direction, but he had committed to opening up. Would revealing more about his lowly background unleash some hitherto-repressed materialistic side to his dream girl and ruin the simplicity of their relationship? Her busy schedule and minority status were on his side when it came to dating expenses, and so far he had escaped with minimal financial outlay in his quest to snare the delectable *débutante*.

'A few years.'

Feeling safe again from marauding eyes, Lynn shuffled closer to her enigmatic stranger and leaned against his thigh, stroking his hairy lower leg. Jeff reached his arm around her shoulders and dragged the slender body downwards onto the rug, so that her head could rest on his chest. Exhaling in pleasure, her hand traced a line along the inside of his thigh, skirting round his testicles and bypassing his growing erection.

'I feel like a fraud,' she continued.

'Why?'

'Because people always talk about me being independent, with the travelling and spending a lot of time away from my family. But I'm not at all, compared to you.'

The teenager giggled as a large right hand swooped on her wandering fingers and snatched them away from his skin. A curl of ash dropped from the cigarette and landed on his broad, tanned chest, just centimetres from her nose, and she blew it away smartly.

'Leave me alone, woman,' her boyfriend mocked gruffly. 'I'm trying to concentrate on your mind, when you're obsessed with my body. That's some gross role reversal, Miss Dyson, and I'm not at all happy with it.'

'Control freak!' the young woman teased. 'Get over it.'

The red-blooded student let out a smoky laugh. 'For Christ's sake! That was uncalled for. Funny though. You're very independent, compared to most Year Twelve students. You've done so many other things that they haven't. And I haven't, obviously. Like winning the US Open, for instance, and having a string of hits all over the world. They're amazing achievements, and you know it. So you're hardly a fraud.'

'I guess not. It's just that I want so much more.'

'Which is a good thing... And you're smart as hell, angel. I love you for that.'

The playful blonde twisted herself round until she was laying half on and half off her prone and exposed lover, tipping towards his face to plant a kiss on his lips. The hunger in his abrasive chuckle, coupled with the quickening of his breath, told her he was ready for more, and she felt her own insides rippling in delightful anticipation. He grabbed her and hugged her tightly, shifting her body until she was completely on top of him, with his stiff penis pressing into her abdomen.

Lynn lifted her face into the sun's rays. 'You love me because of my brain?'

'Not entirely,' Jeff smiled, making his penis twitch and sending shockwaves through the aroused woman's body. 'But guilty, Your Honour.'

'Are you serious? Guys never say that!'

Lynn kissed his smiling mouth again, before sitting up and beginning to stroke him. To her surprise, however, her boyfriend's hands took hold of hers and moved them away from their sublime, sensual task.

'It's true,' his voice sounded suddenly serious, or even a little hurt.

'What's wrong? What did I say?'

'Nothing. Being stunning and sexy on the outside is one thing. Utterly mind-blowing, lady, don't get me wrong! But I love what's in there most of all...'

With his left hand slipping inside her t-shirt, the young man's index finger charted a course from her waist to underneath her right breast, through the delicious dip in the centre and pressing the soft skin that covered her heart, before travelling up over her chin and round her cheek until it reached her furrowed brow, through the wide neck of her top.

'And in here.'

Lynn's eyes immediately filled with tears. 'Are you just saying that because you don't want me to think you're after my money?'

'Yeah,' the boy from Canley Vale smiled impishly, picking up on the thinly-veiled humorous undertone. 'Absolutely.'

The sixteen-year-old slapped his stubbly cheek, bending over and planting another kiss on his lips, and his hand reversed its unhurried route down the same path.

'So why don't you want to be rich? It's got to be better than being poor, hasn't it? You can't tell me you'd rather struggle for the rest of your life.'

'No. Well, obviously,' Jeff confessed, with a half-smile for the home truth she had prised out of him. 'Of course I'd like more money. Who wouldn't? But if I got rich, I'd want to give a lot of it away to people who need it more than me. Take today, for example. How great is this?'

His arms swept round in a wide circle at the landscape surrounding them. The typical Victorian rural landscape of rolling paddocks, with Coldwater Creek just behind them, was lush after the last few days of steady, late summer rainfall. No great wealth was required to enjoy this newfound freedom that the city boy was experiencing, escaping from the inner suburbs and making sweet music with someone so very special.

'How much money does it take to do this?'

Lynn raised her eyebrows, having followed his gaze and re-familiarised herself with its magic. 'Yeah, you're right. My priorities are skewed.'

'That's not what I'm trying to say,' the student countered, grabbing her hand. 'It's just that there's a lot of scope for doing good, and it doesn't take much to have a nice lifestyle. I always look at Gerry's family as a perfect example. Sure, it'd be great to own fast cars and go on extravagant overseas holidays, but they're not leaving an impression on anyone. I think there's a responsibility which should go with having money. To use it well...'

The sixteen-year-old was fascinated, especially since the topic evidently meant so much to her usually rampant lover that in his voice was renewed animation, not to mention the fact that his erection had begun to shrink underneath her. This was a whole new way of looking at the world which the well-heeled daughter had never considered, since she was wholly accustomed to being cocooned in her regimented Dyson life and rarely had the chance to hear about other people. She had a good grasp on elementary economics and was developing more than a passing interest in charitable causes, but the wider distribution of wealth was a subject that intrigued her nascent social conscience deep, deep down. Her eyes urged Jeff to go on.

The ambitious young man wallowed in the attention. It was the type of conversation he longed to have with someone who would listen and not judge based on his or her own preconceived ideas. These were his favourite topics, and ones that he believed were only worth exploring with his soul-mate.

'So my idea of rich is not just having money,' he continued. 'It's money and information and education and opportunities, all given to as many people as possible. That's why I got into computers, because they're the perfect vehicle to deliver information to the masses. And without information and the ability to make sense of it, i.e. education, how can people make sound, life-changing decisions? People don't live in poverty because they want to, but more because they don't know how to change it. And we're going to stop that, aren't we?'

Without warning, Jeff's strong fingers gripped tightly around Lynn's waist, pulling her hips downwards and causing her to tip forward and plant the heels of her hands into his ribs.

'Are we?' she gasped. 'Hey!'

The nineteen-year-old smiled an apology, himself winded by the force of her fall. 'Yes. Sorry, angel. Yes, we are. You and me. Otherwise, they'll just stay stuck in their own disadvantaged ruts forever, and we rich rock stars won't have done right by the world.'

'Wow! You're so passionate about this, aren't you? I love it!' the young beauty purred adoringly and ran her fingers down his front, stopping just short of the swollen head of his penis.

Jeff took the tentative gesture as a signal to lighten up. *Don't push her too far*, his mind taunted. It was important to remember to take it slowly, in case his fevered determination scared her off. He had so many ideas for changing the world, some of which he had been plotting for years, but he shouldn't overburden his gorgeous girlfriend in one fell swoop, and on such a perfect afternoon.

'But of course, as soon as I get some serious money, I'll be buying myself a black Aston Martin.'

The pretty teenager laughed. 'That sounds more like it!'

Leaning over far enough for her t-shirt to reveal her breasts, the young woman kissed her spirited stallion. He had been well behaved all morning, respectful and chivalrous, even though they hadn't seen each other for over a week. Michelle had divulged unwittingly that Jeff had looked particularly out of sorts when he and her best friend had met to exchange homework assignments last Monday morning.

Keen to take advantage of this fresh-air closeness to find out more about her mystery man, Lynn seized her opportunity.

'Tell me about the doors thing,' she invited, fixing him with a stare. 'Please?'

To her astonishment, the orator's mood changed instantly from vehement to withdrawn. Anger was his first reaction to being confronted, as always, and his senses shut down with the precipitous scare. Why had she done that? They were having such a good time. Why did she have to spoil it? He didn't appreciate the ambush one bit and felt his chest tighten with the panic of suddenly being trapped.

Bitterly, the young man cursed his selfish, immature response. Who the fuck did he think he was? Lynn had pandered to his needs and satisfied his desires pretty much as soon as he had arrived this weekend. How could he dare object to her wanting to know more about the person she was trying to help? *Give and take, you bastard*, he challenged himself. Wasn't that what he always preached? It would be good to get things out in the open. He had felt so much better after his first essay, and his beautiful partner certainly deserved to know, particularly since only a few moments ago he had asked her to join him in changing the world...

The thunderclouds gradually dissipated, and Jeff's expression softened from hateful to merely pensive, much to his concerned girlfriend's relief. She had no idea how quickly his dark, twisted mind was being forced to recalibrate to its renewed, clear state.

'Angel, that stuff's so hard for me to talk about,' he responded tentatively, blowing air out through pursed lips. 'Jesus. So bloody hard.'

Lynn kissed the back of his hand, having watched her boyfriend's facial contortions closely and sensing his breathing quicken. She longed to know what was going on in that mercurial head of his.

'I know. I can see by your reaction. I'm sorry. You don't have to tell me. It's OK.'

Flattening the rug out underneath them, Jeff beckoned for his friendly companion to dismount and sit next to him, turning her round so that she faced the view across the eastern paddocks, with the spontaneous idea of allowing the afternoon sun to sink slowly behind them. His long legs splayed out on either side of her hips, in an enticingly similar position to the one they had adopted that first night, sitting at his bedroom window. The frightened adolescent inside couldn't quite muster the courage yet to speak directly to his dream girl's eyes about scars so deep-seated and personal.

'No, baby. You need to know,' a subdued voice acquiesced. 'And God only knows, I need to tell you. It's just I've never told anyone except shrinks about this stuff. And the shrinks are bloody useless.'

The disturbed nineteen-year-old could already feel his blood coming to the boil and wondered about the telepathic signals he must be sending, especially when the woman in front of him reached sideways to pass up one of the water canteens. He drank in large gulps.

'Thanks,' Jeff said, wiping his mouth before kissing the back of her neck.

The coldness of his lips took the teenager by surprise, and a tiny moan of pleasure escaped from her mouth. The anxious young man's heart leaped into his throat, instantly feeling his penis on the rise again. Taking a moment to gather his thoughts, he ingested a huge breath of air and launched forth with another instalment of his untold story.

'OK. Where do I start?' he began, then paused again with his lips pressed against the soft skin of Lynn's neck to offset the predictable dizziness. 'Whoa! Here goes... My mum died when I was fourteen. That's as good a place as any.'

The girl of his dreams had already drawn a sharp breath before she realised she wasn't all that shocked after all. She should have guessed something as serious as this had happened to her troubled man, and the tenebrous revelation made her feel immediately guilty, which of course was by the master communicator's design.

'I'm sorry,' she sighed. 'If it's too difficult, let's not talk about it. I don't want to hurt you, but I really want to help. And can't see how I can help much without knowing more.'

'I know,' Jeff agreed, squeezing her shoulders. 'The paradox as it stands, angel. My instincts are always to stay in the world of denial and frivolous enjoyment, and that's where I've lived up until now. Before you came along, that is... But it's unsustainable for so many reasons.'

'I noticed,' Lynn smiled, slapping both his knees with her hands.

The tired student kissed the back of her head, laughing softly at the interjection and also at the predicament in which they now found themselves. He had conditioned himself to a shield of secrecy, behind which neither of them wanted him to hang out anymore.

'I need to grow up, angel. That's all there is to it. I'm grateful for you pushing me, even though I might not show it.'

'Good,' the playful woman snapped again, with a smile Jeff could hear in her voice.

'So...' he continued, breathing deeply. 'My mother's dead. It's 'sixty-six. But before that, for maybe four years or thereabouts, life had been completely shit for us. Well, it was shit from the word go, really, I suppose. Just the shit factor increased steadily as time went by.'

'Did you ever think of committing suicide?' his dream girl interrupted again, knowing she was trespassing on private and altogether dangerous ground. 'It's just that everything I read about mental trauma seems to be about people who want to kill themselves.'

Groaning deeply and fighting with his acute discomfort, Jeff took another deep breath. How would she react to his honest answer? Would she brand him an ungrateful bastard, as most people did, or would she actually take the time to understand?

'Whoa! You really know how to ask the tough questions, don't you?'

'I'm sorry,' Lynn replied, turning to face him. 'Don't answer if you don't want to. I just can't imagine what it would be like to feel so desperate. I want to understand your world.'

All the air left the young man's lungs at once, panic ringing in his ears. 'Thanks, gorgeous. That's a nice thing to say. And I want to understand your world too. We can learn from each other, I hope. The truthful answer to your question is every day.'

Jeff's dark eyes looked away, desperate to temper the extreme emotions rushing through his head, having fired off an answer to her innocent question with minimal forethought. His brain immediately went into a crazed overdrive. Had he really spoken those words? Why? Normal people didn't talk this way.

The naïve celebrity gasped and immediately felt tears brim in her eyes, and the compassion on her face subdued her boyfriend's wild anxiety.

'Every day?' she repeated hesitantly, turning round to look at her mystery man again. 'Even today?'

Now it was Jeff who felt guilty. He smiled and kissed her forlorn face. He had lived with these terminal thoughts for many years and had become somewhat indifferent towards extinguishing his own life. Confiding in a third party had never been on his agenda until this unplanned detour on their summer's outing, and he had overlooked how reprehensible a concept this was to most people.

'Jesus. Sorry, angel. Don't stress. It's not that bad now. I'm used to it. It's just something you learn to live with over time.'

'But how? How do you learn to live with wanting to die?' Lynn implored, wiping her eyes.

'I don't know,' Jeff answered honestly, turning her powerful shoulders round again to direct her face away from his line of sight. 'I just did. Some days are easier than others. I guess that's why humans don't have an off-switch.'

'Oh,' the young woman sighed, his blatant language painting a vivid picture in her innocent, receptive mind. 'I'm really glad you don't have an off-switch. That's such a horrible idea. What if you changed your mind and decided to try again, and then you couldn't turn yourself back on?'

'Yep,' her mystery man nodded, chuckling gently and resting his chin on her head. 'Exactly what I mean. Every morning I wake up and reach for that switch, but you stop me from flicking it every time. Only you, you gorgeous thing.'

Lynn sobbed in his arms, unable to hold her emotions in check any longer. Silent tears slipped down Jeff's face too, trickling steadily down his neck. They both reached a hand up to wipe their faces at the same time and laughed together. Her sadness at his confession had affected him more than he first thought, making him feel very ungrateful indeed. Such cold, dispassionate truths were as hard to hear as they were to express, especially for someone who genuinely cared.

'I'm sorry, angel. I never wanted to make you cry like this. I didn't drive all the way out here to cast a shadow on your mood this weekend. You don't deserve it and you have too much to do.'

'No,' the starlet objected, leaning back into his chest. 'I'm rapt you're being honest with me. I'm fine. If anything, it makes me want to try harder. I don't want you to feel suicidal ever again.'

Despite his dream girl's apparent acceptance, the amateur psychiatrist was doubtful, knowing how easy it was for the mind to play tricks. He shouldn't assume the conservative teenager would be fine to adjust to his unpleasant stories without some shadows of reconsideration creeping in later. Moreover, he didn't want to take the risk of screwing her up too, for that would be the absolute worst outcome for both of them.

'Do you have someone you can talk to about this?' he asked.

'Yes. You!'

'No. Apart from me.'

'Who, then? Not Mum or Dad. No way am I going to tell them any of this!'

Her boyfriend exhaled, horrified at this prospect. 'No. Please don't. Not even Michelle or your MAC friends. It's got to be someone you can trust to be objective and just listen until your brain's put everything in the right place.'

'This is between us, Jeff,' Lynn reassured him, smiling at another cute metaphor. 'I don't want to give anyone a reason to stop us being together. I love you way too much, and I don't need you to protect me from you. You won't bring me down. I'm going to bring you up.'

Amazement swam in the nineteen-year-old's head, making him almost lose his balance. He lifted his left hand from around his girlfriend's shoulders to rest it on the top of her head and took another huge breath, while a wave of gratitude coursed from his heart to his eyes. Leaning his chin down onto his hand, he found no words adequate to describe the elation he felt. It appeared his wildest dream was coming true, at the oasis in the afternoon sun.

'Thank you,' he croaked. 'That'd be perfect. No. Way more than perfect. But I'm serious. I mean it might be worth talking to someone about how you feel with what I'm telling you, instead of internalising it.'

'A shrink, you mean?' Lynn asked, using the term her tormented boyfriend had used with such derogation earlier.

He laughed. 'Yeah. A psychobabbler. It'd be good insurance, I think. Just in case.'

'OK,' the sixteen-year-old agreed. 'I'll definitely think about it. We have psychobabblers coming out of our ears around here. Dyson Administration is "Shrink Central". Please carry on with your story. I didn't mean to distract you.'

Lifting the canteen to his lips again, Jeff took another long gulp of water and collected his thoughts. Sniffing loudly, he passed the bottle down to his attentive audience and continued.

'I first came to terms with my own feelings when my grandfather died,' he explained. 'I was nine, and remember asking my grandmother what had happened to him. Where had he gone, and all that. Like you do when you're nine.'

Lynn gave a half-hearted chuckle, leaning back into him again. Jeff carried on, pleased he was able to take advantage of his quirky sense of humour to make her feel better.

'She told me he'd gone to a place where he didn't need to worry anymore,' his deep voice cracked, never having put these memories into words before. 'It sounded like a very good place to me. Like a sanctuary, away from all the chaos happening around me. It left a big impression, even at that age, because I suppose I'd always wondered why I even bothered to grace this Earth with my presence.'

As he finished his sentence, the man at her back began to laugh maniacally, which scared the celebrity a little.

'I'm glad you did. Are you OK? You sound weird all of a sudden.'

'I'm sorry,' her boyfriend replied with a palpable sincerity, hanging on to her hand. 'I get very angry, and sometimes it's hard to contain the bitterness. But it's not all doom and gloom, by any means. That's where you come in. There never seemed to be any point for me to be here until you came along. My family didn't see the point of me either, and yet I always felt like I must be here for some reason. To make life better for people like me. I don't know. Sounds pretentious, but there you go... So when I saw you on the TV and you spoke directly to my heart, I just decided you were something to reach for and to focus on through all the crap.'

'Jeff, are you serious?' Lynn asked, finding it hard to believe what she was hearing. 'I was only six when you were nine. I hadn't said anything worthwhile to anyone by that time.'

The lost boy from Canley Vale sniffed in dispute. 'I bet you had! But no... I'm rolling about four years of my life into a few minutes here. This all happened over a long period of time.'

'Oh, I see,' the celebrity replied, her voice soft and welcoming. 'That makes more sense. Although I'm still amazed that you were sitting in Sydney thinking about me in Melbourne, all those years ago, and now here we are together.'

'Well, now it's you who need to be serious,' the young man smiled, running a rough guitarist's fingertip along her arm and teasing her. 'Do you know how many boys fantasise about being in love with you?'

Lynn slapped his leg. 'That's not what I mean. And that's not what you meant either, is it?'

She was clever, there was no doubt about it, Jeff smiled. 'No. True enough. Well, partly true, at least. You know me... Sex always comes into the equation somewhere along the line.'

He received another well-deserved slap. 'Be quiet about that, and tell me more, please.'

Being brought back into line, Jeff immediately felt disconcerted again. 'The doors, you mean?'

Lynn nodded expectantly. Leaving her man nowhere else to go was definitely a tactic which yielded some positive results, now the pair had been together long enough for her to learn the triggers for his various reactions. She watched with interest as his eyes searched the horizon for a possible defence or deflection, knowing he would find none.

'OK,' he hesitated, heart rate quickening. 'Where was I with the doors? No, but before that, I want to finish talking about Lynn Dyson the suicide cure. We never finished that part.'

The beautiful blonde responded with an incredulous stare. 'It makes me sound like I did something special, which I didn't. But alright, tell me.'

'You did, and you better believe it,' Jeff insisted. 'You became like a lighthouse. A steadfast, ever-present lighthouse in my life, guiding me past all the rocks.'

The champion of imagery drew a circle on the rug by his girlfriend's knee, lifted a small stone from the ground nearby and placed it next to himself.

'This is you,' he first tapped her knee and then rested his finger on the pebble, 'and that's me. And here is my life…'

He waved the palm of his hand over the area in between, like it was an expansive ocean.

'There were rocks here, sharks here and pirates over there, but I knew that if I just kept you in my mind's eye, I'd be guided round all the scary shit and eventually I'd find you. So every time I wanted to call it a day, I'd just keep that vision in my head, and somehow it was enough to change my mind for another morning. Crazy, isn't it?'

Lynn was mesmerised by his story, half hoping it wasn't true. 'If this is your crazy, it's a very interesting world,' she remarked. 'I can't believe I was helping you back then. It makes me want to help you now, even more.'

'Please do,' Jeff invited, feeling turmoil washing through him again. 'Nothing would make me happier, angel. And yes, it is interesting, my world. You're right. That's the other way I've learned to deal with my weirdness: by finding myself interesting. It's been a fascinating journey, trying to understand how my mind works and how I can trick it to work differently. I've become something of a lab' rat for doctors, because I'm so determined to find out what's going on that I don't let them give up.'

The celebrity laughed. 'That sounds slightly conceited, but I understand what you mean.'

'Yeah, I guess it does,' he smiled. 'It is easy to get up oneself in this situation, so I'm happy to accept I'm conceited in a very cynical, self-deprecating kind of way. But what I'm trying to say, and you keep interrupting me with insightful observations…'

He leaned forward and kissed her much happier lips.

'…is that I don't want to stay wrapped up in my own world anymore. I'm sick of being surrounded by me and my craziness. I can't do what I want to do with my life while I'm like this, because I'm too caught up in me. So I need you to help me break away from all that noise and concentrate on important things.'

The nineteen-year-old paused and watched Lynn's expression remain unchanged. Did she really understand him that well?

'And now I'll tell you about the doors. But beware,' he warned, putting on an angry face. 'This is not going to be easy for me, so brace yourself.'

The patient schoolgirl shifted back to her original position and remained quiet, just squeezing the heavy arm which was now draped around her neck. Jeff was again thankful for her silent attention and embarked upon his explanation.

'Ever since I remember, dodgy stuff had been going on in our flat that really shouldn't have been. That part I just can't tell you yet.'

'That's OK. I'm happy to hear it in episodes. It's like listening to a serial drama on the radio,' his girlfriend told him childishly.

Jeff chuckled. 'Thanks! I'll put on my best ABC voice,' he continued, sniffing back tears. 'I didn't realise what effect all this was having on me, or even whether there was an initial trigger point, but as the years went by, I just saw way too much as a young bloke. It seemed like whenever I came home, I'd open the front door and there'd be something fucked going on. Sorry for the swearing, but it just makes me so bloody angry. And when I tried to do anything about it, I'd just be blamed for making it worse. So over time, things just built up into this blind, paranoiac fear of going home. I'd do anything not to go home.'

Lynn could tell her man was crying but still kept quiet. Her right hand reached up to his face, searching for his eyes. He caught hold of it and firmly placed it back down in her lap.

'No, you don't,' he scolded, half joking. 'Anyway... I kicked Gerry's parents' kitchen door down once. Can you believe that?'

The aristocratic young lady gasped. 'Really?'

'Yes, really! I felt so bad. I didn't see them after that for ages. Probably a couple of months.'

'So what happened? What made you do it?'

Jeff was becoming a little more relaxed. It truly was liberating to get all these secrets out in such an isolated setting. It was as if he had been transported to another world, from which he could speak freely about his life, as if it belonged to someone else.

'It was about three months after my mum died. I'd hardly been home at all since then. I even spent the night at school sometimes, until one night the security staff found me and reported me to Social Services.'

Lynn interrupted. 'Where were your dad and sister when all this was going on?'

'Oh, my dad was long gone. And Madalena lived with our grandparents, on my mum's side. That's where I should've been too, but I hated them, and they hated me. I never went there. So one day, I'd arranged with Gerry and his sister… Jacinta, that is, the elder one… that I'd come over at night, and to leave the kitchen door unlocked. I'd had a particularly shitty day, and at that point in my life the only emotion I was capable of was blind fury. Well… I got there, and they'd bolted the door, and I couldn't get in, so I kicked it in. At two in the morning.'

His girlfriend was spellbound by the latest in the growing catalogue of revelations. 'Wow! Were they angry?'

'You bet! I was drunk, of course, and you know how pleasant that is…'

Lynn nodded against his chin.

The young man smiled. 'The dog went off, and the whole family was up, trying to figure out what was going on. Gerry's dad was good though. He knew there was no reasoning with me at the time. He gave me a month to pay for the damage, which I paid back in two weeks, and he's never mentioned it since. When they found me, I'd smashed a glass on the kitchen table and was scoring my arm with the broken pieces.'

The schoolgirl gasped again, this time much louder. She turned his right wrist over, but there were no marks.

'No. Nothing to show for it, I'm afraid,' Jeff confirmed. 'Gerry's mum insisted I see a shrink. You can imagine how well that went down with an angry control freak! But I finally agreed. You'd like Gerry's mum… Celia… She's a lot like your mum but less glamorous. They checked me into the loony bin. I couldn't stand that either, so I broke out. They put me on sleeping pills and loony pills, and I started having hallucinations and felt like absolute crap, so *me escapé* and went back home. I've lived on my own since that time, and I've never been able to shake the morbid fear of opening a front door.'

The girl of his dreams sighed, shaking her head. 'God, that's terrible. What a story!'

Still her mystery man continued, relieved to be almost at the end. 'I've kicked my own front door down several times, and only ever when I could afford it the least. I nearly did it again that morning after I met you at the Sportsdrome. I'd been trying to get in for about fifteen minutes and was so fucking sick of it. Anyone's front door will do it, the darker the better. It's fine if it's glass and I can see what's on the other side, but solid doors completely fuck me up. Sometimes I can't even open the back of Suzanne's kennel van, and she looks at me like I'm some kind of retard.'

The young woman's heart was aching with distress at the monstrous narrative and had by now had quite enough of the storyteller talking to the back of her head. She placed both hands on his shaking forearms, feeling them jump in what she assumed to be some sort of shock.

'Jeff, can I turn around, please? Are you alright?'

'Yes, you can,' the student enunciated, syllable by slow syllable. 'I need you to kiss me.'

The sixteen-year-old twisted and knelt in front of her man, keen to indulge him this time. They locked each other's mouths in a kiss which neither wanted to end, until finally the red-blooded man pulled away, breathing heavily and quite clearly still agitated.

'So do you still love me?' he ventured, the words emerging more confidently from his lips than they were issued by his brain. 'This madman you've befriended?'

Suddenly overcome and confused by the juxtaposition of their conversation's nastiness and the intense arousal they were sharing, Lynn wrapped her arms around her handsome stranger and burst into a flood of tears. Jeff was taken aback too, attempting to stem his heavy breathing. He hadn't really counted on her caring to this extent and didn't quite know how to handle the situation.

'Hey! What's going on? That's supposed to be my job.'

He put his hands on the gorgeous woman's shoulders and locked his elbows straight out, so that her face was at arms' length from his. Her eyes were red, but her face was smiling, and her body exuded all the signs of physical longing. He could see pert nipples rubbing against the fabric of her top, and her face and chest were flushed pink. He too was rife with bestial craving.

'Jeff, this only makes me love you more. I can't imagine what your life's been like. I'll never complain again.'

The student was relieved yet fearful too. He knew there was danger in telling his story, because at some stage, pieces of it might reach her father. Then Bart and Marianna would get their people to put two and two together, bringing down the curtains for him. He kissed the corners of his dream girl's teary eyes, like she had done to him several times before.

'I love you so much. All the shit that's happened to me so far... That's history. Being here with you goes a long way towards making everything worthwhile. But listen to me... I'm not under any illusion that we're going to last forever. I'm not the kind of man your parents want you to be with, so I know sooner or later our time'll be up. And Jesus, I don't want it to happen, but when it does, we'll have to deal with it. Until then, let's just be here for each other, huh?'

But Lynn was crying again, sobbing in fact. All the while, she hung on to his arm as if it was saving her life.

'Jeff, I can't possibly think about not being with you. Fuck my parents!' the tennis player flicked her right hand in rejection.

'Hey! Them's fightin' words!' the student teased, never having heard the sophisticated teenager swear before, and a smile flashed across his face.

The celebrity was laughing and crying at the same time. She had surprised herself too, feeling uncharacteristically rebellious. Increasingly excited by the show of solidarity, not to mention the beautiful body which was screaming out for attention, Jeff wrestled her to the ground and pinned her down.

'One more outburst like that, young lady,' he remonstrated, 'and I'll have no choice but to remove your clothes and make you scream!'

'Go on then,' Lynn goaded, responding enthusiastically to his humour. 'Why don't you?'

The virile young man didn't need to be asked twice. They made as much noise as they could because there was no-one around to hear them, their passions thrashing wildly. To the caring lover's delight, Lynn came within moments of his fingers caressing her, grabbing tightly around his ribs as she rode out her orgasm. The naïve girl he had met just a few weeks prior was practically gone, with only a trace of visible innocence when his eyes begged her to climb on top and allow him to massage her breasts in the sunshine.

The pretty teenager screamed out her love, time and time again, rising the whole length of his turgid penis until she almost came free, clenching her muscles around it at the last moment and plunging down again. The intensity of this defiant act made Jeff shout out too, relishing the secluded setting and the ability to rid themselves of all inhibition. When it was over, they lay together on the rug, naked, blissful and totally at home in each other's company, both wishing they could suspend time and stay out in the warm air of their own, private paradise.

Stronger Together

After a while, Lynn broke the spell. 'What time do you think it is?'

Jeff's watch had been left in the ute, and he heaved himself onto his feet, making her smile with his groans of lazy objection. The sight of the beautiful woman's exposed body basking in the late afternoon sun made him glow inside, such was the connection between them. His beautiful woman. For now, at least... He reached for her clothes and tossed them onto her naked stomach before scooping up his own shorts and t-shirt and pulling them on.

'I don't know. Four o'clock or so. I'll see.'

'We should go back anyway,' Lynn decided. 'We haven't got much work done, have we?'

'Nope,' Jeff agreed, walking towards the cab.

He didn't care. This last few hours of openness had been much more productive, he thought, cursing his selfishness. With any luck, he might even sleep through the night tonight. A definite lightness had settled on his shoulders, the like of which he hadn't felt before and had trouble identifying as his own.

'It's quarter-to-four.'

The pair dressed and loaded their stuff into the tray of the ute. After putting up a lacklustre fight, Lynn allowed her boyfriend to drive back along the track to the house, and he showed off by expertly skating the vehicle's wheels across the top of the deep ruts, whistling cheekily as his passenger swooned.

'That's impressive,' the farmer's daughter admitted. 'Are you OK?'

The nineteen-year-old smiled at her. 'Never more so. You know... I'm my own worst enemy really.'

'Why?'

'Because I'm a typical man. Pride gets me every time. I developed this tough shell around me that no-one can penetrate, but then I can't get out either.'

Lynn let out a sunny laugh, kicking her feet up onto the front shelf, under the windscreen. 'That's funny!'

Jeff feigned disgruntlement. 'You might think it's funny...'

The young star gave a half-hearted apology, which was summarily rejected.

'Don't be sorry. I love how we can joke with each other like this. It's been a long time coming. Gerry's mum's the closest I've ever had to a female friend.'

'Gerry's mum?' his girlfriend joked. 'Did you have sex with her too?'

Her boyfriend gave her a stern look. 'Please... Not even I'd go that far. I'm trying to be serious here.'

She apologised again, and his long wingspan swooped its hand down onto her right thigh, rocking it back and forth as the car slewed across the road from side to side, steered by his playful right hand. Again Jeff made his dream girl laugh, and the more she laughed, the higher his tired heart soared.

'You know, angel... Celia never shopped me to the school or anything. She told Social Services that I was living with the Blakes, but I wasn't. I owe her a lot.'

His girlfriend smiled, sensing a more sombre mood than his actions portrayed. 'That's kind of her. I'd like to meet her and say thanks. But why did you stay in the same flat after all this had happened? Wouldn't moving have helped?'

'Tried that,' he answered flatly. 'Didn't work. I moved to another suburb. I also tried leaving my front door open for a while, so I could just walk in. But it didn't make any difference, and it was bloody stupid for security reasons. All the more ability for people to get in and wait for me. It was hell on wheels! I even lived with a woman for two months. What about that? Didn't work either!'

Lynn fell silent, and the atmosphere immediately changed. So that was how her mystery man knew what love was. Of course someone as adept and confident as this handsome Casanova would have seen it all before, perhaps several times. She was on a list. She could hardly have expected anything else, but his admission hurt regardless.

'Were you in love with her?'

'No,' Jeff replied, his voice quiet but emphatic. 'I was not in love with her. Donna, her name was. She was more than ten years older than me. A successful female I was infatuated with for all of a couple of weeks, before I came to my senses. I made the mistake of moving in with her, thinking it might help, as you suggested, but it was a disaster. She watched my every move and became this freaky, possessive cow as soon as I showed signs of disappearing. I don't know what I did in my former lives to deserve all these deviant people around me.'

The sixteen-year-old felt a little better. She had no choice but to believe him, and there was nothing she could do to change the past anyway. The empathetic man sensed her discomfort with this new information. He was used to upsetting women too. This unfortunate side-effect happened to him quite often. However, Lynn Dyson was the very last person he wanted to upset.

'I'm sorry, angel. I don't want to lie to you and I'm not lying to you. I've never been in love before. I was in love with you well before I met Donna, and she knew it. That was another problem between us. When I was in bed with her, I was having sex with you in my mind. Please believe me.'

'Thanks,' the celebrity sighed, sitting up straight while the ute turned into the garage. 'It's so annoying. I wish I didn't flare up with jealousy, but I can't help it. I know you must've been with heaps of women before me, because how else would you be such a sexpert?'

Jeff laughed. 'Sexpert? That's quite good. As long as that's not anything like pervert, I'm happy.'

'No,' his passenger affirmed, smiling again. 'I know. It's just horrible to think about, that's all. Let's change the subject.'

The driver's door slammed before her mouth had closed, and Lynn was smothered through the open passenger window in a tender kiss. The romantic move left her breathless and radiant, realising that her man disliked causing her pain. The door between them opened slowly while they were still locked in the kiss, and soon there were two pairs of feet on the ground, while their two bodies stood either side of the metal frame, lips and hands engaged through it.

'Yeah. I can understand,' the dark-haired stranger murmured, finally breaking away and holding out his hand. 'Men and women are very different in that respect. Men find it hard to link things together, and you strange female creatures find it hard to separate them. How did we ever let this happen, as a human race? Some aspects of our so-called evolution are inexplicable and totally counterintuitive. We don't make it easy for ourselves, do we?'

And so it was that the young woman had already forgiven him. His Pied Piper lyrics were so eloquent and philosophical. After years of taking the blame for things he didn't do, Jeff Diamond had perfected the art of absolving himself from any blame for those he actually had done. She moved on, determined not to let his murky past bother her any further.

'So do you think you'll ever get better?'

'From the doors thing, you mean?'

Lynn nodded. 'And the nightmares.'

'Don't know,' the student shrugged. 'I hope things'll improve, because I can't go on like this for much longer. I really need to find some way of getting regular sleep, at least. And as for getting through my front door, who knows? I've tried everything. But you also have to understand there's a big part of me that doesn't want to be cured either.'

His girlfriend looked puzzled, gathering up their belongings. As if waiting for the words to properly sink in, the couple paused in the garage, facing each other.

'Seriously. It's part of me,' Jeff went on. 'It's made me who I am, and I'm proud of that, in a strange kind of way. It's interesting you used the word "conceited", isn't it? I've come through it, and now look... I'm here with you.'

The tall man reached his laden arms towards her and then turned towards the huge, neo-Georgian mansion, his eyes lighting up.

'It gives me strength and inspiration to know I'm a survivor. I think if I were suddenly to be without all these odd symptoms, I'd lose something of myself. I really believe that.'

Lynn nodded, standing on tiptoe to reach his lips. 'I guess that makes sense, if it's been this way for so long.'

The re-energised nineteen-year-old was on a roll. He led his nubile, new confidante into the courtyard, and they laid down their respective loads and sat at one of the tables while he smoked. Curling a string of little, white clouds sexily upwards, the storyteller opened up yet further.

'And another good side effect is that it's taught me a hell of a lot about people and how to deal with them. In my book, there are two types of relationship: using relationships and respecting relationships. I've had a whole heap of using relationships; the ones in which you just get what you want, then walk away from at any time. And no-one owes anyone anything. D'you know what I mean by reciprocity?'

'I know what a reciprocal arrangement is,' his mesmerised muse offered. 'Like a contract that sets out who does what in a partnership? Is that what you mean?'

'Sort of. In business terms, yes. I'm talking about person-to-person. You understand reciprocity implicitly,' the teacher said, pointing to Lynn's forehead. 'I can see it in how you interact with people, with your family and with me. It's knowing that nothing comes for free.'

'Not in terms of money though,' the rapidly-maturing young woman confirmed. 'Like giving and receiving. Knowing how lucky you are and what you have to do to earn what you have.'

'¡Exactamente!' Jeff cheered, tapping the table twice in approval. 'Stuff you learn growing up, or rather you should learn. Well... As you'd probably guess, I had to learn the spirit of reciprocity bloody fast, because I needed people to help me out when I was left on my own as a kid. I always remember having a big fight with Gerry's baby sister, Tamilla, because she was such a spoiled brat for a while. She used to use up all her favours with everyone... especially her mum... and then just sat there on her arse and sulked when she could no longer get what she wanted.'

Lynn laughed without inhibition, leaning back on the wrought iron chair. 'I've got a few friends like that. They think it's everyone else's fault except their own when things don't go their way, without stopping to think why it happened.'

'Hmm... They're the ones,' her boyfriend agreed with a broad grin. 'I was always keen to give back to Gerry's family, because I liked going to their house and getting roast dinners and a present at Christmas, but Tammy'd give me crap for doing the dishes and washing cars. In her mind, that stuff was sucking up, and she had no room for it. Anyway... What I mean by a using relationship is where the reciprocity's finite and understood, rather than an ongoing investment. Does that make sense?'

The pretty teenager frowned, a little uncertain of herself. 'I think so. You agree to do something specific for each other.'

'Yep, and then it's over,' Jeff picked up a dry, brittle twig that the wind had blown onto the table and snapped it right next to the schoolgirl's ear. 'Clean break. No questions asked. Work is a using relationship for most people. Like, I'll do this list of duties in exchange for this number of dollars per hour, day, week... whatever... with a lunch break and two smokos thrown in, if you're lucky.'

'OK. I see,' Lynn smiled, utterly captivated by the skilful orator. 'Like a coach. Give me fifty push-ups, and you can take a thirty second breather.'

Jeff laughed. 'Perfect reciprocity! But I'd hope you wouldn't only have a using relationship with your coach, because you'd want to both aim for something a little more long-term, I'm assuming. An example for me, back at school, was when my maths teacher had her leather jacket stolen by some shit-kicker kids. Y'see, I needed access to more challenging lessons, so I retrieved her jacket and in return asked her to help me. And she did. She was very grateful, because the jacket was a gift from her boyfriend. But then I teased her by putting the thought into her head that maybe I'd stolen the coat in the first place, so I could get her to help me.'

The young woman's jaw fell open, making him chuckle.

'Did you steal it?' she asked, hoping he hadn't.

'No. And that would've been a using relationship deliberately engineered by one party, wouldn't it?' the bad boy told her. 'It would still get both parties what they needed but it's morally wrong.'

Lynn's eyes widened in wonder. 'Yes, I see. Because there's no respect for the person?'

'Precisely,' Jeff nodded. 'You're damned good, lady! But it's a start, if you want to build it into something more later. So the reciprocity's short-term in a using relationship, but much longer term in a respecting relationship. The promises you make... the clauses in the contract, if you like... aren't based on instant results. It's a shared investment in time and energy into the future, because you want to develop mutual respect.'

'And love,' the young star added, taking his hand and watching her man's deep, dark eyes dance in appreciation. 'I know exactly what that means. Being a parent is the most obvious example, isn't it? Kids don't tend to repay all the effort and heartache until they're adults themselves, and then the payback should go into reverse.'

Jeff stubbed his cigarette out and leaned forward in his chair, until their faces were only inches apart, not wanting this conversation to end. He kissed her tempting mouth, lifting his left hand to stroke her silken cheek. The long, blonde hair belonging to his new friend was untidy and tangled, and her face had slightly reddened from having been out in the sun all afternoon. Brushing a few, stray strands over her shoulder and kissing her again, the kid from the wild, wild west sank into another lengthy, dreamlike interlude, having great difficulty believing that he was sitting and discussing some of his most favourite subjects with Lynn Dyson, of all people.

'Yeah, I guess so,' he nodded. 'I'm painfully aware of the need for reciprocity between us, because you're the first respecting relationship I've allowed myself. Back then, I could never count on getting favours in advance. No-one in their right mind would invest in me, and for good reason a lot of the time. I was an unholy mess and couldn't give a toss about anyone else. I think parents get repaid in other ways in those early years, like having cute photos on their mantelpieces and a hug at bedtime. But perhaps those things are just a representation, an icon serving to remind them of the end game; a symbol of payback yet to come.'

'That's sweet,' the sixteen-year-old smiled, pecking him on the cheek. 'Reciprocity in a respecting relationship's still important though, isn't it? Otherwise, one party gets taken for granted and then they'll dump you.'

Laughing out loud, the boy from Canley Vale lit another cigarette.

'Yeah. Highly likely! It's much *more* important, in my opinion. Everything's more important in a respecting relationship. It's the difference between a job and a career, for example. In a job, you just turn up every day, do your stuff, collect your pay and go home. A career is more of a thing you nurture. You know... Work harder, study, look for promotion, and in return your employers see their business growing and reward you. Hopefully, that is.'

'So, at uni', you just have a job?' Lynn checked her level of understanding.

'Yep. Although I do sometimes make suggestions for how things might work better, which I don't have to do in order to get paid,' the student answered. 'I just can't help myself. But that's how people like me get noticed. That's loading the scales of reciprocity in my favour, if you like.'

'Like stealing your maths teacher's leather jacket. Another immoral act?'

'You don't believe me?' he teased, hoping she did. 'D'you really think I stole it?'

'No, I don't,' she replied. 'But you make it sound like you've got a guilty conscience.'

Jeff shook his head, lighting another cigarette to hide his impulsive fears. 'That's fair. I can see how you'd think that. It helps get my point across. That's my excuse anyway!'

Lynn lifted herself out of her chair and kissed him from across the table. What was going on inside this man's head? Each conversation they shared ended up like a see-saw, his eyes giving away his mood shifts even sooner than his body language, while his smooth mouth continued to charm her as if nothing had changed.

'Carry on,' she urged. 'You were talking about getting noticed at work. Loading the scales.'

'Yeah, thanks. I don't agree that loading the scales that way's immoral. There's nothing dishonest about promoting yourself, as long as you're not exaggerating or lying or unfairly discrediting someone else in the process. You have to remember, I don't have all these sponsors and generous benefactors watching over me, telling my boss how wonderful I am and that he should make me the manager. Like the "old boy network" Gerry lives with. Someone like me'd struggle in that environment, because I didn't go to the right school and my uncle doesn't belong to the right golf club. You know how it is. That's *your* world.'

'This is turning into a political argument!' his girlfriend scoffed. 'I agree with you though. I hate the "old boy network". Dad always says there are so many brainless idiots in high places who've only got there because Uncle Henry put in a good word for them, and they really depend on having good people working for them, otherwise their businesses would fall in a hole. It's upside down, isn't it?'

Jeff thumped the table, pretending to be annoyed. 'It *is* upside down! You're bloody right, angel. *Exactement!* It's been that way for centuries, so it's going to take a long time to change it. But we *will* change it, Lynn.'

The impassioned orator made a lunge for the young star's hands and squeezed them tightly, her squeal of surprise sending shockwaves through his body. He knew he shouldn't push his luck by sharing his grand ambitions with her so soon, but she was a much more receptive audience than he had ever dared to expect. There was a latent world-changer lurking in Lynn Dyson, just as there was in him. He already knew this, and with any luck, she did too.

'You and I'll change it. OK? Meritocracy. That's what we need. At work and at home, everyone brings their own set of traits, skills and experiences to a relationship. Mix 'em all up together in the way that's going to work best and reward everyone appropriately for their part in the success. Not just big fat bonuses for the bosses, when the workers have done all the work and covered up their bosses' failures, and then still have to fight for a two percent pay rise.'

'That reminds me of "Behind every great man, there's a good woman,"' Lynn interjected, becoming more fired up too. 'What a load of rubbish that is! My mum gets really angry when she reads a magazine or newspaper article that describes her as the housewife who raises Bart Dyson's children and keeps the household running. Such an insult! She works just as hard, but people only seem to notice him.'

'Jesus, don't get me started on that!' Jeff laughed. 'I've had so many arguments with Gerry's dad on that topic too. Where are the equal partnerships, huh? Fine in the dark ages, when women didn't get an education.

But even that doesn't make it right, because why did they choose back then not to educate women? Did they think women didn't have brains? And why pay thousands of dollars in private school fees to educate your daughters if all you want them to be is a good housewife to another silver spoon lawyer or accountant? What a waste of money! Better to send you all to cooking classes, I say...'

'Hey! Excuse me?' Lynn stood up and bashed her boyfriend on the head for such a blatantly chauvinistic comment. 'You bastard! And I thought you were on our side?'

Jeff grabbed the irate teenager and pulled her round the table and onto his lap. His hands gripped her ribcage strongly, his thumbs brushing the underside of her breasts while he ground her down onto him. She raised no objection to this equally bad behaviour, so he lifted his left hand and cupped her breast, his lips nipping the side of her neck. His penis hardened almost instantly, pushing against his young lover's buttocks, and her hand squeezed into the tight space underneath to feel it.

'Humping and a good feed. That's all you're good for,' he teased, kissing all over the teenager's face and neck, slowly and with just the right amount of force to drive her crazy with desire. 'There's no point in teaching you girls anything else. And that gets us back to using versus respecting relationships, because if ours was a using relationship, at this point you'd tell me to pack my bags and never darken your door again. But hopefully you know I don't really mean what I say this time.'

Lynn turned to face him and kissed his lips, having witnessed yet another one-hundred-and-eighty degree mood swing. 'No, of course not! Like you didn't steal that leather jacket... You're just illustrating your point. I love having these conversations that can go from serious to funny and back again. It's fantastic!'

'Thanks. So do I. But to get heavy again for a minute,' Jeff continued, 'you must believe me that I've only had one respecting relationship, and that's you and me. Well, perhaps Gerry's family counts as one too these days? They started off with me using them, but I hope that'll gradually change over time. With you, it's all about respecting each other, even right from the start. From before the start, in fact. I want to make you happy, and I'd love you to make me happy. Is that a deal?'

His eyes drilled into hers, begging for agreement. The sixteen-year-old wrapped her arms around his shoulders and leaned into his clamorous embrace. Her temperature was rising again, nearly as fast as Jeff's was, in what she was now easily coming to recognise as sexual arousal. She sensed her vagina craving an absence of fabric between it and his rock-hard erection.

But more than these sure-fire signals, by far the stronger drawcard was the prospect of entering into a respecting relationship with a man so tempestuously indignant about unfairness in the world. If anything, this side of her handsome stranger was even more attractive than his smouldering looks and eager body.

'Yes, it's a deal,' Lynn confirmed, emphatically shaking his hand. 'Let's go in, shall we?'

The nobody from New South Wales felt very good indeed, holding their unused pile of books low in front of his shorts and praying they wouldn't run into any family members between the courtyard and Lynn's bedroom. He had survived another confession, the knowledge of which was tremendously empowering. Walking back into the house in silence, he reflected upon his own comments about being cured. He had read many biographies of successful and famous people who had been affected by depression and other mental illnesses. He wondered which came first, the genius or the craziness. Why had he not accepted his fate at fourteen and gone to live with his grandparents, as his sister had done? Perhaps he might not have had to fight so hard, but then he more than likely would not now be spending the weekend at Benloch with the girl of his dreams either…

Taking a quick look around at the impressive house and grounds, cementing them well and truly into his psyche, Jeff caught a glimpse of Lynn's father at an upstairs window. The Olympian was gazing down at them, as they made their way towards the door. How long had he been there? Had he been watching them talking and larking about? It made the guest feel apprehensive, somehow like an imposter. Perhaps Bart and Marianna were beginning to regret being so free and easy about their daughter's entry into the big, wide world? They probably hadn't banked on her falling in love so soon, and with such an unknown quantity.

'You're very pensive,' the young woman observed, taking his hand as they walked up the stairs.

Her man smiled. 'Just thinking,' he replied, making her laugh again.

'Well, you can stop now. It's the weekend, and we haven't done any work yet. We'll have to do it now.'

The grateful man nudged her shoulder, leaning over and whispering suggestively in her ear. 'Yes, we should, although I'd rather fuck your brains out.'

The celebrity blushed and looked around furtively. 'Wait! Don't say that out here.'

Her boyfriend backed away, his eyes alive with innuendo but his mouth now determinedly shut. She giggled again and blew him a kiss with her free hand. Jeff's expression turned stormy, silently accusing her of being two-faced, and they were both laughing out loud by the time she let them into her room. Dumping their belongings on the dresser just inside the door, the nineteen-year-old swept his quarry up off the floor and locked her lips in another deep, earth-shattering kiss.

'Lynn, thanks for listening to me,' he breathed across her face, setting her feet back down onto the carpet. 'I'm so glad you're you. And remember, I've never loved anyone else before, and I *will* never love anyone else. I'm sure of that.'

They kissed again. 'Thanks. I love you too,' came her breathless reply.

The amorous pair didn't even make it to the bed. Jeff guided the awakening teenager to the couch, and she sank into it at his request, her hands reaching for the waistband of his shorts. The impatient man scolded his muse for being in such a hurry, immediately pulling off his t-shirt and making her laugh again. Their lovemaking was intrepid, their desire to satisfy each other seemingly unquenchable after their very private conversation had bonded them ever firmer in the lazy sunshine of their oasis.

With an orgasm soon upon her, Lynn cried out so loud that her partner felt compelled to cover her mouth with his spare hand, fearing her sister or brother might overhear and come running to investigate the excitement. There seemed to be no end to the stimulation one could give the other, and before long he too was struggling to contain his fervour. Breathing in unison, the lovers stayed still at the end, linked together from top to toe on the sofa.

***

'Now let's talk about you,' the comedian finally announced with aplomb, lifting himself clear of Lynn's spent body and rolling onto the floor. 'I'm sick of talking about me. You remember when we were on our first date at the theatre, you said something about wanting to experience freedom?'

The student beckoned to the beautiful blonde to go ahead of him into the bathroom, collecting the various pieces of clothing which had been discarded so precipitously just a short while ago.

His girlfriend nodded, walking backwards. 'Yes. That's when you kissed me for the first time.'

The boy from Canley Vale smiled, hit with an unexpected and poignant shyness. 'Yeah, that's right. I'm glad you remember that, because it resonated inside me like you wouldn't believe. So what is it you're looking for that means freedom to you?'

Jeff searched her eyes for answers. The teenager stood under the shower, allowing her enigmatic stranger to lather her entire body, slowly and with casual but deliberately caring strokes. She returned the favour, relishing the sensation of taut muscles under hairy skin. He became hard again, pulling her in close and allowing their bodies to shift from side to side together with their slippery, soapy coating. To his surprise, there were tears in the young woman's eyes, and he pulled back to arms' length to make sure she was alright.

'Oh, I don't want to complain. I have a wonderful life with so many opportunities. I feel bad even voicing my opinions, especially after what you told me today.'

'But that's nuts,' her boyfriend assured her, turning off the taps and taking the towel she held out for him. 'Everyone's world has its own priorities. Freedom's very important, whatever form it takes. *Digame...*'

The couple dressed quickly and headed back into the lounge area, originally having intended to settle into some homework. Lynn sat down at her desk and took a number of books out of her school bag, feeling heavy-hearted and not wanting to let her boyfriend know. The university student prepared his own work by spreading it out over the coffee table, whistling one of his new compositions softly to himself. Her heightened level of activity amused him, and he winked when he caught her eye.

'I'm going to make some coffee,' the young woman announced. 'Would you like some?'

Nodding, Jeff got up and followed her, sensing a sudden disquiet between them. 'Hey, what's wrong? Are you still annoyed about me living with someone else?'

Lynn shook her head. 'No. Well, yes, a little bit, but that's not what's bothering me. In fact, I don't really know what's bothering me.'

The empath cuddled her from behind as they waited for the kettle to boil. It was refreshing to find he wasn't the only one with insecurities, and he longed to be granted permission to discover more about this beautiful woman's inner self.

'Well, whatever it is, I'd like to hear it. How can we do anything about it otherwise? You said as much yourself, and not so long ago.'

The sixteen-year-old sighed, leaning back against him. 'Thanks. I know. It's just that the Dyson name and all it stands for can get very stifling sometimes, and I long to be a free agent, like you. But then when I hear all the horror stories that have happened to you, I realise I'm so lucky, compared to you.'

'Hmm...' the worldly student nodded comically, his chin bashing the top of her head. 'That is a very interesting dichotomy. Will you allow me to delve further?'

Lynn laughed. 'Delve? What are you going to delve into?'

'Whatever you'll allow me to,' Jeff answered, kissing the back of her neck and slipping his hand under her t-shirt. 'If you want a preliminary assessment, I'd hazard a guess that you're part jet-lagged, part sick of hearing about my life, part annoyed that you're only sixteen, when all your friends are over that adult threshold, and part stressed about your preparation for the Olympics, given the fact you've been travelling so much.'

Childishly, his girlfriend spun around and kissed him squarely on the lips, her feet leaving the floor in an effort to reach.

'Wow! You're so perceptive,' she declared. 'I'd say that was spot on. I am worried about that stuff. So what am I going to do, doctor?'

The young man smiled. 'Well… If I were a charlatan, I'd recommend a course of physical therapy to be taken over there,' he said, indicating with his head towards the bed. 'Four times a day, six on weekends, progressively building to eight as we get closer to September.'

Lynn sighed, looking exhausted just thinking about it. 'And if you weren't a charlatan?'

'That's the option you like though, isn't it? I can tell,' the red-blooded male persisted, with a flash of his dark, gipsy eyes, 'and I'm just the man to deliver it.'

'Stop!' Lynn bashed him on the chest in frustration. 'Be serious, you sex maniac!'

Feeling sorry for the feisty but frustrated teenager standing in front of him, the comic took her hand and led her back towards the sofa. He watched her hungrily, fighting to extinguish the fire which was fast building inside him yet again, before collecting their drinks and setting them on the floor next to the coffee table. The schoolgirl slumped down heavily.

'Come on, Miss. Spread out on the therapist's couch, and let me delve,' he invited.

Jeff lifted her legs, pausing until Lynn had stretched her long, slender body across the three cushions. He then pushed his piles of books and notes to the far side of the low table and sat on it, staring into her blue eyes.

'OK. Where'll we start?' the surrogate psychologist mused aloud. 'At the end, I think. Olympics. How's the training going?'

The celebrity giggled. 'You *are* serious, aren't you?'

Her boyfriend nodded and shrugged, his smile making her stomach churn. 'Your wish is my command. Come on. Spill the beans, baby.'

'Well, doctor, it's like this…' his patient opened, with a grin on her face.

'Good start,' he smirked, feeding off her humour.

'I've been entered into too many events, Jeff,' she told him, the smile vanishing from her face in a flash. 'The tennis and equestrian events are fine, because they're at either end of the fortnight, but the athletics and the tennis are happening at the same time. I just don't think I'll be able to swap between them easily.'

At first, the practised counsellor steered clear of offering an opinion. 'So is the problem logistics or preparation?'

'Both,' Lynn moaned. 'It's not as easy for me to get around as it is for the others, because I'm more easily recognised. Plus, I'm the only person in the team who's in both, so I'll be on my own going back and forth.'

'Have you told your dad this? Or the team manager, or whoever's responsible for logistics?'

'Yes, Dad and I have talked about it, but I didn't get much of a hearing. I'll have to try again more forcefully. The team manager hasn't been appointed yet.'

'Maybe that's the angle then. Why don't you ask him if he can do anything to speed up the appointment of the logistics people, or find out who you can talk to over in Munich about it?'

The sixteen-year-old smiled. 'That's actually a really good idea, because then it's not my deficiency. He can't just tell me to push harder.'

Jeff put his hand on her forehead, and looked at his watch, making her laugh out loud. 'Eight, nine, ten. Good. Your temperature's a little lower. Your deficiency? Is that really what he'd say? You have no deficiencies, angel. You're perfect. What about the preparation part?'

Lynn reached her head upwards and kissed his hand. 'And you're gorgeous. Thanks for doing this. It does feel good to talk things through, doesn't it?'

'Hey! Lay back, please, Miss. Don't waste time. I'm very expensive. We've only got an hour, and then I have to see my next client.'

Lying flat and giggling softly, the sportswoman thought for a moment. 'My training schedule's pretty full on, I have to admit. It's going to be really hard for us to see each other. I don't want to mention that to Dad, because I'm scared he'll make me stop seeing you altogether.'

Her voice cracked, and the compassionate student saw tears in her eyes. In a second, he felt his chest tightening as a familiar sense of panic crept into his mind too.

'Don't stress about that,' he urged, knowing full well that he would do enough stressing about that for the both of them. 'We can wait until you're home with all those gold medals round your neck. I'm not going anywhere, if I can help it.'

Lynn was pacified a little, although still on the verge of tears. 'That's my main problem though,' she went on. 'It's not good to have priorities other than the glorious victory. It was fine until I met you, but now I'm not so excited by my potential as an athlete or a tennis player. I'm more interested in the music and in all these new ideas you're firing off in my brain. They're like little sparks all around me, and I don't want them to go out. And the conversations we've had today have only reinforced this.'

Jeff inhaled, instinctively reaching over to his pile of homework and unearthing his cigarettes and lighter. This was a worrying sign for the persuasive amateur psychiatrist. He mustn't be seen as the cause of any hindrance to Australia's golden girl realising her potential, due to the knock-on effect it was bound to have on his own potential. His mind referred back to the copious research he had carried out as part of his quest to become a "someone", about the many young Hollywood actors and pop stars who had ruined their lives by pursuing the wrong dream at the wrong time. If he and Lynn were to survive as a couple, he couldn't afford to be partly responsible for, or even perceptibly influential in a similarly spectacular fall from grace. More importantly, not right under Bart Dyson's nose.

'Right. This is more serious,' his tone was now earnest, and Lynn was struck by the same wonder at the apparent depth of his emotions. 'Logistics we can handle, but I said to you when we first got together that I didn't want to stand in your way. We can work around all the training schedules and travel. That's no problem. But if your parents pick up the fact your heart's not in it, there'll definitely be ramifications for us.'

'I know,' the young beauty agreed. 'That's what I'm afraid of. Even though I completely agree with you about speaking my mind and trusting my instincts, I don't think I can get away with it while I'm still under age. There's just no space in my life for free thought.'

Jeff nodded his comprehension. 'That's OK, angel. You can think freely when you're with me. We'll work it out, even if it means we don't get to spend too much time together. We can still talk.'

'That's what I mean... On one hand, I feel guilty about complaining to you,' the modest youngster added, 'but then, one advantage you have over me is that you can make all your own decisions. Even though I really, really hate what you've been through, at least you haven't had to fight for your independence from your family. I can't make my own decisions for another year-and-a-half.'

'Well, you could,' her enigmatic stranger contradicted gently, 'but the consequences would be drastic. Lynn, I'm not going to ask you to disown your family or to decry Dyson principles or anything. I'd be pretty bloody selfish to ask for that. I understand exactly what you mean, and you do need to be careful. Just tell me what you want me to do and say, and I'll fall into line. We can be free after September.'

The glum teenager leaned over towards her handsome counsellor, who met her halfway, giving her a big kiss. The coffee table let out a loud crack under his shifting weight, and they dissolved into laughter as the tall man slid onto the floor in mock alarm.

'Thanks! Are you OK? I really appreciate what you're saying and that you get it. I'm sorry I'm so young and under the thumb.'

'Hey!' her boyfriend replied, showing her the palms of his hands. 'Don't apologise to me. We're all who we are right now. Nothing more, nothing less. The trick is to figure out who we want to be next and then take action at the appropriate time to change. We're both at the mercy of people who don't understand us, angel, but we can work around that.'

'We still haven't done any work, have we?' the schoolgirl sighed, her smile returning as they drank their coffee. 'What were the other things on your list of diagnoses? Jet-lag and sick of hearing about your life?'

'Yep, and not being an adult, but we've already dealt with that one, I s'pose,' Jeff agreed. 'Jet-lag. Can't really do anything about it, except wait until it wears off.'

'Yes, and I'm definitely not sick of hearing about your life,' Lynn insisted. 'You got that one wrong.'

'Seventy-five percent,' the corners of her diligent shrink's mouth turned downwards, receiving an empathetic smack on his knee. 'I'm slipping. Let me see if I can't convince you I'm right. You've got to think on another level, and in fact you already did. You talked about not wanting to complain about your issues, because you don't think they're as big as mine. That's sort of sympathy fatigue, in a way. You know... Like if you go to an art gallery, and by the time you've been round six or seven halls, you never want to see another priceless painting ever again in your whole life...'

The talented musician laughed out loud. 'Yes, I do know that feeling. And that makes me feel guilty too.'

'Bingo!' Jeff chalked up a point in mid-air and then invited a high-five. 'I'm on fire!'

Reluctantly, his partner-in-crime raised her hand to his, but then changed her mind. 'Hold on! Is that what you meant originally? I think you're moving the goal posts.'

The intelligent and hypnotic nineteen-year-old grinned. 'Maybe a bit, yes, although not entirely. What I mean is it's about time you didn't have to deal with my problems and we dealt with yours. Which is exactly why I changed the subject when we got back into the house. It's a stretch, but not a leap.'

Lynn clocked her gorgeous boyfriend lightly on the chin, clambering to a sitting position, and then kissed him on the lips. She was immediately gathered up by two strong arms and pulled closer into his chest. Jeff's love for her was so utterly overt, and she felt exactly the same way about him. What were they going to do?

'OK. I believe you, master manipulator.'

'Eighty-seven-and-a-half percent, then?' the young man bargained. 'Is that fair?'

The pretty celebrity sat with her knees between his legs and reached up to stroke his stubbly cheek. He leaned forwards and kissed her forehead, just as her arms folded around his shoulders.

'Yes, it's perfectly fair. I'd even go ninety. I love you, Jeff.'

'I love you too. So much. And I mean what I say about not getting in the way. I'm in this for as long as I can be, so let's keep talking.'

'Me too,' Lynn echoed, tilting over towards the untidy heap of books. 'I suppose we should finally get down to some work, shouldn't we? It'll be dinner time soon. Which is my pile of reading?'

The undergraduate reached across and picked up a paper folder which was on top of four hefty textbooks. Inside were several scraps of paper, presumably marking passages relevant to the assignments Lynn had on her plate. His girlfriend's eyes spoke volumes, and he could taste the gratitude in her kiss.

'Here you are. Last week's MA Year Twelve summary, courtesy of Michelle and me.'

The famous schoolgirl leafed through the folder. There were references to specific pages and quotes already pulled out, complete with odd cartoon drawings and quirky one-liners which made her giggle. This effort would surely save her a great deal of time. If only all their problems were as easy to solve...

'Wow! This must've taken you ages. Thank you!'

'*De nada, señorita.* It was fun. I enjoyed it. Some bits were a refresher, but not all of it,' Jeff replied, pleased to be able to give back some more.

***

That evening, with her parents having left for Melbourne to attend a function and her older brother playing a late football match at the MCG, Lynn was in charge of the household for Saturday night and Sunday morning. Helen cooked up a storm in the kitchen, making dinner for the three children and their handsome guest, who fitted perfectly into the easy-going environment.

All the years playing the extra child at the Blakes' had made the poor, singleton student appreciative of such an ordinary situation, never having had the benefit of growing up in a loving family of his own. After dinner, the four youngsters headed across the courtyard to the gymnasium, where they played basketball and badminton for a couple of hours. Apart from a single beer before dinner, no alcohol had passed Jeff's lips, and he had only managed to sneak one quick cigarette between buildings.

He didn't mind at all though. The cravings were always there, badgering at the back of his mind, but the good, clean, innocent fun was a welcome change from his normally debauched Saturday night activities. Lynn was totally engaging, never once letting him forget how sexy she was, and it left him as breathless as any long rally might.

New lyrics and tunes filled the creative man's head to bursting point, sometimes spilling out into brief serenades for his enthusiastic lover, or else they sat waiting, lodged in his imagination until he could manage to slip away and write them down. Once Sandy and Anna had retired to bed, he and Lynn sat side-by-side at the Steinway and shaped some more songs from these new beginnings. They raided Bart Dyson's drinks cabinet, helping themselves to whisky on the rocks, and sang out their respective annoyances at the world, encouraging each other at every step.

'I've been waiting so long for this,' Jeff crooned, cradling his dream girl in his lap while his left hand played a selection of emotionally-charged chords. 'I always dreamed about making music with you; that we'd sound good together.'

'We do sound good together,' the young star affirmed. 'Very good. You really need to record some of your songs.'

'Do I?'

She nodded, nuzzling into his warm chest. 'Yes, you do.'

'Thanks, angel. I will. One day, when I get my shit together.'

The happy teenagers kissed passionately, their hands traversing each other's bodies through their clothes, both exhausted from a long day and excited by an equally long night in each other's company. Lynn sighed at the delicious feeling of his fingers fondling her breasts, while she stroked his erection, squeezing its tip and running her long nails down its length, through his track-suit pants.

'Jesus, that's good,' her boyfriend hissed in her ear. 'I can't believe I found you. It's just so unlikely, isn't it?'

'Why?'

The young man shook his head at her *naïvetée*, wondering if it was genuine or if she was doing it deliberately to turn him on further. Either way, it was fine.

'Look, lady… I'm in Lynn Dyson's house, sitting at a grand piano, writing songs with Lynn Dyson, who's wearing next to nothing, with no shoes and hair all messed up from playing sport. With me…'

'And my younger siblings,' the playful sixteen-year-old added.

'Yeah. Them too. Don't tarnish my memories with the whole truth, OK?'

The celebrity giggled, tickling his ribs. 'You're like a little boy inside a grown man's body.'

Jeff paused his kidding around and leaned back, initially offended by her observation. 'What do you mean?'

'Nothing,' Lynn smiled at his defensiveness. 'Just sometimes you act like all you want to do is play, and then other times you're like an old man, spouting wise sayings.'

'I can't believe you said that. That's exactly how I feel on the inside. But how old?'

'Oh, old,' she laughed. 'Really wise and mature. It's lovely. It's a compliment. And I just love how you love everything about me, and about being here. All the simple stuff.'

The boy from Canley Vale shrugged, bewildered by the way this beautiful woman had pinpointed his vulnerabilities so accurately. He kissed the mouth which was so anxious not to put him offside, as if she realised how out of control his emotions were, prowling around behind his polished exterior.

'The simple stuff's all I can afford, but my entire being... physical, spiritual, emotional and sexual... is at your disposal. It's all I have, Lynn. Use it at will, and I'll take whatever I get in return, whether it's a few hours in the State Library doing your homework with you or playing basketball with your baby brother.'

'Shhh,' the celebrity whispered, interlacing the fingers of her right hand into his left. 'I don't need you to spend money on me. I go out all the time, Jeff. This one-on-one is perfect. In fact, it's much nicer doing this than it would be going to dinner in some stuffy restaurant and having to be on our best behaviour.'

The lowly student exhaled, not knowing how to respond.

'There's some kid left in me too, I suppose,' Lynn continued. 'I try to hide it, but I'm not done growing up totally. One day I will be, and I'll get caught up in the party set, like my friends, but I'm actually so happy you agreed to come out here for the weekend. I did wonder if you'd rather stay in the city.'

Jeff's eyes drilled into her clear, blushing face, suddenly overtaken by carnal need, as if a slow-burning fuse had been lit deep within. 'Can I take you to bed?'

How lucky had he got? Good things like this didn't happen to blokes like him. The Sydneysider fought his obsessive cynicism and vowed silently to make the most of the time he could steal from this gorgeous godsend before her parents saw through him and sent him packing. Until then, he would play Prince Charming and give his princess all the love she could take.

Lynn levered herself up off his thighs and beckoned for her handsome songwriter to follow her, which he did, like an eager puppy. The pretty teenager couldn't remember ever feeling so entranced by life, despite all the amazing experiences her privileged position had already brought her. Why had she accepted this fascinating stranger so readily, almost as if she already knew him well?

It reminded the romantic starlet of stories she had read as a child, of young soldiers returning to their wives after years on the battlefield, shell-shocked but much richer for the experience. And like the Vietnam veterans with whom she had spoken during her first brush with this Post-Traumatic Stress syndrome which her boyfriend described, it was as if he was a broken man in need of healing. What had happened to Jeff in his childhood that caused him to be broken at nineteen years old? And why did he choose to latch on to her so tightly at every chance?

Without speaking, the tired pair climbed the sweeping front staircase and soon found themselves behind the second last white door.

'Did you study this hard all year?' the schoolgirl asked, confronted with the two sets of books which they had abandoned on receiving the call for dinner.

Jeff dragged her by both hands, chuckling as she tried her best to resist him. 'Yes, but I'm a study junkie as well as an everything else junkie. I want to know everything. I'm a control freak, remember?'

He gave her arms a deftly camouflaged yank, catching her out while she processed his reply, and their bodies slammed into each other hard. A surge of energy took them both by surprise, and they stood locked together for several seconds, staring into each other's faces.

'Are we supposed to be this close?' Lynn's voice was breathless. 'It feels dangerous, like I'm too young to be this close.'

Her lover shook his head slowly. 'You're not too young. You want it, and neither of us is forcing you into it.'

'That's true,' she nodded.

He watched her eyes react, keen to gauge the young woman's mood. 'You know, it is dangerous for me, because I very much doubt if I figure in your future. That's what scares *me* about being this close.'

'But I want you in my future.'

'At the moment you do.'

The tall, dark, handsome stranger walked backwards, guiding his fair maiden to her bed. His whole self yearned for her; mind, body and soul.

'Can you see into the future?' Lynn asked dreamily.

'No, but I can learn from the past.'

"From the past? What does that mean?'

Jeff could sense a shiver passing through his youthful girlfriend, and he backed off a little. 'We may not always be together, angel, but we'll always want to be together. That's how it is with us.'

'How do you know?'

'I don't know, but that's what I believe. You will never need to doubt I love you, and *vice versa*, I hope. I just know it's not going to be easy.'

Lynn frowned, laying down on the bed and watching her mystery man's naked body looming overhead. 'I think I already know that.'

His penis brushed along the entrance of her vagina, and her hips lifted to make sure he knew she wanted him too. Strong, caring fingers worked to open her up, listening for each irresistibly soft groan of pleasure, and Jeff bent his arms to kiss her wanting mouth.

'I just want to know you're here,' he whispered. 'Even when you're not here. We can each go through our respective lives, doing what we do, knowing we have each other to talk to.'

'And to make love to.'

'Oh, yeah,' the elated student smiled, winking provocatively. 'Definitely to make love to, even if it's only in our minds.'

The lovers moved together, lost in their passion. Lynn climaxed first in a rush of tears, and then for a second time more calmly, her body waiting impatiently for Jeff's to catch up. She was filled with an overwhelming wish to take his sadness away and to make him the happiest man alive. He had taken a chance on her, for whatever reason, and this perfect quintessence they had created together felt bigger than both of them.

'Why didn't you have sex with Dean?' a deep, drowsy voice jolted the teenager awake, a short time after they had settled down to sleep.

'I don't know. Just didn't want to. I wasn't ready, I s'pose.'

The man in her childhood bed kissed her swollen lips. 'I got lucky then.'

Lynn giggled. 'No. We both got lucky. Why do you say that?'

'I came along just when you were ready.'

'No,' his girlfriend countered again. 'You made me ready. I wanted to. I remember writing that in my diary, when I was confused about whether I should or not. Maybe I knew you'd teach me well. I can't imagine how Dean would've been with me. Selfish and rough...'

'OK. That's quite enough,' Jeff put a hand over her babbling mouth. 'I don't need you to imagine how it would've been with him.'

'Are you jealous?'

'Sure am,' the young man turned away, embarrassed by the strength of his feelings.

'But I didn't sleep with him. You don't have to be jealous. I don't care if I never see him again, and that's the truth, the whole truth and nothing but the truth. I love you, and no-one else. Anyway... You brought it up! Now let's not talk anymore.'

As they drifted off to sleep, surrounded by rolling pastures in the remote Victorian countryside, the young woman's thoughts swirled around her head, hoping she wouldn't forget them before she had the chance to complete the diary entry for this amazing day of disclosure and dilemma: death-wishes, Olympic logistics, changing the world, too much homework and a love which promised to triumph over all, as long as her parents didn't intervene.

She loved everything about the way her relationship with Jeff was developing. Above all, she loved how he didn't hold back. Her limited experience with men up until meeting him was one of understatement and macho reserve, where no-one aired their true feelings. What had the promising songwriter said about there being no point speaking if one didn't mean what one said? So was Jeff really the only man she knew who spoke his mind, or was he the only one who acknowledged the importance of emotions? Either one would do.

A torrent of words came rushing into Lynn's head, while she watched her man in peaceful repose. What must it be like to lose a parent as a fourteen-year-old? For him to have acceded to these debilitating psychological symptoms, his mother's death must surely have involved something more sinister than an illness or even an accident. What horrific scenes had he witnessed behind that door as an impressionable teenager? And had this been the trigger for him to want to change the world, or was he born this way?

The teenager vowed not to press for answers just yet. It was clearly very difficult for Jeff to discuss his past and the scars with which it had left him, and yet he was filled with such determination and such passion. And so much love. For her.

***

Lynn woke suddenly to the sound of a man shouting, and the bed was shifting on its castors as she returned to consciousness. Beside her, Jeff's body convulsed, and his eyes were wide open, staring wildly towards the ceiling. Something was spooking her black stallion again, and she startled as a fist shot out from his waist, lifting the sheet from his torso.

At first the celebrity was frightened. Her partner, about whom she had been enjoying a romantic dream until a few moments ago, was swearing profusely in a mixture of languages. His arms lashed out again, so violently that if she hadn't already had this situation explained to her, it might seem as if he were having some sort of epileptic fit.

'Jeff!' the young woman yelled, just as he swung at an opponent on her side of the bed.

Lynn slid backwards, stopping on the very edge of the mattress, and shouted his name again. And again. And again.

'Wake up!' she leaned back into the centre of the bed and dared to grip the biceps of his right arm. 'Wake up, Jeff! You're dreaming!'

Heavy rain was falling outside, battering against the shuttered French windows. The sixteen-year-old's heart raced, unusually uptight owing to the fact that she was in charge of the whole house tonight, and she continued her efforts to rouse the man who was clearly in the middle of a full-on brawl beside her.

Gradually her insistence began to pay off, and the assault appeared to be coming to an end.

'Jeff, sit up,' she instructed more gently, reaching her arms around his boiling, sweat-drenched chest. 'It's over. Wake up.'

'Shit,' her boyfriend hissed, finally returning to the land of the living and coming to terms with what had happened.

He let out a blood-chilling moan and leaped out of bed without even looking round. Apologising gruffly, he made his way round the end of the bed and disappeared into the *en suite*, from where his host heard the strong jet of the shower spring into action. She sank back down onto the pillow and pulled the sheet over her, staring at the same white ceiling that had been painted with such evil scenes for her lover.

By the time Jeff emerged from the bathroom, Lynn was almost asleep again. The sound of the rain against the windows had become louder, now being buffeted by a strong wind. Without speaking and still breathing noisily, the humiliated man stopped briefly to check that his bedfellow hadn't run away, before walking purposefully into the lounge area. She initially feared he may leave and drive home without saying goodbye, but then sighed with relief at the sound of his cigarette lighter sparking.

'Are you OK?' she called out.

'Yeah. Thanks.'

The nineteen-year-old's reply was calmer than she expected, and his girlfriend realised with a smile that he was unlikely to walk out into the driving rain, butt naked and without his car keys, which were sitting along with his wallet in plain view on her dressing table. She decided to let him take his time, neither wishing to panic nor pander to his compulsions. She had no idea whether either strategy was the right one, yet felt surprisingly comfortable, tucked up in bed and listening to the wild weather.

When the smoker returned, Lynn had turned to face away from her partner's side of the bed. She felt the mattress dip as his heavy weight leaned on it and lay down. He groaned softly and shifted closer to her back until he had wrapped his arms needily around her body and engulfed her with his warmth.

'Are you still OK?' Lynn asked with a soft laugh.

'Yeah. Thanks,' he repeated, kissing her neck and squeezing still tighter. 'I'm just lapping you up. You feed me, Lynn.'

'I feed you? That's a lovely thing to say. Thank you too.'

'*De nada.* Are you OK?'

'Yes. I love sleeping when it's raining, and especially thunder storms. Do they bother you?'

'No. They remind me I'm not the only one who's angry.'

His girlfriend said nothing in response to yet another telling comment, simply relishing his hot breath heavy on her neck. It was a strange thing to say, and she longed to ask more but got the distinct impression that her enquiry would be unwelcome. For Jeff's part, he was grateful for the benign line of questioning, still reeling from this latest trip to the dark side. A slender, loving arm reached backwards, and her fingers brushed his hip, sending tingling shivers through his core. His poisoned instincts immediately turned to sex, and an erection sprang up from nowhere, requiring him to retreat a little.

Embarrassed, he unravelled his left arm from Lynn's and took her wandering hand in his. 'Sorry. We don't have to. That felt so good, but the rest of me knows what time it is. You're perfect and you should go back to sleep.'

'I will. I love you,' the relieved woman replied.

'Well, it's time to love sleeping instead,' the dreamer whispered against the sensitive skin underneath her hairline. 'You love sleeping. I've seen it.'

Lynn snuggled backwards, relaxed by the cosy feeling of his softening penis on her buttocks. 'Thanks. You'd love sleeping too, given half the chance, I expect.'

Jeff sniffed, his lingering anger cooled by yet more thoughtful, caring rhetoric from this heavenly friend of his. 'I love sleeping with you.'

From anyone else, the simple observation might have come across as patronising, but from Lynn Dyson, it simply sounded as if she loved him. The tormented soul wished her goodnight for the second time and turned over to face in the opposite direction. He didn't want her to see him crying again.

Then, as if their lives had been rewound by an hour or so, the whole noisy drama was soon happening again, this time even louder. She hoped her siblings wouldn't be woken by the commotion and was now very thankful that her parents were staying in the city overnight. She didn't care to explain Jeff's nightmares to them, fairly confident that he wouldn't either.

The luminous red digits of the alarm clock told the frustrated couple it was three o'clock in the morning. The rain had stopped, but the wind was still whipping through the trees on the rise behind the house. This time, the disruptive visitor had suggested he depart, or at the very least spend the rest of the night in another room, but the patient star wouldn't hear of it.

After following the same ritual as before, Jeff again heaved his exhausted body over onto his left side, expecting Lynn to stay still and drift off. However, half asleep, she spun over and spooned him, kissing his back and sniffing in amusement as the hairs tickled. She scratched her nose, afraid she would sneeze, and then gripped his ribcage playfully. He felt her fingers skim back and forth over a particular spot and instantly tensed up.

'What are these lumps?'

'Ribs,' he answered, almost under his breath.

The celebrity tapped the area again, laughing at his flippant reply. 'No. On your skin, you idiot!'

The student let out a deep sigh, lifting her hand away and stretching it towards his lips. It was his usual avoidance tactic.

'Scars.'

'Hmm… That's what I thought.'

'A fight at school, that's all. OK?'

His girlfriend kissed his rock solid shoulders, wondering why he had reacted so strongly. 'I'm sorry.'

Neither lover spoke for a fair few minutes, regret hanging in the air. Lynn wished she hadn't mentioned anything, and Jeff wished she hadn't found the tell-tale blemishes on his skin. He was so drained and despondent that he had failed to consider how exposed he might be when taking his normal defensive position, not counting on the extent of her desire to relax him back to sleep.

Eventually, he sensed his dream girl descend into slumber again.

'I will tell you, angel.'

She stirred. 'You don't have to. Only when you're ready.'

Her enigmatic stranger scoffed gently. 'I'll tell you before I'm ready.'

'Why?'

'Because I don't think I'll ever be ready but I owe you an explanation, regardless.'

'Oh.'

***

'Jesus!' the nineteen-year-old cursed, becoming aware of a woman's voice calling his name. 'Fucking hell!'

Feral eyes met those of his worried girlfriend, and the angry dreamer broke free of her arms. The third nightmare in a matter of hours. Nausea gripped him, and he could still see the shadows of a fully-clothed man and a naked girl engaged in aggressive entanglement in his parents' bedroom. Lynn cried for him, starting to follow but then stopping short of entering the *en suite* when she realised he was vomiting into the toilet. Instead, she reached for the door handle and closed her dejected lover inside.

'I'm sorry, angel.'

Having drifted off to sleep again, Lynn opened her eyes to find her gorgeous boyfriend crouched down at her bedside, his wet skin shining in the first rays of early morning sunlight seeping through the windows. He had emerged from the bathroom, smelling divinely of toothpaste and soap, but with an earnest look on his face that warned her not to touch him.

'Are you coming back to bed?' she asked, fighting back tears at the glaring contradiction before her. 'We don't have to be up early. You can sleep all morning, if you want. You need to.'

A renewed swathe of anger pervaded the student's brain, causing his jaw to lock painfully, and he thought he might be sick again. Stroking his girlfriend's shoulder through the sheet, he rose to his feet and walked around to the other side of the bed. Lynn wasn't even surprised when he made no attempt to kiss or cuddle her this time. She could only imagine how guilty he was feeling.

'I hope you get some sleep,' she said, turning her head briefly.

Her conclusion had been correct. Jeff had shrunk away to the far edge of the bed, as if he were trying to escape the whole, sorry situation; perhaps as much from himself as from her. The sixteen-year-old tried one more kind gesture, hoping it wouldn't be poorly received by the furious man.

'It's OK, Jeff. Really. How can I convince you it's OK for you to have nightmares with me? Do you want some water?'

The dreamer groaned, sniffing deeply, as if he was trying to stifle a sob. No answer was forthcoming, only a series of long, deep breaths. *Oh, well...* This was all a learning exercise, Lynn thought, for both of them.

But then, just as she had descended into another slumber, her heart leaped into her mouth when suddenly Jeff reached over and bundled her into his chest, swooping on her desperately, as if his senses had been deprived of her for weeks. His needy mouth searched for hers in the dark, their kiss as passionate as any other they had shared, and when they eventually parted, the young woman saw he was smiling broadly.

'Thanks. That'd be great. Get out of bed, because I won't let you go if you don't go right now.'

Lynn laughed, dutifully sliding backwards out of bed and walking over to the sink to fill two glasses with cold water. She could feel lascivious eyes staring at her translucent, white nightdress, not knowing if she should reciprocate or ignore them. Did his mood really change that quickly? If not, which one was the act? The terrified, rejected little boy or the apologetic and super-attentive lover? Her wise man was right about one thing: the continued interruptions were wearing her down a little, and there was probably less than an hour before dawn. She also wondered whether they might be yet in for episode number four before breakfast.

It almost seemed as if the more secure Jeff became in their relationship, the more frequently his mind allowed the nightmares to infringe on their togetherness. The busy celebrity worried whether she could cope with this on a regular basis, especially with the Olympics closing in and her Year Twelve studies requiring her fullest attention. No doubt Jeff would be worrying about this too, which might also account for the increased pressure.

'Why do you always face away from me when you wake up after a bad dream?' Lynn confronted him, sitting both glasses down on the bedside table next to her boyfriend's head.

'I don't know. I guess because I think we need space from each other, to adjust to what just happened.'

The blonde beauty stroked his shoulder, which was still warm and perspiring, watching him drink a whole glass down and flex his jaw once more, attempting to free the muscles of a face wracked by exhaustion. If he was acting, this was an Oscar-winning performance. It was as if the gorgeous, larger-than-life personality, all six-feet- four-inches of virile muscle, had withered to childlike proportions in her bed.

'It's probably a good idea, but you don't have to. If it'd help, I'm more than happy to talk to you and hold you... or leave you alone... whichever makes you recover quicker. I don't want you to think I don't want to share this with you. I do, honestly.'

'Jeez, Lynn, I don't know,' the young man sighed. 'I've never been in this situation before. I've never shared any of this shit with anyone, and I'm sure you'd much rather go back to sleep. For Christ's sake, it's already light. I wish I could give you a sensible answer, but my emotions are all stirred up together. I can't distinguish one from the other in those first few minutes after you wake me.'

'Well, I'm here for whatever you need. I mean it.'

'Thanks, angel. The problem is I don't know what I need. You seem to know what I need much better than I do. I just feel totally empty after waking up like this. I should go and leave you in peace, but I don't want to go.'

'And I don't want you to go either,' the schoolgirl echoed. 'Am I annoying you, forcing you to talk to me?'

The celebrity looked a little frazzled, Jeff's shameful eyes acknowledged, and her body seemed heavier, slumping down onto the mattress as if she lacked the energy to return to her side of the bed. He turned and kissed her forehead, grateful for her consideration, her latest question having caught him unawares.

'No, you're humiliating me.'

'Humiliating you? How? I don't mean to.'

'I know,' he kissed her again. 'You're doing it in the nicest, most helpful way possible, and I love you for it. I'm just a mess who loves you and doesn't want you to have to spend half the night listening to me shouting and screaming, then mopping me up into the bargain. That wasn't what you signed up for, was it?'

The patient celebrity climbed over her man's legs, crawling across the bed and chuckling as she pulled the sheet over her body. A memory stirred from those first few seconds of awareness, before she had jumped up to wrench him back to reality for the third time. Initially, she suppressed it, but after lying in the dark for several minutes, she broached the subject.

'This time you were calling out a woman's name,' she said. 'Layna? Who's Layna?'

Her handsome stranger immediately turned over, hearing the nervousness in the teenager's voice. He propped himself up on his elbow. She was smiling, but her eyes were filled with suspicion. Jeff smiled and stroked her cheek. Thankfully, at the end of a very long night, for once he could quite safely answer with the truth.

'Madalena. She's my sister. It gets shortened to Lena.'

The sixteen-year-old visibly relaxed, sinking deeper into her pillow. 'Oh. Sorry, I should've remembered. Why are you yelling your sister's name? Is she in your nightmares?'

Jeff laid his fingers on penitent lips. 'Not now. I'm sorry, Lynn, but I just can't talk about that with you now. That's exactly what I mean about humiliating. I should tell you, but I can't, and it makes me feel like a rat.'

'It's OK. It doesn't matter. How can I help then? I want you to want to be here, Jeff. I want you to believe in life; in your future. I love who you are and that there are so many sides of you.'

'Whoever I am, you mean,' the young man smirked.

Lynn smacked his chest. 'Shush! Have you ever tried meditation? To relax your mind?'

Her boyfriend sighed, their nocturnal marathon leaving him bereft of all energy and with precious little patience for more good ideas. He rolled over onto his back and invited Lynn to snuggle in close, knowing he was in no position to dictate the play after what he had put her through.

'No. And I'm not going to do it either. It won't work.'

'How do you know? You've already decided?' the young woman teased gently.

'Yeah. I guess I don't believe in myself enough.'

It was Lynn's turn to utter a deep sigh. 'So why, if you keep saying you love how I believe in you, don't you believe in yourself? You *must* believe in yourself.'

Her boyfriend chuckled, reaching his left hand over and taking hold of her right shoulder. The weight of her head on his chest was comforting, and his body shuddered in pleasure at the sensation of an impromptu kiss strategically placed right over his heart.

'Frustrating, isn't it? I'm sorry I'm such an arsehole. We're too tired. But can I ask you yet another favour though?'

'Yes, of course.'

'This is going to sound weird,' he hazarded, 'but I never thought I'd be able to tolerate the feeling of you sleeping on my chest.'

The blonde head lifted, twisting to look at his face. 'Why not? Do you want me...'

Jeff cut her off. 'No. Please stay there. I don't know. I thought it would be like it was too close, but I love it, angel.'

The same blonde head lowered itself back down, and kissed his chest again.

'In fact, I ache for it,' the honest man continued. 'I never thought I'd want to lay myself so open.'

'We're alone together, two people who love each other,' Lynn's voice was calm, belying her tender age. 'We want to be together, no matter what. Isn't that what love is? Now, I want to know why you can believe in being a rock star and changing the world with computers, and yet you don't believe in yourself enough to try meditation to help you sleep. What's with that? Surely you believe in yourself?'

'Not in my ability to control my mind, no,' the weary student explained, his lips brushing the determined woman's forehead. 'I give you permission to believe in me on my behalf.'

The schoolgirl loved his quirky solution. 'OK! I will. I just can't understand how someone can be so confident on the outside and so doubting on the inside?'

'That's just me, Lynn. I can't answer that. I tried hypnotism once.'

'Did you? What was it like?'

'Don't know,' Jeff scoffed. 'You don't remember anything. That's the whole idea.'

Lynn laughed heartily, her amusement a surprise aphrodisiac that set his loins alight again. 'Oh! Was it with a doctor?'

'Yeah. I didn't like losing control,' the embarrassed nineteen-year-old rolled her over, pinned her to the mattress and put his hand over her mouth.

'Oh, really?' the young woman giggled, worming free. 'That surprises me.'

'Shut up and go back to sleep.'

After a long, passionate kiss, with a full erection nagging between them, reluctantly Jeff flopped back onto his side of the bed. Lynn turned away from him too, assorted emotions jangling in her mind.

'Believing in you is the least I can do, as my significant other. Michelle described you that way the other day, to a boy she introduced me to.'

'Which boy?'

'Oh, just someone she met last weekend. He's not significant.'

Jeff smirked, doing his best to put all thoughts of the forbidden female form out of his mind, so that they could both catch up with what little remained of the night. Being informed that he was Lynn Dyson's significant other was hardly going to help.

'*Touché.* That expression's dumb. It's an oxymoron. How can someone who's just other be significant?'

Lynn huffed, her voice muffled by the pillow. 'Stop complicating matters. I like you being my significant other. Am I yours?'

'No. You're my significant one and only.'

'Other. As opposed to my significant self, I guess it is,' the young woman was drifting off rapidly.

Her intelligent boyfriend smiled to himself. 'Whatever. Just as long as I'm significant.'

'You're significant, Jeff. Significantly significant, believe me. Now go to sleep.'

***

'What's your position on Easter eggs?'

The alarm clock now informed them it was already after nine o'clock, and both were secretly relieved that the pressure of surviving the night time was over, even though neither felt particularly rejuvenated. Lynn laughed, her face lighting up at the suggestion. Jeff already had his answer, despite the deadpan reply which sprung forth.

'I don't have a position on Easter eggs. What's yours?'

'Don't know,' the young man sniffed, 'apart from that it needs to be the same as yours, or else one of us'll be disappointed.'

His girlfriend nodded, cuddling in beside him and immediately being swallowed into his eager embrace.

'It feels weird.'

'What feels weird? Talking about Easter eggs?'

'Yeah,' Jeff replied, picking up on the delicate awkwardness radiating through both their bodies. 'I've never shared a religious holiday with anyone before.'

Lynn's fingers traced around his nipples, watching his chest beginning to breathe more deeply and regularly. 'Apart from family, neither have I. We don't typically do Easter eggs, but all my friends do. Do you want one then?'

'Oh, yeah.'

'How normal!' she smiled, kissing his lips quickly. 'Do we want normal?'

'I think so. As much as possible. Don't you?'

Lynn sighed. 'I don't really know what normal's supposed to be like. I keep kidding myself, like yesterday evening. That was pretty normal, wasn't it?'

Loving arms curled around her slender form, and she found herself being transported on top of his warm body, immediately coming into contact with a very large, very hard erection. The young woman wrestled her way out of his tight grip and sat up to take in the enticing view. She couldn't get enough of this man, no matter how many times he might wake her up in the middle of the night.

Jeff's heart soared to see the sexy smile spread across her face. 'Yeah. Pretty normal, in a cute kind of way. Can I take you to breakfast next Sunday?'

'It's Easter though. Everywhere'll be packed.'

The student smiled knowingly, tapping his index finger against his nose. 'I know. I made a reservation.'

The gorgeous blonde bore down on him, letting herself fall far enough that their lips pushed together and her nipples brushed against his chest, Olympian arms resisting the impact. Lynn was laughing, writhing as his hands began to run riot across her back and down her sides. His penis quickly found its favourite place, seeming to need no guidance, and she gasped as his size opened her up with little resistance.

'I don't take you out enough,' he continued.

'I don't need you to take me out. I told you that.'

Breathing heavily against her cheek, Jeff's expert fingers set about raising the stakes still higher. 'Yeah, but you like it. Look at you! You've gone all dreamy on me. It makes me want to fuck you until it makes us late for breakfast.'

Within a few more seconds, Lynn's insides burst into rapturous flames, her face glowing and her hands reaching up to caress her lover's shoulders and neck. The red-blooded teenager groaned and flipped them both over. His initial intention was to slow things down, but the look in his girlfriend's eyes changed his mind. Images of the two younger Dyson children passing through his lust-filled brain served to prolong the sharp sensation of his orgasm, for which he was perversely grateful. He came into her moments later, only just managing to restrain himself from shouting at the top of his voice.

'Making me happy makes you want to have sex, which makes me happy,' Lynn giggled. 'What a virtuous circle that is!'

'Of course. Do you think that happens by accident, angel?'

The Fellowship

'So where are you taking me?' Lynn asked, climbing into the old Fairlane.

It was nine-thirty at night, and the weather was beginning to turn autumnal. Jeff had asked his dream girl to pick a night when she didn't need to be up early the next morning. He had also advised her to wear warm clothes. She had chosen the Thursday before Easter, the thirtieth of March, because her next training session wasn't until Saturday lunchtime, which meant the young lovers had a whole day and a half completely to themselves.

'We're going somewhere to do some good and to exercise some free thought,' the spirited man told her, accelerating quickly back in the direction of the city.

He was soon turning right onto Flinders Street, waiting in a queue of Richmond-bound traffic.

'Your flat?' his girlfriend asked, hoping this not to be the case.

The driver grinned broadly. 'Yeah. Now that's an idea. Why didn't I think of that?'

She smiled back, pleased to be wrong. 'OK. So where then?'

'We're going to a place called "The Fellowship",' he replied. 'Strictly speaking, it's not a place. It's an organisation where people with any and every mental illness can go for help. It's where I go if I get really desperate in the middle of the night, before you were around and when you're away.'

The sixteen-year-old was delighted to find this out. It would give her an opportunity to journey deeper into Jeff's hidden world. Once again, her gorgeously flawed boyfriend had come up with precisely the kind of educational entertainment she had requested, most probably prompted by a recent evening spent dissecting the themes of the classic play they had seen on their first date.

'¡Excelente! That's perfect. I wanted to go somewhere challenging.'

The driver reached over and took hold of her right hand. It had warmed his heart greatly to discover the successful musician and sportswoman ready to learn about such conditions of human frailty from which her family and coaches sought to steer her away. However, not even he was privy to exactly how much analysis and soul-searching the young woman had done while travelling with her diary, once each of her various competitions and television appearances was over.

'I'm glad you're interested. I want to build this place into something much bigger. You know... When I'm a rock star. But for now I'm half client and half worker.'

'Just like at uni'.'

'Yep,' Jeff confirmed. 'I never thought of that, but you're right. I'm making a habit of getting on both sides of the fence these days. Anyway, this is a great place to talk to people and help them understand themselves. I used to go to the one in Sydney when I was a kid. That's where it started. And as I grew to understand me better, it was somewhere I could feel useful during those sleepless nights. People talk to me.'

Lynn nodded. 'People talk to you because you listen. Not many people listen properly. I hope I do.'

Jeff leaned over to grab her hand again and kissed it, which happened to coincide with a left turn that threw him off balance. The car wobbled as he regained control, and they laughed.

'Apologies. They didn't put the autopilot feature in this model,' he lamented. 'You are a very good listener, by the way. That's what I was planning to say before the car took a wrong turn.'

'Excuses, excuses! So what do you want me to do?'

'Nothing,' her tour guide answered. 'Just listen, observe, think. Drink bad instant coffee. And if you want to talk, talk. No pressure. Whatever you want. Even leave.'

Lynn approved. 'Sounds perfect,' she smiled. 'I won't leave. How many people will be there?'

'You never know,' her boyfriend replied. 'Sometimes only one or two. Sometimes twenty or more. It might be busy tonight because it's Easter. Lonely people get lonelier at holiday time, because they typically don't have anyone to holiday with. And a four-day weekend looks like an eternity stretching in front of you if you already know you don't have anything to fill it with.'

'Can I stay with you, please?' the pretty teenager hedged, becoming a little nervous.

She didn't want to be thrown too far into the deep end. She had told her mystery man she was looking for a challenge and was now regretting it slightly. She always had people to holiday with, and in fact was spoiled for choice still more these days, with a boyfriend and a family across whom she must now split the available holiday hours. What would she be able to do to help someone who had no-one? Would she be able to relate well enough not to make things worse for these poor people?

'Sure,' came her boyfriend's cheerful answer. 'I hoped you would. I want to be able to turn round and see your smile or touch your hand. It would make it so much better for me. Positive reinforcement, or some such psychobabble. There are some very intelligent and worldly people whom I'm sure you'll find interesting case studies.'

Lynn was grateful. 'That's good. As interesting as you?'

The handsome man, who was gradually becoming less and less of an enigma, winked but remained silent, pulling up outside a dilapidated, old community hall, one street back from Bridge Road. There were lights on inside, but the gnarled, old tree trunks and long, unpruned branches laden with dry leaves that rustled in the breeze rendered the place eerie and foreboding.

'I'll let you be the judge of that. Put it this way, some of them can tell you every last detail about what they did their whole life, and some of them don't know who they are from one minute to the next. Luck of the draw.'

His smiling passenger opened the door before her chaperone had a chance to get round to her side of the car. The excitement was infectious. In fact, Jeff's mood had been lighter the last few times they had spoken, assisted by a glowing reference from his faculty to mark the end of his probationary period and also because the first royalties for his new songs had been transferred into his bank account. The young woman was very happy for him, and there was clearly nothing to be afraid of here. She would be well looked after as long as her beautiful black stallion was close by.

'Hey! So you want to be all independent now, do you?' he teased.

'Yes,' she answered emphatically. 'You don't have to open and close the door for me every time. Not that I don't think it's very gentlemanly, but you don't have to.'

Her chauffeur pretended to tuck a peaked cap under his arm and saluted, before bending down for an overly familiar peck on the cheek. Lynn walked away from the car, expecting to hear the door close. It didn't, and she turned around and cried out, stamping her foot.

'I knew you'd do that!'

Jeff was standing next to the open car door, with his hands in his pockets, obviously waiting for the independent woman to shut it herself. Obediently, the slim champion returned to complete the job, but just as she got close enough to swing the door, rapid reflexes beat her to it, causing her to tip forward in surprise. He caught her in his arms, and they kissed passionately, laughing all the while.

'Let's go in,' he suggested, dramatically swallowing the divine taste of his favourite friend and wiping the back of his hand across his face. 'And no more smiling, OK? It won't pay to seem too happy, if we want people to identify with us.'

The couple was greeted at the door by two people wearing shirts with "The Fellowship" emblazoned on their breast pockets; a man and a woman, who both obviously knew the good-looking student well. He must have already explained to them why Lynn Dyson was visiting that night, because their synchronised assembly looked suspiciously like a welcoming committee. The staff members were Ruth and Alan, both social workers of many years' experience and totally committed to their vocation.

Lynn gazed past the overawed duo while they gave their special guest a brief introduction to the organisation, her anxiety fading and curiosity on the rise. Half a dozen more people in all, she estimated, not being able to see the entire space. Two dishevelled men sat talking to each other at the far end of the hall, and an aboriginal woman was leafing through a magazine in another corner.

'How's Frances?' Jeff asked. 'Is she talking to anyone today?'

'You probably,' Ruth replied, before turning to their famous visitor. 'They all talk to him, you know. He seems to be able to get through to anyone. This is a very special man.'

'I know,' the celebrity responded with pride. 'I'm really looking forward to seeing Jeff in action. I'm just learning.'

The kindly, middle-aged woman nodded. 'Not many people want to learn, Miss Dyson. Ask any questions you have. We'll be more than happy to answer them.'

'Lynn, please,' she insisted. 'Thanks. Well, people *should* listen. I was pretty ignorant about all this until I met Jeff. I never thought about all the different reasons and conditions that cause mental illness.'

Positively glowing inside, the client-cum-worker took his girlfriend's hand. 'Enough with the small talk, lady. You're not here to cut ribbons. You're here to work. Come over this way. While there aren't many people here, I want to explain some of these to you.'

He was pointing to a wall that was covered in charts, each with one or more names written on the top. The inquisitive schoolgirl presumed these belonged to some of The Fellowship's clients and was keen to find out what the graphs represented.

'That's your handwriting,' she observed.

'Yeah. Illegible, isn't it?'

Alan slapped the tall student on the back, making them both jump out of their skins. 'Need to get that fixed, mate. People will mistake you for a doctor again.'

'Again?' Lynn repeated, looking from her boyfriend to the slight, sandy-haired psychiatrist and back again.

Jeff shrugged modestly, leaving the older man to pick up the story.

'Yes. One time, this bloke was explaining the charts to a visiting politician and a group of donors, and in their farewell address, they thanked the doctor for his interesting presentation.'

The famous songstress chuckled and gave her ever-mysterious friend a loving look. Another layer was gradually peeling off the onion. This work which hadn't yet been explained to her must obviously be valuable in some way if it was used to showcase the organisation to potential philanthropists.

'Doctor Diamond, please go ahead with your presentation.'

With a mixture of pride and humility, Jeff led her over to the far side of the wall, and the social worker left the couple to themselves. Each graph was basically the same, with a vertical axis on the left and several parallel lines across the page. The horizontal axes were graded with days of the week.

'These are people's happiness charts,' the young man began. 'You see this line at zero?'

Lynn nodded, following his hand.

'Well, zero is neutral emotion. You know, kind of indifferent. Not happy and not sad. Above the line is getting happier and below the line is getting sadder, or angrier. Positive emotions and negative emotions.'

'OK. That's easy to understand,' the teenaged star responded with a smile, casting her eyes across a number of the charts.

Her teacher continued. 'When people have been here a few times and they're not scared to open up anymore, we get them to start mapping themselves on the lines by remembering what happened to them during the days since they last came, and drawing their own personal happiness scale. Then we talk about all the highs and lows.'

Lynn's eyes were wide with amazement. Jeff kissed her unexpectedly, and she blushed.

'Stop! You said we couldn't do that.'

'It's OK. There's hardly anybody here.'

'So you can trace patterns for people, to help them learn what triggers depression or happy moods,' the sixteen-year-old offered, her finger tracing one of the graphs.

'*Exactement*,' the intellectual confirmed, pleased but not in the least surprised that his dream girl understood. 'See this bloke here... He's trucking along nicely, just wavering around between neutral and minus three or so, and then... Bang! He slides right down into suicidal. Anything below ten is suicidal.'

'Wow. What happened to him? Poor guy.'

The sometime worker shook his head. 'I'm not going to tell you stuff on behalf of someone else, but in his case it wasn't anything too bad. The purpose of this is to recognise when you respond in a more extreme way than you should, so hopefully next time something happens, your line can be flatter, because you know you recovered last time. It's a way to convince yourself that it won't be so hard to recover again.'

'It's like a graphic equaliser,' Lynn suggested, 'but for minds.'

'*Exactement encore une fois!* That's where I got the idea from.'

'All this is your idea?' his girlfriend asked in wonder. 'I might've known. I thought it was an established technique.'

Jeff's pride shone out of him. 'I'm hoping it's going to become an established technique. You know I told you there wasn't much good information in Australia?'

'Yes.'

'Well… We're starting to create it, right here,' he told her. 'And in Sydney. Bit by bit, we want to collect long-term data from people. But the trouble is that it relies on people continuing to feel vulnerable enough to want to come here over a long period of time. We often joke that we don't want anyone to feel better, because it'll stuff up our research.'

Lynn smiled, daring to sneak a hug with her passionate do-gooder. At first, she had wondered if her boyfriend's ambit claims on changing the world were wild fantasies, but here was a shining example of something tangible. Just as there was nothing half-baked about this guy's song-writing ability, the work he was doing here was the real deal. Jeff Diamond was proving to be much more than a pretty face, for all his bravado. Useful scientific evidence was being gathered here, off the back of a simple happiness gauge. She wondered if her father might allow her to invest some of her trust fund into this very worthy cause.

'Which is your chart?' the blonde starlet dared to ask, scanning for his name along the wall.

Before the sometime client had a chance to point it out, she had found it. Her escort followed, feeling his blood pressure rising predictably. It told a story which might not be so easily explained, given the timing of their relationship.

'Yep, that one's mine. Do you recognise me?'

The student lifted up two sheets which had been stapled one on top of the other, for the weeks since the couple had met had produced a surfeit of precious data. He was both anxious and excited to be able to show Lynn his own profile, even though it cemented still further his status as a madman. Hopefully she would be able to see beyond the bare facts and realise he was not only trying to help himself but others too.

'You see how it flew from top to bottom like that, over and over again?'

The studious woman looked carefully at the peaks and troughs spiking regularly into the no-go zone, below minus ten, and occasionally above plus ten also. She checked the dates, which were from the middle of February to the tenth of March. They had started going out in the middle of February, and the tenth of March was around the time of the now infamous tennis skirt episode.

Jeff noticed her doing the calculation. 'Yeah. Bit of a rollercoaster, isn't it?'

'Certainly is,' Lynn laughed, but in a reserved, almost apologetic way. 'But why?'

Ruth, the plump woman who had greeted them at the door, was standing behind them and listening to the young man's careful explanation. Having formerly worked in the Sydney centre half a decade ago, she had known the young tearaway during the most traumatic period of his life and was particularly proud of his ability to confront his own issues in front of his famous girlfriend.

'Because his troll was having a tug-of-war with you for his heart,' the staff member interrupted.

The beautiful visitor swung round and stared enquiringly at the kind-faced woman. 'His what?'

Now it was Jeff's turn to blush. Lynn had never seen him react that way before and she felt embarrassed for him. His public and private worlds had suddenly collided, for which he hadn't been prepared. As one of Melbourne's most sought after press targets, this fear was something she knew only too well.

'Thanks a lot, Ruth,' he sneered, habitually taking out two cigarettes from the pack in his breast pocket and offering her one. 'I was getting to him. Now Lynn'll know I'm crazy. Until now she only *thought* I was...'

Shaking his head, the dedicated young man regained his composure and his train of thought, doing his best to ignore the older woman peering round his shoulder, listening to every word. This long-suffering social worker had seen the worst of him, violent and obnoxious. He had covered her clothes with the hot, brown, syrupy contents of a coffee mug one night, when she had criticised him for arriving at The Fellowship's Parramatta centre rolling drunk and as high as a kite on amphetamines. Another night, the matronly figure had rocked him in her arms until he fell asleep, wired and rejected after his grandmother's funeral. She was entitled to mock him. She had earned that privilege a million times over.

'Ahem... Where was I? Oh, yeah. That rollercoaster effect,' he carried on, pointing at another similar pattern on someone else's chart, 'is typical of someone who's gone through childhood or adolescent trauma. It's acute manic behaviour. You see this one?'

Lynn followed his finger to another wavy line but smoother, with few highs but a larger number of extreme lows.

'Yes,' she answered, fascinated.

'This person is what they call clinically or chronically depressed. The effect of the trigger is slower to take hold but lasts longer overall, and they don't go into the upper distortion zone at all. In fact, they rarely experience real happiness, but they do go into silence pretty often. And this one here is clinically but acutely depressed, which is another condition again. Still driven by events and still plunging below the line, but lasting for shorter periods.'

The famous musician smiled at the allegory to the graphic equaliser she knew so well from her many hours in the recording studio. What an intuitive way to explain to people how their mind was working! This mystery man of hers was even more special than she had suspected, and every time she saw him, another facet of his complex personality began to reveal itself.

'So how do you turn someone like you into someone whose wave stays within the green zone?'

'Great question!' Jeff exclaimed, seeing Ruth slink away out of the corner of his eye. 'That's my next project, if they let me. Shaving the tops and bottoms off the spikes. Just like too loud is painful and too quiet is useless, there needs to be a compromise position between flat-lining and swimming between the flags that keeps people out of trouble. The difference between non-trauma manic depressives and people like me is that we have way more down-swings than up-swings. That's where the troll theory comes in...'

Lynn laughed again. 'I love all your imagery. What on Earth is the troll theory? You really bring subjects to life, because they're all things that people know about from normal life. It's a real talent.'

The nineteen-year-old was chuffed and kissed her tenderly. 'Thanks. It's good to hear you say things like that. It helps a lot, so don't stop.'

But the spellbound woman was ready with another question. 'So that takes me back to our conversation the other day about not wanting to lose the highs and lows because it stifles your creativity. I'm guessing flat-line's not where you want to be?'

'Correct,' Jeff replied. 'Absolutely. No-one should, but for some people it's the preferable or safe alternative. Not me though. Can you imagine how boring it'd be never to feel any reaction to anything? You'd miss out on so much and you wouldn't be able to relate to anyone else. It's like people with Asperger's Syndrome. Highly intelligent people who can process data lightning fast but can't tell if other people are in a good or bad mood. I don't know which'd be worse: manic depression, where you're super-sensitive to everything, or zero comprehension of feelings.'

'It depends if you knew what you were missing, I suppose,' Lynn suggested.

'Yeah, maybe,' her boyfriend frowned, not buying the idea. 'I know what it's like to be a flat-liner, from when I was heavily medicated after I kicked the Blakes' door down. It was like having cling wrap around my head. I could see and hear, and even touch and smell, but through a layer of semi-permeable haze that dulled everything. It was crap.'

Seeing her lover's brow furrow and his breathing becoming faster, Lynn sensed a *staccato* moment coming on.

'Let's get some coffee,' she suggested, walking away from the chart wall.

The privileged youngster needed a break too. It was somewhat overwhelming to think of all these diverse, new talents she was unearthing in her boyfriend, not to mention the afflictions which life had dealt him. There was a depth to his character that was still uncharted, perhaps even by Jeff himself. They made themselves some tea in stained, chipped mugs and wandered outside to sit on the steps.

'So thanks,' the amateur psychiatrist said flatly but sincerely, lighting another cigarette.

'Thanks for what? For listening or for taking a break?'

'Both. Could you sense I was getting anxious? You're just as empathetic as I am, you know.'

Lynn shrugged. 'I've got a good role model.'

Jeff motioned for her to sit on the step in front of him, so that he could wrap his arms around her. The happy sixteen-year-old snuggled between his legs and rested her elbows on his knees.

'You say all the right things,' he whispered. 'I'm so taking you home tonight.'

His girlfriend kissed his wrist, which was just below her chin, while his right hand gripped tightly around her shoulder.

'Relax,' she reminded him, wriggling a little. 'Tell me about this troll who was having a tug-of-war with me.'

The nervous student released his grip, sniffing at her observation. 'Sorry. I did that the other day too, didn't I? With your hand? I don't know I'm doing it,' he smiled. 'It's Gravity the troll.'

Lynn giggled, but stopped herself quickly, not wanting to humiliate the poor man again. 'Gravity the troll? So who is he?'

'It's OK. You can laugh,' Jeff told her. 'Ruth caught me off guard. She tests me all the time, the bitch! It started back in Sydney, with the social workers up there. Ruth transferred to Melbourne a couple of years before I came down. I didn't even know she was here when I turned up the first time.'

'She's very fond of you,' the celebrity interjected. 'Like a mother, a bit.'

She felt her man tense up again and recalled that parents were a touchy subject. He didn't say anything for a couple of seconds, as if momentarily stunned. Had the frumpy counsellor also treated his mother? That was a possibility... Before she had died? Her heart beat a little faster at the prospect of this strange life story taking yet another unexpected turn.

So how had the nineteen-year-old loner's mum died? Did Ruth know? It irked Lynn to think that someone else might have been let further into her desperate lover's world, even if she was a trained psychologist. Jeff had told her that she was the only one to hear about his afflictions. However, tonight she had found out he was a regular visitor to this godforsaken, run-down church hall. How much detail was it necessary to divulge in order to receive assistance? Especially as a child, presumably arriving alone in the dead of night?

The young woman shivered. Poor Jeff. She ought to put her selfish pride behind her and trust his word. Immediately she felt herself being drawn in closer again. Could he read her mind? Sometimes she was sure he could.

'She's a professional. They all are. Everyone's treated the same. But to bring us back to the plot... We were talking, up in the New South Wales main office... just after we started all this graphing business... about why it's so much quicker and easier to go down the slopes than it is to go up them.'

'Like snakes and ladders,' Lynn ventured. 'The snakes always wind around more, and the ladders don't take you half as close to the end of the game as the snakes take you back to the start.'

Jeff kissed the top of her head, chuckling. 'Hey, that's a good one. Imagery's your thing too. Anyway... So I threw in the idea that when we go through trauma we're given an inner person. Some sort of subconscious being who's intent on sabotaging our happiness, to punish us for whatever we saw or had done to us. One of the others likened this to trolls from the old Scandinavian folklore. D'you know what I mean?'

'Yes,' the schoolgirl nodded her head. 'Of course. He lives under the bridge and scares the shit out of unsuspecting passers-by.'

'Indeed,' her boyfriend laughed at her uncharacteristic use of bad language, kissing her hair again and breathing her calming aura. 'Well... Ours we nicknamed Gravity, only because of the fact that gravity makes things go down more readily than up.'

'Some things come up quite readily,' Lynn countered suggestively, reaching her hand around behind her and searching for his crotch. 'You're not entirely driven by gravity.'

Jeff was mildly shocked by this sudden sexual reference from his butter-wouldn't-melt girlfriend. Her therapeutic techniques were certainly inventive!

'I can't believe you just said that! Next thing I know, you'll be saying, "Fuck my parents" again, and then where will we be?'

'Spanking,' the pretty blonde answered, like a two-year-old repeating a parent's warning.

'Oh, for Christ's sake, please stop,' the red-blooded male moaned. 'This is serious business. I can't afford to get any more distracted than I already am.'

'So continue about Gravity. I'm sorry,' the celebrity apologised, giggling and leaning back against the body which was shielding her nicely from the chilly night air.

'Thank you,' the storyteller snapped officiously. 'So now, when we talk to people about preventing the downward slide, we liken it to a troll coming up and grabbing hold of our heart or our mind or whatever, and wrestling it down into the depths of his despair-ridden cave. He has all these mind-bending skills that we need to master, to counteract his strength, because in our lucid moments we all know we're overreacting, even though when we're actually in the situation all seems lost.'

'I see. That makes perfect sense, but why did you have such a rollercoaster of a time when we first met?'

The handsome man leaned back and tried to twist his dream girl around to face him. He would have found it easier to answer this question inside the centre, surrounded by science and with the spectres of Ruth and Alan listening in. Out here however, there was nothing to protect him from his vulnerabilities.

'Sit here, please,' he asked, placing his hand on the step, next to him. 'I need to look at your face. I need to see what your eyes do.'

Lynn was happy to oblige. This was turning into another evening of fascinating insights.

'What about those chairs down there?' she suggested, pointing to two plastic seats that were facing each other. 'They'd be more comfortable.'

The couple moved to a grubby piece of lawn under one of the twisted, old trees. The chairs were unstable, having been left out in all weathers many times. Light streaming out from the frosted windows of the hall bathed the young beauty in a pale glow, and her eyes were alive with curiosity. Nerves tempered the sexual attraction this time however, and Jeff felt his chest constrict. He took a deep breath in and out to prepare himself. Gravity the troll was not far away. He was making his presence felt, as ever.

'You know you were saying about how hard it was to have a boyfriend, because it disrupted your schedule.'

'Yes,' Lynn was immediately concerned. 'I didn't mean that to hurt you. Did it?'

'No,' the student was keen to stop her going down that path. 'That's not where I was going. I was about to draw a parallel.'

'Oh, good,' she responded, relieved.

'Angel, before I asked you out... Or more accurately, before I had a plan to ask you out, my life just rolled along in the green zone, as you called it. I was as together as I had been for a long time. I'd sold some songs, had a year's rent paid on my flat, some spare cash, uni' was going well. One by one, I'd settled down all the variables in my life, so there was nothing that could fuck me over. I had a nice veneer on things. Non-stick, you know... Nowhere near as dull as taking those god-awful pills, but no particular highs or lows either. And as you rightly point out, that's not enough for me. I moved to Melbourne to meet you, so I couldn't just sit there in my flat, playing it safe.'

His dream girl leaned forward and kissed him. 'No, I can't imagine you playing it safe for long.'

'So that fortnight, from when I asked you out on the Tuesday, we went to the theatre on the Thursday, then I had to wait until the following Friday to see you again, then we spent our first night together and you were a virgin, then I couldn't see you again for over a week... That was a wild, wild time. You told me you loved me, and then there was the mauling after the tennis match. It was a bloody troll convention in here.'

Jeff thumped his chest hard for two purposes: first, to lend effect to his words, and second, to free his lungs from an attack so severe that he had become light-headed and feared he was about to pass out. Without comment, his girlfriend's shining eyes fixed upon him and waited for more.

'It was like God had me as his private yo-yo,' he smiled, clenching his fists. 'One minute I was high as a kite, thinking about how well we'd got on, how good sex was, how exciting it was that you were brand new, then telling you I loved you... Yadda, yadda, yadda. You know what happened. And the next minute I was back on my own, wondering if you'd ever talk to me again, wondering if I'd scared you off, telling myself how dumb I was to reveal my true feelings so soon, punishing myself for having taken your innocence away. You name it, it fucked me up! I surged from euphoria to disaster twice, sometimes three times a day.'

Lynn took his hands in hers, forcing him to unwind his fingers and flex the tension away. 'I wish I'd known. I could've rung you every day or something, because I was definitely thinking about you. All the time. I should have, but I didn't even have your number. I'm sorry.'

'Don't be sorry,' the grateful student told her, desperately trying to remain cool, calm and collected while his insides bled to be held by his gorgeous saviour. 'You shouldn't have. You treated me totally normally. We made arrangements, and you stuck to them. That's perfect. It was me who was impatient and unable to deal with not knowing. Only people like me react that way. This way...'

He lifted her right hand, pulled it towards him and placed it on his chest, so that she could feel how fast his heart was beating. Lynn nodded. She understood what he meant, not from first-hand experience but by drawing her own parallel with being in a tight tennis match against a strong opponent, when the lead was won and then lost and then won again after each passing game. She had been coached by the best on how to conquer her self-doubt, and this was her chance to pass that skill on.

'Yes, I read about that, in one of the articles I found in the library. Something about fear of betrayal or abandonment. Is that what you mean?'

'I guess so,' Jeff answered. 'I'm like two different people going through phases like that. When I'm at the top, there aren't enough hours in the day to do all the things I want to do. And when I'm down, the night's way too long, stretching out as far as I can see. And it tends to go round like that with the daylight. Some people are naturally nocturnal. I'm not, but I'm forced to be both nocturnal and "dayturnal". Whatever the word might be for that... It's *nocturno y diurno en* Spanish.'

'And you have the nightmares on top of all that, which means you can't be dayturnal, even if you weren't on a rollercoaster,' the compassionate woman added, guessing from the complex, rambling sentences that he needed bailing out.

The anxious man nodded, tears filling his eyes again. 'Exactly, angel. It's why I'm always knackered. I tone it right down for you, so you don't see the extremes very often. I'm getting much better at controlling the anger these days, but that doesn't mean it goes away.'

'So is your wavy line getting any smoother now? Now that we've begun to talk about things and we know each other better?'

Lynn hoped for a sign that the relationship that she found so fulfilling was having more constructive than destructive effects on his mental state. However, Jeff's attention was suddenly spirited away by the arrival of a man of about thirty years old, who was jogging towards the building, looking particularly distressed.

'Brian!' the nineteen-year-old jumped up, waving an apology to his beautiful girlfriend. 'Sorry, gorgeous. Hold that thought.'

The two men embraced. Much to the consternation of the young witness, her boyfriend had swapped characters again. Patient had become doctor, with the flick of some internal switch.

'How're you going?' the younger man asked.

'Fucking shit, mate,' the new arrival grunted and pushed the door open.

Jeff caught Lynn's eye and beckoned her to follow them back inside. He stayed several paces behind Brian, who made straight for the kettle. The celebrity watched keenly as the two social workers checked the situation out, apparently content that Brian was likely to be kept under sufficient surveillance, courtesy of their part-time, night-shift assistant.

'D'you want another one?' Jeff asked the stunned teenager, pointing to his empty mug.

'No, thanks.'

Torn between staying with his dream girl and helping this bereft man out, the client-turned-social-worker banged his cup down heavily next to the kettle.

'Make it two, mate.'

To Lynn's surprise, the miserable man lashed out. A tirade of abuse sprang forth from his mouth, and her boyfriend took a punch to the left shoulder, followed by one to the abdomen. The third one he caught with his left hand, as it made for his chin, causing Brian to burst into tears. Jeff put a steadying hand onto the other man's right shoulder.

'Make the coffee, mate, and we can sit down,' was his firm instruction.

The famous bystander glanced over at Alan, who had moved closer, in case he needed to break up the fight. He shrugged back, as if this behaviour was quite normal. Indeed, the tall, dark, enigmatic stranger seemed totally in command of this unusual situation.

'Your man can handle himself. Blokes do that sort of thing. There's no need to worry.'

Lynn stayed out of the way, talking to Alan and Ruth, who proceeded to sing her boyfriend's praises until it became a little boring. All the while, she studied how her mysterious madman moved around Brian, coaxing him into opening up. The pair sat facing the wall, thereby affording the desolate man some privacy. The celebrity thought she could discern fresh scabs on his left wrist. The signs of a recent suicide attempt, she assumed. She shivered as she imagined times when Jeff had turned up at these places, likely in the same state and behaving equally erratically.

'Fuckin' bitch!' Her lover was now laughing at whatever the newcomer was telling him. 'What did you say?'

It transpired that Brian's partner had left him and taken their children with her. The recent expletives, however, were directed at someone who had given him some dubious legal advice. After a few minutes, the older man had calmed down and even began to chuckle at some of the things they were discussing, although Lynn couldn't really hear and didn't want to. It was absorbing enough to watch the body language of the two men. Every time Brian slumped forward, Jeff would lean over too and then gradually sit back. At one stage, both men were pressing the soles of their shoes flat on the wall, about a metre off the ground, and were rocking back in their chairs precariously.

Jeff was firing questions one after the other, encouraging his client to express his feelings and process his wayward thoughts.

'What did you do last time?'

'What are you going to do this time?'

'Do you think that's a good idea?'

The sixteen-year-old noticed that the expert communicator never once forced an opinion on the other man. He had used that tactic on her too, she remembered, during their delving discussion at Benloch. He didn't patronise and he didn't accept any nonsense either. A question never went unanswered, even if it had to be asked in three or four different ways.

Transfixed by the performance, Lynn hardly registered that the two psychiatrists had moved away to talk to other visitors. After ten minutes or so, Jeff's arm suddenly extended towards her. His eyes didn't divert from their task, and she guessed this must be the part where he wanted to be able to turn round and see her smile or touch her hand. Oddly, she was thankful to be needed again, getting to her feet obediently and wandering over.

'Brian, this is Lynn,' her expressive lover introduced her with a welcoming smile.

He didn't attempt to touch her, even though he dearly wanted to. She understood why and left well alone. The other man's eyes had the same crazed look as she had come to know in her black stallion, from back when he had first told her about his nightmares. His head tilted so far downwards that his eyes had to peer out from under his eyebrows, almost as if he didn't have the right to see her.

'Hi, Brian,' she began.

The celebrity was unsure how to follow up, since this was no place for pleasantries. The recent arrival wouldn't be here if he had had a good day, and she could plainly see how he was doing. The half-patient-half-doctor came to her rescue.

'Pull up a chair,' Jeff requested. 'We were just talking about how difficult it is to deal with solicitors, and how expensive they are. They don't realise you're paying them to sort your life out, but they just play with it instead. All they think they're doing is writing letters. Brian builds 'planes, Lynn. Doing a Masters, building 'planes and watching his family walk out the fucking door. Shit, isn't it?'

The young star nodded. 'Yes. Very sad. How old are your children?'

Brian liked her question. 'Three and one. Aren't you Lynn Dyson?'

'No, mate. Only a stunt double,' her boyfriend jumped in before she could answer. 'What would the real Lynn Dyson be doing in a place like this?'

The real Lynn Dyson gave the comic's ankle a gentle kick. He had begun to look tired again, but his smile melted her heart.

'Don't listen to him. Boys or girls?'

'Two boys,' Brian informed her, with tears in his eyes again. 'I saw them on the weekend.'

The younger man took over, not sure whether his pretty sidekick was feeling comfortable or not. 'When'll you see them again, mate? Over Easter?'

'No,' the engineer groaned. 'She's taken them to Apollo Bay with this new wanker.'

Brian kicked the wall hard, leaving a scuff mark on the cream paintwork. Lynn turned round to see if either of the social workers were paying attention, grateful to see both of them look up. There was no problem though. The situation was well under control.

'Are you going to the footy on Saturday?' Jeff asked, winking at her. 'Brian's a fellow Richmond supporter, for our sins.'

'Yeah, maybe,' he replied. 'Some mates were talking about going. I should.'

The student shrugged, looking from one to the other. 'Might be a good idea. When does Junior play this weekend?'

'Saturday night, but in Adelaide,' the sportswoman volunteered. 'What'll you do tomorrow, Brian?'

Jeff shot her an admiring look. She was game, he thought. His heart skipped when she grinned back at him, and he was itching to reach out for her.

'S'posed to go to my mum's, but I can't face it,' the sullen man replied, calming down considerably. 'She just doesn't understand. So many questions. Blaming me for everything. She told me she bought Easter eggs for the kids, and how mean it was that she wasn't going to see them.'

'Do you like chocolate?' the other man interrupted.

'Yeah. Why?'

'Eat the fucking Easter eggs yourself, mate. Your mum'll never know, and the kids'll never know either. Or give them to your next-door neighbour. Just tell your mum you don't want to talk about it. Take her to the movies.'

Lynn shook her head. 'There aren't any movies tomorrow. It's Good Friday. What about working extra hours? Sometimes it's nice getting ahead.'

Brian nodded. 'Not a bad idea, actually. I need a day off next week for study, and to see this bloody lawyer again. Jeff, I don't understand why I can't think clearly.'

'Christ! I know what you mean,' the handsome man agreed. 'I'm the same. I was just saying to Lynn outside, before you arrived, that there was a time a few weeks ago when I was skiing Mount Everest three times a day, not able to make a single rational decision. That's what makes it an illness, mate. There's not much you can do at those times. Just have to ride it out. It's insidious. No-one goes to the doctor saying, "Doc, I'm too happy. I need something to make me sadder."'

His girlfriend chanced a laugh, and so did Brian. He sat up straighter in his chair, and the teenager could see he was a good-looking man too, now that the storm clouds were clearing from his face. Distracted for a second, she allowed herself to wonder if his traumatic event was only recent, or whether the extreme reaction to his family break-up was made worse by the after-effects of some other factor. What sort of curve would this subject have on his happiness chart?

Suitably reinvigorated by his dream girl's able assistance, Jeff was pressing on. 'I suppose there must be people out there who have an equal but opposite problem. But it's not a problem in that case, is it? How unfair is that? It'd be a good problem to have, wouldn't it? I'm just too deliriously fucking happy today. I think I'll eat ice cream all day.'

'But there is such a thing as not sad enough,' Lynn hazarded. 'Or rather, overly optimistic, I should say. Those people who don't see things coming and then get really floored by them when they do. It's better to be in the middle, as you say, so that at least you're sensitive to what might happen. The risks. You know... So you can protect yourself. Be prepared.'

'Yeah. That's good. The Boy Scout theory,' the student smiled, before suggesting a different analogy. 'It's finding that right place to sit to get the best view at a footy match.'

'Depends what you want to look at,' Lynn retorted suggestively, running her hand along her own biceps, as if to refer to strong, muscular male bodies.

'Right! If you say so, lady,' Jeff winked and played along, continuing to take the pressure off the older man. 'If I'm at your tennis match, I want to sit right on the baseline when you're serving, so I can study how your body moves.'

Lynn slapped him hard. Her boyfriend raised his hands, professing his innocence.

'Hey! You started it. What about you, mate? Wouldn't you agree? Those tennis skirts are so short. You've got to get up close to get the full benefit.'

The handsome student exchanged a high-five with Brian, who smiled.

'Thanks. You guys have cheered me up.'

'You're welcome. I'm sure you'll do the same for me soon,' Jeff told him.

The blonde celebrity hoped not. She couldn't bear to think of the next time her gorgeous man might need the support of a place like this. It crossed her mind that they would need to keep a lower profile in the coming months, as the pressure of the sporting calendar and her Year Twelve examinations increased. If not, her parents would definitely seek to put the brakes on their relationship. Given his apparent dependence on her, this might present a reason for him to need The Fellowship's services in the not too distant future. And what about her own dependence? She would be devastated too if she was no longer able to share his inspiring company or feel his arms around her, squeezing the last breath from her lungs in an effort to prove how much he loved her.

Brian stood up, looking altogether a different person. 'Cheers. I'm off home now. I'm going to get up early and go to work, as you suggested, Lynn. It'll stop me from moping about all morning. It was very nice to meet you.'

The dignified celebrity stood up and extended her hand. 'You too, Brian. I hope everything goes better for you soon.'

Jeff shook his hand too, and the pair hugged, slapping each other's backs.

'Stay up, mate.'

The couple watched Brian leave. Another four or five people had arrived since they had come back inside. Some were filling in their charts and talking with Alan and Ruth. The dedicated helper knew a couple of them and went to say hello, with his favourite stunt double in tow. She was tired, but it had been a very worthwhile evening. She had analysed another layer or two of the complex matrix that was her boyfriend and had learned more interesting facts about her fellow humans.

In the car on the way back into the city, Lynn asked which type of wave Brian's chart displayed. The handsome driver considered her question carefully.

'Most likely acute clinical,' he replied. 'He hasn't told me of anything that happened to make him a lifer. I asked him if he'd been in Vietnam... you know, in the Air Force, or something... but he hadn't. Was your dad in 'nam?'

'My dad?' the young woman repeated, for a moment forgetting she had shared the fact that her father had spent some time in the RAAF. 'Oh, yes. Only for a short time. He had to keep coming home for tennis tournaments, so they stopped sending him back after a while.'

Her boyfriend chuckled. It was a stretch to label Bart Dyson as a sufferer of Post-Traumatic Stress Disorder, but he also knew only too well the lengths to which people went to hide their symptoms. Looking across to the passenger seat, it was obvious from the compassionate expression on her face that Lynn was tuning in to his thoughts again.

'He doesn't want to fly himself anymore though. He said he got it out of his system.'

'Did he see anything terrifying?'

The star shook her head. 'No, I don't think so. He said flying was too boring, with long hours of nothing to do but sit and stare at blinking lights or clouds outside.'

Jeff shrugged. 'Yeah. I can understand that. I guess someone like him would find it hard to sit still for long. But as for Brian, I think he'll be OK soon. He just needs to adjust to his new lifestyle. Who knows? I have to be careful though, angel. I'm no psychiatrist.'

'And you're not crazy either,' Lynn told him, leaning across and putting her hand on his left shoulder. 'It was very impressive, watching you deal with Brian. It made me very proud to know you. Shall we go back to your place tonight?'

Jeff's eyes lit up, both at the glowing affirmation and at her magnanimous suggestion. The couple usually ended up back at Admin, to accommodate Lynn's frequent early starts for training or travel commitments. His heart soared when he remembered they still had a whole day and a half ahead of them, before he would need to surrender her back into the Dyson machinery. He struggled to remember what state his flat was in. Who cared?

'Thanks. I'd love that. As long as you open the door for me.'

The lumbering Ford u-turned on Bridge Road, and they sped back towards the MCG, skidding along tram lines which were wet after a short shower. The crowd was spilling out after the pre-Easter, Thursday night football match, and a few local roads had been cordoned off to assist with the traffic flow. They circled the block twice, before being waved through into Jeff's street by a sympathetic policewoman.

Climbing the stairs to the second floor, the celebrity asked another question. 'So have you been to The Fellowship more times as a customer or as a doctor?'

The student chuckled, casting his eyes upwards to think. 'About even, probably. Most times I go as a customer, as you say, and leave as the counsellor. I don't intend to. It just works out that way.'

'Because you understand people so well?'

'Yep,' he replied matter-of-factly. 'Much different in Sydney though. Way more times as a customer.'

This was the first time Lynn had been back to the tiny, dark flat since that mind-boggling night of nights. Accepting her boyfriend's key-ring, she smiled as she revisited the four-pointed, stationary tour she had been granted, not to mention the vivid memory of sitting together and looking out of the bedroom window, in the arms of her first ever lover. Such a lot had happened since that Saturday morning in February, and so many new concepts her mind was grappling with... Already it was Easter, and the ingenuous virgin from that memorable occasion had become totally consumed by her relationship with this flat's sole tenant. She could scarcely remember life before Jeff Diamond, and didn't care to imagine an after...

'I was so unbelievably nervous last time I was here,' she confessed, turning the key in the door. 'I didn't know what to expect.'

'You and me both, angel,' Jeff affirmed, his breathing heavier, though more from anticipation than fear. 'That was a fantastic night. And the first of many fantastic nights, thankfully.'

The grateful student embraced his beautiful, open-minded and open-hearted girlfriend and kissed her mouth hard. Excepting her frequent absences, this new relationship of theirs was pure perfection, and he could hardly contain his excitement at having come full circle. He admitted to being more than a little nervous himself this evening, taking her to a place which would reinforce his status as a defective human being. However, tonight's positive response to being taken out on a most unusual date was gratifying in the extreme.

'Will you stay, Miss Dyson? Or do you want me to drive you home?'

The cute schoolgirl smiled. 'I'd like to sit on the thinking ledge, please, Mister Diamond.'

Jeff liked this idea immensely. 'Anything you say, baby. Naked or clothed?'

'Both, in sequence. Doctor Diamond, I should have said, although I didn't know better at that point. Do you have any wine?'

'Shit! I don't know. You're a minor. You're not meant to ask for it! I'm supposed to ply you with it to get my wicked way. I could go to the bottle shop and get some. Do you have any of those pills?'

'No! It doesn't matter,' the happy woman relented, giving him a slap for his teasing innuendo. 'That would mean you having to come back through the door again.'

Jeff kissed her again, his emotions jangling. 'You're so kind to me. I love how you think. And I love how brave you were with Brian. They were some pretty good questions you came up with on your first time.'

To his surprise, the young woman began to unbutton his jeans, still standing in the hallway, while her other hand stroked his hairy chest inside his t-shirt, winding down over his rippling abs and then tantalisingly along the waistband of his shorts. Their lips found each other's flesh, time and time again, and Jeff lifted his t-shirt over his head and dropped it onto the floor as they made their way to the bed.

'It's not really the first time,' Lynn confessed. 'I've spent much of my life talking to total strangers. I've learned to anticipate what sort of questions people want to answer. I suppose I'm quite well qualified for counselling, in a roundabout way.'

Breaking away from the pleasurable sensations, her boyfriend went to his wardrobe and began to flick through the shirts on their hangers.

'Which shirt will you model for me tonight? Choose one, and I'll check the wine cellar.'

Lynn giggled, working her way through the modest collection. She opted for black, which matched the lingerie she had slipped on earlier that evening. The shirt was the same one that he had worn to the library on the night she had written her special note. Throwing it over her shoulders and threading her arms into the ample sleeves, she stood gazing out of the window, dreaming of what was to come.

By the time her host returned triumphant, carrying an opened bottle and two glasses, the pretty teenager was already sitting on the windowsill, looking out over the distant skyscrapers of Collins and Bourke Streets. She hadn't noticed him enter the room, so he waited quietly and watched her for a few minutes, considering her beauty, both outer and inner.

Finally, his sex-drive calling time, Jeff clinked the two glasses together to prevent his guest from being startled as he approached. She turned round, and her inviting smile warmed him to the core.

'I'm *molto legato esta noche*,' he announced, pouring the wine.

'*Molto bene!* You're mixing your languages up well too.'

'What should we drink to?'

'No more trolls,' the woman in black answered straightaway.

The student laughed. 'Or less persistent ones, at least.'

'Less persistent trolls!' Lynn chanted, and they clinked their glasses together.

The wine hit the tastebuds at the back of their mouths and stung a little on the way down their throats. The fingers of Jeff's left hand were cold as they brushed her skin while unbuttoning the shirt, and he apologised, seeing her flinch. Forgetting that arousal was causing his engine to run hotter than his extremities, he took a while to catch on to the fact that the temperature in the bedroom had fallen sharply since the onset of darkness.

'Great idea,' Jeff declared, savouring another mouthful of wine. 'Are you cold? You need warming up over here.'

Motioning for his dream girl to move along, he climbed onto the window ledge and invited Lynn to sit in front of him, just as they had done at the start of his rollercoaster period. He kissed the back of her neck, instantly transported back to that heady time. Jesus! That night had tested his self-control almost to its limit, what with her being so pristine and untouched, and after having been lured like a charmed snake into their deeply intimate and involuntary connection.

'I love you, Lynn Dyson.'

'I love you too, Jeff Diamond,' her sweet, sultry voice responded. 'Are you OK after tonight?'

The imperfect stranger kissed her neck, folding both arms around her body. 'Very OK, thanks to you. There was someone I wanted you to meet, but he never turned up. He represents the other type of crazy. The type who's totally unpredictable as to which personality you're going to get. I wanted you to experience being in the company of someone like that, because it's totally out there. Fascinating and sometimes a little scary. He's completely in the moment in whichever personality he's come with, completely unaware of the other version of himself. Then something'll cause him to switch, and the stuff you've just been discussing is totally gone.'

'Mid-sentence?'

'No. Something'll usually trigger it, but you don't always see the transition,' the empathetic student responded, relishing her cool lips on his forearm. 'At least, I can't.'

The young woman twisted her head around as far as it would go, to look into her boyfriend's eyes. 'We should go back then. I want to experience everything.'

Jeff hugged her in tight. 'I need you to be my happy troll, if it's not too much to ask.'

'But trolls are never happy,' Lynn refuted, giggling. 'That's why they're trolls. And they're ugly too. You already call me your angel, so maybe angels are the ones who pull upwards?'

'I could go for that,' the appreciative man agreed. 'You know I don't think you're ugly. The world's first stunning troll… But you're right, an angel's much more fitting. My happiness angel.'

The ecstatic happiness angel clinked her glass against his, once more for luck. Sitting wrapped up together, at the end of an evening which had brought them still closer, both minds were fast turning to the physical. Putting his glass down on the windowsill, Jeff rubbed his hands together as if he were trying to start a fire, before slipping them inside the black shirt and beginning to stroke her sides, then her stomach and finally underneath her breasts and between her thighs.

Lynn moaned, shuddering with pleasure, and nestled in closer. 'That feels wonderful.'

The expert lover carried on, feeling her respond to his every movement, as hard as a rock behind her. His dream girl's willingness to embrace his real self energised him no end, to the point where he was poised on an exquisite tipping point. The pressure was deliciously unbearable.

'Baby, this is so good,' Jeff whispered, nipping the sensitive skin of her ear and once more sending convulsions through her body. 'Too good. Coming here was a great idea. Can we go to bed? I've enjoyed the feeling of anticipation building all night, but I'm getting to the stage now where I'm like a racehorse waiting in the blocks. If I don't hear that starter's gun soon, I'm going to throw my jockey and run anyway.'

The farmer's daughter giggled and immediately leaned forward, only too pleased to indulge this gorgeous man, who was so flattering, honest and expressive. They climbed down from the low ledge and fell onto the bed, which hadn't been made since the last time its usual occupant had tried to sleep in it. Rejoicing in the wide-open grin, Lynn was ready for him too and latched on firmly round his waist, pulling him down on top of her.

'Sometimes loose racehorses run the wrong way,' she smiled, reaching for his erect penis and looking at the pleasure written on his face.

Jeff gave a sly wink, his own fingers wrapping around the hand that was stroking him firmly. 'Mmm... And we don't want that, do we? Take me, angel. I'm all yours.'

'I never know whether I can ask you to do things,' the young woman changed the subject somewhat coyly while they moved together. 'You always seem to have a plan that I don't think I can interrupt.'

The hot-blooded lover shook his head, having difficulty concentrating on forming a reply while his tongue traced around her raised nipples. His fingers had slipped inside her, to find her moist and eager to receive more of him. Too right he had a plan!

'Ask for whatever you want, but ask me early, so I can do something about it,' he answered, between sensuous, long breaths. 'It turns me on so much now you're getting more assertive. But if you ask me too late, Doctor Diamond might not have time to fit you in, and you'll have to go on the waiting list for next time.'

Lynn laughed out loud, sending an intense sensation through both bodies.

'Is that just you or all men?' she asked.

Jeff gave her a pained look of consternation, halting in his tracks and shaking his head. Lynn's hands reached up and grabbed around his ribs, enticing him back down again and clenching her pelvic muscles in the way she knew he couldn't resist. They both moaned with shared pleasure, and he growled in pure animal passion.

'All men, I would hope. But you don't need to think about them right now. Only me.'

'Sorry!' Lynn said, levering herself up to kiss his lips. 'It was a theoretical question. For my research paper.'

The handsome man licked his lips in thanks. 'Although that's a bloody good way of buying me more time! That was a troll versus angel moment, and the angel's kiss saved the day...'

The sixteen-year-old was heartened to hear her boyfriend say this. He had put her on a knife-edge of ecstasy too, and over she went. She gasped as the euphoric, floating feeling overtook her and ran her fingers along Jeff's spine until they reached his neck.

'Oh, Jesus! What are you doing to me?' he hissed, coming into her in a series of long, drawn out thrusts of his hips. 'Your timing is sublime.'

After their natural highs had subsided, the enamoured couple lay in the dark, talking about anything and everything and with no early start to constrain them. Then, when the nightmares woke them twice during the night, Lynn dealt with her man's angry frustration without batting an eyelid, forcing him either to pick up the guitar or the keyboard and compose a new song together, or else to use his heightened emotions to make more frenzied, passionate love to her, before relaxing in each other's arms until his heart rate returned to normal for much healthier reasons.

Souls Searching

When the dawn arrived too soon on Good Friday, the two lovers slept on in rebellious decadence. They discovered another common first between them, in that neither had ever eaten breakfast in bed before, so they rustled up a veritable feast to be eaten horizontally and with minimal clothing. Still the conversation never faltered, and Jeff marvelled at their ability to while away hours in each other's company without even trying.

'This is the Goodest Friday I've ever had,' the young man declared, biting the corner off a slice of toast. 'By a long way. You know, I have to confess to being a little scared by the prospect of spending a day and a half with you in one stretch.'

'Me too,' Lynn smiled impishly. 'I said that to Junior yesterday. It's like a test for whether we're more than just sex.'

Pushing his plate to one side, the nineteen-year-old let out an evil laugh, lunging for her naked waist. His prey only just had time to slide her own breakfast onto the bedside table before he had her flipped on top of him, sending his empty plate and cutlery sliding off the mattress and clattering onto the floorboards.

'Who says we need to be more than just sex?' he challenged. 'You wanna see if I can keep it up for thirty-six hours? So you can tell your brother you're going out with a real man?'

Lynn screamed and pulled herself back up to a sitting position, slapping her arrogant lothario's hairy chest.

'No! I don't want that at all,' she objected with a wide smile, 'and I do want to be able to walk tomorrow morning, thank you.'

'Shame,' her boyfriend frowned, reaching down to his erect penis and directing it away from the body it constantly wanted to touch. 'What am I going to do with this then?'

The divine form jumped nimbly off the bed and ran to the window, threatening him not to come any closer. Her protestations were less than half-hearted though, and hence categorically ignored. Smothering her into his arms and feeling her lean into him, Jeff turned themselves around to look out at the blue sky above the dirty and uninspiring buildings, which held much less mystique by the light of day. Christ, this was so perfect! How could he hope to persuade Lynn that their relationship was so much more than sex, when he was having such difficulty even convincing himself? He struggled to rein in his hankering need and focus on how to fully capitalise on the coming twenty-four more hours in her presence.

'OK,' he relented. 'Against my better judgment, let's put extreme carnal rewards to one side for a few hours and get on with the day.'

'Argh!' Lynn groaned. 'You make me feel so guilty for turning you down. Now I feel like a spoilsport.'

'You are a spoilsport,' Jeff smiled, holding his hands high in the air. 'A beautiful, sexy, irresistible spoilsport who's absolutely perfect for me. I need you to tell me when to back off. I don't want you feeling guilty about not wanting to do exactly what I want to do. Stick to your guns or stick to mine. That's your prerogative, angel.'

'Oh, my God! That's the worst attempt at a joke I've ever heard!' the sixteen-year-old couldn't help but laugh. 'Put your gun away, cowboy, once and for all, and let's go out somewhere and enjoy the sunshine before we have to get working.'

'Right you are, ma'am,' the naked student saluted his exquisite young lady, covering his reluctantly softening penis honourably with his spare hand. 'Where do you want to go? I thought you didn't want to run the Tan on Good Friday, because of all the gawking holidaymakers?'

'I don't,' Lynn affirmed, leading him towards the bathroom. 'I've got an idea. Let's get ready.'

She smiled at her compliant boyfriend, and the pair climbed into the bath. Her testosterone-charged lover leaned against the tiles at the far end of the tub, unable to take his eyes off the woman standing under the gushing water. When it was time to change over, she accepted a kiss gratefully while the shampoo rinsed out of her hair. Poor Jeff, she thought, watching him struggle to keep his hands off her while they showered. He did want her so much. She couldn't really understand why, but knew well enough these days that it wouldn't do either of them any good for her to give in to him now.

The schoolgirl looked up into his dark, hypnotic eyes. 'Why is it even called Good Friday?'

'Don't know,' her usually knowledgeable oracle admitted, handing her a towel. 'In Spanish, it's Holy Friday, which makes more sense. Maybe it was translated as Good by someone who was pleased to see the back of Jesus.'

His girlfriend smiled. 'Doubt it! Do you believe in God?'

'I don't think so. Do you?'

'No. We were brought up as non-believers, but I am fascinated with why people do. Not the type of people who just blindly follow what they're told, but intelligent people who are so scientific and analytical in other parts of their life. That's what I don't understand. And now you tell me you don't think so, so that's not a no either.'

The Computer Science undergraduate sniffed, amused at the celebrity's disgruntled air. 'It's more a no than a yes, but I can't rule him out. Or her, I guess.'

Lynn nodded. 'Yes, of course! Could just as easily be a her. That'd be a slap in the face for all those pompous, bearded scripture writers.'

'And how!' Jeff agreed, flashing encouraging eyes. 'I know what you mean though. Gerry's family never questions anything in the Bible, even though his dad'll pick holes in people's business plans with much more hard evidence to go on. It is weird. I guess that's why they call it faith. It's a desire to believe rather than an actual firm belief for a lot of people.'

'Do you mind talking about this?' the eager sixteen-year-old asked. 'I mean, is it too private and personal to talk about religious views?'

Jeff pulled on tracksuit pants and a t-shirt, wondering whether his angel had deliberately started such an in-depth conversation to pour cold water on his rampant ardour. If she had, it was another feather in her cap for learning how to deal with him. And if she hadn't, who cared? The tension was delectable, and the topic another of his favourites.

'No, I don't mind,' the tall, handsome man shook his head. 'Once I find out what my religious views really are, they might end up being private and personal. But for now, I have no clue what I believe. We do however need to suspend this discussion until we get to wherever you're going to ask me to take you.'

'Oh, good. But why?'

'Because it's too claustrophobic in this dark, gloomy hellhole for such big ideas to be given wings,' he told her expectant face. 'We can't have big conversations in small spaces. It just won't be as good.'

Lynn gaped in awe, anxious to hear what this font of wisdom would have to say once they emerged into the open air. She also rejoiced that her earlier choice of location would be perfect for their outing. Every minute she spent in his company, Jeff revealed another facet of his intricate, byzantine self, whether minuscule detail or significant layer. Some traits were cute and appealing, while others gave her goose-bumps for a much more frightening set of reasons.

'Excellent!' she proclaimed. 'Let's get going. We can leave all this washing up for later, can't we?'

'You bet. We're not at Benloch now. You can do whatever you want, in whichever order you want. Good Friday nineteen-seventy-two is the day you're free to make all the decisions. *Allons-y, chef!*'

The blue Ford spat into life and was soon ferrying its owner and his precious passenger northwards towards Collingwood. Lynn explained that she and the rest of the MAC crew had filmed a TV Christmas special at the

Abbotsford Convent a couple of years ago, high above a narrow, winding stretch of the Yarra River. Still an active abbey, it had been under the threat of closure for a number of years, and Lynn remembered the Mother Superior inviting her to use the magnificent grounds whenever she wished.

'Aha!' Jeff grinned. 'So this is all part of your master plan...'

'What do you mean? It truly was a complete co-incidence. I thought of this place a few days ago, well before we started talking about religion.'

'Get outta here!' the young man refused to accept her explanation. 'No way I'm buying that! It's somewhere I can't touch you. Somewhere you knew you could get a rest from me. Tell me I'm not right.'

Lynn lowered her eyes. There was more than a grain of truth to his supposition. His tone was upbeat, but the words hung heavily in the air. The car swung into the driveway, through wrought iron gates, and the tyres scrunched on the gravel before coming to a sharp stop. Her boyfriend's eyes were insistent, almost begging her to challenge him further.

'Yes, you are right,' she confessed with a tentative smile, sticking to her guns, as earlier advised. 'But it's worked out well too, hasn't it?'

Jeff looked up at the imposing, four-storey, gothic building, imagining the history hidden within its walls. It was as magnificent as it was bleak, and the landscaped gardens which swept down towards the river were a perfect substitute for the Garden of Eden, where he quite believed he could be tempted into anything by the most insightful and courageous example of womankind he had ever encountered.

Jumping out of the car, the young man raced round to the passenger side in time to open the door before his dream girl let herself out. She looked apprehensive but determined, and it reinforced his opinion. This aristocratic champion wasn't one for backing down. She had been brought up to take calculated risks and to win at all costs. If it worked in sport, why wouldn't she apply the same principles to the rest of her life too?

'You are just what I need, Lynn Dyson,' the contrite Catholic Argentinean Polish Jew told her, kissing her mouth gently but with enough passion to communicate his sincerity. 'This place is perfect. You're perfect. Don't ever stop punishing me when I get out of line. Please?'

'Shhh,' the relieved teenager whispered, putting her finger on his lips as he finished. 'And you're just what I need too. I love you, Jeff, but this is a convent, so we have to be quiet and keep sins to a minimum.'

With a sly grin, the intrigued student shut the car door as quietly as he could and followed his destiny down the hill and away from the house, aching with suspended anticipation. There were one or two other visitors in the gardens, but no nuns. Presumably they were all inside, deep in contemplation on one of the Roman Catholic Church's most important days of the year.

'Where are the conventionalists?' the playful man enquired, seeing his dream girl pointing towards a flattish piece of grass as a suitable spot for them to sit and resume their conversation.

'Eating fish?' his partner responded in an equally humorous tone. 'That's another weird thing... Why does eating a certain food mean you're closer to God?'

'Maybe a bit like a lucky charm?' Jeff offered, having always wondered about this too. 'Like always wearing the same clothes on match day, because you think it'll bring your team good luck? Catholics don't say only eat fish. Just don't eat meat. It's the Protestants who've extended that to only eating fish, I think. Just like Passover for the Jews, they're only supposed to eat unleavened bread and lamb. Not sure what they expect it'll help with, but it's not working too well for them so far.'

Smiling in appreciation of his irreverent humour, Lynn stretched out on the lawn, enjoying the warm sunlight on her face. Her lover sat a metre from her, determined not to give her any leeway in her quest to straighten out his behaviour. *Game on*, he chuckled to himself, seeing her contemplating his last few sentences.

'That's what I meant earlier,' her serious reply came after a few moments. 'With all the scientific advancement, and with education not being church-based anymore, why haven't people stopped doing these odd things?'

Jeff opened his mouth to reply, then closed it again as his gorgeous girlfriend rolled to her right and propped herself up on her elbow. She looked ashamed, as though her own words had taught her a surprising lesson.

'Go on.'

'Shit!'

'God strike you down, Miss Dyson!' her teacher scolded, crawling forwards and daring to plant a kiss on her forehead. 'I can't believe you're the first one of us to commit a sin, after all that. Now what was I going to say?'

'What were *you* going to say?' the indignant young lady repeated, deliberately trying to keep her voice low. 'You arrogant...'

'Quiet, please,' Jeff grinned, raising his hands to defend himself against her flailing arms. 'I'm sorry. What were you going to say?'

Lynn slumped back down onto the grass and giggled. 'You know what I was going to say. Tradition. The very reason why places like this are closing down. Times are changing.'

'Yep. But not fast enough, angel,' the ambitious philosopher let his muse off the hook. 'Exactly right.'

Gerry and Suzanne had flown back to Sydney for Easter to be with their families, leaving the third musketeer to his own devices for the whole holiday. Jeff's thoughts turned to his mate, probably bored to tears by his very traditional, Irish Catholic relatives. Ever since he had known the Blakes, the intelligent lad from the wrong side of town had tested their faith along with his own. And now here he was with the tables turned, testing the absence of faith, as demonstrated by a member of a family unshackled by any such beliefs, but which drowned in conservatism nevertheless.

An hour went by in the peaceful setting, revisiting the various arguments he had posed to Gerry's parents with his attentive pupil, particularly mentioning the times when he had backed one or other parent into a corner, only to have them drag out the old chestnuts of "He does it to test us," or "The Lord moves in mysterious ways."

'So why don't you know if you believe or not?' Lynn asked. 'What part do you believe?'

'I don't believe in Jesus being the son of God,' the nineteen-year-old answered without hesitation. 'That whole story doesn't stack up, as far as I'm concerned.'

'Why not? Because you're half Jewish?'

'No. Nothing to do with that. Mainly because there've been free spirits or outspoken leaders all through time who've wanted to change things,' he told her. 'So what made this one special enough to say he wasn't made by a man and a woman, like everyone else?'

The young woman shrugged. 'Don't ask me! I don't believe it either, but what about the stories about feeding five thousand people with two loaves and five fish, or whatever it was?'

Jeff lit a cigarette and invited his beautiful companion to sit beside him, curling his arm around her. Nervously, Lynn looked up at the convent windows and wondered how long it would be before someone noticed them and came to enquire as to the purpose of their visit.

'I think there may well have been someone called Jesus of Nazareth, who held the locals to account and put on some rallies to improve behaviour, just like Gandhi or Martin Luther King, or Moses from the Old Testament. I don't have a problem with those guys. They never claimed to be the sons of God, and yet stories still get exaggerated about them. And look at all the crazy preachers in America, claiming they can heal people, when it's really people's own self-belief that heals them.'

'If it really does heal them,' his girlfriend interjected. 'Permanently, I mean.'

'Yeah. And we're talking a long time ago, angel, obviously. No cameras or microphones to verify the truth. Just a whole bunch of excited people who wanted to believe in something new and better than they know. Chinese whispers, maybe.'

Lynn kissed him, grinning at his down-to-earth descriptions. 'But what about all the different religions? Why are there so many versions of God and so many versions of holy book? The Bible, the Quran, Torah, you know...

Aren't they just rules dreamed up by someone, so that people of the same kind can live harmoniously?'

'Most likely. You forgot Wisden, by the way... That's exactly what I believe a religion is. In most civilisations, religion and laws originated from the same place. And that's what I expect these Jesus of Nazareth types were trying to do: changing their societies' moral codes to fit life as it modernised. Exactly the same as I want to do.'

The young woman beamed, raising her hands aloft. 'That's what I wanted to hear you say!'

'Is it? Why?' the long-haired, charismatic student exclaimed, caught unawares.

The celebrity sighed, laughing. 'Wisden... The cricket almanac, you mean? That's actually hilarious! The *Kama Sutra* too... We both forgot that! No, but why did I want you to include yourself? Because you told me the other week that you and I are going to change the world, so I wondered if this had anything to do with religion.'

His cigarette having burned down to the stub, Jeff leaned over and put it out in the soil of the flowerbed. So this was her motive? He had to be careful not to get ahead of himself, because Lynn was impressionable and eager to learn, and her parents would not be best pleased to hear her spouting left-wing, radical ideals at the dinner table in advance of the Munich Olympics. He mustn't be seen to influence the elder Dyson daughter while she was still a minor, and silently he cursed her youth, as she did.

'No,' the nobody from New South Wales answered. 'I'm not motivated by any religion, but I do believe there are ways humans can behave differently that'll lead to a much more equitable world. A better world where everyone has rights and responsibilities to give and receive. But I'm not planning to do it in the name of any God, and neither can I drag you into it yet.'

'But why not?' the teenager asked, almost whining. 'Even if I want to? Because I'm not old enough?'

'Yeah, partly,' Jeff nodded. 'I don't like it any more than you do, but you can't deny your father'd go ape-shit if he found out I'm trying to enlist you onto my social justice bandwagon while he's trying to make you into a multi-gold medallist.'

Lynn sighed. 'Ape-shit's about right.'

'Yep. Agreed. I'll third that, angel,' her boyfriend smiled, kissing her temple. 'I'm with you, but it's too dangerous, isn't it?'

The sixteen-year-old exhaled, turning around and pushing her man's broad shoulders down until he was lying on his back in the grass. She kissed him hard on the lips, her worry at being overlooked temporarily suspended. To her surprise, her boyfriend's strong right hand grabbed her wrist as it sent sensitised fingers inside his t-shirt, and the youthful malcontent took the honourable gentleman's timely reminder with grudging good grace and in the true spirit in which it had been offered.

'Yes, it is,' she was forced to admit. 'But it doesn't mean we can't still talk about this, does it? I just want to know what you think, because I love the way you express all these big ideas that can't grow in small spaces.'

'Ask and ye shall receive, my child,' Jeff dared to play, and received a sharp tap on his chest for his trouble.

'Arsehole,' Lynn moaned.

'Thank you, my child,' he chanted. 'Fucking arsehole, I think is what you meant to say... That'll be four Hail Maries and six Our Fathers, and a spanking when we get home. What else would you like to know?'

The young woman laughed, throwing her head back. 'So if you definitely don't believe in Jesus but you don't know if you believe in God, where's the uncertainty?'

Jeff sighed, putting his hands over his eyes to shield them from the bright sun, as he stared up into the clear blue sky, also trying not to focus on her bouncing breasts, which had seized and reawakened his sedated imagination by their sudden movement.

'Not because of all this,' he began, lifting his hands upwards and waving expansively. 'I certainly don't believe a single God-like being created the cosmos. There's too much scientific evidence against it, as you say, and the religious teachings of all kinds are way too simplistic to be credible.'

'Good. We agree on that then.'

'Good. Thank you again, my child.'

Lynn huffed. 'Shut up! Tell me more.'

'Well, take us, for example...' the nineteen-year-old obliged.

'Us?'

'Yeah. How did I know to find you if something wasn't guiding me?'

The pretty teenager spun round, assuming the comedian was up to his old tricks. His face was not smiling however, and she noticed a familiar melancholy glaze in his eyes; a look that belonged to one so much older than her boyfriend.

'You think God made us fall in love?' she ventured, with a certain amount of disbelief in her voice. 'Are you serious?'

'I don't know,' the young man responded a little more defensively than he had intended. 'Not necessarily *the* God, but *a* god or gods. All I know is I've been driven to meet you for as long as I can remember, and you said yourself that you feel like we've known each other for a long time. What's doing that, angel?'

'Your dick?' Lynn cried out, suddenly stretching across to rub the front of his pants. 'Isn't that what drives men to find women?'

'Hey, stop!' Jeff sat up and grabbed her hand. 'Stop, Lynn. *Calmate.*'

His girlfriend's face was flushed, and her palm was clammy. He had unnerved her; distorted her usual, perfectly round planet into an uneven orbit. Reached too deep perhaps, and now she had embarrassed herself. This was a fascinating reaction which he hadn't anticipated at all, but it instantly made him anxious too. Was Bart Dyson's spectre bearing down on them, or was this latest revelation just a step too far for their fledgling relationship? He watched the teenager retreat, shuffling back a little in the grass.

'Are you OK?'

'Yes,' she replied, kneeling up and hugging him. 'Sorry. I've gone all shivery. I always thought that men and women were attracted physically first, and then they gradually learned what sort of personality they could fall in love with.'

Jeff felt a wave of emotion rush into his heart but refused to let it surface. They were indeed on very dangerous ground, their current location only serving to emphasise it more. Push or pull, the young man wondered.

'You're probably perfectly correct. It's another theory that's just as likely to be true as mine, angel,' he acquiesced, pushing her gently back down onto her haunches. 'Let's not use us as an example then. Take someone like Mother Teresa, for instance.'

'OK,' Lynn nodded, her shoulders sinking as they loosened up again. 'I didn't mean to spoil your argument.'

'You didn't,' the young man shook his head, deciding to use humour to recover the situation quickly. 'I'm not done with it yet! I've had some pretty stiff opposition during my time making these arguments, and I've spent fifty years' worth of nights thinking about it. So what makes Mother Teresa dedicate her whole life to saving the poor and starving? She's no cleverer than any other nurse. No better resourced. Certainly no stronger, faster or higher, if I can be so judgmental...'

The Olympic athlete pulled a face and responded with nothing but a shrug.

Jeff smiled and carried on. 'She has the same religious beliefs as any other nun, and yet she's done so much good and will probably become a saint. Something's given her that drive. The same something that didn't give it to any of the others. What is that, Lynn?'

The young woman drew another blank, seeing her man was not yet done. 'Don't know.'

'And then there's talent,' he continued.

'Talent?' his girlfriend repeated. 'What? Like musical or sporting talent?'

'Yep. But not being good because of a honed skill or years of practice,' the student dared, knowing he was again on treacherous territory with Bart Dyson's daughter. 'I mean natural talent. Times when a kid picks up an instrument and already knows how to play it, or the ability to write poetry or music with no training whatsoever.'

'Or songs,' the spellbound sixteen-year-old interrupted, now getting his drift.

Jeff cocked his head to one side and raised his eyebrows. His Pied Piper talents, whether inherited, gifted or learned, were working to perfection, planting seeds of assertion into his dream girl's inner sensibilities and then subtly helping her to come to her own conclusions. He needed to calm down too. He would push her too far again if he wasn't careful.

'Songs, yeah. And what's with *déjà-vu*?' he trotted out another of his well-worn theories. 'How many times do you think, "Hey, I know exactly what that person's going to say next," and they do. But how the hell can you know? Like it's a warning from someone who's been here before.'

Lynn nodded, laying back down on the ground. 'Yes, I have always wondered about that. It's a bit spooky, that idea... But is it *the* God, or one of several gods or something inside each person that gives them those special powers?'

'Special powers?' her handsome stranger echoed. 'I like that. And whose god is it? That's exactly where my uncertainty lies. Is there some other wisdom guiding us? Is it our own private god lurking inside our mind, who commands us to do what it thinks we should do? Or do the orders come from Head Office?'

Reclining on the lawn and staring up into a round window on the top floor, the young woman laughed out loud. 'From Head Office? That's funny. God's Head Office, One-hundred Collins Street, Heaven. Or Hell? Do you believe in God versus the Devil?'

Jeff shifted onto his side, propping his head up with his hand. It was now his turn to feel uncomfortable, since the battle of good versus evil was a sphere of theological study where he had also spent a good, long while, calibrating and recalibrating his own, frequently misaligned moral compass. The degree of difficulty involved in describing his beliefs on this subject without revealing hidden truths in his past was about to take a quantum leap. Perhaps he should draw this conversation to a close, using their waiting schoolwork as a perfectly valid excuse.

'Whoa! Not sure about that. There's no doubt that some people are motivated by good and some by evil. So if you extend my theory, it follows that the thing that's directing us could be a god or a devil. Shall we get going? We should reserve some time for our assignments today, I guess.'

Lynn rolled over again, sensing a sudden lack of energy in her previously animated boyfriend. 'OK. In a minute. What's wrong? You don't seem interested anymore. Can I ask one more question? Well, two actually.'

The subdued orator invited her to stand up. 'Sure. Let's walk around a bit. We haven't seen half of this place yet.'

The couple walked slowly, hand-in-hand down the steep bank and away from the convent, both admitting to feeling a definite unease. As they descended further along the winding pathway, the buildings appeared to lean over towards them with sombre distrust. Separately, each began to have second thoughts about coming to this place on Good Friday. Lynn was frightened that she may be trying to tame her wild horse too much, and Jeff guessed he was a stone's throw from pushing his saviour away.

'Do you think there's really something like a soul?' the young woman enquired, staring straight out in front of her.

'And is your second question "Do I believe in reincarnation?"?'

'Yes! How did you know?'

Embracing his girlfriend's tense frame and wondering if she could feel his racing heartbeat, the philosopher smiled and kissed her passionately. 'Because the two go together.'

'Do they?'

'Angel, I can't talk about this anymore, because you freak out if I make reference to us,' her mystery man reminded her. 'If I were to tell you my theory on souls and reincarnation, it's hard not to project it onto how it'd work for us.'

Lynn watched her boyfriend's jawline tighten, realising she was pressing her luck. She felt apprehensive too. It seemed as though they were thinking along the same lines, but she couldn't be sure.

'But why, if it's only a theory?' she countered, reaching up and cupping his chin in her hand. 'You believe it, don't you?'

Jeff turned his face to kiss the soft skin on the underside of her fingers. There was more meaning behind her words than perhaps she knew, and he could tell it scared both of them. They stopped and looked out over the view, stuck in the quicksand of their perilous conversation.

'Yes, I do,' her enigmatic stranger affirmed, taking a deep breath. 'But it is only my opinion. What I'd like to be true is that it's our soul which directs our human incarnation, like the individual god we talked about. I believe that souls go round again, and I believe my soul is very, very old.'

Lynn cuddled into his side, almost like a child. 'And do you believe we knew each other in a former life?'

A large left hand travelled up her arm and found its way in front of her mouth. Sensing his girlfriend's pulse quicken and tears pricking behind his own eyes, Jeff turned her around, and they began to trudge back up the hill.

'Two things I believe,' he sighed heavily. 'One, that it's time to go home, and two, that this conversation must wait until your current human incarnation is over eighteen.'

And much to his surprise and relief, Good Friday's decision-maker raised no objection.

***

On Easter Monday, Jeff arrived at the discreetly disguised South Melbourne recording studios ten minutes early and stopped to have a cigarette before going inside. He was so excited at the prospect of a professional recording of his songs at last. He and Lynn had made some demonstration tapes at Benloch a few weekends earlier, and in his enthusiasm, he had temporarily pushed his pride to one side and proclaimed himself prepared to let her take him through the whole process.

A car pulled up next to where the hopeful rock star was standing, and the passenger door swung open. Out stepped Richard Kerr, one of the other MAC stars, an outstanding pianist who had started out as a shy, bespectacled boy but who had in recent years developed into a flamboyant artist. The two men acknowledged one another, just as the famous blonde musician emerged from the back seat, and her boyfriend walked over to meet her, slamming the car door. The driver departed quickly without revealing him- or herself. It was quite Beverley Hills!

Picking up the guitar case and stubbing out his cigarette, Jeff followed the regulars into the studio. Lynn unlocked the doors, turned on the lights and fired up various machines, clearly very much at home. She pointed to a glass-panelled room to their right, which her band-mate had already entered.

'Coffee?' Lynn asked the two men, getting two nods in reply. 'Rich, please could you go through all this with Jeff? I'll be back in a minute.'

Richard Kerr liked Jeff Diamond a great deal. He was more tolerant and open-minded than the average bloke, and the pianist absolutely hated the fact that he was straight. He had been eager to share his fellow child star's first romantic experience, even daring to divulge a few of his own escapades with the equally tolerant and open-minded young woman.

The eight-track sound desk was complicated, exactly like the keen songwriter had seen on many video clips and documentaries about rock bands recording their signature albums, and underneath the desk were four tape drives, side-by-side. Eager to learn, Jeff pored over each bank of knobs, sliders and switches, trying his best to remember everything he was being told: equalisers, phasers, echo and the all-important mixers. Pretty soon, he began to piece the process together.

'Cheers, mate,' the appreciative novice said to his teacher. 'You really know your way around.'

First, they rehearsed the bass and rhythm guitar tracks under Jeff's tentative vocals. Then, for the second take, Lynn sat at the drum kit behind him, also providing backing vocals which immediately caused him to lose concentration. This cracked them all up and required them to start over again. However, on the third go-round, once the lead guitar and keyboards joined in and the sound was at its richest, the song's poetic lyric and strong melody suddenly took flight on their driving accompaniment.

By the time they had repeated the last chorus for the fourth time, the other musicians were nodding approvingly at each other. Jeff handed round cigarettes, while the celebrity disappeared into the sound engineer's den to rewind and replay. She turned the speakers up high and ran excitedly back to re-join her newborn star. "Rock Me Now" had finally been born, some four years after it had been conceived on the hill in Fairfield Park, during one of many hot summer's days spent in teenaged fantasies.

Tapping his feet to the infectious rhythm, Jeff took his dream girl's hands, and they began to dance as he sang along with his own voice. What a buzz! Another ambition achieved in this precarious life. He re-enacted the entire lyric, tasting every word, with its subject dancing and singing background vocals to his song right in front of him. The session musicians clapped and sang along too.

'That's a hit!' Bob, the bass player, assured him, with a genuine pat on the back. 'You're a good performer, sir. A natural, as they say.'

'See?' Lynn positively exuded enthusiasm. 'What did I tell you? People are going to love your stuff, Jeff. Not to mention you!'

'Fuck,' the modest songwriter mumbled. 'Thanks. It felt good, I have to say. What now?'

'What now?' Richard laughed. 'You've just recorded a number one hit. Take the afternoon off, boy! It's a pity we didn't have a movie camera. You need to see yourself when you're playing, to know what works and what doesn't work.'

His fellow MAC superstar waved her hand at her old friend. 'One thing at a time, Rich. What now is you have to do it about twenty more times.'

'No way,' her boyfriend replied, sitting down at the keyboard. 'Twice, maybe, but not twenty. It's got to stay a bit raw at least.'

'OK,' Lynn agreed. 'Play "Last The Night" then. We should record that, Rich. Just wait until you hear it!'

The man at the piano frowned. He wasn't the only impulsive one here, evidently. Hadn't he used up his favours already with these people? Making her boyfriend's dreams come true seemed to give the compassionate beauty great pleasure, which in turn stoked the fire against his raging humility.

'You sure?'

'Yes! Please, Jeff. I want to sing it to Rich. It's an amazing song.'

With a flash of his grateful, gipsy eyes, the songwriter gave the others the key and time signature, then went through the chord structure a couple of times to remind himself. Within a few bars, the songstress' rich, soulful voice chimed in, and he watched her sexily begin to drum along to his accompaniment, while singing at full volume.

Once their second song had started to take shape, Richard and the others picked up various instruments and jammed along, and before too long, a strong bass line had attached itself to the percussion, and the final line was repeated in harmony exactly as a forthcoming MAC single would conclude. Jeff leaned back on the piano stool, allowing his last chord to fade on both pedals and whistling his appreciation for their combined effort.

'Who wrote that?' Bob asked, slapping his bass guitar hard.

'We did,' the proud sixteen-year-old answered.

Staring her down, Jeff spoke over her answer. '*She* did.'

The other players looked from one to the other.

'*You* did,' the first-timer said again, this time urging his girlfriend's assent. 'Didn't you?'

Lynn groaned. Jeff was right. She was under contract, and it was important that her musical director should not be given an opportunity to relay their collaborative antics to her father. Why was he always right? Indeed, since their ominous and compelling conversation on Good Friday, she had begun to feel a little inadequate in his company. Nothing in relation to how he treated her. Quite the opposite, in fact. Their thirty-six hour date had ended as harmoniously as it had begun, with all the promise of a normal romance. However, in the two intervening days, she had been totally preoccupied. She didn't understand her apprehension for admitting to similar feelings about knowing Jeff's soul from a time before. And furthermore, he had been right to forbid her to speak about that too. So completely right, under the circumstances.

'Listen, guys,' the Sydneysider clarified, seeing his beloved was struggling with her conscience. 'I know you're all good friends and I have no doubt you'd back each other to the hilt, but I can't claim any credit for songs that Lynn records. Not now. Just like she can't officially sing bee-vees on mine. Contract or no contract, if people find out, it won't be pretty.'

Richard was nodding. 'OK. That's a good point.'

'Cheers, mate,' Jeff acknowledged the mature young man. 'And besides, I've got more than enough songs I can claim as my own. Shall we do another one, angel?'

The songwriter was inspired now, and he picked up the steel string guitar. He would seek to reward his dream girl for falling into line by laying down one of her favourite tracks. The ebullient piano player leaped off his chair and darted into the sound engineer's room to prepare for more recording, and from behind the glass, he waved for Jeff to start, so that he could check the levels. One of the songs penned on that first trip to the Benloch oasis was about to have its initial public offering, and Lynn cheered without inhibition as soon as she heard the makeshift string melody her talented boyfriend produced on the guitar.

'Hey!' she shouted, immediately making for the drums again. 'I love this one! We can overdub some strings after. You can, I mean...'

Instinctively the composer paused, wondering if his musical soul-mate could already feel the subtle tympanic effect he was looking for to open the track. As soon as Richard gave the thumbs-up from the sound desk, her self-proclaimed special powers gave it to him exactly how he imagined, and his ancient heart glowed with supreme confidence.

With the first few tracks mixed in a single take, the musicians all gathered around the sound desk to hear the playback of the third new song. The athletic lead singer ran back into the main studio and sat at the huge electronic keyboard.

'Open up two more tracks, Rich, please?' she yelled. 'I'll put some piano and strings over it.'

Her co-star did as he was asked, much to Jeff's hesitant joy. The result was magical, especially in the second verse, where the piano riff caught the song's mood perfectly. Bob had also crept back out to quickly conjure up an unassuming bass line. How the newcomer loved this collaborative process! They were literally *making* music.

By the end of their five-hour booking, the happy band had the skin and bones of six songs for the promising performer to use as his first professional demo'. Lynn had an evening training session in front of her, after which she was expected at a family dinner before the start of the new week. The couple waved goodbye to the others, and Lynn locked the studio securely.

'What a weekend!' Jeff shouted, as he grabbed her hips hungrily and pulled her mouth to his. 'I reckon we should have Easter on a monthly basis from now on. Thank you so much, angel. I have no way of thanking you enough.'

'You're going to be a star, Jeff Diamond,' the young woman told him. 'For your first recording session, that was really, really good. You're such a natural performer, Bobby was right. We should definitely get some film of you, because you need to see how sexy you are in front of the mic'.'

The humble student looked at his watch. It was almost five-thirty. He was feeling particularly horny, after all the adulation and having spent so long watching his favourite drummer up closer than he ever dreamed he would. Another night when he would end up at a club looking for cheap action, instead of cavorting with his very own superstar.

'You have to go, don't you?' his face became gloomy. 'Christ! I don't want this weekend to end.'

Lynn stood on tiptoe and kissed him again. 'No. Me neither. Shall we catch up on Tuesday night after work? I'll cook again, if you can stand it.'

'Oh, I can stand it,' Jeff smiled. 'Thanks. That'd be great. You are so good to me, and thank the others again, will you? I love you so much.'

'I love you too. Just as much, Mister Rock Star.'

***

'Thank you, sir,' Gerry said, leaning forwards and reaching for the refilled glass of whisky and soda with which Jeff had returned from the bar. 'Your health.'

'Yours too,' the exhausted man responded, sinking into the sumptuous leather chesterfield.

The billionnaire and his business manager were enjoying a break in a fairly dull program, out of sight in the back of their favourite blues bar, itself hidden in a laneway on the northern side of the CBD. They had spent the entire afternoon shut in a meeting room at Blake & Partners, moving large sums of money between bank accounts and devising tax-effective ways to extract Jeff's interests from various investments held by Paragon Holdings, and had later continued their planning over dinner.

The forty-four-year-old was in a hurry to get home. Kierney was out of town, and he hadn't yet collected the dog from Suzanne after his recent overseas trip. In fact, truth be told, divesting himself of large tranches of his personal wealth had left him feeling more disconnected from the present day than he had felt for the last few weeks.

Plugging the gaps in his evolving autobiography provided a strong motivation to return to their rented house by the Yarra River, with its large, lush gardens surrounded by tall trees, and to the writer's den he had created for himself in one of the ground floor rooms overlooking the lawn. Before driving into the city that lunchtime to meet representatives from a charity in receipt of a substantial bursary from the Diamond Celebration Foundation, Jeff had left the computer on, having very nearly finished his fond description of how he and Lynn had made their first, hesitant foray into the realm of matching souls.

'If these guys' second set looks like more of the same, I'm out of here,' the celebrity announced, offering his old friend a cigar produced from the inside pocket of his leather jacket. 'Do you mind?'

'No, mate. That's fine. Fiona's out with a friend, so I wouldn't mind getting an early night. Can't wait to get back to the book?'

Jeff smiled. 'Am I that transparent?'

'Always, mate.'

'What's the latest with the pre-nup debate?' the widower enquired, puffing on the mellow Cuban and checking his mobile telephone for a message from either child.

'Shit,' Gerry sneered. 'I don't know. She waxes and wanes.'

During a coffee break that afternoon, the executive had confessed to the VIP client that his fiancée had brought the subject of pre-nuptial agreements to his attention, saying that their upcoming union would necessitate full disclosure of each other's considerable asset bases, and her clinical insistence had taken the accountant by surprise. Fiona came from a family of successful solicitors and had also been married to one for twenty years, as Jeff took pleasure in reminding him. It was hardly a surprising move.

'You're entitled to protect yourself just as much as she is,' the superstar pointed out. 'It all depends on how long you think it's going to last. You're both entering into this marriage with more than enough to keep you going. Just use that as the basis. Anything you make from now on, just go halves. If it comes to it, that is.'

'Did you guys ever talk about a pre-nup?' Gerry asked, leaning back and puffing on the chunky Havana. 'This is good, by the way. Very smooth. Where did you get it?'

'Online,' Jeff smiled. 'Somewhere illegal, I expect. Some dodgy e-mail that got through the Cathy filter. Yeah. We did talk about it, and we kind of had one, didn't we? Based around the songs and touring.'

His manager nodded. 'That old thing? That didn't cover much though.'

'Covered everything of real value, mate. Everything else was pretty meaningless to both of us. To be honest, we both wished we didn't even have that, after a while. It always left a sour taste in our mouths whenever either of us referred to it. Neither of us would ever have enacted it, I'm sure.'

Gerry sighed. Even after nine months, his friend's heart was still bleeding. The bereaved husband had opened up to their lunch guests unexpectedly, recounting some of the early conversations he had been documenting over the last few days, from the first few months he and Lynn had spent together as teenagers with lives uncomplicated by profit and loss statements that attracted huge tax bills.

The author crunched the last slithers of ice and emptied his whisky tumbler. 'I was happy enough with nothing back then, mate,' he continued, as if reading his friend's mind. 'It's easier with more than nothing, granted. But not impossible.'

'If we do end up getting divorced, she'll be entitled to half of everything, the way she wants it worded. Everything.'

'Yeah, but apart from the numbers, would that matter? If you halved your assets, would it make much difference to your lifestyle?'

'No, I s'pose not,' Gerry frowned. 'Half of nothing wouldn't have been too hard to handle either, I guess.'

Jeff chuckled. '*Exactamente, amigo.* The numbers are meaningless. Slipping a few rungs on the ladder of Australia's Richest wouldn't hurt the old ego too much. Even yours, mate.'

The accountant stared into space while scruffy band members filed back onto the stage and took up their instruments for the last session of the night. Jeff was perfectly correct, as usual. The intervening years had brought great fortune to both men, pooling one's business acumen with the other's many talents, and then timing their shrewd moves with precision, so much so that Gerry had come to view his own substantial balance sheet with a level of nonchalance until his relationship with Fiona had turned serious enough to consider a wedding.

'True enough, old boy,' the affable man shook his head. 'You bastard. You never cease to prick my conscience. In fact, losing half would be far more painful for Fiona than it would be for me. Lynn'd be proud of you, my man.'

Jeff flinched, the tattoo on his left pectoral muscle stinging sweetly, right on cue. Yes, Lynn was proud of him.

***

'So how's business?' Jeff shouted, as his squash partner loped backwards to retrieve a high-speed return.

'Booming!' Gerry responded, crashing into the wall. 'Beginner's luck.'

The two friends had met after work at the sports club where the businessman had recently become a fully paid-up member, to catch up on each other's news after the Easter break and to take the frustrations of the day out on the little, round ball. Joining such a traditional men's club was *de rigueur* for the ambitious accountant, unaffected by his left-wing buddy's jibes about milking the same "old boy network" which he and Lynn had criticised only the other week.

'Beginner's luck?' the scornful student repeated. 'That I doubt. Any more hot daughters for charming lately?'

His friend laughed, missing another smash by several centimetres. He bent over to catch his breath while he thought of a suitably smart response.

'Fuck you!' was all he could muster. 'What's so wrong with my business model? Can I help it if I go after the low hanging fruit?'

'Your dad'd be so proud,' Jeff shot back. 'Do you want to grab some food? My shout.'

The younger of the two knew only too well that he should hold his tongue, especially since he was quite clearly benefitting from the luxurious facilities the club afforded its members with no financial contribution whatsoever. As much as Gerry was a player in this despicable scene, what sort of bludger did that make his undergraduate guest? He was, however, itching to tell of his first recording studio experience and how chuffed he was with the result.

His mate stood up, a look of amazement spreading over his face. 'Hell, yes! Without further delay, in case this is a flash in the pan. I can't remember the last time you paid for a meal, you bastard. Things must be looking up.'

The pair showered and changed quickly, before installing themselves in the small bar with a beer and a menu each. This new stage of Gerry's career, as Managing Director of the Melbourne branch of Blake & Partners, was indeed going well, largely due to his jovial nature and an outstanding ability to build relationships. The staff had warmed to him after some initial resistance at suddenly having the boss' son imposed on their previously sleepy operation, and he had the Board of Directors eating out of his hand.

The return to Sydney over the long weekend had cemented the older man's resolve to make his mark on the Victorian capital. He and Suzanne had caught up with family and friends, most of whom failed to credit the rival city with anything to offer such sophisticates. Even their respective parents had confessed to being surprised at how well the couple had assimilated into their new environments; particularly Suzanne, who had migrated from the city to the country with barely a hiccough.

Moreover, free from his father's watchful eye, the gregarious party animal had brought a new dimension of client satisfaction to his division of the company, positively encouraging long lunches and boozy evening events. Jeff was keen to add his endorsement for this new tactic, having wined and dined several times at his friend's expense with similarly scant regard to his frequent pangs of guilt.

Over rare fillet steak and a bottle of *Cabernet Sauvignon*, the two men exchanged boastful stories of recent female conquests and robust, largely unqualified opinions about political and economic trends. Gerry had shown little interest in the songwriter's musical exploits, save to nod casually at the suggestion of becoming the performer's manager when he found stardom.

'What do I know about showbiz?' the numbers man scoffed.

'About as much as I do, mate,' his friend answered. 'You know how to make money out of money. That's what I'll need. The rest can take care of itself. I just don't want to waste the opportunity if it comes my way.'

Gerry shrugged. 'Or mine, to be sure! Does Lynn have any pearls of wisdom? I thought you weren't going to let her be involved in your rise to stardom.'

'Yeah, well,' Jeff sniffed. 'I gave in. I bowed to the pressure of an altogether too obvious good idea. It was awesome to work with professional musos, and they gave me some good tips.'

'I bet they did!' the accountant chuckled. 'That Richard Kerr... He'd have been drooling all over the ivories.'

The younger man rolled his eyes. His right-leaning mate's homophobia was no secret, passed down through the generations of bigoted Irish Catholics from whom he was descended. Gayness was nowhere near godliness where the Blakes came from, yet his much more liberal companion bit his lip and refused to rise to the bait. He saw no point in trying to defend his girlfriend's musical associate tonight, especially after three beers and half a bottle of wine, even if it was his turn to pick up the tab.

'He's a good bloke,' the nineteen-year-old said instead. 'I'm sending off a demo' tape to some recording companies. Who knows if they'll think it's any good? Lynn's optimistic though, which must count for something.'

'You'd hope so! She should know, I guess, and she hardly needs to stroke your ego to worm her way into your affections, does she?'

Jeff smiled. 'No. Hardly. I have no issue with her stroking anything, mate. Whatever... It's a weird feeling, being half in her world and half in mine. Sounds arrogant, but I really feel like I'm on the cusp of something great. Poised to leap to previously unscaled heights.'

'Arrogant?' Gerry snorted, causing the men at the next table to look round. 'No, that doesn't sound in the least bit arrogant. Whatever gave you that idea? Fuck me! First you buy me dinner and drinks, and now you're telling me you're poised for greatness. Next you'll be making a takeover bid for my company.'

The student lifted the wine bottle and emptied it into the older man's glass. Maybe he had gone a little too far with his last sentence, and the executive was right to ridicule him. Still, he couldn't deny how he felt, and there was no harm in trying stardom on for size, even if it was somewhat premature. Optimism was a new phenomenon to the boy from Sydney's west.

'*Your* company?' Jeff rebuffed the challenge. 'Since when? Besides, I'm more likely to have a number one hit than you are to have your dad hand over the reins of Blake & Partners. Am I right?'

'Fair point,' the accountant smiled. 'Unless I bump him off...'

'OK. Place your bets, Blake-san,' the ambitious musician picked up his wallet from the table and pulled out a single note. 'Double or quits. Ten bucks says I'll have a song at number one by Christmas.'

Gerry swallowed down his remaining wine and stood up.

'Get out of here,' he sneered. 'I'm not betting with you. I can't think of one thing you haven't achieved when you've said you would. You take me for a fool, Diamond?'

Jeff shrugged, placing a twenty dollar note with the ten to pay their bill and preparing to take it to the counter. His long-time friend was not a fool. Far from it. There were few more astute than Gerry Blake, which was why the young pretender now kept quiet. It was his genuine intention to ask the prodigious businessman to be his manager in the event that he hit the big-time, but tonight was not the night to pursue this idea, for an obscure, subconscious reaction had suddenly filled him with dread.

'Absolutely not, mate. In fact, with all the bravado, something's also fucking scaring me. A sort of foreboding feeling, and I don't understand why. Probably nothing.'

The metallic paint of Gerry's BMW shone brightly under the street lamp. The two men walked slowly through the car park, digressing into less meaningful banter. They drove in a northerly direction up Punt Road, towards Richmond and the student's lowly, second-floor digs.

'So things still going well with you two?' his mate asked.

'Yeah, why?' Jeff responded. 'What about you?'

Gerry raised his eyebrows, flicking his indicator on as they prepared to turn right into Bridge Road. The streets were already dark, with only a few restaurants at the city end still open at nine o'clock on a Tuesday evening.

'Past our sell-by date,' the happy-go-lucky man admitted. 'Living so far apart's making it all a wee bit too hard, to be honest.'

'Shit, Gez,' the sympathetic man responded. 'That's not good. Are you splitting up?'

'No. We keep saying we still want to see each other, but then days go by and neither of us makes contact. It's a kind of marriage of convenience. Have you talked about this with her?'

'No. With Suze?' the peacemaker answered honestly. 'I think she's surprised how much she likes it in the country. Working things out for herself. You know... At least it's likely to be an amicable thing if you decide to go your own way.'

Gerry looked pensive. 'Have you slept with her?'

Jeff let out a derisory laugh. 'No way!'

'She wants to.'

'Well, I don't. Your woman's pissed off at me about the way I treat Lynn anyway. We agree to disagree.'

The city slicker sighed. 'She might sound pissed off with you, but she's not. I was thinking you might like to move out to "Jeff Diamond Creek", so I can shack up with Lynn.'

'Oh, yeah. That's a fantastic idea. Couldn't think of anything better, mate. Fuck off!'

They had reached the narrow driveway to the younger man's drab block of flats, and Gerry pulled the car into the roadside. Thanking his good buddy for the lift home, Jeff reached into the back seat to take hold of his sports bag.

'D'you want to come in for a beer?' he asked, wondering if the normally convivial, overgrown schoolboy wanted to talk.

'Thought you'd never ask, darling,' the accountant laughed. 'No, mate. You're not my type, thanks all the same. I've got an early meeting...'

'And you have to wash your hair. I understand. Them's the breaks. I'll get over it.'

Satisfied that his friend was as right as rain, the nineteen-year-old flicked the door handle and leaned leftwards. He should know better than to make a comparison. The warm and fuzzy stuff of love and relationship security held no importance for the power-hungry businessman, who had grown up greedy for wealth and influence above all else.

'Cheers, mate. See you on Friday.'

'You almost never talk about the wonder of Lynn Dyson anymore,' Gerry blurted out, just as his friend was about to slam the door.

'Don't I?'

'No. Not like before. That's why I wondered if something had gone wrong.'

Jeff grinned. 'No. That's actually a nice concept. I like where you're taking me. Good preparation for a night alone.'

'What are you talking about, you idiot? I'm not taking you anywhere. I thought we already established that much.'

'I'm talking about your observation that I don't talk about Lynn anymore,' the romantic clarified, rolling his eyes. 'I hardly think of her as separate from me these days. It's become normal, I guess. She's inside me.'

The party boy screwed his face up in disgust, wholly unable to relate to his friend's remarks.

'Mate, no,' he scoffed. 'You've got that the wrong way round. You're supposed to be inside her. Go up there and put your imagination to the test. Sometimes I think I haven't taught you anything in all these years.'

The younger man laughed, leaning into the car and reaching across to shake Gerry's outstretched hand.

'*Adiós*, mate.'

Sexual Mercenary

'Hey, I need to talk to you about something,' Jeff announced, as they were driving back from the tennis centre.

Lynn looked across at her boyfriend, gorgeously hot and sweaty after their tough training session. She had stayed in the city all weekend again, mainly because the family's Olympics preparations had stepped up a notch and they needed to make full use of the Sportsdrome's facilities. The couple had managed to sneak out for a few hours on Saturday evening to meet a group of the young woman's friends for another raucous dinner, and had then decided to play safer on Sunday evening and combine training with pleasure.

Their respecting relationship was becoming stronger and closer as the weeks went by, and they were now so comfortable in each other's company that neither teenager needed to think twice to bring up most topics of conversation. They had sorted out the dating politics perfectly, despite both being novices. However, there was one subject that remained unaired and unresolved, and it was eating away at both of them.

'Sure. What?'

Jeff looked sideways, away from the road for a second.

'Sex.'

'Oh, OK!' the young woman laughed, before noticing a more serious expression spread over his face. 'Is something wrong?'

The Fairlane lurched to a stop in the Admin driveway, and her handsome chauffeur snatched the keys out of the ignition.

'No,' he answered, 'but I've been meaning to run something past you for ages and can't put it off any longer.'

Lynn looked puzzled. 'Curiouser and curiouser... Are you pregnant? Are you coming upstairs?'

'You bet!' her boyfriend laughed, closing the passenger door after her and lifting both sports bags from the rear seat. 'And no, I'm not pregnant, although I have felt a bit sick in the mornings lately.'

Inside the familiar, top-floor apartment, Jeff turned to his dream girl and kissed her tenderly. She looked divine, flushed and athletic, and his sex-drive was quickly running away with him.

'My timing's lousy,' he opened, with a look that drilled through her head. 'Now we can't *have* sex until we've talked about it, and right now all I want to do is devour you in the shower.'

'Well, how long a conversation is it likely to be?' the bemused sportswoman asked, smiling at her man's self-inflicted frustration.

He sighed. 'Long.'

'Right,' Lynn frowned, slightly disturbed but determined to keep things light. 'You shower, and I'll make us some food, then we can swap. We'll just have to practise being patient.'

The horny student obeyed reluctantly. His guilt was getting on top of him, in part thanks to Suzanne's endless nagging, but also because his love for Lynn was maturing way beyond anything he had ever imagined. Even his own conscience was beginning to side with Suzanne, despite his body's continuing reservations.

Over dinner, Jeff started to explain himself. 'I need to know what your expectations are around our sexual relationship. You know... Exclusivity and what being faithful means to you.'

To his amazement, Lynn smiled knowingly and nodded. 'You want more than I can give, don't you? Because I'm travelling and busy so often.'

The boy from Sydney's south-west felt like he had been slapped across the face, figuratively speaking at least.

'Whoa! That's to the point!' he groaned. 'I suppose I deserve it for even bringing the subject up.'

The sixteen-year-old shrugged. 'I'm starting to get wise to grown-up things these days.'

'Yes, you certainly are,' her boyfriend replied, taking hold of both her hands. 'It's not only that. This is the first serious relationship I've ever had too, and you're right on the money. Lynn, over the years I've come to use sex as one of the ways to get myself through the night, and I've pretty much become dependent on it.'

'Like an addict, you mean?' she asked with some trepidation. 'Can you be addicted to sex?'

Shamefully, he sighed with a half-smile. 'Angel, I'm addicted to everything. And most of all to you. I'm a hopeless case.'

The young woman nodded in slow motion, silently bidding her man to continue. She didn't much like where this discussion was heading but was prepared to give him the benefit of the doubt. In all honesty, from what she had seen of the effects of his childhood traumas, she was amazed that her scarred boyfriend was able to lead as normal a life as he did.

'That's not to say I want special treatment. I don't,' Jeff added nervously. 'But the truth is that I have still been seeing other women for sex. I have to be straight with you, because it's doing my head in. You mean the world to me, and if you said you couldn't deal with it, then I'd stop.'

'But could you?' Lynn asked, raising her voice and feeling suddenly light-headed from the shock. 'If you *can* stop, then why haven't you already stopped? And if I say no, won't you just go for it anyway? How would I know any different, unless I have you followed?'

All perfectly good questions, the student shuddered. He put his right hand on his heart.

'If you gave me an ultimatum… exclusivity or goodbye… then you win, hands down. But I want to explore the possibilities with you, if you'll let me. Exclusivity and goodbye are at opposite ends of a scale, so I need to find out how long that scale is for you. I'd like us to be able to agree on a point somewhere along it.'

The sixteen-year-old laughed, albeit kindly, scarcely believing she was having this conversation. Jeff was nothing if not irresistibly persuasive, always pushing the boundaries. Where on Earth was he taking her this time?

'That sounds more like a business proposition than a relationship,' she teased.

'You're right, and I'm sorry. I'm not making this too easy on you.'

Lynn shrugged again. 'Too right! Well, I'd have to be pretty naïve not to wonder if you're getting sex elsewhere, given the fact that when we're together you can't go more than a few hours without it. I've been avoiding having to deal with it, I suppose, to be perfectly honest.'

Jeff whistled nervously, shifting in his chair. 'Right again. So have I. I'm already doing it less though, Lynn. Extracurricular sex, I mean. Honestly, if you insisted on exclusivity, I'd just have to find a way. But I wouldn't be able to promise it'd work, just as I can't expect you not to change your mind.'

His patient girlfriend relaxed and poured them both a fresh glass of wine. 'So which possibilities do we explore?'

The student inhaled. 'Whoa. This is hard going. Now I know why it took me so long to bring it up. OK. So can I give you a bit of a character assassination of myself?'

'Yes, of course! Doesn't sound as if it'll help you much though!'

'Probably not, but you need to know,' her mystery man answered, taking another deep breath and feeling sweat forming in his palms. 'I'm a sexual mercenary, I guess.'

'Sexual mercenary?' Lynn exclaimed. 'What does that mean? A prostitute?'

Jeff's eyes widened in horror at the young woman's very logical interpretation of his words.

'Christ, no! Perish the thought. It goes back to what we were talking about before. You know… About using relationships versus respecting relationships.'

She nodded. 'I understand the difference, but what's a sexual mercenary? You make it sound so sinister.'

'It does, but it's not,' her boyfriend acknowledged. 'Angel, meeting you has shown me exactly what the difference is between a respecting sexual relationship and a using one. I kind of hoped it would be this way, but I didn't dare believe it could happen to me. Being who I am, I mean… Ever since I turned thirteen, I've been getting as much sex as I could, from pretty much anyone I could.'

The Olympic athlete lifted both arms to place her hands on either side of her head, not knowing what to make of yet another outrageous story. She hardly needed any more complications in her busy life. Jeff carried on, his heart in his mouth.

'And, let me say, I've never paid for it. But women have often paid *me* for it, in some way or another. Not in cash, *comprendo*, but in other ways. Hence the sexual mercenary label.'

'So how else have you been paid for it?' Lynn enquired, intrigued at the image that was forming of a younger, skinnier teenager sleeping with all and sundry and reaping the benefit somehow.

The handsome cynic laughed. 'Basically with attention and conversation during the day, and occasionally food. Copious quantities of coffee and beer. And at night, with distraction and diversion, and somewhere to go that's not home. I'm proud, angel, but not that proud. And I probably should be ashamed, but I'm past caring. Or at least I was, until I met you.'

The innocent youngster's heart went out to him, totally against her better judgment. This masterful communicator had succeeded in manipulating her again, which annoyed her a great deal, but his stories were always so compelling and painted a picture of a world so alien to her. She had no reason to suspect he was lying, although she feared her own *naïvetée* once again.

'I'm sorry, Jeff. I didn't mean to criticise. Carry on.'

He did. 'Sometimes, if I couldn't be bothered to turn up to particular lessons, I'd hang out in the supermarket and end up talking to women doing their shopping while their kids were at school. I'd help them load their groceries into the car, and then they'd offer to buy me a coffee or a drink, or even lunch. They were looking for company as much as I was. And then more often than not, we'd end up back at their place, in bed. That's where I got my sex education. How I learned what women like and don't like, because they were mostly way more experienced than I was.'

The student raised his shadowy, stygian eyes from where they had been staring at his wine glass, to look into those of his dream girl, in order that he might gauge her reaction. As usual, she was listening intently, and there was no judgment in her expression. He began to relax. It was always so easy to talk to her.

'Several times, I'd see the same woman again, and she'd follow me around the supermarket. I didn't like to repeat anything, in case it became a habit I couldn't honour. Once or twice, I'd have two of them chasing me round with their trolleys at the same time. That was pretty amusing.'

The sophisticated teenager gasped. 'Did they ever find out about each other?'

Her mystery man shook his head. 'Don't think so. That would've been as ugly as sin. Anyway, a few of them figured out I had a brain and used to say, "You could be so much more than this," and stuff like that. But most of them were just out for a good time.'

'So you stopped?' the sixteen-year-old asked, with a sneaking suspicion that there was more to come.

Her boyfriend's body language confirmed there was, with a mixture of macho pride at the number of conquests he had notched up and abject contrition at having to admit it to someone who mattered. He coughed uncomfortably.

'Cruising the supermarkets? Yes, after a while. They thought I was a common street kid, which I was, and I started to resent my own using relationships. But then gradually I just grew out of it too. I suppose when girls closer to my age became more interesting, and when I found a way to make school more of a challenge. You have to know, Lynn, I try to base everything I do on a fundamentally good motive. I never did anyone any harm. Their husbands were none the wiser, the women were happier, and I got what I needed.'

Lynn had to agree he had a point, but she ventured an argument nevertheless. 'But these women were still being unfaithful to their husbands, and you were complicit. That's not a good motive.'

Jeff shrugged. 'Yeah. Good pick-up. I agree now, but back then I just saw it as their problem. If the woman wanted to make it into a problem, she would tell him. If not, no harm done.'

'Well, I'm very grateful to all those women who made you into such a great lover, but what does all this have to do with us?' the famous schoolgirl asked, coming back to his original question. 'Is that what you meant about being resourceful when you go out drinking? So that you don't spend too much money, you get girls to buy them in return for sex?'

'You got it,' he nodded in shame.

'What are you asking me then?'

Perturbed, the student sat forward and put his elbows on the table, flattening out his forearms to take hold of her hands.

'You said it earlier, when we first started. I don't know why I just didn't stop right there,' he sighed with a wry smile, his sunken, smouldering eyes looking out sexily from under a furrowed brow. 'I need more than you can give, and I'm asking your permission to take advantage of these meaningless using relationships when you're not around. You are the most important thing in my life, and I cherish what we have with all my heart and soul. It's the only real relationship I'll ever have, Lynn. I mean that, and I promise I'll give you everything you need, whenever I can. I just have to hear from you what your idea of faithfulness is.'

The pretty teenager looked pensive and paused, perplexed by the frankness of yet another very adult conversation. Her friends would often complain that their boyfriends avoided straight talk, leaving them never quite knowing where they stood. What a contrast to Jeff, who laid everything on the line, time and time again! Moreover, if she were to follow normal dating protocol, she ought rightly to end their relationship here and now. Her boyfriend had been cheating on her all along.

This possibility had often crossed the young woman's mind, but she too had been in denial. She had never wanted to admit to the fact that her mystery man might be taking advantage of her. Lynn's stomach twisted, and she felt sick. Despite how awful his behaviour seemed at face value, how could she possibly give up this adventure? Jeff Diamond consumed every ounce of her emotional energy. Yes, he was manipulative and demanding, but he was also exciting, stimulating and incredibly loving.

As usual, driven by compulsions lurking deep within, the tormented man couldn't wait for her answer. The blood vessels in his forehead were pounding, his pulse echoing in his ears.

'What's being unfaithful anyway? Is it when you have sex, or when you touch someone's hand? Or when you kiss, have a conversation, or when you merely think about someone else? Which is it for you, Lynn? And just think of the scenario we have, where I'm fucking someone meaningless and all I can think of is you? Who's being unfaithful to whom in that case?'

The intelligent youngster considered his statements carefully. Was she a total fool to even be giving this topic air time? Was she really being asked to love a partner enough to share him? That was ridiculous, even to someone so impressionable and infatuated, but by the look on Jeff's face, he was deadly serious. She placed her wine glass onto the dining table and stared into the questioning eyes of her dark-haired, gipsy boy, who was beginning to look far more strained and worried than his smooth, baritone voice let on.

'Wow! I don't know! Exploring the possibilities is always so complicated with you. There's no right answer, is there?'

The reprobate laughed at her refreshing honesty. He flipped the top off his cigarette packet and pulled one out, fumbling in his back pocket for his lighter.

'Nope. There isn't. Life is complicated, angel. People are complicated.'

Staring into space while she listened to these simple phrases, deliberately engineered to absolve her boyfriend's catalogue of sins, Lynn wondered why she didn't feel outrageously offended, upset and angry. She should, shouldn't she? Wasn't that what always happened in television dramas or in newspaper articles about jilted lovers, exacting their revenge or being desperately heartbroken? Whole genres of literature, plays and movies had developed over the years based on these perennial themes.

So what was it about Jeff Diamond which anaesthetised her from this pain? Was she so naïve and starry-eyed that he could walk all over her? The sixteen-year-old hoped not. That wasn't how she had been raised, and certainly not how she viewed herself. Up until this evening's confession, they had been enjoying the most perfect romance. So why had it not immediately turned sour with this latest disclosure?

The blonde schoolgirl stood up again and moved to sit on his lap. A good sign, the anxious man dared to think, wrapping his leaden arms around her. His body radiated a substantial amount of heat; greater still than at the height of their furious doubles tennis match.

'I'm really having the ride of my life with you,' the slender beauty laughed. 'I should be angry, but I'm not and I have no clue why. All my friends have such easy relationships. They go on dates, some of them have sex when their parents are out or go away for sneaky weekends together. Maybe they get stressed because the boy doesn't ring when he said he would. All the normal teenager stuff. They cry when they break up, and then the following week they're going out with someone else. Life goes on... And then there's me... I'm the baby of them all, and I've got the most adult relationship I can imagine.'

Leaning his head back to flex his sore neck, Jeff gave her one of his most heart-warming half-smiles. 'Is that good or bad?'

'It's *really* good,' Lynn insisted, kissing him full on the lips. 'Normally, that is... But it's also a very steep learning curve, and more than a little bit frightening. Please don't take this the wrong way, but it makes me think you really did hypnotise me. Why else wouldn't I be bawling my eyes out now? And why don't I feel like throwing you out?'

'Are you sure you don't?'

'No,' the young woman answered with caution, 'I'm not entirely sure. But if I were to throw you out, it would be because I think I ought to and not because I want to.'

The nineteen-year-old nodded, exhaling slowly again, while his worst fears rang in his ears. He certainly was asking a great deal of someone so special, he realised. Who did he think he was? He regretted even broaching the subject. Why hadn't he just listened to Suzanne in the first place? He wasn't in love with a random, working class girl from the western suburbs. These were Lynn Dyson's affections he was toying with. Exactly what did he think he was worth to her, to expect her to forgive his multitude of indiscretions and let him carry on playing the field?

'Well, that's good,' he sighed, bowing his head onto hers. 'Much better than I deserve, I reckon. I'm very grateful I'm getting a hearing, Lynn. Really I am.'

His dream girl smiled. 'But why *do* you need more sex than other people? There must be hundreds of people in relationships where they only see each other once a week. Or those long-distance romances you hear about that prevail for years. Are you going to tell me that all those men are getting it on the side?'

'Some will be,' the worldly street kid answered. 'Doubtless. But no, I'm not going to tell you they all are. As you said before, there's no right answer. Mister Average, testosterone-laden as most of us are, will without question be more motivated to get sex whenever he can than Miss Average will. That's just how it works. Don't ask me why, because that wasn't my idea.'

'No?' Lynn jeered, in return for his impromptu slide towards insolence.

The charmer went to kiss her, but she backed away just far enough for him to get the message.

'OK,' he continued. 'Fair enough. I deserve that too. What I was on my way to explaining, before I got too cocky, was to say that there are some women who will hunt men down for sport too. And there are, I expect, a whole swag of men who are as good as gold.'

'But not you.'

Her afflicted stranger was determined not to flinch, despite her barb having drawn first blood. He continued his argument instead.

'Lynn, I know this sounds pretty unlikely to you, but I'm willing to bet that a large percentage of these good as gold men'll be fantasising madly about all sorts of carnal exploits, either with people they know or complete strangers. And some'll have their heads buried in porn mags every time they get ten minutes to themselves.'

'Yuk!' the refined young lady grimaced. 'It doesn't sound unlikely. It sounds revolting! I know that sort of thing goes on, but what do all these men have to do with you? Why aren't you one of these good as gold men?'

'Do you want me to be one of those men?' he challenged. 'Judging by your reaction, you didn't think that was too healthy either.'

The star paused for a few seconds, recalling her disgust at the image of fat, bald, ugly men sitting on the toilet or in their shed, masturbating over pictures of girls in lacy underwear. Was that what she would rather Jeff did while she was travelling? Looking at his irresistibly handsome face and picturing his athletic physique, she had to admit that the stereotype didn't fit.

'You're right,' she smiled. 'It's gross. To me, that's what men who can't get sex do, although it's definitely more acceptable to society that they slink away and do something in secret, rather than do what you do. But no, I don't want you to be one of those men.'

'Jesus, Lynn,' Jeff exhaled sharply. 'That's good. That's a big concession, baby. You're an amazing woman, and it just makes me feel even guiltier. Are you sure you're not thirty-six instead of sixteen?'

Initially the schoolgirl laughed, pleased to be told she had acted with a maturity beyond her years. However after a second or two of reflection, she realised that she had once more fallen victim to her enigmatic stranger's considerable guile.

'So we agree that neither of us wants you to lurk in dark corners,' she refocussed, embarrassed and keen to resolve this horrible dilemma without having to take the obvious step.

'Yeah, and I'm not into those peep show places either,' her man chuckled. 'You know? The ones on Swanston Street with all the "X"s in the windows in red, flashing lights.'

'Yes,' Lynn nodded. 'What even goes on in there?'

'You peep,' her boyfriend replied, holding his hands up between their faces and then parting them quickly. 'You gets what you pays for, lovey...'

The celebrity laughed again. 'At what?'

'Girls,' he told her, thinking she couldn't possibly be that innocent. 'What else?'

'Well, yes,' the teenager acknowledged in mock frustration. 'I know that much. What are they doing?'

'I don't know,' Jeff lied unconvincingly. 'Dancing. Feeling themselves up. Anything that's likely to turn a bloke on.'

'Oh,' Lynn responded with a sickly smile. 'And men pay money for looking through a little window. How gross!'

'Absolutely,' the student agreed. 'It's prostitution on the cheap. No touch, small fee. Better for the girl though, I'd imagine. He does all the work, and she doesn't run the risk of getting any diseases or being hurt.'

Lynn frowned and inhaled sharply. 'So is being unfaithful with a prostitute, whether peeping or the whole thing, better than being unfaithful with someone you meet in the pub?'

'Because there's money involved?' her boyfriend checked. 'No. Not in my opinion. But no worse either.'

'I agree,' the objective young woman replied. 'So we're back where we started. But you *are* telling me that you need female company more than I can give you. So is that more than Mister Average needs, or the same?'

Jeff knew this was where he needed to tread carefully. He had told her earlier that he wasn't after special treatment, but in fact, he was. It was in the answer to this question that his truth really lay, but being open about it could swing the argument in entirely the wrong direction. He gripped his temples in consternation at the precarious position he had put himself in. They had been doing better than he had expected by simply concentrating on Mister Average, but generalising wasn't going to cut it with this beautiful, intelligent creature.

'I don't know for sure,' he answered with a half-truth. 'I have a hypothesis, but it's not proven yet. I'm not ready to even offer it up, to be honest, but I want to. When I'm a rock star...'

'What are you talking about?' the musician exclaimed. 'What has this got to do with you being a rock star? You're trying to claim a rock star lifestyle in advance? That's a good hypothesis!'

Lighting another cigarette, the master communicator let out a throaty laugh. 'And why not? Why didn't I think of that?'

He received a sharp slap across the head. Relaxing a little, he ventured another kiss, and this time his lover willingly obliged. Without knowing, she had tipped the scales in his favour yet again, and the grateful empath was not about to point this out just yet.

'When I'm a rock star,' he continued, 'one of the things I'd like to do for myself is to find a psych' researcher who's willing to work with me on my theory.'

'You're serious, aren't you?' the young woman asked in wonderment. 'You have so many theories. I thought you were joking.'

'No, angel,' Jeff responded, more subdued. 'I'm not joking. In fact, it's something I take very seriously. Have you heard of Maslow's Hierarchy of Needs?'

'No. What is it?'

'It's research developed in the forties, based on layers of needs that humans must have satisfied in order to be happy and function normally,' Jeff was at pains to explain, drawing an imaginary triangle on the table and dragging his fingers along its lower edge. 'There are basic ones at the bottom, like food, sex, shelter, *et cetera*. Physical or physiological needs mostly. And then the layers get more specialised, such as meaningful work, the respect of others and owning stuff. The needs on the top layers are all internal. Morals and values, self-confidence, creativity, ability to tolerate and distinguish between fact and fiction, and the motivation to be who you want to be.'

'Have you been talking to my father?' the elder Dyson daughter asked in mock suspicion.

'No, but I'm certain he'll have used Maslow's work on many occasions,' the clever student smiled. 'It's about prioritising the attention you or someone else pays to aspects of your life so that the basic needs are taken care of, thereby allowing you to concentrate on building the capabilities at the top, because they're the ones that'll make you successful. Personally, I have difficulty with the whole hierarchy idea. I don't buy the fact that one type of need is more important than another, but I'm not going to dispute the work I'm aiming to ride on the back of...'

420

'Wow!' Lynn gasped. 'I wonder if my parents ever had one of these conversations when they were dating.'

'Maybe. Are you game to ask?'

'No way! Anyway, carry on. This is interesting. And trust you to have some intellectual link with sex!'

'I'm relieved you think it's interesting. And yes, it is handy to be able to mix business with pleasure for once,' the tired man agreed without smiling.

'Sorry to make light of it,' she wiped the smile off her face. 'It *is* interesting to me, Jeff, particularly if you think it's going to help with PTSD.'

'That's OK, angel. I really appreciate you entering into this as open-minded as you are. That's exactly what I'm hoping to prove. It's encouraging that you're interested, because it's vital for me to get some answers in the not too distant future. I call it my law of compensatory addictions.'

'Law of compensatory addictions? Yikes! That sounds scary,' Lynn echoed, standing up, taking a deep, showbusiness breath and preparing to make a proclamation. '"Diamond's Law of Compensatory Addictions"!'

The amused nineteen-year-old shook his legs out, which were stiff from having Lynn sitting on his lap for so long. Stretching and stifling a nervous yawn, he sat back and watched his gorgeous girlfriend put his name up in lights right in front of them. It gave him some hope that their heavy conversation would not end in disaster after all.

'Thanks,' he smiled. 'It'll never be named after me, although I'm pretty sure I'm onto something. I need a clinician with letters to back me up. Until I do, I'm scared it's going to sound like I'm making excuses for some pretty dodgy, selfish behaviour.'

'That's amazing,' his caring girlfriend told him. 'You should change your degree and study psychiatry instead. Then you can publish your own theory.'

'It crossed my mind,' Jeff nodded, 'but it's too limiting. I don't want to be surrounded by myself any more, baby. There are so many more good things I can do with computer technology for a much larger number of people. Psychiatry is worthwhile, but not as worthwhile as I want to be. But anyway... Where does that put us?'

The young woman stepped gracefully from behind the chair and climbed back onto his lap, almost like a child. At least she felt safe, the nervous man mused. That was good in itself. He kissed her quickly, sensing she was about to speak.

'I don't want to be suspicious but I can't help it, because what you're asking for is not what my friends' boyfriends ask for. Can you imagine me going home to my mum and asking for her advice about my dating issues, asking her what fidelity should mean? She'd go nuts!'

'True enough. When you put it that way, it's definitely not conventional. But conventional's boring, Lynn. By its very nature, we should be looking to evolve it.'

'Should we? Why?' the celebrity countered, fearing she was being manipulated again. 'Isn't that the reason things become conventional to begin with? Because they work well?'

The intelligent man shrugged. This was a good debate, if only there weren't such dire consequences if he should lose.

'In a way, yes,' he agreed, 'but times change. Those conventions suited the first half of this century, when people didn't have the opportunity to have sex before getting married. You got married so you could have sex, because otherwise the risks of ostracisation were too high. Unwanted pregnancies, syphilis, shame on your family name... That's just not the case anymore, with the pill and post-war moral relaxation. Things change, so maybe conventions need to be updated too?'

'So does that mean you think faithfulness only counts in marriage?' his patient girlfriend asked, trying not to sound curt and disapproving.

'No,' Jeff was quick to counter. 'And I can see you don't either! I don't mean that at all. In fact, I think the whole idea of marriage needs redefining too, because of the same reason I just described. You don't have to get married to enjoy a physical relationship anymore.'

'Obviously not! You can be a sexual mercenary,' Lynn snapped back.

The young man's heart sank once more. He released his arms, shaking them to try to relax the sudden tension which had gripped him on hearing his words come back at him. He felt nauseated too.

'Jesus! I walked into that one, didn't I?' he sighed, marshalling his forces for another round of combat. 'What I mean is that there's a scale. It's not just black and white we can choose from these days.'

The stunning teenager reached down with her right hand to take hold of his left. The physical changes that came over this fascinating man whenever his mood altered were remarkable. The blood had instantly drained out of his face, and it was as if he had lost all strength in his arms. Could he do that on demand, as part of his polished chameleon act, or were these genuine physical responses to a real problem?

'So you want me to tell you what I think the convention should be changed to?'

'Yes, I do. At least as it applies to us, which I'd hope would be the same thing.'

Lynn nodded. 'It would. Otherwise I'd be pretty two-faced, wouldn't I? Now you guys have to do this, but Jeff and I are going to do something completely different and get away with it!'

She waved at an imaginary crowd, which made her pale boyfriend laugh and feel slightly optimistic again. Another stomach-churning fairground ride of his own making. Exhaustion washed through his confused mind as his dream girl began to speak again.

'The truth is I don't know,' she admitted. 'All the options you describe could go either way. If I put myself in your position, I'd want to know that you weren't going to be hurt by anything I did with another man, from talking to having sex. So maybe that's what we need to discuss. What would hurt us?'

'That's what I *am* trying to discuss,' Jeff insisted. 'That's where we started!'

Lynn took a deep breath in an effort to force her brain to a conclusion. 'OK, sorry. I need time to think about it. You've obviously given this subject a lot of thought, so I have to catch up. I remember something Suzanne told me about you, at that first dinner we went to with them after the charity tennis tournament.'

The student became nervous again. His long-time friend's opinions on faithfulness were extremely conventional.

'What was that?'

'She told me you'd said to her that you would only ever sleep with one woman you respected, and the rest were all just playtime. I think that's more-or-less the idea. Does that sound right?'

'Yeah. It sounds like me,' the old soul smiled. 'Carry on.'

The celebrity took another deep breath. 'She also said you told her that the only woman you respected was me. She said you'd had heaps of girlfriends, and they all came and went, but you'd only ever talked about a steady relationship with me.'

'That's absolutely right,' he readily agreed. 'I did tell her that. Don't tell her I told you, but she's tried it on with me several times, and I always turned her down. We've had some pretty heated discussions about it, and the whole subject of relationships. She and I have very different views on the world. I've only ever wanted you. It sounds callous and heartless, but all the others are just fillers, Lynn. Playtime, as you say. I never make any promises. Occasionally a girl'll get offended and walk away, because I tell her upfront that there's no future, but most either don't believe me and get offended afterwards, or they just put out because they want to anyway.'

The private school girl laughed, rolling her eyes. 'Your world is such a different world to mine. Sometimes I wonder why you want to be with someone so "conventional" at all,' she said, drawing quotation marks in the air around the word.

The boy with the ancient heart kissed her tenderly. If only she knew.

'Angel, there's a whole litany of things I hate about my world. Not everything, but a lot of it. You coming into my life has transformed it into one I want to like. The fact that you may be conventional has nothing to do with it.

Christ! You're only sixteen. You're a product of your family, of your school, and of all the people who've been put around you to make you into Lynn Dyson. It's much easier for me, as you said yourself the other day. I've always been master of my own destiny. I had no choice but to make up my own rules. But you're only just starting to take control of who you are.'

Lynn loved how passionately her handsome man spoke, and how he could make poetry from her innermost thoughts. She was being manipulated again, but it was impossible not to be drawn in. She felt like a fly being tempted into a spider's web. The most haunting, hypnotic music of folklore would be less effective than Jeff Diamond's persuasive prose.

'But aren't you trying to influence me just as much as the others are?'

Disappointed by her very accurate observation, Jeff shrugged, nodding slowly. 'Yes, I am. You're damned clever, angel. Of course I am. But I'm not forcing you to make up your mind. I said right at the start that if you make me choose between exclusivity and goodbye, I'll renounce all other female contact right now. Just say the word.'

There was no doubting the man's sincerity. His eyes were drilling into hers with a magnetic intensity. The compassionate teenager put her fingers to his lips, which instinctively kissed them.

'Jeff, I can't ask you to do that. It wouldn't be fair. I get what you mean about a scale. No-one could ever be a hundred percent exclusive. There would always be some point where a line was crossed or something would happen to make one of us jealous. I don't understand why you love me so much, but I know you do. And I believe you'd be with me rather than anyone else if I was around.'

'*Bueno*,' he said, hand on heart, 'because that's the God's honest truth, whoever he is. You never have to doubt that.'

'Or she...' Lynn continued with a grin. 'So even though I don't like the thought of you being with anyone else when I'm travelling, I also know you need to get through the sleepless nights. I think I know what you're asking me. You're saying that everyone has a different point on this faithfulness scale you mentioned, for whatever circumstances or reason, and that we need to agree to respect that.'

'I love you,' the troubled man breathed deeply, after listening intently for the answer he needed and knowing he hadn't yet secured it.

'Oh, I love you too. Maybe too much. And I do understand your situation. I'm only going to be travelling more and more over the coming months, so it's good you've brought it up now. I really appreciate your honesty, so thanks.'

The determined obsessive fixed her with a stare. 'So what do you want faithfulness to mean to us?'

'Well...' his girlfriend hesitated, buying herself some final thinking time. 'I would like us to only have one respecting relationship each and I hope it's the same one.'

'Agreed. Completely.'

She smiled at his vehement interjection. 'And as long as the using relationships stay as using relationships and they don't happen while I'm around, I can agree to that.'

The student laughed with relief, although he wanted to cry at the same time. It was as if a stream of air was rushing into the vacuum created by their intense mood, suddenly allowing him to breathe easily again.

'¡Excelente! That's very cleverly put.'

'And if you find someone you like more than me, please tell me straightaway.'

'That won't happen.'

Lynn smiled hesitantly. 'How do you know? Can you promise?'

Jeff kissed her lips. 'Yes. I promise. It won't happen. I just know.'

'Are you really thinking about me when you're with other people?' the teenager asked, also glad the valve on their pressure cooker had been released at last.

'Oh, yeah. Bloody oath, I am. Always have, always will. Angel, I've spent more time walking the streets, ending up in the seediest all-night bars and clubs, than you'd ever believe. I've fucked so many drunk and easy women whom I never, ever want to see again in my life. That's why sex on its own... I mean, without love or respect... is not the big deal with you and me. I can get sex anywhere. It's the rest of you I need.'

The caring blonde held her hand out, immediately having his fold around it. 'You're so gorgeous. I have to believe you, don't I?'

Jeff shook his head from side to side but answered in the affirmative.

'Yes, you do! You can trust me, angel. I'll never lie to you. That's exactly the purpose of these conversations, so that everything's out in the open. You're the only person I'm ever going to love and the only one I'll ever let inside my heart or my head, so please believe me.'

Sighing, the sixteen-year-old threw both arms around her beautiful black stallion's neck and kissed him firmly on the lips.

'Thanks, I do believe you. And I adore you. Did you want to come to bed, o-soldier of fortune?'

Even faster than his normal libidinous reactions to such an invitation, Jeff felt excitement surge through his veins, so relieved was he that the outcome he needed had been secured. He lifted his way too tolerant dream girl from his lap and straightened his legs with hidden strength he did not expect to find.

'Let me show you again what meaningful sex is, my angel. Sex with someone who loves you more than life itself.'

They made love on the floor in front of the television, like a couple who had known each other for years rather than weeks. The connection was palpable, between minds, hearts and bodies. Afterwards, they lingered on the warm rug to continue talking and caressing each other for a long while, content in their togetherness and doing their best to postpone the inevitable arrival of Monday morning.

'Can I ask you a question about your sister?' Lynn asked out of the blue, yawning.

'Yeah, of course,' the satisfied man answered sleepily. 'You don't have to ask if you can ask. Just ask. Too much bureaucracy. It's like getting permission to complete an application form.'

The sixteen-year-old giggled before turning contemplative. 'You said ages ago that your sister only ever called you when she needed an abortion. Were you kidding?'

Jeff shook his head. 'No, it's true. Last time we spoke was sometime last October. She'd got herself pregnant and didn't have any money, so I sent her two hundred dollars to get an abortion.'

His girlfriend looked shocked. 'Wow! That's terrible. Is she OK?'

The boy from the western suburbs shrugged casually, belying the way he truly felt about the situation. 'How should I know? She's never rung back, and I don't have a number for her. I did try calling my grandparents a while afterwards to check on her, and also to see if I was going to get my loan back.'

'But you knew it wasn't really a loan?'

'Right! There's no difference between handout and loan where Lena's concerned.'

'What do *you* think about abortion?' his young muse asked. 'Do you agree with it?'

The bitter man turned onto his back and stared at the ceiling. 'It's very late to be starting this kind of conversation. Are you sure you want to talk about it now?'

The gorgeous woman nodded, putting her hand on his chest.

'Yes, if you're OK talking about it.'

'I'm OK. It might get a bit heavy again, just be aware,' his serious side warned her, but with more than a hint of comedy. 'Thought you'd have had enough heavy for tonight...'

Lynn closed her eyes. Perhaps she should have kept her mouth shut for a few days.

'I'd like to talk about it now. Do you mind?'

Jeff leaned over and kissed her closed eyelids. 'No, I don't mind. Heavy's what I do best, in case you hadn't noticed,' he smiled. 'If you're sure. I do agree with abortion as a last resort option, but not as an excuse for not being careful. You know... "I won't take any precautions, because I know a backstreet abortionist." And it's still killing, Lynn. Killing is basically wrong, isn't it?'

The spellbound teenager nodded again, smiling at his screechy female impersonation.

'Yes, unless you're putting something out of its misery. Like shooting a horse when its leg breaks, because it wouldn't be able to be a horse properly anymore.'

The seasoned communicator laughed. 'That's a great way of putting it. Thou shalt not kill, except when your potential victim is incapable of properly being itself anymore.'

'Yeah,' his girlfriend moaned indignantly, annoyed that her all-knowing boyfriend was making fun of her, especially after the leap of faith she had taken on his behalf only an hour ago. 'What's wrong with that?'

'Nothing at all,' he replied, turning to face her. 'It's great, in fact. I need some time to think about it from different perspectives, but in principle I really like it.'

Thankful that she had misinterpreted his humour, Lynn kissed his nose playfully. 'Good! So what do you think?'

'Well...' Jeff started. 'To follow the line of your argument, you'd have to clearly define what "properly" means. If the horse can't properly be a horse any more, it sounds like it might already be dead, because as long as it's still alive, just because it can't walk doesn't make it not a horse any more. It's just a horse lying down.'

The schoolgirl laughed. 'You're so funny! That's blown my argument completely out of the water.'

'No, it hasn't,' her patient teacher countered. 'If that horse no longer feels like a horse, knowing it can no longer walk, then it might as well not be a horse anymore. It's respecting the person's... or horse's... desire or ability to continue being itself, in whatever capacity it can be happy with itself. We just need to turn your rule around. Let's try, "Thou shalt not kill anyone or anything, except when your potential victim no longer wishes to keep being itself." How does that sound?'

Lynn liked it.

The intellectual carried on, giving her another melting smile. 'Now, in that eleventh commandment, Miss Dyson, you've just given me the argument for voluntary euthanasia. So now back to abortion! That's precisely why, à mon avis, it's so hard to say whether abortion is right or wrong. An embryo of a few weeks old doesn't know what sort of life it's going to have, so killing it won't really take any of its aspirations away, we assume.'

'But we don't know, do we?' the eager pupil interrupted. 'Just because we can't remember what it was like before we were born doesn't mean we didn't have some instinct about who we're going to be.'

'No. Exactly right,' Jeff smiled, now able to fully enjoy the way she was debating, since nothing was at stake for him personally this time. 'So that's the other side. Killing a would-be baby is destroying its potential. It's already a living thing, the combination of its mother and father, with its own life plan, even though it doesn't know it yet. If you think about it, why is it OK to abort a foetus before birth and yet it's not OK to kill a baby in the first few weeks of its life, when all it knows how to do is cry, drink and shit? Just because you can see it?'

'Jeff!' Lynn exclaimed. 'That's a horrible thought.'

'Sorry,' her boyfriend replied. 'But it's true, isn't it? Humans are confronted way more by something that their senses can get hold of, rather than just believing it exists because its mother's getting fatter.'

The sportswoman laughed this time, but shamefully. 'I love you so much. I just love how you express yourself. It's so easy to understand the fundamental principles. You should be a philosophy teacher.'

The young man shrugged modestly, thankful for her affirmation. 'You can teach without being a teacher. It's all about knowing how to communicate.'

'So why did you agree to pay for your sister's abortion?' his amazed girlfriend asked. 'Wasn't that hard for you?'

'Absolutely,' he replied, his heart rate increasing with the prospect of unravelling some more of his life's secrets. 'Much harder for me than it was for her. And she's supposed to be the Catholic.'

Getting tired, the teenager stroked his cheek with her hand and felt his jaw tense up under it. He was fighting back tears, and she felt guilty. It was intriguing how quickly her mystery man's emotions could swing from high to low. Whatever had made his senses so acute?

'We don't have to talk about this if you don't want to.'

Jeff put his own hand on hers and chased it away from his face.

'No. It's good. I need to talk about it. There are many things I need to talk about that I've kept inside forever. I've waited a long, long time to tell you, my gorgeous angel. It's just going to take me a while to summon the courage to get it all out.'

'I wish I could help more. What can I do?'

'Just what you're doing now,' the exhausted man answered, grateful for her support. 'I'll let you into one secret now. My sister makes her living as what you first thought I meant by sexual mercenary.'

'A prostitute?' Lynn exclaimed again, as she had done a little over an hour earlier. 'Really?'

'Yep,' her boyfriend admitted, wondering what his pretty picture of conventionality was thinking now. 'It's all she ever learned how to do. I don't blame her for it, but I hate it all the same.'

Nervous, the teenager smiled. 'So that's why she can't afford to have a child. Bad for business?'

The cynic chuckled. 'Yeah. You could say that. Plus, Lena wouldn't have a clue how to look after another person. I floated the idea with her of having the baby and giving him or her up for adoption, but she didn't want to entertain it. She didn't want to lose any income while she was pregnant, so she went ahead and had the abortion. It was probably better for me that she did, because I'd have to fund their lives too and I can't afford to.'

The wealthy youngster looked shocked. 'Isn't she older than you?'

'Yeah, but that doesn't make any difference,' Jeff answered, a tear running down his cheek. 'It's complicated, angel. I carry a lot of guilt. It's my fault. I should cut her loose, but I can't.'

'Even though she doesn't even give you her 'phone number?'

Her boyfriend got up off the rug and headed for the bathroom. 'Sorry, baby. I've reached my openness threshold for the moment. I just need some time to myself. Is that OK?'

The bewildered woman watched the door close and heard the shower spring into action. She wondered if Jeff was actually standing under it or whether it was merely a convenient way of escaping the situation. Or both. She felt guilty but grateful that they had come this far. While she waited, the inquisitive teenager cleared up their dinner plates and switched on the television. It was coming up for eleven o'clock, and she was feeling very tired indeed.

So her lover was a self-confessed sexual mercenary, and his sister was a prostitute. Boy, Lynn thought, what on Earth would her parents think if they knew? She didn't even know what to think herself. This was a side of life which was very strange to her; the stuff of movies and late night news bulletins. She was beginning to understand why her mystery man had been so reluctant to reveal his past to her, because the closer it came, the more she could appreciate the difference in their backgrounds.

The young star reassured herself with the thought that at least Jeff was trying to escape and make a life in a world much more like her own. But no, actually that wasn't entirely true, she changed her mind, because earlier he had succeeded in making her agree to his sexual mercenary lifestyle. Did that mean he was pulling her into his world? In her circles, such behaviour was known as two-timing, whereas on Jeff's terms, it was using relationship versus respecting relationship. Did changing the name of something wrong make it right?

The stalwart vowed to resist, for the sake of her parents and the reputation her family enjoyed in the public eye for being fine, upstanding members of Australian society. She had a responsibility to uphold the values which had been instilled into her from an early age. Being part of the Dyson dynasty had given her such amazing opportunities so far in her life, so it would be poor form to rebel just because her *avant-garde* boyfriend considered a few conventions outdated.

So complicated! Give him the benefit of the doubt, Lynn resolved. She did believe her passionate beau when he said he would much rather spend time with her, and her travel schedule was definitely much busier than most people's. As far as she knew, he had never chosen to be with someone else over her. Therefore he had the potential to be faithful to her, were it not for his need for diversion during the sleepless nights.

And Lynn was in no doubt that the sleepless nights were real. It would be extremely difficult to fake having the type of nightmare that his poor, afflicted mind experienced, she decided. She had witnessed first-hand the dramatic increase in body temperature, cold sweats and racing heart rate. And why was he driven to confess, when he could easily have continued to see other women behind her back, knowing she would be highly unlikely to find out? She could only assume that on some level he was feeling guilty and didn't want to hurt her.

And so to her boyfriend's sister… Yet another twist in the tale. Jeff had said he hated the fact that his sister was a prostitute. It had been described as "the oldest profession", Lynn had heard, which she took to mean that it was a *bona fide* career of sorts. The paradox made her smile. What a way to earn a living! Fancy having sex with a dozen different men every day! She thought back to her Economics lessons and the law of supply and demand. The so-called profession had clearly only endured because there was a ready demand for such a service. As far as the keen student was aware, there were no government subsidies on offer for ladies of the night.

The sixteen-year-old chuckled to herself. Moreover, if her boyfriend's sister didn't provide this service to her clients, someone else would. Just because she was Jeff's sister didn't make her more or less worthy than the next prostitute. People were paid for providing many weird and wonderful services, so why should sex between two consenting adults be singled out as wrong, simply because money had changed hands? Lynn knew she could never do it, but there were many other things she would never consider as a career, such as cleaning the outside of skyscraper windows or working in an *abattoir*. There were some people who would say that singing or playing tennis weren't valid careers either, but plenty of others were willing to pay a ridiculous amount of money to receive these services from her. Supply and demand, she concluded, was not based on right versus wrong.

Therefore, on that basis, why did Jeff hate the fact that his sister performed this apparently vital service? Because it put her in danger? Or perhaps he thought she was capable of more? The sixteen-year-old decided she wouldn't ask these questions tonight, but this was something she would keep for a future discussion.

After a good ten minutes, the exhausted student emerged from the bathroom. He looked completely drained, and his eyes were sunken and red.

He sat down on the couch next to the girl he loved and put his arm around her shoulders. Silently, they watched the news and attempted to ignore the turgid atmosphere which their unfinished conversation had created.

'Are you OK?' Lynn asked finally, as the closing music from the news was playing.

'Yeah. I'm fine, thanks,' Jeff replied, kissing her temple. 'I get very angry when I think about Lena. She's my main link with the past, and I'd rather shut her out of my head most of the time. The reason I'm OK with my sister having an abortion is the thought of another wretched, no-hoper kid being born into the world with nowhere to go.'

The caring teenager looked at her gorgeous suitor, relieved that she had decided to leave her many questions for another time. His eyes had filled with tears again.

'By another, I assume you include yourself in that category?'

He exhaled deeply, nodding. 'Correct. For most of my life I can remember asking myself why I came. I spent my childhood and adolescence constantly suppressing anger at what people said or did, but that's now under control. For the most part, I can rise above it and just let them get on with their small-mindedness. Though I say so myself, I've come a long way from the hot-headed fifteen-year-old who was convinced he had all the answers. I've matured. Some wouldn't agree, of course, but I now understand the world'll never be perfect. For a long time I wished I didn't exist but, since about the middle of February, I wouldn't give it up for anything. So there's our dilemma right in front of our eyes, angel. If someone had given me the choice to live or die when I was first born, I would most likely taken a quick look around and said, "Thanks, but no thanks." I'd never have known you, but then I wouldn't know what I was missing either.'

Lynn kissed him and wrapped both arms around him, instantly moved to tears too. His words, as always, were as sharp as razor blades. Fleetingly, she wondered what might happen to Jeff's soul-gods if they inhabited an aborted foetus. Would they just go back into the queue and wait for their next baby? She shivered, knowing full well that she must not surface this thought tonight either.

'Well, I'm *really* glad you exist. I can't begin to understand what it feels like not to want to exist, but I'm glad you don't think it anymore.'

'I learned how to take a long-term view,' her boyfriend scoffed. 'Thanks to a sexy, blonde kid on the TV who looked remarkably like you. Out of interest, what brought on your question in the first place?'

It was Lynn's turn to feel uncomfortable with information she needed to share. As this latest discussion had twisted and turned, she had temporarily forgotten the reason why she had started it. She moved across the couch a little and turned to face her handsome lover.

'Dad's told me that if I get pregnant before the Olympics, I'll have to have an abortion.'

'What?' Jeff shouted, shocked and instantly angry again. 'Is he serious?'

The athlete nodded. 'I think so. He's always serious. I wanted to hear your views on the subject before I told you, because I don't think it's only the girl's problem.'

The irate student jumped up, switched off the television and lit a cigarette. Standing and gazing down at his girlfriend, scarcely touched and barely legal, he felt the very same controllable rage that he had decried moments earlier rise up inside him like a wild animal. How dare Bart Dyson make decisions about a child who would be half his?

'Lynn, firstly... If you were to get pregnant, just remember you're not a girl. Only women can have children, and you'd need to take a woman's perspective. A mother's perspective even... You can't just roll over and accept the fate handed to you by your father.'

'I love you, Jeff,' the teenager said softly, 'and I love how you motivate me to act for myself. I'm not used to making decisions for myself, but I dearly want to. That's why I wish I was the same age as my friends, because they're all eighteen and are entitled to speak for themselves. But I can't.'

The tall man crouched down in front of the love of his life, taking her hands. She wasn't at all surprised at how warm they were. He looked as if he were in pain.

'Are you alright?' she asked.

Jeff's legs cramped up, as his anger began to get the better of him, leaving him no alternative but to sit down on the floor at her feet, breathing heavily.

'OK. I understand. But nonetheless, you have the basic human right of choice over what happens to you, as a person. And besides, if you were pregnant, and if it were because of me...'

'Of course it would be yours,' she interrupted.

Her boyfriend smiled. 'I hope so, but what about the conversation we had earlier? If you're kind enough to give me a licence to play while you're away, then I can hardly turn round and deny you the same privilege, can I?'

Lynn shook her head. 'I suppose not, but I wouldn't do it.'

Jeff gripped her wrist harder, before releasing it again.

'I know, and I'm very grateful, because I hate the thought as much as you do. But you're entitled to your place on that scale too. Anyway... Any pregnancy would also be my responsibility, and I'm stoked that you care and want to know my views. But there are more than my views at stake here. Your dad's being a bit fucking naïve to think you'll recover from an abortion quickly enough to be able to go to the Olympics and perform as if nothing had happened.'

The teenager stared with renewed concern at her ever-opinionated boyfriend, whose face was like thunder. 'What do you mean?'

Her teacher sighed with exasperation. 'Lynn, think about it. Don't you think you'd be a little conflicted inside if you had to go through that? We just talked about how hard a decision it would be to kill a potential person whom you and I had created. Even if physically you were unaffected, which would depend which month this was all hypothetically happening in, emotionally you'd still be recovering. I don't think you or he should underestimate the effect it'd have on you.'

Lynn nodded, respecting his impassioned conclusion. 'That's why I was asking about how your sister was.'

Jeff took a long, last drag on his cigarette and extinguished it in the ashtray on the coffee table behind him, blowing a long stream of smoke out to one side. It surprised him to discover that he was unable to picture Madalena's face anymore, so successful had he been at eradicating her from his daily thoughts.

'Please don't compare yourself with my sister, angel. She's nothing like you,' he almost growled. 'Lena couldn't even cast a shadow on you. She's motivated by much baser things than you are. She has no self-respect. Like I was a few years ago, resigned to helplessness. You have everything you could ever want, right in front of you. Make your own choices according to what you believe in, angel, please?'

Australia's darling leaned forward and kissed her handsome stranger, her heart overflowing with love and admiration.

'Thank you. I would want it to be *our* choice.'

Jeff smiled. 'So incidentally, what would happen if you get pregnant *after* the Olympics? What difference do the Olympics make? Surely your parents don't want you to become a mother for years yet.'

'I don't really know,' the sportswoman admitted. 'I suppose because it's our next big goal. But you're right, there's plenty going on after Munich.'

'Well... You know, we shouldn't even be talking about this,' her boyfriend said, giving himself a reality check. 'I need to calm down. I'm sorry. You're not pregnant, are you?'

Lynn giggled, shaking her head. 'No. Not as far as I know.'

Jeff drew his hand across his forehead in mock relief. '¡*Muy bueno, señorita!* You're not going to get pregnant either, because we're both careful. And if it were to happen, I hope we could deal with it between the two of us, and not involve your parents. We won't make it a problem for your dad. He needn't even know.'

'So would you want me to have an abortion?'

The boy from Canley Vale tensed up again. 'Jesus! I don't know. Of course we'd have to consider it as an option. It'd be unbelievably hard for either of us to make that decision, but let me just say that you would have the final word. It's your life that'd be impacted the most.'

The young woman liked what she heard. 'Thanks. You're so gorgeous. Let's hope we don't have to make the decision, because I agree it would be incredibly hard.'

The student looked at his watch. 'Whoa! This has been one of the longest conversations in living memory. I'm knackered. Are you?'

'Yes, very. So should we go to bed now?'

'Do you want to?' the nineteen-year-old asked, with a feeling of uncertainty. 'I'll go home if you want. If you'd rather not take the risk of getting pregnant.'

'Don't joke about it,' Lynn replied. 'Are you going to be less careful in bed than you were on the rug?'

Smiling, Jeff stood up and held out his hands to pull the radiant beauty up off the couch.

'No. It's just that such a serious topic tends to curb the enthusiasm somewhat. Come on. Let's see what magic we can generate from scratch, huh?'

Twenty

'What do you want to do tomorrow night?' Jeff asked the voice at the end of another long telephone line before they signed off their call.

It was Friday the twelfth of May, and the couple was now into the third month of their relationship. The jetsetter was flying back from Sydney the next morning, just in time for the weekend. They had arranged to see each other on Saturday evening and on into Sunday, of course, both of which had been fiercely negotiated with her coaches.

'I'd like to see a film,' Lynn suggested. 'Michelle and Russell are planning to see "The Godfather". Shall we go with them?'

The student paused for a few seconds to let a chill run down his spine. Thus far, the subject of going to the movies had not arisen between them, and he hadn't pressed the issue either. He was sick of always being the one who came up with reasons not to do things. However, two hours in a darkened cinema was not a pastime to which he could look forward with any excitement.

But "The Godfather", the storyteller rued. He so wanted to see it. He had read all of Mario Puzo's books, and the film had received rave reviews since it had been released in the US some weeks prior. It was just the type of story which Jeff could see himself sinking right into. Over the last few years, he had missed out on the various blockbuster releases about which his friends had gushed, only eventually catching up with them whenever they screened on television many months later.

Could he get away with it? It had been four years since the damaged young man had stepped inside a cinema. Surely, with increased maturity and his new guardian angel, he could manage to sit through an absorbing film plot without drawing too much attention to himself.

'Yeah. Why not? That'd be good. We could grab some dinner beforehand, all of us. Did you want me to get tickets?'

Lynn thought she detected a strange tone in her boyfriend's voice, which hadn't been there earlier in their conversation.

'Are you OK? Don't you want to go out with those guys?'

'Yes. It's fine,' Jeff replied, glossing over his concerns. 'I'd love to. It'll be good to meet this bloke finally, after hearing all the gossip second-hand.'

'OK. Great. Yes, please could you get the tickets?' the traveller requested, satisfied with his response. 'I'd better go. I love you, Jeff. Can't wait to see you. I'll ring when I'm back at Admin, probably around four-ish.'

The young man's pulse quickened. He couldn't wait either, despite the fact that his soul-mate had only been away for two days this time. Even though the absences were frequent and sometimes lengthy, there was something very special about the regular reunions and reacquaintances which went some way towards compensating for their periods apart.

'Sounds good. I'll be at the football 'til five, so I'll ring you. I love you too. See you tomorrow, gorgeous.'

That night, the avid reader had gone to bed resolved to enjoy their glimpse inside the Mafia world for what it was: an escape into fictional fantasy. He craved the opportunity to immerse himself in someone else's story, where the violence happened to characters on the screen and not in his mind. However, predictably, within an hour he was awake again and pacing around his flat like a caged lion. Another night when he would resort to calling in a favour from Lynn's blind eye, taking it up on its way too generous offer of turning while he sought alternate female company. Too wound up to focus on anything else, he transformed himself once again into Don Juan, showered, changed and set off for one of the many South Yarra night clubs, feeling guilty and ashamed, and letting his imagination run wild about seeing Lynn the following night.

The distractions were plentiful, and the usual game for the evening was to see how many drinks he could have bought for him by pretty girls who were out for a good time. As always, they hovered around him like wasps to jam, dancing, drinking and all the time vying for the good-looking party animal's attention when the music stopped. He made his choice in less than an hour and spent the early hours of the morning in a share house in Hawthorn, east of the city.

The nineteen-year-old arrived at work at seven o'clock on Saturday morning, dressed in the same clothes and still processing the alcohol through his system. He had caught the tram back to his flat in the morning and jumped straight into the car. His head ached, and his body hurt all over, but he was more relaxed and eagerly anticipating the return of his dream girl. How could anyone describe this arrangement as being unfaithful? He was more devoted to her than he could possibly imagine, fuelled by the gratuitous relief he had obtained from the latest anonymous and entirely insignificant other. As the morning unfolded, even the prospect of a trip to the movies seemed less daunting.

The working hours passed slowly, with only a few uninteresting problems to solve and routine operations to perform. Jeff read the Saturday edition of The Age from cover to cover and caught up on his assignments. No matter how many times he looked at his watch, time refused to go any faster. He wrote out a few lyrics which were floating around in his head, whistling ideas for melodies and gazing out of the window, voraciously short-tempered with the world.

Jeff swung the car into a service station shortly after twelve-thirty, to fill up with petrol and to buy three red roses, one for each completed month of this sublime new life they had been building. He then drove home, left the roses in a sinkful of water and took the tram into the city to pick up the movie tickets. He walked into the cinema on Russell Street to purchase four seats for the evening's showing of "The Godfather", while on his way to meet some friends for a drink before the Saturday afternoon football match. Simply standing in the lobby was enough to make his head spin, waiting in the box office queue. Wayward thoughts drove his eyes towards the theatre doors, where he imagined the rows of people in the dark, sitting immersed in their cinematic experiences. He battled to bring his mind back to the present time and forced himself to think of appropriate dinner venues instead.

A few minutes later, with the tickets in his wallet and his heart rate slowly returning to normal, the nineteen-year-old carried on walking towards the pub near the MCG where he had arranged to meet his mates. The Richmond Tigers were playing the North Melbourne Kangaroos, which promised to be a good contest. His malicious mind travelled back to the last time he had taken a girl to the movies, back when he was fifteen. They were with a group of school friends, watching "You Only Live Twice", the James Bond film starring Sean Connery. As the memory reconstituted itself painfully in his brain, he felt the hackles rising on the back of his neck and sweat forming all over his skin.

Luckily, the lanky teenager had been at the end of a row, on the aisle. As soon as the lights went down and the dramatic opening sequence unfolded, Jeff had been frozen to his seat, locked in a debilitating panic attack. His date, a girl he saw every day at school, quickly became aware of the change that had come over him. Initially he had brushed it off, saying it must have been the alcohol going to his head on an empty stomach. Yet the effects of the loud music and the noise of people chattering, shuffling and eating in the pitch blackness amplified his anxiety until he could barely breathe.

Finally, the fear and embarrassment became too much, giving the youngster no choice but to leave the theatre. He remembered toying with the idea of convincing his date to come with him, so that he could at least recapture what he had planned for the rest of the evening. However at the last minute, he had decided against it, knowing she was bound to subject him to a barrage of questions which he was totally unwilling and unprepared to answer. Desperately trying to contain his anger, he turned to the girl and told her he was leaving. Of course, he was followed out of the darkness and into the lobby, but soon managed to lose her by ducking into the toilets. By the time he reappeared, she had abandoned her search and had presumably returned to her seat to watch the film with the others.

That was the last time the disturbed kid had set foot in a cinema, and now here he was, planning to go through it all again. *Not fair*, he scolded his memories. He didn't relish any more strange behaviour to explain to his new lover, especially now their relationship had stabilised and the focus was at last more evenly spread across both sets of needs. Yet another confession of crazy responses to regular dating activities was hardly the burden he wished to place on their precious hours in the weeks leading up to the French Open tennis tournament.

The frustrated man convinced himself that he must deal with this latest affliction on his own. Lynn Dyson did not exist solely to placate his tortured soul. His rational mind assured him that no-one was likely to storm into a Melbourne cinema looking for him and that the foursome would be quite safe to enjoy their movie. With any luck, there would be absolutely no reason for him to fly off the handle in front of Lynn's best friend and her partner. Above all, his beautiful angel should not be put in the position of having to make excuses to anyone for his freakish tendencies.

The Tigers won, after a close match. A good omen, Jeff wondered, also knowing he was clutching at straws. It was fast approaching five o'clock by the time he got home. Taking no nonsense from his front door, the demons were still tormenting him as he picked up the telephone and dialled the number his fingers now knew by rote.

'Lynn, it's me.'

'Hi, Jeff,' her voice sounded so pleased to hear his. 'Just got in, I hear.'

'Yeah. Can you tell?' he chuckled. 'How're you doing? How did this morning go?'

Lynn could tell he was trying to calm himself down by asking this series of benign questions. It was a game she was always happy to play, imagining his heaving chest and staring eyes.

'Everything went well, thanks. Come over, and I'll tell you. What time's the movie?'

'Thanks, angel,' the student replied. 'Not 'til eight-fifteen. I've booked a table at Florentino's, but downstairs in the casual area. Nothing too flash. I'm just going to take a shower. Be there in half an hour.'

'*¡Excelente!* See you then. Bye.'

'*Adiós, señorita bella.*'

Jeff washed off the sins of the night before once and for all, a sense of excitement building antagonistically against his nerves. While shaving, he asked the face in the mirror if it knew what had happened to the maid, seeing his pile of dirty clothes spreading out from the corner by the bath, but he received no adequate reply. It could wait, he resigned. A trip to the twenty-four hour launderette on Bridge Road would be an entertaining task with which to occupy himself late on Sunday night or early on Monday morning.

Dressed all in black and feeling cleansed inside and out, the young man jumped into the car. Football fans were still trickling out of the MCG and crossing Punt Road, paying no attention to oncoming traffic. He beeped his horn at a couple of staggering North Melbourne fans, who cheerfully gave him the finger, leaving him little option but to steer the Fairlane's front wheel equally cheerfully, yet perilously close to their toes.

Lynn was downstairs in the foyer of the St Kilda Road building when he arrived, talking to her famous parents. Her boyfriend was glad he had dressed up for the occasion. At least it gave the impression that he made an effort for their daughter. It wouldn't be good for them to think she was going out with a common street kid...

His dream girl didn't hide her enthusiasm when she first laid eyes on her black knight. She shouted his name, moving towards him as quickly as she could without losing the grace and poise that was expected of her in public. They longed to throw themselves at each other and for his strong hands to swing her round in a circle, as they often did when greeting her in the confines of her apartment. Instead, the expressive man slipped a reserved arm around her waist and pulled her towards him, kissing her on the lips subtly but nevertheless insistently.

'You look great,' Lynn said, looking him up and down. 'Or are you in mourning?'

Jeff smiled, seeing Bart and Marianna looking on. 'No. It's in honour of the film. My violin case and white tie are in the car.'

Everyone laughed. The sixteen-year-old had obviously already apprised her parents of their movie plans. Each couple wished the other a pleasant evening, and the youngsters ascended to the penthouse floor to herald each other properly. Once behind the closed door, his greedy body grabbed her as she hoped he would, hoisting her high into the air.

'For Christ's sake! It was so hard to resist you down there.'

Within minutes they were breathlessly naked, black clothes shed and blonde hair loose from its ponytail. The ecstatic teenager wondered when the intensity of their lovemaking might *plâteau* and cease to transport them to higher and higher planes every time they met up again after her regular disappearances. Strangely, the more Lynn mastered the art of de-manipulating herself from her man's obsessive physical demands, the more she felt herself longing to feel his touch as soon as they were together. This evening was no exception. The image of her handsome stranger, clean-shaven and dressed in black, was a powerful aphrodisiac which stayed in her mind until well after they orgasmed in absolute raptures.

'You're amazing, Al Capone,' she gasped, kissing him passionately. 'I didn't realise tonight was fancy dress.'

Jeff shrugged, thinking back to his empty wardrobe. 'You can believe that was my intention if you like, but it was more a case of the only clean clothes left to wear,' he confessed.

'Oh, OK,' the young woman replied. 'Shatter my illusions, why don't you?'

They showered and prepared themselves once more for their evening out. Lynn slicked her lover's black hair away from his face, making him look even more like a gangster, but he ruffled it up again. It called to mind some people he didn't care to resemble, one of whom being his father.

'Shall we walk?' he suggested. 'We've got plenty of time, and I want to hear your Sydney tales. How is the old town, by the way? Plus I can have a few drinks before the movie, to get in the mood.'

His girlfriend nodded, none the wiser to his motives. 'Good idea. Sydney's great. It misses you.'

Russell, Michelle's current boyfriend, was in a foul temper when the couple turned up at the restaurant. Lynn and Jeff were enjoying the peace and quiet of their first drink when their friends arrived, glaring at each other. It transpired that the redhead had found out from someone else that the medical student had been two-timing her for the last four weeks. He had sworn it was all over with the other girl, but she didn't believe him.

The boy from Canley Vale smiled at his princess, feeling sheepish that she had probably agonised over his own antics while she was out of town. The stunning sixteen-year-old reached across the table and squeezed his hand, causing him to inhale deeply to fight back his emotions, which were already heightened with the anticipation of a difficult evening. He stood up to offer Russell a handshake and a cigarette.

'Sit down, guys,' he encouraged the new arrivals. 'Let's get the menu and leave all this shit behind.'

Reluctantly, Michelle assented. She removed her coat and handed it to her date, who dutifully hung it on a rack nearby. The waiter arrived to take their drinks order, and the four settled down to peruse the menu.

'Have you read the book of "The Godfather"?' Jeff asked the others.

None had.

'I'll be interested to see how closely they stuck to it for the film.'

'Is there anything you haven't read?' the older woman asked. 'Whenever I see you, you're always telling us about what you've just read.'

Lynn giggled, a hidden glass of wine part-way to relaxing her. 'Well-read and good in bed. The two go hand-in-hand.'

Her boyfriend grinned, taken by surprise. 'Why, thanks!'

Such a solid, gratuitous compliment rendered his guilt even more acute, but somehow it mattered less with each touch that confirmed they were secure. His companion's smile was intoxicating, her inner beauty never more apparent than tonight. What had he done so right lately to deserve this current nirvana?

'You're welcome.'

'Totally uncalled for, but far be it from me to reject your praise,' the handsome man insisted, with a playful nudge.

'Lynn!' Michelle exclaimed. 'You're getting very vocal these days! Whatever happened to the shy, polite girl I grew up with?'

'She grew up a bit more,' Jeff was quick to jump in, kissing the blonde teenager fondly. 'And how!'

Russell was still stewing on their earlier argument and was clearly jealous of the Sydneysider's ability to charm these two women. Each time one of the others tried to draw him into the conversation, he became more stubborn and sullen, until they gave up trying. Lynn got the distinct impression that this was the last they would be seeing of him, judging by the lingering look of disgust on her friend's face. Their meals came, and the conversation ebbed and flowed while they ate. The Computer Science student was drinking quickly, prompting the celebrity to cast him a concerned look.

'Sorry,' he said. 'I need a bit of a kick tonight. I'll slow down.'

Their dinner drew to a close just in time to walk the two blocks to the cinema. On the way, Lynn and Jeff walked behind the other two, who had become involved in a complex decomposition of their earlier argument.

'Are you OK?' the young star asked. 'Why were you drinking so much? Has something happened?'

Jeff's arm was round her shoulder, and he hugged her in closer.

'No,' his due reassurance relatively convincing, or so he thought. 'There is something stressing me out, but I'm determined to deal with it myself tonight. I want you to have a weekend without dealing with anything.'

'What? Like those two?' Lynn laughed, pointing to her long-time buddy up ahead.

The grateful man smiled at the deliberate deflection with which the unselfish teenager had indulged him in her inimitable fashion. Voices were raised in front, and fingers were being pointed.

'I hear the sound of a death knell, don't you?' her boyfriend agreed. 'If you ask me, he's not too much of a catch anyway. Is he always this cantankerous?'

The sportswoman smiled ruefully, shaking her head. 'I've only met him twice before and not for long. He wasn't this bad, but Michelle's giving him a pretty hard time...'

'I want to say thanks,' Jeff interrupted, kissing her temple.

'What for?'

'You know what for. Don't you?'

Lynn nodded and sighed. 'Yes, I suppose so. But how can I resist a man in black with a violin case in his car?'

Her dark knight exhaled, a smile of blessed relief on his face. '*Sí, signorina. Il uomo de Sicilia te ama, pero no se decir mucho mas en italiano.*'

Jeff's insides churned with shame, as his beautiful best friend did her best to hide her pain while glossing over his indiscretions. He didn't deserve this charitable treatment, especially when contrasted with the cold shoulder Russell had received. As expected, a pained expression had spread over the face of the pretty Australian of Dutch descent.

'This multi-lingual conversation is way too confusing! So do you just want me to ignore you tonight if you're stressed?'

'*Oui*,' the nineteen-year-old affirmed, 'I think so. Is that OK?'

'If you want, but you don't sound too sure.'

The tired soul sniffed, staring straight ahead. 'Angel, be quiet. You're encouraging my reliance on you. I need to stand on my own two feet. I'm a Mafia Don tonight. *¡Soy invincible!*'

The blonde bombshell on his arm raised her hand in response to his swashbuckling declaration. 'OK, OK,' she mocked him. 'Anything you say, Mister Capone.'

Suddenly, Russell veered away from his date, crossed the road and broke into a run in the opposite direction. He didn't even turn around to say goodbye to the others. Lynn ran up to her friend, anxious to make sure she was alright.

'Mish, what happened? Are you OK?'

Jeff took his opportunity to light a cigarette, watching his empathetic partner console her schoolmate. She was the best. But damn! Only three for the movie... Now he had lost his chance to spirit Lynn out of the theatre if the atmosphere became unbearable. His braver half was glad to have the additional challenge ahead of him, but its weaker counterpart felt a steady trickle of energy draining out of his heart. He caught the girls up, stepping in between the two of them and putting an arm around each.

'It's my lucky day!' he announced. 'Two beautiful women to entertain me tonight.'

He felt Michelle's arm grip tightly around his waist. She was laughing, but her body language told him the truth.

'Jeff, you're so sweet. Lynn, do you remember that first date, when I said if you didn't like him, you could give him my number?'

The sixteen-year-old laughed. 'Yes.'

'Well, now would be a good time.'

'No, no, no,' the handsome student intervened. 'I'm not going to have anyone doing deals over me. Russ was old news anyway, wasn't he?'

Michelle nodded, and Lynn watched the master at work.

'How many times have you been asked out in the last few weeks?' he continued with his skilful questioning, designed to make her feel good about herself.

'Two or three.'

'Well, then... That's two or three dates you could easily have next week if you want to. Or you could go out with Lynn and leave me alone at home.'

The young star turned the corners of her mouth downwards in jest, grateful for her man's positivity towards her jilted friend.

'Or,' he added with a lecherous grin, 'the three of us could stay in...'

'Hey!' Lynn smacked his chest, seeing the appalled expression on the other woman's face. 'That's disgusting!'

The trio made their way into the theatre and took their seats. Jeff made sure he snagged the one on the aisle and declined the girls' insistence that he sit between them, on the pretext that he would get carried away with so much female distraction around him. Feeling the tension rush to his neck and shoulders almost immediately, he made an excuse to depart on a convenient candy bar run.

Standing on the footpath outside the cinema, the troubled young man smoked another cigarette before buying a selection of edible diversions. He took a deep breath as he reached the doors to the theatre, showing his ticket to the usher for the second time. By the time he reached his seat, the two women were deep in conversation and didn't voice any surprise at the excessive amount of swag he had brought back.

Within a couple of minutes however, Jeff's suspicions were confirmed that his body's vibrations and generally disquieted demeanour would not be lost on his companion. The caring youngster turned away from the friend on her left who had suddenly become single to focus on the stressed out soul-mate to her right. Her eyes asked him if he was OK, to which he nodded and raised enquiring eyebrows, as if wondering what she might be worried about.

'I love you,' Lynn whispered, as he weaved his left hand between the armrest and her body.

Her insides jumped with the sensation of his strong fingers resting on her thigh, with just enough movement to threaten an upward migration. The combination of her man's vulnerability and its humorous disguises ignited a deep desire. He kissed her temple and then her lips, as she turned her head to meet his.

'I love you too,' he replied, loud enough for Michelle to hear.

The ginger-haired schoolgirl rolled her eyes but smiled anyway, because it was clear how happy this pair was. The dark-haired student's blood pressure began to climb quickly during the six or seven trailers which ran before the movie. Jesus, he thought, if this is what it was like during the advertisements, how freaked out was he going to be during the main feature? He practised breathing deeply without Lynn noticing. He doubted he was being all that successful, but she was upholding her end of the bargain and ignoring him fairly definitively.

In the seat next-door, the blonde celebrity was excited for the movie to start. She gripped her boyfriend's sweaty hand as the soundtrack soared and massaged the muscles at the top of his arm once she realised quite how tense he was.

'Relax,' she whispered, kissing him tenderly.

'Thanks. I'm OK.'

The lights were soon turned down, and the music soared through the theatre from the loudspeakers. Jeff felt imaginary eyes boring into the back of his head, coupled with an uncontrollable compulsion to turn around and confirm there was no danger lurking further up the aisle. He knew perfectly well that no-one would be staking him out here, but as usual, his mind was determined to let its irrational thoughts supplant all others.

Still his dream girl kept her word, appearing for all intents and purposes to be engrossed in the plot. And for his part, Jeff was pleased he had read the book, since his concentration was patchy at best. Every now and again, the pretty blonde would glance round to check on him and shoot him another glorious smile. He knew it was impossible to hide anything from someone who knew him this well, finding the pleasant memory of their intense discussion in the convent grounds a much needed antidote to his current alarm. He could feel beads of perspiration on his brow and knew she would only have to touch his thigh or knee for the cramp to shoot through his leg and make it spasm painfully.

However, by far the worst were the images and voices which refused to stop interfering with the dialogue the young man was endeavouring to absorb. He expected at any moment that a deep, gravelly voice would shout directly in his right ear and grab the collar of his shirt, pulling him upwards and outwards with such force that he would be powerless to resist. Again, his rational self told him he was overreacting. He was much taller and stronger than he had been at thirteen; much more street-wise and capable of fighting back.

Jeff duelled with himself for the first half-hour of the movie before coming to the realisation that he was gradually making peace with his circumstance. He remained jumpy and constantly surveyed his territory, but his heart rate was no longer audible, and he finally found his concentration returning, no longer impeded by the ad-libbing of unscripted bit-parts.

Stretching his spine, the tall, dark, handsome stranger leaned back in his seat and extended his legs into his neighbour's footwell, rubbing his shin against her calf.

'You're feeling better,' Lynn whispered, during a break in the dialogue.

The man in black nodded. 'I think so,' he replied, crossing the fingers on both hands, 'but keep ignoring me.'

He dared to wonder if any subsequent cinematic outing might now be easier. Was there a whole new mode of entertainment open to them, where it was easy for his famous companion to remain unidentified and unmolested among her fans? Lynn ran her hand up and down his left arm, which was leaning on the velvet rest between their two highly-charged bodies. The ongoing mystery was gnawing at her curiosity, but she resolved to speak not a word about this latest batch of peculiar conduct, nor the fact that he seemed to have conquered whatever had been bothering him.

'OK,' she smiled and shrugged. 'Who said that?'

***

'What would you like to do for your birthday?' Lynn asked.

The couple had been out playing badminton with Michelle and Keith, her latest boyfriend. Jeff had just stepped out of the shower, with evidently only one thing on his mind.

'What?' he cried out, taken by surprise. 'I can't discuss that now. Far more important things to take care of...'

Although he noticed her eyes scanning his nude, muscular form up and down, his girlfriend's face nonetheless wore the determined look which he was coming to understand required his fullest attention. He reached his hands out for her to come closer, waiting for her reply. She looked unbelievably sexy, as she teased him by turning her back and making herself comfortable on the bed.

'Second of June, isn't it? Please will you let me organise something?' the nubile beauty thumped the mattress as a signal for him to sit down and come to order.

Jeff wasn't having any of it, however. He lay down beside her and proceeded to stroke her legs, hips and abdomen. His penis was hard and throbbing, and his impatient libido willed Lynn's fingers to touch it and stroke it, which they did, almost on autopilot. A few soft moans escaped from her mouth while they kissed, even though he knew she would be fighting her own arousal in order to revert him from the subject at hand.

'Stop a minute!' the determined teenager smacked his leg when he defiantly climbed on top, smiling at her frustrated expression. 'Are you listening? I'm trying to do something nice for you.'

'I'm sorry,' her boyfriend laughed, sitting up and fondling her breasts instead, 'and *I'm* trying to do something nice for *you*.'

'Argh!' she was becoming exasperated. 'I'll start again. God, I sound like my mother!'

Suddenly wide-eyed, it was Jeff who smacked the palm of his hand down on the mattress this time, mimicking his gorgeous bedfellow.

'What the hell did you say that for? Now I'll never be able to get it back up.'

'Good! Then I might get a straight answer, for once.'

Understanding exactly how far he could abuse her good humour, the horny student gave up the charade. Could he really give himself permission to admit that his dream girl was making plans to celebrate his birthday? He had certainly never taken his fantasies that far in all his years of waiting.

'Skiing,' he decided in a flash. 'If you mean it, I'd really like to try skiing.'

Gravity the troll predictably punched his host in the stomach for being so impertinent, and for a blinding few seconds the lost boy's confidence deserted him. The habitual power drug released by an impending sexual encounter had once more pushed him to overreach, and he cursed his own impulsiveness.

The sportswoman definitely hadn't expected this suggestion either, yet considered it to be a great idea, and both were momentarily left in limbo while they wrestled with the legitimacy of his spur of the moment request. A smile crept across her face, kneeling up so that she could work her way closer, and her hand eagerly reached for his genitals.

'Excellent! Thank you. Now we can play.'

Welcoming her advances without hesitation, Jeff couldn't help but feel guilty for pressing his luck and having her so readily agree. He was even being a control freak without trying, such was his inherent crusade to seize whatever he wanted whenever he wanted.

'Are you serious?' he checked, kissing her breasts lovingly.

'Yes! Why not? It's much better than I'd have come up with on my own.'

Next, the poor man felt pride rear its ugly head, although now typically too late. He gritted his teeth and exhaled through them, feeling ashamed. He ought to know by now never to go with his first response. It always got him into trouble, leaving his conscience to battle with the intense feelings of inadequacy which skulked in the hidden reaches of his mind.

'Angel, you can't pay for us to go skiing? At least, I hope it's us and not just me…'

Lynn giggled. 'Yes, of course. It'll be tricky to get a leave pass from Dad, but I'd love it. You know what I think we should do?'

'What? It's got to be cheap.'

'Oh, shut up about the money! It'll be my treat. When you're a rock star, you can take me skiing. This is my investment in our respecting relationship. I think we should go with Gerry and Suzanne for a long weekend.'

As his birthday plans developed in tandem with their lovemaking, Jeff found himself warming to the idea. After all, it had been his in the first place, despite the fact that this irresistible and big-hearted creature had expanded and embellished it somewhat in the succeeding half-hour. Nevertheless, he remained averse to being paid for. He had always been so insistent about paying his own way, even when he could ill afford to.

'Lynn,' the guilty man said, cupping her face in his hand. 'I'm really uncomfortable with this. I love the idea but not the fact that you'd be paying for me. You don't propose to pay for the others too, I hope?'

The young star felt sorry for him. She didn't want to embarrass her very honourable gentleman, knowing he had a limited source of income from his part-time jobs. She was quite sure that much of his recent windfall from song-writing royalties was being directed to her entertainment, since his generosity had stepped up several notches in the last few weeks. Still, as someone who had never gone without, Lynn had a fairly good idea of how expensive it must be for someone to live alone in an apartment so close to the city, and also how vital it was that her mystery man retained the ability to live that way.

'That would depend if they offered. I expect they would, don't you?'

Jeff nodded. 'Yeah. Gerry'd pay for them. I don't know though. It's a lot of money.'

'Do you want sex tonight?' Lynn asked, pretending to lose interest in their sublime encounter.

'Oh, no, you don't... Don't you dare do this to me, you minx,' the nineteen-year-old chastised her bare buttocks, thinking how unfair this latest tactic was. 'You can't hold me to ransom like that. I can't believe you'd be so mean.'

'No, I wouldn't, but it got you going, didn't it?' his playful girlfriend hugged him. 'Have a think about it. Please?'

Jeff rolled the delectable, slim frame over on the bed and held it down forcibly, staring into Lynn's blue eyes. To his surprise, she didn't object to his show of dominance, turning him on still further. He presumed by her actions that their conversation had gone far enough at this point, as it had for him. They had both laid their intentions on the table, and the rest would unfold over time. Now for more compelling issues, he decided.

'Christ! You are so amazing. I love the way you are. Please don't ever change.'

Having fallen into a deep slumber soon after their passions let loose, the couple slept peacefully for a few hours. In fact, it was not until four o'clock in the morning that Jeff's arms began to flail and Lynn was woken by a fist in the small of her back.

'Ow!' she yelped, shaking the writhing man awake. 'Stop! Wake up.'

At first, her pleas failed to penetrate the soundtrack inside his head, and Jeff's long limbs continued to lash out, as if he were trying to grab hold of something or someone. His fingers would snatch at the air, and his muffled voice swore out loud. Then, whipping his head from one side to the other, he suddenly yelled out in Spanish.

His lover touched his burning cheek with two fingers, just firmly enough for him to register the sensation. She had now had ample opportunity to employ a variety of tricks and was gradually coming to understand which triggers were likely to work for each stage of this ever-recurring dream.

'Jeff, it's OK. There's nothing happening. Wake up.'

Still the wild man continued to toss and turn, and his girlfriend redoubled her attempts at rousing him. It wasn't usually this difficult. This must be a deep-seated nightmare, perhaps because he had been asleep for longer than normal. Lynn wiped the beads of sweat off his forehead and spoke to him yet again, this time much louder.

'Jeff, please wake up.'

Finally, the dreamer began to emerge from his subconscious turmoil. Feeling helpless, the patient woman watched him switch the struggle to his own emotions as he began to realise where he was. What must it be like to live with this, night after night after night? Her heart went out to him. What unspeakable things had he experienced to bring about such an extreme reaction? And so frequently?

'Are you OK?' Lynn asked, loudly enough that he was unable to drift back into the unconscious. 'Talk to me.'

Her dazed bedfellow reached out and pulled her towards him, eyes wild with fear and his lungs sucking in air. Even though fury was written all over his face, he was crying in abject frustration.

'I can't do this anymore. Jesus Christ!' he muttered under his breath, clinging on to her hand. 'I'm sorry, angel. When's this going to end? I'm so fucking sick of waking you up. Did I hit you? I remember hearing you shout out.'

Lynn kissed him on the forehead. 'Yes, you punched me in the back. I can't believe you can be in the dream and in reality at the same time. But it's good, because hopefully it means I can wake you up quicklier that way.'

Her boyfriend stood up to shake the cramp out of his legs, smiling at her childish, made-up word. His right leg was so numb that he almost fell back onto the bed.

'For fuck's sake!' he shouted, slapping his tingling thigh muscles to rid them of the debilitating sensation.

Lynn saw a chance and took it. 'Jeff, do you see how you are now? How you're suffering? If anyone deserves to be treated on his birthday, it's you. Please let me take you skiing?'

Feeling desperate and so grateful for his girlfriend's compassion and steadfastness, the exhausted man slumped down onto the mattress and lay on his back across it. His hands stretched over to make certain she was really there, and not another cruel mirage. He would be mad to pass up this opportunity. It was most likely the only chance he would ever have to go away for a weekend with the girl of his dreams. Hell! If he had his way, they may well never come back! And going to the snow with his best mate would be an unbelievable experience too.

'You know what? You're right,' he capitulated. 'Why not?'

'It doesn't make this into a using relationship, does it?'

Jeff turned over. His sanity was returning, and with it his appreciation for the sixteen-year-old's adoption of his language.

'Marginal.'

Lynn frowned in jest, rubbing his hairy stomach and leaning over to kiss him. She was ecstatic to get his agreement.

'Then tell me if there are any weekends when you can't go,' the young star schemed aloud, 'and leave me Gerry's phone number. I'll ring him to see if we can arrange something. It'll be great.'

'Thanks, angel. One day I'll pay you back.'

His girlfriend shook her head. 'I don't see it as payback. It'll be your turn to spoil me with something special on my birthday. Let's try and get back to sleep.'

They lay together in the dark until Jeff's heart rate had dropped. His naked counsellor told him to visualise skiing down the mountain side, twisting and turning through the trees and feeling the wind rush past his face, cool and crisp. The old coaching technique worked a treat, and within fifteen minutes he was asleep again. Their pooled skills at dealing with this affliction were becoming progressively more effective, even though its manifestations were no less frequent. Lynn was glad to be able to help him, however long it might take.

***

Jeff Diamond woke up in his own bed on his birthday. Lynn and he had ordered *pizza* the night before, after another trip to the recording studio to finalise some of the backing tracks for his would-be album. The session had gone really well, and the budding rock star was over the moon with the result. A producer friend of Bob, the MAC bass player, had offered to work on the record for free, in exchange for a small percentage of sales, such was the faith the young musicians were showing in the newcomer's talent.

On top of this, his gorgeous companion had managed to suppress his dreaming overnight before it developed into the usual total body experience, and the birthday boy woke up feeling marvellously refreshed. He turned over to check out the picture of perfection in his bed, still not quite able to believe how much she loved him.

Today was his twentieth birthday. The nineteenth, just like the rest of his teenage birthdays, had passed by unacknowledged, apart from a quick telephone call from Gerry's mother. He cast his mind back to that previous year, remembering having gone out drinking with some UNSW friends and ending up in bed with a nameless girl, smoking a joint or two after way too much whisky.

This year was already so, so different. It had been the celebrity's suggestion to wake up at his place, which the young man had initially resisted.

However, the more he contemplated the idea, the more it had grown on him. She had arrived with a couple of bags containing unknown items in brightly coloured wrapping paper, which he guessed were part of the birthday proceedings. He had learned from the Blake sisters that girls liked to make a fuss on birthdays, and he wasn't averse to being the centre of Lynn Dyson's attention, in the privacy of his home at least... He was almost ashamed to admit to being really quite childishly excited.

Lynn stirred and opened her eyes to find a handsome, smiling face staring back at her. She beamed, immediately noticing an abnormal liveliness in his eyes.

'*Buenos días*,' Jeff said in a typically husky, first-thing-in-the-morning voice, kissing her tenderly on the lips.

'Happy birthday!' she replied, pulling both hands out from under the quilt and wrapping them around his neck. 'Twenty! You're officially old.'

'Thanks. Is that all? Only twenty?'

The smiling sex-god began to run his hands over her body, and the one left in her teens responded eagerly. It shocked her, albeit pleasantly, how much more relaxed and positive he seemed, without the usual pull of depression doing its best to keep him in a dark mood. Twenty looked about right this morning.

'What time were you born?' Lynn enquired, between clamorous kisses.

Her boyfriend exhaled and shook his head. 'I have no idea.'

His reaction told her to leave the topic alone, realising that there were some aspects of her mystery man's life which were not worth exploring, especially on his birthday. Sex between them was these days both tender and intense. Jeff had been a patient and thorough teacher, and the young woman's self-confidence as a lover had grown in leaps and bounds. They made a good team, she thought. If sex were an Olympic sport, she had no doubt they would both be medallists!

Afterwards, pulling on a t-shirt and some boxer shorts, the satisfied man got up quickly to put the kettle on. The kitchen window, which had been broken since he moved in, was letting in a stream of water from the pouring rain outside, and the towel he had used last night to mop up the mess was now completely sodden. He scooped it up and wrung it out in the sink. No amount of petty annoyance was going to interfere with his enjoyment of this extra-special morning.

'I was supposed to do that,' the pretty teenager whined, when he returned with two cups of tea. 'Thanks, anyway. Would you like your presents now?'

'Presents?' the birthday boy responded, emphasising the plural noun.

'Yes,' she affirmed. 'Presents.'

The sixteen-year-old swung her long legs out from under the covers and pulled on a pair of panties under the t-shirt which her boyfriend had lent her overnight. Throwing her hair up into a rough ponytail, she went to retrieve the mysterious bags from the living room, all the while singing "Happy Birthday". Jeff sat on the window ledge with his steaming mug, staring out at the grey, wintry sky to which Melbourne was waking up, and gave thanks again. Happiness personified, the returning celebrity dropped the bags onto his bed and beckoned to him to take a peek.

'I hope you like them.'

The student felt sure he would like anything his amazing, new friend were to give him for his birthday. He had become accustomed to Blake family Christmases, when everyone would be opening gifts at the same time. However for this event, he was the one being made a fuss of for a change, which actually made him feel overly conspicuous.

Lynn sensed his hesitation. 'Open them! This one first…'

She pointed to the smaller of the two bags. With a tender kiss of gratitude on her forehead, the student tipped the contents out onto the quilt and began to unwrap. A winter sweater, because the native Victorian had come to the conclusion that her boyfriend's Sydney wardrobe was not coping too well with the colder Melbourne weather, then two large blocks of dark chocolate and a bottle of Glenfiddich scotch whisky.

'Great! Thanks heaps,' Jeff kissed her again, this time full on the lips. 'For winter nights, when you're not here.'

Lynn nodded, slightly melancholy. The last item remaining in this first batch was an envelope, which the student tore open and sat reading for a few seconds. He kissed her again, and they hugged each other tightly. It was a letter from the recording studios, informing him that he had ten hours booked in advance, to use whenever he wanted, with sound engineer included.

'You are too good,' her favourite songwriter shook his head, embarrassed by her generosity.

'Jeff, you said yourself… ages ago… that money should be put to good use,' the star responded. 'It's not about the cost. It's about the value we get for it. I love spending money on you, because I know you'll appreciate it. And it's money well spent. You're going to be a star soon. Plus, it's your birthday and I love you, so let me invest in you, please. Enough good reasons?'

The young man said nothing. How could he possibly take issue when her sermon sounded like one of his own? Sighing, he moved on to the second bag. A pair of thick, black ski gloves and a woollen hat. Laughing, he put the gloves on and pretended to strangle his squealing bedfellow, pushing her down onto the pillow and smothering her with grateful kisses and caresses that tickled terribly. This was a much better outlook than most mornings, Lynn thought. Her tormented soul-mate was free of the blues for another twenty-four hours.

'Aha... I can see a theme,' he joked, sitting back up again and spreading the jumper, gloves and beanie out on the bed, arranging them in the shape of a person.

Another envelope fell out of the second bag, bigger and heavier than the first. The peasant boy felt his throat tighten, and the back of his eyes were stinging. It was a card. A birthday card from Lynn Dyson. How good was that? For how long had he been dreaming about receiving one of these? The message inside was simple:

"Jeff, these last four months have been the best of my life. Happy 20th birthday. All my love, Lynn. 2nd June, 1972."

The words "best" and "All" were underlined in girlish, red, squiggly lines. A tear dropped onto the card as he read it, and the boy from Canley Vale sniffed, wiping his eyes.

'It's beautiful, angel. *You*'re beautiful. Thank you, and I love you too,' he croaked.

The pair kissed once more, locked in a firm embrace and only moving after the schoolgirl picked up the rest of the envelope's contents and held them under her boyfriend's nose. There was a picture of the photogenic couple taken at Benloch. The blonde beauty was sitting on his lap in the family's large lounge room, and they both looked very relaxed.

'When was this taken?' he asked, overwhelmed by a memento that captured two people who quite clearly belonged together.

'Sandy took it,' Lynn answered. 'Not last time we were there, but the time before, I think. You look gorgeous. You'd just had your hair cut. It's good, isn't it?'

Yes, it was good. Very good, in fact. The framed picture which Jeff already had in his possession, taken at Robert McLean's twenty-first, was fantastic enough, because it was proof for all to see that they had been at the party together, yet this new photograph captured them perfectly. He and Lynn Dyson looked like lovers. No, he thought again, they looked like best friends who were also lovers.

'It's perfect, angel. Please thank him for me. He's a good photographer.'

The proud sister smiled. This was exactly the reaction she had hoped for. This man's happiness was worth all the money in the world to her. Despite the fact that she had never celebrated a boyfriend's birthday before, the teenager wanted to let her first love know how much he meant to her, particularly since they would be spending less and less time together over the coming months.

'I'm glad you like it,' she smiled brightly, lifting yet another item that had also spilled out onto the sheets.

'Jesus, woman! This goes on and on!' the unworthy recipient accepted it reluctantly, his uneasiness beginning to subside.

The white window envelope contained four ski passes, a brochure of a resort hotel and some flimsy paper documents. The virgin traveller couldn't work out what they were at first. He read the red text, noting his own name and those of each of his friends, together with what looked like some sort of timetable. His stomach flipped. These were airline tickets. Where were they going? He had assumed they would simply drive the few hours to Mount Hotham or Bulla in the Victorian ski fields.

Jeff fixed his girlfriend with a hard stare. 'What have you done?'

'Gerry chose the hotel, and I booked the flights,' the young star answered, seeing his confusion and smiling. 'I suggested New Zealand, and he loved the idea. He and Suzanne picked Queenstown, so I asked our travel agent to come up with some accommodation choices. Hopefully it'll be good. You have got a passport now, haven't you?'

'You've been scheming with my mate behind my back.'

He couldn't believe it, waving a finger to scold her. His first flight, and his first journey outside Australia. He had known this gem of a woman for just over four months, and already his life was changing beyond recognition: recording his own songs, socialising with famous musicians and sports personalities, and now waking up with Lynn Dyson on his birthday, only to be treated to an overseas holiday. It couldn't be much more of a contrast to his miserable half-life back in Sydney's south-west.

'I'm still not sure I'm totally OK with this, but thank you,' the student whispered, taking her hand. 'Yes, I did apply for a passport, on your recommendation. It's never been anywhere, mind you. I'm amazed. I can't believe we're actually going to fly somewhere.'

One gift to go... The last bulky package was wrapped in the same colourful birthday paper as the jumper. Jeff ripped it open and hoisted up a heavy, black leather jacket. It was one he had seen at David Keith's, when they had dropped in a few weeks ago for Lynn to visit the family tailor. She was certainly observant, he thought. He hadn't expressed an opinion at the time, but she must have noticed him admiring the item on the rack. It smelled heavenly and felt classy, its price tag etched in his avaricious memory.

'How did you know? Did you see me looking at this?' he asked, emotional again.

'Yes. I was watching you stroking it and sniffing it. I could tell you really liked it, and I love it too. I knew you'd never buy it for yourself, so somebody had to. You'll look so sexy in it. Put it on!'

A leather jacket on top of boxer shorts and a faded, shapeless t-shirt was not exactly the look either of them had envisaged, but the size was perfect and its substantial weight made the ambitious man feel somehow very important.

He took it off again and hung it on the back of the door before taking the generous teenager in his arms and steering her to the window ledge.

Together they sat, wrapped in the quilt to protect them from the chilly autumn air, and planned their long weekend in Queenstown. So happy with the way the morning had unfolded, Lynn was sorely tempted to skip school and tempt the birthday boy into spending the whole day together. She was dying to know if he was thinking the same, but dared not ask. If he were to accept, she would be in big trouble. And if he didn't accept, she would love him all the more, because he would have only resisted in order to prevent her from getting into big trouble.

The duo took turns at a quick shower in the draughty second-floor bathroom, after another necessarily rapid sexual interlude, groaning as they rushed to get dressed and warm again. Jeff drove his dream girl to school, flagrantly dropping her off at the gate, right in front of several of her friends and a few teachers. Neither lover cared if they were spotted that morning, and they waved to each other cheerfully as the blue Ford sped off.

The new twenty-year-old wore his new, luxurious leather jacket to university with some dark trousers and a collared shirt, attracting a great deal of attention. He admitted to looking mighty fine, dressed in the *accoûtrements* of the rich and famous. He pretended he could see into his future and lost himself in fantasies of life as a rock star; fantasies that were no longer so far out of reach. What a stupendous birthday this was!

By lunchtime, the dreamer had another hit song written, scribbled furtively during one of Professor Martin's lectures. He turned down two drinks invitations from disappointed female students who had swooned over his tasteful turnout and left work to meet Gerry for a gym' session, before working the late night shift at the pub. Even if his rock star career were never to take off, the direction his life had taken over the last four months was nothing short of a miracle. Why would he ask for anything else? Jeff Diamond was filled with an alien, peaceful feeling. Someone cared about him. No. Much better than that... Lynn Dyson cared about him. Apart from a little more sleep, what more did he need?

On the other side of town, the tennis champion reached the Sportsdrome by four o'clock that afternoon, feeling guilty at having skipped her morning training session on account of Jeff's birthday. Her coach had not been too pleased when she had made her excuses, but the potential medal-winning athlete was as committed as she needed to be to her own success, so he could hardly begrudge her one morning off.

School had dragged unusually slowly that day after the breakfast-time high. Lynn's mind continually drifted back to her gorgeous black stallion's sincere reaction to being spoiled, and to the raw emotions that had been expressed so openly in response. This man, whom she hardly knew but who felt like her oldest friend, had entered his third decade, and her under-aged heart was heavy with the news she vowed to hide until his birthday celebrations were over.

Up So High

Jeff was unbelievably excited! Air travel, New Zealand, skiing, staying in a hotel with a superstar... Everything about the coming weekend would be new. He hadn't slept all night, finishing his university assignments and all required reading for the coming week. He had packed a suitcase and filled the remaining hour with song-writing, before Gerry was due to pick them all up to drive to the airport. All three Sydneysiders were greatly looking forward to this short break from their individual and highly diverse routines.

At Dyson Administration, Lynn, on the other hand, was downhearted. She had endured a very serious conversation with her parents and coaches the previous evening over dinner, during which they had issued her an ultimatum to break the news to her boyfriend. The normally truthful teenager had lied through her teeth several times the previous day; both to her parents, that the trip was not going to interfere with her Olympics preparation, and then to Jeff, when he had expressed surprise that her father was allowing her to travel for pleasure this close to the enormously important sporting events.

The seasoned traveller fastened the zips on her bag, feeling sure she would brighten up soon enough, once the others' enthusiasm rubbed off on her. The telephone rang on the dresser, and she ran to pick it up. It was her beloved, enigmatic stranger, from down at the reception desk, and his voice was so upbeat that it nearly made her cry. It sounded as unlike the normal Jeff as she felt like the normal Lynn.

'We're here, gorgeous! Shall I come up?'

'Morning, Jeff. Are you all there?' she asked, sensing the anticipation. 'Don't come up. I can easily bring my bag down. It's not too heavy.'

'OK,' he replied. 'What are you waiting for then? We've got a 'plane to catch!'

The foursome sped to the airport in the purring, gold, German panther. The autumn weather was fresh and biting, and it definitely felt like they were heading off on a winter holiday. In the driver's seat, Gerry was whistling one of MAC's biggest hits over and over again until Lynn put a stop to it.

'Gerry, please! Stop whistling that tune. It's driving me crazy.'

The indomitable accountant only whistled louder, turning and grinning at the blonde singer in the back. To help her out, Jeff clocked his friend round the back of the head from the passenger seat.

'Shut up, mate! Let's play nicely this weekend.'

Once they had parked the car in the long-term car park and piled their luggage onto an abandoned trolley, the first-timer became even jumpier when they reached the terminal building. His manic eyes darted around the unfamiliar layout of the check-in area, desperate to understand how air travel worked. If he were soon to be touring, he would need to become *au fait* with Departures and Arrivals, not to mention what went on behind the sliding doors. The bright lights, glossy posters and myriad desks staffed with heavily made-up ground crew put him in mind of a corny American disaster movie.

'Are you OK?' Lynn asked him quietly. 'You seem so edgy.'

'I'm just looking forward to the weekend,' he responded with a dismissive shrug. 'This is fantastic. Sorry. I'll calm down. There's nothing wrong, except I'm as horny as all hell! Everything's great. Are you?'

The young woman played along, although inside she was far from OK. She hoped she would manage to act as convincingly later on, when it came time to assuage her man's desires.

'Yes, I am. It'll be so much fun. I can't wait to see you on the snow for the first time.'

Jeff grinned and stole a quick kiss. 'Making an arse of myself, you mean? Prepare to be amazed at my natural skill.'

Suzanne scoffed. 'Yeah, right, Mister Wonderful. Just you wait!'

His old friend was an expert skier. Her parents had taken her and her brother on skiing holidays many times throughout their childhood, and her boyfriend was equally adept on the slopes. There wouldn't have been a single child at their local primary school who hadn't spent at least every other winter school holidays at Thredbo or Perisher.

Soon it was time to board the aeroplane bound for Queenstown, the picturesque resort town high up in the mountains that formed the backbone of New Zealand's South Island. The passengers made their way from the cafeteria to the gate, where it was the older couple's turn to wonder at the level of attention their famous companion was attracting. By now, the adulation was all but second nature to Jeff, who nudged Lynn's arm when he saw his mate's gawking stare. The celebrity shrugged and kissed him furtively, which stoked both his inner fire and his outer ego at the same time.

Finding seats in the empty rows of an adjacent departure gate, Suzanne and Lynn sat down and waited for the boarding announcement, chatting idly about their weeks. The men wandered over to the window to check out the runway and the steady stream of aircraft landing and taking off. Every now and again, the twenty-year-old would turn around to make sure his famous charge wasn't being subjected to any unwanted scrutiny.

Despite his girlfriend's frequent reassurance, Jeff was unable to relax while so far away. He left Gerry charming a pair of frivolous females and plonked himself down on the floor at her feet. The gesture won the weekend's guest of honour a heart-steadying smile from the musician, and when they were finally called to stand in line, both women laughed at the sorry sight of his boarding pass, which had been wound round his fingers over and over again.

'What?' he laughed when he caught his dream girl's amused gaze. 'I can't smoke, so I've got to do something with my fingers. Or would you prefer me to do something else with them?'

'Jeff!' Suzanne bellowed from behind her friends in the queue. 'Keep your voice down. That's disgusting.'

Lynn cringed coyly and said nothing. Slowly, they shuffled their way through the boarding pass check and finally found themselves inside the aeroplane, when again the first-time flyer's senses were inundated with a multitude of new stimuli, all of which he drank in thirstily. He let his beautiful companion go ahead of him through the door and followed his three best friends down the fuselage.

'Here's us,' Gerry shouted from a few rows further on. 'Who wants the window?'

The blonde teenager motioned to her dark-haired companion to sit by the window, but he objected, preferring to shield her as much as he could from onlookers. However, the famous youngster shook her head insistently, making it quite clear that he was here to enjoy his first flight as much as possible. Both men squeezed their tall frames into the narrow gap between the rows, and their respective partners slipped into the seats next to them. Jeff became suspicious when the doors were closed with neither aisle seat occupied, but opted not to air his regret at the amount of money which had been spent on his extended birthday celebrations.

'Jeez,' Gerry moaned at the lack of legroom. 'This is luxurious. We'll all need massages when we get there.'

His friend looked up from the safety instruction card, immediately interested. 'Oh, yeah? I'm up for that.'

Lynn jabbed his ribcage sharply. 'Shhh!'

Leaning his head leftwards onto hers, the twenty-year-old apologised and mentally drew the latest line on his happiness chart. Well into the distortion zone this morning, he admitted, thinking that his gorgeous girlfriend was uncharacteristically quiet and subdued. Jeff took her hand, concerned there was something on her mind that was important for his elation not to gloss over.

'Are you sure you're OK?' he asked. 'You're behaving like I normally feel in the mornings. We've gone through some weird role reversal process.'

'I'm fine,' Lynn responded in a positive tone. 'I think it's just because you're so hyper. Don't worry about me. Just concentrate on enjoying yourself. This is your weekend, remember?'

Jeff was happy enough with her answer, particularly when it came with a kiss. Perhaps she was right. He could still scarcely accept that the next four days were all about him, and yet somehow this morning, such notions of unworthiness had dissipated. He was surrounded by the only people who mattered in his life and was all set to appreciate his first ever flight.

'So can I have a massage when we get there?'

'Of course you can,' Lynn answered. 'I'll make sure he's big and beefy, covered in tattoos and gay.'

'Cool! Look forward to it. Please will you fasten my seatbelt for me?'

This time, the sixteen-year-old gave him a scolding glare, its ferocity taking them both by surprise and causing them to burst out laughing. The celebrity slapped her impetuous boyfriend's forearm.

'Just because you've never been on a 'plane before! I don't know... You're like a little kid. Haven't you seen seatbelts on the telly? If you wait until we start moving, the pretty lady over there'll show you.'

The young man looked over at the uniformed stewardess, who was bending over another passenger. Yet another tantalising experience for the freshman to avidly consume, which he did without compunction.

'Hmm... Will she? But I like this pretty lady better,' he disputed, kissing his dream girl tenderly. 'Thanks for humouring me. I love you so much.'

The last of the passengers were filing down the aisle, and the sound of overhead locker doors slamming shut echoed through the cabin. Lynn was in the process of explaining where the first class seats were located and showing her favourite companion how to turn on his reading light or the jet of cool air above his head when Suzanne's face appeared over the top of the seat in front, also keen to check on the new traveller.

'Is he behaving himself yet?' she asked. 'Stop kicking my seat, you horrible little boy.'

Jeff stuck his tongue out at the haughty woman, who flopped back down into her seat. He then reached up to ruffle the hair on the top of her head and received a barrage of abuse in return.

'I don't think she likes me,' the overgrown child complained.

Lynn nodded in agreement, putting her finger to her mouth to request his silence. The engines were now revving harder, which she recognised as the sign that they were about to reverse off their stand and taxi to the runway. After startling at an initial sharp jerk, the novice traveller sat back and gazed out of the small, oval window in awe while the aeroplane joined the long line of crawling aircraft.

'I wish I were in the driving seat,' he declared, staring at the buildings trundling by.

'Fuck! I don't!' came Gerry's booming voice from the row ahead.

A number of passengers must have overheard Jeff's comment too, because there was a ripple of laughter. The younger couple smiled at each other, on hearing their friends exchanging terse words.

'No dramas, mate,' the comic relented. 'On the way home then.'

Lumbering far closer to the end of the runway than the sudden expert considered ideal, the Boeing 737 eventually lifted its passengers into the air. Whispering his amazement to his nonplussed neighbour, he took the incredible acceleration and the sight of buildings and trees becoming rapidly smaller and smaller in his enthusiastic stride. His senses were assaulted by these new experiences, leaving him quite washed out, waiting for the aircraft to level off just underneath the clouds.

Lyrics began to swirl around the songwriter's head, as if the altitude had unleashed all his pent-up creativity at once. Jeff closed his eyes and leaned his head back, willing the words to assemble themselves into something meaningful which could be committed to memory for whenever he next had access to a piece of paper and a pen.

The flight itself was smooth and uneventful. Gerry and Suzanne immediately fell asleep, leaving the others to amuse themselves. It was nice just to sit and read, once the novelty had worn off, knowing they had the whole long weekend ahead of them. This would set a new record for the young lovers as the longest period spent in each other's company, but the prospect didn't faze either of them. Notwithstanding, the student remained slightly concerned that the normally unfailingly sunny sixteen-year-old was upset about something. He figured he was able to read her pretty well by now, but his gentle questioning yielded nothing. Giving up and focussing back on his novel, he resigned to taking her at her word and forced his mind to stop its incessant worrying.

'Hey! Wake up, Gez,' the birthday boy's sonorous voice announced, pressing his knee into the back of the seat in front of him. 'It's lunchtime.'

The handsome man's first trip in a flying machine was a substantial tick on his life's checklist, and he was even managing to have fun in the droning monotony. He had read up on their destination, situated on the shore of Lake Wakatipu, and couldn't wait to see the famous location through his own eyes. Within another two hours, they had crossed the coastline of South Island and were flying above the mountainous countryside around Queenstown. Seeing the frozen lakes and brilliant white slopes from above was awe-inspiring, and his attention began to drift to the moment when he would discover what it felt like to drop out of the sky. The regular holidaymakers around him had warned that the popular skiing destination's airport was notorious for buffeting approaches, and he wasn't disappointed when a shaky landing sent their hearts into their mouths.

'Phew! That wasn't too bad,' Lynn said, checking on her man. 'Landings aren't usually that bumpy.'

'Welcome to Queenstown,' the thrilled student whispered against her cheek, kissing it and sending delicious shivers across her skin. 'That was absolutely effing fantastic, angel! Thanks again. I owe you, big-time.'

His overflowing gratitude warmed the young woman's heart, coupled with the tingling sensation that rushed through her body. She had asked that the others hang back until the rest of the passengers had disembarked, so as to minimise any interaction with over-eager fans. Gerry and Suzanne obediently remained seated, criticising the ridiculous amount of cabin luggage with which some travellers flew. Several people leaned over and asked Lynn to autograph their boarding passes, only to meet the steely glare of her handsome minder. The aeroplane took quite a while to vacate, and the foursome eventually traipsed out, only to come to a stop again at the baggage carousel, waiting for their luggage.

'I can't believe I'm overseas,' Jeff joked, 'even if it is only New Zealand.'

'Be quiet!' Suzanne scolded him. 'Some of these folks actually like it here.'

The empathetic man laughed out loud as he scanned the vexed expressions on some of the nearby faces. No matter how good a job the average affluent Mosman parent made of bringing up young ladies and gentlemen, their offspring invariably let the side down at the most inopportune moments with their unwittingly superior rhetoric. His own refined and reserved aristocrat would never have uttered such tactless words, he was sure.

'That was good for diplomatic relations, Miss Crozier. Where are we going now?'

Gerry held out the rental car paperwork and the map to the ski resort in his hands for the others to pore over. Between them, they identified their luggage and loaded it onto a couple of trolleys, ready to locate their means of transport. Soon they were on the road, driving through the winding streets and up into the mountains. The older couple had visited Queenstown twice before in their time together, making them reasonably familiar with navigating around the resort town.

More than happy to let his old friend take control on this leg of their journey, Jeff sat back and invited his beautiful girlfriend to cuddle into him. It was already well into the afternoon, after over four hours on the flight and with the two-hour time difference. Every now and again, the car would round a corner to reveal a steep, jagged slope, at the top of which they could see skiers weaving this way and that. Jeff wound down his window in preparation for lighting a cigarette, only to be hit with a blast of freezing air, shortly followed by two icy female voices of dissent.

'Jeez, it's cold!' the birthday boy smiled, reversing the direction of the window handle, his eyes wide with a drug-like euphoria. 'I'd like to come back and drive these roads in the summer. We should bring the rally car over here when we get one.'

'Good idea, mate,' his friend scoffed. 'When *who* gets one?'

The hotel selected by the Dysons' travel agent was luxuriously appointed and located just a few minutes' walk from the vibrant town centre. A smartly-dressed *concièrge* recognised Lynn immediately and lavished special attention on the new arrivals, once again leaving Gerry and Suzanne bewildered. After registering for their adjacent rooms, the attendant ushered the small party and their baggage up to the fourth floor, and the couples each made themselves comfortable in their new digs.

Allowing his dream girl to open the door for him by way of a magnanimously overstated bow, Jeff whistled his appreciation at their room, and again even louder when he saw the view from their window. The lake glistened in the falling sun, flat calm and surrounded by majestic mountains. The primæval backdrop overwhelmed him, the ancient scenery appealing to the city boy's senses more deeply than he had ever imagined.

'This place is fantastic, angel. Thanks again for bringing us here.'

'You're welcome,' Lynn replied, locking their door and placing the key on the chest of drawers. 'I thought you'd be impressed. So do you want that massage now?'

'Oh, I'm impressed alright. Blown away. How could I not be?' Jeff grinned at her, holding his arms out. 'Is it my birthday again?'

'Yes, it is!'

Happily, the celebrity began to undo his belt, running her other hand around his side and over the tight muscles in his back. Pressing herself against his body, amorous vibes gushed from the young woman's every gesture, making Jeff's heart rate shoot through the roof. As slowly as they could, each piece of clothing was shed in a mesmeric dance, and they fell breathlessly onto crisp, starched sheets, the like of which the boy from the western suburbs had never slept on before.

'Your wish is my command,' the sixteen-year-old's newly confident voice insisted, turning the tables on her ever attentive seducer.

With the light fading on the magnificent view outside, the devoted lovers combined for what they hoped would be the first of many encounters this weekend, precariously balanced between patience and frenzy. Lynn had tears in her eyes as her tongue caressed the tip of her man's aching penis, and again he dismissed his nagging doubt as the antidote to his hyperactivity.

As the hours ticked by, this afternoon and evening was to inspire countless new songs from both musicians. As he came inside his very best friend, Jeff had melodies galore swirling around his head. They were songs about sex with love, about healing and rebirth, and a fervent wish for time to stand still, none of which he fully understood but somehow suspected had been introduced by the old men of the mountain outside.

And for Lynn, she had successfully satiated her gorgeous partner without giving away the sadness in her heart. She thought she had sensed a question brewing a few times, courtesy of his expressive eyes, but was grateful to have been spared the inquisition. Perhaps he knew already? It wouldn't have surprised her, particularly as someone so sensitive would also know not to ask. She had tamed his inner child well enough today, having subjected it to a feast of intoxicating catalysts, and felt doubly sorry that their journey was shortly to come to a most unsatisfactory end.

***

The telephone in the hotel room rang while Lynn was in the shower. Jeff was dozing in the darkness, and the shrill warbling startled him. Beyond the window, streetlights reflecting on the water served to remind the contented man exactly where he was.

'Hello?' he answered blurrily.

'Jeff, GB here,' Gerry barked from the room next door. 'We'd better get a move on. The ski rental shop closes in under an hour.'

The younger man shook his head awake. 'Hey, mate! Slow down. What are you so strung out about? That's OK. We'll meet you downstairs in twenty minutes.'

The businessman huffed. 'Yeah. Good. But as quick as you can. I'm in the dog house for letting us fall asleep. What are you guys doing?'

'I was enjoying a relaxing, post-coital snooze too,' Jeff told him honestly. 'Until the 'phone went, anyway. Lynn's in the shower. We won't be long.'

The young woman emerged to see her boyfriend putting the receiver back on the hook. He grinned at her, immediately jumping up and grabbing his clothes.

'Was that them?'

'Yep,' he replied with a military salute, already halfway to the bathroom. 'Sergeant Major Blake on patrol. Apparently we're in the shit, because the ski hire place is about to close.'

'Oh, right,' the teenager laughed at the naked man's antics, turning round to look at the bedside clock. 'That's true, actually. We'll waste a lot of valuable skiing time if we leave all that measuring and fitting until tomorrow. Go on then. Get going!'

Jeff saluted her again and made haste. Within fifteen minutes, all four musketeers were assembled in the lobby of the hotel, ready to be kitted out with suits, boots and skis. The temperature was a few degrees above freezing and quickly falling as the last remnants of light dissolved into the clear sky. Buzzing inside from the sheer enormity of their situation, the student grabbed Lynn's gloved hand with his.

'This is so effin' exciting!' he hugged her, swinging her arm upwards to search for her fingers. 'Are you sure there are hands in here? I can't feel a bloody thing through these.'

'Haven't you ever worn gloves before?' Lynn asked, amazed.

'Na!' Jeff laughed, absorbing the spectacular view. 'I'm a glove virgin. Why would I have had to wear gloves? This is my first real winter, remember?'

Snow was falling in a light dust as they reached the ski shop. Fortunately, the queue for returns was much longer than the queue for hire, and the foursome was served quickly, especially once the assistants behind the counter realised who was among them. In no time flat, it seemed as though the entire staff was on hand to make sure they were measured, fitted and issued with everything they required.

'How the hell do you walk in these boots?' the newcomer complained. 'We're like Frankenstein's monsters, stomping about like uncoordinated morons.'

Gerry laughed. 'Just you wait until we get out on the snow, mate. Then we'll see who's the uncoordinated moron!'

The girls grinned at each other. Boys were always so competitive, Lynn thought. Poor Jeff! He didn't have a clue how hard it was going to be to keep up with the rest of them, even though he now looked the part in his ski gear. The outwardly-confident novice was clutching his extra-long pair of skis tightly, attempting to keep their undersides stuck together, following advice from the surrounding know-alls.

'Now,' the patient schoolgirl began, with a determined expression on her face which caused her boyfriend to snap to attention obediently. 'Up to you, but I think you should book in for a lesson in the morning. Just to get the feel of stopping and turning in a controlled way. To get some ground rules, *et cetera*. Otherwise you'll end up making straight for a person or a tree with no way of getting out of trouble. Other people have a chance of jumping out of your way, but trees don't!'

Their friends looked on in amusement, anticipating a typically macho reply from their long-time amigo. True to form, the control freak didn't disappoint them.

'The basics, you mean?' he replied gruffly.

'Yes, I suppose so,' his girlfriend responded, not backing down. 'Skiing's not natural, Jeff. You're not three years old, you know. We all learned years ago. Learning to ski as an adult's not easy.'

The arrogant twenty-year-old scoffed. 'And how would you know, pray? If you're all such experts, how would you know how easy it's not?'

'What?' Suzanne interjected. 'Don't talk in riddles. Lynn's right, but you can take your chances if you like.'

'No,' the sixteen-year-old chimed back in, reverting to her original suggestion. 'I'm serious. You'll come up to speed much more quickly, believe me.'

Jeff shrugged, putting on the agony while they all navigated the shop's narrow doorway and steps with their bulky paraphernalia. Gerry was doing his usual, manly best not to get involved in the persuasive tactics. Unbeknown to the others, the crafty young man was pitting them against each other, quietly enjoying the pre-dinner sport.

'OK. If you insist,' he moaned. 'I'll go to kiddies' corner while you guys piss off and have fun on the grown-up slopes. Don't worry about me. It's only my birthday.'

'Bloody hell!' the businessman exclaimed, throwing his hands in the air. 'What a fucking drama queen. Just do as she says, man.'

Lynn took her boyfriend's hand and began to lead him on towards the main part of town. 'Come on, guys. Let's go and get a drink.'

They trudged off through a fresh, new layer of snow which had fallen during their time in the shop. Gerry and Suzanne walked on ahead, and Lynn deliberately held back until they were out of earshot, to talk to her petulant charge.

'I've got a plan,' she told him, slightly tentative, 'if you let me.'

Jeff hugged her. 'I'm just jerking around. I love to wind those guys up. I know exactly how hard it's going to be. I'm prepared to make a fool of myself, don't you worry.'

The blonde sportswoman was relieved. 'Well, you did a good job of winding us all up! My plan is for the two of us to go out early, before the others get up. I'll teach you how to put everything together so you can get the feel of snow-ploughing to stop. Then you can slot into an intermediate class. That way, you'll learn proper turning techniques and things like that before we all go out together.'

The beginner was all in favour of the idea. 'Sounds perfect, thanks.'

'And it won't be kids anyway,' his coach added, giggling. 'There are separate children's lessons. Unless you want to, of course! They play follow-my-leader and picking up pine cones and other entertaining games.'

'Really? You're right to advise me not to dismiss it, angel. The other entertaining games interest me,' the playful joker smiled, squeezing her tightly. 'But probably an entirely different set of entertaining games from the ones I'm thinking of.'

The bar eventually chosen by the four friends was warm and cosy, with a log fire blazing in one corner. The three from Sydney managed to hide their pet celebrity well enough for her to enjoy a glass of mulled wine, and they whiled away two hours, exercising their impeded brains by playing Scrabble using some very dubious rules. After a leisurely dinner, they played cards until midnight, which was still only ten o'clock Melbourne time.

The long day of travelling was catching up with them all however, mixed with the stuffy air in the low-beamed room and the alcohol they had consumed on top of their full stomachs. Suzanne was the first to suggest going to bed.

'We need an early start to make sure we get to the lifts before the queues build up,' she urged defensively, hearing the boys' protestations.

After a last, quick nightcap, the relaxed quartet left the warmth of the roaring fire and emerged into the street. There were people everywhere, enjoying the Friday night entertainment; all ages and all nationalities. Still voraciously taking everything in, Jeff was like a child in the deep covering of snow on their way back to the hotel, throwing snowballs and sliding along the footpath at break-neck speed. He was full of wonder at this new weather experience, and Lynn enjoyed seeing his high spirits much more than she enjoyed the feeling of snow being shoved down the back of her coat.

'You're lucky it's your first time,' she berated him, dodging to avoid a snowball down the front of her coat as well.

'That's what I said to you not so long ago,' retorted her boyfriend, who withdrew his attack chivalrously.

'Oh, my God, Jeff!' Suzanne pounced. 'You never miss an opportunity to big-note your sexual prowess, do you?'

The tall, handsome man put his hands up in innocence. 'Hey! Wait a minute. I didn't say anything of the sort. That's wishful thinking, Suzie. How d'you know I'm not referring to Lynn's driving lessons?'

The older woman was embarrassed, and the others laughed, even though they all suspected she had been on the right track all along. The handsome student turned his newly acquired snowballing skills on his old mate, who was more than happy to reciprocate in his drunken state. The two females wandered on ahead, hands in pockets and their collars pulled up to protect them from the chill wind.

'How are you two going these days?' Suzanne asked. 'You're very good at standing up to him.'

'I'm learning,' Lynn smiled. 'He's gorgeous. I never have to fight for too long. Half the time he's just teasing, which I used to find annoying, but I've got used to it now.'

'Well...' the twenty-two-year-old replied, diverting to one side as both men hared past their girlfriends, nearly knocking them over. 'I've never known him so laid back and happy. He was telling me about recording some of his songs. I can't wait to hear them. Are they good?'

'Brilliant,' the proud teenager answered without hesitation. 'He's such a natural performer. He studies everything so closely. He's learned all the moves that work for Elvis and Jim Morrison, and even some of the blues players. He can take them off pretty accurately.'

The country girl's eyes gave away her jealousy. 'That'd be right! Jacinta always raved about Jeff's Elvis impersonations. What is it about him? Whatever he tries, he always does really well. And now look! He's going out with you while I'm stuck in the middle of nowhere with a bunch of smelly dogs.'

Lynn laughed, anxious to change the subject. 'You enjoy running the kennels though, don't you?'

Suzanne nodded and smiled, but didn't have the chance to elaborate owing to a whirlwind of male attention which suddenly descended on the two women. Their energy expended, both men were panting and red in the face, having shed their gloves and unfastened their jackets. They collected their keys from reception when finally at their hotel, soon reaching their rooms and disappearing inside with arrangements to meet at eight o'clock for breakfast the next morning.

As was now customary, the young beauty held her hand out for the key and let her rowdy companion inside. She peeled off her gloves and coat, draping them over a chair, and used the large mirror to check how red her frozen cheeks were. She thought of her parents and what they might be prepared to tolerate in terms of late nights and unwholesome activities this close to competition. It had been a fun evening. The noisy but good-natured company of these very close friends was most enjoyable, and she loved how well they had accepted her into their *milieu.* She was also sure she would be extremely tired by the end of the weekend.

***

Lynn and Jeff were up and running two hours before breakfast, already out on the nursery slopes in advance of first light. The morning was cold but dry, and the student was keen to learn, having had remarkably little trouble dragging himself out of bed. Within an hour, they had progressed to the top of the short hill, where the gradient was a little steeper, and they had even begun to tackle parallel turns. Turning left was mastered far better than turning right, for some inexplicable reason, unleashing great amusement in both of them.

'It's easier just to jump,' the eager pupil offered, after demonstrating and ending up in the snow again.

'At the speed you're going now, yes,' his teacher chuckled, 'but I don't think you'll be jumping down a black run.'

At breakfast, Jeff proudly recounted his progress, to the amazement of his old friends. His lesson was over by lunchtime, and he had already been up and down the green runs several times, so was ready to attempt something more challenging, particularly after a few beers. To satisfy his curiosity, Gerry and Jeff headed off to an intermediate run, leaving the two girls in the cafeteria.

They talked over dessert and hot chocolate before venturing back out to the slopes, not expecting to see the boys again until after dark.

'So do you like Melbourne, now you've been here for half a year?' the famous teenager asked, as they were propping up their skis in the cage outside the café where they had agreed to meet the others.

'I like my life,' the older woman replied, 'but I hardly know Melbourne. Where I'm living, I could be anywhere. Some people living near me never even visit the city.'

'That's true,' Lynn agreed. 'It's the same around where my family's farm is. The nearest big towns, if you can call them that, are Lancefield and Kyneton, and that's as cosmopolitan as it gets for some people.'

'I don't regret coming down here though,' Suzanne was keen to add. 'I'm much more relaxed than I was in Sydney, in the rat race.'

'I don't even know what you used to do,' the schoolgirl admitted. 'Jeff's never mentioned it.'

'Oh, that's probably because I didn't really do anything. I graduated from uni' in 'seventy but only had dead-end jobs. I never knew what I wanted to do. Not like the boys. They always had so much drive, but I didn't have a clue. When my auntie left me the kennels, it was like, "Oh, OK then. That's what I'll do."'

While the two young women shared a laugh, a group of lively teenagers came rushing up to their favourite singing sensation, pestering her for autographs and photographs. Lynn apologised to her companion, who marvelled again at the sudden gathering, before standing up and being swallowed into the group by animated fans. This noisy activity only generated more interest, once other patrons realised who was frequenting the popular ski resort.

It took a long time to see off the last of the unruly queue which quickly built up at their table, since the diligent showbusiness sensation felt obliged to make sure she spent enough time with each person. Then, just as she sat back down to drink the last few sips of her now cold hot chocolate, Suzanne bashfully pulled out a camera of her own.

'Lynn, would you mind if I ask that man over there to take our 'photo?' she asked, suddenly tongue-tied. 'I've been wanting to ask you all weekend but was too scared.'

'Of course!' the pretty teenager exclaimed. 'You should've asked Jeff to take one of us.'

The older woman shook her head, turning to the next table to make her request. 'No, he would've given me heaps.'

Laughing at the accurate summation, Lynn waited for her friend to give a quick lesson to the obliging photographer, moving along the wooden bench so that the pair could sit close together. Suzanne quickly took her position, and they posed for the camera a few times, until the kind man was happy that he had captured them properly. As the Sydneysider zipped up the camera case and slotted it back into her ski suit pocket, Lynn turned to her with a serious look on her face.

'Suzanne, I have to ask you to keep the photo' to yourself, if you don't mind.'

'Oh, OK,' the surprised woman nodded. 'Can I show a few of my friends?'

'Oh, sure,' the celebrity affirmed. 'It's just that we can't have photographs of us being copied and sent around, in case they get into the wrong hands. Sorry. It's a pain, I know, but I always have to ask.'

The other woman smiled, glad to be given a glimpse into the world of these famous people. The child star was so natural to talk to that it was easy to forget she was from such a high-profile family. This had been a topic of conversation between the three musketeers when their new amigo had first come onto the scene, while Jeff had been going through the same transition, yet now their relationship seemed so rock solid that the older couple had begun to treat his new love like part of the furniture.

'No worries. That's fine. I'll only have one print developed.'

'Thanks,' the teenager said. 'It's especially hard at the moment, with the Olympics coming up and VCE exams after that. I can't afford to be seen out enjoying myself, when I should be in training. I had to fight really hard for permission to come on this trip, to be honest. But please don't tell Jeff that.'

'I won't. It's so nice to see you two getting on well these days,' the kennel owner told her. 'You seem so relaxed around each other.'

'We are. He's completely gorgeous to me. I'm very lucky. Every day's an adventure. Sometimes he gets too intense, but then we have a few days off because I'm travelling, and I'm ready for more intensity when I next see him. I just love him to bits.'

'And he loves you to bits too,' Suzanne echoed. 'I've never seen him so happy. He's funny though. Because he knows I'll be jealous, he never talks about you until I ask him a question, and then I can't shut him up!'

'Really?' Lynn exclaimed. 'That is funny. What I find so amazing is how much capacity he has for everything. He never seems to reach a limit, either for work, for play, for loving or hating. Does that make sense?'

Her boyfriend's long-time friend shook her head. 'He and Gerry have always been like that. I don't know how they keep up with their lifestyles. Jeff's just a bundle of sexiness, as far as I'm concerned. And doesn't he know it?'

Lynn laughed. 'I *will* tell him you said that! Gerry's funny too though. He's got such a bombastic turn of phrase. He reminds me of my dad; always wanting to be the centre of attention.'

Suzanne grunted. 'Yeah. Tell me about it. I get pretty, bloody tired of it, actually. He's just not at all subtle, is he?'

'No,' the starlet had to agree. 'You could never describe him as subtle. As subtle as a slap in the face, as Jeff would say! He'd be a trombone or tuba or something, if he were a musical instrument.'

It was the accountant's girlfriend's turn to laugh. She didn't know much about classical music, but understood these brass instruments to be particularly harsh, loud and overpowering.

'Perfect! What would Jeff be then?'

Lynn looked up towards the ceiling, thinking as she spoke. 'I don't know. I just came up with the analogy on the spur of the moment. What *would* Jeff be? A piano, I think, because of the versatility.'

'He certainly is versatile,' Suzanne confirmed. 'I've never met someone who can turn his hand to so many things. He just seems to know how to do everything, and if he doesn't, he learns really quick. I remember when Gerry taught him to drive, it only took him about three kilometres to master the gears, and he was away. It took me about six months to get comfortable changing gear.'

'He loves cars though,' Lynn said. 'It helps when you're interested in something. But then again, there aren't many things he's not interested in either.'

The two girls continued to swap notes about their men, sitting on the balcony and drinking more steaming hot chocolate while they waited for the intrepid snowmen to return from their long afternoon on the mountainside. The more Lynn put the joys of her romance into words, the greater the melancholy grew inside her. Chatting away cheerfully nevertheless, her friend was none the wiser and devoured the many insights into the multi-talented woman's life.

'Hey!' the celebrity cried out, once the pair of tall skiers came into view, both apparently unscathed. 'How did you go?'

Catching sight of their partners, the exhausted duo waved and wove their way through the bunches of people, all of whom seemed to have had enough at the same time and were removing skis, gloves and hats in front of the resort's eateries and shops. With his sunglasses perched on top of his head and his beanie sticking out of an unzipped pocket in his suit, Jeff slid quickly up to the cage and barrelled into it, causing his right ski to ping off his boot.

'Great!' he gasped, out of breath. 'It's fantastic! Not too elegant in parts, but I managed. This bloke's awesome. I couldn't keep up most of the time.'

The energised twenty-year-old scaled the wooden structure to greet Lynn up close and personally, and she kissed his icy cold but sunburned, unshaven face. She had never seen him so happy.

'What do you expect? It's your first day. No broken limbs is a good result.'

After shedding their bulky clothing and Frankenstein footwear, the foursome passed another cosy evening playing board games and drinking. The longer they spent together, the closer Lynn and Jeff wound around each other until their overt displays of affection became too much for Suzanne to bear, especially while her own boyfriend remained typically oblivious of everyone else but himself.

'Go to your room, guys,' she sneered, nudging Jeff's arm as he went in for another kiss.

The recent birthday boy grinned, deliberately adjusting his jeans to needle his old friend even further.

'Good idea,' he agreed. 'Why didn't I think of that?'

The six-year couple ordered another round of drinks, bidding their passionate companions a good night. Jeff shook Gerry's hand warmly and gave Suzanne a peck on the cheek, thanking them for sharing in his most enjoyable weekend, before pointing the object of his ardent affections towards the door. Lynn slotted her gloved hand into his, and they jogged back to the hotel, trying not to slip on the patches of black ice.

The young cynic teased his girlfriend about her rigorous pre-Olympic training regimen, receiving a thump on a tense shoulder in return. In this luxurious, rustic setting, the absent athlete didn't wish to be reminded of her father or to be forced to calculate how much extra spare time she would need to forfeit to catch up next week. Their day had in fact been very strenuous at times, even though what had passed between her lips could not exactly pass for the prescribed diet of an *élite* sportswoman.

At first, the sixteen-year-old jokingly refused to accept the duty of door opener, to serve her boyfriend right for the disrespect he had shown towards her family name. However, their individual needs to get into the bathroom soon hastened her acquiescence. Laughing, they fought each other for first access, and Jeff won narrowly.

'Do you want that real massage now?' the young woman suggested, watching her beautiful black stallion drop backwards onto the bed and hearing him let out a huge groan.

'From you or the beefy gay guy you described yesterday?'

Lynn leaped onto the bed, bouncing down beside him to stare up at the ceiling too. 'Your choice. It's your weekend.'

The happy man smiled, keeping his eyes closed as she slipped her hand inside his jumper and began to unfasten his shirt buttons. He had enjoyed the evening immensely, with the disconsolate mood he had detected earlier in the weekend now vanished from his dream girl's demeanour.

'What if I were to say the latter? Would you be able to deliver the goods?'

Lynn scoffed, backing off. 'Leave it with me.'

Jeff rolled over and quickly caught hold of her leg as it was retreating off the side of the bed. 'Not so fast!' he yelled. 'It'd be just like you to be able to call my bluff, so I'll choose you, if it's all the same to you?'

'Well, it's not all the same to me,' the sexy teenager chided. 'There's nothing the same about it. You think you can chop and change on a whim, and I'm not going to feel spurned? I don't know. The things I do for you.'

They lay in each other's arms fully clothed, their tongues searching, and feeling each other's excitement growing. It felt healthy for them to be in a strange town and far away from their normal lives; a chance to leave reality behind and get lost in each other.

'So can I try to free up some of the knots in your shoulders first?' Lynn asked, as they pulled back the heavy blankets on the massive, king-sized bed. 'I've been taking lessons from our physio'. I don't expect to be able to fix them completely, but it might make a difference. And if it does, we can keep doing it.'

'I'd love that,' her partner agreed. 'Do you mind? Will it hurt?'

'Yes, it will hurt,' the temptress nodded. 'Mine do, and I'm not all knotted up like you. Just tell me to stop if it hurts too much.'

Stripped to the waist, the lean, muscular man lay face down on the bed. Lynn sat across his back and covered his shoulders and neck in massage oil, spreading it everywhere with her strong hands.

Jeff groaned, this time in pure contentment. 'That feels fantastic.'

'Hold that thought, sir,' the enthusiastic *masseuse* smiled. 'Everything's about to change.'

Starting with gentle movements, Lynn gradually increased the pressure as she painstakingly located the knots on her lover's scapulæ, along his spine and in the muscles across the top of his shoulders and towards his neck. Each time she pushed into his flesh, she watched the muscles twitch curiously, imagining the sensation radiating away from the spot she was working.

'Exhale if it hurts,' she instructed her uncharacteristically quiet boyfriend. 'You're supposed to inhale before I put the pressure on and exhale while it's there.'

His head nodded, and he did his best to obey her instructions.

'Jesus, it does hurt,' he complained.

Lynn didn't let up. She could feel how deep the crystallised grains were, and in so many places. Her physiotherapist had given her a muscle map, marked with the places where tension tended to build up in people with nervous conditions, and Jeff's body had them all covered. After alternating around each set, focussing first on the right and then on the left side, she then switched her attention to his neck and to the base of his skull, pressing one thumb at a time into his skin.

The patient's breathing deepened considerably, but not once did he ask her to stop. The sportswoman knew he would be keen to withstand any measure she thought might help treat his pain. It made her feel super-close to him, and once more the sad thoughts drifted across her mind. Out of her man's line of sight, she uttered a silent vow to make the most of every moment from now on.

'Are you OK?' Lynn asked after a while. 'You're being the perfect client.'

'It's bloody agony,' a croaky voice answered, with a mix of humour and defeatism. 'It feels like there's a long way to go. You can stop if you like. You're on holiday too, in case you forgot.'

She continued undaunted. 'No. I'm determined to make some progress. Can I press harder?'

'No!' her victim exclaimed, as she moved his arms from under the pillow and positioned them straight down at his sides. 'Is it humanly possible to press any harder? This is a great cure for an erection, I have to tell you. I always wondered how a bloke could get through a massage without succumbing to desires of the flesh, but now I see it's perfectly feasible.'

Giggling, Lynn flicked the back of her man's head with her fingers.

'Stop thinking about sex!'

She worked her magic on his upper arms, one after the other. Drilling into the pressure points made him wince as the referred pain shot from his elbow right into his brain. Despite the incredible discomfort, Jeff couldn't deny how lucky he was to be in this position. The woman he had sought out to transform his life was currently sitting across his half-naked body, using up what must be the last drops of the day's energy on solving another of his irksome problems.

'Sorry,' the strong teenager murmured, seeing him jump again. 'I hate hurting you, but it feels a bit looser.'

The fortunate man surrendered gradually to the almost unbearable burning. After a while, his tormenter turned him around, so that he could flop his head over the end of the bed and stretch his shoulders out still further. At one point, her foot was levered against the end of the bed, not ten centimetres from her patient's face, almost pulling his arms out of their sockets.

'Are you sure you know what you're doing?' the squirming man groaned, both dissolving into fits of laughter. 'Are you trying to sabotage my skiing holiday altogether?'

'No. I'm trying to help you!' his feisty lover answered, collapsing down onto the floor, then twisting herself round to kiss his lips. 'Trust me, won't you? Just trust me.'

Jeff exhaled loudly. The simple but unexpected words from this gorgeous creature arrived like manna from heaven, the last straw for the troubled boy from the Stones Road. He had been hanging on by his emotional fingernails for the last fifteen minutes or so. He let out a blood-curdling moan, and Lynn watched him take in a whole chestful of air at once.

'Christ! I want to trust you so badly,' he told her, with huge tears dropping noisily onto the carpet beneath his gaze. 'I need this so badly too, and not just for the physical remedy. It's all linked; the mental with the physical. I can't stand the pain any longer, but I need you to keep going. I want you to unlock all these stupid fears that are inside me.'

Lynn felt awful, and not only for the distress she was inflicting on him at this moment. This adorable man clearly needed a great deal of reparation, and who knew how long the process would take? Did she have enough time between now and leaving for Munich to make a lasting difference? Somehow she doubted her ability to deliver sufficient improvement between now and then. She slid backwards off the bed and fetched the tissue box from the table, leaving it on the floor under her patient's chin. He thanked her and blew his nose clear, in order that he might continue breathing relatively normally for what remained of his torture.

'I really want to help you, Jeff. Let me do it, please?'

'Go for your life,' the young man gasped, sniffing back the tears. 'I love you so much. Do your worst, lady.'

She did her worst. The Olympian's knuckles, fingertips and thumbs worked deep into each pressure point, causing her man to shout out loud and swear profusely. After a while however, he began to feel a weird change; a cool, viscous liquid slowly slinking around like mercury inside the muscles of his shoulders and neck. An element of sensation began to return into his tingling fingers, and his upper spine crunched audibly when he flexed it. He hadn't been able to turn his head this far round in either direction for a number of years.

Lost in their own world, the couple was startled by the sound of the telephone ringing and immediately fell silent, as if they had been caught in some illicit act. Lynn crossed to the bedside table to answer the call while her patient took a long-awaited opportunity to stand up and roll his shoulders.

'Hello?'

'What the hell's going on in there?'

It was Gerry, of course. The pair grinned at each other guiltily, noticing how late it was.

'Nothing,' the perpetrator replied innocently, chuckling. 'Jeff's getting a massage.'

The young woman had to move the receiver away from her ear while their indomitable friend yelled in surprise.

'A massage? Jesus Christ! Who's doing it? Brunhilde the Great?'

'No. I am!'

By now, her boyfriend was in hysterics, able to hear every word his friend was saying from the room next door. He signalled for the receiver.

'Mate, you're missing something special in here,' he recounted. 'I'm going to be nine foot tall by the end of this!'

'Get dressed,' Gerry ordered. 'We're coming in.'

'I *am* dressed,' the younger man exclaimed, 'if you can believe that. Well, half anyway...'

The line went dead, and within a few seconds came a fierce pounding on their door. Lynn opened it, cloaked in a bathrobe, and there stood the neighbours, open-mouthed at the sight of their third musketeer back in his prior position, spread-eagled on the bed with his head hanging over the edge, bare above the waist and his back completely covered in red welts.

'And you claim to love him?' the businessman remonstrated to the blonde beauty. 'Looks like we arrived just in time, Suze.'

Suzanne was aghast, running her fingers over the marks on their old friend's skin.

'Does it sting?'

'Bloody oath, it stings!' Jeff gave a desperate laugh, rolling over onto his back and sitting up, 'but it's working a treat.'

'Is it?' Lynn asked, genuinely surprised. 'That's great!'

The young lovers hadn't swapped notes for several minutes leading up to the time when the telephone had interrupted them, meaning she had yet to receive the progress report which would have mentioned the new fluid sensations her client was experiencing.

'Who wants coffee?' asked Suzanne, now that the volume had returned to normal. 'I'll go and bring our cups in.'

The willing victim rolled off the bed, pretending to have lost the ability to stand up straight, which actually wasn't too much of an exaggeration. He felt wonderful though, now that the pain had reduced into a dull soreness. His back was loose, and his arms seemed at once longer and lighter. Was this how normal people felt? Damned good.

'If I can crawl that far, I'll make it. It's nice to see you guys,' he laughed.

Lynn sat on the bed, a little frustrated that her good work had ended prematurely.

'We'll have to start again now,' she moaned.

Gerry sat beside his friend's irresistible, school-aged lover and took hold of her arm, measuring the strength in her biceps. 'You *are* Brunhilde the Great! No wonder he's so scared of you.'

'We don't have to stop, angel,' the protective man said, motioning with a flick of his index finger to the lecherous accountant that he should move away from his precious property. 'I want more pain. I've got a lot to update my research file with.'

'OK,' his girlfriend replied, bolstered by his enthusiasm but also concerned for his privacy. 'Lie back down again. Let me at you!'

With refreshed vigour, albeit mostly for show, the superstar physiotherapist oiled the palms of her hands again, and Gerry gasped in delight.

'Hey! Now we're going to get a floorshow, Suzanne. Don't want to interfere, mate, but I always find it pays to get your pants off first. It saves on the dry cleaning.'

'Fuck off!' the arrogant man sneered.

'Shush!' Lynn warned, bashing the show-off on the back with the heels of both fists. 'You're supposed to be calm and relaxed, not swearing.'

'Sorry, gorgeous,' Jeff apologised, cowering theatrically beneath his *masseuse*'s looming hands. 'Anything you say, Brunhilde.'

The youngster slapped him again, harder this time, before sweeping her hands round in grand arcs from the small of his back to his neck. Since he had informed her that her efforts were paying off, she had taken on renewed confidence, which of course also meant renewed pressure.

'Jesus, Lynn, you're a sadist,' the patient did his best to laugh without choking. 'She wasn't doing it this hard earlier.'

'Concentrate,' the athlete instructed firmly. 'You've got to focus on getting rid of the knots just as much as I have.'

Unfortunately for both, the momentum had been lost. This was not an operation that could be properly executed in front of onlookers. The patient tried very hard to get back into the zone, but it was impossible with their friends sitting right there beside them. He sighed heavily, because he knew his caring dream girl would be disheartened at not being able to finish the job.

'Angel, you might as well stop. We can't do this with an audience, can we? I'm sorry. I can't concentrate.'

The sixteen-year-old realised her boyfriend felt genuinely thwarted too, but there was little point forcing the issue now that Gerry and Suzanne were with them. Jeff was right.

'OK. I'll let you off this time,' the generous young woman agreed, hauling him up to a sitting position by his pulsating deltoids. 'It's probably enough for a first session anyway.'

The grateful man kissed her tenderly, grabbed his coffee cup and some fresh clothes and disappeared into the bathroom to soap the greasy oil off his skin. Under the shower, he wept like a child, unable to fathom the complex, raging ecstasy swirling around his brain. Lynn Dyson had fixed the persistent, foggy headache he remembered lurking in his brain since primary school. In less than an hour, this enchanting woman had made him feel healthier than he had felt for as long as he could recall. Maybe he might even enjoy a full night's sleep…

When the emotional wreck had recovered sufficiently to return to his friends, he propped a few of the huge pillows up against the mahogany headboard and invited Lynn to sit in front of him, leaning her against his pummelled but now particularly libidinous body. It was half-past midnight in Queenstown, and the quartet sat watching a movie on the enormous bed. On the other side, their friends had adopted the same position, and pretty soon, Jeff was the only one left awake. He smiled at the sight of his sleeping *compadres*.

'Time for bed,' he suggested, rocking Gerry's shoulder. 'Get out of here, you guys.'

His sleepy saviour reached her arms up towards her boyfriend's face, and he kissed her hard-working fingers with love that immediately seeped through her skin.

'Do I have to go too?'

'Yes!' the older man pounced. 'You come and join us next door. That'd be fun.'

'Oh, no, you don't!' his mate snarled. 'The *masseuse* stays with me. I need more pain.'

Wishing each other goodnight after a very successful day, Suzanne and Gerry returned to their room. The half-naked, creaky patient gave his partner an apologetic smile, guessing she was perturbed that his friends had invited themselves in.

'That didn't quite go according to plan, did it?' he shrugged. 'Thanks for trying again. It was most definitely helping. I feel much more mobile already.'

Lynn gave him a rueful smile. 'That's OK. I could see how disgruntled you were too. It was annoying, but never mind. I don't want you to be too sore for tomorrow's skiing anyway.'

'Are you tired?' her boyfriend asked, downing another glass of water. 'I've lost track of how tired we should be now.'

'That's an odd thing to say,' the young woman chuckled, stretching and rearranging the pillows. 'I'm as tired as I should be already. Are you really feeling more mobile?'

'Absolutely. Look!' Jeff turned his head from right to left. 'But it's noisy as hell in my head. You should put your ear to my neck and see if you can hear what I can. It's a bit nauseous, to tell you the truth.'

The amateur physiotherapist did her boyfriend's bidding and was indeed able to hear the crystals in his deeply stressed muscles grinding as he moved his head from side to side.

She grimaced. 'Yuk! I can. What does it feel like?'

'Just like it sounds,' Jeff smiled, kissing her adorable, childlike face. 'Crunchy. You're right about having to concentrate. It took me a while to figure out what I was feeling, but I was getting the hang of relaxing the tension out of each muscle after the immediate pressure subsided. Can we try again when we get back to Melbourne?'

'Great! Yes,' Lynn happily agreed. 'I'm so glad. I wasn't sure how well it'd work.'

Her gorgeous enigma hugged her tightly. 'You just have to have faith. Believe in yourself. You should know that by now, Miss Dyson.'

'Let's go to bed,' the teenager invited, heading towards the bathroom. 'I think you'll be pretty sore in the morning.'

Waiting for her return, Jeff stared out of the window at the eerie mountain shadows, which stretched away into the distance behind the hotel. He took stock of where he was, both physically and emotionally. How did somebody like him end up receiving a therapeutic massage from Lynn Dyson in a luxury ski resort in New Zealand? What had happened to turn his life around so completely? Give thanks and keep quiet, he vowed.

'Beautiful, isn't it?' his girlfriend whispered, leaning against his tall frame.

'Yes, you are,' he replied. '*Es muy hermosa, señorita. Ven a la cama, cariña mia.*'

The lovers returned to their vast bed, pulling the sheets and blankets over themselves. Climbing on top, Jeff leaned down and kissed his dream girl with the passion he had been saving up all evening. Their undulations were slow and gentle, but the energy became almost violent in their feverish desire to give each other the utmost pleasure. The sublime act was over in less than ten minutes, leaving them spent, replete and ready to surrender to what remained of the night.

'Sorry I was such hard work on the way over here,' the elated man whispered, kissing the top of Lynn's head, which was resting on his heaving chest.

'You weren't that bad. It was interesting.'

'Interesting? There's that word again.'

The sixteen-year-old lifted her head and leaned back until she could see into her stallion's dark eyes. 'Like you were vacuuming everything up.

'I was,' Jeff smiled. 'That's a good analogy.'

The celebrity's eyes danced at the compliment. She hugged his body close, and he pulled the quilt higher, until it covered her shoulders completely. She reached up and tapped his forehead a couple of times.

'But where does it all go?'

'In there,' her boyfriend confirmed, nodding. 'For future reference.'

Switching off the bedside lamp, after several failed attempts at locating the correct switch from the array on the headboard had resulted in almost every light in the room flashing on and then off again, Jeff wrapped the giggling schoolgirl up in his arms and smothered her in late night kisses.

'Was flying what you expected?' she asked, yawning as she spoke.

'Yeah, pretty much. Still amazing though. I just can't fathom, even though I get physics,' the young man mused, 'how a couple of hundred people in a heavy metal object can stay in the air.'

Lynn chuckled again. 'Me neither! I just take it for granted, I s'pose.'

The boy from Canley Vale exhaled, hit by another sudden bout of unworthiness. What was he doing here? Valiantly, he struggled to purge his mind of such negativity, eager to continue on his journey towards "someoneness".

'I'll take it for granted soon too.'

His beautiful best friend's right hand swept lightly down his hairy chest and rocked his stomach.

'Good,' she sounded pleased with him. 'I'm so stoked to hear you say that!'

'You are the best,' Jeff whispered, his face so close to hers. 'Do you know how much I love you?'

Lynn kissed his nose. 'A lot?'

'No,' her handsome stranger countered. 'Way more than that.'

***

Bright shafts of light pierced the drowsy holidaymakers' eyelids almost simultaneously, the sun having climbed high enough in the sky to cast its rays on their hotel room window and around the edges of the heavy, flocked velvet curtains. Day Three of Jeff's birthday weekend! He shielded his eyes while he scanned the sumptuous furnishings again, pushing his mind to counteract the blues by imagining another fun day in the snow.

Realising that her gorgeous companion had awoken naturally, Lynn flipped herself over to kiss him a good morning, the one-nightmare night having been an additional blessing for the loving pair. His hair stuck out in various directions, and an imprint of a fold in the starched pillowcase was stamped into his cheek. He looked irresistibly hers, and love surged through her body from top to toe.

'Whoa, it's late!' the young man exclaimed, glancing over her shoulder to the clock on her bedside table. "We'd better get going. You're turning me into a sleep junkie.'

'You need it,' the happy teenager was overjoyed to take responsibility for this new habit.

'And I like it!'

The horny twenty-year-old let out an almighty roar, turned towards her pyjama-clad body and smothered it until she squealed with delight. He couldn't wait to get her out of these restrictive nightclothes, his own body radiating its usual heat and warming them both up nicely. Before long however, a need of a whole different nature reared its ugly head.

'The pressure from my bladder's waking me up these days,' he chuckled, sitting up. 'That's a new phenomenon! I can't even think about sex without seeing to that first.'

Lynn laughed, shouting after him as he made for the bathroom. 'See? There is a hierarchy of needs!'

'Yeah. OK, smart-arse,' his deep voice floated back through the door, 'but I still need to satisfy them all.'

The lovers took their sweet time in pleasing each other, with another, uninterrupted day of togetherness stretching ahead of them. They even schemed about dodging their next-door neighbours for a while after lunch, such was the pull to be alone.

As the agreed meeting time for breakfast rolled around, Lynn coaxed her eager but slothful partner into the shower, shivering while the water warmed up.

'Don't you ever feel cold?'

'Yeah, sometimes,' Jeff smiled, directing the powerful jet onto the sexy being of whose raptures he was certain he would never tire. 'Being around you makes me heat up. Passion is heat.'

She giggled. 'I heat you up so that you can heat me up!'

'*Cierto*, angel. Symbiosis, between friends.'

The rest of their long weekend was perfect. The snow on the Sunday morning was wetter and softer than the previous day's, and the determined novice spent more time buried in it than skimming the top of it. On the chair lift, ascending for their last run, the two couples spent a few minutes suspended in mid-air, one behind the other, due to some unknown problem.

'I wouldn't mind staying up here for a few hours,' the unusually becalmed dreamer admitted, noting the delay was equally welcome for his dream girl. 'Look how amazing this scenery is.'

Lynn nodded, leaning into his side. 'Yes, it's stunning.'

'*Como tú*,' her boyfriend responded, planting a kiss on her cold lips.

'Jeff, I won't be able to see you all next week,' the young star suddenly blurted out, as if she had been frightened to tell him. 'I'm just not going to get a chance to escape.'

Her impulsive statement caught the compassionate man off guard, such was the desperation in her voice. Perhaps she was becoming as dependent on their relationship as he was? How good would that be! Apart from the havoc it would play with her hectic life...

'That's OK. Let's not talk about it up here. Patience is a virtue, they tell me.'

The chair lift jolted and began to move again. Lynn smiled sweetly and caught a layer of snowflakes in the palm of her glove, blowing them towards her poetic and supportive boyfriend.

'Yeah,' she rued. 'And I used to think I had some.'

'Patience? You still do, I'm sure. There are different levels of patience for different things,' the student went on, a little anxious and confused by her tone. 'I have endless patience for this current journey, and even for the 'plane trip home, but none whatsoever when it comes to our week apart.'

'Oh, that's so true,' the pretty teenager exhaled. 'That's exactly how I feel. I've had such a fantastic time with you this weekend. I really don't want to go back to Melbourne tomorrow. How ungrateful am I?'

Jeff scoffed. 'About as ungrateful as me, by the sound of it.'

They dismounted from the wobbling chairlift and skied off to follow Gerry and Suzanne, who were already lining up to take another blue route. Putting their heavy hearts away, the younger pair prepared for their last set of exhilarating twists and turns down the steep hillside before they would have to surrender their expired ski passes and return the rented equipment.

After a shower and a change of clothes, the revellers soon found themselves outside in the fresh air again, looking for somewhere memorable for dinner. They ended up on Cow Lane, in a tiny Italian restaurant, where the staff sported huge personalities that complemented their guests' perfectly. On their last evening, the four friends mixed with the locals in the bar, and Lynn succeeded in blending with the crowd, well protected by her posse.

Every now and again, Jeff thought he caught that melancholy look in her deep, blue eyes again, choosing each time to ignore it. That was a feat in itself, given his paranoia, but he took the view that the gorgeous woman would share whatever it was with him whenever the time was right. They would need to pack and check out first thing the next morning, and he knew she would be anxious to return to her whirling hamster-wheel of a schedule.

When the holidaymakers reached Melbourne's CBD from the airport on Monday lunchtime, the celebrity asked Gerry to divert to the recording studios and drop them off there because she had an idea for a song that she wanted Jeff to hear. Not being in any rush to say goodbye after such a blissful weekend, the student was only too happy to indulge her, and made himself comfortable on the floor while she played the piano and sang.

'I love how I feel with you,' her sweet voice murmured, picking out a new chord sequence.

'Me too. With you, I mean.'

Lynn smiled and caught her breath. 'I've had the best time these last few days. Just the thought of going back to Admin on my own makes me dizzy.'

Jeff hauled his string of aching muscles upright and took a seat at the piano next to his favourite singer, putting his arm around her and kissing her temple. Was this ever-increasing desire to stay together simply due to the passage of time or to the fact that they had enjoyed their short holiday so much? He hoped that at least one of these might be true, because he couldn't bear the third alternative, in that his formerly irrepressible ray of sunshine appeared to be harbouring some inner darkness of her own these days.

'You're just hungry,' he nudged her playfully and banged out some loud, major cadences in return. 'Eat some ice cream with chocolate sauce before bed, and you'll be as right as rain in the morning.'

The tired sportswoman rested her head on his shoulder, making him flinch again. 'Oh, sorry! Is that Doctor Diamond's remedy?'

'Sure is. Failsafe, angel.'

Long Way Down

There was no easy way to tell him what she needed to tell him. Lynn had agonised over several different phrases during the last few days, but this morning had opted for the direct approach. Her devoted *paramour* would appreciate the plain truth, and it would allow them to express their emotions freely, with no hidden agendas.

'Jeff, I'm going away.'

The perceptive young man had suspected something was wrong from the moment he caught sight of her. Although instantly recognisable in her smart school uniform and with her long, golden hair tied up in a ponytail, there was a certain absence in the way his normally statuesque maiden was standing... no, leaning... against the wall. Lynn Dyson lacked her trademarked energy and poise.

The tall, athletic student jogged up to his waiting girlfriend, annoyed that she had arrived before him. It was also unusual for the celebrity to be loitering outside early and alone. He always liked to beat her to any arranged meeting point, hating the thought of her ever being placed in danger. With a broad smile, he opened the glass door, ushered her into the café and watched her lackadaisically drop her heavy school bag onto the floor. Something was definitely wrong.

The couple had talked for an hour on the telephone the previous afternoon, after their long week apart, and had agreed to meet for breakfast in the Botanic Gardens. Being the last Monday morning in July, the Melbourne Academy gates were open again after the winter break, and Lynn had been driven back from Benloch the previous evening by both parents. She had woken up petrified of what this day would bring. She picked a table in the corner, pleased to see there was no-one else in the café. Greeting the sixteen-year-old with a tender kiss as she passed him, her boyfriend motioned for her to sit down and signalled politely to the woman behind the counter.

'What did you say?' her boyfriend asked, having clearly heard the first time.

Lynn's eyes welled up, and she could feel a huge lump swelling in her throat.

'I'm going away,' she repeated, coughing and trying to maintain her composure. 'Dad's taking me out of school at the end of this term. I'm finishing Year Twelve remotely.'

Jeff's heart sank like a stone. 'Why? How remotely?'

'I'm going to the US. I've been enrolled in a sports programme at UCLA and I'm going to be making a string of movies. It's a great opportunity,' she issued her rehearsed yet lacklustre answer, trying her best to smile.

Anger, as ever, was the young man's initial and unavoidable reaction. So he had been right to pay attention to the bizarre sense of foreboding which had gripped him in Queenstown; the mad scramble of words he had been unable to mould into anything lucid until this moment. As it turned out, it had been a perfect example of the ethereal *déjà-vu* he had described to Lynn at the convent but then had comprehensively failed to act upon.

'Is it?' he asked through gritted teeth. 'For whom?'

This was the day the ambitious student from New South Wales had been dreading ever since he had first made contact with the girls of his dreams.

No warning. Here it was.

Lynn reached for her boyfriend's hand. He initially recoiled but checked himself just in time, thinking better of it. *Don't be so selfish*, he scolded his mean streak.

'It's a great opportunity for me,' the starlet continued, drawing on the characteristic resolve instilled in her from an early age, although her words sounded hollow when she imagined how her passionate lover would hear them.

'Mmm... How long have you known?'

Lynn sighed and bit her lip, brushing a lone tear from the corner of her right eye and looking anywhere but into his eyes. 'Oh, God, Jeff. It's been the hardest, hardest thing. About six weeks ago, my parents told me it was all confirmed. I was hoping it would fall through and that I'd never have to break the news, but it didn't. Then I wanted to wait until we came back from New Zealand. I didn't want to spoil your birthday.'

The young star's breathing was laboured, desperate not to dissolve into tears in a public place. This was clearly no easier a conversation for her to initiate than it was for him to accept. Jeff thumped the table with both fists and pushed back on his chair, making the coffee cups and spoons rattle on their saucers.

'Christ!' he exclaimed.

'Shhh,' Lynn urged. 'Do you want to go somewhere else?'

Her magnificently ferocious man drew his chair back in. 'No. I'm sorry. It's not your fault,' he responded, doing his best to appear conciliatory.

'It's nobody's fault.'

The teenager's heart became heavier with every utterance and with each vain attempt made by her gallant gentleman to hide his true feelings. She began to reach her hand across the table again, dying to touch him, but something in his eyes this time told her to back off.

'Oh, yeah?' his sarcastic voice challenged. 'Let me think about that for a minute.'

The schoolgirl drank her coffee quietly, staring at the table. She wanted to give him time for the news to sink in. She had had over a month to stew over her situation. His dark eyes made no effort to hide his emotions, staring wildly as fumbling fingers held the cup to her mouth, and she found his predictable reaction both edifying and withering. Would this be the last time she saw the wonderful Jeff Diamond? She really hoped not but certainly wouldn't blame him.

Jeff looked across the table and caught her eyes in his, so menacingly that she almost turned away. 'So how long have we got?'

Lynn wondered whether he could read her mind, for this was exactly the information she was now silently rehearsing.

'I leave for the Olympics at the beginning of September, and then go to California straight from Munich,' she answered. 'It'll give me a week or so to settle in before the college year starts over there.'

The twenty-year-old fell silent, gazing out of the window at nothing in particular. After a while, he stood up and swallowed down the remainder of his coffee. Almost throwing the empty cup down onto its saucer, he spoke gruffly.

'I can't stand this; sitting here, pretending everything's fine. Can we go?'

Obediently, the young woman donned her blazer and picked up her bag. Her boyfriend offered to take it from her, but she declined with an apologetic smile. They walked out of the café and onto the path which led behind the Herbarium. It was a cloudy day in Melbourne, though not cold enough to encourage them to move with any haste. Leaning on the railing by the rose garden, Jeff lit a cigarette and turned to the famous schoolgirl, blowing a plume of smoke into the cool air.

'So what's the plan?'

Her man was calmer than Lynn had expected. His hot, Latin temper was well under control, even though she was sure he would be seething inside. She leaned on the fence beside him, but neither acted on the acute pull to touch each other. There were quite a number of people around, on their way to work or school, or out for their morning jog. She felt like she had been transported into a parallel world, where she could see and hear everything around her, but where only she and Jeff existed at that precise moment.

'Well… That's up to us,' she ventured sadly. 'Up to you, I mean.'

'Up to *me*?' the student exclaimed, anger boiling up again. 'If it were up to me, you wouldn't be going in the first place.'

'Come with me to school, please?' the dignified young lady requested, pushing her lethargic body off the railings. 'It's too horrible to stay here. I feel like I'm stuck in a bad dream.'

Sympathetic to the familiar observation, her dazed boyfriend put an arm around her shoulder generously, and the dejected couple headed off towards Domain Road. They walked in silence for a few minutes, mired in their individual sadness, while horns beeped and voices shouted the usual morning greetings from the locals who regularly spied Lynn Dyson on her way to school.

'Are you alright?' the teenager glanced up and asked. 'I'm sorry this has to happen. I wish there was some way we could carry on.'

'Yes, well…' he answered, avoiding making eye contact. 'I assume by that you mean we have to break up. Completely, that is.'

Lynn sighed. 'How else? I can't expect you to wait for me while I'm off in California doing all these things. We're talking about two years here.'

The manic depressive stopped in his tracks, this latest piece of news sending shock waves through his ear drums. His stomach was seized by a painful cramp that made him want to bend double. It hadn't occurred to him to enquire after the timeframe. Two years was an eternity.

'Two years? That's a fucking long time to be away from your family,' he deflected his distress back onto its messenger as passively as he could. 'How do you feel about all this?'

The young woman dealt him the party line. Now that their fate was out in the open, she saw no value in doing anything else. It didn't make much difference how she felt. The decision had been made, and they had no choice but to live with it.

'Jeff, it's not about how I feel. It's about the opportunities I get to do things that so few other people get to do. It'd be stupid of me to pass this up. I had hoped I'd be able to go to uni' here or even in Sydney, but Dad chose this programme, so I have to do it.'

Disappointed by her apparent capitulation, the irate rebel took hold of his lover's strong shoulders roughly and spun her round to face him. A passer-by gave them a concerned look, but the celebrity smiled at her, and she walked on.

'Lynn, it's your life. What do *you* want?' he raised his voice.

'No, it's not my life yet, remember?' the sixteen-year-old replied, with tears in her eyes. 'I'm still under age, and my parents are giving me the best start in life they can. I need to do this. I don't want to split up. I really, really don't. But we have to.'

Jeff stepped off the footpath and down a driveway leading to a pair of huge, black-painted, wrought iron gates that led back into the Botanic Gardens. The celebrity followed him through the entrance and down one of the winding pathways, through the long-established shrubberies and flowerbeds.

'Come over here,' he invited, waving her towards him.

The teenager obeyed, and they sat on a park bench together. Initially, she had positioned herself at the opposite end of the slatted, wooden seat from her smouldering companion, but he immediately slid across to be close to her. She felt almost embarrassed, rather like the hesitation she had felt on that first night in his apartment when she had realised she could well be in danger.

'I'm going to be late for school,' she said, hazarding a smile.

Jeff leaned over and kissed her. 'You won't. We can go in a minute.'

Hating herself for presuming the worst, Lynn dissolved into tears, sobbing in the arms of her kind, devoted ally, which in turn ripped his heart out. For his part, the student was far too angry to cry. He simply wanted to grab Bart Dyson by the throat and force him to change his mind, but he knew he couldn't divert this new tangential shift in the champion's life. Despite everything, Jeff Diamond was a man of his word.

'Angel, when we first met, I promised you I wouldn't stand in your way. If this is something you need to do, then you have to do it. Just understand though, please, that I'm never going to like it unless you can prove to me it's what you *want*. But regardless of what I believe or don't believe, I have to respect your decision.'

'Thanks,' his girlfriend sniffed, drying her eyes with a pressed, white handkerchief that she pulled from her blazer pocket and kissed him tenderly. 'Can we keep seeing each other until I go? Please?'

The forlorn student nodded. 'I hope so. I guarantee I'm going to be lousy company between today and when you leave, but let's see how good we can make it, huh? I love you and I'm going to treasure every moment we have left together. How does that sound?'

'It sounds as good as anything could, under the circumstances,' the young woman acknowledged. 'Thanks for being so understanding. I was dreading having to tell you.'

The tortured soul from the wrong side of town was nothing if not understanding. He had been understanding all his life. It was his best and worst trait, he concluded. The couple strolled hand-in-hand the rest of the way to Melbourne Academy, the schoolgirl having this time allowed her gallant suitor to carry her bag, each searching for topics of conversation to lift the mood. She was a little sceptical of how well he had accepted their fate, and neither did she expect this to be the end of his anger, grateful to be at least parting on peaceful terms this morning.

Michelle England caught them up just before the school gates, excited about something which she could hardly wait to share with her close friend. Unaware of the pair's heartrending start to the day, she waved cheerfully to the tall, handsome man she had come to know fairly well. Taking his cue, Jeff kissed the famous beauty goodbye, judging that a quick exit would be best for everyone.

'I don't think we should see each other tonight,' he whispered, momentarily steering her away from Michelle. 'We need time to sort things out in our heads. Or in my head, anyway. Is that OK?'

Lynn nodded, fighting back the tears once more.

'OK,' she agreed, before a horrific thought immediately caused her head to spin. 'Are you going to see someone else tonight?'

Her lover's eyes turned thunderous again. 'No,' he answered without hesitation. 'Nothing could be further from my mind. And besides, I'd have hoped you'd think better of me, if I want any chance of seeing you again before you go.'

Lynn forced a weak smile. They each knew this was a question and answer combination that they both deserved.

'Thank you. I'm sorry. I had to ask.'

Jeff shrugged. 'I'll ring you tomorrow after work. I love you. Please don't forget.'

The young lady sniffed, straightening her stance to better befit her status. 'I won't. I love you too.'

The couple kissed for a long time, well able to hear Michelle huffing and puffing in disgust behind them. Then, stepping back, Lynn joined her friend and walked through the gates, turning once for a final wave, only to see her mystery man already marching in the other direction without looking round.

'Did you tell him?' the older teenager asked, suddenly noticing her schoolmate's red eyes. 'Oh, my God. You just did?'

'Yes,' the sporting star replied, unable to prevent herself from crying again. 'And I don't want to talk about it, if you don't mind. It's a horrible, horrible day, and I just want to forget about it.'

The saddened redhead put her arms around her best friend's shoulders and hugged her.

'Sorry. I'll shut up.'

***

Anger was a powerful emotion. Anger on top of a breaking heart was worse.

The hurt felt disappointingly familiar to Jeff as he walked back along the river towards Richmond. And what was more, he recognised, its full force couldn't possibly have been felt yet, because his mind was still racing and the bad news hadn't been properly classified, categorised and filed into his highly analytical brain.

What the fuck would he do right now? The lost boy's head was spinning. He didn't have to work this morning and he certainly wasn't in the mood to study. He didn't trust himself to drive anywhere either, scared he might go crazy and end up crashing into a wall or even harm someone else. Feeling spaced out and utterly hollow, he turned around and headed across to Flinders Street station, where he bought a ticket and picked a platform at random.

The student sat on the train, with his elbows on his knees and his head in his hands. As he counted the suburban stations by, the impact of Lynn's news began to hit home. His heart was pounding, and his lungs felt like they were too big for his rib cage. He was losing control drastically, and he tried his hardest to steady his breathing, sitting back and staring out of the window as the scenery trundled along. After nearly five months of sublime happiness, he was suddenly facing the future alone again.

The old paranoia was back too. Their horrific fate was all his fault. In his anguish, Jeff convinced himself it was. Why else would Bart Dyson rip his daughter away from everything she knew and loved and send her to bloody America? What did UCLA have that Melbourne Uni' didn't? For Christ's sake, the big man had his own fucking sports programme down on the farm.

The dejected man punished himself for neglecting to insure against this eventuality. How many times had he casually mentioned the high probability of their relationship coming to an end? He had forgotten to invoke his self-preservation plan, so perfect had the match been. Why had he let himself get so close to Lynn? He had always known this day would come and yet, for all his professed intelligence and self-awareness, he had failed to protect himself. He had become so wrapped up in her perfection, drawing her into his innermost dreams and fears. He had knowingly built a dependence on her, and now this great void would leave him high and dry in less than two months' time. How stupid was he? How absolutely fucking stupid! Yes, he considered himself a survivor, but this was going to be one hell of a survival exercise.

And where was Lynn in all this, while he was dishing out the blame? No, the scarred man chided, she was faultless. She was doing what she thought she should. But then again, she had been harbouring this terrible secret for a month without giving anything away. His instincts had been accurate when they had picked up a strange signal or two while away in Queenstown, but otherwise the gorgeous teenager had kept everything to herself. That showed some hardness of heart, Jeff decided. Perhaps his dream girl wasn't as blameless as his blind, lovelorn heart would have him believe? Perhaps this was all a game for her? Puppy love which she had now outgrown. Bloody hell! He despised himself for falling so hard.

The student felt suddenly sick. The train pulled into an outer suburban station, and he rushed to jump off. He vomited into a litter bin on the platform, surrounded by disgusted senior citizens who were setting off for a day's shopping. He could hear them muttering about alcoholics and describing him as a delinquent. Hey, great! He was back in his old world again. *Welcome home, you fucking waste of space*, he sneered. The lowlife had enjoyed his brief sojourn on the Riviera, putting on a suit and a smile and sharing Lynn

Dyson's rarefied air, but now he was being reminded in no uncertain terms that he didn't belong.

The boy from Sydney's west wandered out of the station and into the street. He had no idea where he was and hadn't even bothered to check the name of the station. It was nearly nine-thirty, so he must have travelled quite a distance. He bought a coffee and a copy of The Age and sat down outside the run-down café, aware that he needed to get himself straight. And fast. He tried his best to concentrate on reading the newspaper and gradually began to feel human again, smoking one cigarette and then another to calm his nerves. And then another coffee and another cigarette.

The lady behind the counter asked the attractive but very pale man if he was feeling alright. He wondered what he must look like, to garner such sympathy from a total stranger. With the coolest of half-smiles, Jeff assured her he was fine, lying from the very core.

After an hour or so, the wretched twenty-year-old walked back to the station and waited next to the opposite track for a train returning to the city. His shift in the computer room was due to commence at one o'clock, and thankfully his creative juices were flowing again, spurred on by his hyperactive and over-emotional mind. By the time he was back at Flinders Street, he already had the seeds of several new songs. All desperately sad songs, of course, but the sad songs were also the ones which made the most money.

The student made a pact with himself while walking home along the river. In the two years of Lynn's immersion in the American Dream, he would transform himself into a "someone". Someone she couldn't resist, and someone who could thumb his nose at Bart and Marianna Dyson when their adult daughter chose him in spite of it all.

This was the same way the tormented kid had survived his teenage years, setting himself a series of goals and putting every ounce of his being into their achievement, using any means at his disposal to get what he wanted. The other choice was unthinkable in this apparently finite scenario, no matter how tempting a picture Gravity the troll tried to paint. If he ended his life, which was the course of action he craved more than anything right at that moment, he would never know whether his dream girl really loved him or if they might rekindle a future together beyond this ominous and suffocating two-year sentence.

Taking a long-term view must become his new imperative. The old soul had told his teenaged muse that four months of her love had counteracted nineteen years of childhood unhappiness. Time to put that resolution to the test! He only needed to endure another twenty-four months to secure the chance to start again with his beautiful best friend, who by then would be a grown woman and in charge of her own destiny.

Waiting at a set of traffic lights for the opportunity to cross the busy highway, Jeff's gaze alighted on the tall buildings in the distance, looming a grey-brown colour against the heavily overcast sky. Lynn's tearful face filled the foreground of his mind's eye. How quickly their state of grace had been torn down... He clenched both fists, hit by extreme feelings of hatred for the Dyson parents, who would have done better never to have let their beautiful princess out to play if they wished to protect her from discovering the world outside their castle walls.

Australia's high society family had placed their bets, just as the humble, State-sponsored nobody had. To assist their cause however, they had an abundance of the very commodity he lacked: the power to manage the consequential loss. They would sail on, safe in the knowledge that a man like him was unlikely to possess the means to pursue their daughter, whereas he was left to pick up the pieces and work out how to put them back together again and shrink the gaping hole in the puzzle's centre.

And Lynn? She would be OK after the initial shock wore off, the abandoned lover reluctantly acknowledged. She was made of stern stuff, and therefore, so must he be. If they couldn't have what they wanted right now, they must ride out the next two years by taking their pleasure anyway they could. To pass the time, as his dream girl had said. Again, her rational alternative was by far the more sensible solution: two more years of turning on the charm and losing themselves in other people's embraces until they could be together again. Jeff chuckled bitterly. Was Lynn Dyson destined to become a sexual mercenary too, surrounded by West Coast college boys? Fancy that!

Only another two years... The young man examined his reflection in a shop window as he walked along Bridge Road, dragging his lead-filled shoes. The sun's reflection made the contrast too stark to see his face clearly, but he was sure it didn't look good.

'OK, mate,' he muttered to the shadow in the glass. 'That's a good enough plan. Now stop feeling sorry for yourself and get on with it.'

Mercifully, the hours at the university that afternoon were busy. Several final year students needed his help, and their difficult problems provided a welcome distraction for the intelligent technologist. Arriving home though, the temptation to destroy his own front door was overwhelming, such was the residual anger, and the young man struggled with his morbid fears for five minutes or so before unlocking the door and fighting through the screams of pain and ugly intruders to face quite the bleakest of futures. He drank steadily from Lynn's birthday bottle of Glenfiddich and began to work out some chords and melodies for the jumble of songs churning around in his mind.

The empathetic twenty-year-old dared to wonder how his stunning temptress would be feeling this evening. She had immense powers of concentration and would have used them wisely to forget about their predicament for the day. His compulsive self wanted so much to call her or to see her, needing to capitalise on however many precious hours he could persuade her to allocate his way. One thing was peculiar though: there was now no sexual urgency whatsoever percolating through his thoughts, as if his body had already withdrawn from their physical relationship.

This reaction was totally unrecognisable for the red-blooded adolescent, and yet he felt strangely comforted. Perhaps it might be easier not to resort to pleading with Lynn to stay if his libido were for once not leading the charge. Easier to pretend that he wasn't addicted to everything she had brought him over the last few months. Wouldn't her father love to know the damage his daughter would be leaving in her slipstream as she flew out of Tullamarine!

***

The next day, Jeff spent the morning in the computer laboratory and attended classes in the afternoon. His head was heavy after spending a dark night with the whisky bottle, but he managed to drum up sufficient enthusiasm to ensure no questions were asked. Still prepared for the potential of a further descent into his mind's foggy dungeon, the young man reactivated his well-practised self-defence mechanisms with monotonous deliberation.

The answering machine light was already flashing when the student arrived home at five-thirty that evening, having also successfully negotiated some extra shifts at the pub to assist with his new mission of passing the time. His heart clutched at the brittle straws of fantasy, hoping that Lynn had called to tell him the trip had been cancelled and that their previous conversation had all been a big mistake. Sadly, this was not the case.

'Jeff, it's me. Are you OK? I'm really worried about you. Please ring me when you get this message. I love you.'

The bitter man's first thought was to make her wait. He wanted the privileged and ambitious superstar to know how much her street kid was hurting. The dependant inside needed her to know exactly how serious this was.

Let her sweat, he vexed while taking a shower, only to have guilt get the better of him fairly soon while standing under the hot water. He castigated himself for being such a selfish pig. As usual, his primal impulse was far from the mature attitude of someone who considered himself an expert communicator. The sixteen-year-old's message sounded genuinely concerned for his welfare, as he hoped she would be, and if the shoe were on the other foot, he would hate not knowing. Dressing quickly, Jeff returned to the sofa, picked up the telephone and dialled the top-floor apartment at Dyson Administration.

'Hey, Lynn. How are you?'

'Oh, thank God! I was getting really worried. Where are you?'

He could almost feel the relief in her voice.

'At home,' he answered, endeavouring to regulate the boiling cauldron inside.

Don't take it out on her, you fucking idiot, he cursed under his breath. This special woman cared about him, leaving aside the unpalatable situation that was about to tear them apart. Did he want to spoil what little time they had left together?

'And how are you?' Lynn asked her tentative follow-up question. 'It was so hard not to ring last night, and then my brain started to panic that I should've.'

The downhearted student scoffed. 'You sound like me. No wonder you're leaving.'

'Jeff, don't say that,' his girlfriend insisted, groaning in objection. 'That's not fair. Andrea said she saw you yesterday on the station platform at Mitcham, and you looked terrible. It made me even more worried because I didn't know why you'd be in Mitcham.'

The twenty-year-old instantly became defensive. Now her friends were spying on him. He hardly wanted their imminent break-up to be turned into a soap opera for his girlfriend's squawking private school buddies.

'I was bloody ropable, Lynn. I just got on the first train out of Flinders Street. I don't even know where Mitcham is. I got off, walked around, read the paper with a coffee and then came back again, that's all.'

The teenager was placated to a degree. She could picture her enigmatic stranger doing exactly as he described, and the image made her cry. All her genuine plans for fixing sore shoulders and nightmares, abating his addictions and being around to see the launch of his rock star career were fading fast into the sunset, which itself was cloaked in dark clouds. Would his train even still be running by the time she was ready to jump back on board?

'OK. That's good, I suppose. So how are you? You didn't answer before.'

'How do you think I am?' he responded, trying not to sound too bitter.

'Unhappy, like me. And angry. Have you been at uni'?'

'Yes,' her boyfriend snapped this time. 'Please stop asking me questions, angel. I'll cope, OK? It'll just take me a few days to get my shit together and work out what happens next. Tell me about you instead.'

His girlfriend sighed. 'OK. You're right. I'm sorry. I just don't want you to do anything horrible.'

'You mean kill myself?' the tired man riled at the poorly camouflaged euphemism, his sarcasm too raw to conceal. 'You can say it, Lynn. Christ knows, I'm thinking about it. Don't bother about making it sound nice. It's not nice, right? But *c'est la vie*, baby.'

By now, his dream girl was weeping into the telephone without inhibition. 'Jeff, please. I'm so sad about this too. I'm worried about you.'

'Hey, I'm sorry,' the dejected student capitulated, somehow still unable to feel guilty about causing her additional stress, despite taking strength from the honest emotional outpouring. 'Please don't cry. I'm being an arsehole. Just ignore me. Thanks for caring, angel. I don't want to hurt you.'

'Thanks,' Lynn sniffed back the tears and put her game face back on. 'Do you feel like doing something tonight? I'd really like to talk to you in person.'

'Sure. What'd you like to do?'

'How about the movies? There must be a few good ones to choose from.'

Jeff resisted the temptation to laugh at the irony of her unwitting punishment. 'We can't talk much in the movies, but I don't think we've got much to talk about anyway.'

'No, I know,' the sixteen-year-old sighed. 'It'll help pass the time, as I said before. Find our feet, I think. I'd like to figure out how we're going to spend the next two months.'

'Yeah. You're right. That's important. Although I'm not sure I subscribe to the time-passing option. I'd rather make it stand still, to be honest. Shall I come to Admin? We can work it all out from there.'

Disconcerted by the voice of reason she had come to respect so highly now scarcely hidden behind the blind terror of Little Boy Blue, Lynn was grateful for his co-operation. How could she let this latent genius disappear from her world? There was no hiding the fact that they were both distraught over their respective new and wholly independent futures, but if they were going to stay together for the remaining months, somehow they both needed to learn how to focus on the positives.

'OK. Just turn up when you can. I'll be here. Thanks, Jeff.'

'See you later then. About half an hour. Hey, and I'm sorry, OK?'

'That's alright,' the sympathetic teenager replied. 'So am I. It's going to be hard for both of us over the next few weeks. See you soon.'

They hung up, the air in both homes thick with despondency. Months had already turned to weeks, and soon the remnants of their respecting relationship would be measured in days. Jeff lay back on the couch for a few minutes, detesting his predicament and the negativity it was causing him to unload onto his beautiful saving grace. He vowed to be agreeable towards her from now on, and to show her that he was bigger than this godforsaken wreck of a man. They weren't talking about another lifetime here...

***

The usual anticipation Jeff felt when driving the four kilometres from home to Dyson Administration was notably absent that evening. His testosterone production plant had shut down in sympathy with his heart. Not a bad thing, on reflection, he decided, since it would allow him to focus better on getting the best outcome he could for the next few weeks. He didn't want his sex-drive to force him into behaviour he might later regret.

Alastair, the dour, Scottish security guard, was on duty. 'Good evening, Jeff,' he said, letting the tired-looking man through the barrier. 'Miss Lynn's expecting you.'

'Great, thanks,' the regular visitor acknowledged without ceremony.

Indeed she was. The lift opened on the penthouse floor, and Jeff made his way down the quiet corridor, wondering if her parents were also in residence. Inside the apartment, the sixteen-year-old was working at her desk and immediately jumped up and ran into his arms.

'Oh, it's so good to see you,' the schoolgirl gushed, hugging him tightly.

'You too,' Jeff agreed. 'Sorry I was such a shit to you on the 'phone. I promise I'll be more helpful going forward.'

'It doesn't matter. I don't blame you and I'd much rather know how you really feel. I rang for film session times. They're written down on the pad, over there. What would you like to see? Your choice.'

Taking off his leather jacket and draping it across the arm of the couch, the new arrival sat and scanned down the list, letting out a long sigh. 'To tell you the truth, angel, I'd rather not go to the pictures. I'd prefer to do something more active. I'm like a rifle waiting to release both barrels.'

'Oh, OK. What about badminton?' his girlfriend suggested. 'We should get a court if I ring now. Have you got shorts and stuff in the car?'

'Yeah, I have, actually. I didn't know what we'd end up doing. How are you, anyway?'

'Alright,' she answered. 'Considering... I keep finding myself crying.'

Jeff nodded, signalling for her to join him on the couch. 'Know what you mean! Did you tell your parents I was angry?'

'No,' Lynn responded with defiance. 'I'm not going to tell them anything, apart from the fact that you know I'm going overseas. I just don't want to give them any reason to stop us seeing each other for the remaining time. And I don't want to give them the satisfaction...'

'Satisfaction for what?' the furious man interrupted. 'To know they've got rid of the nuisance that was hanging round their daughter?'

The young woman glared in frustration, ruing the very short duration of his promised helpfulness, and he put his hands up in apology. This type of exchange wasn't going to get them anywhere.

'You know what? I don't want to hear about it. Let's just go, shall we?'

Relieved, Lynn held her hands out and led him into the bedroom, accepting a contrite kiss. She changed quickly into sports gear, and the couple were soon on their way to Albert Park. During the drive there, they swapped stories about the mundanery of their ordinary days and skirted around the heartbreaking topic hanging over them.

'This was a much better idea,' the famous athlete admitted, audaciously holding her boyfriend's hand and walking through the crowded foyer with her head high.

'Yep. Gives us a chance to vent our aggression.'

Fortunately, theirs was the only court in use on one side of the large sports hall, which gave both players a chance to properly let off steam. The sixteen-year-old smashed a low shot over the net and watched her opponent scramble forwards to reach the shuttlecock before it hit the boards. Jeff nodded in appreciation of the cleverly-disguised drop-shot after emitting a loud groan, retrieving the inanimate object from the floor and hitting it back over for the slender schoolgirl to serve again.

'What's Mitcham like?' the nervous teenager dared to tease him. 'I don't know anyone who lives there.'

'Non-descript,' the young man replied, being forced to run backwards to return a very long serve. 'They have newspapers and bad coffee. That's all I noticed. And a kind woman who asked me if I was feeling alright.'

Lynn put on a sad face. 'That's nice.'

Her boyfriend laughed bitterly. 'That is, as opposed to the other women, who accused me of being a drunken slob when I threw up in a rubbish bin.'

'Did you?' his girlfriend gasped. 'That's not good.'

'No. I didn't enjoy it,' his sarcasm sliced through the air as the resentful man began to feel angry again. 'It's OK though. I pushed them in front of the next train.'

The famous teenager stood mortified for a few seconds before chancing a chuckle at the effusive man's sharp wit. How she was going to miss this, she rued. She had never met anyone else with such a keen sense of timing and a way with words that frequently took her breath away.

'What? That's not funny.'

'Yes, it is,' her partner insisted, gradually feeling his self-control slipping away. 'This whole thing's fucking hilarious. Isn't that how we're going to have to act now? All happy faces and being grateful for good opportunities coming our way?'

'Stop!' Lynn warned, running round to the other side of the court and pointing her racquet at him. 'There *will* be good opportunities. For both of us. What's happening with your record?'

'It's finished,' the songwriter told her with some reluctance, flicking the shuttle out to her left-hand side. 'All ready to go. How many should I order?'

'Oh, three or four,' the young woman joked, running back to her side by ducking under the net. 'One for you too.'

'Bitch!' Jeff snapped in jest, glad of her persistence in the face of such unnecessary vitriol. 'I'm ordering fifty thou'.'

Lynn gave him an approving look, for the beginnings of a smile were spreading across her man's face. She was going to have to work hard to keep both sets of spirits up, she realised. That was fair enough. It hadn't been his idea to split, had it?

'That's a good first pressing,' she agreed. 'What about international? Did anyone talk to you about US or UK numbers?'

'Come on, Miss Platinum,' he jeered. 'Let's not get ahead of ourselves. I'm not you, remember?'

The sportswoman let her opponent's shot fall to the floor just in front of her toes. 'Let's stop for a while, shall we? Let's get a drink from upstairs.'

Collecting their belongings, the pair embraced strongly before vacating their court. Another ten minutes or so remained on their booking, but neither felt like continuing. There were too many words to say and not enough time in which to say them. Both felt the pressure mounting by the time they reached the cafeteria and purchased some soft drinks.

'Are you hungry?' Jeff asked.

'Not really. My stomach's in knots.'

Her boyfriend smiled in sympathy. 'We should eat something,' he encouraged. 'Especially you. You can't compromise your training.'

Sitting amongst members of the public, most of whom were parents collecting their children from swimming or *karate* lessons, the good-looking youngsters blended into the background with minimal fuss. Once in a while, they picked up a hushed voice whispering the celebrity's name and pointing in their direction, but for the most part, they were left alone.

'Have you had enough aggression venting?' Lynn asked the ashen-faced student, after they had finished their drinks.

'Yeah. Have you?' he responded, the sugar hit having calmed him somewhat. 'I'm going to insist that we eat, Miss Dyson, because I have to keep this body of mine in peak condition. Yours can go to hell, but I need nourishment.'

The Olympian forced herself to laugh. There it was again. She was going to have to memorise these priceless examples of her boyfriend's sense of humour and quirky turn of phrase. Not to mention the extent to which he continued to prioritise her best interests, regardless of how disillusioned he must be feeling.

'OK. You win. I can't believe you still want to look after me after everything. Thank you. Let's go to South Melbourne. The Paper Shop Deli might still be serving hot food.'

Jeff shrugged. 'It's called love, I think you'll find.'

The lovers ran down the stairs at the back of the Sportsdrome, letting themselves out through a fire exit which Lynn knew led directly to the car park. The old Fairlane was waiting patiently for them, and they jumped in before anyone could spot them. Lucky to find a parking space on Clarendon Street, not far from the Deli, the pair squeezed into a corner table, and the chivalrous man positioned his chair so that his very own superstar wasn't easily identified. It was a trick he wouldn't be needing for much longer.

'So,' Jeff began, placing the palms of his hands on the table and stretching out his tense fingers. 'What do we do now? Apart from remain calm and try to slow down time.'

His girlfriend smiled wistfully. 'That's a really nice idea. I'd be happy for time to stand still too. Groundhog Day. Have you heard that expression?'

He nodded. 'Keep living the same day until you get it right?'

'Yes. Except how do you know when you get it right?' the teenager asked, latching on to the light-hearted topic, intent on keeping it going for as long as possible.

'I wouldn't want to know,' her partner loaded the scales. 'I'm happy to be wrong forever if it means you stay here.'

Too late. The mood was lost again. Lynn's eyes filled with tears, and her gaze turned down towards the table. This positivity thing was a much harder skill to master than she had expected.

'I'm sorry, baby,' the young man said in a low voice, feeling his own throat tighten. 'I can't bring myself to speak encouraging words about you leaving the country. There's no point in me even trying. Can you understand?'

The gracious teenager reached across the table and stroked the back of his huge, dark-skinned hand. 'Yes, I do understand. It's going to be a long, sad two months though, if we just mope around in each other's company.'

'That's true,' the twenty-year-old agreed. 'It's not even as if I can come over and visit you, I suppose? Total break in contact. Why is that? Do you know specifically why?'

'No. Honestly, I don't. My suspicion is they think you're influencing me too much away from sport... my goals... you know...'

'But that's complete crap,' her boyfriend disputed. 'Isn't it even worth making a case? Or is it a done deal? Not necessarily the trip itself, but the no contact part. Or do you agree with them?'

'It's a done deal, Jeff,' the stalwart stood her ground, trying not to cry again. 'Dad told me I have to forget you until I'm eighteen and have finished my studies.'

'But that doesn't add up either,' he persisted. 'It's only just over a year 'til you're eighteen. So does that mean on your eighteenth birthday, I can come to LA, and we can party?'

Lynn smiled and dropped her guard for a second. 'Oh, that sounds perfect. I wish. I've made the commitment though and I have to honour it. Can't cut off my nose to spite my face, whatever that stupid saying's supposed to mean.'

Her boyfriend laughed, caught unawares by the old fashioned expression and the look of confusion on the pretty schoolgirl's face. She was strong, this one, and his heavy heart filled with remorseful admiration for her fortitude.

'Yeah. What *does* that mean?' he winked. 'I've never been able to work that one out.'

'Of course, it's one my mother used, when I objected to all of this,' she continued, deflating once more.

'Of course,' Jeff repeated, before directing her back on track. 'You didn't answer my question about making a case for staying in contact.'

'Do I agree you're influencing me?' the sixteen-year-old replayed his line and received a solemn nod in reply.

His dream girl couldn't bring herself to lie. 'Yes, but I *want* to be influenced, that's the problem. I let you influence me. I'm sorry, Jeff. I know you think I brought this on us, and I s'pose I did. Like you, I have to be true to myself, and I obviously didn't hide the fact that my priorities were changing well enough. I'm really sorry.'

The intelligent man rolled his eyes but stopped short of pressing her. He could see she was hurting too. Lynn had jumped heart-first into his life; a fate which up until only a few days ago had completely delighted him. However, as the ever-present Miss Irony was quick to point out, the closeness he had craved had ultimately been his undoing.

Before long their meals arrived, and the young couple began to eat slowly and silently. Jeff ordered a second beer, finishing his first with an enormous mouthful. He sighed heavily at his lack of appetite and, judging by her sickly facial expression, at Lynn's too.

'So at least now we know why it wasn't an issue for you to get pregnant after the Olympics.'

The young champion looked up in surprise, having been steered towards this conclusion for the first time. She had nothing to say in reply, so the impatient man continued.

'I always thought there was more to that little episode than we'd found out. Didn't you?'

The naïve celebrity shook her head. 'No. It honestly never crossed my mind. I suppose I just took Dad at face value. Probably expected him to issue some new edict after the Olympics. Am I that naïve?'

Seeing the non-committal expression on her boyfriend's face, Lynn guessed in the affirmative. She sighed, loading another unwanted mouthful of food onto her fork and swallowing it down. Jeff placed his cutlery roughly on the sides of his plate, shaking his head in resentment, and planted both elbows on the table. He rested his chin on his hands, and his dark eyes drilled into hers.

'Maybe we *should* get you pregnant,' the vindictive lover suggested. 'Then you'd have to miss the Olympics, and we'd get a chance to write our own history book.'

Lifting her napkin elegantly to her lips, the starlet's eyes filled with a new batch of tears. This was a particularly spiteful thing for her boyfriend to say, even though she understood exactly why he had said it. Did she dare even answer? Whatever she might say, whether in her parents' defence or to back him up, would undoubtedly lead to another angry outburst, so the elegant teenager chose once again to stay silent, simply forcing another fork-load into her mouth.

Her boyfriend's empathy overrode his rage in response to her discomfort, and he quickly apologised for the callous proposition. The young woman, still upset, excused herself politely and made her way to the back of the café to find the ladies' room. He took the opportunity to smoke a quick cigarette outside on the street, never once taking his eyes off the door through which his dream girl had vanished. That was enough, he decided. He had to stop being so selfish and punishing the innocent beauty for a decision to which he hoped she had not been an assenting party.

Watching as the graceful young lady navigated the other guests on the way back to their table, her suitably subdued dinner companion swung the steamy glass door open and returned on cue to pull out her chair. Lynn's fingers brushed his cheek softly in forgiveness, and they kissed and hugged each other quickly before sitting down again for another go at civility.

'Well... You'll be pleased to hear that I've finalised the sequence for my second album,' Jeff told her, as positively as he could. 'And I've got a preliminary release date of the eighth of September for the first one. They want to start a promotional tour a week afterwards, so with any luck I'll have that to occupy me for the first few weeks after you go.'

'Wow! That's amazing news!' Lynn exclaimed, a little too loud to sound entirely natural.

'See? I'm not a completely hopeless case,' the songwriter smiled. 'You can stop worrying about me.'

His caring girlfriend frowned. 'I'm never going to stop worrying about you, but it's great that you've got all that mapped out. Once you get on the road, you won't have time to miss me.'

'That's right,' he smirked, giving her a blank look. 'Lynn who?'

The sixteen-year-old smiled sweetly. 'So how can we stop behaving like this?' she asked. 'I've known I've been leaving for a while and managed to pretend everything was OK. Would you have preferred I didn't tell you until the day I was leaving?'

Jeff sighed, staring out of the window at the people walking along the footpath. 'In some ways, yes. There is something to be said for "What you don't know can't hurt you." And in answer to your previous question...'

'Can we manage to pretend everything's OK?' Lynn paraphrased.

'Yeah,' the student nodded. 'That's called denial, baby. It's not healthy, but then again, is this?'

The celebrity glanced furtively around at the other tables, hoping no-one was listening in on their conversation. She imagined there to be a host of well-meaning people ready and waiting to provide her with some much-needed advice. Other couples must have been forced to break up as a result of moving cities to go to university or changing jobs, for instance. She longed to know how they had figured out a way to make the best of the situation, because she could surely do with a few hints right now.

'I know, but what about "Live for the moment"? Isn't that what the *Kama Sutra* preaches? When you can't control what's going to happen in the future, you might as well carry on as you would've done before your future arrives.'

'To screw things up...' Jeff smiled, as he further qualified her wholly reasonable statement. 'Very clever. I agree. That's exactly what we should do, although I can't guarantee I'm going to be any good at it. I want you in my future, angel, and I guess I let myself get too far ahead. I've always known we couldn't possibly last forever, but Jesus, I hoped it'd be a bit longer than this! And I'd much rather one of *us* had pulled the pin. Then at least we would've let our relationship run its natural course. This way, it just feels wide open and unfinished.'

'I'm sorry,' the young woman lamented. 'That's how I feel too, except I would never have been able to describe it so well. Cut off in its prime. I don't know why I'm full of all these old sayings today. It's like we only just got started. I feel like we reached a really comfortable stage, and now it's all disruption and highs and lows again.'

'Amen to that!' the twenty-year-old declared, gripping her wrist lovingly. 'I love you so much for saying that. Even superstar tennis players need happiness charts on occasion, don't they? But getting back to whether I wish you hadn't told me until the day before you leave, overall I would prefer to know ahead of time.'

Lynn smiled, feeling a little better. Forcing the issue had played to the introvert's strengths and allowed him to express himself constructively for the first time in a while.

'That's good. I thought so.'

'There's no right answer to all this, angel,' her boyfriend continued on his philosophical path of mutual reassurance. 'I'm realistic enough to know that, even though I'll fight it to the end. You're too important to me to do anything less, just so you know... It'd hardly be doing what we have justice if I turned around and said, "OK, whatever. Thanks for the sex, and I'll see you around."'

The young woman caught her breath, listening to the callous cast-off. That would truly be an unbearable phrase to hear from the man she adored.

Her lover squeezed her hand again. 'And I'm pretty sure if you'd told me at the last minute, I'd be even more in the shit when you go, because I'd have to deal with raw grief as well as adjusting to the fact that you're gone. At least this way, I can get a head start on the grief part.'

'Yeah, but it still doesn't sound much better,' the young woman sighed. 'Shall we go?'

The couple finished their drinks, and instead of heading back to Admin straightaway, Jeff turned the car southwards and drove to St Kilda. They walked to the end of the pier and then along the promenade for a while before it became too difficult to dodge the attention. Back in the city and climbing up the steps into the building, the normally irrepressible male was becoming increasingly concerned that his body wasn't showing any interest in the nubile female form which invariably dominated his thoughts at this stage of an evening.

'Do you want me to go home?' he asked, hesitating outside the revolving doors.

Pain and shock were instantly plastered all over his companion's face, and the empathetic man saw his shadow before him. This was the clearest sign he had received in recent days, furthering his tenuous belief that Lynn genuinely didn't want to leave him behind.

Her voice reflected her instinctive reaction too. 'No. Why? Do you want to go home?'

'I'm not sure,' he confessed. 'I'm ashamed to admit that my body appears to have gone on strike. I don't think it can be persuaded to play tonight.'

Lynn put her arms around his waist, and they kissed tenderly. 'That doesn't matter. I'd much rather you stayed here, if you can stand it.'

Jeff gestured chivalrously for her to enter the building ahead of him, a long arm starting the doors turning from behind. The circumspect pair travelled up in the lift, and he pondered over what the night might have in store for them. He had never been to bed with a woman without having sex before and didn't relish the thought of making tonight the first time. It just didn't seem right, especially under the circumstances. With the clock now ticking on their time left together, he found it impossible to come to terms with the sardonic injustice of being incapable of taking advantage of every pleasurable opportunity they could lay their hands on.

'Did you want something to drink?' his girlfriend asked, heading towards the kitchen area. 'Tea or coffee?'

'Yeah. Coffee, please. How's the workload?'

'Same,' the schoolgirl replied in a dismissive tone. 'At least I haven't got any travel next week. How about going to the library on Sunday evening? I have to go to the farm on Saturday, but I'll be back sometime in the afternoon on Sunday.'

'Why not?' the worried man responded coolly, already feeling their meagre time allocation frittering away. 'Tell you what would be good...'

The teenager looked over. 'What would be good?'

'To sit down and map out a calendar of events between now and D-day,' her man elaborated with a sigh. 'I'd much rather know in advance, so I can set things up for myself for all other times. It's better than finding you're going to be out of town at the last minute.'

'Like this weekend, you mean?' Lynn interjected, feeling guilty. 'Sorry. I should have told you earlier. I was going to ask you to come to Benloch with me, but I get the impression you wouldn't want to. Am I right?'

Jeff nodded, suddenly angered again. 'You're damned right,' he sneered, unable to stop himself in time. 'I don't want to have to play Mister Nice-Guy with your mum and dad, thanks very much. Plus, I don't know if I could be trusted to keep my mouth shut, to tell you the truth, the way I feel just now.'

Lynn hugged him close. 'I understand. I have to go though. We've got all sorts of meetings about the US Open and the Olympics.'

'And I expect your parents don't want to see me anyway, after their ultimatum,' he added. 'Did they think I'd piss off straightaway?'

'I don't know what they thought. I haven't spoken to them about it. I'm sort of on strike myself.'

Her boyfriend smiled, pleased to hear a modicum of opposition. 'That's good to know. Sometimes I get the idea you're quite happy with this new arrangement.'

The patient host placed two mugs of steaming coffee on the coffee table, exhaling in resignation. Again, her boyfriend's bitterness had taken the smooth edges off the ambiance in the apartment, and the onus was clearly back on her to keep things pleasant between them.

'For God's sake, I'm not. Please believe me. It's just that I know I have to go through with it. I'm not at all happy with it.'

Reaching his hand around her waist, Jeff leaned into her face and kissed her lips tenderly. Closing her eyes and giving in to the welcome warmth, the celebrity forgave him again. She switched on the television, and the young lovers sat side-by-side on the couch. The busy sportswoman showed the student her diary, and he jotted down the dates when she would be in Melbourne and free. There weren't very many.

'Jesus, Lynn,' he complained, folding the piece of paper and slotting it into his wallet. 'That's not much time. Can you let me know if anything changes, please? I don't want to miss out on anything.'

Lynn took his hand, sensing his desperation. 'Come to bed.'

'Already?' he questioned in astonishment, unusually unsure of himself. 'You might be disappointed.'

'You really think I care about that?' his girlfriend shot back, trying to laugh. 'I just want to cuddle into you and see what happens. Skin-on-skin. You know...'

Full of apprehension, Jeff switched off the television and followed the lithe frame into the bedroom, feeling a definite chill in the air. Secretly fascinated by the physical manifestations of his impending loss, he realised how warm his body must run in its normal state of arousal.

The couple undressed and climbed under the quilt. The bewildered young man lay on his back, like a fish out of water, and was suddenly hit with a wave of anxiety at the uncertainty within him. What would he do? He couldn't face the idea of simply waiting for Lynn to fall asleep. This lonely scenario was so utterly alien to him. Sex relaxed his tormented mind, and without it he would be left to lie motionless all night, wound up like a spring.

Lying in Lynn Dyson's bed on this winter's night, the economics of time had never been so real, so clear or so terrifying, with all the interminable hours the boy from Sydney's west spent awake and in the company of his destructive memories and tenacious demons, and with the prospect of many more nights stretching out in front of him. Moreover, if this dismal impotence persisted, he would be unable even to enjoy the precious few hours that remained. How dare he do this to himself?

Lynn began to stroke his dormant genitals, lifting his hand and placing it on her breast. The act felt weird; almost dirty. His panic attack subsiding, the expert lover reached down between her legs and began to work his magic, not wanting her to go without because he couldn't rise to the occasion. Their bodies moved steadily closer together while they kissed for a long, long time.

'Thanks, angel,' he whispered. 'I'm not sure this is going to work. You don't have to. Let me concentrate on you.'

Lynn leaned her head on his chest and kissed the hairs that tickled her face. 'Let's just enjoy each other. Who knows what might happen?'

The sixteen-year-old spoke with a maturity beyond her years, a gift bestowed upon her by this gorgeous Argentinean Jewish mystery man. Her voice resonated inside him, and the depth of his feelings frightened him still more. Doing his best to ignore the descending clouds, he brought his smiling dream girl to orgasm, and she gripped onto him tightly, writhing and moaning in pleasure.

They lay quietly for a few minutes, allowing Lynn to float back to Earth after her delicious escape. Throughout the build-up and even in the knowledge that his fingers had given her the breathtaking thrill, still an erection eluded the forlorn student.

'Fuck, Lynn!' the despairing man almost shouted, by now obsessed by the scarce, invaluable and irretrievable minutes steadily trickling away. 'What a waste of bloody time! Only twenty shopping days 'til Christmas, and I'm out of money already.'

Jeff sat up suddenly and started to get out of bed. Jumping up and pulling him back down by the shoulders, his bedfellow laughed.

'Would you please relax? Do you want another Brunhilde special?'

Flopping back down next to the stunning creature who was trying so hard to compensate for everything, the impetuous twenty-year-old sighed loudly. He felt guilty that his anger and frustration was dominating their time together and vowed to find some way to rid himself of the negativity. Lynn didn't deserve this. He knew she was attempting to work out a tolerable *dénouement* for their relationship.

'You're right. I'm sorry. I've never…'

'Be quiet,' the celebrity commanded, fondly kissing his lips. 'It doesn't matter. We're together. You love me, and I love you.'

Her fingers wandered over his abdomen and on to stroke his testicles again, while her mouth followed the line and wrapped itself around her boyfriend's uncharacteristically flaccid penis. Jeff did his best to picture her in his flat on that first night, keen to recapture the extreme level of excitement which he had been at last ditch pains to control. How keyed-up he had been that night, with Lynn Dyson on his window ledge, wearing nothing but his shirt! Turning onto his side to remind himself of just how exquisite the sight was, he ran the fingers of his left hand down her back and felt her shiver. If his mind could play tricks on him, surely he should be able to call its bluff occasionally too.

After a while, with Lynn's tongue caressing the shaft and tip, keeping him guessing as to where she might go next, her lover's ragged senses signalled to his hormones that it was about time they abandoned their protest and joined in. He raised his head off the pillow, coaxing her to sit up, and his hungry mouth found hers.

'I love you so much,' he whispered.

'Welcome back,' the teenager replied, grinning as she felt his erection growing in her hand. 'I love you too. We'll get through this.'

Jeff rolled his beautiful partner over onto her back, entering her moist vagina before his fears had a chance to chase the stimulation away. He rose up and down steadily, drinking in her beauty, while he brought her gently to another climax. The sadness written on her face was tough to ignore.

'Don't cry, gorgeous,' he urged, leaning down and kissing the corners of her eyes, like she had done to him so many times. 'You're supposed to be enjoying this.'

'I am. That's the trouble. I want to keep enjoying it.'

The morose man thrust as far inside her as he could and lay down gently on top, keeping the pressure of regular movement going. Her tears were contagious, and he was in grave danger of losing all motivation to continue.

'Me too, angel,' he hissed in her ear. '*Para siempre.*'

Several minutes of sustained rhythm finally induced the necessary spark in both of them, which once ignited was preordained to burst into flames. Lynn resisted against his deliberate motion as she came, sending Jeff straight to the point of no return.

'You are fantastic!' he cried aloud. 'You can make me feel good in spite of everything.'

The relieved lover orgasmed into her, the struggle rendering its force all the more powerful once the payoff finally arrived. Its sublime sensation seemed to linger for a long time, and he made sure he savoured every delicious second. Drained from the stress of the last few days, the couple drifted off to sleep in each other's arms, as if nothing was amiss.

And it was a similar story for the ensuing nightmare, not two hours later. Jeff woke himself up, such was the volume of the screaming and shouting in his head. Lynn woke a few moments later to find her man already sitting up, swearing and fighting for breath. She felt totally helpless.

'Are you OK?'

'Sure. Wonderful,' he snapped, getting up and going into the bathroom.

The young star turned over in the bed and waited for her belligerent partner to return, knowing there was little point in trying to cheer him up. She had a fairly good idea about the themes that must be coursing through his head. All the effort he had expended and the courage he had found to open up and seek help must now seem worthless. She felt as though she was betraying the trust he had battled so hard to give her.

About ten minutes later, the refreshed and clean-smelling dreamer returned to bed. He pushed the quilt to one side, lay back down and attempted to cool down, both outside and in. His girlfriend, who had fallen back to sleep in the meantime, stirred quietly once again and turned to face him.

'Can I hold you?'

'Yeah,' the sheepish man agreed.

Lynn held back, sensing some hesitation. 'Do you want me to?'

'Yes. Do you?'

'Yes. Of course! I love you,' she smiled.

'Sometimes I wonder why.'

The sixteen-year-old sighed heavily, feeling the schism in her heart splitting a little further apart. 'Because sometimes you wonder why.'

The morose man paused, feeling surprisingly grateful for where they now found themselves. He reached his right hand across and placed it on top of the bedclothes which were draped over her shoulder, overwhelmed by her poignant but perfect answer.

'Thank you. Sorry for shouting at you.'

'Shhh… We need a new rule,' the wise woman said, smiling. 'No more apologising. I know you don't mean to hurt me, and I hope you know I'm the same. Let's just agree to express ourselves in the best way we know how.'

Jeff kissed her. 'That's a deal. I'm going to sit and watch TV for a while, if that's OK. I don't think I'm going to sleep. Do you mind?'

Lynn shook her head, already drifting off again. She needed to conserve as much energy as possible for the hectic day ahead.

'Alright. As long as you don't leave without saying goodbye.'

Her devoted boyfriend shook his head at the ghastly thought. 'Now why would I do that?'

'Good,' the drowsy teenager whispered. ''Night.'

The tormented soul kissed her once more, then put on his t-shirt and boxers and went to stretch out on the couch, feeling the cold again now that his engine had returned to idle speed. He turned the television's volume down low and forced his mind to become absorbed in the night time shows. Still uncomfortable in the chilly spring temperature, he decided to fetch his towel from the *en suite* and wrapped it around his shoulders. The restless student felt centuries of wear and tear calcifying in his bones, having left twenty behind in the bedroom.

On the way back to the lounge, Jeff lingered for a moment by the bank of wardrobes separating Lynn's bed from the rest of the apartment and watched her sleeping peacefully. Would it take too long for her to forget him? Part of him hoped not, benevolently dismissing the soul-mate notion, for her sake. The best programme he could find at that time of night was an old black and white Western, with actors he recognised but couldn't name. A good hour later, he reclined across the couch and began to feel sleepy again.

The next thing he knew, his dream girl was shaking his shoulders and shouting at him to wake up. The movie had finished, and a bright, white screen lit up the room. She switched off the television, standing in front of it, totally naked and shivering in the cold.

'Jesus Christ,' the outcast muttered under his breath, waking up quickly at the sound of her voice so loud in his ear. 'Again? I'm sorry. Do you want me to go?'

Why were they putting themselves through this agony? Surely it would be better just to call it quits now. That way, Lynn could concentrate on preparing for the Olympics, and he could scream to his heart's content in the comfort of his own home.

'No. Please don't,' the young woman insisted. 'Come back to bed. Do you want a drink? Tea or a glass of water?'

Jeff helped himself to water and drank the entire glassful down in only a couple of gulps. Climbing into bed again, he wrapped his dream girl up in his arms, and they both cried again. The goodness was fast draining out of their worlds, as each realised they would have to set the other free.

'I feel like the sun won't come out tomorrow all day,' his girlfriend said, reaching for the tissue box and offering them over her shoulder.

'I hope we get out of this mode soon,' the supportive man whispered, rocking back and forth and kissing her neck fondly. 'I don't want to cry for two months.'

'Me neither,' Lynn replied, trying to smile.

Every Precious Moment

The blue Ford sedan slowed down as it reached a sharp bend, the first in several kilometres. Jeff and Lynn had been on the road for almost two hours, initially stuck in the Friday evening traffic radiating out from the city. They were making a break for the countryside, at Suzanne's invitation, looking forward to a few hours of frivolous diversion before the sportswoman resubmitted herself to the intensity of another weekend's training.

'It's left,' the driver decided, after coming to an unsigned intersection that he failed to recognise in the dark. 'I always get lost right about now.'

His girlfriend laughed. 'I hope you get lost tomorrow morning too.'

Jeff forced a smile. 'Could be arranged.'

Within a few more minutes, a familiar set of whitewashed and weathered tractor tyres came into view, marking the gateway into the boarding kennels. Jeff sped up as the headlights illuminated the tree-lined drive, and the car fish-tailed around the corner on the gravel. Lynn gripped the handle on the passenger door, not seeking to deny her man his rev-head pleasures tonight.

A cacophony of barks, howls and yelps greeted the couple once they drew close to the cluster of buildings, which consisted of a small cottage, some ramshackle outhouses and three rows of roofed enclosures. Suzanne emerged through the front door, yelling for quiet from her canine doorbells. The Fairlane came to a standstill under a lighted window, and both passengers disembarked and collected their bags from the boot.

'Come in, guys,' their host invited. 'It's cold tonight. Hope you brought your flannelettes.'

'I did,' the famous teenager raised her eyebrows at her boyfriend, who she knew had no time for such unflattering nightwear. 'My pyjamas were a big hit in Queenstown.'

Jeff chuckled, standing back to let both women into the house ahead of him. 'Gerry not here yet?'

'No,' Suzanne shook her head. 'Typical. Always last to arrive when there's work to be done. Dump your stuff there, and I'll show you to your room in a minute. Did you want wine or beer?'

The student took charge of the drinks preparation, leaving the women to swap their respective news items. Lynn was in good spirits tonight, which would surely save the day, since Suzanne looked almost as hacked off as he felt. He downed an entire can of Victoria Bitter in the time it took to fill three glasses with warmed Cabernet Sauvignon, then paused before taking them into the kitchen to open and sink another one down his throat.

'Cheers,' he toasted, raising his glass to the others. 'What's for dinner? It smells good, Suzie.'

'Thanks. I did a roast. A premonition that we'd have to wait. I'm so pissed off that he's late, the bastard.'

'There was an accident, I think,' Lynn came to Gerry's defence. 'It took us a long time to get here.'

'I don't care,' Suzanne scowled. 'You managed to get here on time! And he promised he'd leave early to help me get dinner ready. He could've come with you. I asked him to stay for the weekend, but I know he won't. I don't know why we're still going out, for God's sake. I've had a gutful of him.'

Being left in the lurch by her busy executive was an all too common occurrence for Jeff's long-time friend. He put his arm around her, steering her up the stairs and towards the small bedroom that had been made up for him and his dream girl. Lynn made appropriate noises of admiration at the cosy space under a sloping roof, and was immediately jumped upon and pinned to the mattress by her amorous partner. The jealous woman groaned and turned tail, feigning a need to return to the source of the delicious aroma, after almost being reduced to tears by the sight of the loving pair. The celebrity levered herself free of Jeff's forceful grasp, shouting an apology through the open door and down the stairs, promising to be there soon to lay the table.

'She doesn't know the half of it,' the twenty-year-old shrugged at his girlfriend's scolding glare. 'It's not our fault Gerry's a heartless fucker.'

'I know,' Lynn gave in, although determined to hide their own agony from their friends. 'But let's not touch each other and seem too over the top. No yukky stuff before he gets here and hopefully tries to make up, OK? Do you want to see what I've got for you to take off this time?'

Jeff's attention was immediately drawn to the sound of a zip opening on the famous teenager's overnight bag, egged on by her suggestive tone. 'Jesus! Not another full body suit? It won't be on for long, so I don't know why you bothered to pack it.'

Without responding to his light-hearted sarcasm, the young woman reached into her suitcase and twisted her hand around for a couple of seconds, finally pulling clear with a bundle of shimmering white fabric, shifting and slithering in her fingers as she went to hold it aloft. Her boyfriend's face immediately lit up, and his hands shoved themselves deep into his pockets, as they always did when driven to force himself to slow down.

Lynn smiled, her eyes moving from his hungry grin to the impatient hands and a bulge becoming very apparent between them. On a recent shopping trip with Michelle, thinking of their night away, she had purchased an expensive silk *negligée* and a matching robe that descended no lower than the tops of her thighs, confident that it would meet with her hot-blooded man's approval. They were already having the desired effect, she was sure, even imagining steam to be rising off his shoulders, chest and head in the chilly, damp air.

Downstairs, the stout, old front door creaked to admit the latecomer inside, and the lovers were momentarily distracted by their host's foreseeable berating. Suzanne's voice was shrill, and Gerry matched her volume with the excuses of late appointments and heavy traffic. The lustrous, satiny aphrodisiac slipped out of the celebrity's hand and dropped onto the floor, prompting both to bend down and retrieve it, while the fiery dispute reduced in volume in the background.

'Wait!' the blonde teenager laughed.

'Why?' her boyfriend asked in horror, deliberately dumbfounded.

The shiny garment was gathered up again and held out for Jeff to take a sneak peek. The cool, sheer fabric moved between his fingers as if it had a life of its own, divine inspiration for his heightened senses. He took hold of the teddy's narrow straps and let its hem fall from his hands, admiring the sheer translucence, wide-eyed and starving. The young star's heart felt as if it were being constrained by the same desperate grip, and she fought back tears, grateful to be able to elicit such a reaction from the man who was already in mourning for their shortening future.

Jeff exhaled, stepping forward to pin a strap on each of Lynn's shoulders and leaning in for a long kiss. Words failed him. It was the sexiest nightdress he had ever seen, and he couldn't wait to see the tanned, long-limbed beauty wrapped in it, beseeching him not to take it off while he struggled with vital disobedience.

'Jeez,' he hissed. 'I so want you pressing up against me with this in between us. You drive me crazy, d'you know that? How am I supposed to give you up?'

'I wanted to seem mature and sophisticated,' the sixteen-year-old smiled, dispelling the latest serve of gloom with a gentle squeeze of his wrists.

Loving arms embraced her tightly, and the couple kissed again, with the silk lingerie suspended between their clothed bodies. Lynn shuddered as her lover's strong, purposeful hand drove up her back, round her neck and on to brush the hair aside from her cheek. He knew how much she loved the rasp of his stubble on the soft skin of her face.

'Well, it'll work. I guarantee you,' he told her, inviting her to test how hard he was. 'It's already working. You are mature and sophisticated, and I'll love the cosmo' you as much as I love the regular you. Thanks, angel. Can we put it on now?'

'No! It's for later. Stop!'

An authoritative but tempered burst of Gerry's normally booming voice wafted up from the bottom of the stairs to shatter their romantic interlude, and the couple exchanged a silent, shared joke at the subservience it masked. They imagined their friend to have received a thorough dressing-down by his long-time girlfriend, and knew the improved behaviour would last as long as, but no longer than the time they were under the same roof.

'It's how I'm going to help you,' the blonde continued, watching Jeff's fingertips glide over their delicate, new sex toy and noticing him mouth a silent *à bientôt*. 'I thought it'd help you with sleeping at someone else's house. We have to make the best of a bad situation.'

The pair descended to the ground floor and to the smell of freshly carved lamb and roast potatoes. The exhausted undergraduate had confessed during the long drive out beyond the city limits that he was fearful of the others overhearing his nightmares, and that this was likely to further increase the level of disturbance for his patient companion. Lynn was not particularly surprised to discover that accepting Suzanne's overnight invitation was another first for her troubled boyfriend.

'Agreed,' Jeff nodded. 'You just have, and I love you.'

The meal and the easy company carried the evening along merrily, and the foursome hailed the new weekend in cheerful drunkenness. Gerry had compensated for his tardy arrival by supplying half a dozen bottles of an award-winning Penfold's Bin, more than meeting the approval of the assembled discerning palates.

Later, with the dinner cleared away amid a fertile conversation ranging from the rise of Gough Whitlam in Australian Federal politics to the eagerly-awaited showdown for Richard Nixon in the United States' Presidential race, both of which would be decided before the end of the year, Lynn happily took her place on Jeff's lap while the friends played cards. He had been extraordinarily well behaved during the three, long courses and had even restrained himself when the liqueurs were brought to the table, evidently keen to signal to his girlfriend that he had prioritised their promised liaison ahead of his usual zeal around alcohol.

The young woman experienced mixed emotions at this realisation, foreshadowing the descent into depravity to which her boyfriend would undoubtedly submit after her departure. The back of her left hand stroked his thigh, catching his appreciative gaze from time to time, while her right hand held her cards away from his line of sight. Playfully, the twenty-year-old kept shifting and leaning to one side, trying to catch a glimpse of her cards, causing the others to laugh and Lynn's insides to churn with pleasure.

Suzanne appeared to have forgiven her charming executive sufficiently to ensure their night would also end amorously, and neither couple was paying much attention to their game of Blackjack. Feeling Jeff's temperature rising around her, which was welcome due to the cold draught blowing in under the front door, Lynn let her knuckles occasionally slip closer to the crease between the top of her man's thigh and his crotch, and they brushed his testicles through the heavy denim fabric. Whenever she needed to play a hand, she would quickly rush her fingers out and break the sublime contact.

'Hey! I was enjoying that,' the young man whined.

Every now and then, the tease would extend to the teenager's fingers sliding smartly away from their warm resting place and dragging themselves across where she imagined an erection to be swelling in the confined space of his jeans. Sure enough, by the quickening of the handsome man's breath, she could tell his poker face was having to work very hard to disguise how turned-on he was.

'OK, that's far enough, lady,' Jeff announced suddenly, gripping the tops of Lynn's arms and lifting her to her feet. 'Excuse us, guys, but we've got things to attend to upstairs.'

Gerry grinned lasciviously, most probably waiting for his mate to lose his cool first, so that he could carry through with his same intentions without incurring the host's wrath again. Sure enough, Suzanne was immediately and far less gracefully jettisoned, almost tripping and falling against the edge of the dining table. The red wine haze prevented her from feeling any pain or embarrassment, while the Olympian winced on her behalf, thankful for her relative abstemiousness. Sobriety this late in the evening was ordinarily a scarce commodity for her boyfriend too, and it was especially pleasing not to be subjected to his rougher edges tonight.

In fact, the languid tenderness he displayed sent the celebrity reeling with joy once the youngsters had shut themselves into their bedroom in the eaves, which Jeff had humorously labelled "the servants' quarters" earlier, much to his old friend's amusement. The habitual rush to disrobe each other and to drench himself in carnal pleasure with the body he desired so strongly was now replaced by a slow dance to subliminal, stereo serenades that might very well have been precisely the same melody, judging by how far under each other's spell they had fallen.

Suddenly, the delectable romance was disturbed by the harsh sounds of thirty dogs barking, some high-pitched and others deep and menacing. Suzanne had stepped outside to complete a last check on her boarders before turning in, and she shouted equally earsplittingly loud to silence them. The amorous pair looked into each other's eyes, dismayed that their private peace had been impaired, and slowly set about unbuttoning their clothing to reclaim the moment. However, as if this cacophony wasn't enough, Gerry then yelled his own diatribe from the house, just below the couple's window.

Lynn's hands extended towards her man's belt, and the twenty-year-old allowed her to unfasten it and unzip his fly without breaking eye contact for a second. Shrugging in amiable resignation, he released his lover's fingers from his waistband, where she had been poised to push his trousers and undies down to free his erection. Pulling his legs out of his jeans one at a time, he hopped over to the window and flung it open.

'Keep the fucking noise down!'

'Fuck you!' was Suzanne's immediate retort. 'Are you starkers? You're lucky I'm short-sighted!'

Her boyfriend guffawed from underneath, gazing up at the lead-light window under the eaves. 'I'm not, and there's not much to talk about, Suze. Go put it back where it belongs, mate.'

The accountant's instruction drew a groan from the kennel maid, and the lovers heard the front door slam below them. The whole house shook with the vibration, causing the sixteen-year-old to grimace in mock alarm. Sighing, Jeff pulled the rotting window frame closed again, threading the handle into its latch. Gerry's words had hit home more than he cared to let on, and he found himself choking up with the knowledge that no part of him would belong in this divine place for much longer.

The slender celebrity had joined him at the window and was laughing, pointing to a smear on the window which was backlit by the exterior light. Her boyfriend fought to smile too, seeing that his jutting penis had drawn a pattern in the condensation, and he returned to make something more meaningful of his accidental artwork. Then, lurching back, he quickly wrapped his beautiful best friend into his arms, encouraging her downwards, to where her mouth could thaw out the freezing tip.

'Jesus, that's cold!'

'What did you write?' Lynn asked, doing as she was asked without complaint, while her eyes darted sideways to see. 'Oh, that's gorgeous. Thanks. I love you too.'

The hot-blooded man sought to distract her, struggling with his own emotions at having fashioned a heart with an "L" and a "J" on either side. His fingers caressed her cheek, gently coaxing her willing mouth back to the task at hand, moaning as she flicked the end of her tongue over the most sensitive part of his penis, on down its shaft, finally kissing and stroking the delicate skin around its base.

'You're gorgeous,' Jeff countered, leaning into her and massaging her strong shoulders. 'That feels so good.'

As their sensuous lovemaking continued, plunged back into the melodious stillness they had shared before the stark interruption, Lynn felt herself succumb to the secret messages exuded by the expressiveness of her lover's breath, and stretched up beyond her full height to kiss his waiting mouth. His hands and his groin pressed insistently against her abdomen, making the muscles around her vagina convulse with anticipation. Her clothes were peeled off gently, one by one, until she stood between the bed and the angled skylight completely nude, in front of an admirer with hands swathed in white silk. As they looked up into the starry sky, the nightdress was threaded over her head and allowed to float down until it accentuated her breasts, and his loud, measured breathing ignited a fire so deep within her that tears immediately sprang to her eyes.

The handsome man said nothing, for once choosing not to remind his dream girl of his own unhappiness, simply manœuvering her into the lamplight to reveal her in all her glorious splendour. Softly whistling in patent awe, he took hold of his girlfriend's right hand and encouraged her to draw her fingernails along the length of his erection, as his own traced a line through the fabric, generating static electricity from her navel to the opening of her vagina. The bristling friction made him cry out, and the exhilarated teenager gripped hard and embraced his red-hot, naked body. Gluttonous arms pulled her even closer, and his hands shifted the silk against their skin like a layer of foamy water between them. Still no words were spoken and their dance resumed, turning in slow circles until Jeff had covered every centimetre of fabric, investigated every fold and pressed every delicate seam into his lover's sensitised flesh.

With his right hand sliding its fingers along the narrow shoulder straps and following them with firm, passionate kisses, the virtuoso's left hand travelled downwards and paused on the outer side of the translucent veil, so that it merely flashed against her pubic hair. A powerful orgasm streamed out of the entranced woman without warning, bringing forth sobs of desire and almost leaving him without control of his own carefully moderated progress.

'Jesus, baby!' the elated man broke the silence through gritted teeth, overcome by the intensity of her reaction. 'Where did that come from? You are so unbelievably sexy. Come again for me. Please?'

'Hold me,' Lynn begged, dragging him backwards until they both collapsed onto the bed, which creaked noisily with their combined weight. 'I want to feel us sliding together again, as if we're in danger of slipping apart. It's the most amazing feeling I've ever felt. You held me so tight.'

No longer capable of restraining his own emotions, Jeff's tears fell onto his girlfriend's face as his lips closed around hers, and his tongue forbade her to speak another word. His thumb alighted on her clitoris, moving so slowly that the sixteen-year-old groaned long and low until it unleashed another, equally deep climax. While she was coming, he thrust himself inside her, prolonging her pleasure for as long as he could and then following quickly after, with a roar so primitive that it reverberated around the room like distant thunder.

'That was wonderful,' the silk-clad beauty cried softly. 'I'm going to miss you so much.'

Her boyfriend kissed her again, his fingers refusing to leave the shimmering material alone. 'It was. You're the best, angel. *La mejor en el mundo entero.* And me too. Missing you, that is.'

'Let's not think about it.'

'I can't not think about it,' her boyfriend replied, exhaling heavily. 'You're asking the impossible.'

The celebrity sighed too. 'We have to try.'

Her boyfriend collapsed down onto the bed beside her, shaking his head. 'That's denial.'

'No, it's not,' Lynn countered, determined to save some of the heavenly aura before reality chased it away again. 'It's making the best of the time we have left. Just another way of looking at life, Jeff.'

The student raised himself up and settled onto his haunches, gazing at the stunning vision with whom he had been transported to paradise just moments ago. She looked raw, like a real woman, and it shocked him, because for the first time he realised what Bart and Marianna Dyson must see. He was stealing the little girl from their daughter, day by day and night by night. Her blonde hair was strewn over the candy-striped pillowcase, the garish tones of which he had failed to register until now, and her nipples and navel had left impressions in the sheer fabric, now damp from the heat of fevered hands and endless kisses. This embodiment of female perfection was not likely to vanish from his mind without a trace, no matter which way he looked at life.

'Thanks for not drinking so much tonight,' Lynn interrupted his *rêverie*. 'I hope it was worth it.'

Jeff exhaled through his nose, looking around for the blankets, which had fallen off the end of the bed during their furious activity. 'You're welcome. It was worth it. More than worth it, if you force me to admit it.'

The young woman giggled, and with relief, her boyfriend sensed the girl returning in the nick of time.

'I did it because you care enough to make it special,' he continued, 'and not just because I want it to be special.'

'I know,' the teenager smiled, stifling a yawn.

'Good. I hoped you would.'

Lynn shuffled across the bed, planting a kiss on her lover's forehead with her deep crimson, swollen lips, before wrapping the silk robe around her and disappearing into the passageway to visit the bathroom.

'I love you.'

'I love you too,' Jeff said to a door which was latched abruptly to stop a blast of icy air from cooling down their private hothouse.

With his hands levered against the frame of the skylight, the boy from Canley Vale wiped a smear of steam from the glass and stared through tearful eyes at a night that was much darker in the countryside than in the city. And also much darker for him and his beautiful starlet than for their friends on the other side of the wall. The end of the line was imminent for them too, he guessed, although it appeared that their long relationship had had its day. The same could not possibly be said for the one that could exude such rapturous fervour as had been evident in this very room.

The door opened and closed behind him, and he turned to see Lynn return and hop into bed, shivering and chattering her teeth in fun. Her arms beckoned for him to return and warm her up, which was a duty he was only too happy to fulfill.

'You can put your pee-jays on,' the human heater smiled, being dragged under the covers most forcefully.

'I might.'

'You looked exquisite tonight, like forbidden fruit. The most beautiful woman in the world, if you'll forgive me for repeating myself.'

'Thank you,' she kissed him, beginning to weep from a combination of tiredness and despondency.

Her boyfriend shrugged, cradling her head under his chin and rolling onto his back to hide his own tears. 'Thank you. Don't cry, angel.'

'I can't help it.'

'Makes two of us. I just want to love you, that's all. Nothing else.'

'I know, Jeff. I'm sorry.'

The couple fell asleep to the sound of the bed on the other side of the wall rocking on its casters. The amused student went to thump hard on the plaster, only to have his wrist snared and dragged back under the blankets by his pyjama-clad partner. They had no idea how long their next-door neighbours' noisy session had lasted, because their next waking memory was Jeff fighting for breath, springing bolt upright and straining to grab hold of an invisible being in front of him.

The dream had begun pleasantly enough, as if the twenty-year-old hadn't yet fallen asleep in Suzanne's upstairs spare room. He was walking back from the bathroom carrying two glasses of water when he noticed the door of their bedroom had been closed since he left, and he froze at the sound of loud voices coming from within.

Gripped by fear, more for her boyfriend's embarrassment, should their hosts hear him yelling expletives and the huge gasps of breath which would shake the very foundations of this lowly cottage, Lynn tried to wake him up before the full force of his nightmare took hold. Still deep in the unconscious however, Jeff grappled with the two full glasses, cursing as most of their contents spilled onto the floor in his frantic effort to open the door. Inside, now drenched with sweat and still unaware of Lynn's attempts to rouse him, he came face-to-face with a livid Bart Dyson, who was attempting to drag his daughter out of the bedroom, through some previously undiscovered door which the young man swore had not been there earlier.

His defenceless lover's screams ripped through the street kid's psyche, at once wanting to block the sound with his hands over his ears while lashing out at the Australian hero, whose commands were bloodthirsty and meeting fierce resistance from the young woman. Somehow his dreaming feet wouldn't move, now glued to the floorboards of his second-floor flat in Canley Vale.

'How the fuck did you get in here?' he shouted at the top of his voice.

Jeff reeled back, feeling a hand grab round his shoulders and then another slap across his face.

'Wake up!' the celebrity hissed in his ear, smothering his mouth as best she could. 'Wake up, Jeff. You're dreaming! You don't want to wake Gerry.'

Six-feet-four-inches of solid muscle swung around, ripping the sleeve of her pyjama top clear of the shoulder seam and drawing clawlike fingernails across the teenager's upper arm. She yelped, temporarily disoriented, before standing up on the mattress and pushing hard down on her boyfriend's shoulders until finally he crumbled into the dishevelled bedding, biting at the hand which continued to block his airway.

'Jeff, stop!' the determined woman shouted. 'Stop, for God's sake. It's me! Lynn! You're hurting me.'

Staring eyes almost burst free of their sockets, and the rasping sound of air being pumped from already empty lungs vibrated against the sixteen-year-old's chest. Her tormented soul-mate was finally coming out of the wilderness and returning to the servants' quarters, and she described the scene thus to the disintegrating fighter in an effort to calm him down. Hurriedly recomposing their evening's entertainment with her silk *negligée*, to keep the commentary flowing, Lynn rocked her lover back and forth until his faculties returned.

The girl of his dreams was softly crying when Jeff finally woke up and realised where he was; her warmly-clad figure reclining just as he had last seen her, shortly before they had fallen asleep. They both sat still in each other's arms, anxiously waiting for the others to knock on their door or give some other clue that the nocturnal interruption had disturbed them.

'Are you OK?' the drenched man asked, first seeing his companion rubbing her arm and then the torn armhole of her pyjama jacket. 'Did I do that?'

Lynn nodded, swiftly covering three parallel lines of reddening scratches. 'It's nothing. I didn't expect you to wheel round so fast. Your nails are sharp!'

She was smiling at her wayward lover, who failed to see the funny side of anything at this precise moment. Thankfully though, there were no signs of life from the room next door, and he broke away and let himself out of the room with the intentions of splashing some water on his face and reclaiming some equilibrium.

Jesus! These violent dreams were spiralling more and more out of control. Bart Dyson had somehow found his way to the Stones Road, and Lynn had taken his sister's place. Whatever was going on with his messed-up head now? Not content with reconstituting real events from his childhood, his twisted mental state now sought to further pollute his scant hours of repose by feeding off his current agonies too.

Climbing back into bed, Jeff found his long-suffering, sympathetic beauty attired aptly in the costume of an angel, hands outstretched and eyes watery. The sheen of the white fabric had been nearly washed out by the perspiration of their earlier passions, which lent even heavier weight to the strung-out addict's need to enjoy her in it again. His hard penis penetrated with next to no foreplay, and he gasped in indebted pleasure to find her more than ready to receive him, both sets of hands gripping each other's hips insistently as they moved together to combined orgasms.

The quenched *inamorati* collapsed together onto the bed, their mood enlightened by another full dose of hormones and endorphins so violently unleashed. They laughed at how soundly their friends must be sleeping, presumably as a result of full-bodied red wine and the sugary dessert which Suzanne had served. Lynn reached over the side of the mattress to pull up her pyjamas, holding them up in front of her man's eyes to check that he had no objection to her clothing herself in them again.

He shrugged, knowing he was in absolutely no position to bargain against her warmth and doggedly refusing to tell the gorgeous creature about the latest extraneous journey on which his mind had taken him. What good would it do to share it? She didn't need the image of her own father manhandling her like a pimp prising her out of the hands of a penniless customer. He was learning, at least, the young man realised. He would maintain the *status quo* and make the best of a bad situation.

'What do you want for your birthday?' he turned the tables instead.

His girlfriend chuckled, caught by surprise. 'My birthday? That's ages away. I want to celebrate it with you, two weeks early.'

'Thanks,' the student gathered his flannelette-encased girlfriend up in his arms. 'Hmm… Not quite the same effect, this, huh? I want to celebrate it with you on the day.'

Lynn giggled, squirming in his tight hold. 'I know. But we can't. We should go to sleep.'

'I love you so much,' Jeff lifted his head and kissed her forehead.

Exhaling deeply, she flexed her neck backwards until their mouths met. 'I love you too. That's what I want for my birthday.'

Her boyfriend sniffed, pulling the sheet up to their necks to block the cold air's path. 'You can have that on your birthday, and on every other day, before and after.'

'Thanks, Jeff. I accept,' she replied. 'You know the soul-mates thing that we were talking about a few weeks ago?'

'Yes,' the young man flashed his eyebrows to signal a dangerous diversion.

His lover laughed again. 'Shut up. Do you think it's always two? Is it possible to be more than two?'

'What are you talking about? I hope not. I don't want to share you.'

'No?' she tested him gently, determined to fall asleep on a light note. 'I thought men always wanted to have sex with more than one woman.'

Jeff's mouth smothered her playful grin, refusing to let it go for several seconds. Finally, breathing heavily, he answered in typical, romantic fashion, making Lynn's heart soar.

'That's mating bodies, angel, not mating souls. Change the subject, huh?'

The sleepy schoolgirl smiled and kissed the end of his nose, snuggling into his radiating body. 'I really hope you don't have another nightmare.'

'Are you going to wake me up if I do?'

The sportswoman rolled over, reminded of her scratches. 'I hope I don't have to.'

'I hope you don't either, but I expect you will.'

The pair lay on their backs, touching at the shoulder, hip and calf, in the position they had adopted as their own. Both felt silently and perfectly connected, despite the clouds suspended above, and drowsiness was soon upon them. Neither wanted to drift apart, either physically or emotionally.

'Your biceps are twitching,' the sixteen-year-old murmured, running her fingers along his strong arm.

'Yeah. They do that. So do my legs,' he replied, coughing his vocal chords into action. 'That's why I go running in the middle of the night, because when I'm in bed, it's as if I'm running anyway. When I'm really tired, especially.'

Lynn leaned across and planted a kiss on his shoulder. 'Wow. That's awful. No wonder you can't relax.'

'Tell me about it!'

'Have you thought any more about meditation?'

Jeff sighed, giving a low chuckle. 'I've thought about it but I can't empty my mind. It's too active. Just won't stop.'

'Go and see someone who can teach you,' the sportswoman suggested.

'A yogi?'

'Yeah. Guru, yogi... I'm not sure.'

The skeptic chuckled. 'Yogi Bear, more like. Jellystone Park must have a whole area devoted to the *Kama Sutra*. Drugs work well...'

His humorous aversion tactics weren't working, judging by the expression on his dream girl's face. Not wishing to be psychoanalysed any further, the student rolled leftwards and swung his legs out of bed, deciding to diffuse the atmosphere by visiting the bathroom instead.

'Put the light on,' his girlfriend urged. 'You'll fall down the stairs. I don't mind.'

'No, it's OK. Don't need it. I can see in the dark pretty well these days.'

'Go on! You don't have to be that selfless.'

Pausing in the doorway, Jeff gave a cruel laugh, taking the caring woman by surprise. 'I'm not. I'm being selfish, Lynn. Purely selfish. It kills me to turn the light on and find out what time it is. Kills me.'

The door bobbed against the catch but didn't close, thankfully. Tears pricked at the corners of the young woman's eyes as she prepared to leave the comfort of the bedclothes and reopen it for her troubled man's return, relieved that she didn't need to. This decaying relationship was as anguished as it was passionate, lately spiked with equal parts bitterness and tenderness. She knew they would both feel completely drained in the morning, but only she was likely to suffer anyone's wrath when her performance at training delivered less than one hundred percent.

Jeff's hand found the wall in the dark, his eyes having become accustomed to the fluorescent light in Suzanne's bathroom, and felt his way back to the guest bedroom. He could see a slither of light coming through the door, and smiled to himself, imagining Lynn to have upended or hidden Suzanne's clock. Sure enough, when he crept back into bed as quietly as he could, knowing how tired Lynn must be, he saw the luminous red digits of the electric radio-alarm had been planted face-down on the bedside table.

His compassionate lover was not asleep however, and turned to greet him, looking thoroughly consumed and contented. At least he scored one out of two, he joked in passing, commenting on how appealing the sight was. He received a sharp slap on the shoulder for his trouble.

'I shouldn't be here,' the sixteen-year-old rued, gazing at the ceiling.

'I know. D'you want me to drive you home?'

'No.'

The dreamer kissed her forehead, settling down under the blankets. 'Good. I love you so much.'

'I love you too.'

'I don't want you to go,' he dared, after a long pause.

'No, I know,' she sighed. 'I don't want me to go either.'

Another ten seconds must have passed before the next words were spoken, the air thick with regret. Of all the words the young man wanted to say, he could think of only two that would make his point clearly while inflicting the least damage.

'Thank you.'

Lynn rejoiced inside, despite the trepidation she felt at disobeying her parents' wishes. Australia's darling had become the rebellious teenager few believed she could ever be. Herself included, she admitted. Junior had tried to give her some advice concerning the best and worst independence muscles to flex, but his warnings had gone unheeded. Only Jeff had seen her defiant streak coming, of course. He had chosen his own, vastly accelerated pace towards adulthood, because he could. The wise man living in his youthful body had predicted that his saviour would want to grow up faster than the world would let her.

Things were different for Lynn Dyson, and she was beginning to understand why. For her, two years ahead in school and precocious in so many other ways, her normal teenaged angst, according to her handsome sage, was made more acute because she was not a normal teenager. *Your angst is metered out on a stage*, he had said.

To her boyfriend's *chagrin*, the awakening starlet propped herself up on her elbow and fixed him with a hugely melancholy stare. 'Thank you too. You're breaking my heart.'

'It's mutual, angel.'

'Does Gerry know I'm leaving?'

The handsome man nodded, his eyes firmly shut. 'Yep.'

'What did he say?'

'Ah, you know... You'll get over it, old chap.'

The teenager couldn't help but chuckle, so accurate an impression of the rambunctious accountant having been rendered without a change in her boyfriend's facial expression.

'We will. He's right.'

'Yep.'

'You will, Jeff.'

'Will I?'

***

Conductor and orchestra of Bedlam's morning symphony were on hand to wish their guests goodbye before first light the following morning. The youngsters needed to be back at the Sportsdrome in advance of Lynn's father's arrival, in order not to arouse suspicion that she had spent the night in anything other than peaceful slumber. Jeff was in predictably poor humour and manfully tried to hide it from Suzanne and also from his companion. Her smile warmed his ancient heart, while he took yet more liberties by spinning the car's rear tyres on the gravel.

One of the new songwriter's recent compositions suddenly floated across the airwaves from the car radio, played by an early morning disc jockey, and was met with a mixture of pride and embarrassment by its creator and with whoops of joy by the gorgeous groupie in his passenger seat. The song had been recorded by an emerging rock band from Texas whose roots were in country music. Even though the single was racing up the charts in several northern hemisphere markets as well as in Australia, Lynn didn't like it half as much as her boyfriend's version. To her mind, the hit was nowhere near as raunchy or as soulful as the rendition to which her sexy showman had treated her by the dam at Benloch.

After they had been driving for fifteen minutes, still outside the perimeter of the city's outer suburbs, the blonde Olympian suddenly requested the driver to stop the car in a secluded spot away from the roadside. Automatically jumping to an enticing conclusion, Jeff was more than happy to oblige, his mood lifting at the prospect.

'I want to have sex in the car.'

'I know you do,' her boyfriend smiled.

Lynn let out a squeal, and buried her face in her hands. 'How?'

A reassuring left hand alighted gently but firmly on her right shoulder and wove its way around her back and up towards the base of her skull, sending shivers down her arms and butterflies into flight in her stomach.

'Why else would you ask me to pull the car over here? Or are you intending to put me out of my misery?'

The teenager sighed deeply, wondering if she had done the right thing. She wanted so much to distract her man from the despair that had descended on him as soon as they left the kennels. Yet perhaps on reflection, resorting to sex to cheer him up might be perceived by the self-confessed sexual mercenary as a slap in the face. Turning off the engine once they had hidden the old sedan behind a thick clump of bushes, Jeff gamely threw the keys into the driver's footwell and leaned over towards his passenger.

'What are you doing?' the young woman asked, a little worried.

Her boyfriend scoffed. 'Sorry. Old trick, that's all.'

'Oh.'

But before she could voice her objection to another story from past conquests, the student deftly reached across her body and flicked the handle on the side of her seat. She dropped backwards, until she was lying nearly flat, with the Fairlane's grimy roof lining in plain view. Giggling at the sudden change of position, her fingers fumbled to unfasten her seatbelt, which was now straining at full stretch from its bolt on the door pillar.

'I left the keys on the dashboard once, behind the steering wheel,' Jeff explained, while reaching up inside her jumper and taking her right breast in his caring and purposeful hand, flicking it free of her bra with his middle finger. 'With all the action and the car's vibrations, they fell down a crack between the seat and the console and vanished without a trace. It was a lesson well learned, let me tell you.'

Even though she tried not to let it show and spoil the moment, the empathetic but bitter lover knew Lynn was saddened at hearing him describe the prior sexual encounter. He was also ashamed to admit that his main motivation for telling her was for payback. By now, he was straddling her hips, with his knees precariously balanced on the very edges of the passenger seat, while she grappled with his belt buckle. It took all his core strength to lean forward without falling onto her, and both smiled at the dangerous manœuvre.

'Sorry, baby,' he kissed his fingers and brushed them across her denuded abdomen. 'It's just a funny story.'

'That's OK. It doesn't matter.'

Jeff continued, now smiling at the paradox of being turned on faster by the unusually rough treatment his erection was receiving from his girlfriend's scorned hands. His eyes asked her to take it easy, which only made matters worse, and he dropped onto her in defeat, smothering her mouth with his for several long, intense kisses.

'I can't remember a single thing about who I was with, you know. I just remember taking a bloody long time to retrieve the keys afterwards, and I don't want to cause you to be late for training by the same thing happening again.'

Lynn groaned, laughing and pulling on his hipbones to lower him on top of her. 'Oh, for God's sake, shut it! You're just making it worse, you idiot.'

'OK. I'll stop,' he gasped, losing himself in the incredibly warm sensation of being inside her while the chilled air from the partly open windows drifted across his back. 'I don't want to keep these things to myself, but I will, if you prefer. Your wish is my command. Now come for me, angel, please.'

As if to honour his pledge, the young woman climaxed almost instantly, powerless to resist and crying out in pleasure. The animal attraction between the two desperate lovers transported them to ecstasy, magnified by the ever-present danger of being discovered.

'No, you're right,' the celebrity said, feeling another orgasm fast approaching. 'It is a funny story, and I'm glad you shared it with me. I just can't compete.'

Her man rose up until his arms locked straight, leaving her right on the brink. 'Compete? Who's competing?'

'You bastard!' the sixteen-year-old shouted. 'Bring it back!'

Jeff laughed out loud, her face an absolute picture of desolation. 'Oh, I'll bring it back. Never fear. I want it just as much as you do! Who said sex had to be a competition? We're a team, angel. You said so yourself.'

A muffled scream burst through pursed lips as his fingers sent her clitoris into overload again. A determined hand grabbed around the back of her head, and the expert lover held her against him as he came feverishly straight afterwards. Riding her until the last vestige of blissful sensation was released, he pressed her for an answer, as if it had the power to prolong the feeling yet more.

'I can't compete with all your touring stories,' he countered, 'but I still want to hear them.'

'Yet...' the celebrity snapped back, shuffling down the seat until they were able to sit up.

Condensation was running down the steam-covered windows, and rising breath billowed as white smoke from their panting mouths. Again Jeff called her bluff, this time making no apology, by reaching behind him and flicking open the glove compartment to reveal a box of tissues. Snatching a handful with a disdainful snort, Lynn shrugged and gave up her fight.

'OK, yet! But I can't, can I?'

The twenty-year-old kissed the top of her head just as his right knee finally lost its tenuous grip on the edge of the seat. He yelped, uttering a number of choice words, and levered himself free again.

'This was a damned fine idea,' he declared, blowing his lover a kiss.

Knowing he shouldn't change the subject so soon, the satisfied student flopped back down into the driving seat, narrowly missing the gear lever with his other shin. He wound the window down further to let more cool air in.

'Hey, world!' he yelled into the misty dawn air. 'Lynn Dyson's in here, and I'm never going to let her go.'

The shared passion first thing in the morning, trapped in their confined space, had unleashed the creativity in both musicians. By the time they had reached the inner suburbs, they had two new songs nearly completed. The blue Fairlane dropped its secret passenger off at the Sportsdrome at ten minutes before six o'clock, stopping a good distance from the entrance, so as not to arouse unnecessary suspicion. The couple kissed furtively, and the famous, long-legged blonde ran inside, leaving the anonymous driver to speed away.

That night, arriving home from a game of squash with Gerry, Jeff found a card from Lynn in his mailbox. It initially sent him into a panic, since he feared it might be a warning note saying they had been sprung and that she had been henceforth totally grounded. Instead of waiting to open it inside his flat and thereby running the risk of rendering entry through his front door even more difficult, the nervous student walked down to the river and sat on a bench next to the towpath. Gingerly, he peeled open the envelope to see what was inside.

On the front of the card was a picture of a black horse, which made the tired man smile. Inside, his dream girl had begun to write on the right-hand page in large lettering, obviously not intending to write too much. However, the text had become smaller and smaller with each line, as inspiration had begun to flow and space ran out, finally ending with a tiny signature and two kisses squeezed in at the bottom of the left-hand page.

The boy from Canley Vale smiled again as he imagined his gorgeous girlfriend writing it in an uncharacteristically impulsive mood.

> "To my beautiful black stallion. Jeff, I wanted to send this because this morning I feel so terrible, terrible, terrible. I feel like I've betrayed you. You put your trust in me, and I was pleased to be trusted with your innermost confidences. It makes me feel very special and respected. I can just imagine how you must be feeling, now that our amazing relationship must come to an end.
>
> I'm really so sorry for what has happened, and please believe me that I don't want to break up. I argued for a long time with my parents, but nothing will change their minds. I hope you can understand that I'm still their child and they still control me.
>
> Being in love with you is so wonderful, and I wouldn't have missed what we have for the world, but they are saying I need to suspend love until I've built a solid career for myself, because love will wait but career will not. I'm not sure I agree, but I can't convince them.
>
> I was very happy to hear about your plans for releasing your albums. I look forward to hearing more of your songs on the radio, and sung by you, obviously. They will make me sad too though, because I know so many of them speak of your hard times which might now come back. (I didn't mean for that to sound big-headed, by the way, but too late, it's written!) I really wanted to help you get cured of the nightmares, etc. I also think I will hear many sad songs about us over the next two years, as you will from me.
>
> Anyway, running out of space! I love you, Jeff, and I thank you so much for hanging in there with me. I hope we can spend as much time together as poss in time left. See you Sun. Lots of love, Lynn xx"

A long sigh of relief emanated from the old soul, his heartbeat thumping through his temples. The letter was good, he thought, under the circumstances. It didn't change anything, but at least the situation hadn't deteriorated. That was about as much as he could hope for. He closed the card and tucked it into the side pocket of his sports bag, as one more souvenir of his very special time with Lynn Dyson.

Earlier that evening, Jeff had taken a chance by confiding in Gerry over a few beers about his fears for Lynn's impending departure and had been surprised to receive a sympathetic hearing. Even the easy-come, easy-go man about town was not totally insensitive to how much his friend adored the sweet-natured, blonde bombshell. Even the hardest heart could see how natural they were together and how happy the younger man had been to find out that meeting the stunning star in the flesh was every bit as rewarding as his long-held fantasies had promised.

'Two years, mate?' Gerry had almost shouted, when the details emerged one at a time. 'Bummer. It sounds like a long time but it'll fly by, especially if your record deal comes off. Your feet won't touch the ground for two years anyway. Sex, drugs and rock'n'roll, Jeff. You'll soon forget about her.'

Yes, that was the plan. The intelligent amateur philosopher could envision what lay ahead of him quite clearly these days. He would go the way of many a tortured and lovelorn poet before him. Unrequited love commanded a high price tag. People were willing to pay dearly for despair, as long as it wasn't their own. And perversely, the songwriter understood, even more so if it gave them a way to transfer their own painful loss to someone else.

The wannabe rock star had joked with the junior partner that if he were going to be lonely and crazy, he might as well be lonely and crazy and stinking rich. They had raised their glasses of malt whisky to this pretentious claim, luxuriating on dark green chesterfields in a corner of the swanky sports club.

Wandering back to his flat at the end of the night, chilly in his shirt sleeves after the alcohol had begun to wear off, Jeff formulated a suitable response to his guilt-ridden girlfriend. There was still a part of him that wanted her to suffer, as if it might somehow cause his suffering to diminish. Not constructive, he concluded. Would he put his response in writing too, seeing that she was out of town for a few days now anyway? It would be nice for Lynn to receive something she could open on her return.

Depending what he put in it, of course... Trolls were devilish beings. All the way home, the young man wrestled with the many things he wanted to say. Should he hedge his bets and make the best of the remaining time, and thereby leave the door open for their relationship to continue in two years' time? Or should he speak his mind about Bart Dyson's argument that she couldn't possibly combine love with her career? It was wholly unfair to make Lynn choose between her boyfriend and her father, leading him to conclude that the latter approach could easily jeopardise any potential reconciliation in the future.

Jeff knew the maturing youngster always sought his honest opinion. It was one of the things he loved most about her. One of the many things. This was the basis for their respecting relationship after all; the unadulterated truth. It only remained for the wordsmith to phrase his reply carefully. No point in descending into placid indifference with such a short time to go. That was only cheating both of them.

The confused and lonely man stood outside his front door for twenty minutes or so, becoming colder and colder. For some unknown reason, the alarming incursion of childhood images appeared outside the door this time, urging him to get lost and not even attempt to breach their imaginary lines. In the end, he managed to direct his mounting anger towards opening the door, and he fought and swore his way through the hallway, endeavouring to defy his demons and block out the interminable screaming in his head. He jumped straight into the shower and leaned against the tiled wall until he almost fell asleep, with another new song churning endlessly in his head.

Perfect, the young man thought. The words had arrived completely out of the blue, with the name of its subject having been with him for years as his codename for Lynn when he hadn't wished to identify her: Regala, the one bestowed. This torrential lyric had come from deep within, a product of his grief and frustration, but it was also a sound variation on a familiar plight. In fact, it presented the ideal response for the woman who was about to desert him.

With his long hair still dripping, and sporting the bizarre fashion statement of towel and leather jacket, it took less than five minutes for the inspired songwriter to pen his new composition. He sat on the bed, with his guitar on his knees and the primitive tape recorder beside him on the mattress. When he was done and satisfied with the result, he picked up the telephone and dialled the young star's number, waiting for the answering machine to beep. The catharsis of writing had left him in a more optimistic frame of mind, and he was anxious to record this fact and to ease his girlfriend's concerned mind.

'Lynn, it's me. Thanks for the card. It's great, and I understand everything in it. I know it's hard to argue with your parents' theory, but I could give you countless arguments for the coexistence of love and career. One needn't preclude the other. It's been done before. And don't sweat, because I don't feel betrayed. Not by you, angel. I betrayed myself, if anything, by thinking we'd last. Whatever... In the spirit of "Let's say exactly what's on our mind," I do feel deserted, abandoned. Not yet, but soon to be. Anyway... "The Graduate" with Dustin Hoffman and Anne Bancroft's opening on Thursday. Did you want to go next Friday? Hope you had a good trip. See you Sunday. I love you. *Adiós.*'

Jeff replaced the receiver and stretched out along the couch. Sitting in the dark and quietly strumming the chords that went with his new lyric, he felt his stomach churn in melancholic fury. He was beginning to feel stronger though. Gerry's support had helped, so good on him. His mate was useful for something. The astute businessman was also in the process of devising a very sound structure for a management company to administer the fortune which would soon be streaming in from the aspiring rock star's recording contract and his arrogantly-anticipated stream of royalties.

Over the last few days, another concept had been forming in the indefatigable intellectual's head, this time for a novel. He had never previously taken himself for an author and deemed the protracted process of creative writing to be the antithesis of his usual short-term, fast yield *modus operandi*. However, some hidden force appeared to be shepherding him towards this exercise, and his rabid curiosity had already been galvanised. Why not? Perhaps he could lose himself in a work of fiction for around twenty-four months? Its theme was dark, of course, but the plot was taking shape, and he was keen to start writing down all these random ideas. Suzanne had a typewriter which she hardly ever used, so he planned to borrow it over the weekend in exchange for company walking her pack of assorted pets in the early mornings.

The news was now official that she and Gerry were also splitting up, although without sorrow or animosity. The two had simply grown apart in their respective new Victorian homes; he in inner suburban luxury, and she on the verge of the countryside, in the ramshackle cottage in the woods. Suzanne would not be sympathetic to someone else's heartbreak, which dissuaded the young man from sharing the pain of the love of his life leaving, at least until the departure date was upon them. Still nagging regularly about his unfaithfulness and sleeping around, the conservative woman would more than likely assume these to be the reasons behind Lynn's throwing in the towel and siding with her parents. Jeff didn't care to tackle that particular argument this weekend.

The thoughtful artist lay down on the bed, desperately tired and longing for some peace. He had been disturbed by the aggressive cluster of his least favourite personalities appearing on the landing tonight. Did this mean that eventually they would be following him around wherever he went, no longer satisfied with meeting him at the door? Just when he thought things might improve... Their taunting and cackling had put the manic depressive in mind of the time, when as a child on the promise of a treat from his absent father, he had gone running after him as he left their squalid, second-floor flat, only to have the door slammed in his face. If the rejection he felt at being left behind wasn't damaging enough to the six-year-old, there were also the cold-blooded hoots of laughter coming from the group of men in the stairwell, the evil dispassion of which still haunted him to this day.

His was such an ironic set of symptoms, the student rued bitterly, thinking back to the wicked events of the night at Suzanne's, when Lynn had been forced to cover his mouth in order to silence his nightmares. Dog-tired and yet plagued with sleep-depriving dreams; so much ambition but obsessed by bringing about his own demise.

Perhaps it was a good thing that the beautiful celebrity was being taken away. Had her parents been snooping around in his old medical or police records? The Sydneysider guessed Bart Dyson would be able to find out pretty much anything merely by pulling a few of his well-connected strings. For Christ's sake, he had been standing next to the Deputy Chief of Police at the bar at Benloch just a few months ago. At least his admittance to the psychiatric clinic, courtesy of the Blakes, had been classed as voluntary, thereby mercifully saving him from a section record. Such an indelible watermark underlining the rest of his life would have given him even more of a problem than he already had.

How did people with more serious mental conditions than his ever get the opportunity to lead a normal life? Society simply didn't cater for rehabilitated schizophrenics or people with a history of violent disturbance. Those who once fell off life's treadmill had no easy way to get back on, so long as their records travelled with them and while mainstream decision-makers remained unprepared to take the risk of giving them a second chance.

And the young man cursed his father's unassuming parents for allowing the original Polish spelling of their surname to be altered to such an ostentatious and memorable English noun. It would not be much of a stretch for the New South Wales State Records Office to trace this Jeff Diamond of Canley Vale to one Paul Diamond of neighbouring Fairfield. Why the hell hadn't he changed his name when he moved to Melbourne? With a little less brute pride and much greater foresight, he could have introduced himself to Lynn and her family as John Smith, and they would have been none the wiser as to the dubious past he had left behind. True, it would have been inconvenient to change all his examination certificates and his driving licence, *et cetera*, but that was all administrative bureaucracy which would only have been disruptive for a short time.

Jeff laughed to himself in the dark, thinking of the new John Smith albums about to be released onto the unsuspecting Australian music market. He had decided on a title for the first, "Road of Stones", which was taken from the name of the notorious and neglected street on which he had grown up. Its title track was a song he had written for his sister, although she didn't yet know it. The pretender preferred to wait for Madalena to hear it on the radio. There... He was nothing if not presumptuous, wasn't he?

It was also the sentimental songwriter's intention to call the second double album "Regala", to serve as a reminder for Lynn that the majority of its songs had been conceived because of her. It wouldn't be difficult for her to work it out. Jeff wondered if she might attend one of his concerts if things were to go well and he was granted a tour in the United States. That would certainly be surreal and more than a little acrid, he lamented, imagining the sudden role reversal: he on stage and she in the audience. At some point over the next two years, Lynn Dyson might rock up to a Jeff Diamond gig, when he had never been to one of hers in all these years of being her Number One Fan. Yet another irony to keep him company in the dark.

The disillusioned but determined dreamer slipped into a shallow slumber at last. As expected, however, what started as a pleasant dream involving his sister in their childhood years quickly turned vile and brutal on the Stones Road, and soon he was once more sitting on the couch with a beer, his cigarettes and the faithful fifty dollar guitar. Predictable but no less harrowing than usual. Such was life.

Long Shadow Cast

With the colours seeping gradually out of Jeff's world, the next few weeks took turns to fly or drag, depending on Lynn's busy schedule. Despite their ongoing gloom at the approach of her departure date, the pair managed to remain loving and reasonably positive as the weeks went by.

The young celebrity had not confirmed her boyfriend's paranoiac suspicions that her father had been digging around in Sydney for information contributing to the downfall of their relationship. She probably hadn't been told, he decided. Indeed, the twenty-year-old could hardly imagine being too keen to pass on such disturbing facts to a daughter of his, if he were ever to have one.

And in the moments when the pair was seen together in public, one might have been forgiven for thinking that the gregarious, fun-loving student had rationalised his dream girl's exodus. He had declined her misguided invitation to attend the pre-Olympics team dinner together, saying it was inappropriate for him to be her guest in front of her parents, team-mates and those other partners who evidently weren't seen to be interfering with the athletes' quest for glory. Reluctantly, Lynn had seen his point of view and understood his refusal to be for the best, even though she had secretly been disappointed at losing an opportunity to thumb her nose at the establishment.

In contrast however, they had both attended a farewell party which the MAC crew had thrown for their favourite singer, and Jeff had cracked jokes and danced the night away with the people with whom his girlfriend shared the greatest affinity. The highly-regarded musicians waxed lyrical about the success the emerging artist was bound to have with his new recordings, and the teenaged idol told him how proud she was to publicly project that he would be a very big star by the time she returned to Australia.

There were now only two weeks to go until Lynn left for Munich with the rest of her family, and from there she would fly to Los Angeles to commence her studies at the beginning of October. Her training schedule remained intense, the Year Twelve workload demanding, and there had been precious little time for relaxation. Most downtime was spent eating or sleeping, or practising the visualisation techniques which brought the sportswoman ever closer to her sporting goals each time she pictured herself on the gold medal rostrum.

'Do you think that stuff really works?' Jeff had asked her cynically, driving back from the Sportsdrome, where she had sneaked out without her coach noticing and jumped into the waiting Ford parked around the back.

'Yes,' Lynn answered without hesitation. 'Definitely. We've been using visualisation for years now. It helps focus your mind on what you're trying to achieve and less on all the things that could go wrong.'

'Would you teach me then, please?' her boyfriend requested. 'I could do with some help focusing less on the things that could go wrong.'

The sportswoman looked across at the handsome but exhausted driver, who had come straight from work to pick her up and who hadn't shaved for at least two days. He looked just like he sounded; dispirited, resentful and worn out. She imagined him to have been out all night drinking and most likely in the arms of a nameless woman about whom she preferred to remain ignorant.

With her head bent forward in her hands, the heartbroken teenager was unable to stop herself bursting into tears. She was trying so hard to stay upbeat and to be all that her parents, team and country expected her to be.

'Angel, I'm sorry,' Jeff said, hearing her crying next to him. 'Forget I said anything. I don't mean to make you cry. Let's get something to eat, shall we? There's an interesting-looking noodle house just opened up on Victoria Street that I ran past this morning.'

The famous schoolgirl was grateful for his attempts to find pleasure in what was turning into a torturous situation for both of them. She had been forced to cancel a planned date earlier in the week, and her smarting boyfriend had done his utmost to remain understanding. She was testing his tolerance to the limit and knew he was bound to take it out on her tonight, even though he wouldn't really mean to. It was just the way he was, this fascinating man with whom she had fallen head over heels in love. Breaking up this way was never going to be easy, but their open communication was raw and honest and utterly, utterly unmissable.

'Thanks. That sounds good. I'd like that.'

The student parked the car in a side street on the northern side of the bustling, multi-cultural thoroughfare, and the couple jogged across the road and ducked into the small Vietnamese restaurant that he had in mind, before the blonde celebrity could be spotted. The owners, who like most of their patrons were not native to Australia, didn't recognise their special guest, which meant that few among them would care that a member of their adopted country's sporting dynasty had taken a seat at one of the pale green plastic and chrome tables.

'This menu's huge,' Lynn laughed, flicking through the various sections. 'How do you choose from all these dishes?'

Jeff pushed the plastic-coated pages downwards in her hands until they were flat on the table. 'Close your eyes.'

His girlfriend did as she was told with a smile on her face. She let the playful man take hold of her right hand and start it moving in a circular motion.

'Visualise something tasty,' he teased, somewhat sarcastically, 'and your finger'll land on it.'

The smile lessening and still with her eyes tightly shut, Lynn turned over a couple of laminated leaves and allowed her finger to fall onto the left-hand side. She opened her eyes to learn her culinary fate.

'Euch!' she exclaimed in a fairly subdued voice. 'Braised quail eggs with bean curd and vegetables. That's not quite what I was picturing in my mind.'

Her partner raised his eyebrows and shrugged. 'See? All this psychobabble... Not too reliable, is it?'

'That's not fair,' the young woman replied, not knowing whether to hold her nerve or to sympathise with her melancholy dinner companion.

'Cheap shot?' he asked, knowing full well it had been. 'Sorry. Couldn't resist. Choose the conventional way. It's safer.'

After much consideration, during which Jeff downed two full bottles of beer, they plumped for two of the Chef's Specials, and the waiter soon brought their next round of drinks. The contaminated soul drank quickly, straight from the bottle, while his girlfriend sipped on some very refreshing, clean and pure jasmine tea.

'I can teach you,' Lynn returned to their earlier topic, 'if you like. There might be some visualisation techniques that'll at least give you ideas of how to modify them to suit.'

The student was genuinely interested, although he played it cool. 'Mmm... Are you sure you won't be giving away any official secrets?'

'No! Why? Are you going to sell the information to other teams or something?'

Her boyfriend shook his head. 'Nope. And neither am I about to enter any last minute events against you guys.'

'Good,' she smiled at him emptying the last few mouthfuls of beer down his throat and immediately catching the waitress' eye for yet another. 'Although by the looks of you, your training schedule's falling a little bit behind.'

Now that's a cheap shot, Jeff thought, *if ever there was one*. Probably well deserved, since he had been abusing his body greatly over the past few weeks, but still not too supportive under the circumstances.

'Thanks for your vote of confidence,' he responded in a caustic tone. 'Is that what you really think? You want to stop me taking myself down? It's a bit late for that, isn't it?'

The pretty teenager frowned. 'Sorry. That was mean of me. It was supposed to be a joke, but I realise it wasn't at all funny.'

Jeff put his left hand on her right wrist and squeezed it gently. There was no point in fighting. Her observation was an accurate one, and they were on borrowed time.

'That's OK, angel. It's true enough. I just can't bring myself to be positive about anything, given how fast the clock's ticking and how pathetic this situation is.'

'Well, let me help you then,' Lynn suggested anew. 'Alcohol's not the only way. Your album's sounding great, and everything's on track for your launch, so you should start getting yourself ready for all the hype.'

Their food arrived, yet as it turned out, neither had much appetite for it. The songwriter knew the seasoned campaigner's words were sensible and well-meant, and the Olympian realised that it was a tall order for her to convince the longstanding addict to put his faith in an approach based on her father's doctrine. They both began to eat in silence.

'Thanks,' the young man said calmly, after a few moments lost in their own thoughts. 'You're right. I need to get my act together. I do want to go through with everything, angel. I really do. It's just so damned hard to think good thoughts about the future.'

The athlete smiled. 'I know what you mean. I don't want to stop seeing each other now though, do you? Do you think it'd be better, rather than eking out the time left?'

Shaking his head, her perturbed boyfriend finished his mouthful quickly. 'No, absolutely not. Although sometimes I think it might be easier overall. More for you than for me. That's why the alcohol option is preferable. Or other mind-altering substances, even better. Pity you're so young, gorgeous. You can't take advantage of my miracle cure snake oil.'

Lynn chuckled, raising a delicate china tea cup to her gorgeous and eloquent mind-bender. 'OK. You win! Let's eat. Mine's delicious, after all that. Is yours?'

With a hot meal inside him and one more bottle of beer to chase it down, Jeff began to feel better. His caring girlfriend was right not to let him off the hook. She was so good to him, despite his best efforts to ruin their last few times together.

'So, teacher...' he invited, putting his chopsticks down onto a clean plate. 'Where do I start?'

'Serious?'

The student nodded. 'Yep. Just ignore my vindictiveness. I need a good talking-to.'

'You do!' the celebrity laughed. 'And a good seeing-to, later.'

'Now there's a concept I can subscribe to,' he told her, managing a glint in his tired eye. 'Maybe we should just skip straight to that part?'

The well-bred youngster tutted like a schoolmistress, watching her good-looking boyfriend leave the table to pay at the counter. They left the restaurant and walked hand-in-hand towards the car. Catching him frowning at his watch, Lynn once again felt like crying. This in-between zone was so difficult to deal with. Neither wanted to miss out on the remaining hours, so they would simply have to put up with life's cumbrous overtones bearing down on them.

The driver turned the car round and pushed their way into the busy traffic on Victoria Street, crossing the eastbound lanes before turning left down Hoddle Street, towards the river and back to Admin. The radio was turned up loud, in an effort to disperse the gloomy air pressure.

Once inside the celebrity's apartment, Jeff pulled his beautiful girlfriend close and kissed her hard. They were both crying this time, no longer embarrassed about airing their misery.

'OK,' the sportswoman began, signalling for her flagging pupil to sit beside her on the couch.

Jeff removed his leather jacket and tossed it onto the dining table, making a detour to the bathroom. By the time he returned, his personal trainer had laid out a notepad and some coloured pens on the coffee table and had begun to draw rows and columns on the top sheet of paper. He slumped down heavily, hoping he was giving the impression of being inquisitive.

'What are you doing? This table's going to change my life?'

The studious teenager nodded. 'Be patient. I was going to start with focus and the triggers that create the right thought processes, but you know all that stuff anyway.'

'Do I?' he asked. 'Not sure I do. If I do, it's not working, put it that way.'

Lynn chuckled. 'OK. Well, there's nothing I can do about that.'

Jeff gave her a blistering stare and raised his eyebrows, his rebuke carving through the dense air like a Samurai's sword.

'Is that right?'

The young woman looked away.

The eyes of her enigmatic stranger never missed a chance to ask her not to go, even though he had not directly put the request into words for some weeks now. They had even shared a joke recently, wherein he threatened to kidnap her and whisk her off to France or Spain. On complaining half-heartedly that neither her French nor her Spanish was good enough, he had been unable to stifle a sinister laugh when telling her not to worry, since she wouldn't be setting foot outside the door. This image had not scared her half as much as it should have.

'No, there isn't,' she confirmed, gently touching his hand, determined to move on. 'You already know that learning's reinforced by whatever your senses are experiencing at the time, don't you? You're the most sensual person I've ever come across, so there's no way you wouldn't have already made that connection.'

The gifted intellectual nodded. 'Yeah. I've read heaps about those concepts. Are you going to "mind over matter" then?'

'Yes,' his mentor sighed, fully expecting another smart retort. 'I'm not finding it too easy either, just at the moment, I confess. But I believe in the theory. If you focus on the emotional triggers that remind you of what your goals are... what you're interested in... they'll happen. If you focus on all the things you don't want to happen, then they'll be more likely to happen instead.'

'Sure. I understand all that. They say that ninety percent of your brain responds to sensual perception and only ten percent to learned, factual memory. Who knows if that's really true though?'

The young beauty leaned into her struggling stallion, grateful to find him amenable to discussing these ideas constructively. For her own peace of mind over the coming months, she needed so much to help him prepare for the inevitable. There was nothing she was looking forward to more than being back in his embrace in two years' time, no matter what her family's attitude might be by then.

Jeff's arm draped itself around her shoulder, and his lips kissed her hair. And their eyes shed some more tears.

'Christ Almighty,' he moaned. 'Do you have a cure for crying in that do-it-yourself Dyson kit of yours? That's really what we need, isn't it?'

'No, obviously not!' Lynn sniffed, wiping her eyes with her sleeve. 'Otherwise I'd be using it now. Do you want some wine?'

The dependent laughed out loud, cupping her tearful face in his hands and kissing her soft, moist lips. 'What? Doctor, you're supposed to be steering me away from alcoholism and into good, wholesome psychobabble. Stop with the temptation.'

His girlfriend slapped his leg, determined not to descend too far into the doldrums. 'Shut up! I just thought you'd like a glass while we go through this stuff.'

Jeff backed off. 'Yes, I would. Of course I would, but I also want to make the best of my time with you without getting shitfaced. I can do that tomorrow. And I will, most likely.'

Lynn nodded, becoming instantly more circumspect again. 'Alright. But it's there if you change your mind.'

'Thanks, angel,' the young man replied, leaning back on the couch and staring straight into her gorgeous blue eyes. 'So what I need to do is find something that looks, sounds, smells, tastes and feels nice and reminds me that I need to be a rock star. Is that it?'

'Yes!' the sixteen-year-old giggled. '¡Exactamente!'

Before the last Spanish syllable had finished escaping from her mouth, her insatiable suitor turned her face towards his and kissed her passionately, his tongue caressing hers with its usual vigour. As she gave in to the comforting sensation of his hand on her breast, she opened her eyes to see two dark pools of desire focussed intently on hers.

'Found it!' he announced in triumph, breaking away. 'I'll be able to remember this fairly easily. Going to be a touch hard to trigger though, over twelve and a half thousand kilometres. Still… Aim high, huh?'

The teenager nodded. 'Yes. Aim high.'

Jeff exhaled, suddenly bereft of all energy. 'Right. What next? Lesson three.'

'Lesson three? What was one? Oh, sensory input. Yeah. Next, you have to be clear on your stakeholders. Who are you going to make happy by achieving your goals?'

The student leaned back on the couch and lit a cigarette, prising the shoes off his heels one after the other and kicking them under the coffee table. Lynn handed him the notepad onto which she had ruled the criss-crossed lines of blank rows and columns.

'My stakeholders?' he repeated, dragging hard and playing provocatively with the smoke. 'That's actually pretty interesting. Who am I doing this for?'

Lynn's dancing eyes concentrated back on his, guiding them down to the piece of paper on his lap. 'I'm not going to answer for you.'

A sigh accompanied the next cloudy stream from his lungs. 'Well, you, obviously. First and foremost.'

'Write it down then,' the sportswoman encouraged. 'Although I'm not sure I should be first and foremost.'

'Angel,' the attentive and amorous scholar gave her a mischievous nudge, 'you said you weren't going to answer for me, so butt out.'

A welcome wave of relief washed through the teenager. For the first time that evening, she felt as though she had managed to break the man she loved out of his moribund demeanour. Hopefully, this exercise would go some way towards igniting his limitless imagination sufficiently well to keep him going for a few more days.

'Good,' she replied, slipping off the couch and heading towards the kitchenette. 'Coffee?'

'Yeah, thanks. What am I supposed to do next?'

His teacher shouted over the noise of the kettle. 'Identify each stakeholder in your success and write down why they have a stake in your success and why you want to make it happen for each of them.'

'Cheers,' he acknowledged, already sounding more positive.

While the water was boiling, the celebrity disappeared into the bathroom for a few minutes. Behind closed doors, she let go another batch of pent-up tears, while donning another new piece of lingerie she had rushed out to buy that afternoon after school. It was a superficial gesture, but she knew the virile hot-head would appreciate it for what it was.

To her delight, Lynn returned with two steaming mugs to a page of boxes already filled with scribbled entries.

'Hey!' she exclaimed, putting their drinks down onto the coffee table, along with a packet of TimTams that had been tucked under one arm. 'That's excellent! So the idea is, when you're happy with it, you should read it whenever you need inspiration, to remind you to focus on the people who'll benefit when you're a rich and famous rock star.'

'TimTams,' Jeff observed, reaching two out of the opened packet of chocolaty goodness. 'Since when are you allowed to have TimTams before the Olympics?'

'I'm not,' the dedicated athlete answered sadly. 'They're for you.'

'Thanks, angel. Don't mind if I do,' he smiled in sympathy, taking two more on her behalf. 'Bummer they're all for me...'

Chuckling and rolling her eyes, the teenager took her place again on the couch and attempted to peer over his arm and onto the busy page of notes. Warm, coffee-flavoured lips met her cheek as it leaned in towards him and they pushed her head away.

'Oh, no, you don't,' he smirked. 'This is between me and my stakeholders.'

'I thought I was one of your stakeholders,' the feisty coach responded, refusing to go on the defensive.

'You are, but you already know why I'm doing what I'm doing, don't you?'

Lynn shook her head. 'Not really,' she admitted. 'I don't need you to be a rock star.'

'Yeah, OK,' Jeff gazed into her beautiful face and felt the tears stinging his eyes again. 'But without it, you know I'm not going to get through these two years, and I need to come out the other side as someone who's worthy of you.'

The sixteen-year-old gasped. 'No! What are you talking about? You're already worthy of me.'

'I don't think so,' he answered, taking a large gulp of coffee to counteract the depth of his emotions. 'And your parents don't think so either.'

The sixteen-year-old breathed out slowly, reaching for her mug too. The headstrong student's last phrase was certainly true. What would become of this mystery man who had bewitched her for the last six months? She had no reason to doubt his sincerity. She had read many accounts of talented and capable people committing suicide when faced with obstacles they had no motive or desire to surmount. She had no doubt he had what it took to be a star, only hoping its rewards would be sufficient to keep him from following the terminal course to which his warped mind continually drove him.

With such a small number of days to go before they were no longer boyfriend and girlfriend, Lynn was hit for the first time with an unbridled urge to cast away everything she had worked for. What was so important about being an Olympic champion? So what if she only had a degree from Melbourne University? A degree was a degree, and the local tertiary institution had a perfectly respectable reputation. She focussed her mind on those others who would have made it to Jeff's stakeholder list: poor kids from decaying city suburbs, people in remote places with no power to stand up to tyranny, ordinary citizens who were denied a basic education and access to information that would help them make their lives better. A degree from a cashed-up Californian seat of learning meant little in comparison to changing these otherwise undervalued lives.

Did she even deserve a place on this man's stakeholder list? The star's own goals didn't contribute to anything remotely as noble. Undeniably, bringing glory to one's country was laudable, and her various ambassadorial duties and endeavours while performing overseas would indirectly attract more investment into Australia. Yet how much of that contribution would make a material difference to any individual human being in need? What small-minded goals they were, the naïve celebrity concluded.

The pretty teenager felt her face redden as these new ideas germinated, along with the knowledge that her own stakeholder list was incomplete by necessity, so as not to alert her father to this apparent shift in her motivations. No, she was not immune to being influenced. Moreover, God damn it, she needed some influencing.

'What's wrong?' Jeff asked, seeing her suddenly deflate. 'You look worried.'

Lynn dissolved once more into floods of tears and lurched forwards on the couch into his arms. Tossing his notes and pen onto the cushion and catching her willingly, Jeff held her close into his chest and felt her lungs fill and empty while she sobbed. Why the hell were they putting themselves through this purgatory?

'I should go, angel,' he whispered, his chin resting on the top of her head. 'You need to rest and forget about us as best you can. I don't want to cause you to suffer like this and potentially damage your chances in Munich.'

His dream girl clung onto him still tighter. 'No. I don't want you to go. I hate this. I hate this so much.'

'Me too, baby,' the despondent young man replied and stroked her wet face. 'Me too.'

'You're not even on my stakeholder list,' the teenager blurted out, pulling back and looking into his dark, soulful eyes.

'No. I guessed that,' he reassured her quietly. 'That's OK. It's not appropriate, and what would I do with a gold medal anyway?'

The sportswoman gave an uninspired laugh and leaned back down onto his chest again. She had stopped crying, grudgingly preparing herself once more to continue being the staunch and tenacious daughter of Bart Dyson, and not Jeff Diamond's idealistic dream girl.

'You're so gorgeous, and I feel like such a selfish cow.'

'Stop that,' her boyfriend objected firmly. 'I don't want to hear you describe yourself that way. You're doing what you have to do. Let's have this conversation again in two years' time and see where we are, OK?'

Pleased to finally play a helpful part in this grotesque charade, the student suddenly tipped forwards, with her limp, miserable body balanced precariously half on his lap and half on the couch, while he attempted to reach for the box of tissues on the far side of the coffee table. As his dream girl's head came to rest relatively softly on the glass table top, his lips locked hers in a passionate kiss. The transfer of emotions made them both cry again, and they lingered in the one position for several minutes, staring into each others' tearful eyes.

'Promise me you'll still be here in two years' time,' Lynn begged.

The desolate man shook his head, pulling themselves back upright, handing out tissues to his beautiful girlfriend and taking a few for himself.

'If you are, I will be,' he assured her. 'I promise.'

'I'm not sure I know what that means.'

'Neither am I. My stakeholders'll have to want me to succeed a great deal, or I might not make it.'

The athlete nodded. 'They will.'

'That's good,' Jeff forced a smile. 'OK. What's next on my rescue plan?'

'Thanks. Let's see…' his trainer answered, taking a deep breath in and regrouping on his instruction. 'Not self-sabotaging.'

'Ha!' the tearaway from the wild, wild west scoffed. 'You've got the wrong man for that gig, lady!'

'No, I haven't,' the Melbourne girl contradicted, tapping his forehead. 'It's "thinking leads to behaviour leads to results." Convince yourself you're a champion.'

'A champion what?' her boyfriend chided, throwing his hands in the air. 'I'm not sure I want to be a champion anything. I just want to make the world a better place.'

'No, that's just an example. You already do it,' the famous schoolgirl continued, undeterred. 'It's picking friends like Gerry and Suzanne, for example.'

Jeff nodded, capitulating with a sarcastic sigh. He understood the allusion only too well and already believed in this latest technique. It was one he had employed throughout his teens and it had been the overriding factor in his so-called success thus far.

'Associating with the right people?' he checked. 'Mimic a millionnaire, play in his world and you'll stand a better chance of becoming one?'

'Yes. Precisely!' Lynn answered, pleased that he could still be bothered to think laterally this evening. 'Don't be bound by the things that seem like limits and restrictions. That's where the visualisation comes in. Try, before you go to sleep, to picture being in the world you want to be in, rather than surrounded by all the things you're trying to overcome to get there. Picture yourself already there.'

'In my Aston Martin,' the lowly student began, pretending his hands were on a steering wheel, 'with you in the passenger seat, speeding away from Benloch at a hundred-and-fifty "K"s an hour, with my middle finger in the air?'

Following the grand mime enacted by his explicit and emphatic hand, the young woman's eyes gave away the fact that she didn't entirely approve of this image, but nevertheless she was excited to hear some positivity again.

'Something like that,' she smiled. 'If you keep over-analysing the problem, all you'll wake up with is a bigger problem.'

'And a headache.'

'Or a nightmare,' Lynn added, putting on a sad face.

'*Si. Te entiendo,*' her man replied, wearing his cynicism proudly on his sleeve. 'Whereas if I go to sleep with the vision of us together in two years' time, I'll wake up, and it'll still only be tomorrow. And that's if I'm lucky... More than likely, it'll still be today, and the thrashing and yelling will have scared you away again.'

The teenager sighed, slumping down against his side once again. Despite everything she believed, she couldn't deny that Jeff's description of the ensuing scenario was infinitely more plausible in the present circumstances.

'I'm sorry.'

'Why? What are you sorry for?' he asked, tilting his head sideways so that it rested against hers.

'It sounds really simplistic, doesn't it?' the wistful young woman murmured. 'What a superficial world I live in... I'm the one who's not worthy.'

'Yeah. Maybe so,' Jeff couldn't help but agree, smiling at her apparent *renaissance*. 'And it's that kind of statement that got us into this shit in the first place. Regardless, it's getting to that simplicity that's the secret, angel. Reaching the point where there are no other factors governing your life except those you can control. I understand exactly what you're saying, but it's a hell of a long way from where I am right now.'

Lynn gave a big yawn, holding her hand over her mouth and laughing.

'Sorry! You're not boring me,' she smiled. 'I'm really tired.'

'Right, Miss Freud,' the young man shook his head. 'Let's stop now anyway. Did you want me to get out of here soon? I've had a good lesson tonight, and I promise you I'll figure out what I have to behave like to get through and become who I want to be. And somehow I'll find motivation, just as long as I can still feel you with me. I've done it before.'

'Great,' his girlfriend said, kissing him tenderly.

'I heard a good quote once,' her resident oracle continued, stroking the delectable body through her clothes and feeling himself quickly becoming aroused. 'From a bloke called Earl Shoaff, I think, who died a few years ago. He was into making millionnaires out of ordinary folk. He said, "Don't wish things were easier. Wish you were better." Everything's in our power to achieve. We just need to work for it.'

'That's good. Do you believe in it?'

Jeff lifted his left hand and rocked it from side to side, indicating that his jury was still out, before returning it inside the waistband of her jeans, which had been unzipped to reveal pale pink underwear. He leaned down and placed a soft kiss on her belly button, while his fingers stroked the sensitive skin along her panty line.

'Not entirely. It's basically capitalist doctrine. There's no collective achievement in it. There was nothing in Schoaff's work that encouraged people to do things for others.'

The sixteen-year-old frowned, pushing his hand away and kneeling up to wrap her arms around his neck. Her knowledgeable boyfriend had made her feel very selfish and over-privileged again, and it embarrassed her. She still had a lot of learning to do about the big, wide world.

'I'm annoyed with how I just accept things without considering them more carefully,' she admitted with a resigned grunt. 'I agree with you and hate that I don't think like you do of my own accord.'

'Angel, you're tired and you have a mission to accomplish,' her patient lover told her, running his fingers down the side of her face, then her neck and on towards her breasts. 'Don't beat yourself up. Concentrate on what you need to concentrate on to get the immediate job done. There's heaps of time to save ourselves from the Earl Shoaffs of this world.'

'Will you stay? Please? I mean after...'

'If you're sure,' the horny student replied. 'I'd love to.'

Also turned on by the lavish attention her body was receiving while her brain was undergoing its education, the pretty athlete swivelled round and off the couch, pulling the tall man up onto his feet. They were soon in bed, once more faced with the ticking clock telling them how few chances remained to connect their mesmerised bodies together. They held each other tight while they made love, stretching each pleasurable sensation for as long as they possibly could.

A few hours later however, after the second nightmare of the night, Jeff slid out of bed and left the exhausted celebrity to sleep the last hour and a half alone before she needed to be back at the Sportsdrome once again. She had objected vehemently, but he insisted, even though it was the very last thing he wanted to do. He dressed quickly, picked up his stakeholder plan and drew a large smiley face on a blank page in Lynn's notebook, scribbling, "I love you, Jxxx" underneath.

In the quiet of the pre-dawn darkness, messed up in more ways than one, the twenty-year-old emerged from the lift to find none other than Bart Dyson waiting in the lobby. The older man was dressed in sports clothes but was not sweating or breathing hard, so Jeff could only guess he had forgotten something and was heading back up to his suite on the penthouse floor. The two men stood eye to eye as the doors opened.

Intrigued, the student couldn't help but wonder where the upstanding pillar of Melbourne society was off to this late at night and dressed only in a tracksuit? It put him in mind of the conversation he and his beautiful best friend had shared about faithfulness and Maslow's Hierarchy of Needs. Who knew what the illustrious Bart Dyson got up to while his good lady wife was safely ensconced in their sumptuous homestead?

Startled, Lynn's father coughed uncomfortably and took a step back. What was the protocol when using lifts in one's own building? He hadn't expected to have to wait for someone to get out at this time of night. With a perfunctory nod, Jeff stood to one side and invited his adversary into the lift. Bart entered, but stood across the sensor light in order to prevent the doors from closing.

'Good morning, Jeff.'

'Morning, sir. Out late or out early?'

Big D gave his daughter's boyfriend a slight smile. 'Not sure. I've been on the 'phone for a long time. I don't even know what time it is.'

'Just after three-thirty.'

'Are you leaving? Is Lynn upstairs?'

'Yes to both,' the boy from Canley Vale answered, with suspicion in his deep voice. 'She's still breathing. You don't need to worry.'

'What does that mean?' his girlfriend's father snapped. 'I don't appreciate that sort of humour. Why are you leaving at this hour? Have you two been awake until this time?'

Jeff sighed, knowing he had no right to be insolent to the great man. Of all the delicious phrases which came into his head to say right at this moment, he played it safe. For the sake of an angel.

'No, sir. Lynn's asleep. She's been in bed for hours,' came his perfectly honest account. 'I'm going home because I couldn't sleep. I didn't want to disturb her.'

Bart nodded, seeming satisfied. 'Good. I apologise. I didn't mean to sound accusatory.'

'Right. No offence taken. G'day.'

The dark-haired man stepped through the lift doors, only to be stopped again.

'Jeff,' the elder statesman barked, as his daughter's lover passed him.

'Yes?'

'Jeff, I trust you're going to stick to our agreement.'

'Which agreement is that, sir?' the smart pretender asked. 'I'm not aware of any agreement between you and me. My agreement is with Lynn. And yes, I'll honour it.'

'Fair enough,' Bart extended his right hand towards the angry visitor. 'That's kind of you.'

But the swarthy university student from New South Wales opted not to accept the big man's gesture of conciliation. Instead he turned away and strode purposefully towards the security barrier.

'It's not out of kindness, sir,' he shouted back, as calmly as he could.

Not waiting to hear his girlfriend's father's response, the twenty-year-old slammed the release button for the revolving doors hard with the heel of his clenched fist, and the glass panels slowly swept around, launching him into what remained of the night. As if he wasn't feeling disconsolate enough on leaving Lynn's bed for almost the last time, his surprise encounter with Big D had plunged him right down into the lower reaches of his happiness scale. He took his aggression out on the world on the way home, yelling at the top of his voice at the bats and the occasional tramp as he drove with the car window open, down Alexandra Gardens and towards the Swan Street Bridge.

While the scenery accepted his verbal onslaught without mounting a defence, the furious philosopher reflected on his parting shot at the dealer of his despair. He had lied to him. He *had* agreed out of kindness. Why else? His weakened mind confronted endless morbid thoughts of jumping in front of an oncoming train or off a nearby tall building, or going home via the pharmacy and rinsing a whole packet of strong painkillers down with the tiny amount of Glenfiddich left in his birthday bottle. As a matter of fact, kindness towards his dream girl was the only reason he had agreed to their separation. He didn't want Lynn to suffer. Far better for him to suffer than her. This was his lot in life, evidently, and he had better get used to it.

***

The hesitant author took a deep breath and lifted the loose sheets of paper which had been folded into Lynn's nineteen-seventy-two diary between the pages for the twenty-fifth and twenty-sixth of August. During one of many, many particularly romantic getaways in the early years of their marriage, his beautiful best friend had confessed to an outpouring of emotion after the night spent at Suzanne's kennels.

Exhausted from a hard day's physical training and mental application, his new wife had described how she had fallen onto her bed and cried herself to sleep, fully clothed and with her hair still tied up in a ponytail. She had later told her adoring husband, tears in her eyes and limbs entangled with his, that she had woken an hour or so later with a dull throbbing at the back of her head where the knot of her hair elastic had been digging into her skull. The beauty smiled as she depicted her teenaged self swinging her heavy legs off the side of the bed and padding across the carpet in the dark, in order to fetch her secret diary from her bag. Once back at her bedside, she had switched on the lamp and propped the pillow against the headboard, settling down to complete the previous two days' entries.

So great was the young celebrity's wish to purge the sadness from her heart, that the torrent of words flowed over four full pages from her ruled foolscap notepad. Tears fell onto the lines as she wrote, and the ink smudged a little when she brushed the first few away, causing her to refrain from any further drying attempts. She had held back absolutely nothing, so the story had gone; writing paragraph upon paragraph of the account she dearly wanted her parents to read and yet knew they must never see.

And now, twenty-four years later almost to the day, the lover she had left behind for a second time was finally about to read these same pages. Their autobiography would be incomplete without them. His heart was pounding in his ears.

Lynn had begun the Friday night's entry with an expression of gratitude that her boyfriend did not possess Gerry's carefree attitude to other people's feelings, which made Jeff laugh out loud. Earlier that very same evening, the two men, true brothers-in-arms who had seen the Diamond empire grow from nothing to a multi-billion dollar, global enterprise, had shared an animated and very frank discourse concerning his manager's upcoming nuptials, during which the younger had been at pains to remind him several times of either his fiancée's or his mother's duly-expressed wishes.

'Nothing's changed there, angel,' the grieving husband said into the smoky air above his head.

However, his attention was quickly diverted from the immediate past and back into the couple's history when the following paragraph commenced with, "I expect I will cry for forty days and forty nights on the day I say goodbye to Jeff."

'Jesus,' he whispered, tears immediately brimming over the lower lids of his own eyes and starting to run down his cheeks. 'I'm sorry, Lynn. Did you? I know I did.'

The great man read on, already lost in the depths of his wife's innocent and powerless despair. It was not a surprise to him, since they had talked about it several times over the years, but the anguish that burned out of her blue, ballpoint handwriting was like a vice gripping his temples.

> "Why can't my first love be my last? Why is that so wrong? If this is my first love, whatever will my second and third love be like? Surely nothing can be as good as this, as powerful. No way! What am I supposed to want? A relationship with someone more like me? Straightforward and with no chinks, creases or pages deliberately stuck together? Would a less complicated affair be anywhere near as fulfilling? No, no, no, no, no.........
>
> I don't care about the smoking and drinking, the interruptions to my sleep, the missing parts to the story. I care about not knowing when I'm going to see him again. I care about him and I care about me. We belong together. I don't want him to have to battle every day until I come back just to stay alive. What if he can't take it? What if he gives up too soon? I hope he contacts me somehow, if he gets that desperate. That would be worth risking everything for. I don't want him to die because of me. I don't want him to die, full stop. It would make me want to die too. Would it? I don't know, but perhaps it should."

Finally bearing witness to the inky blotches of Lynn's tear stains which had been preserved for over twenty years, Jeff's fingers traced the indentations each word had made in the diary's stiff page, filled with amazement that the woman he loved had written so blatantly about his suicidal bent. He wasn't sure if he now regretted sharing these frightening facts with someone who was only on the cusp of adulthood at the time, but there was no point in thinking about that now. He had opened up to a tender sixteen-year-old, and Lynn had taken him in, lock, stock and barrel.

The next few paragraphs, still written into the diary itself at this point, outlined how the teenager had put her pen down for several minutes and seriously contemplated lifting the telephone and dialling the number of the tiny, dark flat in Richmond. The reader breathed deeply, remembering with trembling hands and a dagger slicing through his heart that her call would have gone unanswered. That night, as went the way of countless others back in those days, he had chosen to visit a city nightclub and had most certainly not returned until well after daybreak.

What if he had been at home? And what if she had placed that call? Blinking, watery eyes alighted on the first extra page, where the desolate woman wrote that she had momentarily decided, as a rare detour into the colloquial now reported, to "chuck everything in": her Olympic goals, her

Hollywood movie career and her place at UCLA. Jeff breathed deeply, easily able to identify with the turmoil she had obviously been going through. The young star had fleetingly been willing to give all this up for her tortured lover, but went on to add that all she could see in her mind's eye was her wise man's compassionate face telling her not to do it. Was it good or bad fortune that had steered events that night? Good fortune, they both would have admitted as mature adults.

> "'Just think about all those American college boys,' Michelle waxed lyrical at school the other day. She simply refuses to believe that I'm so loathe to leave my first boyfriend behind. What does she know about love? She hasn't found that special person yet. Perhaps she'll understand when she does?
>
> I don't want some middle-class, squeaky clean jock. How boring would that be? Like going out with my brother. A boy on a basketball scholarship might share some of Jeff's qualities learned from struggling, but would he write songs or speak to me about changing the world? No, I doubt it. Probably only wants to go to parties and be rich and drive a Corvette. It doesn't matter to me that whenever Jeff and I share a bottle of wine, it's one glass for me and four for him. It also doesn't matter that my clothes stink of smoke when I take them out of my bag and throw them in the washing basket.
>
> What I will miss is his tight grip on my arm, his eyes that talk to me and ask questions of me all the time, and his mouth that kisses me as if I'm the only woman who matters. The hand in the small of my back when I wake up, the hand casually resting on my shoulder while we talk to friends, and the feeling of him inside me most of all. And I don't just mean sex. But I do mean sex too!"

Again the superstar laughed aloud. The private school virgin had indeed been a willing pupil in bed, that was for sure! His lessons had been well learned, and they had grown together as true lovers during that heady seven-month period, exploring themselves as much as they had explored each other. Of all his hundreds of teenaged sexual conquests, Jeff could put hand on heart without a shred of doubt, to swear that pleasures of the flesh had never been so satisfying as with the girl who had known the least but who had adored him the most.

By now, Lynn's adolescent ramblings had overflowed onto the second sheet of notepaper, torn from the pad in her school folder. The same pad from which his stakeholder plan had been drafted, the widower recalled. The years melted away as he tentatively unfolded the flimsy leaves, their jagged edges having become smoothed and straightened from being stowed inside the leather-bound book for over two decades. It was hard to believe they had not been disturbed in all that time, locked in the bottom drawer of the filing cabinet in the couple's home office.

On and on the paragraphs wound back through their short but intense relationship, justifying their love and reiterating time and again that the young woman expected never to find a bond so all-consuming with another man. Jeff nodded to the photograph on his desk, whence his dearly departed wife smiled back. She had been right. They had both been right. In a few more days, as outlined in the heavyweight missive on flimsy paper, they would have been setting each other free. His teenaged girlfriend had questioned what being set free might mean, and her middle-aged husband echoed her unanswered thought. They had again been set free in the human world, yet continued to cling together like fridge and magnet in the spiritual world.

'Nothing's changed there either,' the forty-four-year-old chuckled. 'True to type forever, angel.'

Lynn next burrowed deep into the introversion of her soul to wonder how it would feel when the time actually came to say their final goodbye. "It scares me to the core," she wrote, telling of her fears at being stuck with that awful feeling of abandonment about which she had read in the library books on Post-Traumatic Stress Disorder. This sense of dread also reminded her of another early conversation, the meaning of which she had barely grasped, when Jeff had ardently professed that her psychological state would be weakened far more than her physical state after an abortion. Another shiver ran down the author's spine. He had written about that episode too.

Of course, the sensible schoolgirl was not about to completely deny the possibility of finding someone she loved even more. However, immediately after this confession, which was especially hard for her grieving husband to accept, she then described another pause from writing while she buried her head in her hands and wept, not knowing if she was crying for Jeff or for herself at this prospect. She couldn't want anyone else, she insisted. She only wanted Jeff Diamond.

> "'Naïve, starry-eyed puppy love,' my father said today, pouring scorn on my feeble objections. 'Too caught up in your first romance,' Mum also said much more sympathetically, but it made my blood boil anyway. They were each others' first loves, so is there a message there? Do they regret not spreading their wings? Is that why they're putting us through this horror story?"

'Woah, angel,' her husband sighed. 'You really went to town that night. Did you get any sleep at all?'

To Jeff's delight, the tattooed skin on his chest stung sweetly, and he thanked Lynn's spirit by blowing a kiss towards the ceiling. There was still more thorough deliberation to come, on pages three and four. She explained to her diary that her boyfriend would not be able to join her in Los Angeles, because he would need a visa and a ready supply of money to enrol as an international student. She then went on to list the pros and cons of running away to Europe, as her fanciful highwayman had suggested. What would she do or be in either of those places? She had worked all her life to become Lynn Dyson.

The teenager declared that she didn't want to wash dishes, teach English to foreigners or pack endless boxes of fruit as a backpacker for the next two years. She didn't doubt it would be fun for a few weeks, living under a pseudonym and stretching out a meagre living with their shared earnings, but that wasn't who she was destined to be, and neither was it her ambitious boyfriend's plan, as the annals of time were reliably informed. Of that she was sure, no matter how tempting the idea had been when he had broached the subject.

Said ambitious boyfriend assured the young woman from the early 'seventies, from his position of affluence in the mid-'nineties, that reluctantly he had to agree, with the benefit of hindsight and after twenty years of undivided attention from her soothing voice and healing hands.

> "Who is this amazing man who wears his leather jacket on sunny days as a sign of his love, who sings with me at the piano when he'd much rather take my clothes off, who helps with my homework when I'm travelling, who shows up in a suit and tie, smelling like a distinguished thirty-five-year-old whenever we're going somewhere formal and who smells like a divine but sweaty athlete in the heat of passion?"

It was probably this long, convoluted question which pleased the tired, voyeuristic biographer the most, nearing the end of the youthful ode to exhilaration. He had taught his dream girl to use her senses, and how she had loved to ply this trade on him! Animal passion it had been, the union of two bodies whose souls had found each other in a bygone era and had worked their way back together through the rough and the smooth.'

Jeff Diamond, the world-changer turned documentarian, had almost finished the chapters which would impart previously obfuscated details to its readership, whether fan or sceptic, of the famous couple's first, prolonged absence. He pushed back on his office chair, twisting his spine and flexing his shoulders, once more relishing the tingling in his chest, and speculated on what he and Kierney would do for dinner.

Right on cue, the boisterous golden retriever bounded into the room, serving to announce the dark-haired teenager's homecoming. Still not yet having perfected the art of putting on the brakes in time to prevent himself from ploughing into unsuspecting knees, Indie responded eagerly to his master's invitation to jump up and lick his chin.

'Enough for now,' Jeff said to Lynn's ghost, rubbing his pectoral muscle. 'To be continued, angel.'

LORRAINE PESTELL

Act One Finalé

Ryan slapped the two covers of his parents' autobiography together with a resounding thwack, before dropping it down onto the coffee table in his sister's apartment. He had only popped in to borrow a telephone charger and to use her computer to check his e-mails, since he hadn't yet had a landline connected next-door. However, after enjoying a quick cup of coffee together, he had ended up immersed in his father's account of "the big break-up". The Diamond teenagers thought they knew every nuance of this painful separation already, but the seventeen-year-old had warned her brother how the unmistakably categorical language had evoked strange and conflicting emotions towards their grandfather on reading this chapter.

'Jeez,' the twenty-year-old gasped. 'I feel exactly like you said I would. I'm gobsmacked, because I really didn't think it'd affect me.'

The dark-haired, willowy teenager walked over to her brother and sat down next to him. She lifted the book and caressed its front cover on her lap, her fingers pausing over the couple's photograph, as if she could feel the whiskers on her papá's chin.

'How does it make you feel then?' she asked the muscle-bound cricketer, whose frame spread over the majority of her two-seater couch. 'About G and G?'

Ryan shrugged. 'About all of us. Dad then and me now. We're pretty much the same age, but I have no clue what it feels like to want someone that much. I'd like to, in a way, but then I also don't want to, because it obviously hurts heaps if it doesn't work out. And I can understand how two years'd seem like forever, even though he looked back on it and said it didn't feel very long after all, in the grand scheme of things.'

'And Grandpa?' Kierney pressed, opening the book at the page where her brother had slotted a stray *pizza* menu that he had found sitting on the table, to discover which part of the story he had just skimmed over.

'Yeah. Don't know. I need to think about it. What you said before, about maybe he learned a lesson from that time too... I never find him that heartless. He's pretty easy to talk to, and lenient too occasionally.'

The *élite* sportsman chuckled at the horrified expression on his sister's face. She always took her beloved papá's side. She too was a complete sucker when it came to romance.

'Big D isn't the ogre Dad makes him out to be,' he insisted. 'Come on. Not to us, anyway.'

'Alright,' the teenager acquiesced, 'you're right about how he is now. He's mellowed with age, and so did Papá, but to know how much they loved each other and still to rip them apart totally was heartless. At the time… You know, without e-mail and mobiles. It'd be impossible to enforce a "no contact" rule these days. I'm just glad I haven't met my soul-mate yet, in case my last few months of childhood mean I can't control what happens to me either.'

'I wasn't expecting such frankness and pathos from Mum's diaries though,' Ryan admitted. 'It was even a bit embarrassing to read all that sex stuff.'

Kierney nodded. 'I know. Me too. Still, we're the product of that sex stuff, so I s'pose we should be glad they felt that strongly. If they'd got over each other, we'd be someone else's children.'

'Yeah. True,' her brother gestured for the thick volume again, which was passed over readily. 'There's a bit in here that really got to me…'

'Which bit?'

'When they were in that Vietnamese restaurant, and Mum made that bitchy comment about Dad being soaked up and unfit.'

The seventeen-year-old frowned. 'Why did that get to you? I would've thought you'd agree with her. You were his personal trainer last year. I seem to remember you were pretty hard on him.'

'OK. True enough, again,' the cricketer nodded, smiling at the bittersweet memories of putting his widowed father through his paces, running through the streets of Paris at first light. 'Not quite the same though. I wasn't sleeping with him.'

'I don't remember reading anything about that meal in her diary, do you? I wonder what she thought about his drinking back then?' Kierney asked, giggling at the absurd suggestion. 'Why do you think they were spiteful towards each other?'

'No-one else to take their anger out on, I s'pose.'

'At least they both understood how each other felt. Can you imagine how horrible it'd have been if only one of them was upset at having to split up?'

Ryan gave a shrug and a nod. 'Nightmare. But probably easier to close out. Even Dad would've given up if Mum said she didn't want to be with him.'

'Literally. So where d'you think Grandpa was going that night?'

'Nowhere. You know what he's like… Just needed to stretch his legs after one of those long IOC conference calls or whatever.'

His sister wasn't convinced. 'Yeah, maybe.'

'Yeah, definitely!' the blond sportsman wagged a finger. '*Cierto, pequeñita.*'

He pushed himself up to a standing position, his hands pressing down on his knees, to let strong thighs lever his body to its full height. Six feet and four inches; the same as his father. The nineteen-year-old was downplaying his reaction, truth be told, growing more and more like the old man with each passing year. His own progress through "A Life Singular" had been slow in recent weeks, given his finals were not too far away and that the English cricket season was in full swing.

And furthermore, he was not yet fully ready to read it. Family and friends had rallied around Kierney after the events of New Year's Day, considering her to be the more vulnerable of the Diamond siblings. The bombastic student hadn't taken issue with this at the time, both to protect his sister and also to give himself some space to come to terms with the situation privately. Now however, eight months later and back in Melbourne for their grandparents' combined sixty-fifth birthday party, he too found himself in need of an emotional handrail every now and again.

'People didn't have depression in the 'seventies,' his sister smiled. 'That's the way I prefer to rationalise it. Especially not men. Papá told me Grandma apologised for not picking up the signs.'

'Would they have relented, d'you think, if she had?'

'I think they might've let them stay in contact.'

'Really? Why?'

'Because Papá needed her just as much as he loved her back then. He would've played by the rules. He did anyway. And he wouldn't have spoiled anything for Mamá. He loved her too much not to respect her wishes.'

'Lessons learned all round then,' her brother nodded. 'I guess that's the whole point of the book. Open your eyes, open your minds, open your hearts, open your wallets. Just one big, bloody tin-opener really, our dad! What are you doing tonight?'

Kierney followed the fair-haired giant through the hallway and waited while he turned the latch and pulled the front door towards him. 'Having dinner with Sophie and a couple of other friends from school. You? What time do you fly out?'

'Two-ish, I think. I was going to get a taxi to pick me up from here at eleven-thirty. Did you want to share it?'

'OK. Yes,' the Sydney University first-year accepted his offer. 'Thanks. That works for me. I'll sit in the lounge and answer e-mails. My flight's at three-thirty. You are doing something tonight, bro, aren't you? You seemed a bit lost last night.'

Ryan dipped his head and gave his kid sister a peck on the cheek. 'Yes. Don't mother me, woman. I'm doing *déjà-vu* with Nicola. Plenty to look forward to.'

Kierney giggled at his lewd actions. 'Again?'

'Yes, again,' her brother sneered. 'She's hot and single. What's wrong with that?'

'Nothing's wrong with it. Are you single?'

'While I'm here I am.'

'*Bien sûr, mon ami,*' the seventeen-year-old impersonated their father's oft-used playboy accent. '*De quoi, hein?* I thought she might be sick of being used.'

The young man smiled. 'Cheers. *Au contraire*, she appreciates it.'

'Really? Your arrogance knows no bounds.'

Ryan shrugged, a broad grin on his face. 'It is impossible to be out of contact these days though, isn't it? You pricked my conscience, wench. The idea of Mum being forced to get experience with other men as a sideline to their time apart was ahead of its time though. They obviously didn't subscribe to "No sex before marriage." I'm surprised Grandma admitted it'd been one of their not-so-hidden agenda items.'

The young woman nudged him towards the door. 'Are you going or not?'

'Yes. Sorry. I'm processing what I've read.'

This latest slip into introversion was not a surprise to either sibling. In the months leading up to their father's graceful, understated exit, the threesome had discussed endlessly the importance of balancing thoughts and deeds. Even Action Man himself had come to endorse the performance enhancing qualities of due consideration, even using it to the cricket team's advantage now that he had been installed as its captain.

'*Bueno.* I don't think G and G were necessarily thinking about sexual experience,' Kierney teased her brother. 'They wanted her to fall in love with someone more like Bart Dyson or Junior.'

'Without having sex,' Ryan appended, with equal sarcasm.

'Yes. *Bien sûr, mon ami,*' the teenager waved across the landing. 'Have fun tonight. I'll see you *mañana mañana.*'

***

Only Jeff and Lynn knew the hell they were living through each time they returned to Admin and fought to maintain brave faces for one another. They had paid a visit to The Fellowship in their last week together and had sat with Alan for a long time, talking through their individual coping strategies.

Not once did the student mention that he would prefer his beautiful best friend not to leave, and not once had the celebrity aired the feelings of regret she had about going. Her stint in the US was a *fait accompli*, and they had both accepted their imposed separation with alacrity. The philosopher maintained his position on visiting Benloch, and the Olympian invited him to stay overnight every time she was in the city. Exquisitely passionate trysts and twice- or thrice-nightly nightmares were to be the overriding memory of this frantic time in their life.

Lynn had made sure her last night in Australia was kept for the enigmatic stranger, unbeknown to her parents. After a final breakfast with some school friends, she had spent the whole day at the Sportsdrome. Putting on a smile and an optimistic, excited outlook, she had managed to convince everyone that she was able to leave Jeff Diamond behind, including the man himself.

'Are you going to miss me?' he almost shouted as he rode up and down, thrashing in a mixture of ecstasy and agony. 'Tell me you're going to miss me.'

'Jeff, stop,' she urged him. 'You're hurting me.'

The passionate man carried on, close to the edge in more ways than one.

'Well, you're hurting me too.'

The desperate man came into the woman he loved so much with tears in his eyes and torment on his face, falling down and kissing her hard on the mouth. Pinned underneath, his girlfriend turned her head from side to side, trying to break free of his vice-like grip.

'No, I'm not hurting you. You're hurting yourself. Calm down a bit, please?'

'Hey, I'm calm,' he hissed, relenting. 'I'm sorry if I hurt you.'

The celebrity couldn't be angry with her boyfriend, although she knew she ought to be. They were both highly emotional, bordering on hysterical at times. Her flight left the next morning at ten-thirty, and this was their final hours together. Probably forever, if her parents had anything to do with it.

'Please... I'm trying to make a bad situation as good as I can. You're just making it worse.'

Her lover looked his beautiful girlfriend in the eyes, apologetic and totally miserable. 'I know. I'm sorry, angel. I'm not sure I can do anything else. It feels like I'm stuck in some bad opera. I just can't believe this is happening to us. It's as if I want you to tell your father that you're going to throw yourself off a bridge, like in Madame Butterfly or some other posh pantomime. *Digame...* Is it eighteen-seventy-two or seventeen-seventy-two, baby?'

Caught between a furious abhorrence of the Dysons' decision and flagrant pity for himself and his dream girl, the morose songwriter climbed off the bed and headed into the bathroom. He couldn't quite come to terms with the fact that this was the last time he would see Lynn in his flat, or anywhere for that matter. His heart was thumping so loudly in his head that it was scrambling his thoughts. The combination of anger and sadness was a lethal cocktail, and he felt as if he might explode at any moment. It had been a long time since he had experienced such extreme destructive emotions.

Jeff splashed some water on his face and drank a glassful from the tap. He swore quietly at his reflection, which by the look of it was feeling the same misery. Why was this happening? Couldn't he do anything about it? Wasn't he the one who always got his own way?

The bathroom door opened behind him, and the flushed and dishevelled teenager stood there naked, stunning and concerned.

'Are you alright?' her kind voice asked, wrapping her arms around her lover's waist and hugging into his warm body.

The boy from Canley Vale nodded, unable to say anything. Twisting around in Lynn's grasp, he embraced her too. He took her outstretched hand in silence, and she led him back to bed, where they lay together without exchanging any further conclusions while the last light faded out of the sky. The number of hours remaining was already a single digit.

'Don't take it out on us, Jeff,' Lynn begged, as he rolled away from her onto his back.

His hostility towards the world was palpable. This handsome man who only wanted to do good in the world appeared to have reached the limit of his tolerance, and yet she continued to sense his devotion radiating out and warming her in the chill of the night. It was breaking her heart to think they might part under such a dark cloud.

'I love you and I always will. We have some amazing memories to take with us.'

Groaning loudly, her boyfriend turned back towards her and kissed her lips.

'Yeah, I know,' he croaked, sobbing against her shoulder.

His words and actions triggered the same response in the young star, and they hung on to each other tightly. After a few minutes of calmer silence, his stare became keener again, as if he was about to address whomever cared to listen.

'How the fuck am I going to go back to how I was before I met you? Reapply the old veneer and off I go, staying between the flags. It's just not going to happen, is it?'

Lynn kissed the corners of his tearful eyes. 'You just need to look forwards. You're going to release your single and become a rock star overnight. Then your album'll go to the top of the charts, and you're going to do all the things you want to do, because they're good things that need doing. You'll be really proud of what you do, and so will I.'

It was a good speech, Jeff realised, and probably well-rehearsed too, yet it was wasted on him. He didn't have the heart to tell her, but there was little hope of a warm reception for her words of wisdom, the way he felt right at this moment.

'Thanks. But why should I do it? You're the only reason I want to do all that stuff.'

'No, I'm not. I don't have to tell you why,' his girlfriend smiled, sounding surprisingly didactic all of a sudden. 'You know why. It's just now it doesn't feel like a good idea.'

'You're not wrong there,' the twenty-year-old snapped back, trying not to be angry at her and failing.

He knew what the celebrity was trying to do. Motivation was her byword; her stock in trade. He simply didn't want to hear it. He wanted to hear that she had changed her mind about leaving the country and quitting their relationship, but he knew these words were not going to come out of her enticing mouth tonight. It was too late for mounting a dramatic last stand.

Lynn continued, a slender index finger weaving its way up his arm and towards his face. 'You're going to do all these things for yourself, for your own self-respect, because you owe it to yourself. Not for me. For you. And for all those people you want to help.'

Jeff sat up on the bed without warning and sank his head into the palms of his hands. His tank was empty. He was all cried out, with merely the omnipresent bitterness simmering away inside. He took a few deep breaths in and out before lifting his head to see the teenager about to speak again.

'Come on... You can move on from this. You know you can, because you've done it before. You're the strongest person I know. You're my beautiful black stallion, remember? Record your songs, perform them, get out all those raw emotions, and people'll love you. Everyone will. Put everything into The Fellowship, even if you are a customer again for a while. Do it in my name, if you like, but do it for you. Promise me?'

The young man sniffed sarcastically. 'I'll do it for all the other poor bastards like me.'

His wilting bedfellow sat up and leaned against him, cuddling him in close and kissing his concrete shoulders. 'OK. That sounds good too. Let's not alienate each other so late. That's not who we are, is it?'

'Nope,' Jeff affirmed, coughing his vocal chords clear and reaching for his packet of cigarettes, which were sitting on the bedside table.

Ignoring the sigh of ineffectively-masked disappointment beside him, he lifted his head to scan up and down the lithe, young body which was slipping rapidly out of his life. His stomach churned when he felt his penis begin to engorge for the third time that evening. How was he ever going to rid his system of her inner and outer beauty, her instinctive counterpoise for every act of love and her boundless compassion for him, flaws notwithstanding?

'No, it's not, angel.'

'Thanks,' the teenager whispered, gratefully accepting a kiss. 'You said you didn't want an arm's length relationship. Let's ride out the last few hours together. We can both be angry or sad or both, but let's be together while we can.'

'I love you, Lynn Dyson,' the bereft student told her, in as positive a tone as he could summon. 'You're amazing. I wish I had your maturity. Will you still be my metaphysical lighthouse, even though I won't be able to see you in the real world?'

'Of course I will, if you'll always be my beautiful black stallion.'

'Sure thing. We'll live with this invisible elastic connection. It'll just be pulled very tight.'

The young star's eyes filled with tears again, but there was a smile on her face. 'That's a lovely image. I hope it doesn't pull so tight that it snaps. Of course I'll be your lighthouse, if I can,' she choked a little, catching her breath. 'Any time, Jeff Diamond, and I really appreciate that you haven't asked me not to go. I couldn't stand that.'

The student managed a smile too, but words would not come.

'That's the greatest show of respect I can imagine,' his girlfriend continued, 'under the circumstances. That's your strength. You can do the most painful thing, because you know it's the right thing to do. We can help each other to be strong for tomorrow.'

'Thanks, I guess.'

Lynn sighed, leaning the side of her head onto his bony shoulder again. 'You've taught me more about my place in the world than I ever thought there was to know.'

'And we only just got started,' the young man sniffed, brushing her hair away from her face. 'You taught me too.'

'Have I? What?'

'Things I didn't want to know, like how to survive, to overcome and to focus on something other than what I want right now.'

'Oh,' the sixteen-year-old smiled, feeling his warm lips through her hair as he kissed her head. 'That's good. I'm glad.'

Fed up with being cooped up in the tiny bedroom, with its low ceiling and grey walls, the couple dressed and went out into the night air for a walk. They wandered along Bridge Road and into the city, past the northern stands of the MCG. With the breeze fresh on their faces, they zigzagged through the streets and parks with no particular destination in mind, and after twenty minutes, they found themselves at the eastern end of Bourke Street. Calling into Pellegrini's for a coffee, the bartender engaged the couple with his banal banter, but neither the regular philosopher nor his famous girlfriend fancied embarking on their customary animated discourse with the staff and other late-night patrons.

They politely made their excuses and left as soon as their cups were empty, wending their way up Exhibition Street, turning right onto La Trobe Street and continuing in an easterly direction until they arrived at Carlton Gardens and the Royal Exhibition Building, which was glowing an eerie amber among the tall trees.

'Look, angel... I know I'm not very good company,' Jeff began.

He sat the brave, young woman down on a wooden bench out of sight from the surrounding streets and stood behind her, massaging her strong shoulders. It had turned quite cold as evening merged with night. Tears were rolling steadily down his cheeks again, and he didn't want her to see them.

'If you want to go back to Admin tonight, that's OK. It makes little difference now, does it?'

The heartbroken athlete reached up and held onto his hands, leaning her head back onto his hipbone. 'No, I don't want to. We can't expect each other to be good company. I think we just need each others' company, plain and simple, however it comes. I understand how you feel, and I'm exactly the same. I don't want to go back yet. Really, I don't.'

Above all, the teenager couldn't bear to think of her tormented boyfriend returning to his flat alone. That would really make her feel awful, imagining him struggling with the front door demons, having just said their final farewell. She couldn't possibly be that heartless and wasn't even prepared to voice such thoughts. It would be like hammering another nail into his hand.

The pair walked some more, northwards towards the university. A group of students on their way out for the night recognised their favourite star and were keen to stop and talk. Lynn gave them autographs, answered a few quick questions and then briskly walked on. With no part to play in these proceedings, as anonymous as ever, her companion was lost for words, barely even hanging on to the ability to stand upright. She tried her best to maintain conversation, but her efforts at keeping the channels of communication open were singularly consigned as a one-way street. The young Olympian didn't much care. She knew this whole *fiasco* was her doing.

Finally, they ended up back at the humble, second-floor flat, after walking for almost two hours. Its tenant made a last ditch show of ceremoniously handing over his key-ring, and his kind-hearted girlfriend curtsied as she accepted it. Once inside, he embraced her tenderly, knowing there was little to be gained by remonstrating in anger any longer. There was nothing either of them could do now to make things better.

He just needed to look forwards, she had said.

Yeah, sure. Easy.

At just after one o'clock in the morning, Lynn stood up from his bed. One last desperate and hollow lovemaking session had used up the best part of another hour, since both were spent of all energy and emotion. In the dull silver light of the moon through his window, Jeff watched her rise to her feet.

His head was immediately gripped by a numb terror, and his heart sank like a stone. This was it, he understood.

'Don't come to the door,' the young woman made him promise.

She was crying, but he was not. The man who had dreaded this moment for so long had entered a type of detached, stuporous zone, probably similar to being in shock. He stretched his right hand out towards the blonde vision, who held it briefly to her lips before picking up her bag and kneeling onto the bed for one last, long, lingering kiss.

'Thanks for everything, angel. You will always be the most beautiful woman in the world, whatever happens... I love you,' his ancient heart assured her from deep within. 'More than anyone else will ever love you. Don't ever forget it.'

'I won't, Jeff, and I love you too,' she answered in a weak, trembling voice, clutching his hand to her chest. 'So very much. Thanks for spending the best months of my life with me. I will always feel your love in here.'

Neither uttered the word "Goodbye". Lynn walked out of the bedroom, down the short hallway and through the front door. Jeff heard it click shut, followed by her footsteps on the landing and down the first flight of stairs.

His soul-mate was gone.

Two-hundred-and-four days.

Just over twenty-nine weeks.

Almost seven months.

Over, just like that.

The young man's numbness melted away as quickly as it had arrived, and he lay face-up on his bed as naked and unprotected as he had ever felt. He wept for what seemed like hours, until his ribcage ached and his eyes stung. All the time, his sick, unstable mind repeated, "Are you going to miss me? Are you going to miss me?" taunting him and fuelling the anger left over from his childhood. The voice reminded him of a little boy seeking the reassurance of a parent reading the same bedtime story time and time again. He had never been granted this special experience which most children take for granted, yet right now he craved it more than ever.

He merely needed to look forwards, his dream girl had said, but the bereft student already knew how difficult this was going to be. As he saw it, prostrate and cold in the dark, there were two choices. Well, three, actually; the third being his usual below-the-line response to any crisis. However, even to a dyed-in-the-wool manic depressive as damaged as he was, checking out after giving himself no more than half an hour to acclimatise to his new state was too weak and defeatist to contemplate. He must look forwards, he resolved. Lynn was right. He owed it to himself to give these next two years his best shot, because that was what made him him.

Jeff dragged his clothes back onto his tired, sore body and grabbed his car keys. He didn't close the apartment door, racing down the stairs as if escaping a fire. He had no idea where he might go but started the car anyway, turning onto the main road and driving away from the city. He drove eastwards for about thirty minutes, well past Doncaster, before turning north through Heidelberg, then towards Greensborough and Eltham, weaving through the residential streets without the slightest inkling of a destination.

One cigarette after the other was stubbed out into the ashtray until the packet was empty. The driver pulled into a service station to buy some more and fill the petrol tank. For the first time in a year, he purchased a girlie magazine. Just for the hell of it, he decided. He didn't know how long it might be until he was able to face real, live female company again. Even the King of Smooth himself would find it impossible to make even the brusquest of flirtatious conversations while in his current frame of mind.

In the middle of nowhere, the twenty-year-old eased the rattly, blue Ford into a parking lane and drew up the handbrake. The radio was playing a mixture of songs requested by similarly lonely people, which offered him no consolation whatsoever, so he switched it off. The fading interior light did its best to illuminate the magazine's full-colour pages as he flicked over the glossy photographs one by one. Nothing gave him any inspiration, and he tossed it into the passenger footwell, on top of the empty cigarette packet.

Tilting the driver's seat back, Jeff replayed some of the motivational words Lynn had expounded during their last evening while he lay staring up at nothing. Recalling the one and only time they had had sex in this old car brought a sequence of brief happy memories to mind before the inevitable tears of loss overtook him again. He needed to find some way to believe his lover's words, because he recognised the truth they contained.

If this nobody was to become a somebody between now and the star's return to Melbourne, he must not allow himself to be defined by her. Simply being Lynn Dyson's boyfriend was hardly how he would prefer to go down in history.

Lynn Dyson's ex-boyfriend, as the mournful student corrected himself.

Jeff Diamond, whoever he was, had been the Australian darling's first lover, and a very good one to boot. Of this he was supremely confident. He was not overly concerned about being her only lover. With a reputation like his, how could he be? Yet over the last six months, he had set his sights on being her last lover, and at this rate its likelihood was rapidly diminishing, splintering his heart into tiny pieces.

A fresh wave of emotion rushed over him, and the exhausted man sniffed back the tears. How could one head contain so much water? Regardless of the intermittent but ongoing deluges, his response to losing his dream girl was infinitely more peaceful than the violence and destruction that had followed his mother's sordid demise. Jeff allowed himself a moment of self-congratulation that he was not currently blind drunk, sitting outside the Dyson Administration building and yelling profanities at the family's penthouse windows.

You've grown up, the boy from the western suburbs sneered, *even if you didn't want to, chico.*

The lonely night-bird must have drifted off to sleep shortly afterwards, because the salt on his face had dried and it cracked when he next opened his eyes. No nightmare tonight? Be grateful for small mercies. Demonic nightmare on top of living nightmare would have been very ugly indeed. Perhaps his tormentors could tell he was already in sufficient distress.

Lynn would be fast asleep by now, Jeff suspected. She could always fall asleep. The sign of a clear conscience, his grandmother used to say. He wondered if her parents' decision to ship her overseas for two years may possibly have been welcomed by their daughter on some level. Could it be that he was simply too intense for her after all? Maybe she had been looking for a way to get out? He wouldn't blame her for that. He wasn't the easiest person to love. For Christ's sake, he found it hard enough.

No. Stop, mate. Don't go there. The knowledgeable amateur counsellor knew he could ill afford to send himself crashing down even further. He was also sure the tears in his girlfriend's eyes had been genuine. He trusted her word. She was beautiful and innocent and courageous. She had no reason to lie to him. If she had wanted to say goodbye, she of all people would have found the strength to do it without engineering such an elaborate exit clause.

Jeff turned the key in the ignition, and the creaky Fairlane spluttered into life in the cold air. He drove in a large arc around the northern perimeter of Greater Melbourne, finally reaching the airport. He was halfway to Benloch, in fact. Look! There was Miss Irony again, out on a hot date with Gravity the troll. Smiling to himself, he envisioned breaking into Bart and Marianna's bedroom and smothering them both with pillows, suffocating them as they slept.

How good it would be for Lynn to be free to make her own choices! That way, he would soon find out whether or not she was complicit in her removal.

The distraught driver dismissed this dangerous design, although pleased to find his weird sense of humour hadn't completely deserted him. Planning to drift citywards in a southerly direction, he remembered his open front door. He ought to go home. How would he occupy himself out here anyway? It was almost four o'clock in the morning. Six hours before Lynn's flight was to take off and soar into the sky right above his present location. Did he really want to watch the flying kangaroo spirit her away to far-off lands?

No, he did not. His beautiful best friend's memory was doing its level best to wrestle some optimism away from Gravity, and the egotist fed off his over-inflated and vainglorious prowess as best he could. The Fairlane headed into the city's outskirts and on towards the next chapter in his life. There were songs to write and record, albums to sell, concerts to organise, television interviews to conduct, fan mail to receive and answer and groupies to cavort with. As he neared home, the songwriter had reconstructed the sequence of tracks for his second album. He would release "Rock Me Now" as a single as soon as he could, impulsively deciding not to wait for the main record deal to come into force. This was an easy song to perform and talk about while still smarting from Lynn's departure.

The rising star had transformed himself into an almost positive mood by the time the blue sedan crawled back into the car park. The flat was undisturbed, of course. Who would think to rob a second-floor, one-bedroomed flat behind the MCG, when they could have their pick of mansions in Toorak or drug dens in Carlton or Fitzroy? Besides, the only thing of any value had already been stolen earlier that morning.

Later on at work, Jeff managed to keep it together despite being sapped of all energy. At a few minutes to ten o'clock, he took a cigarette break and stood outside to formally observe a minute's silence for the country's loss of its first daughter. Daylight and diversion had brought more rational thought and very few hard feelings.

A Qantas jet flew overhead on a steep ascent, even before his cigarette was finished, with its engines straining and bright sunshine glinting on its wings. It may or may not have been bound for Frankfurt, but all the same, the young man pictured the smiling beauty fastening her seatbelt for take-off and wished the best for his high-flying lady from her old friend stuck at sea level.

***

Lynn Dyson's seventeenth birthday had come and gone, amid a flurry of good wishes on the radio and television. On the night of the twentieth of September, Jeff had raised a glass of whisky to her, then another and another, fondly remembering the most special of birthday celebrations which she had lavished on him. The Munich Olympics received such abundant coverage across all press and popular media that it was impossible to ignore. There were photographs of the Dyson family on the front and back pages of each newspaper on most days that fortnight, along with other pictures of racial protests and the proud black athletes who were raising their fists and their profiles in order to stamp their equal and often greater capability into the record books.

The Wednesday before Grand Final weekend, the RMIT student turned on the radio for the drive home from work, intending to catch the evening news and the pre-match analysis. His adopted team, the Richmond Tigers, were running out against the Carlton Blues for the Premiership flag, and it promised to be a great spectacle. Jeff didn't have a ticket for the match but was planning to watch it at a local hotel with some mates. Driving along in the slow evening traffic while waiting for the football commentary to begin, he caught the last thirty seconds of a song which immediately grabbed his attention, turning the volume up just as a sweeping guitar solo drew it to a close. He could have sworn it was Lynn's voice. It must be a new single. Brand new, in fact, since he didn't recognise it from anything she had shared with him.

Sure enough, at four in the morning, the sleepless man heard the song again, this time the whole way through. He hadn't switched the radio off all night, such was his compulsion to confirm his suspicions. *You're sick, man*, he chastised himself, but at least he now knew.

It was a bittersweet feeling for his lonely soul to hear something pointed and mournful from someone he had known so well. The song proved Lynn still existed, and its words suggested her memory of him was alive and even causing her some pain too. Part of him was relieved not to be suffering alone, and the other half hated the thought of his former angel suffering at all.

The single, which was soon added to the young man's select music collection, possessed a lyric more melancholy than the starlet had ever recorded before. Her grieving ex-lover was surprised that her musical director would have sanctioned such a release, knowing how tightly her *répertoire* was controlled. She must have used all her recently-acquired persuasive powers to convince him to put it out.

Over on the other side of the world, in the most aptly-named City of Angels, life was very different for Lynn Dyson. If she thought she had been busy in Melbourne, the pace had been verging on idle in comparison with her schedule across the Pacific in California. Fresh from her medal-winning performances at the Olympic Games, the stunning teenager had been treated like royalty upon her arrival in the USA, and after spending a week in a luxury hotel and being ferried anonymously from place to place in limousines, she had been relieved to move into her college residence and mix with other students.

The newcomer's first dinner invitation came from the Associate Professor of Sports Psychology, the same one to have visited Benloch at the end of the southern hemisphere summer to deliver the famous family a dose of what Lynn had originally dubbed "psychobabble". David Hall was a former Melbourne Academy student who had also been an Olympic medal-winner, a rower, and who had been handsomely rewarded for securing Miss Dyson's enrolment at UCLA.

The attractive student arrived at the restaurant to find David alone at a table. She was no stranger to the showbiz city and had therefore insisted on meeting him there, rather than having a car pick her up from her apartment block, as he had offered. It hadn't previously occurred to her that his agenda would be anything other than professional, but he stood up to present her with a bouquet of flowers and a kiss on the cheek. She hid her surprise well and cursed her *naïvetée* once more.

While they dined in the sumptuous restaurant setting and shared experiences of international travel, mutual acquaintances, their country and its most recent sporting successes, the young woman's mind constantly flashed back to happier times with her enigmatic stranger: nights spent ensconced in the State Library with their homework; a socked foot caressing her calf under the table, or her own wandering hand being slapped playfully as it found its way to a thigh or some other special place; outdoor song-writing on a rug by the creek; walking through Melbourne's streets after dark, hand-in-hand and talking, talking, talking. These were memories all facilitated by a single common commodity, which was not legal tender but possessed a far greater value for the teenaged celebrity.

'Are you seeing anyone at the moment?' the perfect gentleman asked her over dessert.

'A boyfriend, you mean? No, I don't have time.'

'That's a shame,' David sighed. 'I was hoping we could go out again.'

Lynn smiled graciously. 'Thanks, but I really can't. Not at the moment. I'm still finishing my VCE, on top of everything else. Every minute's accounted for up until Christmas.'

The Antipodean sophisticates finished their coffee in the bustling downtown Los Angeles street, and the handsome academic made sure his special guest found a taxi back to her accommodation. He had asked her out for a third time while they were waiting and was disappointed to be turned down again. Lynn wondered whether her father had given him some indication of her availability. David was a person wholly dedicated to his cause, whom the big man admired and who would tick all the right boxes as a suitor for his errant offspring. The very thought made her shudder.

The truth was that the pretty teenager could not bring herself to start a new romantic relationship, for more reasons than she had given her Associate Professor. Her fresh wounds still stang after her break-up with Jeff, and she simply couldn't entertain the prospect of replacing him in her bed, let alone in her heart. It had required every gram of her mental strength to concentrate on winning her Olympic events, and upon arriving in California, she had spent over a week recovering from her heightened state of detachment. The young woman had cried for hours, wishing she could pick up the telephone and hear her mystery man's sexy, dark chocolate voice at the other end of the line.

Nevertheless, Lynn was determined to honour her commitment to her parents and to focus on the present instead of the past. She had deliberately brought no photographs or mementos with her, so that her resolve would not be weakened by attacks on her senses. By daylight, she felt happy and eager to participate in college life, recording and filming, but enduring the night-time hours was a whole different matter. Her overwhelming sorrow gave her a much keener appreciation for her former boyfriend's afflictions, and she often pictured him sitting on the couch in the early hours of the morning, strumming his guitar or reading drowsily, dreading the next time he awoke prematurely.

By contrast, sleep was sweet respite for the busy young woman and fortunately it never evaded her. She could only imagine how desperate it would be not to be afforded the escape that peaceful slumber brought from their shared heartache. Waking from dreams of happier times and finding the space next to her empty and undisturbed, she finally understood the concept of "sexual mercenary" and hoped that Jeff was finding pleasant distraction in whichever way he could.

The ambitious songwriter's first single, "Rock Me Now", was due for release in the United States the following week, Lynn recalled. How long would it be until she heard it on the radio? She wondered if he had heard her own latest single, and whether it had a positive or negative effect on how he was coping. Anticipating her talented former lover's instant success, she was very disappointed at not being able to share in it, taking solace from knowing it had been his wish to make it big without her help. She longed to be able to congratulate him on becoming the "someone" she knew he desperately needed to be.

Telephone conversations with her parents remained brief and strained, and the Australian celebrity had no desire to warm them up yet. "Relations in Gaspacho", her sardonic poet had fittingly characterised them during the pair's last week together. How she missed the expressive richness of his language, which would leap from highly cryptic and subtle to downright in-your-face in the space of a single sentence; such a stark contrast to the typical American, who used straightforward phrases and left nothing to the imagination.

Her close-knit group of Melbourne friends were gradually spreading out across the globe too, which was comforting, because they could all relate to the considerable level of displacement to which each was subjected. Michelle and Lynn's fellow MAC members had sworn not to mention the name of their pet starlet's tall, dark, handsome stranger in their correspondence, and none had dared to ask how she was faring since the happiest couple had split up. Only Richard Kerr possessed sufficient sensitivity to really empathise with the young musician's situation, often providing simple messages of support for which she was very grateful.

The Dyson siblings also kept their sister informed about goings-on back in the Victorian capital, and Michelle was already planning a trip to visit her in California over the Easter break. Richard, John Betts and some other regular band members were jetting out to join her for a US tour over the southern hemisphere summer, after the group of high achievers had graduated from school and while they waited for their respective new university terms to start. The concert series out of the way, Richard would then be flying to London to commence a course at the Royal Academy of Music, and John was off to do the same in Sydney. Lloyd had secured a place at Juilliard in New York to study dramatic arts and music, and Andrea, Anthony and Jenny had planned a year's volunteer work in South-east Asia, before taking up their various university places.

Still, despite her hectic workload and welcome stimulation from friends old and new, Lynn still felt lost and adrift without Jeff's unswerving and inspiring devotion. She longed for his tight hold, both physical and metaphysical, constantly reminding her of how important she was to him. And he to her.

Twenty-three months to go, the young star rued.

***

'So whose bodies will we occupy next, angel?'

Writing this latest, heartbreaking chapter had taken a great deal of energy from the forty-four-year-old celebrity, struggling with feelings of loss on top of feelings of loss. With any luck, he would soon be setting himself back on the path to finding love again, initially by sinking his teeth into Act Two of their autobiography. He let his mind wander to the longer term, unable to imagine either his or Lynn's new incarnation as anyone other than the people they had been in this era.

'Do we come back the same?' he spoke aloud, positive that his beautiful best ghost was on this journey alongside him. 'Me as a man, you as a woman? Me as the incredibly suave, handsome genius who repays the hours of time you invest in me with the occasional burst of consummate pleasure, and you as the knockout blonde who lights my fire every night and helps me get out of bed every morning? Bloody well hope so, huh?'

So what lessons would he and his dream girl take from this generation into the next? Probably the most valuable gift would be a sound understanding of how much effort one needed to expend to effect only a small fraction of the change required, and that persistent care and attention can overcome the greatest obstacles.

Love and wisdom, the great man scribbled in the top left-hand corner of his notepad. Which came first? And could one exist without the other? Certainly Jeff Diamond had been born with more wisdom than he knew how to handle, certainly in those early, troubled years. His wife too. As the first collection of chapters in "A Life Singular" described, the teenaged Lynn Dyson had been blessed with an innate prudence and astute judgment well exceeding that which might have been termed "common sense". Beyond even "women's intuition", the thinker acknowledged.

Moreover, they had both proven themselves worthy in the game of love, countless times and in a great many ways. Their charitable organisations had touched millions of hearts over the years, and their music and their individual acts of kindness had brought many people closer together. They had raised two happy and healthy children, brimming with a symmetry of self-esteem and humility and who were now primed to pass on their individual brands of love and wisdom to the people nominated on their own stakeholder plans.

But it was in their love for each other, above all, where the famous couple had absolutely excelled. From the very first date in February nineteen-seventy-two to that most final of mornings in the same month, twenty-four years later, when Juan Antonio García had brought their marriage to a crashing halt, neither lover had harboured a single wayward thought for pastures new. And, as Act Two of their autobiography would soon articulate, Jeff chuckled, most definitely not for lack of opportunity!

Perhaps this was another inbuilt warning his new incarnation would do well to observe, whether man or woman? Life for the average rock star was fraught with dangers of the most tempting kind, and it was with a fair degree of perverted optimism that the author looked forward to documenting the next phase of the story. What secrets would Lynn's diaries hold for the next two years? And which of his own experiences would he be brazen enough to commit to print? By all expectations, the scores for the next few chapters' sexual conquests were destined to be heavily stacked in his favour, even if they had all left him completely cold.

'Whatever, angel,' he sighed. 'It passed the time.'

The widower rolled his chair back from the huge mahogany desk, switching off the computer screen to give his eyes a rest. The room was immediately plunged into darkness, lit only by a slither of light coming in under the door. He glanced down at the luminescent hands on his watch, having started writing in broad daylight, and wondered how late it was. After midnight. Whoa. That was a long session, and painful too.

'Out?' the tired man called to Indie, whose ears pricked up immediately.

All six legs were stiff from being in the same position for so long, and the billionnaire groaned as he stretched back up to his full height. Where was his gipsy girl tonight? Out enjoying herself, as she should be.

The Labrador retriever was obviously glad to be outside, rushing to the nearest bush and cocking his leg. It put the writer in mind of the same overdue bodily function, given how long the inseparable pair had been holed up in the study, and he took his place in the garden too. Neither his wife nor their daughter was on hand to remind him that he shouldn't really be pissing in the flowerbed like the dog, so he did.

Back in the house, the widower picked up his mobile telephone and peeled a yellow sticky note off the pad in the hallway. On it was written "Grandma mobile", followed by a set of digits in Kierney's handwriting. He was about to finish the final chapter in Act One of their autobiography and had a few questions to ask Lynn's mother, in order that he might clear up some last, outstanding details. He keyed the number into his telephone, knowing his parents-in-law were away in London at the moment.

'Marianna, it's Jeff,' he said, when the call was answered. 'Are you free to talk?'

The sophisticated woman's voice replied, sounding eerily like his wife's, and all the gloomy memories which had been extruded from the celebrity's brain over the last few hours came flooding back. How desperate those months apart had been... A bit like now, in fact. Back then however, he had lacked the maturity to see into the future the way he could these days. At twenty years old, the tortured man he used to be hadn't learned to put his faith in happier days to come anywhere near as well as Lynn had.

'Of course, darling,' his mother-in-law responded. 'I got your message. How are you? Shouldn't you be in bed by now?'

'Ah, same, same,' the night owl responded. 'I've been writing. The house is nice and quiet. Listen, I was hoping you could shed some light on something that I want to get right in the book.'

'Yes. Absolutely. What would you like to know?'

Jeff paused, inhaling slowly and wiping tears from his eyes. 'I never said thank you for checking on me after Lynn left for California in 'seventy-two,' he croaked.

'Oh, you did, dear,' Marianna insisted in all innocence. 'Many times. Particularly after you'd had a bit too much to drink.'

The forty-four-year-old laughed politely at the subtle dig from a virtuous woman. 'That'd be right. Well... Thanks again anyway, from someone who's sober for a change.'

'You're welcome,' the kindly woman chuckled too. 'You never quite forgave me though, did you?'

Jeff could hear a deep voice and papers rustling in the background. The stately couple was attending a conference this week, he recalled. He would be quick, imagining Bart frowning and tapping his foot impatiently while his wife chit-chatted.

'No,' he admitted. 'That's true, but it hardly matters now. It's just that I never quite understood why you did it.'

Marianna sighed a little. 'Neither did I at the time, dear. I did it because Lynn was so upset. She'd told me she was worried about you, so I decided I'd better find out if you were alright.'

The tired author felt a chilling surge of shock run through his veins. This wasn't the answer he had been expecting, that was for sure. For all these years, he had been under the impression that his mother-in-law had either been overcome with curiosity about her daughter's outspoken lover and his dented pride, or else she had been sent to spy on him by her husband, to make sure he wasn't planning any nefarious deeds to get his own back for the affair torn asunder.

As it turned out, the older woman's motivation had been neither of these things. Rather, it had been his guardian angel's fault, although presumably, and judging by the itching sensation in his chest, she too had only just become aware of her mother's conscience having got the better of her. It appeared that Lynn had been protecting him back then, all the way from the other side of the world, just as she was now, from who knows where. The widower rubbed the tattoo under his t-shirt, mouthing his thanks into the air.

'Are you there, Jeff?' the high-classed female voice enquired. 'Did the line drop out?'

'No, Marianna,' her son-in-law answered promptly. 'Sorry. I was thinking about what you said. You never told Lynn you'd seen me though, did you?'

Again the woman sighed. 'Oh, no, dear. I couldn't have done that. You know her father wouldn't have allowed it. I remember wondering what I might do if you hadn't been coping. It would've been for the best not to pass that on. I didn't want to make her even more upset.'

Jeff curled the fingers of his left hand until his nails dug into its palm, attempting to quell his growing anger. He now regretted making the telephone call altogether, wishing he had left well alone. The memory he was about to document was from too long ago to worry about, and his readers would forgive a factual inaccuracy in the unlikely event that they ever uncovered the means to prove it.

'No,' the listless man agreed. 'Guess not. Thanks. On Lynn's behalf, that is...'

Fortunately, Marianna didn't pick up on his sarcasm, already off on another tangent. Decades of plenty had seen the last dregs of bleeding-heart liberal cleansed from the dignified woman's psyche. Despite spending a great deal of time attending charity functions, smiling benignly for the cameras and delivering prepared speeches, she rarely came into contact with the very real people with the very real issues her worthy causes sought to remedy. Such sympathies, these days, were reserved for herself and those closest to her.

'You were extremely kind to us when Sandy passed away, darling,' she gushed. 'As you have been these last few months... As son-in-laws, both you and Brandon have been everything we could've wished for for our daughters.'

The elderly woman paused, either to take a breath or to receive an acknowledgement to ensure the new-fangled, cordless piece of telephonic wizardry had not lost its connection. The lonely man at the other end of the call said nothing, waiting for her to make her point.

'Exemplary, in fact. And as men too.'

The caller inhaled and slowly exhaled. 'Thanks again, Marianna.'

'But as a leader, Jeff,' she rolled on, 'there's none better than you. I only wish there were more like you.'

The great man chuckled as Miss Irony kicked him where it hurt, at exactly the same time as his left pectoral muscle experienced a sharp twinge. Here he was, ringing his mother-in-law to find out what had happened after she and her husband had chased him away from their daughter as a hot-headed troublemaker, only to receive such adulation as a middle-aged, twice-decorated Australian of the Year and Nobel Prize recipient.

'Why are you laughing?' Marianna asked with a typical lightness in her tone. 'I'm serious.'

'Oh, no reason really. If you read the book when it comes out, you'll probably find it funny too.'

'I'm looking forward to it, dear,' Lynn's mother affirmed. 'We expect you to be honest. Bart and I were only talking about that on the 'plane over here.'

Once again, Jeff was taken aback somewhat. He hadn't spent much time while writing to consider how his beautiful best friend's parents would receive the couple's autobiography and now felt a pang of guilt at how frankly the last few chapters had been worded. Still, he wasn't about to change anything. The past was the past, and he was reporting it against the backdrop of its day and not washed with rosy hindsight.

'You were probably right to take the stance you did,' the mature peacemaker offered, deciding discretion to be the better part of valour. 'I must've seemed pretty destructive and unreliable to you at the time.'

His mother-in-law took a few seconds to consider his comment, and the superstar philanthropist dared to imagine her being transported back to the strange meeting they had shared in the ostentatious cafeteria. He was about to describe this event in perpetuity, and it was sweet charity indeed to have received a gratuitous testimony into the bargain.

Yet as it happened, the dowager wasn't yet finished. Again hearing Bart Dyson mumbling in the background, the younger man prepared to sign off, only to be stopped in his tracks.

'Lynn saw something we couldn't see in those days, darling,' Marianna stated clearly, almost as if her lines had been rehearsed specifically for the call. 'All we saw was the danger of your family background and radical ideas. I'm sorry, Jeff. *We're* sorry.'

Unusually, no involuntary wave of emotion rose up to drench the successful man as a result of this belated affirmation, and for once he was left uncomfortably impassive. Not only was it neither pity nor guilt that had motivated Lynn to keep seeing him right until the last minute. Rather, it had been a *bona fide* miracle, Jeff realised, that she had been able to look past the wild compulsion and wilful maltreatment to which he had subjected her just prior to her departure for the United States. Her formidable parents had sought to eradicate the very attributes which had encouraged his dream girl to give him the benefit of the doubt throughout those agonising few weeks.

'I should let you go, Marianna,' the calm writer replied. 'I don't want to hold you guys up. And don't be sorry. Things worked out OK.'

Terminating the call and placing the handset onto the table, the author shook his head and wandered back into the study. Should this brief, long-distance conversation with his mother-in-law change anything he had written so far? No, Jeff sighed. In fact, he felt oddly vindicated at having not diluted the truth to save the Dysons' reputation. They were expecting the truth, and that was exactly what they were going to get. In future chapters also, come to that...

Scratching the singing skin through his shirt, the author felt confident that his guardian angel was of the same opinion. Things had worked out OK. That much was true enough, but he would never know why. Not in this lifetime anyway...

***

'Science and Engineering Faculty. Jeff Diamond speaking,' the deep voice announced, answering the computer room telephone.

It was the middle of October, and the student was just over a month into his new, old, solitary lifestyle. His career as a rock star had catapulted him to instant fame and certain fortune, with his second single already at number one in the charts. "Road of Stones", the first album, already occupied the same spot on the LP chart at home and in New Zealand, on its way to similar trans-Pacific and European successes. Such was the hype with which he was now inundated that the young man oddly found himself enjoying the mundane work at the university as a sojourn back in the real world.

'Good morning, Jeff. It's Marianna Dyson here,' came a voice the twenty-year-old recognised.

His heart skipped several beats. Had something happened to Lynn? Why would her mother being ringing him? He was *persona non grata*, wasn't he?

'Good morning,' the young man replied, gritting his teeth as angry memories reignited. 'This is a surprise. What can I do for you?'

A wild idea spread across the student's mind: Lynn was pregnant and had kept her silence too long for a termination to be advisable. Was he was about to be asked to do the decent thing? It was highly unlikely to be true. The Australian team doctors kept a very close eye on her medication and the regularity of her periods. There had been no secrets to hide, but how superbly ironic that would be!

'How are you?' a kind voice asked. 'I've been meaning to give you a ring for a while, to see how you're getting on.'

'Ah, you know,' the impatient man answered, not wishing to engage in a discussion about his broken heart with his ex-girlfriend's mother. 'Life's a ball. How about you?'

Marianna was not perturbed, doubtless expecting a cool response or even outright rejection. Jeff felt less animosity towards her than for Lynn's formidable father, even though it was widely publicised that she supported her husband's conservative position on all matters. Surely she must miss her daughter too? Or had she been brainwashed so well into the Dyson way to ensure all attachment was easily suspended in the name of Australia. The team must win at any cost.

'I'm very well, thank you, dear. I wondered whether we could meet for lunch today. I'm going to be in the city.'

What a ridiculous suggestion, Jeff thought. Why on Earth should he have lunch with Lynn's mother when she had been co-architect of their dissolution? What did she want to talk about? To be forced to make polite small-talk for the duration of a whole meal would place great strain on his diplomatic powers.

'Can I ask why?' he replied. 'Is Lynn OK?'

'Oh, yes, thank you. Lynn's fine. I'm keen to hear about your record launch.'

The suspicious young man didn't believe her for a second, but how could he refuse? There was absolutely no way he could turn the invitation down, as Gravity the troll was quick to point out, with his masochistic curiosity so cruelly awakened. Did Melbourne's First Lady have the slightest clue how irresistible an offer she had made to an obsessive-compulsive addict who was desperate to feed his dependencies?

'OK,' he agreed coolly. 'I'm not sure I have anything interesting to tell you, but where do you want to meet?'

Marianna was obviously pleased. 'Thank you, Jeff. What about at the Georges' food hall at twelve-thirty?'

'Fine. I can do that. See you there, Marianna.'

'Very good. Thank you,' the refined voice responded. 'Bye, Jeff.'

Churlishly, the furious songwriter hung up without saying goodbye. Rude, he acknowledged, but this was the best he could do under the circumstances. It was now just after ten o'clock, and he took a cigarette break outside, pondering over the real reason for the elegant lady's call. Was Lynn's mother honestly inquisitive about his career? Why?

His shift over, and with three hours until his next lecture, Jeff reached the large department store on Collins Street about ten minutes early. He wandered around, searching for his fellow diner and perusing the wide selection of foodstuffs on offer. He had never set foot inside the famed gourmet Mecca until now and immediately realised why. It was full of Marianna Dysons! Well-to-do ladies who lunched.

The unshaven student who worked had left home that morning in jeans and an unironed, checked shirt, having been up for most of the night rehearsing with his new band before making his backing singer's day by offering to take her home. Not very professional, the compulsive musician understood, but he had already lost out on the best female vocalist in the world, and there would be plenty more talent to choose from if things became too awkward.

Satisfied at least physically and creatively, the budding star had run home just before dawn from a crowded share house in Prahran, a far cry from the dignified atmosphere in which he now found himself. Heads turned, and tongues wagged, as he walked by the old birds in their fine plumage. Jeff amused himself by hazarding a guess or two at what the offended women might be saying to each other in their haughty voices: "Truly disgusting how such riff-raff feel free to roam around our territory," or "It must be a socialist conspiracy from the Labor government."

Care factor? Zero, smiled the boy from Sydney's south-west.

A few minutes after twelve-thirty, in walked the lady herself. Fashionably late, of course. More heads turned, but for different and much more approving reasons. The student remarked to himself how much like her mother Lynn was becoming. Slender, beautifully coiffured and graceful, Marianna still had the poise gained during her former career with the Australian Ballet. She had different facial features from her daughter's, more pointed and a little harsher. All four Dyson children bore an even stronger resemblance to their father.

The waiting student saw Lynn's mother before she saw him and began to walk towards her. His active imagination again took flight with the unspoken fears of the other patrons while he stalked the elegant woman, catching up to her from behind as if he were intending to snatch her handbag.

'Missus Dyson,' he called, sensing she was about to head in the wrong direction.

'Oh, Jeff!' she answered, turning round. 'Hello there! Thank you for agreeing to meet me. I'm sorry it was such short notice.'

The twenty-year-old said nothing, standing tall and motioning towards a table at which he had already ordered an expensive bottle of imported beer. Striking for a woman now into middle-age, Marianna was wearing a dark blue business suit and a brightly coloured scarf around her long dancer's neck, with flawless make-up and her nails subtly varnished. She smiled, sat down opposite him and picked up the menu.

'Thank you. Have you chosen already?'

Here we go, thought Jeff. *Here starteth the small talk.*

'I was only going to have a sandwich,' he answered, going with the flow. 'I need to get back soon for a couple of classes, and then I'm doing the early evening shift at the pub I work in, so I can't stay out too long.'

You know, lady, his rancorous mind longed to tease, *the sort of things that your sort of people don't have to do. Like watch the time...* Unfair, he realised, since Lynn had frequently described how hard her mother worked for the various organisations of which she was Patron. But now she was here to patronise him, he presumed. Or matronise perhaps, if there was such a word.

The odd couple placed their food orders, and the waitress laid their table with silver-plated cutlery and iced water served in a crystal jug. The handsome gentleman did the honours with their two glasses.

'Thank you,' the gracious woman said. 'Now, tell me how you're going. You look tired.'

Jeff smiled and cocked his head to one side. 'How am I going? Marianna, what do you want to know?' he answered, trying his best not to sound angry. 'Forgive me, but it's more than a little bizarre to receive a 'phone call from you, under the circumstances.'

His ex-girlfriend's mother shifted uneasily in her chair, sipping her Chardonnay. She looked around at the other tables with a benevolent, almost righteous smile while she unfolded her napkin and placed it in her lap.

'Yes, I suppose it is,' she agreed. 'I've been thinking about you a lot recently and feel somewhat guilty about the way we forced you and Lynn to bring your relationship to an end. I suppose I'm just being a mother hen and fussing over my brood.'

The words rolled off the well-bred tongue as if they were meant truthfully, but even so, it was extremely difficult for the young man to hide his feelings. The lost boy checked his eyes before they had a chance to glare wildly at the woman who had issued this last, outlandish statement. How dare she?

'Forgive me again, but I have no idea what that means,' Jeff told her in no uncertain terms. 'You're not my mother, luckily for you. And I apologise if this sounds somewhat cynical, but you can't stick a knife in with one hand, then pull it out with the other and expect the wound to disappear.'

Marianna shook her head, thrown off guard by his directness and by the powerful imagery evoked through his barb-laden words. At this juncture, it probably became apparent to her that the meeting was a mistake, and yet here they were, waiting for their food to arrive and surrounded by Melbourne's nosiest. Her eyes grew moist, which made the young man feel guilty too.

'I understand, Jeff,' she replied, with typical aristocratic composure. 'And I appreciate your honesty. I didn't expect you to be happy to see me.'

So why had she come then? The student bit his tongue and lightened up on the well-meaning parent, feeling ashamed for his aggression. He shouldn't jump to conclusions that her motives weren't honourable. Up until recently, he had quite liked Marianna Dyson. She was empathetic and worldly, and he was struck by a similar projection of his dream girl with a few more years of ripening under her belt.

'I apologise. What would you like to know? How is my gorgeous goddess of an ex-girlfriend, by the way?'

'Lynn's well, thank you,' the elegant socialite responded to the loaded sarcasm of the discourteous peasant littering the food hall. 'She's still fairly terse in her communication with us but has settled in well to her course, and I believe she's currently filming in LA. I'm not sure when the movie will be released, or even what it's about, to be frank.'

'That's good,' Jeff nodded.

He was genuinely pleased to hear that his beautiful former best friend was adjusting to her new, States-side life. He particularly liked the part about the paucity of her parental *communiqués*. Good on her! That was the best piece of information he had received for weeks. And how he craved more, hungry for the smallest glimmer of hope that Lynn's plans might change...

'I expect you miss her too,' the loner added, trying to be diplomatic. 'I look forward to reading the reviews when the film comes out.'

'I hope you'll go and see it,' Marianna suggested.

'Look, Marianna,' her daughter's handsome suitor continued, with a flash of his dark, sultry eyes as a cursory acknowledgement. 'Grateful as I am for the hospitality you and Mister Dyson extended me during those weekends at Benloch, I'm not part of your brood, and you don't have to fuss over me. Initially I was welcomed with open arms, and then everything fell over, and no-one's had the courtesy to tell me why. Or Lynn, for that matter. Does she even know the real reason?'

'There were a number of reasons,' the famous wife and mother replied, sitting up straight and matching the fearless man's tone quite well.

Marianna had already figured Lynn's first love as a formidable opponent in an argument on any topic, but his passion for this one in particular was only too evident. Jeff waited patiently, his fingernails flicking the edges of the label on his beer bottle, which the condensation was causing to peel off. He averted his gaze to take the pressure off his luncheon companion a little. He didn't want to turn this into a shouting match. It wouldn't be the done thing to embarrass her in front of her peers, many of whom would surely be doing their best to eavesdrop. Whatever was the Honourable Lady Marianna doing, having a clandestine meeting with a Catholic Argentinean Polish Jew? The whole scene was kind of funny really, he confessed.

'Lynn's still under eighteen, you see,' the matriarch continued. 'Our main concerns were for her reputation and for her education.'

'Really?' the former tearaway interjected, offering no defence. 'And what else?'

The refined socialite took a deep breath, pausing while their food was delivered. Both diners thanked the waitress, and their plates were put down on the table in front of them. The student was looking forward to a square meal, especially after his long night and lack of breakfast. He picked up his fork and stabbed a couple of hot chips, putting them into his mouth as the lady opposite prepared to tackle a chicken salad.

Before taking her first mouthful, she answered his question. 'Lynn's future is well planned, Jeff. Her goals... all our goals... are designed to achieve great things for our country. We were concerned that your influence was diverting her from those goals.'

Nodding, Jeff gave her a wry half-smile. 'I see. So you sent her to America as an act of patriotism? To get her away from her dissident rebel? I feel like I've ended up in a Victor Hugo novel. How romantic!'

'Please, Jeff,' Marianna warned under her breath. 'It's you who are romanticising it.'

576

'Sure. Quite possibly. That's what I do best,' the songwriter confirmed. 'That's what dissidents tend to do. What did you think I'd get her to do? Deliberately throw her first round tennis match to dishonour the Australian flag? Poison the equestrian team's horses? Or march the wrong way in the Opening Ceremony?'

Marianna couldn't help but laugh at the preposterous suggestions. 'Don't be ridiculous, dear.'

Don't matronise me, the twenty-year-old urged in his head, knowing all the while that considerable chemistry was at work between the two of them. In her mid-forties, the former ballerina remained a very attractive woman, and the virile, good-looking gipsy could tell by the regular toss of her hair and slightly heavy eyelids that she was not immune to his charms.

'I'm sorry,' he responded, as sincerely has he thought the situation merited. 'But from where I sit, forcing your daughter into exile because she happens to be sharing her bed with an aspiring musician from the common classes is also pretty damned ridiculous. It's the nineteen-seventies, Marianna. You're a hundred and fifty years too late.'

No doubt about it, his adversary acknowledged in silence, Jeff Diamond was an impressive and articulate young man; fervent and cultured. Just the type she herself would have longed to meet at Lynn's age. She nodded slowly, allowing the indignant man to say his piece.

'You're a woman of the arts,' he continued in a more conciliatory tone, 'and I understand it was due to your influence that Lynn ended up in the music world in the first place. So have you changed your tune or are you just bowing to pressure?'

Both knew this was an astute and very brave question. Marianna declined to furnish him with an answer, and therefore Jeff surmised that he didn't need one. Letting each other off the hook, they took a few moments to eat their lunches, retreating with their respective opinions. Thoughts keen to be expressed formed a restless queue behind the perceptive poet's mouth, which in the end was unable to remain silent.

'Marianna, I believe as much as you do that sport and music can be used as forces for good. God knows, I'm embarking on a music career myself for exactly that purpose,' he explained. 'And once the genie's out of the bottle, it's bloody hard to get it back in if it doesn't want to go. Lynn's an entertainer with a social conscience, as well as a sportswoman of record-breaking capability. That's not my fault. That's your fault.'

The emphatic twenty-year-old was grateful to be holding food in his hand, because it rid him of the temptation to point a menacing finger towards his distinguished eating partner. The reason for this peculiar social call was still abundantly unclear to him, and he saw no reason not to take full advantage of the opportunity to speak his mind.

'I freely admit she may be writing a whole different kind of song these days, and yes, that's partly because of my influence. But she would've got there eventually anyway, in a few more years. That's why I was so strongly attracted to her in the first place. We're kindred spirits, your daughter and I. And I know that sounds hopelessly romantic and not what you want to hear, but there's no denying her impatience with the true blue, silver spoon world, is there?'

'No, there isn't,' Marianna agreed, after a short pause. 'You're right.'

'Thanks,' Jeff responded quietly, nudging the argument skilfully where he wanted it to go. 'And I'm not sure you don't share some of those sensibilities, given the fact you didn't answer my question about bowing to pressure. Does your husband know you've crossed the barricades and are fraternising with the enemy?'

'That's quite enough now,' the maternal disciplinarian stated firmly, tapping the table with her painted nails.

'I apologise,' her daughter's former beau replied without hesitation, raising his hands in front of his face, palms opened towards his most civil of opponents. 'That was out of order. I respect your silence, and that's the last you'll hear from me on that topic. I'd just like to know what you expected to achieve from this meeting, that's all.'

'Nothing specific,' the stylish lady answered. 'I was concerned for you.'

'OK, thanks. So is your curiosity satisfied?' the songwriter asked with a shrug, knowing both were intentionally skirting around the truth. 'Do I deserve your concern? You know, I do my best to put on the airs and graces of the noble classes, but scratch the surface, and I'm still an angry, motherless rat-bag from the western suburbs of Sydney.'

'No, Jeff. That's not what...'

'I know that. I can't change who I was, but I have enormous capacity to change who I will be. Ironic, isn't it? As Lynn once told my best mate, "Jeff's a control freak, just like my father." I won't quit until I become who I want to be, and that hopefully includes being by your daughter's side.'

Marianna exhaled, affected by the young student's tenacity. 'Did she really say that?' she asked, smiling. 'She'd never say that to his face.'

All his shots fired, Jeff leaned back in his chair. There was an air of vulnerability in the older woman's voice, appealing and reminiscent of someone he once knew. His heart ached, and his senses cried out for attention, yet he was determined to play it cool. Like Lynn, the fiercely independent man didn't want to give the Dysons the satisfaction of knowing how far they had thrown his life into disarray, regardless of his burgeoning fame and fortune.

'No, I expect not. Lynn loves you and her dad, and she's proud to represent Australia. She wanted to do the right thing by you. She'll have all the success you want her to have in the next two years, and no doubt she'll change along the way. But I'm prepared to wait and see who she is when she comes back to Melbourne.'

The determined philosopher's eyes had filled with tears, which he fought back valiantly but unsuccessfully. His ex-girlfriend's mother looked on, rendered temporarily speechless by his candour.

'And in the meantime, we'll all change a bit too,' he added. 'Or a lot, in some cases. Maybe she won't want to come home to any of us? Who knows? It's a big, wide world out there.'

The young man folded his serviette roughly and placed it on the table. He then took twenty dollars out of his wallet and slapped it down next to his empty beer bottle before standing up and waiting for Marianna to follow suit. He couldn't help but smile as his evil twin subliminally suggested he might take the sophisticated lady to a hotel room, both to encourage her to admit the truth she had avoided so easily and to exact some sweet revenge on her husband. But of course he would never go through with it.

Would he?

'Missus Dyson, I hope I haven't offended you too much. Please wish Lynn well from me, if that's allowed.'

'It's not allowed, I'm afraid,' the adroit woman was unequivocal in her reply, suddenly uneasy in the young man's presence. 'Thank you for coming here. I have a better appreciation now of where you stand, and I wish you every success with your career. Are you graduating at the end of this year, by the way?'

Jeff coughed, banishing his preposterous, perverted idea to the dark side of his brain whence it came. He had succeeded in raising the dignified stateswoman's blood pressure though, which boosted his ego nicely. Yet not even the eternal angel relegated to his fantasies would forgive such an antagonistic mercenary act.

'No,' he answered. 'Another year yet. I'll send Lynn a ticket to the ceremony, care of Admin, shall I?'

Marianna chuckled, seeing the sly look on his face. The tall, elegant woman rose to her feet and looped her handbag over her arm. A few inquisitive sets of eyes surreptitiously fixed on the pair as they made to leave, and the nobody from New South Wales was struck again by the familiar easy manner of politely dismissing onlookers that his dream girl had inherited and employed so naturally.

'Good luck, Jeff. Keep well.'

'Thanks. You too,' he replied, offering her his hand to shake.

To his astonishment, the famous lady offered him her cheek to kiss. He obliged, having been left no option in such a public place. Gravity and Irony danced another quick jig, and this time the lost soul joined in.

Back at the university, during a quiet moment between classes that afternoon, Jeff Diamond slipped out for a cigarette break and reflected on the strange assignation with his former girlfriend's mother. Her answers had confirmed his suspicions once and for all that he had been the main reason that the teenager had left the country before she had even finished high school. The lovers had made the ultimate sacrifice for his desire and her willingness to open her mind, and consequently it depressed him no end to realise that he would have to shoulder ninety-nine percent of the blame for their relationship coming to a premature end. Another injustice had been done, and there was nothing he could do about it.

The tormented soul had often assumed there to be a sign saying "Blame me" hovering above his head wherever he went, visible to everyone except him. What had happened to make him into the world's favourite scapegoat? He oughtn't to be surprised. He had predicted this eventuality all along, but it was hard to bear nevertheless. This was the price one paid when one tried to rise above one's station, the poor student concluded. He should have known better than to pursue his dream girl in the first place. His immediate destiny was to be condemned to habitual fuck-and-run relationships, in which girls had no interest in cultivating the assets between their ears or behind their ribs, and to keep his ambitious intellectual pursuits well and truly to himself.

People like Jeff Diamond obviously didn't deserve a soul-mate from the upper strata of life. Gerry's sisters had told him so, teasing him mercilessly about his infatuation for a certain blonde starlet who would remain out of reach. He had been able to thumb his nose at them for a short time, and what a magnificent ride the lovers had taken together! He had wormed his way into her neophyte, compassionate heart and given her everything he had for as long as he was permitted.

It was bound to come crashing down eventually though, wasn't it? Boys who grew up alone on the Stones Road had no business stealing time from a girl as singularly perfect as Lynn Dyson. Mummy and Daddy had seen through him pretty quickly, hadn't they?

Espérame, Regala, Jeff whispered into the sky, testing the strain on their invisible elastic connection. Sooner or later, their star-crossed souls would find a way to reunite. It would take more than an ocean and twenty-four months to extinguish a fire that had burned for so long.

End of Part Two

If you enjoyed reading this book, please take the time to tell your friends and leave a review on Amazon and Goodreads.

Book 3 in the series, "A Life Entwined", was published in June 2014. Full details can be found at http://lorrainepestell.com.

Fame and fortune beckoned. Jeff Diamond was a success, whatever that meant… Fans followed him everywhere, reporters and photographers hid around every corner and journalists recorded his many indiscretions. A whole different world to the downtrodden streets of Sydney's south-west, where vices were satisfied by using people to one's best advantage.

The star had more money than he could spend, his opinion suddenly counted, and the opportunities to feed his ever-hungry mind were plentiful. Yet the demons continued to torment him, no longer protected by the guardian angel who had been spirited away as soon as her family found out who Jeff Diamond was and where he had come from.

Suddenly the ambitious businessman and philanthropist found himself in the fight of his life. He would win Lynn's heart by showing her father he was worthy, and by convincing his dream girl that they had something worth fighting for. Would she risk throwing her privileged lifestyle away for a man whose public persona depended on alcohol, drugs and a string of pretty girls?

Jeff had nothing to lose. The trappings of his new life held little significance until the soul-mates were reunited. This was where their life singular would really begin. Up until this point, there had only been playtime. Now they must step up and take responsibility. It was up to them.

www.ingramcontent.com/pod-product-compliance
Lightning Source LLC
Chambersburg PA
CBHW030741030726
47497CB00001B/84